M

28 DAY BOOK

12/13   3+3R   2013

USEFUL ENEMIES

USEFUL ENEMIES

JOHN DEMJANJUK AND AMERICA'S
OPEN-DOOR POLICY FOR NAZI WAR CRIMINALS

Richard Rashke

DELPHINIUM BOOKS
Harrison, New York • Encino, California

USEFUL ENEMIES

Copyright © 2013 by Richard Rashke

All rights reserved

Printed in the United States of America

For information, address DELPHINIUM BOOKS, Inc.,
P.O. Box 703, Harrison, New York 10528

Jacket and interior design by Greg Mortimer

Library of Congress Cataloguing-in-Publication Data
is available upon request.

ISBN 978-1-88-328551-7

13 14 15 RRD 10 9 8 7 6 5 4 3 2 1

Photo credits:

Page 351: U.S. Holocaust Museum
Page 353: U.S. Holocaust Museum
Page 385: Reuters/Landov
Page 430: U.S. Holocaust Museum
Page 433: U.S. Holocaust Museum
Page 514: Reuters/Landov

To Paula
my essential

CONTENTS

INTRODUCTION

History, Like Life, Is Messy

NO EASY ANSWERS

In November 2009, orderlies wheeled an eighty-nine-year-old former American citizen, John Demjanjuk, into a Munich courtroom on a gurney to face charges that he helped the Nazis murder 29,060 Jews at the Sobibor death camp in eastern Poland during World War II.

Why did it take almost sixty years for the United States to find and extradite John Demjanjuk for trial in Germany as a Nazi collaborator?

Finding an answer to this often-asked question is like trying to solve a Rubik's Cube. Historical forces, moral behaviors, legal issues, and matters of survival must be separated and realigned—a daunting task when an individual's wartime actions and a country's postwar judgments of those actions are so intertwined.

In the United States, Israel, and finally in Germany, John Demjanjuk stood accused of being a Nazi collaborator. Yet if war is as much about survival as it is about killing, does wartime create its own version of what is right and wrong, based on an individual's right of survival? If so, was John Demjanjuk a collaborator or simply a survivor?

At the same time that postwar America was pursuing John Demjanjuk and other alleged Nazi collaborators in the courts, it was also employing and protecting former Nazis and Nazi collaborators. Was America's use and shielding of these war criminals a repugnant but necessary and pragmatic choice to secure the nation during the Cold War? Or was it illegal, unethical, and immoral? And were its pick-and-choose decisions about which Nazi "collaborators" to try, deport, or extradite an exercise in cynicism and hypocrisy?

If the end justifies the means, does a morally acceptable end justify *any means?* Is there a line of pragmatism and political expediency, albeit fuzzy and shifting, that an individual or a nation should not cross? If so, who decides where to draw that line?

The panel of seven judges in Munich rendered a final answer—subject to appeal—in the case of John Demjanjuk and established a war crimes precedent in the process. For the first time, a German court convicted a Nazi-era war criminal without either documentary or eyewitness evidence that he had personally killed anyone. That precedent sent German prosecutors scurrying back to their file cabinets in search of other alleged Nazi collaborators who had "aided and abetted" in the murder of civilians, without proof that they had ever pulled a trigger. As a result of the Demjanjuk conviction, there may be more war crimes trials in Germany.

For John Demjanjuk the long journey to Munich began in 1920 in a tiny Ukrainian village.

IN HIS OWN WORDS

Fleshed out with the history of the times, here is John Demjanjuk's story. It is cobbled from official records bearing his signature and his sworn statements to prosecutors and courts in the United States and Israel.

Iwan Demjanjuk* was born on April 3, 1920, in the Ukrainian village of Dubovi Makharintsi. With a population of about three hundred, it was not on any map. The village was near Kiev, one of the oldest cultural centers in Eastern Europe. But as important as Kiev was to Ukrainian national identity, it offered nothing to a barefoot boy born into a farming family and destined to be a farmer himself.

Iwan never had a chance to attend Kiev's famous Taras Shevchenko National University, or the Kiev Polytechnic Institute, or the Kiev-Mohyla Academy. He got as far as fourth grade in the village school before being drafted to work on a communist collective farm (*kolkhoz*), where he slowly advanced from horse and plow to tractor.

Iwan was the epitome of a survivor. He lived through Joseph Stalin's artificially created famine of 1932–33 (the Holodomor), during which three to four million Ukrainians died of starvation. The famine hit chil-

---

* *Iwan* is the spelling of the common name *Ivan*.

dren like Iwan the hardest. As one observer described them: "You could see each bone in their arms and legs protruding from the skin, how bones joined, and [how] the entire skeleton was stretched over with skin that was like yellow gauze. And the children's faces were tormented, just as if they were seventy years old . . . . And the eyes. Oh, Lord!"

The famine kept the Demjanjuk family teetering on the brink of starvation for fifteen months and made a lasting impression on thirteen-year-old Iwan. It became a compass point in his life's journey, toughened his will to live, and taught him skills he would need to survive the Nazi earthquake about to tear Europe apart. Iwan also managed to dodge Stalin's maniacal purges of the 1930s and early 1940s, during which an estimated 3.3 million intellectuals, political activists, and Communist Party leaders, whose loyalty was under suspicion, were executed or imprisoned in the Siberian gulags. Among them were thousands of Ukrainian journalists, poets, teachers, wealthy landowners, and clergymen. Iwan survived the purges because Stalin feared the pen and the tongue, not the tractor and its driver.

In the end, the dictator paid a heavy price for raping Ukraine. The Holodomor, the purges, and state-mandated atheism sowed the seeds of hatred deep in Ukraine's Christian heart.

Like his father, Nikolai, before him, Iwan was drafted into an artillery division of the Red Army. It galled the young man that he was forced to defend Stalin and communism, but the alternative was death as a traitor. And like his father, who lost several fingers during World War I (probably from frostbite), Iwan too was scarred by war. He suffered a shrapnel wound in the back from the premature explosion of an artillery shell. The paralyzing wound was so serious that he spent nearly a year in hospitals before being sent back into battle at Kerch, a Ukrainian harbor city in Crimea.

For the German Reich, the Kerch port was a tempting plum. After heavy fighting, it captured the city in November 1941. But not for long. Mounting a surprise attack from the sea, the Reds recaptured Kerch a month later, only to have the German navy retake it once again the following spring. During the battles for Kerch, the Germans killed or took as prisoners more than 160,000 Red Army soldiers. Iwan was one of the survivors.

Because Stalin distrusted the loyalty of his Christian soldiers, Soviet military law required Iwan to kill himself rather than be taken prisoner. POWs could be tortured for military information, flipped to fight against the Red Army, or used as labor cogs in the Reich's war machine. For twenty-two-year-old Iwan, suicide was not only a sin; it was the ultimate act of loyalty to the atheistic government he hated. As a matter of conscience and survival, Iwan chose to take his chances as a German POW.

The capture of Soviet soldiers presented the Reich with a huge problem. It had several million Russian POWs but no system to process them, not enough shelters and food, and no medicine or doctors. Conditions in the jerry-built POW camps in western Ukraine and eastern Poland were so atrocious that prisoners resorted to digging holes in the ground to keep warm and to eating the frozen dead for dinner.

In an attempt to buy time, the German SS (Schutzstaffel), a nonmilitary protection squad, opened a transit camp in Rovno, a rail transportation hub in western Ukraine, which offered the Reich army easy access to Germany and its occupied territories. During the winter of 1941–42, an estimated two million Red Army POWs died in Rovno from starvation, exposure, typhus, and dysentery before Berlin decided to put them to work, as Stalin had feared.

Adolf Hitler assigned the task of building and managing the Reich's more than six thousand transit, POW, concentration, labor, and death camps to the SS. SS officers selected the healthiest POWs and penned them inside hastily constructed camps in the Reich-occupied territories until they could be placed in proper labor camps. Iwan was sent first to Rovno in June 1942, then to an outdoor holding camp in Chelm, Poland, a historic city founded in the ninth century and only a twenty-minute train ride from the Bug River, which divided Poland and the Soviet Union. Chelm served as a cultural center for both Poles and Jews, who had lived in relative harmony until Hitler made it legal to rob and kill Jews.

The Soviet army occupied Chelm for eleven days in 1939, before retreating back across the Bug as the German army advanced eastward. Many Chelm Jews, who feared the Nazis more than they loved their homes, fled into the Soviet Union behind the Red Army. After the war, the majority stayed there.

The Nazis eventually killed, or sent to work camps and death camps, all but a few Chelm Jews, who managed to hide. The Chelm holding camp for Soviet POWs (including Iwan Demjanjuk) is not to be confused with the tiny village of Chelmno, the site of a not-so-secret Nazi extermination camp in northern Poland. It was at Chelmno that the Nazis experimented with gas as a murder weapon, first in sealed vans, then in two primitive gas chambers with adjacent crematoria. The Chelmno guinea pigs were mostly Polish Jews, Gypsies (Roma), and Russian POWs.

The Chelm prisoner holding camp was a corral without barracks, ringed with rolls of barbed wire. Prisoners who tried to escape got caught in the wire and were left to die of exposure and dehydration. During the 1942–43 winter, the SS gave the camp's first sixty thousand Soviet POWs wood and tools, and ordered them to build their own barracks. Most died of starvation or sickness. The following winter was almost as cruel. The only survivors were prisoners who were selected to work in labor camps or who "volunteered" to serve as camp guards. Iwan survived the winter.

Late in 1943, the SS sent Iwan to Graz, Austria, to be inducted into an all-Ukrainian unit of the Waffen SS (armed SS) to fight the Red Army. At Graz, a doctor tattooed Iwan's blood type on his upper left arm in case he was wounded and needed a blood transfusion. A few weeks later, the SS transferred Iwan to Heuberg, Germany, where he was inducted into the Russian Liberation Army (RLA). Given his hatred of the communists as a Ukrainian and as a Christian, young Iwan saw his service in the RLA as both an honor and a patriotic duty.

The RLA was under the command of Andrei Vlasov, a Red Army general whom the Germans had taken prisoner a few months after Iwan. To the Reich, General Vlasov was a public relations coup—a Soviet war hero because of his brilliant defense of Moscow and Leningrad in the deadly winter of 1941. In reality, Vlasov was, like Iwan, an anti-Stalinist.

When Vlasov offered to collaborate with the German army against the Soviet Union, Berlin accepted. In September 1944, as the Red Army relentlessly drove the Germans west, the Reich incorporated the RLA into the German army.

Although most RLA soldiers (*Vlasovtsy*) saw action in the final year of the war and suffered heavy casualties, Iwan survived. General Vlasov never called up Iwan's unit, so he sat out the last days of the war far from the front.

When Germany surrendered in May 1945, there were more than ten million uprooted and starving men, women, and children in Western Europe. They poured through the gates of displaced persons (DP) camps in the American, British, and French military sectors like a human tsunami. Most were former slave laborers, concentration camp inmates, and POWs. Among them was Iwan Demjanjuk.

Iwan entered a DP camp in Landshut, the former site of a slave labor subcamp of the infamous Dachau prison complex. While in Landshut, he joined the camp's uniformed police force and met Vera Kowlowa, a fellow Ukrainian whom the Germans had uprooted to work as a domestic. They married in September 1947, then moved to the much larger, American-run DP camp in Regensburg, Bavaria, hoping to find better food and living conditions. As an insurance policy, Iwan worked for the U.S. Army as a truck driver, hauling wood, coal, and other camp supplies.

Postwar Europe offered three choices to DPs like Iwan: return to one's home country, create a new life in Western Europe, or emigrate to a country outside Europe. Iwan chose emigration. As a first step in the process, he requested refugee status from the International Refugee Organization. That step posed a moral problem. If Iwan told refugee officials that he was a former Russian POW who had served in the RLA, he could be handed over to the Red Army for extradition back to the Soviet Union. The 1945 Yalta Agreement between the United States, Britain, and the Soviet Union stipulated that all Soviet POWs had to be remanded to Soviet authorities along with any Soviet citizen who had lived in the Soviet Union before 1937. Iwan Demjanjuk was both a POW and someone who had lived in the Soviet Union before 1937.

Iwan knew that if he were handed over to the Soviets, he was a dead man. Word had drifted across the Bug River that Stalin was trying POWs as Nazi collaborators. Some were executed. Most were sentenced to a slow death in Siberia. *Vlasovtsy* officers got special handling. Stalin summarily hung them publicly as traitors, including General Vlasov himself, whom the Red Army had captured during the waning months of the war.

• • •

In March 1948, Iwan wrote on his refugee application form that from 1937 to 1943 he had worked as a farmer in Sobibor, a tiny village in eastern Poland near the Bug River. That lie put him beyond the legal reach of the Soviet Union. Iwan chose the town of Sobibor as his fake residence because there was a sizable Ukrainian colony there, a fact that would make his story realistic if anyone bothered to check. To account for the months between 1943 and the end of the war in June 1945, Iwan wrote on his application that he had worked as a stevedore on the docks of Pillau, a German port on the Baltic Sea, and as a laborer in Munich.

Refugee officials accepted Iwan's application without challenge. They had to process millions of forms, didn't have time to check details, and had no access to records.

. . .

In 1950, Iwan and Vera had their first child, Lydia. Hoping to create a better life for his new family, Iwan applied for and received a visa to the United States, based on a sworn statement that he had spent the years 1937–45 working in Sobibor, Pillau, and Munich, and that he had taken no part in the persecution of any person due to race, religion, or national origin. Under the aegis of the Displaced Persons Act of 1948, Iwan, Vera and Lydia Demjanjuk steamed into New York harbor on the *USS General W. G. Haan* on February 9, 1952. Vera cried when she caught sight of the Statue of Liberty.

The Demjanjuks were only three of approximately one hundred thousand war refugees who entered the United States that year. Between four and five hundred thousand European refugees would eventually sink new roots in America after World War II.

For both Iwan and Vera, New York was the end of a harrowing journey of cunning and luck. Burying their painful memories under a comforter of hope, they settled into the harsh life of a penniless immigrant family. With all their possessions crammed into two boxes, they boarded a train for Decatur, Indiana, where a farmer and a spare room were waiting.

Iwan (now Ivan) began his new life in America tending pigs. Unable to speak English, the life of the Demjanjuks in rural Indiana was isolated and depressing until they made friends with a neighboring Polish family. When his new friends learned that Ivan was a mechanic, they found him a full-time job at a garage in Decatur. It didn't pay well, but it was a step up from castrating piglets.

Fortunately for him and his family, Ivan had a Ukrainian friend who lived in Cleveland and worked at the new Ford Motor Company plant in the suburbs. The friend, whom Ivan had met at a DP camp in Germany, invited the Demjanjuks to Cleveland, promising to help them get settled and find Ivan a good job at Ford. Given Ivan's experience as a mechanic, Ford quickly hired him as a hot-engine tester, a responsible job that required both mechanical and analytical skills. It was a well-paying, secure job, with the United Auto Workers union watching his back while he listened to motors purr on the assembly line. Vera got a job in a nearby General Electric plant.

Like thousands of immigrants before them, the Demjanjuks lived in a series of cheap, two-room flats and apartments and pinched nickels and dimes. Then, in 1956, four years after reaching New York, they bought a small, fixer-upper house. As their family grew—they had a second daughter, Irene, and a son, John—they bought and moved to a second home, then a third. Each move brought them one step closer to the American dream.

Ohio had the largest Ukrainian population in the country, and western Cleveland was its cultural and religious heart. The Orthodox-Byzantine Church of Sts. Peter and Paul was the mother church from which radiated a string of parishes and parochial schools that taught Ukrainian language, culture, and catechism. There were Ukrainian newspapers, youth organizations, and music academies that taught traditional Ukrainian instruments, dances, and folk songs. In fact, the Cleveland Ukrainian community offered so many services in the native language that fluency in English, although an asset, was not a necessity.

Ivan felt at home among his fellow anticommunist Ukrainians, many of whom had fought the Reds in Ukraine's 1917–21 civil war. He enrolled his children in Ukrainian language and culture classes, he and Vera became American citizens, and he legally changed his name to the quintessentially American "John."

The Demjanjuks worshipped at St. Vladimir's Ukrainian Orthodox Church, built in 1924 by Ukrainians who had fled Europe after the communist revolution. John served on its advisory board and his son became an altar boy. When "refugees" from Appalachia began flooding the old Ukrainian neighborhood in search of cheap housing and work, St. Vladimir's parish fled to Parma, a southwestern suburb of Cleveland. The Demjanjuks followed their church.

In 1974, after more than twenty years of steady, hard work at Ford, the Demjanjuks could finally afford to buy their dream house—a brick ranch on Meadow Lane in Seven Hills, a typical Cleveland suburb of safe, tree-lined streets shading well-kept bungalows and houses, with bikes and roller skates on the front porch, and picnic tables and barbecue grills out back. The Demjanjuk home had a huge backyard, where John could do what he was born to do—grow things. He planted vegetables, trimmed his fruit trees, and tended the rosebushes.

To his neighbors, John Demjanjuk was a kind, quiet man, always willing to help a neighbor fix a lawn mower motor, as well as a hardworking provider, a dedicated Christian, a caring husband and father, and a true anticommunist patriot who had been wounded in battle, hung tough as a POW, and served the Ukrainian cause of independence.

John Demjanjuk was finally living the hard-won American dream.

• • •

That dream was shattered in 1977 when John Demjanjuk received a subpoena from the U.S. Department of Justice, charging him with fraudulently acquiring a U.S. visa in 1951 and illegally entering America the following year. That legal action ignited a war of words and deadly violence between Jews and émigrés over three issues:

Was John Demjanjuk the victim of a Jewish witch hunt?

Did the Soviet Union set him up for a fall?

Did the United States, Israel, and Germany use him for political reasons?

The search for answers to those and other questions raised here begins with America's pre–World War II immigration policy.

PART ONE

Opening the Door

CHAPTER ONE

Anywhere But Here

By all standards of fairness, the U.S. record on World War II refugees is embarrassing for a country that prides itself on its generosity. Beginning with the Evian Conference in 1938 and culminating in the Displaced Persons Act of 1948, the United States was blatantly selfish, timid, callous, and discriminatory. It is a chapter of history that Americans would prefer to leave resting in the coffin of ancient history.

If the United States was slow to admit World War II refugees from Europe, it was a tortoise in the hunt to find and expel thousands of former Nazis and Nazi collaborators hiding among the 400,000–500,000 refugees it had been shamed into accepting. American sentiment was to "let sleeping Nazis lie" and the United States only entered the hunt, bickering and screaming, in the late 1970s—more than thirty years after the war. The reasons it took so long are clear: Most Americans couldn't have cared less about a bunch of former Nazis as long as they behaved themselves; some felt that old Nazis were better than Jews; the U.S. government didn't want to take time from the Cold War to smoke out former Nazis who were now loyal, contributing members of American society; and America had dark secrets to protect.

• • •

The first time the United States showed its hand in the refugee poker game was at the international, invitation-only conference in Evian-les-Bains, France, in the summer of 1938, six months before Kristallnacht, Hitler's first major salvo in his war against Jews. More than 150,000 German Jews had anticipated the murder and mayhem of Kristallnacht and fled Germany in the vain hope of finding a home elsewhere. When Hitler annexed Austria (in the forcible union known as the Anschluss) in March 1938, another 200,000 Jews became either homeless or at risk.

Most of the wandering German and Austrian Jews wanted to settle in Palestine, but the British, who controlled that territory, had set a rigid quota. Great Britain was not about to turn Palestine into a dumping ground for European Jews whom other countries, including the United States, didn't want. To do so would risk yet another Palestinian Arab uprising.

Chaim Weizmann, a Zionist who would later become the first president of Israel, parsed the Jewish problem with laser precision. In an address to an international refugee conference in London, he said: "The world seemed to be divided into two parts—those places where Jews could not live and those where they could not enter."

All eyes were on America, and President Franklin D. Roosevelt didn't relish the spotlight. Most Americans were nervous isolationists who didn't want to be drawn into someone else's war, and a good part of the working classes and WASP intellectuals were openly anti-Semitic. Roosevelt knew he had to do something. But what?

Ten days after the Anschluss, Roosevelt called for an international conference to address the growing refugee problem, which he foresaw was much larger than a few hundred thousand homeless Jews. France volunteered to host the meeting at Evian.

The call to action was more political than humanitarian. America was slowly emerging from the Great Depression and, although unemployment was gradually dipping, it still stood at a staggering 19 percent. Roosevelt found himself facing the twin pressures of isolationism and overt anti-Semitism. The latter had spiked in the 1930s with the advent of a string of anti-Semitic publications and the popular anti-Semitic radio addresses of Charles Coughlin, a Detroit Catholic priest. Father Coughlin had a following of more than forty million, and the Catholic hierarchy made no attempt to silence him.

Opinion polls at the time illustrate Roosevelt's political dilemma. A 1938 American Institute of Public Opinion poll asked the following question: "Should we allow a larger number of Jewish exiles from Germany to come to the United States to live?" Seventy-seven percent said no. Other polls reported that one-third of Americans thought the government should economically restrict Jews and one out of ten favored racially segregating Jews as well as deporting them. Many members of Congress and the State Department, including U.S. consulate officials who had great discretionary powers in granting visas, reflected the nation's anti-Semitism. The Veterans of Foreign Wars opposed the Evian Conference and called for the end of *all* immigration. And the American Coalition of Patriotic Societies challenged Roosevelt to "stop the leak before it became a flood."

What was a president to do?

If he sought to admit more Jews into the country, Roosevelt knew he would be pouring gas on the embers of isolationism and anti-Semitism, thus running the risk of losing the upcoming presidential election. A consummate politician, Roosevelt called for a high-profile conference. It was a deft sleight of hand that would simultaneously make the United States appear humanitarian, offer a sop to Jewish voters, win applause from the majority of Americans for not caving in to international pressure, and discourage the unemployed from staging angry demonstrations. Roosevelt invited thirty-three other countries to Evian. Only Italy and South Africa declined.

A lone *New York Times* reporter, Anne O'Hare McCormick, sought to challenge Roosevelt, the conference attendees, and the American public. With amazing insight and clarity, she wrote:

> It is heartbreaking to think of the queues of desperate human beings around our consulates in Vienna and other cities waiting in suspense for what happens at Evian. . . . It is not a question of how many unemployed this country can safely add to its own unemployed millions. It is a test of civilization.... Can America live with itself if it lets Germany get away with this policy of extermination?

Roosevelt wasn't listening. His invitation to Evian had reduced the conference to a cruel charade even before the first tap of the gavel. It said in part: "No country would be expected or asked to receive a greater number of immigrants than is permitted by its existing legislation." Having said that, the conference challenged the participating countries to accept more German and Austrian (Jewish) refugees either under their quota systems or current immigration laws, something the United States itself was unwilling to do.

Evian was little more than a ten-day paid vacation at the Royal Hotel, a luxury resort on Lake Geneva. Casino gambling, pleasure cruises on the lake, outings to Chamonix for summer skiing, five-star dining, mineral baths, massages, golf . . . In the end, the conference turned out to be historic, but not in the way Roosevelt had anticipated or hoped.

Hitler believed that Western democracies were cowardly and hypocritical. Evian proved him right. The United States did not send a single government official, high or low, to represent it at the conference because it didn't want to antagonize Hitler. Instead, Roosevelt chose a friend, steel tycoon Myron C. Taylor, and gave him the title of "Ambassador Extraordinary Plenipotentiary." One of Taylor's mandates was to ban the use of the words *German . . . Hitler . . . Jew* during the conference, to which Third Reich observers had been invited. Roosevelt didn't want to upset them.

Prior to the conference, the United States and Great Britain struck an under-the-table deal: Britain agreed not to bring up the fact that the United States was not even filling its *legal* German-Austrian emigration quota, if America would not propose that Palestine accept more Jews. As a result, the word *Palestine* was added to the list of verboten words. Also verboten would be any mention of the fact that out of its 1938 combined German-Austrian emigration quota of 27,370, the United States had only granted 18,000 visas so far that year. Of course, any Jew from these two countries could apply for a visa at the appropriate U.S. consulate. But there was a hitch. The United States required a certificate of good conduct from the German police from whom the Jews were fleeing.

Ambassador Taylor tried to put a positive spin on U.S. reluctance to admit more refugees. He promised that more German and Austrian refugees would be accepted under its existing quota and that U.S. consuls would be instructed to make it easier for them to acquire visas. In effect, the United States offered nothing. Taylor was hoping, of course, that countries with large territories and small populations, like Australia, Canada, and New Zealand, would open their borders.

One by one the conference delegates took the microphone and repeated the same message as if rehearsed before the conference: We are saturated with refugees and, therefore, regrettably cannot accept any more; we are willing to accept refugees as long as they are agricultural experts (by law there were no Jewish farmers in Germany and Austria); and we already have too many merchants and intellectuals and, regretfully, cannot accept any more (thus eliminating most Jews). Although the underlying anti-Semitism in the country-by-country refusal was unspoken in most instances, it was blatant in the responses of several countries:

- Australia said it currently had no real racial problem and was not eager to import one.
- Brazil said it would accept refugees if a Christian baptismal certificate were attached to the visa application.
- Great Britain promised to accept refugee children but not their parents out of fear of an anti-Semitic backlash. It did eventually accept nine thousand Jewish children.
- New Zealand noted its policy of admitting only immigrants of British birth or heritage. Since the conference invitation said participating countries were not expected to change their immigration laws, New Zealand said it wouldn't.
- Switzerland brazenly stated that it had as little use for Jews as Germany had and promised to adopt measures to protect Switzerland from being swamped by Jewish refugees. Switzerland would soon require all German Jewish passports to be stamped with a large *J*.

None of the Evian attendees seemed to understand the scope of the refugee problem confronting them. It was not just about a few thousand homeless German and Austrian Jews. It was about the soon-to-be millions of homeless non-Jewish refugees who were certain to overwhelm Europe. As one analyst at the time put it: "Viewed as a whole . . . this potential problem is vast and almost unimaginable."

The conference ended with a resolution to establish a permanent Intergovernmental Committee on Refugees to study the problem and design a framework to deal with it. The only one who thought Evian was a success was Myron Taylor, who reported to the State Department: "I am satisfied that we accomplished the purpose for which . . . the meeting at Evian was called."

The Evian Conference was a bonanza for the Third Reich. The pro-Nazi German press interpreted it as a tacit approval of the Reich's handling of the Jewish problem. And Hitler laughed all the way to Auschwitz. Evian only proved what Hitler had suspected all along: He could do anything he wanted to European Jews and the Western democracies would turn a blind eye. To some Jewish observers, Evian had become "Hitler's Green Light to Genocide."

No one explained the Jewish perception of Evian clearer or better than Golda Meir, a conference observer who would later become prime minister of Israel. In her memoir, *My Life*, she wrote with great angst:

> I don't think that anyone who didn't live through it can understand what I felt at Evian—a mixture of sorrow, rage, frustration and horror. I wanted to get up and scream at them all. "Don't you know that these numbers are human beings, people who may spend the rest of their lives in concentration camps or wandering around the world like lepers, if you won't let them in?"

In sum, the Evian Conference of July 1938 betrayed the Jews who trusted in world humanity, rendered them worse off than before, and opened the door to genocide. As one Jewish analyst put it: The thirty-two countries met, ostensibly, to help the Jews out of the jaws of the German beast; instead they tossed them to the sharks.

Four months after Evian, the Nazis celebrated Kristallnacht, during which thousands of Jewish businesses and shops were destroyed, hundreds beaten to within an inch of their lives, and hundreds more imprisoned and killed. Hitler was right. The world responded to Kristallnacht as it did at Evian—with shock, condemnation, and no action.

In May of the following year, 1939, the German transatlantic liner *St. Louis* steamed down the Elbe River into the North Atlantic. Flags were flapping in the wind and well-wishers waved from the Hamburg pier. On board the eight-deck ship were 938 paying passengers, all but one of whom were Jews fleeing Germany for their lives. They had all purchased landing permits from the Cuban government. Several had relatives, spouses, or children waiting for them in Havana. Most were on the waiting list for visas to the United States and planned to stay in Cuba until America granted them entry.

The voyage was a setup. Cuba had no intention of letting them off the ship. Caving in to anti-Semitic pressure, Cuban president Federico Laredo Bru signed "Decree 938" eight days before the ship departed Germany. The decree invalidated the landing permits. No one had told the passengers.

It was more than hiding the truth. The Reich was playing an espionage game and the *St. Louis* passengers were its pawns. Havana was the center of German intelligence and espionage activities directed against the United States. Nazi intelligence officers there had purchased top-secret documents detailing U.S. submarine designs and needed a way to smuggle them into Germany. The plan was simple: A Nazi agent, planted as a *St. Louis* crewman, would disembark in Havana, rendezvous with a Nazi intelligence agent there, carry the documents back to the ship, and deliver them to Berlin as soon as the *St. Louis* returned to Hamburg with its Jewish cargo.

Over and above the espionage payoff was the PR factor. Nazi propaganda minister Joseph Goebbels couldn't pass up the opportunity to make the United States look like a hypocrite in the eyes of the world. The *St. Louis* would show the German people that the Reich was serious about ridding the country of its Jews. Then it would demonstrate to the world that the Reich was allowing Jews to leave freely and unharmed. And finally, it would make concrete in human terms what Evian had told the world in theoretical terms: Nobody, especially the United States, was willing to take German and Austrian Jews.

To make sure Cuban president Bru would not change his mind under pressure from the United States and the world community, Goebbels sent fourteen Nazi propagandists to Cuba to stoke the smoldering flames of anti-Semitism. The strategy worked. Five days before the *St. Louis* steamed out of Hamburg harbor, the streets of Havana boiled over with forty thousand angry demonstrators, the largest anti-Semitic demonstration in Cuban history.

To command the *St. Louis*, the Hamburg-Amerika line, operating under the direction of the Reich, had chosen Gustav Schroeder, an experienced seaman and staunch anti-Nazi, to captain the ship. Even though the Reich didn't trust him, he was perfect window dressing for the charade.

The *St. Louis* reached Cuban territorial waters in mid-May. To the shock and anger of Captain Schroeder and the passengers, Cuba refused to allow passengers to disembark until a sales transaction was completed. President Bru put a price of five hundred dollars on the head of each passenger. The bill came to about half a million dollars (nearly $8 million today). It was a bluff. Bru knew the passengers didn't have that kind of money, and he gambled on the assumption that no one else would come to their rescue. Then, when an international coalition of Jewish and non-Jewish leaders called his bluff and deposited the money in the Chase National Bank of Cuba, Bru raised the ante to $650 per head. When an international negotiator tried to bargain, Bru abruptly removed his offer from the table.

President Bru's denial of entry left Captain Schroeder with two choices: return to Hamburg as ordered by the Hamburg-Amerika line or find another country willing to accept more than nine hundred refugees. Gambling on the generosity of America, Schroeder sailed north into international waters off the coast of Miami and aimlessly cruised up and down waiting for either a change of heart from Bru or a message of welcome from the United States. From the decks of the wandering ship, passengers could see blinking lights of hope from the luxury hotels lining Miami's beaches. A Coast Guard cutter shadowed the ship, not so much to prevent it from docking as to "rescue" any passenger desperate enough to try to swim to freedom, and to keep the ship in sight in case President Bru had a change of heart.

Captain Schroeder sent a message to Roosevelt. He didn't answer. The *St. Louis's* children cabled a plea for help to First Lady Eleanor Roosevelt. She didn't answer, either.

President Roosevelt's hands were not completely tied. Although U.S. immigration law prevented the *St. Louis* passengers from entering the country, he could have issued an executive order to accept them, a politically dangerous move. It would have been unfair to the 2,500 Jews already waiting in Cuba for visas, as well as to the many more thousands in Europe, all of whom were in line ahead of the *St. Louis* passengers. It would have triggered a wave of protest from the anti-immigrant lobby and encouraged the other ships filled with Jews roaming the seas in search of a home to head for the United States.

To complicate the issue even more, the U.S. unemployment rate was still over 17 percent and national feelings of isolationism and anti-Semitism had not changed since the conference at Evian the previous year. Courage aside, Roosevelt was not prone to commit political suicide.

The State Department visa division didn't keep Captain Schroeder waiting very long. "The German refugees," it ruled, "must wait their turn before they may be admissible to the United States." And immigration officials in Miami cabled the following blunt message to the German captain: "The *St. Louis* will not be allowed to dock here, or at any U.S. port." To further encourage the problem to go away, the United States offered the ship no water, food, or fuel.

The international press followed the *St. Louis* story with great sympathy, as Goebbels had hoped. The United States was no better than Nazi Germany, they wrote. It didn't want German and Austrian Jews, either. As the *St. Louis* pointed its bow back toward Germany and the lights of Miami faded like a dream, hope turned to despair. The passengers cabled President Roosevelt one last plea: "Repeating urgent appeal for help for the passengers of the *St. Louis*. Help them, Mr. President." There was no response.

The passengers knew with awful certainty that a return to Hamburg was a death sentence. Fearing mass suicides, Captain Schroeder set up suicide watch patrols. In a wild attempt to save themselves, a small group of refugees forcefully commandeered the ship. Schroeder talked them out of their futile mutiny and never pressed charges.

After Canada and Great Britain also refused entry and the other European countries did not volunteer to accept any of the refugees, Captain Schroeder devised plan B. He would shipwreck the *St. Louis* off the coast of England and set the vessel on fire. Under international law, Great Britain would be forced to accept the refugees as shipwrecked passengers. The plan, however, never came to fruition. Before he could execute it, Great Britain, Belgium, Holland, and France agreed to divide up the passengers.

The voyage of the *St. Louis* was an espionage and public relations success for the Reich. As for Captain Schroeder, the Federal Republic of Germany awarded him its Order of Merit medal after the war, and Israel posthumously honored him as a Righteous Among the Nations. But 254 of the *St. Louis* Jews in Europe weren't so lucky. They were murdered in the Holocaust, most in the killing camps of Auschwitz and Sobibor.

The Evian Conference and the *St. Louis* affair firmly established the first two planks in U.S. refugee policy. First, the United States did not want European refugees, especially Jews. Second, if it had to accept some refugees under its strict quota system to save face, it would make it as difficult as possible for Jews to enter the country even if denial meant death. And if a few thousand Nazi collaborators ended up in the U.S. refugee potpourri, better them than Jews, who belonged in Palestine.

CHAPTER TWO

The Triumph of Bigotry

The United States entered the war after the bombing of Pearl Harbor in December 1941 with its "no refugees—especially Jews" policy intact. When Sweden requested help in rescuing Jewish children, and when England proposed a bilateral conference to discuss the refugee problem, America stalled and stalled, then stalled some more.

Neutral Sweden came up with a plan in early 1943 to save 20,000 Jewish children. At the time, it had good relations with Germany and felt confident that if it asked Hitler to release the children, he would, if only to keep Sweden sweet. Already bursting with 42,000 Jewish refugees, including almost all of neighboring Denmark's Jews, tiny Sweden turned to England and the United States for help. It would welcome the 20,000 children, Sweden said, if England and the United States would share food and medical expenses and agree to resettle the children after the war. How could the two great countries refuse?

The British Foreign Office accepted the Swedish proposal immediately. The U.S. State Department waited five months to respond even though it knew, without a doubt, that Hitler was gassing Jews in death camps in Poland, that millions had already been murdered including 85 percent (2.8 million) of Polish Jews, and that Hitler didn't plan to stop until he made Europe *Judenrein*, cleansed of Jews. Polish emissary Jan

Karski, a Catholic, had made those facts clear to President Roosevelt during a visit to the Oval Office the previous year.

• • •

The Jewish underground had smuggled Karski into the Warsaw Ghetto and, disguised as a Ukrainian guard, into Izbica Lubelska, a concentration camp for Jews in eastern Poland. With the accuracy and coldness of a camera, Karski described to Roosevelt the atrocities he witnessed. When he finished he said: "I am convinced that there is no exaggeration in the accounts of the plight of the Jews. Our underground authorities are absolutely sure that the Germans are out to exterminate the entire Jewish population of Europe."

After stalling Sweden for five months, the State Department made a face-saving counterproposal: The United States would accept the Swedish plan only if it would include in the 20,000 Jewish children some Norwegian, non-Jewish orphans. The United States was worried about an anti-Semitic American outcry—*our soldiers are dying just to save Jews.*

By the time the amended U.S. plan finally reached Sweden—eight months after the original plan was proposed—Sweden's relationship with Germany had become strained. Convinced that Hitler would never release the children, Sweden scuttled the plan. No one knows how many of the twenty thousand children Sweden had hoped to save were murdered.

Around the same time Sweden proposed its save-the-children plan, the British Foreign Office suggested a British-American conference in Bermuda to discuss both the Jewish and looming non-Jewish refugee problem. Once again, the United States stalled. When it couldn't delay any longer, it tried to take credit for the idea, angering the British Foreign Office, which was in dire need of good press.

The tentative U.S. plan was to ask Hitler, through neutral intermediaries, to release several million Jewish refugees who were in German-occupied territory. If Hitler refused, the reasoning went, his moral position would be further compromised. When visiting British foreign secretary Anthony Eden was informed of the plan, he observed that any attempt to ask Hitler for anything fell into the realm of the "absolutely fantastic."

In light of Eden's criticism, Washington scuttled its tentative plan.

Ultimately, the United States gave its conference negotiators the following secret orders:

- Do not offer to accept any more Jews into the United States.
- Do not pledge funds for any rescue operations.
- Do not offer naval escorts for ships carrying any kind of refugees.
- Do not offer any refugee space on empty U.S. ships.

The Bermuda Conference was doomed to shame. It was structured by diplomats in the U.S. Department of State and the British Foreign Office who, to put it kindly, had little if any desire to help Jews. To them, Bermuda was like Evian, another sop to the "sob sister" crowd and "the wailing Jews." The two countries built the conference on a false dichotomy that no one could possibly challenge: Winning the war was primary; saving Jews was secondary. No one dared say publicly what they privately believed: Saving Jews would actually delay winning the war.

When the conference was over, the United States and England jointly announced that the delegates had passed a number of concrete recommendations to help refugees of *all* nationalities, but the recommendations must remain secret because of the war. The top-secret recommendations were to revive the totally ineffective Evian Conference's Intergovernmental Committee on Refugees so that it could study the problem in depth, and to ship twenty-one thousand Jews *already* safe in Spain to North Africa to make room for more refugees in Spain.

World opinion saw through the not-so-clever smoke screen. The general consensus was that the Bermuda Conference was a dismal failure. Both the international press and liberal American politicians called it a *farce . . . perfidy . . . an exercise in futility . . . a distortion of civilized values . . . diplomatic mockery . . . a yoke of shame . . . complicity with the Nazis.*

• • •

By 1948, more than two years after the war ended, the European refugee problem had reached critical mass. International refugee agencies had already settled 90 percent of the refugees in their Western European countries of origin outside the new Iron Curtain. But that still left more than a million refugees whose countries of origin were now behind the Iron Curtain. Even the United States recognized that Western Europe could not be expected to absorb them all. For these refugees to go back home would mean harassment, imprisonment, or death. Most of them were either Polish Catholics or Christians from Ukraine and the Baltic countries of Estonia, Latvia, and Lithuania. It was time for the United

States to step up to the plate. At bat was President Harry "the buck stops here" Truman.

The majority of Americans were still antirefugee after the war. A 1946 American Institute of Public Opinion Poll asked: "About a million Polish people, Jews, and other displaced persons must find new homes in different countries. Do you think the United States should let any of these displaced persons enter the country?" Fifty-eight percent said *no* even though U.S. unemployment was low. There were limited exceptions, such as religious and ethnic relief organizations who welcomed only their fellow religionists and countrymen.

Truman was not Roosevelt. Where Roosevelt chose to deal with the refugee issue as a political problem, Truman confronted it as a humanitarian problem. Where Roosevelt asked, "What is expedient?" Truman asked, "What is right?"

With typical bluntness, Truman challenged the Eightieth Congress in his 1947 State of the Union address. He said he didn't think the United States had done its share in accepting European refugees, and that new immigration legislation was necessary to admit more. It was not a popular stance. Nevertheless, the president asked Congress for a swift, fair, and generous American response to an international humanitarian crisis.

What he got was congressional silence.

In July 1947, six months *after* his call to action, Truman sent Congress a special message. "We are dealing with a human problem, a world tragedy," he said. "I urge the Congress to press forward . . . and to pass legislation as soon as possible."

Congress adjourned for the summer.

In January 1948, a full *year* after he first asked for new legislation, Truman again prodded Congress to ante up "at once so that this nation may do its share in caring for homeless and suffering refugees of all faiths."

Congress crept forward like a garden slug.

On June 2, 1948, nearly seventeen months after Truman's 1947 State of the Union address, the Senate finally passed a refugee bill; the House followed with its version ten days later. Neither chamber held a single hearing on its respective bill. Then, anxious to adjourn for the summer, Congress hastily merged both bills and, in a late night session, passed the Displaced Persons Act of 1948, which authorized the entry of two hundred thousand refugees over the next two years. The bill managed to incorporate the worst of the Senate and the House versions. The devil lurked in the details.

To begin with, the Displaced Persons Act of 1948 created an artificial "device" to discriminate against Jewish refugees. U.S. visas could be granted, the act stipulated, only to displaced persons who had entered refugee camps in Austria, Germany, and Italy *before* December 22, 1945. That seemingly innocuous, random date rendered ineligible more than 90 percent of the mostly Polish Jews who survived the Holocaust, since they sought safety in the West *after* that date. Then, to make it nearly impossible for the eligible remaining 10 percent to secure visas, the bill added a list of financial, occupational, and good conduct restrictions. Just as the United States had blocked the entry of the more than nine hundred *St. Louis* refugees under an old immigration law, it now blocked the entry of Jewish refugees under the new 1948 legislation. The reason for the bigotry was obvious: It was an election year.

The Eightieth Congress didn't stop with Jews. It used the same date "device" to block the entry of middle European Catholics, many of whom refused to live under communism both as a matter of conscience and out of fear of persecution. Most of these anticommunist Catholics had fled west after 1945, when it was clear that their homelands would become "independent" communist countries under the sway of the Soviet Union.

The Displaced Persons Act of 1948 further stipulated that 30 percent of the refugees admitted to the United States had to be farmers, a regulation that further discriminated against Jews, who couldn't own land, and favored Ukrainians who could and did. The bill went on to reserve fifty thousand slots to *Volksdeutsche*, mostly the descendants of seventeenth-century German settlers in Ukraine who maintained cultural and emotional ties to Germany. With one foot still in Germany, the *Volksdeutsche* had been perfect candidates for Nazi collaboration.

Finally, the act not only used the December 22, 1945, device to discriminate against Catholics and Jews; it also favored refugees from the countries "annexed by a foreign power" (the Soviet Union). The act mandated that 40 percent of the refugees to be admitted into the United States under the bill had to come from the countries now behind the Iron Curtain. It was generally known by 1946 that thousands of Belorussians, Estonians, Ukrainians, Latvians, and Lithuanians had volunteered to help the Nazi Gestapo and Einsatzgruppen identify, round up, and execute more than one million Jews, mostly Ukrainians and Belorussians, living in their communities.

• • •

Not only had Hitler given the SS the task of building and managing the Reich's string of camps; he also had put it in charge of the Final Solution plan to exterminate the Jews and Gypsies of Europe as well as the Reich's political enemies. To get that massive job done, the SS created Einsatzgruppen or death squads commissioned to liquidate the Jews, Gypsies, and upper- and mid-level communist commissars in German-occupied territories. These squads mopped up behind the German army as it marched east across Europe toward Moscow in Operation Barbarossa. Although they murdered all the Gypsies and communist bureaucrats they could find, the Einsatzgruppen specialized in unarmed, sitting-duck Jews. As the Nuremberg War Crimes Tribunal succinctly put it: "The purpose of the Einsatzgruppen was to murder Jews and deprive them of their property."

Given communication barriers and limited manpower, there was no way the Germans could identify, round up, and shoot more than a million Baltic, Belorussian, and Ukrainian Jews without help. To solve the dual problem, the SS recruited volunteers from local populations called *Hilfswillige* (*Hiwis* for short), who were more than willing to kill Jews. As one German army officer put it: "We were actually frightened at the bloodthirstiness of these people."

Hundreds of Einsatzgruppen field reports found by the U.S. Army and the Red Army in files in Berlin, as well as Nazi war crimes testimony, detail the work of the Nazi collaborators. Two examples serve to illustrate the degree of their complicity:

- Einsatzgruppe C engaged in an anti-Jewish action near the Ukrainian town of Korosten in September 1941. The group commander divided his unit into squads of thirty men, one of which was made up exclusively of Ukrainian volunteers. He ordered the Jewish victims to kneel in small groups at the edge of a mass grave. Each squad shot at them for about an hour before being replaced by a fresh squad.
- Einsatzgruppe A received orders in October 1941 to liquidate all

the Jews in the Belorussian town of Sluzk. The group commander divided his battalion into four companies, two of which were
made up entirely of Lithuanian volunteers. After the operation
was completed, the commander reported to Berlin "with deepest
regrets" that the action "bordered on sadism . . . with indescrib-
able brutality on the part of both the German police and, particularly, the Lithuanian partisans."

Heinrich Himmler, commander in chief of the Einsatzgruppen, witnessed a group C commando unit execute one hundred Jews in Minsk,
Belorussia, in August 1941, two months after Germany invaded the Soviet Union. According to an eyewitness:

> As the firing started, Himmler became more and more nervous. At each vol-
> ley, he looked down at the ground . . . The other witness was [General Erich]
> von dem Bach-Zelewski . . . Von dem Bach addressed Himmler: "Reichs-
> fuehrer, those were only a hundred. . . . Look at the eyes of the men in this
> commando, how deeply shaken they are. Those men are finished for the rest
> of their lives. What kind of followers are we training here? Either neurotics
> or savages."

Historians estimate that the Einsatzgruppen operating in the Soviet-
occupied countries murdered between 1.3 and 1.5 million Jews, Gypsies,
and communist leaders. Scholars also agree that the thousands of Baltic,
Belorussian, and Ukrainian volunteers from local police, partisans, and
militia groups were "indispensable" to the slaughter.

• • •

Joseph Stalin had no love for Nazi collaborators, whether real or sus-
pected. As a consequence, an estimated two hundred thousand cold-
blooded Nazi collaborators followed the German army west as the Red
Army forced it to retreat, according to German historian Dieter Pohl.
After the war, the displaced persons camps in Germany, Austria, and
Italy were bulging with Nazi collaborators.

In effect, the Displaced Persons Act of 1948 had a not-so-hidden
consequence obvious to anyone who bothered to look for it. More than
70 percent of the refugees eventually admitted under the act (around
280,000) were born in countries occupied or dominated by the Soviet
Union. By disproportionately favoring Ukrainians, Belorussians, and

Baltic citizens, the bill made it relatively easy for the Nazi collaborators among them to get visas to the United States. The net result? An estimated three to five thousand Nazi collaborators from Iron Curtain countries entered the United States between 1949 and 1953. Some would raise that estimate to as many as ten thousand.

As subsequent chapters will document, the FBI and the CIA welcomed and protected these Nazi collaborators like long-lost relatives. FBI director J. Edgar Hoover used them as spies, informants, and anticommunist leaders in their respective émigré communities. And the CIA encouraged and secretly funded their governments-in-exile that were taking root in America.

CHAPTER THREE

Dealer's Choice

As members of Congress began slinking home after passing the Displaced Persons Act, President Truman greeted the new bill with anger and disgust. Congress had delivered an embarrassing piece of legislation founded on "abhorrent intolerance" and left him little choice. The clock was ticking on the refugee bomb and Congress was on summer vacation. Convinced that a flawed act was better than no act, Truman signed the bill, then verbally took the Eightieth "Do Nothing Congress" to the woodshed.

"If Congress were still in session," he said, "I would return this bill without my approval and urge that a fairer, more humane bill be passed. In its present form, this bill is flagrantly discriminatory. It mocks the American tradition of fair play."

Truman hoped that special-interest opposition to the bill, mostly from Jews and middle European Catholics, would shame lawmakers into approving a series of corrective amendments. With that in mind, he called a special session of Congress a month after passage of the act and laid out an eleven-point legislative agenda. One point asked for an amended Displaced Persons Act that would eliminate the discriminatory regulations.

Congress failed to act for two years.

Finally, in 1950, Congress extended the act for two more years in a new bill that admitted another two hundred thousand refugees, eliminated the anti-Jewish and anti-Catholic "device," and erased the preference for farmers and Baltic immigrants. By that time, however, more than one hundred thousand Belorussian, Estonian, Latvian, Lithuanian, and Ukrainian refugees had already entered the country.

The 1950 act charged the Immigration and Naturalization Service (INS) with deporting refugees who had entered the country illegally and/or had become American citizens illegally. Although the act did not specifically exclude former Nazis and Nazi collaborators, it did bar "any person who advocated or assisted in the persecution of any person because of race, religion, or national origin." Important for the future case against John Demjanjuk, the act also excluded refugees who lied "to make themselves eligible for admission."

It sounded simple on paper. The reality was something else. INS investigators had to find the estimated three to five thousand illegal *Hiwis* hiding in communities across the country, collect incriminating documents from the Soviet Union and its satellites, pierce the Iron Curtain to find and interview eyewitnesses, and persuade the Soviet Union to allow willing witnesses to testify in the United States.

To ensure enforcement of the law, the 1950 act also mandated "thorough" investigations of European visa applicants and written reports about their "character, history and eligibility." It was a logical first step. Unfortunately, the task of investigating more than six hundred thousand visa applicants landed on the overburdened shoulders of the U.S. Army forces stationed in the American Sector of Berlin. The assignment was more than a logistical nightmare. It was impossible, given the conditions in postwar Germany.

• • •

It would be difficult to overestimate the confusion and misery that all but swallowed Germany in the months after the war. The sheer number of homeless and displaced persons was staggering. Besides the millions of German soldiers who had to be screened for Nazi affiliation and the more than two hundred thousand SS officers who had to be investigated for possible war crimes, civilian armies of tramps clogged the roads. Ten million were fleeing the rubble and starvation of bombed cities. Another ten million were concentration camp survivors and former slave laborers from Eastern Europe. Another seven million were *Volksdeutsche*, mostly from the farmlands of Poland and Ukraine.

Add to this starving, sick, and anxious horde of humanity a German currency that was next to worthless and Western Europe had a problem of gargantuan proportions. Food was more precious than a wedding ring. Virgins could be had for a candy bar. As one German police report described the desperation: "It is impossible to distinguish between good girls and bad girls in Germany. Even nice girls of good families, good education, and fine backgrounds have discovered that their bodies afford the only real living."

To make displaced-person investigations even more difficult, the U.S. Army in Berlin had few investigative tools. True, it had access to a card index of SS officers, which it had found on the floor of a Munich paper mill waiting to be pulped. But as valuable as the index was, it offered no help in identifying Nazi collaborators who were not members of the SS. Their records were either in filing cabinets behind the Iron Curtain in their countries of origin or in the hands of the Soviet secret police, who had lucked upon a treasure trove of Gestapo records containing documents and files on thousands of *Hiwis* when the Red Army entered Berlin from the east in the spring of 1945.

• • •

To prevent dangerous persons from entering the United States, the Displaced Persons Act created a special Displaced Persons Commission (DPC) with the authority to determine which European organizations were "inimical" to the United States. Members of those organizations would be denied U.S. visas. By 1951, the DPC had developed an official country-by-country "Inimical List" of more than 275 organizations. U.S. officials responsible for screening visa applicants used the list to make eligibility decisions.

One organization defined as criminal by the Nuremberg International Military Tribunal and as inimical by the DPC was the German Waffen SS (armed SS), whose battalions were made up of mostly non-German volunteers. Besides fighting the Soviet army, Waffen SS volunteers executed Soviet POWs and assisted the Nazi Einsatzgruppen in rounding up, robbing, and killing Jews, Gypsies, and communists.

In September 1950, the DPC made a controversial decision that opened America's door for a group of Latvian and Estonian Waffen SS who had survived the war. In so doing, the DPC was following the lead of both the Nuremberg tribunal and the U.S. High Commission in

Germany. Both bodies had ruled that the 30,000 Estonian and 60,000 Latvian soldiers who had served in the Baltic Legions were conscripts, not volunteers. For that reason, Nuremberg and the High Commission defined them as freedom fighters protecting their homelands from a Soviet invasion and another Soviet communist occupation. As such, they were not true members of the criminal Waffen SS.

With that distinction in mind and with the full support of both Nuremberg and the High Commission, the DPC ruled: "The Baltic Waffen-SS units (Baltic Legions) are to be considered as separate and distinct in purpose, ideology, activities, and qualifications for membership from the German SS, and therefore the Commission holds them not to be a movement hostile to the Government of the United States."

The decision was as complex as it was controversial.

It is clear that the Baltic Legions did not collaborate with the Nazis in rounding up, robbing, and killing Jews and Gypsies for a simple reason—by 1944 there were few if any left to kill. At the same time, no one could possibly deny that there were war criminals guilty of genocide among the ninety thousand Baltic Legion soldiers. But how many? Hundreds? Thousands? No one knew in 1950, when the DPC ruled, and estimates today would be mere guesses.

It was also true that the vast majority of the Baltic Legion conscripts were not war criminals before being drafted. So why punish the innocent majority because of the crimes of the minority? Implicit in the DPC ruling was a decision to separate war crimes from *forced* membership in a Baltic Legion.

In sum, if it could be shown that a member of a Baltic Legion had committed war crimes as a member of an organization inimical to the United States *before* being conscripted into a Baltic Legion, he would be denied a U.S. visa. Otherwise, he would be welcomed to America as a valued, anticommunist freedom fighter.

American émigrés and their national and international organizations, such as Latvian Relief, Inc., were basically pleased with the DPC ruling. So was the U.S. Catholic Church because the majority of Latvians living in the eastern part of the country were Catholic. Jews, on the other hand, considered the ruling anti-Semitic. DPC commissioner Harry N. Rosenfield gave voice to the fierce objection of his fellow Jews in his dissenting vote (there were two votes in favor).

The argument of the Jewish community against the ruling was logical, to a point. Although most members of the Estonian 20th SS Division (30,000) and the Latvian Legion (60,000) were forcibly drafted into the Waffen SS, their ranks were populated with police and militia volunteers who had collaborated with the Nazis to round up, rob, and murder Jews, Gypsies, communists, and Soviet POWs *before* the January 1944 general conscription order. (Latvians argue that the conscription began in mid-1943.) Also in the ranks of the Baltic Legions were men who had *voluntarily* joined the Waffen SS—defined as a criminal organization by Nuremberg and as inimical by the DPC—before conscription began.

By exempting former members of the Baltic Legions, the Jewish community argued, the DPC unfairly opened America's door for the war criminals in their ranks. Hadn't the DPC blocked all former members of the Waffen SS in other European countries from entering the United States, knowing full well that not every Waffen SS member had volunteered, or, if he did volunteer, had actually committed a war crime? Why should Estonia and Latvia get special treatment?

A brief review of the scope and brutality of Estonian and Latvian collaboration with the Nazis helps explain the angry reaction of the Jewish community to the problematic Baltic Legion decision and the impact the ruling had on U.S. immigration policy.

In the end, the argument of the Jewish community turned out to be legally correct. Thirty years after the Baltic Legions decision, the U.S. Supreme Court ruled that involuntary induction into a criminal Nazi organization *was not* an extenuating circumstance to be considered in granting a visa to the United States.

• • •

The German army entered Estonia and Latvia in July 1942, a few weeks after it invaded the Soviet Union. By July 1943—long before conscription into the Baltic Legions began—nearly 100 percent of Estonian Jews, 80 percent of Latvian Jews, and 80 percent of Estonian and Latvian Gypsies had been executed and their property stolen.

In the last fifteen years, historical researchers and research institutes in the Baltic countries and in the West have confirmed in some detail what was already known in 1950 when the DPC ruled that the Baltic Legions were not criminal organizations: 1) Estonian and Latvian militia and police collaborated with the Nazis in the execution of their Jewish and Gypsy populations; 2) without their assistance, making those countries virtually *Judenfrei* would not have been possible; 3) the motives for this indigenous collaboration were varied; and 4) Estonia and Latvia are still struggling to understand and accept responsibility for their part in the genocides.

Estonia was unique among nations. With a population well under two million, it was the smallest nation in the east, with the smallest number of Jews (one thousand). It had a history of peaceful coexistence and cooperation with the Jews who lived in the major Estonian cities of Tartu and Tallinn.

Estonia also had the highest World War II death rate of any country— an estimated 25 percent of its total population. And it was the first country the Nazis declared *Judenfrei*. With the help of Estonian volunteers, the Nazis managed to wipe out the entire Jewish population in one year.

Those numbers, however, do not tell the whole story.

Before the Nazis finished building the death camps of Belzec, Sobibor, and Treblinka in eastern Poland, they transported to Estonia for execution an estimated ten thousand Jews, mostly Germans and Czechoslovakians. At the same time, the Nazis built a string of work camps in Estonia to house another estimated twenty thousand Jewish slave laborers from the west to work in the country's strategically important shale-oil mines.

The Nazis relied on volunteers from the Estonian Home Guard (Omakaitse) and Security Police to serve as guards to round up the country's Jews and Gypsies, and then to execute them along with the foreign Jews sent to Estonia to die. Most victims were taken to trenches in the woods and shot by six- or eight-man teams of German soldiers, SS officers, and Estonian volunteers.

Based on the testimony of eyewitnesses during the war crimes trials conducted in Estonia in the 1960s, the Nazi collaborators were brutal. They raped and forced women to work as sex slaves, then killed them when they were worn-out; they tossed babies in the air for target practice; and they buried wounded victims alive.

Just before the Soviets retook Estonia in 1944, the Nazis loaded onto ships the remaining Western European Jews who had been deported to work in the mines. The vessels brought them to Germany for reassignment at work camps. Those unable to work were executed. A few survived the war and were liberated by the Allies.

In neighboring Latvia, anti-Semites didn't bother to wait for the Germans to arrive. After the Soviets withdrew, they began hunting and executing Jews with enthusiasm. Once the Germans arrived in July

1941, these anti-Semitic Latvians helped them "incite other Latvians to a Jewish action without much prodding," according to American historian Valdis O. Lumans. In less than two years, the Nazis and their Latvian collaborators—mostly volunteers from self-defense and police units—murdered 90 percent of Latvia's 95,000 Jews.

According to Lumans, two of the most rabid Latvian Nazi collaborators were Voldemars Veiss, a lieutenant colonel in the Latvian national army, and Viktors Arajs, a Latvian policeman. Veiss, who was probably an ethnic German (*Volksdeutsche*), organized an initial auxiliary police unit of about four hundred Latvian volunteers to find and execute communists and Jews. Arajs organized a similar unit of two to three hundred thugs known as "Arajs' Boys." Both leaders took out newspaper ads seeking volunteers "to participate in the cleansing of our country of destructive elements."

Arajs soon became known as the "Jew Killer," a sobriquet he wore with great pride. His gang of Latvian terrorists, generally known as the Latvian Security Police, embarked on "drunken orgies of looting, murder, torture and rape," according to Lumans.

"[Arajs] seized as headquarters for himself, the luxurious [Riga] residence of a Jewish banker on Valdemars Street," Lumans wrote, "and turned it into a house of horrors for Jews, a veritable robbers' den, where he and his 'boys' tortured and murdered Jews for sport and kept Jewish women for sexual entertainment."

Over time, Arajs' Boys grew to more than a thousand. Not satisfied with killing Jews in big cities like Riga, they went Jew-hunting from town to town in blue, Swedish-built buses. Their hatred of Jews took them on raids into neighboring Lithuania and Belorussia as well. Scholars estimate that the Arajs' Boys murdered twenty-six thousand Latvians. They had no counterpart in any other land or region under German rule. Arajs' Boys were eventually conscripted into a Baltic Legion before fleeing west just before the Soviets retook Estonia.

One of the largest wholesale slaughters of Jews in Latvia was the liquidation of the Riga ghetto in late 1942, eighteen months after the Germans occupied Latvia. Approximately thirty thousand Jews were executed. Of those, six thousand were children under the age of fourteen.

For the sake of efficiency, the Nazis divided the ghetto in half. The evacuation of the first fifteen thousand Jews began at six on the morning of November 30. Sensing that death was about to "liberate" them, the victims were in a state of panic and despair. As Latvian policemen and execution commandos stormed their half of the ghetto, some single mothers, whose husbands had already been murdered, killed their children and then themselves. Riga survivor and historian Bernhard Press described the round up that freezing November morning:

> First the policemen, rolling drunk, forced their way into the old-age home and the neighboring houses. In the old-age home, they machine-gunned old people, sick people, and invalids in their beds. They drove out of apartments . . . people who were still in the midst of their preparations for the supposed evacuation, with truncheon blows and shots, curses and threats. Anyone who did not obey fast enough was shot on the spot. Small children were hurled out of windows onto the street.
>
> In the dark of night, Latvian policemen on foot and on horseback . . . drove people down the street like a panicky herd of animals. According to an eyewitness report, Herberts Cukurs [the Butcher of Riga] tore an infant from its mother's arms and smashed the baby's head against the curbstone. As the mother threw herself with a wild scream on the lifeless, bleeding body, he riddled her head with bullets from his revolver. Anyone who couldn't keep up was killed with a shot in the neck.

The column of Jews marched two hours to a forest in Rumbula, a dot on the map with a railway station. Older Jews arrived by bus. The killing began at 8:15 A.M. and ended at 7:45 P.M., when the last of the fifteen thousand Jews had been shot.

Latvian volunteers ringed the field in front of the killing site in the forest to prevent Jews from escaping and unauthorized persons—potential eyewitnesses—from entering. The exhausted victims were herded into the forest through a tube made up of two lines of Germans and Latvian police. There was little resistance. Those who had resisted were already dead.

Once through the tube, the Jews passed three stations. At the first, they deposited their suitcases and other belongings. At the second, they stripped. At the third station, they placed all the valuables they were wearing in a wooden box—watches, jewelry, rings. Then Nazi SS officers and Latvian collaborators led them down wooden ramps into pits dug by Soviet POWs.

Once in the pits, the Jews were ordered to lie down in rows "like sardines." The SS and Latvian executioners assigned to the smaller pits shot their victims from the rims above. Those assigned to the larger pits walked down the rows and shot each victim in the neck.

After the first layer of Jews was shot, the Nazis ordered another group to enter the pit and lie on top of those who had just been murdered.

When the executioners tired, they were relieved by others. A dozen Soviet POWs stood ready to fill in the pits with dirt when the massacre was over. The Nazis and their Latvian collaborators killed the remaining fifteen thousand Riga ghetto Jews in the same fashion a week later.

How many of the Latvians who had voluntarily participated in the extermination of more than eighty-five thousand Latvian Jews ended up serving in the Baltic Legions in 1944, survived the war, and were granted U.S. visas is unknown. How many were hired by the CIA after the war as saboteurs, spies, and informants is also unknown. And it is unlikely that the numbers will ever be calculated with any degree of accuracy even after information stored in Eastern European archives has been sifted and digested, and the responsibility for the genocide is debated, fixed, and accepted.

Given the voluntary collaboration of Estonians and Latvians in the wholesale butchery of Jews in their countries, one can readily understand why the Jewish community was cynical and angry at the Displaced Persons Commission decision to open America's door for former members of the Baltic Legions.

• • •

In June 1950, Congress passed the Lodge Act, which authorized the U.S. armed forces to recruit up to 12,500 aliens into the U.S. Army to help fight the Cold War. The recruitment drive was part of the National Security Council's Psychwar-2 program, which was to be implemented by the army in collaboration with the CIA and with the full approval of the Department of State. The White House and military had found an eager legislative ally in Senator Henry Cabot Lodge Jr. of Massachusetts, a moderate Republican and decorated war hero.

A military man from collar to boot straps, Lodge was a perfect choice to introduce the bill. While still a U.S. senator, he served as a major in a 1st Armored Division tank unit and fought in North Africa. In late 1942, he returned to the United States to campaign for reelection, which he won, only to give up his seat in 1944 to resume active duty in Italy and France. In 1945, he retired from the military as a lieutenant colonel with French Legion of Honor and Croix de Guerre medals pinned to his chest. He was reelected to the Senate in 1946. As an army officer during World War II, Lodge became convinced of the need for an indigenous reconnaissance and intelligence corps made up of soldiers who spoke the local language, understood local customs, and knew local topography. Could the army ask for anyone better to introduce an innocent-sounding alien recruitment bill?

The Lodge Act left it up to the military to set additional enlistment criteria besides age and marital status. It did not forbid the hiring of Nazi war criminals.

When the Displaced Persons Act of 1948—which was amended and extended for two more years in 1950—finally expired in 1952, Congress passed Public Law 414, the Immigration and Naturalization Act. Missing from Section 212 of the new law, which dealt with who should be excluded from the United States, was a critical sentence present in the old law: "any person who advocated or assisted in the persecution of any person because of race, religion, or national origin" would be ineligible for a U.S. visa.

The omission slipped through Congress with hardly a ripple of protest and without public debate. The implications of the deliberate deletion, however, were far-reaching. In effect, a Nazi war criminal could *only* be refused admission to the United States, or deported if already living in America, if he had already been *convicted* of a war crime. In so ruling, Public Law 414 set a new immigration policy. The door to America was now wide open to every stripe and brand of former Nazi and Nazi collaborator, but it was closed to the feeble-minded, insane, polygamists, prostitutes, pedophiles, rapists, drug dealers, anarchists, and especially communists.

To make it even easier for former Nazis and Nazi collaborators to become American citizens, the State Department refused to accept the legality of a raft of Nazi war crimes convictions in the Soviet Union and its satellites because the United States did not recognize Soviet bloc countries as legitimate.

In sum, Congress and the State Department sent Europe a clear message in 1952: The United States was passionate about keeping *communists* out, but not *war criminals* eager to salute the stars and stripes and eat hot dogs with yellow mustard on the Fourth of July.

• • •

The Displaced Persons Act of 1948 and its 1950 revision, the Displaced Persons Commission decision to grant U.S. visas to former members of the Baltic Legions, the Lodge Act, and Public Law 414 solidified long-standing U.S. immigration policy and practice. The United States would accept Western European refugees only with great reluctance and little generosity. It would do whatever it could to exclude Jews and middle European Catholics. At the same time, it would welcome their murderers. Virtually every Belorussian, Estonian, Latvian, Lithuanian, and Ukrainian was eligible for an unchallenged U.S. visa. All a Nazi collaborator had to do was to spin a credible yarn, then swear to it.

As a result, the White House, State Department, and Congress had stacked the deck to favor Europe's Nazi collaborators in the immigration game—easy visas, anonymity, safe places to hide, an immigration law nearly impossible to enforce, and the near-total indifference of the American public.

Given those odds, John Demjanjuk should have lived the rest of his life in the peace and comfort of Seven Hills, Ohio, surrounded by his family and Ukrainian friends, under the protection of U.S. law. But his luck was about to change.

It all began with Hermine Braunsteiner, a Nazi war criminal living quietly on Long Island.

CHAPTER FOUR

The First Domino

Hermine Braunsteiner's calling card was a pair of steel-studded boots. Her specialty was using them to stomp women and children at Majdanek, a concentration and death camp in eastern Poland where the Nazis murdered an estimated 1.5 million people, half of them Jewish. Braunsteiner was the vice commandant of the women's sector there.

"I've seen cruel men and cruel women," recalled a Majdanek survivor. "And Hermine Braunsteiner was one of the most vicious I ever met." Prisoners called her *Stute von Majdanek* (Mare from Majdanek).

When the SS began to evacuate the camp in 1944 in advance of the Red Army, they sent Braunsteiner to supervise a small German labor camp for women and children just outside Berlin. It was a subcamp of the larger Ravensbrück prison for Polish, Jewish, and Gypsy women. Her war crimes there would one day come back to haunt her.

In 1958, Braunsteiner immigrated to Nova Scotia, Canada, to marry Russell Ryan, an American Air Force enlisted man whom she had met in Austria, her homeland. In 1959, the couple moved to Maspeth in Queens, New York, where Hermine took a job as a machinist in a clothing factory. *New York Times* reporter Joseph Lelyveld found her in Maspeth in 1964 living a frugal life.

Based on information supplied by Nazi hunter Simon Wiesenthal, Lelyveld wrote an article, "Former Nazi Camp Guard Is Now a Housewife in Queens." The piece turned out to be an important story because it served to remind Americans that there actually were former Nazis hiding in America and not a single one had ever been deported. The story was the first domino to tumble in a row that would lead eventually to John Demjanjuk, and its falling prompted the building of a wall of government resistance and obstruction.

After the *Times* story appeared, the INS promised to review the Braunsteiner case. But when it thought interest in her story had waned, the INS closed its "investigation," claiming there wasn't enough evidence to strip Braunsteiner of her citizenship. Not that it ever tried to find any. INS never bothered to ask officials in Berlin, Tel Aviv, Warsaw, or Vienna for any evidence that might be sitting in their files, and it seemed to have conveniently forgotten that Austria had already convicted Braunsteiner of a war crime, which made her ineligible for U.S. citizenship.

When the media wouldn't let go of the mildly sensational story, the INS reopened the case in 1971—seven years later—because of "periodic and highly vocal interest." It assigned the Braunsteiner case to Anthony DeVito, an INS investigator in the New York regional office, which had jurisdiction over Long Island cases.

DeVito had spent most of his twenty years at the INS looking in closets for suspected communist subversives. Braunsteiner was his first alleged Nazi assignment and it changed his life. From the day he wrote "Braunsteiner" on his case file folder, DeVito hardly had a good night's sleep.

It all began with the list of eyewitnesses DeVito found with the help of Otto Karbach, an old Nazi hunter on the staff of the World Jewish Congress. At first, DeVito was pleased. With a dozen eyewitnesses to Braunsteiner's war crimes, the case was turning out to be a slam dunk. But once the eyewitnesses agreed to actually testify against Braunsteiner, the investigation honeymoon abruptly ended. The government started mistreating and harassing the witnesses. It was as if Washington wanted to scare them off.

Besides witness intimidation, there were veiled phone threats to DeVito's wife—made in German. Only the INS knew she was German and had her unlisted number. Since witness tampering was a federal crime, DeVito called the FBI. If the bureau ever investigated his allegations, it never bothered to interview him (the complainant), or his wife, or the Braunsteiner witnesses (the victims).

Then there was the money that mysteriously appeared. Enough for Russell and Hermine Ryan to hire a high-priced law firm that specialized in immigration cases. The Ryans were just scraping by. So who was paying their legal bills? DeVito concluded that the cash came from Odessa, the international Nazi network dedicated to hiding and protecting fellow Nazis from prosecution. But he was reluctant to air his suspicion publicly, for fear of being labeled a conspiracy fruitcake. Frederick Forsyth had just published his sensational novel, *The Odessa File*, and most people considered Odessa a myth. DeVito and Wiesenthal did not.

As it turned out, DeVito was partially right. A mystery person had set up a Braunsteiner-Ryan Legal Defense Fund, which collected thousands of dollars from right-wingers and neo-Nazis. Who knew? Maybe even from Odessa.

Strange phone calls, harassment, and untraceable money aside, it was the missing investigation reports that convinced DeVito that the INS was actually working *for* the Braunsteiner defense team. He had meticulously prepared summaries of his interviews with twelve Majdanek survivors who had identified Mrs. Ryan as Hermine Braunsteiner of Majdanek. He placed the investigative reports in the bottom drawer of a filing cabinet in the office of the prosecutor the INS had assigned to the case. Because the papers were essential to the Braunsteiner case, DeVito locked the drawer with a combination lock before he went home. When he opened the drawer the next morning, seven of the twelve summaries were missing. Only three people knew the combination to the lock— DeVito; the Braunsteiner prosecutor, Vincent Schiano; and Schiano's chief clerk.

The thief had to be the clerk, and the why was obvious. Either the INS wanted the names, addresses, and phone numbers of the witnesses so it could intimidate them, which would be witness tampering, or the INS wanted to give the information to Braunsteiner's defense team so they could harass the witnesses and/or prepare a strong defense, which would be obstruction of justice.

More troubling was the question of who told the clerk to filch the papers. DeVito's boss? Some suit at INS headquarters? If it was someone in Washington, how high? Hoover? Henry Kissinger? DeVito reported the theft to his regional boss, Sol Marks.

Marks yawned.

Prosecutor Vincent Schiano was just as frustrated and suspicious as

DeVito, but for an added reason. The Braunsteiner case was not his first Nazi assignment. That dubious honor went to Nicolae Malaxa. And INS's gross mishandling of his case left a bitter taste in Schiano's mouth.

• • •

Malaxa was a Romanian industrialist and arms manufacturer whose only allegiance was to money, which he amassed with ruthless cunning. One of the fattest and richest cats in Europe, he was the éminence grise behind the Romanian Iron Guard. The fascist group was a pro-Nazi, anticommunist, and anti-Semitic brotherhood of young killers who specialized in murdering Jews. Malaxa was such an Iron Guard fan that he flew the Guardist flag over his factories and required his five thousand workers to wear the green shirts of the Iron Guard, according to recently declassified FBI and CIA files. The Displaced Persons Commission had found the Iron Guard inimical and barred its members from entering the United States.

Malaxa provided the Iron Guard with the cash, guns, trucks, and cannons it needed for its January 1941 military coup and pogrom, during which five hundred to one thousand Bucharest Jews were butchered in a three-day bloodbath. Malaxa's stone mansion served as the Iron Guard command center and arms depot.

After the coup failed, Malaxa went to work directly for the Nazis. He partnered with Albert Goering, brother of Field Marshal Hermann Goering, who was later convicted of war crimes and sentenced to be hanged. The Goering-Malaxa enterprise produced hundreds of tons of Romanian steel for the Reich war machine, making an already rich Malaxa even richer. And when the Soviet Union occupied Romania, he sold steel to Stalin.

After the war, Malaxa bribed Grady McClaussen, head of the U.S. Office of Strategic Services (OSS) in Romania, to get him to America, according to recently declassified FBI and CIA files. With a renewable, three-month residence permit in his vest pocket, Malaxa entered the United States as a member of a Romanian trade commission whose mission was to convince the Truman administration to sell oil drilling equipment to Romania. Malaxa never went home. Too smart to seek U.S. citizenship, for fear that his Iron Guard-Nazi-Communist background would surface, he opted for permanent residency, which didn't require such a rigorous investigation. What it did require was political juice. And Nicolae Malaxa had plenty of juice. An estimated $500 million worth (roughly $4.5 billion today).

Whispers rippled through the Romanian émigré community that if you needed help in the United States, the guys to see were Senator Richard Nixon, soon to be vice president, and Allen Dulles, a former OSS spy and future director of the CIA. Malaxa aimed his wallet at them. Then the Washington merry-go-round began to spin.

Malaxa hired Dulles's New York law firm and Nixon's old California law firm, which still bore his name. Dulles in turn recruited Congressman John Davis Lodge of Connecticut to introduce a bill granting Malaxa permanent residency. The Dulles and Lodge families had been friends for years. (Lodge was the brother of Henry Cabot Lodge Jr.)

Lodge introduced the save-Malaxa bill in the House in August 1948, while the Eightieth Congress was preoccupied with plans for its summer recess. Lodge was hoping the bill would sneak through without notice. He ran out of time and it died in committee. That suited the CIA just fine. The agency had been watching Malaxa from the moment his toe touched U.S. soil, and it had long since concluded he was a communist agent and should be expelled from America.

"As Malaxa is extremely clever, efficient, perfectly self-controlled, very discreet, of an unbelievable perfidy, and a master in the art of bribery," the CIA concluded, "he must be considered as one of the most dangerous agents."

Next, it was Richard Nixon's turn. To sweeten the pot, Malaxa slipped Nixon one hundred thousand dollars, according to investigative journalist Seymour Hersh. In exchange, Nixon tried to do what Lodge couldn't. Too smart to introduce a bill himself, he asked his red-baiting buddy Senator Pat McCarran, chairman of the Senate Judiciary Committee, to add Malaxa's name to McCarran's 1953 joint congressional resolution granting permanent residency to a list of displaced persons whose visas were about to expire.

The Justice Department joined Nixon and began to pressure McCarran to sponsor Malaxa as well. Almost overnight, the most "dangerous" communist in America became the darling of Washington. The only contrary voice was the CIA, which still viewed Malaxa as a smart, powerful, conniving communist agent.

McCarran buckled under the pressure. Like Nixon, he was too smart to add Malaxa's name to his resolution. He asked his friend and fellow senator William Langer to do it for him. "Wild Bill" Langer was no stranger to dirty work. The beloved son of North Dakota had spent two years in a federal prison for taking bribes as the governor of the state. Langer offered Malaxa's name as an amendment to the McCarran resolution. Both the resolution and the amendment passed the Senate. It looked like Malaxa was in.

When the McCarran bill reached the House with the blessing of the Justice Department, however, Congressman Emanuel Celler spotted Malaxa's name tucked in near the end of the list. A Jew from Brooklyn, Celler was outraged. The guy was a Nazi collaborator and a communist to boot, and no matter how much money he had, he would never find a home in the United States of America if Celler could help it. As chairman of the House Subcommittee on Immigration, Celler legislated Malaxa's name off the list.

It was time for plan B. Malaxa would approach the government with a proposal to build a factory in Whittier, California (Nixon's hometown), to manufacture seamless tubes for oil wells. The timing couldn't have been better. The United States was embroiled in the Korean War and oil was in great demand. At the same time, Senator Nixon himself would argue that Malaxa was critical to the success of the factory and, therefore, should be a "first priority" candidate for permanent residency.

The plan worked. Malaxa got a rush order to build the factory, a fat tax break, and permanent residency. Malaxa took the tax break, but never built a factory. He never hired an architect to design one. He never bought or leased a building site.

A few years later, Malaxa made an extended trip to Argentina, a hotbed of Iron Guard activity that he had continued to support. Malaxa went to Argentina to seek government approval for a munitions plant he wanted to build there. The trip raised a problem that neither he nor his handlers anticipated. Under pressure from a chorus of anticommunist and anti-Nazi congressmen, the INS reluctantly revoked Malaxa's reentry visa on the grounds that he had fraudulently obtained his permanent residency by not disclosing his ties to the Iron Guard, the Nazis, and the communists.

During the sixty-day INS trial that followed, Malaxa refused to answer a single question Vincent Schiano put to him. He broke his silence only once, when he lost his characteristic cool and threatened to have Schiano fired.

While Malaxa was giving Schiano the legal finger, his money was hard at work. An anonymous Romanian dropped in to say hello to Schiano. He told the prosecutor he had some loose change—around $200,000. "What would it take to dispose of the problem?" Meanwhile, Malaxa's son-in-law offered $20,000 to a witness on Schiano's trial list to disappear in California, all expenses paid, according to recently declassified FBI documents.

When the courtroom circus finally ended, the immigration hearing officer found Malaxa guilty on all counts and ordered him to be deported. Malaxa took his case to the Board of Immigration Appeals. BIA overturned the ruling because, it claimed, the evidence was insufficient to support alleged Nazi-Guardist ties and the hearing officer had inferred too much from Malaxa's silence.

Nixon, now vice president, didn't want to take any chances. What if the INS challenged the BIA ruling? What if Malaxa was deported after all and leaked the hundred-thousand-dollar bribe out of revenge? Nixon knew the scandal would kill him politically. To protect his presidential ambitions, he asked his friend and advisor, Attorney General William Rogers, to intervene. As final arbiter in INS cases, Rogers upheld the BIA ruling.

Insulated with a warm blanket of cash, Nicolae Malaxa lived out the rest of his life in his luxurious Fifth Avenue apartment. He took his hundred-thousand-dollar secret to the grave in 1965. The INS didn't fire Schiano as Malaxa had predicted in his courtroom outburst. Instead it ordered him to report to his new assignment—the INS regional office in Alaska. Schiano quit in disgust. To him, the Malaxa legal fiasco was about more than losing a case he had clearly won. Something smelled terribly rotten. Washington was protecting Malaxa, a Nazi collaborator living illegally in the United States. Why?

There was no way Schiano could have known in the early 1950s that Malaxa was a double agent. He was working for communist Romania's interests in the United States. As a 1953 U.S. Navy communiqué to the FBI put it: "Mr. Malaxa is undoubtedly one of the top communist agents in the country." At the same time, Malaxa was operating undercover for the Naval Intelligence Agency on a project so sensitive that the navy hid it from both the CIA and the FBI.

When J. Edgar Hoover got wind that Naval Intelligence had a valuable Romanian source, the FBI director wanted to borrow him. He made his request to Rear Admiral Carl F. Espe, director of Naval Intelligence, who replied: "In view of the fact that an operation is involved which must not be jeopardized, I cannot disclose [the name of] this source [Malaxa] without his concurrence."

Malaxa had the last laugh. What Hoover didn't know was that the Navy's nameless secret agent was already an FBI informant.*

• • •

Nicolae Malaxa still stuck in Schiano's craw nearly twenty years later, when he rejoined the INS and got the Braunsteiner case. Like DeVito, he found the agency blocking his every move. First, there was the budget—just enough to "buy coffee and doughnuts for the visiting press." Then there was the office phone. Or rather, the lack of one. Schiano had to use the pay phone in the building or the one outside across the street. Next, there was the oppressive office he and DeVito shared.

"We were placed in a cubicle which shrunk from week to week," Schiano later testified before the House Subcommittee on Immigration. "For two of us to occupy that office, one of us would have to climb over the desk. This is where we interviewed the witnesses, and also the representatives of foreign governments."

At first, Schiano was baffled. In other cases, his boss Sol Marks usually gave him whatever he asked for, and without argument. The first day on the Braunsteiner case, Marks was enthusiastic and told Schiano to forge full steam ahead. The next day he "rescinded the order." And when Schiano asked Marks for a team to help build the case against Braunsteiner, all he got was DeVito.

Since the eyewitnesses on DeVito's list were critical to prosecuting Braunsteiner, Schiano began making phone calls to U.S. embassies in Bonn, Warsaw, and Vienna for help in locating the witnesses. One day, Europe simply stopped returning his calls. It was obvious to Schiano that Washington had warned the U.S. posts not to help him any further. In one instance, the INS wouldn't even pay the hotel bill of an eyewitness. Schiano and DeVito had to pass the hat.

The roadblocks continued. The Polish government had sent a package of Braunsteiner documents to the INS in Washington earmarked

---

*The FBI refused to release Malaxa's classified file under my Freedom of Information Act request. And the U.S. Department of the Navy said that its records do not go back to the 1950s. It suggested a review of CIA files. Under the circumstances, one can safely conclude that Malaxa's extended trip to Argentina was an undercover intelligence mission for the U.S. Navy.

for Vincent Schiano. Someone returned the package to the Polish embassy as unneeded.

Finally, there was the leak of a CIA document vital to Schiano's case. Austrian police had arrested Braunsteiner after the war on charges of beating female prisoners at the Ravensbrück subcamp. She was tried, convicted, and sentenced to three years in prison. When she had applied for a visa to the United States, she failed to disclose her prior conviction. Under American immigration law, she could be deported if she had obtained her visa illegally or fraudulently. To prove either, the INS would need a copy of her conviction record. Vienna was reluctant to release it, citing privacy reasons.

Schiano and DeVito found a way around the Viennese stonewall. They convinced a covert CIA agent to get the record of Braunsteiner's conviction for them. In return, the INS found a way around Schiano and DeVito. Someone leaked the conviction record to the Braunsteiner defense team. Now its lawyers were preparing to argue that the document was inadmissible because it was obtained illegally.

If supplying both the gun and the ammunition to the other side wasn't obstruction of justice by the INS or the Justice Department or whoever, what was?

When Vienna eventually relented and gave the INS a certified copy of Braunsteiner's conviction record, she knew she was in trouble. She cut a deal. She would voluntarily surrender her U.S. citizenship—no hearings, no witnesses, no public trial—if the government promised not to deport her. The government agreed and Hermine Braunsteiner went home to Queens.

As far as Schiano and DeVito were concerned, the "deal" was a fix, and both the INS and the Justice Department were in it up to their elbows. In effect, they had said to the defense team: "Go ahead and consent to denaturalization. We'll go through a superficial deportation hearing. Your client will be granted a waiver. Deportation will be suspended and she'll be able to regain citizenship several years later."

If that was the plan, the government grossly miscalculated the media and public response. The Braunsteiner deal only added more wattage to the spotlights already focused on her case. Americans finally seemed to be getting the message. How could a woman accused of stomping women and children to death be allowed to stay in the United States?

Under renewed media pressure, the INS once again reopened the Braunsteiner case. Eyewitnesses from Queens, Brooklyn, and Warsaw publicly testified about the steel-studded boots of the "Mare from Majdanek." The open-and-shut case dragged on until West German prosecutors lobbed a grenade into the Brooklyn courtroom. West Germany was preparing to try a group of Majdanek guards, mostly women, for war crimes against humanity. One of them was Hermine Braunsteiner. West Germany asked the United States to extradite her for trial. To grease the wheels of justice, German prosecutors gave the INS an additional three hundred pages of information about Braunsteiner and her crimes.

The evidence was overwhelming. On May 1, 1973—nine years after the first *Times* article appeared—Judge Jacob Mishler ruled that Braunsteiner should be deported to West Germany.

DeVito was shocked. After all the interference, harassment, and obstruction, the INS *actually won* the case it was trying to block. Maybe it was his imagination, but when DeVito returned to his office he was greeted with stone-faced silence. No handshakes or congratulations. No slaps on the back. No pink champagne or Kentucky bourbon in paper cups. Just hostile silence. He felt like he had walked into "an enemy camp."

For DeVito and Schiano, the Braunsteiner story had a "happy" ending. A Düsseldorf court convicted her of murdering eighty women and children, abetting the murder of another 202 children, and collaborating in the murder of still another one thousand prisoners. She was sentenced to life in prison but won release after fifteen years due to a severe case of diabetes and a resulting leg amputation. She died at home in Germany in 1999, at the age of seventy-nine.

Schiano's story did not have such a satisfying ending. The INS wanted to silence him once and for all. This time, it didn't reassign him to Alaska. Instead it threatened to open a public investigation into alleged "irregularities" in his conduct during the Braunsteiner case. The INS never specified what irregularities. More than likely, they were Schiano's unauthorized requests to Bonn, Vienna, and Warsaw. Win or lose, public hearings would smear Schiano's reputation, kill any future career in government, and seriously hurt his chances of landing a decent job as a private attorney. Schiano understood the all-too-familiar Washington game. If he quit, the threat would go away.

He quit. Again.

Schiano went to Wall Street. In his office, he kept his well-fingered file on Nicolae Malaxa and a huge Nazi SS organizational chart.

CHAPTER FIVE

The Second Domino

One morning in 1972, Anthony DeVito got a cryptic phone call from Otto Karbach. The Braunsteiner case was still bogged down in court. "I have some useful information," Karbach said. As an INS investigator, DeVito was used to calls from whistle-blowers convinced their phones were tapped. Given the way the Braunsteiner case was going, maybe Karbach's actually was. But if Karbach said he had "useful information," DeVito knew he did. Every Braunsteiner lead the Nazi hunter had given him had turned out to be gold.

DeVito canceled an important lunch date with Schiano and agreed to meet Karbach at an East Side restaurant. After some small talk, the Nazi hunter got to the point. He had been following the Braunsteiner case with both interest and skepticism, he said. And he simply didn't trust the INS. Why should he? Immigration had done nothing about Nazi war criminals living in America for nearly twenty years, and now when it had an indisputable deportation case with Braunsteiner, it was doing everything it possibly could not to deport her. If the United States ever did send her packing back to Germany or Austria, it would be because of DeVito, not the INS.

What troubled Karbach was *why* DeVito was being such a bulldog on the Braunsteiner case. Unlike Karbach, the investigator wasn't a Jew who had lost family in the Holocaust. So why would an Italian Catholic from Brooklyn be so committed to smoking out a Nazi war criminal when his INS bosses, his church, and the majority of non-Jewish Americans couldn't care less? Could DeVito be trusted with a secret?

"Why do you care so much?" Karbach asked.

DeVito's answer was as painful as it was personal. Long before working on the Braunsteiner case, he had concluded that the Immigration Service was filled with thieves who made all the honest, hardworking grunts like himself look bad. A 1972 multi-agency investigation, codenamed Operation Clean Sweep, made that as clear as Polish vodka. Dozens of INS officials were indicted on charges of selling border crossing cards, smuggling heroin, stealing government property, and accepting bribes. It was a typical political investigation. It caught enough guppies to appear credible while letting the barracudas swim away.

As far as DeVito was concerned, Clean Sweep was nothing more than a diversionary tactic. It publicly tarred and feathered border agents in California, New Mexico, Arizona, and Texas, and left Washington INS bureaucrats dressed in their immaculately pressed suits. It never asked: Is INS management engaged in obstruction of justice? Or why were the State Department, the White House, and the Justice Department constantly interfering in the workings of the INS? Or who was running the damn agency anyway?

DeVito had an even more personal reason behind his passion for deporting Braunsteiner. During World War II, he had served as an investigator in the U.S. Army's Criminal Investigation Division (CID), arresting disruptive army drunks and petty thieves. One of his cases involved a rape, and he was driving around the Munich outskirts looking for witnesses. He stopped for a free warm lunch at the Seventh Army encampment in Augsburg. Everyone there seemed to be talking about Dachau, a concentration camp the army had liberated several hours earlier. DeVito decided to see for himself after chow.

As the very first Nazi concentration camp, Dachau was an experimental model for the thousands of camps that followed. The prison was located inside the town of Dachau, close to the railway station. Prisoners were marched from the station through the village to the taunts of residents who were ordered to jeer and spit or pay the consequences. Over the gate leading into Dachau hung the Nazis' first wrought iron sign that read ARBEIT MACHT FREI (Work Makes One Free). Near the prison barracks was Himmler's SS training school for raw recruits and for the seasoned SS officers he chose to run his T-4 string of "euthanasia" killing centers in Germany and Austria.

General Dwight Eisenhower had diverted the 45th Infantry Division of the Seventh Army to Dachau in the closing days of the war with orders to seize the camp, but not to disturb or destroy any war crimes evidence. When the first U.S. soldiers crept through the gate on Sunday, April 29, 1945, they found more than thirty-two thousand starved, sick, and crazed prisoners—nearly all Jewish—as well as three hundred SS guards. Himmler had ordered the guards to kill all the prisoners, then flee. In such a hurry to leave, they skipped the killing. What happened next became a closely guarded military secret.

Angry, shocked, and disgusted by what they found at Dachau, some American soldiers began shooting the SS guards who remained, including those who surrendered. Prisoners joined in the lust for revenge. In the end, fifty of the three hundred SS men were killed, in violation of American and international law. The irony of the slaughter was that they killed the wrong men. The SS war criminals who ran Dachau had already fled. The SS guards that the Seventh Army found were new recruits, some as young as seventeen.

Eisenhower reported: "The 300 SS camp guards were quickly neutralized."

When DeVito arrived at Dachau after lunch, he found five gas chambers, one lined with a tile-like finish and false showerheads. Above the door to that chamber hung a sign reading BRAUSEBAD (Shower Room). In a large room nearby, he found four furnaces with metal trays on iron wheels. Standing in front of one furnace was an American soldier pushing the conveyor in and out, over and over, in disbelief.

DeVito found piles of bodies inside and outside the crematorium waiting for the final indignity. Wandering around in the roll-call *Platz* were thousands of prisoners with color-coded patches on their gray rags identifying them as Poles, Czechs, Jews, homosexuals, political enemies, common criminals, or Jehovah's Witnesses. They chattered and shouted in a babel of tongues. One group was stoning to death a fellow prisoner who apparently had been a stoolie. The stench of rot, blood, and death hung over the camp like mustard gas.

The evil DeVito saw that April day in 1945 was beyond his comprehension. More than twenty-five years later, he could still smell Dachau in the East Side restaurant as he told Karbach his story. The Jew understood. He was ready to take a chance on the Italian Catholic who *knew*. He slid two pieces of paper across the lunch table.

"A list of fifty-nine names," the Nazi hunter said. All are living openly in the United States, he explained, and there are eyewitnesses willing to testify against many of them. "We are counting on you."

DeVito knew that if he passed Karbach's list up the line, his boss would get orders from Washington to bury the names so deep that no one would ever find them. So he devised a three-point plan to protect the list. First, he would keep a copy in a secure place. Second, he would create an internal INS paper trail that would prevent the service from asking later, "What list?" Third, he would investigate the names on the list on his own, hoping to build strong cases against them—cases that could not be denied.

If all else failed, there was always the *New York Times*.

John Demjanjuk was not on the Karbach list. If anyone in his Ukrainian community in Cleveland knew of any war crimes he may have committed, no one had reported the fact to the INS, or to Nazi hunter Simon Wiesenthal, or to the World Jewish Congress. And unlike the Braunsteiner case, no alleged victim had asked Wiesenthal or Karbach to hunt for him.

Even though Demjanjuk was not on it, the Karbach list still constituted an important domino, the second to tumble in the row leading ultimately to him.

CHAPTER SIX

The Third Domino

Publicity in the Braunsteiner case flushed more whistle-blowers into the sunlight. Two of them brought their Nazi collaboration cases to DeVito because, like Karbach, they knew he would take them seriously. Each had built an impressive file on a Nazi collaborator. One was Boleslavs Maikovskis. The other was Tscherim Soobzokov. Both were on the Karbach list.

• • •

During the war, Boleslavs Maikovskis was a policeman and the captain of the second precinct in Rezekne, a medium-sized town in eastern Latvia. The Displaced Persons Commission ruled that the Latvian police were inimical and barred its members from the United States.

As a Nazi collaborator, Maikovskis brutally rounded up Jewish and Christian civilians for execution by Einsatzgruppe A and burned their homes. In one purge, he delivered Jewish children from the Daugavpils ghetto to the SS to be shot and buried in a mass grave in the Pogulanka Woods.

An eyewitness at the roundup explained the role Maikovskis played. He described how Maikovskis dragged and shoved two Jewish women and two children into the group selected to die in the woods:

> I saw him lead two small children out of the ghetto and he pushed them to-
> ward the whole group that was standing there. The children were grimy with

black coal. They had been hiding. Maikovskis found them. . . . He beat them with the wooden end of the gun. They were crying, "Mama, Mama," and the tears streamed down their dirty cheeks. And then the mother ran out from somewhere. Maikovskis pushed her. He kicked her. She fell down. She got up. He pushed her and the children to the other side where the people were standing. . . . They took out all the children and liquidated them.

In another action, he supervised the mass arrest and execution of the entire village of Audrini, with a population of two to three hundred, for allegedly hiding two Soviet soldiers, according to court documents and recently declassified CIA files.

To make a point, Maikovskis marched the Audrini men to nearby Rezekne and ordered the entire town to gather in the square to watch. He lined up the men in two rows of ten each. The front knelt, the rear stood. Then he gave the order to shoot. The bullets passed through the heads of those on their knees into the stomachs of those standing behind them.

Back in Audrini, an Einsatzgruppe death squad took the women and children into the forest and executed them. Then they burned the village to the ground. For his efficiency and dedication, the SS awarded Maikovskis the German Order of Merit and the German Cross.

Maikovskis entered the United States in 1951, swearing on his visa application that he had spent the war years as a civilian bookkeeper for the Latvian state highway commission. He settled in Mineola, Long Island, where he worked as a carpenter for fifteen years. When he wasn't sawing wood, he tended his garden, went to Mass every morning, and served as an officer in Latvian American organizations until 1965, when the Soviet Union made a formal request to the United States for his extradition, on behalf of Latvia, to stand trial for war crimes. When the State Department refused to give up Maikovskis, the *Times* pounced on the story. To keep the media quiet, the INS opened an investigation into Maikovskis's alleged Nazi background, then secretly slammed the file shut when publicity evaporated.

DeVito knew none of this when, a few months after he had met Karbach for lunch, a whistle-blower came to him with a file folder and some old black-and-white film footage featuring Maikovskis as a Latvian cop. The evidence in the file was so convincing that DeVito immediately ran a check to see what, if anything, the INS had on the Nazi collaborator. He found a reference to an investigative file in the INS New York office, but the file was missing.

DeVito began to call around to other INS offices. He eventually found the missing folder in Detroit. Why the hell did a New York investigative file end up in the Detroit office when Maikovskis lived in New York state and had no apparent connection to Michigan? The answer was buried in the file itself—an internal INS memo from the assistant director of investigations in Washington to Sid Fass, the Maikovskis investigator, ordering Fass to drop the case. Fass was so upset with the deep-six order that he made sure the incriminating memo got into the file before the file was hidden in Michigan.

If the INS wanted to play games, DeVito was ready. He baited a trap. First, he notified his superior, Sol Marks, that he was poking into the Maikovskis case based on new and compelling information. After making a copy for himself, he put the Maikovskis file from Detroit in the same drawer where earlier he had placed the Braunsteiner papers, then locked the drawer with the same combination lock. The next time he checked, the file was gone. And it stayed gone for more than two months, until the *Times* was about to run a Maikovskis exposé by Max H. Seigel. Like a good reporter, Seigel called Sol Marks for comment.

All of a sudden, Maikovskis was back under investigation, and Marks gave the case to DeVito, "the famous Nazi investigator" who had nailed Braunsteiner. At the same time, Marks blitzed DeVito with a caseload of alleged communist subversives, each marked "priority." The only case in the pile on DeVito's desk that *wasn't* priority was Maikovskis. When DeVito opened the Maikovskis folder, the incriminating memo was missing.

What DeVito didn't know in 1973, but probably suspected, was that the CIA had recruited Boleslavs Maikovskis as a soldier in its psychological war against communism. He was the vice president of the American Latvian Association, a leader in the Committee for a Free Latvia, and a member of the International Peasant Union. All three groups were anticommunist, and the latter two were secretly bankrolled by the CIA.

His leadership in the Latvian international community placed Maikovskis in a unique position to spy on his fellow Latvians for communist sympathizers, hunt for subversive plots, strengthen anticommunism in the patriotic groups, and promote a Latvian government-in-exile. And as a member of the international Hawks of the Daugava River, the Daugavas Vanagi, or Vanagis for short, his outreach was exponential. An anti-Soviet organization with a reputation of assassinating Latvian communist sympathizers in Europe after the war, the Vanagis had fifty-five chapters in the United States established to assist Latvian orphans and widows. In short, Boleslavs Maikovskis was a CIA case handler's dream.

In November 1965, a Riga court tried Maikovskis and four others Latvians in absentia and sentenced them to death. The United States declined to extradite Maikovskis. Of course the CIA wanted to protect Maikovskis. Through Radio Free Europe and Radio Liberty (RL), the agency had illegally laundered up to a billion dollars, which it funneled to the Latvian organizations Maikovskis spied on as well as to scores of other anticommunist émigré groups. Deportation hearings on Maikovskis might accidentally expose the CIA's illegal use of funds and place it under the microscope of a congressional investigation. The United States was at war. What choice did Langley have but to shield Maikovskis?

• • •

The subject of DeVito's other whistle-blower case was Tscherim Soobzokov, a Russian from Circassia, a mountainous region of the Soviet Union between the Black and Caspian seas. Like Maikovskis, Soobzokov was a lieutenant in a Circassian unit of the Waffen SS (armed SS), which he helped organize to fight the Red Army. The Displaced Persons Commission ruled that the Waffen SS was inimical and barred its members from the United States.

After the war, Soobzokov made his way to the United States and was living in Paterson, New Jersey, where he worked as Passaic County's chief purchasing inspector. He soon became a leader in Circassian American organizations.

Reuben Fier, a retired New York City cop-turned-investigator for the Social Security Administration, stumbled on Soobzokov's Nazi background while checking a complaint that Soobzokov was bribing someone in the SSA to accept forged birth certificates of fellow Circassians, making them eligible for Social Security benefits.

For the next three years, Fier used all his cop savvy and government clearances to compile a fat dossier on Soobzokov. Armed with enough information to have the Nazi collaborator stripped of his U.S. citizenship and deported, Fier approached the New Jersey INS office. It treated him to a bum's rush. When he read about DeVito's work on the Braunsteiner case, Fier offered him the dossier.

After reading Fier's file, DeVito pronounced Soobzokov a slam dunk. Since the man lived outside his New York jurisdiction, DeVito gave the file to the New Jersey office, investigator to investigator. When he called a few weeks later to check on the status of the case, he was greeted with "What file?" There was a dossier filed under S, all right, but it was empty.

What DeVito didn't know in 1973, but probably suspected, was that the CIA had also recruited Tscherim Soobzokov. They first noticed him in Amman, Jordan, where he finally settled after the war. For him, Jordan was a logical choice. It was the home of a deeply rooted Circassian Muslim community of eighteen thousand that dated back to the late 1800s.

The CIA noted several characteristics about Soobzokov that made him a good prospect. He was bitterly anticommunist, a leader in the Circassian community (both feared and respected), and nearly destitute, with little hope of ever finding a well-paying job. The CIA also noted that he liked to show Jordanian Arabs his Einsatzgruppe ID card and brag about how many Jews he had killed, according to recently released CIA files.

Soobzokov was eager to work for the CIA, especially since it assured him that it didn't care if he had a war crimes history or had committed "moral lapses." Most important, the agency suggested that U.S. citizenship was always possible after his tour of duty. As part of its vetting process, the CIA put Soobzokov through a series of polygraph tests in its Beirut safe house to find out what he did during the war and how it could best use him as a clandestine operative.

After the vetting, the CIA gave Soobzokov the code name Nostril and trained him as a "spotter" in Operation Redsox, a joint American and British espionage operation. The agency housed, fed, clothed, and paid him. His job was to look for communist sympathizers among his fellow Circassians and to identify those who were so anticommunist— or desperate for money—that they would be willing to sneak back into their home country and perform dirty tricks for the CIA as assassins and saboteurs. Soobzokov himself went on at least one spy mission to the Soviet Union.

When his two-year contract was up, the CIA disbanded Redsox in Jordan, cut Soobzokov loose, and arranged for him to emigrate to America. It settled him in New Jersey, which had a small Circassian community, and before long his house became the meeting place for local and international Circassian leaders.

The CIA reemployed Soobzokov briefly and recommended his services to the FBI. The agencies sent him to the national intelligence center at Fort Meade, Maryland, outside Washington, for specialized training as a "Hot War Agent." He studied clandestine field craft and leadership. After graduation, the CIA sent him back to Jordan for three months, this time to spot, train, and send Circassian agents across the border into Syria.

The CIA decided to cut Soobzokov loose permanently in 1960 because of "discrepancies" in his war biography that he couldn't clarify. That was bureaucratese for "the guy was a liar." He continued to do odd jobs for the FBI, supplying the bureau with "valuable information on numerous" individuals of interest.

Naturally, when DeVito began sniffing around Soobzokov's Nazi background, Washington got very nervous. The FBI and CIA were still running illegal clandestine operations in the early 1970s and they needed to make the Soobzokov investigation go away.

• • •

The Maikovskis and Soobzokov cases pushed DeVito over the edge. As a Nazi investigator, he felt trapped inside a vicious circle. The INS had blocked his every move in three Nazi collaborator cases. The agency failed to investigate itself with even a show of integrity. The FBI either looked the other way or gave the INS a cursory glance and pronounced it clean. And the Justice Department itself seemed to be working for the other side.

Disgusted and bruised, DeVito told his boss to go to hell and took early retirement. Then he and Schiano teamed up to play their trump card. Using media pressure had worked in the past, maybe it would again. They described to the *New York Times*, point by point, how their boss Sol Marks and his Washington shadow-superior had "hampered" their investigation into, and prosecution of, Hermine Braunsteiner.

Brushing their allegations aside like a piece of lint, Marks simply dismissed DeVito and Schiano as "romantics." If he expected the issue to go away, he was wrong. The *Times* article about DeVito, Schiano, and the government's obstruction of the Braunsteiner case became the third domino to topple in the row leading to John Demjanjuk.

CHAPTER SEVEN

The Fourth Domino

Elizabeth Holtzman smelled a rat. A representative from Brooklyn and the youngest woman ever elected to Congress, she was in office only a few months when she got an anonymous phone call from a mid-level INS bureaucrat requesting a confidential meeting. The man was calling her because she was both Jewish and a member of the House Subcommittee on Immigration, which monitored the workings of the INS. Not sure what to expect, Holtzman invited her administrative assistant to sit in as a witness. The year was 1973. Schiano had just quit and DeVito had just retired.

"There is a matter that is troubling me greatly," the man said. He did not give his name and Holtzman did not ask for it. "The Immigration Service has a list of Nazi war criminals living in America, and it is doing nothing about them."

Holtzman didn't know what to think. The whistle-blower was clearly agitated and appeared deeply ashamed of what he considered an INS cover-up. Holtzman could almost feel his moral outrage. Of Armenian descent, the man was no stranger to ethnic cleansing. The Turks had systematically murdered more than one million of his ancestors before and during World War I.

At first blush, the allegation seemed impossible. If there was a list, as the whistle-blower said, where did it come from? Who at INS was sitting on it? Why would an enforcement agency under the aegis of the

Justice Department protect the criminals it was supposed to keep out of the country? If there was a cover-up, it would have to involve the highest levels of the INS and perhaps the Justice Department itself.

"If the man was right," Holtzman thought, "the information was explosive."

As a junior member on the Immigration Subcommittee with about as much clout as a secretary in a basement office, Holtzman knew she would have to pick her time and place carefully if she was going to allege INS obstruction of justice. She tucked the information in the back of her mind and waited for the right moment. It would be a short wait. The subcommittee would soon be holding its annual INS oversight hearing.

Three months before the April 1974 subcommittee hearing, the *New York Times* had published its article about DeVito and Schiano leaving the INS and why. Their allegations confirmed what the whistle-blower had told Holtzman months before. She found Sol Marks's rebuttal—they're "romantics"—arrogant. She was surprised, therefore, when a much-humbled Marks confessed to the *Times* in a second article three weeks later that the INS indeed had a list of thirty-eight alleged Nazi collaborators living in the United States. This was essentially the Karbach list minus twenty-one names the INS had culled—either because they had died or the service said it couldn't find them.

At the April subcommittee oversight hearing, the new INS commissioner, General Leonard Chapman, retired commandant of the Marine Corps, was just finishing his testimony about a group of Haitian refugees trying get into the United States when Holtzman requested the floor. Although she was primed to hunt bear, she put on a nice face. She had no grievance with the newly appointed Chapman. It was the INS bureaucracy she was after.

"I would like to welcome the new commissioner," she said, "and am pleased that after four months you still seem pretty optimistic."

Holtzman then called Chapman's attention to the two *Times* articles and the INS list of thirty-eight names. "Can you tell me whether any of these ... have been deported since the article appeared last December?" she asked.

Since Chapman was still learning his way around the INS, Deputy Commissioner James F. Greene, an INS old-timer, was present at the hearing to answer questions Chapman could not.

"None," Greene said.

"Do you intend in the near future to commence deportation hearings in any case, or has any case been developed to the point at which deportation proceedings can commence in the next few months?"

"Not to my knowledge," Greene said.

"Have any witnesses in any of these thirty-eight cases been interviewed?"

"I cannot give you specifics on the cases because they have not passed over my desk," Greene said.

At that point, INS general counsel Charles Gordon piped up. "We are in the process of developing that information," he said.

Holtzman was getting angrier by the minute. "What does that mean 'in the process of developing'?"

"Whether the witnesses are still around and—"

"Have you taken statements from any witnesses in these thirty-eight cases?"

"I can't tell you about the thirty-eight," Gordon said.

"I am surprised that since December 1973, not a single witness has been interviewed by the service. . . . Can I have some assurance of a timetable?"

"I am really unable to do so," Gordon said.

Holtzman zeroed in on DeVito and Schiano. "There were two officers mentioned in the *Times* article who indicated that pressure was put on them not to pursue these alleged war criminals. Have you or the service done any investigation with respect to their claims?"

Greene fielded that question. "The district director [Sol Marks] called the man in and said, 'I want the list.' . . . It was taken from him."

"When was that list taken?"

"Sometime last fall," Greene said.

"Can you explain why, since last fall, we are sitting here today and we see no investigation of any witnesses?"

Holtzman wasn't sure what to make of the Gordon-Greene game of dodgeball. Were they trying to cover their backsides or did they not even know what the hell was going on in their own agency? Or both? She now understood why Schiano and DeVito had cleared out their desks in disgust. Gordon and Greene were smothering the hearing room under a blanket of words.

Convinced that if she wanted honest answers she'd have to dig, Holtzman asked to see the thirty-eight case files. It was a long shot, outside the realm of proper procedure for a junior congresswoman. To her surprise, and before Gordon or Greene could object, INS commissioner Chapman told her the files would be ready for her in the INS New York office.

Chapman's response was the only straight answer Holtzman got that day.

The files were waiting for Holtzman the following weekend, thirty-eight folders stacked neatly on a metal table, each labeled with the name of an alleged Nazi collaborator. The more she read, the sicker she felt. Each file told the same story over and over: negligence in locating alleged Nazi collaborators; failure to interview eyewitnesses named in the files; refusal to seek help from Germany, Israel, and the Soviet Union and its satellites; interference in opening new cases, reopening old ones, and aggressively pursuing those already in play.

Holtzman came to the same conclusion as Anthony DeVito, Vincent Schiano, Otto Karbach, and the anonymous INS whistle-blower. To open the INS files was to come "face-to-face with evil and indifference to evil." Where was the national moral outrage?

There was no simple answer. No single explanation.

• • •

Americans felt a deep need to forget. Although World War II had been fought in Europe and Asia, it touched most of them. If they hadn't lost a member of their family on the battlefields or in the jungles and the seas, their next-door neighbors had. To some extent, the country was in deep denial, caught in the vise of post-traumatic shock. Supreme Court justice Felix Frankfurter summed it up in four simple words. "I can't believe you," he told Jan Karski after the Polish emissary described the gassing of Jews in death camps.

Karski's message was so big, so tragic, and so far outside the realm of human experience that Frankfurter simply couldn't digest it. Neither could the rest of America. The numbers were numbing, and Americans felt there was nothing they could do about them but plant white crosses and begin to rebuild their families and their country.

At the same time, America had just shifted from a hot to a cold war without missing a step and without taking time to reflect. The United States had a new enemy dedicated to destroying the very freedoms that half a million of its young soldiers had just died for. And this threat was not across an ocean in countries that were, for most Americans, just colored shapes on a world globe. The enemy was inside America, in classrooms and government offices, in labor unions and movie studios. A hundred rabid J. Edgar Hoovers and Joe McCarthys sprouted up overnight, riveting the attention of Americans on today's "enemy within"— not on yesterday's leftover Nazis. The only colors their demagoguery could see were red and pink.

In the face of this new threat, who had time to worry about former war criminals who posed no danger to America and who were, for the most part, staunch anticommunists and valued members of their communities?

Finally, many Americans chose to view the Nazi issue as a Jewish problem. If Jewish organizations wanted to hunt down the killers of their people, good luck. Their hunt was not relevant to the rest of Americans, who had more important things to do.

The argument was as ignorant as it was specious. Those who used it either did not know, or chose to forget, that the Nazi war machine killed more than thirty million European civilians who weren't Jews, either directly through execution, deliberate starvation, and overwork, or indirectly through hunger and disease. Thirty million was more than the combined population of New York, Los Angeles, Chicago, Houston, Phoenix, Philadelphia, San Antonio, Dallas, San Diego, Detroit, and San Francisco. They were men, women, and children from the countries of Americans' Christian grandparents: Poland, Bohemia, Germany, Hungary, Croatia, Serbia, Slovenia, and Ukraine. That fact alone made Nazi war crimes everybody's problem.

• • •

After she finished reading the files, Elizabeth Holtzman felt an anger so intense that she made a promise to devote herself to getting as many Nazi criminals as she could deported, hopefully to stand trial for war crimes. Time was running out. Anger aside, Holtzman was a pragmatist. To find, prosecute, and deport even a thousand of the Nazi collaborators hiding in America would be a miracle. A hundred would be a victory.

When she got back to Capitol Hill, Holtzman called a press conference. The United States had wasted nearly thirty precious years. Six alleged Nazi collaborators on the Karbach list were already dead, and war criminals were literally getting away with mass murder. The rat in the woodpile was beginning to stink.

With cannons of outrage blazing, Holtzman accused the INS of "appalling laxness and superficiality . . . creating a safe haven for alleged Nazi war criminals" and of being "haphazard, uncoordinated and unprofessional."

The release of the INS files to Holtzman, resulting in the fiery press conference, was the fourth domino to tumble in the row leading to John Demjanjuk. Three names on the Karbach list troubled Holtzman deeply. They sat festering under her skin like slivers. Two were alleged Nazi collaborators—Andrija Artukovic and Valerian Trifa. The third was a German scientist named Hubertus Strughold.

CHAPTER EIGHT

Welcome to the Big Leagues

A ndrija Artukovic was a leader in the Croatian Ustasha, whose fascist thugs (Ustashi) killed, or delivered to the SS, every Jew, communist, and Gypsy they could find. Their specialty was the slaughter of Orthodox Christian Serbs. Their brutality reached a new low in a war that was no stranger to inhumanity.

"Some Ustashi collected the eyes of the Serbs they had killed... proudly displaying them and other human organs in the cafes of Zagreb," one observer wrote. "Even their German and Italian allies were dismayed at their excesses."

The Displaced Persons Commission ruled that the Ustashi were inimical and barred them from entering the United States.

At first, the Catholic-based ethnic cleansing of Serbs followed a calculated rule of thumb: Kill a third, deport a third, convert a third. The formula didn't work. So many Serbs chose conversion that "Catholic priests were besieged by crowds of panic-stricken men, women, and children clamoring for admission to the Church of Rome."

With conversion no longer practical, the Ustashi simply murdered between 330,000 and 390,000 Serbs, numbers roughly equivalent to the entire population of Minneapolis. Much of the killing of Serbs, Jews, Gypsies, and communists took place in the Jasenovac concentration camp, whose commandant was a Ustasha Franciscan priest, one of dozens of Ustasha Franciscans who took part in the ethnic cleansing.

As Ustasha minister of the interior and minister of justice and religion in the Nazi puppet government of the Independent State of Croatia, Andrija Artukovic was frequently called the "Himmler of Croatia," responsible for implementing the genocides. After the war, Yugoslavia tried and sentenced him in absentia to life in prison.

Artukovic entered the United States with his wife, Anamaria, and their three children in 1948 on a ninety-day visa under the name Alois Anich. He joined his brother John in Surfside, California, where Andrija worked as a bookkeeper for John's sewer and road construction company. When his visa expired, Artukovic never bothered to renew it. To make sure his brother wouldn't be deported, John borrowed a move from the Nicolae Malaxa playbook. He and his rich friends "convinced" their congressman to introduce a private bill requesting that the Justice Department grant Andrija Artukovic permanent U.S. residency.

The bill was killed by Emanuel Celler, chairman of the House Subcommittee on Immigration, who was no more welcoming to Artukovic than he had been to Malaxa. But in spite of congressional refusal to grant Artukovic permanent residency and an eventual INS investigation into his wartime activities, Artukovic remained in the United States.

When Elizabeth Holtzman closed Artukovic's incomplete file, she was torn between puzzlement and righteous anger. An alleged notorious Ustasha war criminal was basking in the California sun. He wasn't a U.S. citizen, didn't enjoy permanent residency, and lacked a valid visa.

Was someone protecting Andrija Artukovic? If so, who? And why?

• • •

Viorel Trifa was a top-echelon Romanian Iron Guardist and the beneficiary of Nicolae Malaxa's guns and cash. A theologian, historian, and Gestapo school graduate, he was editor of the anti-Semitic Iron Guard newspaper *Libertatea* and leader of the nationwide National Union of Romanian Christian Students. The group was an anticommunist and anti-Semitic fraternity of university students and one of the Iron Guard's most rabid cadres. An adjunct commander in the Iron Guard, Trifa was a charismatic speaker. Like Hitler, he could whip a crowd into a frenzy. But unlike Hitler, who used anti-Semitism as political glue, Trifa actually *believed* that communism was a worldwide Jewish conspiracy.

The Nuremberg Tribunal defined propagandists like Trifa as war criminals because they made genocide palatable to the public.

Trifa and the Iron Guard presented Hitler with two dilemmas. Although the Führer applauded their anti-Semitic zeal, he didn't trust them because he couldn't control them. Because Germany had no oil fields of its own, the oil deposits in Romania were critical to the Reich. To keep the oil flowing, however, Hitler needed political stability in that country. The Iron Guard was about as stable as nitro in a jar.

Hitler assigned SS officer Otto von Bolschwing, chief of the SS intelligence corps in Romania (Sicherheitsdienst, or SD), to keep an eye on the Guard. Baron von Bolschwing was a good choice. He was a loyal Nazi and an aide to Adolf Eichmann, the architect of the Holocaust. Bolschwing's job was to craft solutions to the Jewish problem. His new assignment in Bucharest was to win the confidence of the Iron Guard, then report its every political move back to Berlin.

Nuremberg defined the SD as a criminal organization and the Displaced Persons Commission ruled its members to be inimical and barred them from entering the United States.

As a counterintelligence officer, Bolschwing knew that if he befriended the twenty-one-year-old Trifa, he would have entry into the inner sanctum of the Iron Guard (also called Legionnaires). Bolschwing stuck to Trifa like Liquid Nails.

Hitler's worst Romanian nightmare became real in January 1941. On January 20, Trifa signed and issued an anti-Semitic and antigovernment manifesto prompted by the assassination of a high-ranking German officer in Bucharest. The manifesto, which was proclaimed over the radio on January 20, condemned the political regime of Marshal Ion Antonescu for protecting the "Satanic" assassins who had murdered the German officer and for allowing Jews in his government.

"We beseech General Antonescu," the manifesto concluded, "to do justice by [the] Romanians. We demand the replacement of all Masonic and Judized persons in the government.

"We demand a Legionnaire Government."

The next night, January 21, between three thousand and ten thousand Iron Guard students rallied in the square in front of the state university to hear Trifa deliver a rousing, thirty-minute speech over a loudspeaker expanding the incendiary themes of his manifesto. He demanded the overthrow of the Antonescu regime and the establishment of a new Iron Guard government. He went on to praise Hitler as the savior of the world and demanded the execution of all Jews and Freemasons, whom the Iron Guard considered antifascist and pro-Jewish.

After the speech, Trifa led an orderly column of Iron Guard students through the streets of Bucharest singing Legionnaire songs and chanting "Death to Freemasons and Kikes." As they passed the German legation, where von Bolschwing lived, they shouted "Sieg heil!" and "Long live Germany!" By the time they reached Antonescu's headquarters, the crowd had swelled to twenty thousand angry, chanting students.

Trifa's call to action ignited a military coup and a three-day, anti-Semitic pogrom in Bucharest that quickly spread to eleven other Romanian cities. Iron Guard Green Shirts attacked the regular army and stormed into the capital's Jewish quarters.

Besides the usual burning of synagogues and the desecration of sacred Torah scrolls, Iron Guardists hung Jews on hooks in a meatpacking plant and skinned them alive, later using the skin for trophy lampshades and shoes. They cut throats in a parody of the kosher killing of chickens and hung "Kosher Meat" signs around the necks of the dead. They raped, stoned, and decapitated. One eyewitness described a group of Green Shirts kicking three naked Jewish women into a temple they had set on fire: "The wretched victims' shrieks of despair tore through the sky." When the four-day carnage finally ended, between five hundred and one thousand Bucharest Jews had been tortured and butchered.

After government soldiers quashed the leaderless coup, thousands of Iron Guardists scurried off to European capitals to set up intelligence cells and to plot the eventual liberation of Romania. They skipped town so fast that they left behind two hundred trucks filled with plundered jewels and cash, and a very unhappy Marshal Antonescu. In retaliation, he ordered the execution of every Iron Guardist foolish enough not to flee. Trifa was at the top of the hit list, but Antonescu couldn't find him. Von Bolschwing was hiding his friend in the German legation.

The Reich welcomed the exiled pro-Nazi Guardists into Germany and provided them protective custody. Trifa ended up in Dachau. Not in the Dachau prison, but in the prison's guesthouse, where he enjoyed a private room with heat, free access to a community lounge with a radio, and a monthly stipend for cigarettes, books, and movies. When he developed bleeding ulcers, the Nazis sent him to the best German hospitals and health spas.

In August 1944, the SS released Trifa from Dachau. He eventually made his way to Italy, where he taught history at a Catholic college.

Meanwhile, Romania sentenced him to death in absentia. Eyewitnesses testified at the trial that Viorel Trifa was more than just an instigator of carnage. He personally gave execution orders, they said. In one instance, according to an eyewitness interviewed by the FBI, Trifa ordered a squad of Green Shirts to cut out the tongues and pluck out the eyes of three families of Jews, then toss the bodies out a three-story window one at a time. The eyewitness accounts have never been independently authenticated.

• • •

Trifa received a visa to the United States in 1950, two years before John Demjanjuk. He told immigration officials that he had been the editor of a religious newspaper but was arrested by the Gestapo and sent to Dachau, where he spent four years before escaping. He denied being a member of the Iron Guard, which would have excluded him from U.S. citizenship.

The U.S. Army Counter Intelligence Corps (CIC) knew that Trifa was lying. In its background check, it had learned that he was indeed an Iron Guard member and a propagandist ineligible for a U.S. visa. How and why the United States granted him a visa, given his known Nazi collaboration, is not clear.

Like Demjanjuk, Trifa settled in Cleveland, home to the oldest and largest Romanian community in America and its Romanian Orthodox Church (ROC). While editing the church's newspaper, *Solia* (Herald), Trifa found himself caught in the middle of an unholy episcopal war that would both define and destroy him.

The ROC was hopelessly split over the authority of its spiritual head, Romanian patriarch Justinian Marina. The problem was that Justinian, who claimed an unbroken episcopal bloodline back to the apostles, was a puppet of the Romanian communist government. It was no secret that Romania wanted control over the fifty-five ROC parishes in the United States and Canada. The majority of Romanian Americans, who were more anticommunist than religious purists, rejected the "Red Patriarch"; a minority led by Father Andrei Moldovan accepted him as their true spiritual leader.

At the invitation of Justinian and with the approval of Romania's communist government, Father Moldovan went to Romania, where the patriarch anointed him bishop. Back in the United States, he declared himself the valid leader of the ROC. The Romanian American majority immediately elected Viorel Trifa to oppose him. That choice posed a major problem. To be a bishop, one had to be a priest. Trifa was a lay-man, and Moldovan and his fellow bishops refused to either ordain him a priest or consecrate him a bishop.

To solve the problem, Trifa supporters went to other U.S. Orthodox episcopates looking for someone willing to do the job. They ultimately settled on the Ukrainian Orthodox metropolitan, head of John Demjan-juk's church. The Ukrainian archbishop agreed to ordain and consecrate the Romanian Trifa even though the Moldovan faction warned him that Trifa "was a Nazi collaborator responsible for the murderer [*sic*] of thou-sands of Romanian Jews." The archbishop couldn't have cared less. To him, Trifa was a loyal anticommunist and a war hero.

In shotgun fashion, the archbishop ordained Trifa subdeacon, then deacon, then priest. He received Trifa's vows as a monk, then conse-crated him Bishop *Valerian* Trifa. The feast of St. Valerian is January 21, the day the pogrom took place. The newly minted bishop moved from Cleveland to the Romanian American episcopate's headquarters, a 250-acre farm in Grass Lake, Michigan, fifty miles west of Detroit.

Before long, Trifa was nationally recognized as a religious leader. As head of the forty-five-thousand-member ROC, he became a governor on the board of the National Council of Churches. And at the recom-mendation of Nicolae Malaxa, his and Richard Nixon's friend, he deliv-ered the opening prayer of the 1955 session of the United States Senate.

• • •

While *Bishop Valerian* was caring for the spiritual welfare of his Roma-nian Orthodox flock, including dozens if not hundreds of Iron Guard war criminals, Charles Kremer, a Romanian American Jew, was building a file on *Viorel Trifa*. Like Javert chasing Jean Valjean through the sewers of Paris, Kremer had been on Trifa's trail for more than thirty years in between filling teeth as a Manhattan dentist.

Then, one day in the early 1970s, Bishop Moldovan whispered in Kremer's ear that the balding and bespectacled Archbishop Valerian was none other than the Viorel Trifa he was looking for. Kremer wasted no time. He wrote to President Nixon demanding an immediate investiga-tion of Trifa, unaware that Nixon was tied to the bishop through Malaxa. INS deputy commissioner James Greene—the same Greene who tried to snow Holtzman during the congressional oversight hearing—an-swered Kremer's letter. "These charges were exhaustively examined and extensively investigated by this Service over a period of years," Greene wrote. "The conclusion was reached that grounds for deportation proceedings—or that he was excludible at the time of his entry—had not been established."

Kremer then fed the story to the *New York Times*. When the INS got wind of the soon-to-be-published article, it opened a deportation investigation faster than it could say "Nazi collaborator." Once exposed in the media, Bishop Trifa admitted he had been a member of the Iron Guard, but hastened to add that he had never "killed anyone, neither Jew nor Christian, nor a member of my Faith."

• • •

Elizabeth Holtzman was more than troubled by what she learned from Trifa's INS file. If the bishop admitted he was a card-carrying leader in the Iron Guard—a highly documented Nazi bedfellow like the Ustasha—why wasn't he deported? As DeVito would have said, it was a slam-dunk case. The guy had lied on his visa application.

Was someone protecting Bishop Trifa as well? Who and why?

When she closed the Artukovic and Trifa files in 1974, Holtzman probably suspected that the "who" was the FBI and the CIA. The "why" was mired in Cold War politics.

CHAPTER NINE

Cold War Chess

J. Edgar Hoover certainly wasn't asleep at the helm during the Romanian American episcopate battle. As soon as his agents reported that Father Moldovan had gone to Romania to be consecrated bishop by the Red Patriarch and that Trifa opposed him, Hoover opened an espionage investigation of both men.

From the start, Hoover knew that Trifa was an alleged Nazi collaborator, Iron Guard leader, signer of the manifesto calling for the deaths of civilians, and instigator of the pogrom that butchered who knew how many Jews. His agents even provided the names of Canadian Jewish eyewitnesses to Trifa's war crimes. Hoover wasn't interested in any of this. The job of the FBI wasn't to investigate immigration fraud, unless requested by the INS or the Justice Department. Neither was it the bureau's job to hunt war criminals hiding in America, unless they were a threat to national security. Cold War focused, all Hoover wanted to know was whether Trifa and Moldovan were communists, communist sympathizers, or anticommunists.

After two years of FBI interviews with Romanians in the United States and Canada, Hoover concluded that neither Trifa nor Moldovan posed a threat. Nor did he recommend a deportation investigation of Trifa for immigration fraud to either the INS or the Justice Department. For a very good reason.

Hoover and Bishop Trifa were on the same side. Both wanted the same thing—to keep communist Romania from gaining control over the U.S. Romanian Orthodox Church. For that reason, Hoover applauded Trifa's plan to install anticommunist former Iron Guard priests as pastors of his parishes, according to recently declassified FBI documents. If Trifa were deported, Hoover would lose an important watchdog in the Romanian community and an eyeball inside the American cell of Iron Guardists.

To Hoover, Trifa was more than just an anticommunist Doberman with a keen sense of smell. FBI field agents advised their FBI chief that the bishop could furnish "invaluable information" about American Iron Guardists and the political orientation of new Romanian immigrants. Trifa also had Iron Guard contacts abroad, especially in Argentina, home of a large contingent of Guardists dreaming of the liberation of Romania.

When Elizabeth Holtzman and the media began sniffing down Trifa's war crimes trail, the FBI quickly moved to protect him. Since he lived in Michigan, his FBI file was kept in the bureau's Detroit office. Before INS investigators and prosecutors could ask for it, the Detroit office shredded the papers. That allowed the bureau to later say with a straight face: "Trifa is not, nor has he been an asset of the Bureau. He has provided information and the same has been accepted." Without paper proof, who could allege otherwise?

• • •

Instead of investigating Valerian Trifa, the FBI began dogging the bishop's nemesis, Charles Kremer, according to Kremer's bureau file obtained under my Freedom of Information Act (FOIA) request. The investigation began in January 1967, when Kremer wrote to President Lyndon Johnson—as he did later to President Nixon—asking him to order the INS to open an investigation of Bishop Trifa for war crimes, which Kremer described in his letter.

> Mr. President, since this man has been able to get away with the murder of thousands of Jews, since he has been accorded the honor of becoming a bishop here in the United States, and since he has become friends of so many influential people who know nothing of his past, I fear the day that I shall see him a welcome guest in your presence . . . I have a complete file with undisputed evidence and corroboration of every statement I have made. . . . I am eagerly awaiting your reply and am grateful for your interest in this matter.

The White House immediately sent the request to the FBI. It asked the bureau to investigate Charles Kremer.

For the FBI, Kremer's accusations against Trifa were old news. "There have been numerous allegations against Bishop Trifa indicating that he may have been associated with the Romanian Iron Guard, a profascist group, when he was in Romania in the early 1940s," the FBI immediately reported back to the White House. "It has also been alleged he may have participated in atrocities against the followers of the Jewish religion." The FBI went on to say that the allegations were nothing more than an internal smear campaign orchestrated by Bishop Trifa's Orthodox Church enemies.

The FBI then opened a ten-year investigation of Kremer, the primary purpose of which was to determine whether he was a communist or a communist agent. The secondary purpose was to learn why Kremer was so determined to see Bishop Trifa deported. The bureau had a jump-start on its probe. It already knew a lot about Kremer and had once considered developing him as a confidential source, but ultimately decided against it.

"The NYO, after careful consideration of the personality of Dr. Kremer," the New York FBI office reported to headquarters, "concluded he does not appear to possess the qualities desired in a Confidential Source or a Security Informant." That was bureaucratese for "He's too independent and, therefore, not trustworthy."

Using its string of Romanian sources already in place, the FBI followed Kremer's every move—whom he visited and what they told him; whom he contacted at the Romanian embassy in Washington; what he said in speeches and the television shows he appeared on; which Romanian-sponsored concerts and ballets he attended; when he went to Romania and why; and whom he visited on his trips there. The FBI became suspicious when Kremer began lobbying Congress to grant most-favored-nation trading status to Romania and making plans to produce a Romanian cultural hour on a New York radio station "to be covertly sponsored" by the Romanian Tourist Office and the Romanian embassy Commercial Office, both in New York.

Ten years later, the FBI concluded that Kremer was not a threat to the security of the United States. On the contrary, he was a dedicated anticommunist interested in helping to reunite Romanian Jewish families and win concessions from the Romanian communist government favorable to Romanian Jews. Despite its findings, the FBI put Kremer's obsession to expose and deport Bishop Trifa in the worst possible light. "Dr. Kremer has two compelling motivations," the FBI concluded: "to be or feel important, and to harass Bishop Valerian Trifa."

The FBI also investigated the bishop. In an interview with bureau agents, Trifa admitted being the head of the Romanian Iron Guard student organization before the attempted coup in January 1941, but he disclaimed "responsibility" for any atrocities against Romanian Jews.

End of FBI investigation.

• • •

For Elizabeth Holtzman, the greatest insult to the memory of Trifa's victims was the lengthy interview the bishop gave in Romanian to Radio Free Europe in 1980 on the occasion of the fiftieth anniversary of the Romanian Orthodox Church in America. The interview was approved by Paul Henze, director of RFE and a former CIA agent, and it was beamed from Munich into communist Romania.

The Trifa broadcast made an already angry Holtzman spitting-mad. To have a Nazi war criminal represent the United States of America in the very country where he committed war crimes was not only insensitive and cynical. It insulted thousands of Trifa's Jewish victims and mocked the value of their lives. "It is outrageous," she told the *New York Times.* "Simply inexcusable."

Holtzman wrote a blistering letter to President Jimmy Carter demanding RFE director Henze's head on a White House platter. In response, Henze made bad worse. After admitting in a private meeting of the RFE supervisory board that the forty-five-minute Trifa interview was a mistake, he called Holtzman's reaction to it "silly." Someone leaked the minutes of the meeting to syndicated columnist Jack Anderson, Drew Pearson's successor as Washington gadfly. Feathers soon began to fly all over town.

The heat of Holtzman's anger reached Carter's national security advisor, Zbigniew Brzezinski, who had worked with Henze at RFE in Munich in the 1960s. Brzezinski reprimanded his friend—not for airing the broadcast, but for involving the White House in the flap. He then attacked Holtzman. "She is blowing this up into an enormous issue, practically painting Henze as a Nazi—McCarthyism of the left."

To Holtzman, it was an enormous issue. Radio Free Europe had been founded and secretly funded by the CIA in the years after the war. That the agency was still using its airwaves in 1980 was a safe bet, and the Trifa broadcast served to illustrate RFE's brazen pattern of hiring a string of Nazi collaborators and paying them with U.S. tax dollars, above and under the table. In the end, Paul Henze was not fired. Two whistleblowers from RFE's Romanian Broadcast Division who leaked word of the Trifa broadcast to Holtzman weren't so lucky.

Having received the FBI's support for more than twenty years, Bishop Trifa was a great fan of J. Edgar Hoover. In the name of his church, Trifa wrote the director: "The clergy and laity of the Romanian Orthodox parishes in the United States are unanimously inspired and grateful to you for your outstanding preservation of our democratic system and your efforts to keep out of our country subversives and subversive activities."

While Hoover and the FBI were busy protecting Trifa, the CIA was shielding his old Nazi friend, SS captain Otto von Bolschwing. The baron had turned out to be as much of a chameleon as Nicolae Malaxa. When he realized the Reich's days were numbered, he offered his services to the U.S. Army, provided valuable inside information about German troop movements and military strength, and led reconnaissance patrols, personally capturing over twenty high-ranking Nazis and fifty-five lesser officers, according to recently declassified CIA files. Most important, he supplied critical details about Germany's secret weapon, the V-2 rocket, and its closely guarded location. The army found him "virtually indispensable."

After the war Bolschwing joined the Gehlen Organization, code name Zipper, a U.S. spy network run by former German intelligence officer Reinhard Gehlen. (There will be more about the Gehlen Organization in part four.) In 1950, the CIA hired Bolschwing, first in Salzburg, Austria, then in Vienna under code names Unrest, Usage, and Grossbahn. He traveled on CIA missions in Western Europe as U.S. Army Captain Albert A. Eisner.

The CIA was both cautious and somewhat ambivalent about Otto von Bolschwing. It found him a shady, self-seeking, and egotistical adventurer and lover of intrigue with shifting loyalties, according to the declassified files. On the other hand, it deemed him extremely intelligent and experienced in espionage, with a wide circle of well-connected friends and sources. His understanding of Balkan politics was superb, and he had excellent Romanian Iron Guard contacts.

The CIA concluded that Bolschwing was "a valuable man we must control." Over the next three years, Bolschwing would run spy nets of Romanian Iron Guardists and members of the Hungarian Arrow Cross, another anti-Semitic, pro-Nazi group of thugs whom the Displaced Persons Commission defined as inimical to the United States. He undertook secret missions to Italy, Romania, Hungary, and Czechoslovakia.

By 1953, everybody in the intelligence world, from the French to the Soviets, knew that "Grossbahn" was a CIA agent whose real name was Otto Albrecht Alfred von Bolschwing. Not only was he no longer useful to the United States, but he was a security risk because he could be kidnapped and tortured for information. It was time to help Bolschwing realize his dream—to become a citizen of the United States of America.

While preparing Bolschwing's biography for the INS, which included Bolschwing's membership in the Nazi Party and the SD, the CIA uncovered a deeply buried secret. Bolschwing had once worked on the staff of Adolf Eichmann, the architect of the Holocaust and one of the most sought-after former Nazis in hiding. It was like digging up unexploded ordnance in the backyard.

The CIA hid the Eichmann connection from the INS and cautioned Bolschwing that, once settled in America, he should not contact anyone in the CIA unless it was a dire emergency. Nor should he apply for a sensitive civilian job or U.S. government job that would require a security check. Above all, he should zip his lips. If the media ever learned about the Eichmann connection, there would be such a storm of protest that the government would have to deport him.

Over the objections of the INS, the Department of State granted Otto von Bolschwing, his wife, and their two children U.S. visas. Bolschwing was so grateful that upon arrival in the United States, he wrote a note to his CIA contact from the Henry Hudson Hotel in New York: "I wish to express my thanks for the excellent arrangements with immigration authorities."

Like Artukovic, Bolschwing settled in sunny California, where he lived quietly for six years working as an international executive for the Warner-Lambert pharmaceutical company, until the Israelis captured his former boss, Adolf Eichmann, in Argentina in 1960. Worried that its former ace agent might be investigated and called as a witness in the

Eichmann trial or, God forbid, be indicted along with Eichmann, the CIA warned the baron to prepare a defense. Luckily for Bolschwing, Israeli prosecutors showed no interest in him. They hanged Eichmann in 1962. Bolschwing lived undetected for nearly twenty more years, until his name surfaced during a Trifa investigation in 1980.

• • •

Once the INS found Andrija Artukovic living illegally in California in 1948 without a visa, the Justice Department, State Department, and FBI buried his case for more than a year, until someone leaked the news to Yugoslavia that the Ustasha leader was living the good life in California under the protection of the U.S. government.

Right after the war, Yugoslavia had asked the United States to keep its eyes open for Artukovic, who was number two on its most-wanted-war-criminal list, just below his boss, Ante Pavelic, who like Eichmann was living in Argentina. To say Yugoslavia was miffed to learn that Washington was hiding Artukovic would be the polite way of putting it. Yugoslavia requested Artukovic's immediate extradition. It even gave the State Department his home address.

The United States ignored the request for more than a decade.

In response to the brush-off, Yugoslavia eventually fed the "Nazi-hiding-in-California" story to columnist Drew Pearson. Hoover was not pleased when he learned—probably through a wiretap—that Pearson was about to publish a nationally syndicated column on Artukovic. Besides summarizing the war crime facts in the Nazi collaborator's case, Pearson would be calling on President John F. Kennedy to scrutinize other war criminals living in the United States. That call to action threatened the bureau's string of war criminal informants in émigré communities. After alerting Kennedy about the article, Hoover advised the president not to answer any questions about Artukovic during an upcoming press conference, hoping that the Pearson story would fade into yesterday's news.

It didn't.

Yugoslavia responded to the latest U.S. stall with intense media pressure in the form of an eighty-three-page publication titled *This Is Artukovic*. The slick, eight-by-twelve-inch magazine, written and published by a New York public relations firm, was seasoned with snippets from incriminating documents, photos of charred bodies, and excerpts from

Artukovic's speeches, among them exhortations to his Ustashi thugs: "If you can't kill a Serb or a Jew, you are the enemy of the state." "Don't come to me unless you have killed two hundred Serbs." "Kill all Serbs."

Hoover was so unhappy with *This Is Artukovic*, which he considered pure Cold War propaganda, that he assigned a team of bloodhounds to find out who paid for it. Hoover was betting that it was the Yugoslav Information Agency, the mouthpiece of that country's U.S. embassy. If so, Yugoslavia would be in violation of the Foreign Agents Registration Act.

FBI agents spent months contacting and interviewing every news organization and American leader who had received a copy of the booklet. They duly recorded the postmark on each envelope and filed the envelopes away in the hope that Yugoslavia had illegally used the U.S. postal service. In the end, it was huff-and-puff drama. The embassy of Yugoslavia never faced a judge, and the FBI failed to convert *This Is Artukovic* into a public relations windfall.

• • •

The *This Is Artukovic* teapot tempest demonstrated Hoover's (and Washington's) mind-set about former Nazis and Nazi collaborators hiding in America. While investigating the alleged illegal funding of a booklet and the alleged fraudulent use of the postal service, the FBI showed no interest in learning whether the publication's war crimes allegations were accurate or not.

Hoover had long since made up his mind that Yugoslavian president Josip Broz Tito was using Artukovic for Cold War propaganda. A public execution of a much-hated Croatian would be a popular move in Serbia and would increase Tito's shaky credibility there. Hoover advised the State Department not to take "appropriate action" against Artukovic. The FBI chief was not about to help a commie like Tito.

In the light of intense media pressure, the State Department decided otherwise. It instructed the INS to open dog-and-pony-show deportation hearings against Artukovic, angering both Croatian and non-Croatian Catholic organizations. They began lobbying Washington not to extradite Artukovic, alleging without evidence that the charges against him were blatantly counterfeit. Even Francis Cardinal Spellman of New York, a leading spokesman for the Catholic Church in America, quietly lobbied against extradition, most certainly with the blessing of the Vatican. At stake was the World War II reputation of the Catholic Church in Yugoslavia, segments of which had openly supported and collaborated with the Nazis.

Artukovic's Ustashi supporters in the United States set up an Andrija Artukovic Defense Fund, just as Hermine Braunsteiner's friends had done for her. Dozens of Croatian Franciscan priests went door-to-door asking for donations, according to recently declassified FBI documents. The Justice Department turned the legal proceedings into an eight-year tug of war between Yugoslavia and the United States. Yugoslavia lost when the INS finally ruled that Andrija Artukovic was welcome to stay in the United States even though his presence was clearly unlawful.

While INS prosecutors and defense lawyers were pushing paper around Washington, Hoover was evaluating Artukovic as a confidential source. Soon after Artukovic settled in California, Hoover concluded that the Ustasha boss was "the uncrowned leader of the Croatian movement" in the United States, which was planning to establish an independent Croatia. As such, Artukovic had "considerable knowledge" about the major players in the current communist government of Yugoslavia and could provide information about Yugoslav espionage activities in the United States.

Hoover sent agents to California to pump Artukovic and to ask him to keep his ear to the ground for the footsteps of Croatian terrorists, real or imaginary. In return, Hoover would warn Artukovic about Serbian and Israeli plots to assassinate him as required by law.

Artukovic took the threat of assassination seriously. He isolated himself in his Surfside beach house. When members of the Jewish Defense League (JDL) couldn't get to him, they went after his brother John, chanting outside his home in Sherman Oaks, California:

"What do we want?

"Artukovic!

"How do we want him?

"Dead . . .

"Deportation now!"

The peaceful demonstrations soon grew violent when someone fired shotgun blasts through three of John's front windows in December 1974, narrowly missing his daughter. A month later, someone placed a bomb under the car sitting in his carport. It exploded at two o'clock in the morning. The flames scorched the side of his house.

There was no doubt in Artukovic's mind that the JDL wanted him dead and he was grateful to Hoover for literally saving his life. He wrote Hoover to express his "deep appreciation for the FBI's interest in his safety."

· · ·

The government resisted and blocked efforts to find former Nazis like Baron von Bolschwing and Nazi collaborators like Andrija Artukovic and Bishop Valerian Trifa because it was not eager for Americans to know that, while it was trying some Nazi war criminals at Nuremberg, it was paying others to spy for the United States and using them as sources and community stabilizers in the Cold War.

Former Nazis working for the United States aside, there was a more cynical and morally troubling reason for the U.S. government's reluctance to search for, try, and deport former Nazis and Nazi collaborators. The Pentagon was sitting on a nasty secret that was bound to shock Americans if it ever leaked out. That secret began with the third name on the Karbach list that had disturbed Elizabeth Holtzman's sleep— Hubertus Strughold—and ended in a secret army chemical research lab buried deep in the woods of Maryland.

CHAPTER TEN

To the Victor the Spoils

Months before the war in Europe ended in June 1945, the Pentagon was anticipating both an opportunity and a problem. The Allies had long since concluded that Germany was years ahead of them in weapon, rocket, submarine, radar, airplane, tank, and chemical warfare development. What should be done with the estimated nine thousand German and Austrian scientists and technicians who had designed and created Hitler's weapons of mass destruction? What should be done with their laboratories and factories, and the advanced rockets and airplanes, and tanks and subs they were bound to leave behind? What should be done with the tons of research housed in universities and laboratories or buried in mine shafts like pirate's treasure? What should be done with the seventy thousand tons of uranium ore and radium products stored throughout Germany?

The opportunity was to snatch them as war loot. The problem was how to prevent the Soviet Union from grabbing them first and how to prevent German scientists from rebuilding a Nazi movement in Nazi-friendly South America. What followed was a wild scramble for brains, documents, and materiel, the likes of which the world had never seen.

To make sure it got the lion's share, the United States planned its hunt for loot as it would a vital military campaign—clearly defined, totally funded, and fully manned. It set up T-teams (T meaning "Target"), or T-forces, composed of specialists who posed as civilians when needed—three thousand men trained in languages, document retrieval, and every scientific discipline from chemistry to physics. There were troops for kidnapping, doctors for interrogation, engineers for dismantling labs, bomb squads for disarming. The teams were given unprecedented authority to commandeer planes, ships, trains, trucks, and cash. Each team received a specific target—a named scientist, a university, a factory or lab. Mobile units directed the teams to their targets, even dropping kidnap squads behind enemy lines.

The initial idea in the months before the war ended was to vacuum the brains of important scientists. But the program quickly changed after the war. Why just interview? Why not offer these people high-paying jobs in America, guarantee them and their families U.S. citizenship, and set them to work on tempting new projects? You were a war criminal? Not a problem. We will protect you.

The Soviets were doing the same thing in what was called Operation Osavakim, but with a twist. They arrested as war criminals all the Reich scientists they could find, then loaded them on trains. Once in Moscow, they gave their war spoils a choice. Work for us and we'll pay you twice as much as a Soviet scientist gets, or go to Siberia and work for bread and soup.

"Competition is fierce," one observer put it mildly. Highly trained American teams would sneak into French, British, and Soviet zones in Germany and Austria to kidnap scientists. And the army, air force, and navy began "stealing from" each other in competing operations with code names like Backfire, Safehaven, Overcast, Lusty, and National Interest.

In the end, the United States came out the big winner. It captured prototypes of every conceivable war vehicle, weapon, and device—Walter submarines, thirty-nine different airplanes, partially assembled V-2 rockets, sophisticated bombsights. It took samples of poison gas and dismantled and reassembled whole chemical warfare labs. It appropriated nearly four hundred tons of documents and it microfilmed another four million pages, including patent applications.

While the highly funded and focused T-teams were finding, kidnapping, and interrogating German and Austrian scientists for their export value, the Army's Counter Intelligence Corps (CIC) was wrestling with two interrelated tasks: to denazify more than 120,000 SS officers, Gestapo, and high-ranking military leaders in the American zone, and to find the suspected war criminals among them. In contrast to the planning, urgency, and organization of war spoils operations, both CIC tasks were underplanned, understaffed, underfunded, and underled.

On paper, denazification was simple. Find the SS officers, Gestapo, and high-ranking military officers, secure and interview them, then place them in one of five categories: major war crimes offender, offender, lesser offender, follower, and exonerated person. The CIC used the Seventh Army to conduct Nazi sweeps in the American zone under code names like Tally Ho, Lifebuoy, and Choo Choo.

The sheer magnitude of the effort was daunting.

So was the mandate to find suspected war criminals. Thousands of them had strolled out of makeshift and underguarded holding pens. They wandered back home or hitched rides on ratlines to the Middle East and South America. Furthermore, the Pentagon failed to design a system to locate and question the hundreds of thousands of war crimes eyewitnesses trapped in DP camps. There were no T-teams with specific targets, no mobile units to guide them, no top-priority status with the authority to commandeer. The task was impossible. And that was no accident.

Even before the war was over, the Pentagon approached the war crimes issue with amoral pragmatism. It instructed General Eisenhower, commander of U.S. forces in Europe, to arrest and hold all war criminals. Then it instructed him to *exempt* those war criminals who could be used for "intelligence and military reasons."

This clear, deliberate dichotomy between finding, shielding, and employing Nazi scientists with urgency, efficiency and capital on the one hand, and finding, exposing, and punishing war criminals with confusion, disorganization, and lack of resources on the other became the postwar mind-set of the Washington bureaucracy dominated by the military. It was the root of U.S. hostility toward finding and investigating Nazis hiding in America.

CIC investigators worked with dedication and speed. A U.S. denazification tally issued in September 1946—sixteen months after the war ended—reported that the CIC had registered and categorized more than eleven million Germans. Of those, more than one hundred thousand were eventually charged with war crimes. Few, if any, of the hundred thousand were Nazi collaborators or other war criminals living in DP camps in the American zone.

• • •

Needless to say, it wasn't the prototype subs, airplanes, nerve gas, and weaponry that the United States lusted after, as useful as they were. The

War Department wanted the scientists who had created them. Once it found them, it had to craft a subterfuge to sneak them into the United States. To cover their tracks, the military and the State Department sent covert agents dressed in army and air force uniforms to infiltrate the CIC in Europe. Their job was to "smoothly and conspiratorially" expunge the names of its targeted scientists from the Central Registry of War Criminals and Security Suspects (CROWCASS) and to make sure that the CIC did not issue any "derogatory information" reports on them. (*Derogatory information* was bureaucratese for suspicion of war crimes.) Then, to make sure there would be no embarrassing problems later on, the covert agents created false employment histories and political bios for each target. Scrubbed clean and with new identities, the scientists were loaded on planes, listed as "cargo," and flown to the United States.

In approving the postwar military talent grab, President Truman made a clear distinction between Nazis and SS officers who had committed war crimes, and "normal" Nazis who had joined the party merely to advance their careers or who had accepted positions as a reward for their achievements. This latter group fell in the CIC category of "follower."

Truman welcomed followers to the United States, and then authorized the military to make the scientist program public. Three months after the war ended, the Department of War issued a press release: "The Secretary of War has approved a project whereby certain outstanding German scientists and technicians are being brought to this country to ensure that we take full advantage of those significant developments which are deemed vital to our national security." The War Department also released photos of smiling American and German scientists working side by side.

Other than short-lived shouts of anger from Jewish organizations that suspected there was more to the German scientists than science, Americans accepted the employment of German and Austrian scientists with can-do pragmatism. The old war was over. The new war had begun. It was time for all anticommunists to work together with determination and harmony to defeat the new enemy. Let's put a man on the moon. And God bless America.

Thus began "the biggest, longest-running operation involving Nazis in our country's history." The air force got the biggest slice of the pie for its missile, space, and jet fighter program. The navy came in second.

Worried that other countries, especially the Soviet Union, would hire or kidnap valuable scientists, the State-War-Navy Coordinating Committee (SWNCC)—the predecessor of the National Security Council—approved an expanded scientist plan in May 1946, eleven months after the war ended. In one of a series of top secret reports, SWNCC recommended that the United States bring up to one thousand German and Nazi scientists to America to work for the military as well as private industry, and to teach and conduct research in U.S. universities. SWNCC called the expanded program Operation Paperclip.

"It is the policy of the Government to exploit selected German and Austrian specialists in the United States, and thereby *deny* to the nations other than Great Britain access to these specialists," SWNCC ruled in May 1946, one year after the war in Europe ended. "This policy does not limit in any way, but rather supplements the existing procedure under which the War and Navy Departments are bringing German specialists to the United States."

In formulating that policy, SWNCC expressed a concern that the American public might suspect that Operation Paperclip condoned the use of Nazis war criminals. To forestall criticism and perhaps outrage, the committee ruled that any German or Austrian scientist who fell into CIC's "automatic arrest category" (major offender) be barred from the program.

As a result, the Operation Paperclip recommendation that SWNCC sent to President Truman for his approval in August 1946 contained a tough anti-Nazi clause. "The War Department," the top secret recommendation said, "should be responsible for...excluding from the program persons with Nazi or militarist records." The mandate not only looked good on paper, it also provided plausible deniability to the White House and the Department of State in case Americans ever learned that their government was secretly employing Nazi war criminals.

In approving the SWNCC Paperclip recommendation, President Truman was either naïve or duplicitous. The U.S. military establishment had no intention of excluding Nazi war criminals from the program. And to make sure that they could be employed, SWNCC created three giant loopholes. First, it gave the U.S. European military command the authority to remove the name of any Nazi or Nazi collaborator from the major offender category, rendering the exclusion clause impotent. Next, SWNCC declined to bar from Operation Paperclip the use of Nazi scientists in the *offender* and *lesser offender* categories. Finally, SWNCC gave the military's ever resourceful Joint Intelligence Objectives Agency the final say over which scientists would be welcomed to America and which ones would be barred.

In effect, the Truman anti-Nazi policy was no policy at all. It was merely window dressing. If the military wanted a scientist who was a suspected Nazi war criminal, it had plenty of room to wiggle around the law. As a result, an estimated 80 percent of the scientists brought to the United States by the military to be employed by the military were former Nazis and SS officers. Among them were "some of the world's vilest war criminals."

Besides the U.S. Air Force and Navy, universities like Yale, Michigan State, Wisconsin, Oregon State, Chicago, and Ohio State were among the winners. As were companies like Boeing, RAND, Lockheed, Dow Chemical, Raytheon, GE, Northrop, Westinghouse, and RCA.

Even Congress got into the spoils race. Tucked inside its CIA Act of 1949 was a provision that slid through the Capitol as smoothly as a puck on ice. The bill authorized the INS to grant permanent residency for up to one hundred individuals and their families per year in the interest of national security and intelligence gathering, and "without regard to their admissibility"—code for Nazis scientists and high-ranking military officers. The act further authorized the CIA to hire three of these individuals annually, even specifying their salary range. The act had no accountability provision for the "one hundred" program, making it a secret Nazi carte blanche.*

Among the most precious Paperclip "cargo" landing in America was Hubertus Strughold, a doctor linked to Nazi medical experiments on humans.

• • •

Dr. Strughold had been the director of the Institute for Aviation Medicine in Berlin, a civilian research center under contract with the German Air Force (Luftwaffe). His boss was Reich Marshal Hermann Goering, who was later convicted of war crimes and sentenced to death. Goering beat the noose with a cyanide capsule. Dr. Strughold was neither a Nazi nor a Luftwaffe officer, as some have stated. He resisted the pressure to become either, he claimed, to preserve his scientific objectivity.

In reality, Dr. Strughold was a closet Nazi who believed that the party had done much for Germany. He was also anti-Semitic, complain-

* Citing national security, the CIA rejected my FOIA request for the names of the scientists and intelligence specialists it brought into the country under the "one hundred" program.

ing that "Jews had crowded the medical schools and it had been nearly impossible for others to enter."

War crimes investigators named Strughold, a specialist in high-altitude medicine, as one of ninety-five German doctors who attended an October 1942 conference in Nuremberg at the Deutscher Hof Hotel. The topic of the two-day meeting was "Winter Hardship and Distress at Sea." Two of Dr. Strughold's colleagues delivered papers based on their medical experiments on humans. The participating doctors discussed the lectures afterward.

The idea to experiment on humans belonged to Strughold's associate, Dr. Sigmund Rascher. As Rascher explained to his boss, Heinrich Himmler, hypothermia and high-altitude experiments on animals furnished limited data. The best results came from primates, which were next to impossible to get under war conditions. How about a few humans? Would it bother you if some died?

Himmler gave him Dachau.

Rascher and his colleagues randomly selected as their primates: 1,000 Russians, 500 Poles, 200 Jews, and 50 Gypsies. They conducted three kinds of experiments at the camp: hypothermia, high-altitude, and saltwater. Dr. Rascher directed the first two, which turned out to be "astonishing acts of cruelty." Rascher's fellow doctors described him as a brute—ambitious, greedy, sadistic, and perverted.

The purpose of the hypothermia experiments was to answer the question: What is the best way to warm a German pilot downed in the icy waters of the North Sea or a soldier suffering from hypothermia on the eastern front? In one experiment, Rascher dressed victims in life vests and a flying uniform. He then submerged them in a wooden tank of ice water for three to five hours. Sometimes he allowed their brain stems to protrude above the water; sometimes he submerged them, which caused death within minutes. In another experiment, he forced victims to stand naked outside in 27–29 degree Fahrenheit temperatures for nine to fourteen hours.

"Victims screamed in pain as parts of their bodies froze," the Nuremberg War Crimes Tribunal later reported.

Rascher monitored body temperatures at regular intervals, recorded the time it took for loss of consciousness and for death, and performed autopsies to collect data. He used two kinds of warming techniques for those who survived the ice tank and the winter weather: submersion in warm water and animal warming—sandwiching the victim between two naked Gypsy women who were "volunteers" from the Ravensbrück camp, where Hermine Braunsteiner worked for a time. Rascher duly recorded the progress and the times of the rewarming. As part of the experiment, he forced the subjects to have intercourse while he watched. One-third of the hypothermia victims died.

The purpose of the high-altitude experiments was to answer the question: How much atmospheric pressure can a German pilot withstand after ejecting from his airplane at high altitudes? The experiments took place in a round, airtight, low-pressure chamber that Rascher and Strughold codesigned. Dachau victims called it the Skyride Machine.

Dr. Rascher would lock the victims in the chamber, then manipulate the pressure inside to simulate atmospheric pressures at 35,000–66,000 feet. The lower number was somewhat safe. The higher number was certain death. Rascher designed four different experiments: slow parachute descent with oxygen, then without oxygen; free-fall descent with oxygen, then without. Rascher would carefully measure how long it took to lose consciousness, how long to die.

Death was not easy.

In an April 1942 report to Himmler, Dr. Rascher described the murder of a thirty-seven-year-old Jew who took a trip in the Skyride Machine—first with oxygen, then without it—at sixty thousand feet. At four minutes he began perspiring and wagging his head; at five minutes, he had cramps; at six to ten minutes, fast breathing and unconsciousness; at thirty minutes, death.

Death was painful.

"Some experiments gave men such pressure in their heads that they would go mad," Rascher reported to Himmler. "They would tear at their hair and faces with their hands and scream in an effort to relieve the pressure on their eardrums." After each experiment, Rascher and his assistants would open the chamber, haul out the victims, some of whom were still breathing, and dissect them for data. One-third of the high altitude victims were murdered.

Once Germany's ultimate defeat became obvious, Himmler made sure that Rascher would never implicate him in the war crimes trials that were sure to come. Just weeks before the Seventh Army liberated Dachau, he ordered the SS to execute Rascher and, with a twist of irony, to shoot him inside the camp. They did.

U.S. Army Intelligence placed Dr. Strughold on the Central Registry of War Criminals and Security Suspects. Investigators wanted to question him. What did he know about the Dachau experiments? What was his relationship to Dr. Rascher and other Dachau doctors? Did he initiate the experiments? Did he help design experiment protocols? Was he privy to the results? If so, did he use the results in his work and writings?

The U.S. Air Force saw to it that Nuremberg investigators never got to interview Strughold. He was easy enough to find at the U.S. Aero Medical Center in Heidelberg, where he was directing a contingent of about two hundred German scientists, all working for America. Five of those scientists were already awaiting trial at Nuremberg for medical war crimes. All five had been screened and selected to work at Wright Field in Dayton, Ohio, but the air force screwed up. Nuremberg investigators nabbed the quintet before the military could erase their names from the Central Registry.

Dr. Strughold's major task at the Aero Medical Center was to synthesize all data on high-altitude experiments, both animal and human, into a compendium on aviation medicine for use by the U.S. Air Force. An important part of that job was to integrate the Dachau experiment findings without revealing where the data came from. The Pentagon was not eager for Americans to know that while it was prosecuting Nazi doctors in Nuremberg for killing prisoners to get scientific data, it secretly was using the data.

Nuremberg prosecutors tried twenty-three German doctors and medical administrators during the "Doctors Trial" in December 1946. Missing from the list was Dr. Hubertus Strughold. On the list were all the Dachau-related scientists and administrators above and below him. Among them: Dr. Sigfried Ruff, who reported directly to Strughold; and Drs. Hans Romberg and Georg Weltz, who both reported to Ruff. During the Doctors Trial, these three along with other defendants suggested that Strughold not only knew about the Dachau experiments, but also received written and oral reports on the results. Since Strughold was not on trial, prosecutors did not dig deeper into his role in the experiments.

The doctors also testified that, as director of the Institute for Aviation Medicine, which sponsored the experiments, Strughold could have either objected to them on moral grounds or stopped them. But if he had done either, they hastened to add, his life and career would have been at the mercy of Goering and Himmler.

In the end, it was Heinrich Himmler and the U.S. Air Force who saved the necks of Ruff, Romberg, and Weltz. Only three people could have definitely implicated them in medical crimes at Dachau: Himmler, who committed suicide before he could be questioned; Rausch, whom Himmler executed; and Strughold, whom the air force was shielding. As a result, the Nuremberg panel acquitted all three doctors, on the grounds of reasonable doubt. It was, the panel said, a close call. In the end, sixteen of the twenty-three doctors/administrators were found guilty. Seven of those were sentenced to death.

The air force immediately put Ruff, Romberg, and Weltz back on the U.S. payroll. It had special plans for its war treasure, Dr. Strughold. Worried that the Soviets might kidnap him, the air force forged Strughold's way into the United States in 1947 on the first wave of Paperclip scientists to hit the shores of America.

The air force sent Dr. Strughold to Randolph Field, Texas, where he created the first ever American department of space medicine, earning him the title "Father of Space Medicine." Strugi, as his friends called him, went on to pioneer the next generation of low-pressure chambers, space simulators, and pressure suits, all of which helped put Neil Armstrong on the moon.

As a result of his groundbreaking research, Dr. Strughold was inducted into the International Space Hall of Fame. The Daughters of the American Revolution awarded him the Americanism Medal. The Aerospace Medical Association created the "Hubertus Strughold Award." The Texas State Senate declared a "Dr. Hubertus Strughold Day." And Ohio State University included his portrait in a mural of medical heroes alongside Hippocrates and Marie Curie. The university removed Strughold's portrait from the group after he died.

In 1958, eleven years after Strughold entered the United States, the INS received a complaint about him and checked his background. It began by asking the air force if it had any "derogatory information" on its famous employee. The air force said no, Dr. Strughold had been "appropriately investigated." Case closed.

When Strughold's name appeared on the published Karbach list in 1974, Texas congressman Henry Gonzalez was upset. Anxious not to see a famous son of Texas smeared by reckless war crimes innuendo, Gonzalez complained to the INS. The congressman said his constituent had told him he first heard about Nazi medical experiments on humans after the war. So what was the flap all about?

INS commissioner General Chapman reassured Gonzalez: "Our inquiries [about Dr. Strughold] were terminated. . . . We consider the matter closed." For its part, the Justice Department opened an investigation into Strughold's wartime activity, but it didn't find enough clear and convincing evidence to charge him. Dr. Hubertus Strughold died a free man in San Antonio in 1978 under a cloud of suspicion and with a slightly tarnished name.

Dr. Strughold's alleged complicity in the medical experiments on Dachau prisoners, as terrible as they were, was a "minor" war crime compared to the role other Paperclip scientists played in a secret SS camp hidden in a remote mountain valley and code-named Dora.

Greek for "gift."

CHAPTER ELEVEN

Waiting in Hell

Bivouacked just inside the western border of Germany, U.S. Army Private John Galione smelled death. The stench came from somewhere up ahead, from the east. It was an odor the 104th Infantry Timberwolf—a veteran of the battle for Remagen Bridge—had smelled many times before. Galione had heard rumors about Soviet soldiers finding concentration camps filled with corpses and the walking dead as they pushed across Poland toward Berlin. He had a hunch that if he followed the stench, it would lead him to such a camp. The problem was—the smell was coming from territory still held by the German army.

Galione told his platoon leader about his suspicion and asked if he could have a couple of guys for reconnaissance. There may be some American prisoners there, he argued. Maybe pilots shot down and captured.

Although the platoon sergeant didn't disagree, he said no. A reconnaissance mission would be too risky. If there is a concentration camp up ahead, he said, it'll have to wait another week.

Galione couldn't sleep that night. A week was a long time; men would die. The more he thought about the camp—now a reality in his mind—a plan began to take shape. If there was a Nazi camp farther east, it would have to be next to a railroad. How else could they move thousands of prisoners in and out? All he had to do was follow the train tracks east, deeper into Germany, and they would lead him to the camp.

Galione woke up a buddy and told him he was going to have a look up ahead and why. He expected to be back by morning, he said, but if he wasn't, would his buddy tell the sarge that he hadn't deserted? Galione didn't want to be branded a coward if he got captured or killed.

At nine thirty on the night of April 5, 1945, Private Galione began to follow the rail tracks southeast. He felt at home traveling under the stars. For a Timberwolf, specially trained in nighttime fighting in America's rugged Northwest, darkness was a friend.

Galione never made it back by morning. When the sun rose, he continued following the tracks and the smell. For five days, over one hundred miles, along the tracks at night and in the woods during the day, no sleep, just a few hours of rest against a tree. He was surrounded by German soldiers and retreating convoys of trucks and jeeps. To sleep was dangerous.

Exhausted and weak from hunger, Galione was also in pain. Walking had chaffed raw the unhealed leg wound he suffered at Remagen. But he kept on going, pushed by an invisible hand (was it God?) and pulled by the fear that there might be Americans in the camp. God or no God, he was worried. Would he face court-martial when he got back to camp? If he got back?

With each step, it seemed, the smell of death got stronger. On the fifth day of trekking, he spotted another Timberwolf camp a mile or so from the tracks with a road leading to it. He thought about going for help, then dismissed the idea. Lives were at stake; every minute was a life.

A few hours after he passed the Timberwolf bivouac, he found a spur trailing off north from the main tracks. The stench was now overpowering. He followed the spur and soon found an abandoned boxcar. It was empty, the straw-strewn floor fetid from blood, urine, and feces.

The spur curved and the tracks stretched toward the mouths of two openings in the mountainside, camouflaged with netting. In the valley, on a flat plain, stood a huge, silent camp with empty guard towers and a gate with a large lock. A lone soldier was loading a truck. Galione knew he had stumbled onto something big.

On the tracks near the first opening sat another boxcar. The smell coming from it was even riper. He didn't have to guess what he would find inside—dead bodies dressed in prison rags. He began poking around the five-day-old corpses with his rifle, hoping to find out who the dead men were, how they died, and whether any were Americans. The only identifications he found were colored armbands sewn onto the prison pajamas—red, green, yellow, blue. He knew that "yellow" meant Jew. What did the others signify? While turning corpses, his gun made a steel-on-steel clang. He silently cursed. If he weren't so tired, he would never had made such a rookie mistake.

The first shot pinged off the boxcar. Galione ducked. The soldier he had seen earlier was running toward him with a rifle. Galione jumped from the boxcar and scampered up the mountainside as fast as loose rocks would allow. Bullets whizzed by his ear and ricocheted off the granite rocks as he dove into the camouflage above the first opening.

Unable to see the American with the green and silver Timberwolf patch on his shoulder, the soldier lost interest, jumped in his truck, and drove off. As soon as he disappeared around the curve, Galione relaxed and scanned the camp below. The barbed-wired prison was as quiet as a ghost town.

Attracted by the gunfire, curious prisoners began to gather at the gate. They knew the Allies were advancing. For days they had heard the sounds of battle, closer every daybreak. Was this liberation day? There was no cheering. Just an eerie silence.

The openings in the mountain were calling to Galione like sirens. What were the Nazis hiding inside? Fuel? Bombs? Tanks? How deep into the mountain did the openings go? As curious as he was, he was too smart to explore. There might be Germans hiding inside or the place might be booby-trapped. One step into the darkness and the mountain could explode into piles of rock. Instead Galione picked his way down to the prison gate. The least he could do was free the prisoners.

It was four thirty in the afternoon on April 10, 1945. The men he found waiting inside the gate were "skeletons wrapped in skin," with an average man weighing less than sixty pounds. Private John Galione had just discovered Camp Dora.

Galione tried to break the lock while the men watched mutely. Without tools, he couldn't force it open. He could shoot it, of course, but that would be nearly as dumb as exploring the mountain. What if there were guards still inside the camp? As a lone soldier standing in the open, he'd be an easy target.

Galione decided to go for help. But first, he needed sleep. He climbed back up the mountainside to a clump of trees above the mine openings. From there he had a clear view of the camp and road and would hear anyone climbing over loose rocks. He quickly fell asleep and awoke in the dark. Perfect for a prowling Timberwolf.

Galione began to hike back up the tracks to the American camp he had spotted on the way to Dora. He was not up to walking five more days to his own camp, if it was still where he left it. Besides, judging from what he had seen, the prisoners in the camp could die waiting for rescue.

A miracle was waiting for him when he got to the road leading to the Timberwolf bivouac, at two o'clock that morning. Sitting on the road was a stalled jeep and a tired driver. Galione tried to use his basic knowledge of auto mechanics as a bargaining chip. He told the driver about the secret openings in the mountain and the camp. He'd fix the jeep, he said, if the driver would take him back there, help him break the lock, and free the prisoners. The driver said he couldn't. He was on a personal assignment for his commanding officer and needed his permission. He offered to take the private to his superior. Galione found a disconnected wire under the Jeep's hood and fixed it.

The Timberwolf battalion leader not only agreed to give Galione a ride back to Dora; he insisted on going to the ghost camp himself along with one of his men. Just as the spring sun was about to rise, the three Timberwolves rounded the curve to the camp. Within minutes they broke the lock and opened the gate. A wave of prisoners swallowed them up, grabbing their hands and kissing them over and over. Like DeVito at Dachau and hundreds of other liberators in camps across Europe, the three Timberwolves could not process what they saw.

The rising sun slowly lit a scene from a horror movie. Men so thin "you could see their back bones through their stomachs." Rotting bodies in open trenches and piled outside buildings. A prisoner led Galione to the "infirmary," where a hundred men lay on straw in their own excrement, the dying next to the already dead. The French Resistance fighters among the living began singing "La Marseillaise" when they saw the American soldiers.

Worried that there were still guards in Dora, the Timberwolves raced back down the road to their camp to radio for backup and medical help. Then the commander drove Galione back to his platoon to face charges.

The next day, army medics, German civilian health workers, and the Red Cross streamed into Camp Dora with trucks full of medicine and bandages, blankets and sheets, and food fit for an SS officer—cold meats and cheese, coffee and milk, bread and butter and jam. They found about twelve hundred men and boys still alive, gave them first aid, then loaded them into field ambulances and trucks for transport to nearby hospitals. For some it was too late.

With tanks as backup, U.S. soldiers explored what turned out to be three camps—Dora and two sister camps. Except for prisoners and the dead, all three camps were empty. The soldiers found torture chambers. A crematorium with the smoldering corpses of men and boys as young as ten. Men hanging by their necks, some by their genitals. And corpses around every corner and in every building. Five thousand of them. Battle-hardened soldiers wept and retched along the barbed-wire fences.

One of the SS officers responsible for Camp Dora and the deaths of its slave laborers would become the crown jewel in the treasure chest of Paperclip scientists hired by the Pentagon to send the first U.S. satellite into orbit.

His name was SS Major Wernher von Braun.

CHAPTER TWELVE

Hitler's Last Hope

Wernher von Braun was a dreamer. Ever since he studied rocket science at the Technical University of Berlin in the early 1930s, he wanted to build rockets that would carry men into space. When the war shattered his dream, he turned his genius to designing for the Reich a rocket of mass destruction—the V-2 (V for *Vergeltung*, or Vengeance). As the first long-range ballistic missile ever built, the giant V-2 was destined to replace the small V-1 "buzz bomb" that destroyed much of London.

Von Braun's problem was that his superiors, distracted by bickering and power-playing, didn't believe in his new and as yet unproven rocket. Fortunately for the Allies, their indecision delayed the development of the V-2 for several months of the war. With the future of his rocket in jeopardy, von Braun leapfrogged his military superiors and took his case directly to the Führer.

Armed with optimism and film to justify it, von Braun visited Hitler and Albert Speer, Reich minister of armament and war production, in July 1943. With Germany caught in a squeeze, his timing was impeccable. The Red Army was steadily pushing west toward Berlin and the Allies were planning an invasion. The only question was when and where. Although he was still optimistic, Hitler was looking for a reason to give his discouraged military officers a straw of hope.

Von Braun, Hitler, and Speer sat in a darkened room at Wolf's Lair, the Führer's hideaway, on an ordinary summer day in 1943, ten months before the Allies hit the beaches of Normandy. Von Braun turned on the projector and the film began to roll. It featured, as Speer recalled, "the majestic spectacle of a great rocket rising from its pad and disappearing into the stratosphere." Hitler was so impressed, he called the V-2 a weapon that could "decide the war." If the Reich could rain V-2s on England—and eventually the United States—war momentum would most certainly shift. The rockets would make an Allied invasion too risky, perhaps impossible. Hitler could then use the V-2 as Truman would later use the atom bomb—to bring his enemies to their knees.

Hitler made V-2 production a top priority.

So did the British Royal Air Force. Based on solid intelligence, the RAF launched Operation Hydra, which destroyed or crippled much of von Braun's rocket factory, lab, and launch sites at Peenemünde, a village in northern Germany on the Baltic Sea. Before the Peenemünde ashes could cool, Hitler gave the order to move V-2 production out of range of the RAF and into the very heart of Germany. He commissioned the SS to find a secret site. They settled on an abandoned gypsum mine in Mount Kohnstein, in the Harz mountain range. All they had to do was remove the fuel and chemical tanks stored inside the mine and expand the space. To dupe Allied intelligence, Berlin gave the future underground factory complex the bland name of Mittelwerk (Central Works).

The first stage of Mittelwerk construction was to excavate two tunnels and build two factories inside them, one to assemble V-1s for immediate launch against England, and the other to make V-2s for testing. To dig the tunnels and build the underground factories, the SS would use slave laborers from the neighboring Buchenwald concentration camp. If they needed more men than Buchenwald could supply, there were hundreds of other camps to draw from.

Usually, the SS built their camps with logic: roads and utilities first, then SS barracks, followed by camp fences and watchtowers, and finally prisoner barracks and workshops. But there was no time for logic at Mittelwerk. When the first prisoners arrived, there were no barracks, no tents, no electricity, and above all, no safe drinking water, making conditions at Camp Dora the worst of any SS camp, including Auschwitz, which became the symbol of Nazi evil.

The main excavation job of the slave laborers was to load the rock that had been blasted or drilled out of the mountain into mine wagons, then push them down narrow tracks to empty railroad cars at the mouth of the tunnel. They worked in twelve-hour shifts in constant dampness and cold—59 degrees Fahrenheit was the warmest it ever got inside the mountain. The only light came from miner lamps.

The slave miners worked in clouds of ammonia-filled dust from the blasts, without ventilation or protective clothing. After a few weeks, they turned gray-black, the color of the rocks they carried. The SS and trusted inmates known as Kapos—mostly career criminals—drove the prisoners "at an infernal speed" with clubs and cords of rubber-covered copper wire, cursing and taunting and shouting "faster, faster, you pieces of shit."

The only liquid the slave miners got was a daily ration of soup. Sometimes not even that. If a prisoner was lucky, he might find moisture dripping from the rocks. If a slave was driven to drink the polluted water used for mixing cement, he would soon die of typhus or dysentery. Thirst drove some of the men insane. Dora survivor Jean Michel, a former French Resistance leader, recalled a crazed miner gulping rocket fuel. "He died in agony."

At first, while the camp was still under construction, the Dora miners slept inside the mountain in granite chambers on four-tiered bunk beds with lice-infested straw pallets. The smell and the noise assaulted them constantly: the warning bell before a blast, the explosion with falling rocks, the shouts of the guards, the sounds of drills and machines, of stone clanging in metal boxcars, of the cars rolling down tracks—all bouncing off the walls, turning the tunnels into echo chambers. "Over a thousand despairing men," recalled one Dora survivor, "at the limit of their resistance and racked with thirst, lie there hoping for sleep which never comes."

The slave miners saw daylight only on Sundays during roll call. The SS needed to know how many men they had lost during the week so they could replace them with fresh bodies. The human moles were marched out of the tunnels in rows of five, arms linked, the strong holding up the weak. Suddenly exposed to bright light, many of the men permanently injured their eyes, a death sentence. Unable to see well, if at all, they were bound to make a mistake. Their replacements were waiting a few miles away at Buchenwald.

There was no medical help for the men injured by falling rocks. They either bled to death or died of infection. Exhausted and weak, men fell off scaffolds. Some were crushed to death by falling stones or by the heavy machinery they carried from the trains into the mine. A slave worker task force (Kommando) stacked the dead outside the tunnel, an average of one hundred a day. A lorry from Buchenwald would pick up the corpses after the SS logged their prison numbers in a ledger and take them back to the crematorium at Buchenwald.

The lucky ones died in boxcars on the way to Dora. Those who arrived alive but unable to work were promptly killed. "I had to deal with the sick who could no longer get out of the railway cars," one Nazi guard confessed. "They didn't want to stand up. I had to crush their larynxes by stomping on them with my boots to finish them off."

Albert Speer inspected the Mittelwerk tunnels a few months after work had begun. "The conditions of these prisoners were in fact barbarous," he wrote in his memoirs, "and a sense of profound involvement and personal guilt seizes me whenever I think of them." Speer's staff became so ill that "they had to be forcibly sent off on vacations to restore their nerves."

Some relief came for the slave miners when the barracks were completed in March 1944—seven months after the work had begun. By then, the slave labor population had grown from 1,000 to 12,000. And when Dora became too small because Speer decided to dig more tunnels in the Harz Mountains for more factories, the SS constructed two neighboring camps—Ellrich and Harzungen—and added a crematorium to dispose of the growing number of corpses. The population of the new three-camp complex, now called Mittelbau-Dora, climbed steadily to 30,000—French, Poles, Czechs, Ukrainians, Russian and Italian POWs, Slovenians, and Gypsies. The largest groups were the French and Russians. Jews were a minority, and the SS reserved the worst jobs and most brutal treatment for them and the Russians.

The first group of mostly young Hungarian Jews arrived at Mittelbau-Dora in the spring of 1944, among them children ages eleven to fifteen. Broken by work, starvation, and haunting despair, they didn't last long. For one survivor, their nighttime cries and whimpers became his "most distressing memories" of the camp. A second group of several thousand Jews began to arrive early in 1945. They were the last of the Polish Jews at Auschwitz, evacuated in advance of the Soviet army.

• • •

The V-2 factory inside the mountain mine was completed in December 1943, an incredible four months after the first thousand slave laborers began digging. It was a marvel of German engineering. Reinforced with concrete and steel, it was forty-six feet wide and thirty-three feet high. Brilliantly lit and powered by electric generators, it stretched nearly two miles north to south, from one end of Mount Kohnstein to the other. Branching off from the main tunnel were smaller connecting tunnels and a string of side chambers, some as high as 125 feet to accommodate the giant V-2 rockets. Two silent electric trains ran down the entire length of the tunnel.

On the left side of the tunnel was a conveyor belt that carried V-2 rocket parts for assemblage. At the mouth of the tunnel stood a huge crane that transferred the finished missiles onto flat railcars for transport to testing sites. A description by survivor Abraham Biderman of his first day on an assembly line would have made Henry Ford proud.

Biderman worked in Kommando 147 under the supervision of a German civilian called *Meister*. His job was to insert a metal box in a cavity near the V-2 fuselage and fix it in place with two bolts. The next Kommando connected wires inside the box, and a third Kommando covered the box with a metal plate, then screwed it in place. All the while, the camp symphony orchestra at the mouth of the tunnel played a Mozart violin concerto.

As soon as the conveyor belts began to roll, Mittelbau-Dora became a tale of two cities. In one, slave miners worked digging tunnels 3, 4, and 5, driven to exhaustion and death by starvation or accident. In the other were "skilled" slave workers—welders, solderers, drillers—who assembled rockets in a comfortably heated tunnel equipped with pumps to replace the air. They ate better, lived in cleaner barracks, received some medical care, and had time to rest between shifts. Nothing could illustrate the difference between the two "cities" better than the latrines.

Assembly line workers used clean, white-tiled bathrooms. The miners used empty fuel tanks, which they cut in half with hammers and chisels. The half-tanks sat in a row inside the tunnel, a wood plank resting on the rims. Every hour, a latrine Kommando would pour chlorine over the waste, and when a tank was full, the Kommando would carry it outside and empty it in a hole. From time to time, bored or angry guards and SS officers would topple a slave miner off the plank into the waste. Some miners were so weak from work or dysentery they couldn't climb back out. They drowned in shit. Those who were strong enough to hoist themselves out cleaned off as best they could by rolling in the mine dust before going back to work.

Work on the assembly line could be dangerous as well. Always worried about sabotage, especially by the French Resistance fighters and the Russian POWs, the Gestapo planted spies everywhere and "interviewed" suspects in their special torture chambers. Anything unusual could be interpreted as sabotage. Dropping a screw, missing a beat as the pieces rolled by, whispering. Or having money, which spelled bribery to the Gestapo.

Suspected saboteurs were hanged each day either on the gallows in the roll-call platz, six at a time, or from the construction crane gallows, an even dozen at a time, while the entire camp watched in silence. Workers entering or leaving the tunnel where the crane stood had to pass through the bodies dangling only five feet off the ground, puddles of urine under them. March 12, 1945, was a typical Dora day. The SS hung fifty-eight "saboteurs": fifty Russians, five Poles, two Czechs, and one Lithuanian.

The relentless driving of the mine and assembly line slaves turned out to be a two-edged sword. Von Braun tested the first batch of V-2s on an island in the Baltic Sea in April 1944, two months before the Allied invasion of Normandy and just nine frantic months after tunnel digging had begun. But the sword had cut too deeply. Due to haste, sabotage, and untrained workers, the rockets were defective: bad welds, poor connections, and faulty parts caused tail explosions, engine cutoffs, in-flight breakups, erratic trajectories, and crashes.

Von Braun rushed back to his blueprints and made a "blizzard" of changes. Four months later, in September, the Reich launched the first V-2s into West London from Holland. Not five thousand at a crack as Hitler had dreamed of doing, but twenty-five over a ten-day stretch, causing only scattered damage and few deaths. The Allies lucked out. The V-2s were too late to change or delay the course of the war.

Once it was clear that the Americans would soon be at Dora's gate, the SS evacuated the camp, as they had at Majdanek and Auschwitz in Poland. The plan was to herd all the prisoners into the tunnels, pump in poison gas, then blow up the evidence, but they ran out of time, as they had at Dachau. Five days before Private Galione discovered Dora, and just as he began his hundred-mile hike, the SS crammed most of the thirty thousand Mittelbau-Dora prisoners into trains and trucks, or formed them into death-march columns. Most were destined for Bergen-Belsen, another hellhole, a hundred miles north.

While the twelve hundred prisoners remaining at the Dora camp waited for death or liberation, von Braun gathered his precious rocket blueprints and plans and buried them deep inside a nearby abandoned mine. For insurance, he blew up the mine entrance before fleeing to the Bavarian Alps. Like the Dora prisoners, he was waiting. For a chance to surrender to the Allies. For a job in America.

American army ordnance scavengers led by Major Robert Starver, an intelligence officer in the Ordnance Corps, arrived at Dora a week after Private Galione discovered it and the site had been secured. Starver pretty much knew what to expect at Mittelwerk based on intelligence provided by Otto von Bolschwing and other informants. The liberation of prisoners was not his objective. The V-2s were, and Starver didn't have much time. The Soviet army was less than two weeks away and eager to claim the spoils in its postwar zone.

Starver and his crew picked the tunnels clean of partially assembled V-2s, fully assembled V-1s, rocket parts, and machinery. An informant led him to the mine where von Braun had buried his blueprints. Soldiers dug them out. Then they loaded the loot on a train, blew up any buildings the Soviets might find useful, and chugged off. When the Soviets finally arrived at Dora in early July, they found Mittelwerk stripped. It was one of the biggest heists of the war, and Starver laughed with his spoils all the way to the White Sands Proving Grounds in New Mexico.

Private John Galione wasn't laughing. To his relief, the army did not court-martial him, for fear that a trial would publicize the Dora atrocities and the role that von Braun and other Paperclip scientists played in them. Instead, the army swore him to silence. Galione took his secret to the grave—with one exception. He told his story to his daughter, who published it in 2004, nearly sixty years after her father discovered the hidden camp. Testimonials in the book from Galione's Timberwolf colleagues substantiate his story.

Von Braun and his colleagues on the V-2 project—SS Major General Walter Dornberger and Arthur Rudolph—all eventually came to the United States as part of the Paperclip program. Because they were never actually tried for war crimes, evidence and eyewitness testimony against them has never been fully explored. What is known about their role at Dora is, therefore, sketchy but damning.

All three were responsible for the use and abuse of the slave laborers they needed to do their jobs: as production director of Mittelwerk, Rudolph needed slaves to assemble the V-2s; as chief rocket designer, von Braun needed slaves to deliver V-2s for testing; and as chief rocket military officer, Dornberger needed perfected V-2s to launch against the Allies. All three sat in on meetings where the use of slave laborers was discussed. All three supported the decision to use them, first at Peenemünde, then at Camp Dora. From time to time, all three asked for more skilled laborers. All three visited the tunnels to check on excavation progress and witnessed the abuse of prisoners, as Albert Speer had. Rudolph permanently moved to Mittelwerk in January 1944. Dornberger and von Braun spent chunks of time there. All three witnessed the hangings. And like Bishop Trifa, all three would later argue: "But I never killed anyone."

There were several Camp Dora trials in Germany. In the end, five Nazis were hanged and more than twenty received prison sentences. For his part in approving the use of slave laborers, among other crimes, Albert Speer—who also never killed anyone—was sentenced to twenty years in prison. He served his full term and was released.

The United States brought von Braun and Rudolph to the White Sands Proving Grounds immediately after the war. Then it sent them to the space center in Huntsville, Alabama, to spearhead NASA's man-in-space program.

Like his friend von Braun, Dornberger had surrendered to the Allies. He was imprisoned and questioned by the British, then released to U.S. Army intelligence, which had asked for him. He worked for the CIC in Germany, then for the U.S. military at Wright-Patterson Air Force Base in Dayton, Ohio, with a yearly salary of $8,004, the equivalent of about ten times that today. The U.S. Air Force transferred him to NASA's guided missile program in Huntsville, where he became a member of von Braun's team. Later Dornberger went to work for Bell Aircraft.

When Dora survivors began publishing memoirs and Paperclip was finally making news in the early 1980s, the spotlight focused on Rudolph. Von Braun and Dornberger were already dead. Rather than face a public deportation trial for immigration fraud, Rudolf struck a deal with U.S. prosecutors. Like Hermine Braunsteiner, he agreed to voluntarily relinquish his U.S. citizenship and move to Germany if the United States would not prosecute him. Once Rudolf was settled in Hamburg, the German government declined to try him for war crimes, claiming that the evidence provided by U.S. prosecutors and investigators was insufficient.

The government knew that von Braun was a dangerous man. The

Joint Intelligence Objectives Agency, which oversaw Operation Paper-clip, warned in a secret 1947 memo that von Braun posed "potential or actual threats to the security of the United States." In spite of his war criminal background, von Braun was awarded the National Medal of Science and the President's Award for Distinguished Service, the high-est honor the nation confers on its civil servants. NASA gave Rudolph medals for Exceptional Service and Distinguished Service. West Ger-many awarded Dornberger the Eugen Saenger Medal, named after a famed German space scientist. All three died free men.

• • •

Some may argue that the use of Nazi war criminals to protect Ameri-cans from the Soviet Union was a distasteful but necessary compromise. After all, truth and morality are the first casualties of war. Others will counter that by all human standards, the United States crossed a moral divide that even the most pragmatic American would find difficult to justify.

The fact is that, long before it put Nazi doctors on trial at Nurem-berg for medical experiments on humans at Dachau and Auschwitz, the U.S. military was conducting similar medical experiments on its own servicemen. To continue and advance those experiments, it hired some Nazi war criminals under the Paperclip project and put them to work at secret locations.

CHAPTER THIRTEEN

The Nasty Little Secret

The experiments on U.S. soldiers began in the early 1920s at the Naval Research Laboratory in Anacostia, a section of Washington, D.C., where the military maintained a gas chamber not unlike the Nazi gas chambers at Dachau. Servicemen were conned into volunteering as guinea pigs, then given a dose of mustard gas. The "volunteers" were never told the true nature of the experiments or warned of the dangers.

Unlike the Nazis, who didn't care if they killed their victims for the sake of science, American doctors and scientists were more sensitive. They worked hard to bring their victims to the point of death, without crossing the line, for a pragmatic reason. They didn't want the public to know what they were doing behind barbed-wire fences or in hideaways in the woods. They could always cover up an occasional mishap by explaining that "he died during a training exercise." But hundreds of deaths?

The U.S. Army also built a gas chamber at its Edgewood Arsenal, camouflaged deep in the woods of Maryland near the Chesapeake Bay. In 1941, the arsenal was under the command of the 2nd Special Chemical Battalion, which included Companies B and C and a "medical detachment." The Edgewood battalion was part of an offensive chemical warfare unit created in 1917 by the War Department.

• • •

While Nazi doctor Sigmund Rascher was experimenting on Dachau prisoners in his Skyride Machine and ice tanks, American doctors and scientists were giving sailors like Nathan Schnurman heavy doses of mustard gas at Edgewood.

When the navy put out a call in 1940 for sailors to test a new line of summer clothing, seventeen-year-old Schnurman volunteered. He had just finished basic training at the naval station in Bainbridge, Maryland, on the Susquehanna River just north of Baltimore. The three-day pass the navy offered as a reward was too sweet for the young sailor to pass up.

Schnurman and four other volunteers, who were never told where they were going, boarded a bus and headed south. After about an hour on mostly back roads, the bus turned onto a dirt lane winding through the woods. It stopped in front of two Quonset huts. The ground was covered with snow. There was no sign of life, not even a barking dog. Attached to one of the huts, like an afterthought, was a smaller structure.

Army soldiers led Schnurman into a Quonset and dressed him in protective clothes, rubber boots, and a gas mask. Then they led him through a steel door and locked him inside a bare, windowless, ten-by-fifteen-foot concrete chamber. There was no place to sit.

As Schnurman stood inside, wondering why he was wearing a gas mask if he was testing new summer clothes, technicians released a fifty-fifty mixture of sulfur-mustard gas and lewisite, which contains arsenic, known to cause heart attacks. Both gases, which are vesicants, or blistering agents, are absorbed into the body through the lungs and the skin. They burned moist tissue—sweaty areas like skin folds and testicles, lungs and mucous membranes, windpipes and eyes. Each daily experiment lasted sixty minutes. On the sixth day, Schnurman started to get nauseated, then very ill. He asked to be released. The technicians refused. Then he demanded to be released. The technicians still refused. Seconds later, he passed out. When he came to, he was lying outside on a snowbank still wearing his gas mask, which was full of vomit.

"I was presumed dead," he testified before Congress after more than forty years of illnesses. The next day, seventeen-year-old Schnurman got his first heart attack.

Since he was no longer useful, two soldiers dressed him, carried him onto the bus, and drove him to a train station at the end of a one-way track. They threatened him with a long vacation in Leavenworth for treason if he ever revealed the experiment, and they warned him never to come back. "You wouldn't know where to find us anyway," they said before carrying him into the train—an engine and three coach cars.

Back at his base in Bainbridge, Schnurman's superiors took one look at him and sent him home for a week of rest. He needed it. He was suffering from pneumonia and laryngitis. He had blisters on his body and blood in his stool. The damage was permanent.

Like Private Galione, Seaman Schnurman kept the secret. The first time he brought up the gas experiment was during a physical exam more than forty years after the gassing, when his doctor asked if he had ever been exposed to chemicals.

Schnurman was just one of more than four thousand servicemen who received dangerous doses of mustard gas and lewisite during the 1940s and who died as a result or suffered permanent damage. The U.S. military used them to test the reliability and longevity of gas masks and protective clothing and to calculate how long it took for subjects to be seriously injured.

To assist in its experiments, the U.S. military recruited at least six Paperclip chemists and chemical engineers—war criminals who, like Rascher, had experimented on concentration camp prisoners.* Sent to Edgewood, they continued the mustard/lewisite experiments before moving on to nerve gases like tabun and sarin, which they themselves had created. Waiting for them to work with at Edgewood and other chemical warfare centers in the United States were ten tons of the gases—the spoils of war.

Between 1950 and 1975, Nazi Paperclip and American scientists experimented on nearly seven thousand American servicemen, exposing them to as many as 254 different chemicals. Before long, the military and the CIA expanded the medical experiments to include unwitting and vulnerable civilians—veterans, orphans, prisoners, mentally handicapped children, and poor pregnant women. They were radiated and exposed to, fed, and injected with plutonium. They were treated to heavy doses of LSD and PCP, among other mind-altering drugs. As with the gases, the physical and psychic damage was permanent.

In 1994, more than fifty years after the secret medical experiments

---

* In response to my FOIA request for the roster of military and civilian personnel who worked at Edgewood from 1950 to 1960, the U.S. military personnel center in St. Louis claimed that it could not find a single roster containing the names of civilians stationed at the army base during that time period.

had begun, the General Accounting Office (GAO) reported: "Precise information on the number of tests, experiments, and participants is not available . . . and the exact numbers may never be known. However, we have identified . . . experiments in which *hundreds of thousands* of people were used as test subjects."

Texas congressman Martin Frost, who heard Nathan Schnurman's testimony, spoke for the entire congressional committee when he said: "Experiments like these happened in Nazi Germany . . . Not here."

• • •

The first question raised in this book was, Why did it take almost sixty years for the United States to find and extradite John Demjanjuk for trial in Germany as a Nazi collaborator? It is the question that is asked most often in discussions of the Demjanjuk case. A partial answer is now clear.

A small group of powerful and unaccountable military and intelligence officers resisted and blocked the investigation of former Nazis and Nazi collaborators hiding in America because they had secrets to protect: obstruction of justice, illegal use of funds to hire former Nazis and Nazi collaborators as spies, fraudulent whitewashing of the records of former Nazis, illegally helping former Nazis acquire U.S. citizenship, and criminally experimenting on U.S. servicemen and civilians. Every single Nazi or Nazi collaborator hiding in America posed a potential threat to those secrets. Exposing them and the war crimes they committed might raise embarrassing questions.

But no secret is forever. Strands of the government cover-ups started to unravel in the late 1970s, as the tide of American indifference began to shift. There were several reasons for the change in attitude. The old entrenched layer of bureaucrats at the Pentagon, State Department, and Justice Department began to retire. The Cold War rants of McCarthyites had turned to hoarse whispers. The nation was no longer "distracted" by Korea and Vietnam. The Watergate scandal and the resignation of Richard Nixon no longer riveted the nation, and perhaps even inspired a new demand for accountability in government. Millions saw the *Holocaust* TV miniseries, starring a young Meryl Streep.

In sum, there was a new generation of Americans for whom World War II was a chapter in a history book, not a traumatic personal experience. They were curious and willing to question.

Nazi war criminals in America? You've got to be kidding. Where?

With that new awareness dawning on America, the dominoes leading to John Demjanjuk began to tumble with increasing speed. And Elizabeth Holtzman caused most of the tumbling.

CHAPTER FOURTEEN

The Last Domino

Elizabeth Holtzman had a razor mind and a rapier tongue. Although she knew exactly what had to be done to bring Nazis and Nazi collaborators hiding in America to justice, she was handicapped. In 1973, as a junior member and the only woman on the House Immigration Subcommittee, she had limited clout. So she relied on a bit of wisdom she had gleaned from her years at Radcliffe and at Harvard Law.

Screw the rules.

As Holtzman saw it, there were five things that needed to be done yesterday: formally request Bonn and Tel Aviv to supply information about the alleged Nazis on the Karbach list; forge an anti-Nazi alliance with Moscow and the Iron Curtain countries; investigate the INS for obstruction of justice; close a major loophole in immigration law; and move the investigation of suspected Nazis from the compromised INS to a special, independent Nazi unit in the Justice Department.

It would take an iron fist and seven years to get the job done.

A critical first step was to penetrate the Iron Curtain. All but one of the alleged Nazis on the Karbach list were from the Soviet bloc countries of Eastern Europe. At least six of them were either about to be tried in absentia for war crimes committed in their countries of origin— Latvia, Estonia, Lithuania, Ukraine, Yugoslavia, and Romania—or had already been convicted of such crimes in absentia. Assuming the investigations into their Nazi collaboration were not frame-ups and their trials were not conducted in kangaroo courts, there had to be documentary evidence of their crimes and credible eyewitnesses. The question was: Why didn't the State Department ask the Soviet Union for cooperation on an issue that both countries presumably agreed on—namely, that former Nazis and their collaborators should be punished for their crimes against humanity?

Holtzman sent blistering letters to INS commissioner Leonard Chapman and Secretary of State Henry Kissinger in April 1975 demanding that they open channels to Bonn, Tel Aviv, and Moscow. Under pressure from her and the chairman of the Immigration Subcommittee, Representative Joshua Eilberg of Pennsylvania, Kissinger caved in. He agreed to review the names on the Karbach list, one by one, then ask Bonn to provide what information it had on each.

Kissinger's promise was an empty one because all but one of the people named on the Karbach list were Eastern Europeans. It was highly unlikely that West Germany would have any useful information on them as it had on Braunsteiner, a Western European. And, in fact, it turned out that Bonn couldn't help.

A month later, in May 1975, Holtzman was part of a congressional delegation to the National Conference on Soviet Jewry (NCSJ), held in Moscow. The conference focused on the Soviet campaign of intimidation to prevent Jews from joining their families living outside the Iron Curtain. NCSJ did not pull any political punches. It accused the Soviet Union of firing Jews who applied for emigration permits, evicting them from their subsidized apartments, kicking them out of school, arresting them on trumped-up charges, and drafting them into the army as punishment. Soviet officials did not take kindly to NCSJ's public lashing. The atmosphere in the conference room was palpably hostile.

While attending the conference, Holtzman asked for a private meeting with Mikhail Malyarov, deputy procurator of the Soviet Union and one of the country's ranking legal officers, to discuss an issue not on the NCSJ agenda—Soviet help in finding and deporting Nazi collaborators. Given that Holtzman did not have the blessing of the State Department to make such a request in the name of the United States, the unofficial meeting was a gamble. Would she make the State Department so angry that it would punish her subcommittee with an even colder shoulder? Would she kill the possibility of cooperation by making a hostile Soviet leader even more hostile?

When Holtzman brought up the Nazi issue with Deputy Malyarov, the atmosphere in the conference room immediately changed "from night to day." Not only was Malyarov willing to cooperate with the United States, he was in fact eager. "We'll help in any way we can," he said. Then he went on to promise Holtzman the bright side of the moon: documents from its extensive archives, names and addresses of eyewitnesses, a welcome mat for American officials who wanted to interview them, and visas for witnesses to testify in the United States if requested. It was almost as if Malyarov were saying: Where have you been for the last thirty years? We've been waiting.

Malyarov placed one condition on his surprising offer. He wanted to see Henry Kissinger on his knees. The request for help, he stipulated, had to come through official channels. That was bureaucratese for not through a congresswoman, or an unenthusiastic INS, or a compromised Justice Department, but through Henry Kissinger and the U.S. Department of State.

There was the rub.

Kissinger had consistently refused to ask for Soviet assistance. To begin with, he was constitutionally suspicious of any Soviet promise. If the communists offered to help, there must be something in it for them. And what was in it for them was clear. If the Soviet Union helped, it would want extradition rights in return. A public Soviet trial of a Nazi collaborator would send a message to the rest of the world: We communists care about crimes against humanity while the United States does not. It would also send a political message: Collaborating with the enemy was high treason, and if a Soviet citizen ever committed treason, Moscow would chase him down and punish him even if it took thirty years.

Finally, cooperating with the Soviet Union would help Moscow disguise a not-so-subtle hypocrisy. Moscow was offering to help the United States find and expel Eastern Europeans who killed Jews as members of Einsatzgruppen. Truth be told, the Soviets had been happy to get rid of those Jews. And now, while its right hand was ready to try Nazi collaborators for murdering Jews in the past, its left hand was depriving Jews of their human rights and punishing them in the present.

Cold War politics aside, Holtzman knew what she had to do.

Washington bureaucrats did not respond to right and wrong, or the golden rule, or to justice and fair play. The higher moral ground was for angels. The only arguments they understood were political pressure and public embarrassment. So Holtzman tossed Kissinger and the State Department into the most powerful pressure cooker in America—the *New York Times*. Again, it was a ploy a junior congresswoman was not supposed to use. Juniors were expected to go through proper channels before launching public assaults on high government officials with the power to retaliate.

In an article published soon after she returned from Moscow, Holtzman accused the State Department of "making every effort to *avoid* contacting countries, including the Soviet Union," for information about alleged Nazi collaborators. "Plainly dilatory," she cried, "incomprehensible . . . at a loss to explain . . . an affront to Congress and the American people."

The media whipping worked. Kissinger authorized a tentative overture to Moscow, requesting information about fourteen names on the Karbach list. And with the approval of the State Department, the INS sent four attorneys to Israel to interview witnesses of alleged Nazi collaborators on the Karbach list. They returned home with thirty-two signed affidavits and thirty-two promises to come to the United States to testify, if asked.

The breaking of the Cold War logjam was the fifth domino to tumble.

In an attempt to make sure that Holtzman would remain happy and quiet, the INS tossed her a bone—a new office totally dedicated to investigating alleged Nazis and Nazi collaborators. The new office was.... Sam Zutty. The INS gave him virtually no staff and forbade him to approach any foreign country for documents without the unanimous approval of a committee of fourteen INS bureaucrats. The last thing the INS wanted was another loose cannon like Anthony DeVito or Vincent Schiano.

The INS also released the Karbach list to the public, and it was no mere bone. Encouraged by the INS's newfound "interest" in enforcing U.S. immigration law, individual whistle-blowers and organizations volunteered more names. The INS list quickly grew to more than two hundred. The last domino had finally tumbled.

One of the names on the new INS list was Iwan Demjanjuk.

CHAPTER FIFTEEN

Iwan Who?

Sam Zutty got a letter from New York senator Jacob Javits late in 1975, soon after he became the titular INS Nazi hunter without a full staff and a puny budget of ninety thousand dollars. Accompanying the Javits letter was a list of seventy alleged Ukrainian war criminals in the United States, a dozen of whom lived in Cleveland. The list had been compiled by Michael Hanusiak, a native-born American of Ukrainian descent and the editor of the *Ukrainian Daily News.*

Like Karbach, Hanusiak didn't trust the INS. Wouldn't a powerful New York Jewish senator like Jacob Javits command more attention than the editor of an obscure four-page ethnic newspaper?

The Hanusiak list was suspect from the start. It was no secret in the Ukrainian American community that the *Ukrainian Daily News* was a pro-Soviet rag, if not an actual mouthpiece of the Soviet government. It was also no secret that Hanusiak himself was a member of the Communist Party USA (CPUSA).

The FBI had been closely watching Michael Hanusiak since the mid-1950s and compiled a 534-page file on him and his communist activities based on interviews with reliable confidential sources. I acquired a copy of that file under an FOIA request. Although half of the pages were still classified, the reports in the file paint a profile of Hanusiak and his relationship to the Soviet government.

. . .

Hanusiak was a member of the Communist Party (CP) and later the Communist Party USA (CPUSA) beginning as early as 1941, when he held weekly CP meetings at his home in Pittsburgh. He was a leader in the America-Slav Congress, a paid field director for the International Workers Organization, and a sponsor of the Civil Rights Congress. All three groups were defined as communist by the U.S. Attorney General.

In the late 1940s, Hanusiak left the CP, disillusioned with its aims and disgusted with its insider politics. The FBI attempted to recruit him in the mid-1950s as a confidential source, but he politely declined to supply the FBI with names of known communists or to spy for the bureau. Sometime around 1972, Hanusiak rejoined the CPUSA and became a member of its National Committee and president of its Nationalities Department. The FBI noted that he made yearly trips to Ukraine, paid for by the Soviet government.

A series of FBI reports, written between February and May 1987 and based on information supplied by confidential sources, were directly related to the Demjanjuk case. It was Michael Hanusiak who "fingered" Demjanjuk (February 13) and was a conduit for the Soviets, who used him to provide "the initial information used against John Demjanjuk... to the Department of Justice, Office of Special Investigation" (April 13). Former OSI director Allan Ryan revealed in his book, *Quiet Neighbors*, that OSI had relied on a Ukrainian source whom he fictitiously called Wasyl Yachenko. The source's real name was Michael Hanusiak (April 20).

• • •

It was obvious from reading the list that the Soviet government had directly or indirectly helped Hanusiak compile both the list and the summaries of alleged crimes it contained: who, what, where, and when.

The suspicion of Soviet complicity in compiling what would become known as the "Ukrainian list" was confirmed the following year with the publication of *Lest We Forget*, a book about Ukrainian civilian collaboration with the Nazis. Edited by Hanusiak and published in Canada, home to more Ukrainians than the United States, the book featured more than 150 pages of field reports and photos of alleged Ukrainian atrocities against Jews; some reports were written in German and some in Cyrillic script. Assuming the documents were not KGB forgeries, they had to come from the closely guarded Soviet archives.

Zutty found himself impaled on the horns of skepticism and pragmatism. The Soviets had consistently denied accredited journalists and
international organizations access to the Nazi files it had captured in
Berlin and on its long march to get there. Skepticism asked: Why would
the Soviets grant rummaging privileges to a Ukrainian American? And
why now? Could it be that Hanusiak didn't rummage? That maybe the
KGB prepared the list and gave it to him? Like the CIA, the Soviet spy
agency was no stranger to dirty tricks. It was a toss of the coin as to who
played dirtier.

Hanusiak himself was no help solving the who-gave-what-to-whom
puzzle. He claimed he composed the list from Ukrainian newspaper articles, interviews with editors and journalists, and addresses on letters
mailed from America to Ukraine. The explanations limped. How could
Hanusiak and communist newspapers know where each of the seventy
alleged Nazi collaborators had committed war crimes and which crimes
they had committed? How could addresses on letters mailed from the
United States provide such information? Either the KGB gave the list
to Hanusiak, or it helped him compile it, or it fed the information to the
newspapers, editors, and journalists Hanusiak consulted. Simply put, the
Ukrainian list had KGB fingerprints all over it.

Pragmatism asked: So what? The names were just leads, like those on
the Karbach list. As leads, they were either true or false. Zutty's job was
to figure out which, then to develop solid cases built on the strict rules
of evidence required in deportation and denaturalization cases, regardless of where the information came from.

With no investigative staff or budget to speak of, however, it would
be impossible for Zutty to open seventy new investigations while jug-
gling a handful of active ones. So he pared down Hanusiak's Ukrainian
list to a more manageable nine names. Two were especially promising—
Feodor Fedorenko and Iwan Demjanjuk, both alleged SS death camp
guards in Poland. Hanusiak had described Fedorenko as a guard at Treblinka, where he allegedly beat and murdered Jews, and Demjanjuk as
a guard at Sobibor. Hanusiak had not, however, attributed any specific
war crimes to Demjanjuk as he had to Fedorenko.

If Hanusiak was right, Zutty believed both men were ideal candidates
for denaturalization because both had lied on their visa applications.
Fedorenko swore he spent the war years farming in the Polish village
of Sarny before being deported to Germany as a forced factory worker.

And Demjanjuk swore he was a farmer living in the Polish village of Sobibor, not a guard at the camp there.

Fedorenko and Demjanjuk were promising targets for another reason. There were dozens of Treblinka and Sobibor survivors living in the United States and Israel who should be relatively easy to find. They would either recognize the two alleged guards or not, know them by name or not. The other seven targets on the Ukrainian short list had allegedly collaborated with the Nazis in Ukraine as local police officers or members of SS death squads (Einsatzkommandos). Evidence against those seven would require a lot of legwork inside the Soviet Union, and Zutty was short on legs.

There was another positive development for Zutty and his small staff. The State Department had asked Israel for help in collecting evidence against Nazi collaborators in America, and Israel had agreed. Perhaps the Israeli police could find survivors who would positively identify Fedorenko and Demjanjuk as SS camp guards. Gambling on that hope, Zutty asked his new regional boss (Sol Marks had retired) to submit a request to the INS control board for Israeli assistance. To Zutty's surprise, the board approved, and the pared-down Ukrainian list of nine names with the photographs of eighteen men accused of alleged war crimes left for Jerusalem tucked inside a diplomatic pouch. When the package arrived, the Israeli police made up a photo spread by pasting the eighteen pictures on three pieces of brown cardboard.

• • •

The photos Zutty sent to Israel were deeply flawed and would come back to bite U.S. prosecutors during the 1978 trial of Feodor Fedorenko in Fort Lauderdale, Florida. In 1977, the year before the Fedorenko trial opened, the U.S. Supreme Court set strict rules for the use of photo spreads in American trials and proceedings. In essence, the court ruled that no single picture should call attention to itself. Photos should be the same size and color, and be uniform in appearance, with no single photo brighter or clearer than the others. No single photo should be labeled or highlighted or matched with unfocused pictures. And all photo subjects should have somewhat similar distinguishing characteristics such as age and race. If the alleged criminal was a twenty-year-old Caucasian, the other photos must also be of young Caucasians.

Unfortunately, Zutty's photos—and consequently the Israeli photo spread—failed to comply with the specifications set by the U.S. Supreme Court. The first six photos on page one of the spread, for example, were smaller than Fedorenko's (no. 17) and Demjanjuk's (no. 16). Each photo in the spread was blurred or shadowed except three—Fedorenko's, Demjanjuk's, and photo nine on page two, which was also smaller. If that wasn't invalidating enough, the Fedorenko and Demjanjuk photos were the only two in the spread with large borders, which made them leap off the page.

• • •

The Israeli police had their own Nazi Crimes Unit, whose main job was to help other countries like the United States build cases. The Nazi unit assigned the nine Ukrainians to its ace investigator, Miriam Radiwker, a Ukrainian-born attorney who had fled to the Soviet Union early in the war to escape the Nazis, and who had practiced law in both Poland and the Soviet Union before immigrating to Israel in 1964. Radiwker studied Zutty's report and arrived at the same conclusion he had and for the same reasons. Fedorenko and Demjanjuk were the two most promising targets on the list.

Radiwker began her preliminary investigation with Feodor Fedorenko, a seventy-year-old retired welder living in Waterbury, Connecticut. He was the easier target because there were more Treblinka survivors living in Israel than Sobibor survivors, and the alleged crimes against Fedorenko were specific—beating and murdering—while those against Demjanjuk were vague.

In May 1976, while Congresswoman Elizabeth Holtzman was meeting with the Soviets over U.S.-Moscow cooperation, Radiwker placed ads in Israeli newspapers asking Sobibor and Treblinka survivors for help in a Nazi collaboration investigation. She also contacted three Treblinka survivors whom she knew from a previous investigation. All three had escaped from Treblinka during the uprising there in the summer of 1943. She made it a point not to tell them Fedorenko and Demjanjuk were the subjects of the investigation.

Radiwker's interviews with survivor-witnesses followed a protocol provided by Zutty: Show each witness at least three photos; if the witness recognizes anyone in the spread, get a physical description of the subject at the time the witness knew him; have the witness describe the uniform the subject wore at the camp; and most important, find out whether the survivor had *personally* seen the subject commit acts of violence on civilians (if so, from what vantage point) and had *personally* suffered at the hands of the subject.

Radiwker's first witness was Treblinka survivor Eugen Turowsky. Before presenting the photos, Radiwker asked Turowsky if he could recall the last name of any guard at Treblinka. He could not. She then placed the three-page photo spread in front of him. Each of the eighteen photos was a visa picture of a young Ukrainian.

"Please, sir," she asked. "Look and see whether you find someone you know."

An experienced lawyer and investigator, Radiwker made it a point of asking this unembellished question lest she be accused of prompting or trying to influence the witness.

Turowsky didn't recognize anyone on the first or second cardboard pages. But when he came to the third page, featuring photos sixteen and seventeen, he became visibly agitated, then pointed to number sixteen, the visa picture of a round-faced, well-fed Ivan Demjanjuk dressed in a dark suit and tie.

"Iwan," he shouted. "Iwan from Treblinka. Iwan Grozny."

Iwan of Treblinka was well-known to Nazi hunters worldwide as the guard who operated Treblinka's gas chambers. He sat at the top of Simon Wiesenthal's most-wanted list of Nazi collaborators. Treblinka prisoners gave him the name Ivan the Terrible (Grozny). The historical Ivan the Terrible was Ivan IV (Vasilyevich), who became the first czar of Russia.

Radiwker's first reaction to Turowsky's identification was that the survivor had to be mistaken. Iwan Demjanjuk had been a guard at Sobibor, not Treblinka. Information from America was always accurate, in her experience, and she didn't have the slightest doubt that it might be wrong this time. Since Turowsky was emotionally shaken, Radiwker chose not to probe his memory, however gently. Instead she asked him to describe Iwan Grozny, as the INS had requested.

"He was of medium height, solidly built, with a round, full face," Turowsky said. "He had a short broad neck, high forehead with the beginning of baldness . . . He could have been 23–24 years old at most."

Turowsky did not work near the Treblinka gas chamber in camp two, but he saw Iwan almost daily as he passed from one camp to another. Given her witness's emotional state, Radiwker decided to end the interview. "Mr. Turowsky," she said, "we can talk about this more tomorrow." Then she wrote up what Turowsky had told her, as the INS had requested. When Turowsky returned the next morning, she showed him the photo spread a second time.

"Look at the pictures," she said. "Perhaps you will find someone you know."

"The man in photograph seventeen is familiar to me," Turowsky said. "This could be Fedorenko. I am almost certain of it, but I must comment that I always saw him in uniform and here he is in civilian clothes."

The more he studied photo seventeen, the more certain Turowsky became. "This is Fedorenko. I am sure of this. I don't remember his first name. . . . I saw him almost daily. . . . He was tall, about 180 cm [five feet, nine inches], age about 30, with broad shoulders. . . . He committed crimes. He murdered Jews on his own."

Radiwker added the new information to her report and offered it to Turowsky, who read and signed it. That afternoon, she placed the same three pages of photos on the table in front of Treblinka survivor Avraham Goldfarb.

"Please, sir. Look and see whether you find someone you know."

Like Turowsky, Goldfarb picked out Demjanjuk as Iwan of Treblinka. But unlike Turowsky, he was not visibly agitated. He was certain the man in photo sixteen was Ivan the Terrible, he told Radiwker, because he worked only a few yards from the gas chamber and could see Iwan drive the prisoners into the chambers, then enter the building that housed the motors that delivered the lethal carbon monoxide gas.

"We workers called him Iwan Grozny," Goldfarb said. "Ivan the Terrible."

Either the information Zutty had given Radiwker was wrong or Goldfarb was wrong. Faced with the dilemma, Radiwker decided to probe. She pointed to photo sixteen, Demjanjuk.

"This man was at *Sobibor*, not Treblinka," she said.

Goldfarb was adamant. "When I came, he was already at Treblinka," he said.

Next, Radiwker showed the photos to Eliyahu Rosenberg. Like Turowsky and Goldfarb before him, he pointed to photo sixteen, but was more cautious.

"The man in this photo," he said, "is very similar to the Ukrainian Iwan who . . . was called Iwan Grozny."

Without any prompting from Radiwker, Rosenberg went on to describe Iwan. "He had a round face, full. . . . He had a high forehead with the beginning of baldness. He also had very short hair. His neck was short, fat....I remember that he had prominent ears....He was 22–23 years old."

Rosenberg hastened to add that he was not 100 percent sure. "I refuse to say that I identify him with certainty," he said. "This photo apparently originates from a much later period. Here he is dressed in civilian clothes while I always saw him in . . . a black uniform."

Rosenberg's point was valid. Demjanjuk's visa application photo was taken in 1951, eight years after the SS liquidated Treblinka.

Rosenberg then went on to positively identify Fedorenko as a guard at Treblinka. Once again, Radiwker decided to probe. According to the information she had, she told Rosenberg, the man in photo sixteen was a guard at Sobibor, not Treblinka.

"Madam, I know the face, and I am telling you he was at Treblinka," Rosenberg replied. "In the course of 1942, several prisoners—construction workers—were sent to Sobibor together with some Ukrainians who did not return from there. However, I saw Ivan the Terrible until the last day."

Radiwker concluded that the two positive (and one probable) identifications of Demjanjuk as Ivan the Terrible were hardly a coincidence. All three Treblinka survivors had based their identification on the same set of physical characteristics—round face, premature receding hairline, short bull neck, protruding ears, and age. There was some discrepancy on Iwan's height. Was Demjanjuk Iwan Grozny, Radiwker asked herself, or did he just look like Iwan Grozny?

As requested, Radiwker sent the INS a report summarizing her interviews and presenting a concise description of each witness—age, state of mental and physical health, ability to travel, and willingness to testify in the United States. Then she went back to interviewing Treblinka and Sobibor survivors. Maybe she could solve the apparent contradiction.

• • •

Back in New York, Zutty couldn't have been more pleased. All three Treblinka survivors had positively identified Fedorenko as a camp guard and a murderer. As far as eyewitnesses go, they were a category three, *la crème de la crème*. In the first category were those who had personally known the alleged war criminal—as schoolmate, neighbor, coworker—and knew that he collaborated with the Nazis because they saw him in uniform. They had not, however, actually seen the person commit a war crime. These eyewitnesses were useful because there was little chance of mistaken identity.

Next, there were eyewitnesses who had neither known the alleged war criminal nor had seen him commit a crime. But they had witnessed local Nazi collaborators rounding up victims, brutalizing them, and, sometimes, killing them. These witnesses could testify that the organization the alleged collaborator belonged to habitually committed such war crimes.

Finally, there were eyewitnesses who both had known the alleged war criminal and had actually seen him commit crimes against humanity. The three Treblinka survivors fell into this category. They each had known Fedorenko as an SS auxiliary guard in uniform and armed with a gun. And they had witnessed him beating prisoners with whips and shooting them to death. Important to Zutty was that each eyewitness appeared—at least on paper—as convincing and credible, and each was specific about Fedorenko's crimes. Who could ask for more?

The three Treblinka survivors, however, surprised Zutty as much as they had Radiwker. Each had paused at the visa photo of Iwan Demjanjuk. Each had pointed to it and said that he was Iwan the Terrible, the most hated and feared man at Treblinka. They had lived with his image in their heads every day for more than thirty years. How could they possibly be mistaken?

In August 1977, two years after the INS received the Ukrainian list, the U.S. attorney's office in Cleveland filed the complaint: *United States of America v. John Demjanjuk, AKA Iwan Demjanjuk, AKA Iwan Grozny (Ivan the Terrible)*. The charges were clear and simple: Demjanjuk had served as a Treblinka death camp guard and lied about it; and as Ivan the Terrible he had engaged in the "cruel, inhumane and bestial treatment of Jewish prisoners."

At the same time, the U.S. attorney's office in Fort Lauderdale filed a similar suit against Fedorenko, who had retired and moved to Florida; it alleged he had been a guard at Treblinka as well. Since the case against him was stronger, Fedorenko faced a judge first.

In July 1978, three years after the INS received the Ukrainian list, six Treblinka survivors confronted Fedorenko in a Florida courtroom. As the first alleged Nazi collaborator to be tried under the rules of the Displaced Persons Act (DPA), his trial turned out to be a watershed case that prepared the legal ground for the prosecution of John Demjanjuk.

CHAPTER SIXTEEN

Paving the Way

E motions erupted in the grassy courtyard outside the Fort Lauderdale courtroom as twenty-year-old Brett Becker, executive director of the Jewish Defense League (JDL) in Miami, led a group of demonstrators in a chant.

"What do we want?" Becker shouted through a bullhorn.

"Fedorenko!" the crowd screamed back like "avenging cheerleaders," as the *Miami Herald* described them.

"How do we want him?"

"Dead!"

The chanting was so loud that Judge Norman Roettger interrupted the trial twice, ordering Becker to muzzle the bullhorn and silence the crowd. When he refused, Roettger told U.S. marshals to arrest him. The handcuffs silenced the bullhorn, but the sight of police dragging away a young Jew evoked images of the Gestapo and only inflamed the crowd even more. The arrest and handcuffs also gave the JDL another excuse to ask a federal appeals court to remove Roettger for bias. The court refused.

A group of Holocaust survivors from Miami joined the JDL in the courtyard, adding blind fury to the emotional mix. Members of the Ben Gurion Culture Club, they carried signs reading "Impeach the Judge" and "Remember 6 Million Jews Murdered by the Nazis." Besides joining in Becker's chant, they conducted a memorial service in the courtyard.

"We are Jews," they chanted.

"We couldn't be prouder.

"If you cannot hear us,

"We'll yell louder."

Protected by a cordon of U.S. marshals, one lone Holocaust denier braved the anger of the mob. He carried a sign that said, "The Jews Live a Lie . . . Six Million Lies." A female survivor managed to break through the cordon. She ripped the placard from the denier's hands and stomped on it. Marshals restrained her before she could punch him.

For Fedorenko, entering and leaving the courthouse past jostling demonstrators screaming "Death to Fedorenko!" was an emotional ordeal. One Holocaust survivor broke through the ring of U.S. marshals who escorted him to and from the courthouse and landed a blow before they could pull her away.

Things were just as emotional inside the courtroom during the fourteen-day trial. The tension was, as Judge Roettger put it, "so thick you could almost touch it." And when Fedorenko took the stand after days of verbal abuse, he was visibly pale and shaken.

At issue in the trial were four questions that went to the heart of the Fedorenko and Demjanjuk cases:

- Did merely serving as a camp guard constitute assisting the enemy?
- Did Fedorenko deliberately lie on his visa application form?
- If so, was it a "material" lie, that is, the suppressing of facts which, if known, either would have made him excludable from the United States, or would have led to the uncovering of facts making him excludable?
- Did it matter whether he volunteered for the guard duty or was drafted?

Recognizing that U.S. citizenship is a priceless treasure, the Supreme Court had deliberately drafted evidentiary standards for denaturalization cases that were stricter than those governing other civil cases. It ruled that the evidence must be "clear, unequivocal, and convincing [and] not leave the issue in doubt." Those narrow rules are especially necessary, the Court further ruled, when charges of immigration fraud are made long after citizenship or a visa has been granted, and when the accused has met his obligations as an American citizen and has committed no crimes.

Charges against Fedorenko and Demjanjuk were made more than thirty years after their visa applications had been approved. And neither man had a criminal record as an American citizen.

In spite of the heavy burden of proof, the U.S. attorneys assigned to try Fedorenko believed they had an airtight case. Six eyewitnesses from Israel testified that they had identified Fedorenko from a photo spread. All six eyewitnesses also testified that they had seen Fedorenko shoot and beat prisoners with a metal-studded whip. Three eyewitnesses positively identified him in the courtroom as the brutal Treblinka guard they described from the witness stand. A visa application was offered into evidence in which Fedorenko swore he had been a farmer in Poland and a forced factory worker in Germany during the war. A former U.S. vice consul testified that he would not have granted Fedorenko a visa permitting him to enter the United States in 1949 if he had known that Fedorenko had been a guard at Treblinka.

Testifying in his own behalf, Fedorenko stole much of the government's thunder. He frankly admitted that he had been a perimeter guard at Treblinka, but denied he volunteered for the job. The SS had drafted him, he said, and he would have been executed had he refused to serve. He knew that prisoners were being gassed at Treblinka because, one day, he was posted to camp two, where the gas chambers were located. What he saw, he said, so sickened him that he refused to work there again. He never beat or killed anyone. The only time he ever fired his rifle, he testified, was when the SS ordered him to shoot during the uprising, quickly adding that he fired over the heads of the fleeing prisoners.

Fedorenko also frankly admitted that he had lied on his visa application. Not to deceive the office of the U.S. consul, he said, but out of fear for his life. If he admitted he had been a POW, he would have been turned over to the Soviets for repatriation and executed as a deserter. And if he admitted he had been a guard at Treblinka, the Soviets would have executed him for collaborating with the enemy, an act of treason.

Judge Roettger, who presided over the juryless civil trial as mandated by Congress, was clearly sympathetic toward Fedorenko. In his written decision, he described the case as a David and Goliath legal battle. Four attorneys with an oversized budget sat at the prosecution table. That much legal firepower, he pointed out, was generally reserved for Mafia dons, serial killers, and drug lords. A single attorney sat at the defense table, and he was one attorney more than Fedorenko could afford. The retired welder was living on Social Security and a modest pension. He didn't own a home or a car and had only five thousand dollars in the bank. The only thing the man actually owned, Roettger noted, was a cemetery plot.

Roettger went on to condemn what he called the "Hollywood spectacle" staged outside his courtroom. He noted that the Jewish Defense League advertised in Miami newspapers offering free chartered bus rides to Fort Lauderdale for the trial.

If Roettger was harsh on the crowd outside his courtroom, he was merciless on the prosecution inside. In essence, he disemboweled the government's entire case because, he ruled, it failed to prove the case without a doubt. Since the government did not offer any *documentary* evidence that Fedorenko had committed crimes as a Treblinka guard, Roettger observed, witness identification was "the heart" of the trial. And witness identification relied on a photo spread that Roettger characterized as "impermissibly suggestive [and that] did not pass muster under American law."

After noting that only three of the six eyewitnesses positively identified Fedorenko in court, Roettger went on to say that the three identifications were tainted because their testimony and body language suggested that the survivors had discussed the case among themselves and had been coached. Both indiscretions violated the rules of the court.

Roettger also attacked eyewitness testimony about Fedorenko's alleged shooting and beating of prisoners. He found the survivor testimony both disturbing and heartrending and never doubted that they were at Treblinka and suffered horrors there. But he characterized their identification of Fedorenko as a brutal guard at Treblinka as inconsistent and, therefore, unconvincing. And he found the testimony of former U.S. vice consul Kempton Jenkins unconvincing as well. Although Jenkins told the court that every camp guard he had ever interviewed claimed he did not volunteer for the job, Roettger did not consider that unsupported statement as proof that Fedorenko lied when he testified that the SS had drafted him for guard duty.

If he was hard on the prosecution, Roettger went easy on the defense. As a judge, he prided himself on being a keen observer of courtroom body language and vocal innuendos that he used to help determine witness credibility. He found Fedorenko a credible witness. Unlike his survivor-accusers, who were "combative, hostile and intensive," he said, Fedorenko was calm and guileless and spoke with a firm, sincere voice.

In the absence of any specific evidence to the contrary, he believed Fedorenko when he said he did not volunteer for guard duty at Treblinka.

Roettger further pointed out that the defense had drawn an uncontested picture of Fedorenko as a model American citizen. Fellow foundry workers and union bosses testified that he was hardworking and reliable, and that he never filed a single grievance with the union or had one filed against him. Neighbors testified that he was a gentle man without any apparent prejudices. And his attorney presented evidence that he had no criminal record and only one traffic ticket after twenty-nine years in America.

In the end, Judge Roettger ruled that the government failed to present "clear, unequivocal, and convincing" evidence that Fedorenko had committed any crimes against civilians, or that he had volunteered for guard duty at Treblinka, or that his lie masked material facts or was an act of "willful deceit."

Roettger also wrote that there were two "equitable considerations," or extenuating circumstances, critical to the case and his decision: 1) if Fedorenko had refused to serve at Treblinka, the SS would have executed him; 2) if Fedorenko had told visa officials the truth, his life would have been in danger. Roettger therefore ruled: "Because the Government failed to meet its burden of proof, judgement is entered for the defendant. Under the circumstances of this case equitable considerations would also require the same result."

Fedorenko cried. The JDL fumed.

Chant leader Brett Becker told the press: "This decision is indicative of the fact that Nazi war criminals will be allowed to live in America in comfort. This decision strengthens our belief in the philosophy of the JDL, which states there is no justice for the Jew, except that which he takes himself."

In New York, Bonnie Pechter, the national director of the JDL, said: "We are going to start a large campaign against this judge and . . . demand a new trial. There is no prosecution for Nazi war criminals in America."

Morton Mattel, a Treblinka survivor never called to the stand, expressed his shock at Roettger's decision. "How can it be that he goes free as you and me," he told a reporter. "I was with him for four months. I can't forget. I woke up last night screaming."

Mattel, who lived near Fort Lauderdale, had been prepared to testify that Fedorenko beat him with his whip and that he had a scar on his scalp to prove it, but prosecutors never called him to the stand. Arguing that six eyewitnesses were enough, Roettger asked the government not to call any more. The government agreed.

Although Roettger's decision appeared cold and uncaring, the trial had affected him deeply. "It was the most gruesome testimony I've ever heard," he told the *Fort Lauderdale News*. "I just couldn't get it out of my mind. The testimony kept creeping into my dreams. I dropped a couple of pounds because I couldn't eat. Food had no taste."

The government didn't waste any time filing an appeal, which it won. And Fedorenko wasted no time filing a counterappeal to the U.S. Supreme Court, which he lost. Attorney General Benjamin Civiletti himself argued the government's case before the High Court, sending a clear message to America and the rest of the world that the era of protecting Nazi collaborators in the United States was over. Civiletti argued: "armed guard service, with a uniform, with epaulets, with a black tie, with boots, with a pistol, with a rifle in a death camp . . . was such conduct that it amounted to assistance of the enemy in the persecution of civilian population."

For the High Court, the Fedorenko case was a simple application of the Displaced Persons Act of 1948 (DPA). Congress had passed the law, as was its right under the Constitution. Congress could have stipulated that assistance to the enemy had to be *voluntary* to warrant exclusion from the United States, but it deliberately chose not to do so. Therefore, the justices ruled, involuntary forced service was not a valid consideration.

The High Court further pointed out that the DPA did not grant the government the right to use equity considerations in making its denaturalization decisions. Therefore, the Court held, Judge Roettger erred when he ruled in favor of Fedorenko based on extenuating circumstances.

In sum, the Supreme Court ruled: Whether Fedorenko's guard service was voluntary or involuntary was irrelevant; Fedorenko's lie hid material facts; and if visa officers had known that Fedorenko had been a guard at Treblinka, they would have denied him a visa. Therefore, the government could strip Fedorenko of his U.S. citizenship.

Even though he faced deportation, Feodor Fedorenko held no grudge against the United States. "I am happy and satisfied with America," he said. "America is not to blame that Jewish groups have brought this up."

Fedorenko had learned that his first wife and son, whom he thought died during the war, were alive and living in Ukraine. He asked to be deported to the Soviet Union to join them. He left for Ukraine in 1984, six years after his trial in Fort Lauderdale and nine years after the INS received the Ukrainian list from Michael Hanusiak.

CHAPTER SEVENTEEN

The Smart Thorn

While the government was preparing for the trial of John Demjanjuk in Cleveland, Elizabeth Holtzman was sparring with Congress and the Department of Justice in Washington. At issue were three items on her to-be-done-yesterday list.

As a lawyer, Holtzman recognized that the Immigration and Naturalization Act of 1952 (Public Law 414) had a loophole big enough for any Nazi who wasn't brain dead to skate through. The congresswoman closed that loophole in 1978 with what would be called the Holtzman Amendment. It made inadmissible to the United States "*participants* in Nazi persecution, genocide, or the commission of any act of torture or extrajudicial killing."

As a result of the Holtzman Amendment, the names of sixty thousand known Nazis and Nazi collaborators were placed on a U.S. immigration watch list. Hundreds were eventually blocked from entering the United States. The amendment also made prosecutable those Nazis and Nazi collaborators who entered the United States after 1952, and closed a loophole whereby those ordered deported could avoid deportation by seeking "discretionary relief" from the court under a hardship provision in immigration law.

• • •

Holtzman also knew that the FBI and the CIA were protecting former Nazis already in the United States. Although she was eager for proof of federal meddling, she wasn't about to waste even a day trying to find it. Let historians unravel the tangled strands of cover-up, conspiracy, and obstruction. Her mission was to help deport Nazi war criminals. Along with Immigration Subcommittee chairman Eilberg, Holtzman lobbied for a General Accounting Office investigation into the INS bureaucratic disaster.

The GAO opened its investigation of the INS in 1977, three years after Holtzman had asked to read the Karbach list files. The subcommittee had given the GAO a clear, no-nonsense mandate: Find out whether INS's lack of Nazi deportations was "due to a conspiracy involving INS personnel and possibly other Federal agencies," as Anthony DeVito alleged.

From the moment they opened the first INS file folder, GAO investigators ran into their own "iron curtain." Citing national security, both the FBI and the CIA had refused to deliver the Nazi files and documents the GAO had requested. Tossing the GAO a crumb, the agencies did offer to provide good-faith summaries of files and documents, if they had any.

With one hand stapled to its back, the GAO selected fifty-seven INS Nazi cases for review. The findings were so totally predicable they constituted a nonevent. Only five, or less than 10 percent of the total, appeared to be thorough INS investigations. The real issue: Why was the INS record so shoddy? Was it because the FBI, CIA, and INS were protecting Nazi war criminals?

To answer those questions, the GAO relied exclusively on self-reporting from the three agencies:

- Without revealing any names for national security reasons, the CIA reported that it had used twenty-one former Nazis as "sources," seven of whom had been paid. *None* of the twenty-one, the agency hastened to add, was a suspected war criminal.
- Also without revealing any names, the FBI admitted to having had a "confidential relationship" with two former Nazis who were not paid. It hastened to add, however, that it never "intervened in or obstructed any INS investigation or prosecution."
- And the INS claimed that no government official ever attempted to "interfere" in any Nazi case.

Accepting those reports without challenge, the GAO concluded: "It is unlikely that widespread conspiracy has existed in Federal agencies—

especially the INS—to obstruct investigation of allegations that individuals, now residents of the United States, committed atrocities before or during World War II."

Holtzman wasn't displeased. Even though its investigators had allowed the FBI and CIA to hide behind the shield of national security, the U.S. government had publicly admitted for the first time that it both coddled and employed former Nazis. The cat was now out of the bag.

If Holtzman was reasonably satisfied with the GAO report, former INS staffers Tony DeVito and Vincent Schiano were not. During an Immigration Subcommittee hearing, they accused the INS of caving in to the FBI and the CIA by accepting agency summaries and denials without even a hint of skepticism. They told the subcommittee that the FBI, CIA, and INS had made fools of the GAO and called its report a "whitewash."

What really upset DeVito and Schiano was that GAO investigators hadn't even bothered to interview either one of them, when it was their sworn testimony that had sparked the investigation to begin with. As far as they were concerned, the GAO had tarred them as liars and fruitcakes.

Despite its severe limitations, the GAO report had an important, albeit quiet, impact on both Americans and foreigners who were watching the Nazis-in-America drama unfold. It whetted their appetite for more details about government use and protection of former Nazis and Nazi collaborators. It increased international pressure to find and deport them. And it showed the world that America was finally serious about facing its own war crimes hypocrisy.

• • •

In keeping with her promise to do whatever she could to expel Nazis from the United States, Elizabeth Holtzman began to lobby for a special unit of prosecutors dedicated exclusively to finding, investigating, and trying alleged Nazis and Nazi collaborators for immigration fraud. Unlike the Zutty team at the INS, the new unit would have to be independent and have its own budget. Given the Justice Department's reluctance to pursue former Nazis, Holtzman's six-year struggle for a dedicated Nazi unit was greeted with hostility. In 1978, the department finally gave in to the constant nagging and created the Special Litigation Unit (SLU), a five-attorney team inside the Justice Department responsible for preparing alleged Nazi cases for trial. Local U.S. attorneys would conduct the courtroom prosecutions. Fedorenko had been one of SLU's first cases.

In the fall of 1978, while the government was licking its Fedorenko trial wounds, the winds of congressional power unexpectedly shifted. Facing indictment charges for bribery, Joshua Eilberg failed to get re-elected in a stunning upset. Elizabeth Holtzman became the chairperson of the Immigration Subcommittee. With new congressional teeth and muscle, she was ready to play serious Washington hardball.

Not one to crawl or beg, Holtzman simply told the Justice Department she wanted an independent Nazi office with a respectable budget inside its Criminal Division, which was the department's strongest and least subject to manipulation. The Justice Department responded: Over our dead body. Holtzman parried: Do it voluntarily or I'll introduce a law mandating the office and I'll hold public hearings. You'll come out smelling, and it won't be of roses.

Justice buckled.

The new Office of Special Investigations (OSI), with a budget of $2.3 million, quickly fielded a staff of twenty lawyers, seven historians, four investigators, and a raft of support personnel with a wide range of language skills—secretaries, paralegals, researchers, and analysts. It was a long leap from the days when DeVito and Schiano had to crawl over each other's desks to reach the door in an office without even a telephone.

If the INS dragged its feet, lacked direction and leadership, and was compromised, OSI was dogged, focused, ably led, and independent. Most important, it was driven by a deeply felt sense of urgency. Nazi war criminals and eyewitnesses were getting old and sick and were dying. Memories were fading. OSI hit the road running. In the fall of 1979, its team of attorneys gathered in its new office to review more than two hundred case files and twelve pending cases, and to parcel out assignments. Four of the hot targets were names on the original Karbach list: Bishop Valerian Trifa and Andrija Artukovic, friends of the FBI; and Tscherim Soobzokov and Boleslavs Maikovskis, friends of the CIA. There were other big targets not on the original Karbach list, among them Baron Otto von Bolschwing, who had worked for the OSS and CIA, and John Demjanjuk.

Because of its inexperience in trying forty-year-old Nazi cold cases, the pressure to prove itself, and its haste to get alleged Nazi collaborators into court before they and witnesses died, OSI would stumble badly.

CHAPTER EIGHTEEN

Himmler's Helpers

W hile preparing to try John Demjanjuk as Ivan the Terrible of Treblinka, government attorneys learned that a former Ukrainian SS guard had identified Demjanjuk as a fellow guard at Sobibor, not Treblinka. Michael Hanusiak, who had included Demjanjuk's name on his Ukrainian list of Nazi collaborators, reported the allegation in the *Ukrainian Daily News* in 1976, the year Miriam Radiwker began interviewing Treblinka survivors in Israel. So did *Visti z Ukrainy* (*News from Ukraine*), a communist newspaper for Ukrainians living outside the Soviet Union that was published in Kiev in Ukrainian and in the United States in English.

The Ukrainian guard's name was Ignat Danilchenko. In 1949, a Soviet court in Kiev had sentenced him to twenty-five years of hard labor in a Siberian gulag for collaborating with the Nazis. He served eight years of that sentence and was released. When the news articles appeared in Ukrainian papers in 1976, he was living and working in Siberia.

News from Ukraine said: "Demjanjuk went over to the other side, betraying the fatherland." It went on to quote Danilchenko as saying that he had served at Sobibor with Iwan Demjanjuk. And for the first time, the newspaper referred to an official Certificate of Service, or ID card, that the SS had allegedly issued to Iwan Demjanjuk in 1942. According to the newspaper, the card, which included a photo, indicated that Demjanjuk had been posted to Sobibor in March 1943. The card made no mention of Treblinka. If it was authentic, the ID card confirmed what Danilchenko alleged.

The following year, *News from Ukraine* quoted Danilchenko at length in an article with the threatening title "Punishment Will Come." Somehow the newspaper had gotten a copy of Danilchenko's 1949 Soviet trial testimony.

> I first met and became acquainted with [Iwan Demjanjuk] in March 1943 in the Sobibor death camp where he served in the secret SS forces as a guard. He wore the uniform of a soldier of the German SS . . . and carried a firearm.
>
> As an SS guard Demjanjuk participated in mass annihilation of persons of Jewish nationality . . . guarded them from possible escape before executions, and conveyed them to the [gas chambers] in which these people were executed by suffocation with exhaust from a special motor.
>
> In the spring of 1944, together with me, he was sent to Flossenbürg [Germany] and then to Regensburg [Germany] where he guarded concentration camps of arrested Soviets and other citizens and conveyed them to various jobs.

The newspaper even printed Demjanjuk's home address in Parma, Ohio. "Today the residents of the city of Parma in the USA know Mr. Demjanjuk as an ordinary automobile inspector," the article said. "And probably they do not know that in greeting him, they are extending their hands to a murderer of innocent people who has escaped just punishment."

Most important, the newspaper published two pictures of the ID card called "Certificate of Service No. 1393." Given that the newspaper was a communist publication, the authenticity of the card was immediately suspect. It would soon go on trial along with Demjanjuk and become, as one government attorney put it, "the most analyzed document of the twentieth century."

Because official archival documents like "Certificate of Service No. 1393" are carefully guarded, the Soviet government or the KGB must have given photos of the card to *News from Ukraine*. The leaked photos raised two critical questions. Was the card an authentic document captured by the Red Army from German files, or a clever KGB forgery? And why did the Soviets wait until 1976 to release photos of the card when they knew as early as 1953 that Iwan Demjanjuk had survived the war and was living in Cleveland? In fact, it was John Demjanjuk himself who was indirectly responsible for giving the Soviet government his home address.

• • •

One day in 1953, Iwan Demjanjuk's mother got a letter from America. It was posted from Cleveland and it was from her son. She must have been shocked, for Soviet officials had informed her soon after the war that her son was missing in action and that she was entitled to his military pension. A niece read her the letter from Ohio because Mrs. Demjanjuk was illiterate. It said that her son had a good job, was safe and healthy, and that she had a daughter-in-law, Vera, and a granddaughter, Lydia. Demjanjuk continued writing to his mother and sending care packages to her home in the tiny village where he was born. The niece wrote back in his mother's name. Then, in the mid-1960s, Vera traveled to Ukraine to visit her own mother and her mother-in-law. Vera's visa application required her to state the reason for her visit and to give her home address. If the KGB ever wanted to find Iwan Demjanjuk, a Red Army deserter, and assassinate him, they certainly knew where to look.

• • •

The two newspaper pictures of the ID card, bearing Iwan Demjanjuk's alleged signature, showed the front and back of an official-looking German document. The front described the German organization that issued the document. In the left-hand corner on the back side of the card was a wallet-size head and shoulders photo of a young, hatless man with an oval face and short hair, dressed in black or dark clothes. The card identified the man as Iwan Demjanjuk, a Ukrainian, son of Nicolai, born on April 3, 1920, in Duboimarchariwzi. Actually, Demjanjuk was born in Dubovi Makharintsi. The card said the village was in the district of Sporosche. Actually, Demjanjuk's village was in the Vinitsaya district. The card said he was 175 centimeters tall (about five feet, eight inches). Actually, he was six feet, one inch tall. The card said he had dark blond hair and a scar on his back. The color of his hair would later be disputed.

The card listed two service postings: Okszow, a work-camp farm estate maintained by Jewish women, beginning in September 1942; and the Sobibor death camp, beginning in March 1943. Written on the card was a word-for-word translation of the German into Russian.

The ID card bore two official-looking stamps and the signatures of three men: Karl Streibel, Ernst Teufel, and Iwan Demjanjuk. Streibel

Росси

Grösse: 175 cm
лицо овальное
Gesichtsform: oval
волосы темнорусые
Haarfarbe: dklblond
глаза серые
Augenfarbe: grau
Особые приметы
Besondere Merkmale:
шрам на спине
Narbe auf dem
Rücken
ДЕМБЯНЮК
Familienname: D e m s a n j u k
Иван Николаевич
Vor-und Vatersname: Iwan/Nikolai
род
geboren am: 3.4.20
в губ. Махаривци Запорожской обл.
geboren in: Duboimachariwzi/Saporosch
украинец
Nationalität: Ukrainer в колонне Округ
Abkommandiert am 22.9.42 zu L.G.Okzow
Abkommandiert am 27.3. zu Lublin
Abkommandiert am _____ zu _____
Abkommandiert am _____ zu _____
Abkommandiert am _____ zu _____

Empfangene Ausrüstungsgegenstände:

Mütze:	1	Koppel:	
Mantel:	1	Seitengewehrtasche:	
Bluse:	1	Handschuhe:	
Hose:	1	Unterhemd:	1
Stiefel:	1	Unterhosen:	1
Schnurschuhe:	1	Wollweste:	
Socken:	1		Badehose
Fusslappen:		Brikab	1
Essgeschirr:			
Brotbeutel:			
Trinkbecher:			
Feldflasche:			
Wolldecken:	1		
Gewehr Nr.:			
Seitengewehr Nr.:			

Ausgegeben: _____ Richtig empfangen: _____

Raum für Anmerkungen der Dienststelle:
WIRD DER INHABER DIESES AUSWEISES
AUSSERHALB DES ANGEGEBENEN STAN-
DES ANGETROFFEN IST ER FE T Z
NEHMEN UND DER DIENSTELLE ZU MELDE

Если владелец данного свидетельства
будет обнаружен вне указанного гарни-
зона, его следует задержать и сообщить
в часть.
переводчик 4 Упр. МГБ СССР
12/IV-48 г.

уполномоченный рейхсфюрера СС по созданию
СС-и полицейских опорных пунктов в нов...
Der Beauftragte des Reichsführers-SS
für die Errichtung der SS- und Polizeistützpunkte
im neuen Ostraum

DIENSTSITZ LUBLIN
AUSBILDUNGSLAGER TRAWNIKI
Свидетельство о прохождении службы
Dienstausweis Nr. 1393
ДЕМБЯНЮК ИВАН
Der D e m s a n j u k , Iwan
(Name des Inhabers)

ist in den Wachmannschaften des Beauftragten des
RF-SS für die Errichtung der SS- und Polizeistützpunkte
im neuen Ostraum als Wachmann tätig.
служит в командах уполномоченного рейхс-
СС по созданию СС- и полицейских опорных
пунктов в новых областях на востоке.
i. A.

SS-Hauptsturmführer
гауптштурмфюрер
Штрайбел

was the SS commandant of a camp called Trawniki. Teufel was a Trawniki camp supply officer, and Demjanjuk was a Trawniki graduate.

• • •

The village of Trawniki is a few miles northwest of the village of Sobibor, where, on his visa application, Demjanjuk had sworn he worked as a farmer before and during the early part of the war. Trawniki's landmark was an abandoned sugar refinery near the railroad tracks. The SS established a school for auxiliary guards on the site. In 1942, the year Demjanjuk was captured by the German army during the battle of Kerch, nearly all of the auxiliary guards in training at Trawniki were Red Army prisoners recruited from POW camps in eastern Poland and western Ukraine, especially from Rovno and Chelm, where Demjanjuk said he had been held prisoner.

Just as the SS could not round up, rob, and kill the 2.1 million Jews in Russia and the Soviet-occupied territories east of the Bug River without the help of volunteers (*Hiwis*), it also couldn't round up, transport, rob, and kill the 3.3 million Polish Jews in Operation Reinhard without help. Nor could the SS guard the thousands of labor and concentration camps it had built throughout Poland and Western Europe without help that included civilian employees like Hermine Braunsteiner, the Mare of Majdanek. In the fall of 1941, while German and *Hiwi* Einsatzkommandos were shooting Jews by the thousands in the forests of the Soviet-occupied territories and loading their stolen valuables onto lorries destined for the Reich, the SS opened the Trawniki school.

The SS envisioned a disciplined corps of one hundred thousand guards but ultimately fell far short of that goal. By July 1944, when the Red Army captured the town of Trawniki, the school had only trained approximately five thousand, and they were far from disciplined.

The SS deliberately chose Soviet POWs to become "Trawniki men," as they were called, because they already had military training, had seen action, and were no strangers to death and killing. Most were Ukrainians, the largest ethnic group among the prisoners. The SS favorites were ethnic Germans (*Volksdeutsche*) from eastern Poland, Belorussia, and Ukraine. They were loyal to Germany—therefore they could be trusted—and they spoke both German and Ukrainian.

Major General Odilo Globocnik, the SS officer and police leader who ran Operation Reinhard and its death camps in the Lublin district of Poland, appointed SS Captain Karl Streibel as Trawniki's first and only commandant. Initially, Streibel personally visited the POW camps to select candidates for his new school.

Before Streibel or his recruiters visited a POW site, camp security personnel conducted a preliminary screening of potential candidates. That narrowed the number of prisoners Streibel and the doctor he brought with him had to interview and evaluate.

The first selection criterion was good health. If a Soviet POW was in reasonably good physical shape under starvation conditions, he would be cheaper to maintain, and easier to train and deploy. Furthermore, good health more than likely signaled that the prisoner had received extra rations for providing a service to the camp staff. That meant he had already crossed a line by collaborating with the enemy to stay alive.

Besides healthy men, Streibel wanted anticommunists who would be less likely to desert to the Red Army, and anti-Semites who would find it easier to brutalize and kill Jews. The ability to understand and speak German and the skill to drive a transport truck made a candidate especially valuable to the SS and its mission in Poland to capture, rob, and kill all Polish Jews with speed and efficiency.

The vast majority of the POW Trawniki men, most in their early twenties or younger, did not volunteer. They were recruited to collaborate without being specifically told for what. As an inducement to work with the Germans, they were promised better food and warm clothes. If the SS had asked for volunteers, however, they would have been deluged. Life in a POW camp in 1941–42 (especially 1941) was a virtual death sentence. The Germans shot hundreds of thousands of Soviet prisoners they didn't know what to do with. Starvation and disease were rampant. Soviet POWs would volunteer for almost anything for an extra crust of bread.

"Because we were all starving," a former Trawniki man recalled after the war, "no one . . . who had been selected, refused."

Of course, if a POW was selected to collaborate, he could always refuse. If he did, depending on who was the recruiter that day, he could be killed or sent back into the prison ranks, where he had less than a 20 percent chance of surviving. There is at least one recorded instance of a group of Soviet POWs refusing the offer to collaborate and *not being shot*.

Most trainees from the POW camps arrived at Trawniki relatively healthy, but undernourished and in rags. They were cleaned up, deloused, given a haircut, and clothed in recycled military uniforms—

black ones made from old SS uniforms or Polish army uniforms dyed black, or earth-brown Belgian military uniforms appropriated from the warehouses of Reich-occupied Belgium.

Most of the time, an SS officer would explain to the new recruit—through a *Volksdeutsche* interpreter—that he would be trained at Trawniki for guard duty and that he would not be asked to fight against Soviet soldiers. When his training as an SS guard was completed, the officer would explain, he could be assigned guard duty at a factory, airport, labor camp, or concentration camp. He might also be ordered to help the police round up and transport Jews to camps.

After the lecture, the new recruit would be given the choice to accept the assignment or return to a POW camp. "No one wanted to return," a former Trawniki man from Chelm (Stalag 319) explained after the war. The POWs feared they would either be shot if they said no or would starve to death in a camp. Although camp conditions had improved after the terrible winter of 1941–42 because the Germans decided to use Soviet POWs as forced laborers, the fear of starvation was still very real.

An ethnic German interviewed the recruits and recorded their data on a personnel form (*Personalbogen*) that included their name, birth date and place of birth, language and occupational skills, military service, and marital status. The interviewer looked the new recruit over, then recorded the color of his hair and eyes and his height. A print was made of his right thumb. A photographer took his picture. Then, based on the information on his personnel record, he received an identification number and an ID card (service pass).

The identification number was important in the German human accounting system. It was the number, not the name, that administrators used on most routine documents such as personnel rosters. The service pass was equally important. How else would a Trawniki man explain to a local police officer why he was wearing an unusual uniform, carrying a gun, unable to speak German, and walking in a restricted area?

The new recruit had to sign a service obligation form swearing allegiance to the SS and promising to abide by the rules, regulations, and disciplines of the guard service (*Wachmannschaften*) under the supervision of the SS and German police. He also had to swear that he did not have Jewish blood and that he had not been a member of the Communist Party or the Komsomol communist youth organization.

The Trawniki students received specialized training of no predetermined length of time. It could last several months or several weeks depending on the SS need for auxiliary guards. The training included: general guard procedures; German language lessons focusing on understanding basic commands in German; firearms instruction in the use and care of German-issued rifles, pistols, machine guns, submachine guns, and grenades; crowd control and roundup techniques; and German ideology. Like all military units, the recruits marched and sang (German songs).

The SS organized the trainees into platoons of from 35 to 40 men, and companies of from 90 to 120. Whenever possible, company commanders and platoon leaders were ethnic Germans. As an incentive, Streibel established a ranking system with appropriate pay increases from private (*Wachmann*) to private first class, to sergeant, to staff sergeant, and to senior noncommissioned officer (*Oberzugwachmann*). Streibel also established an NCO training program for conscientious and disciplined Trawniki men and issued special citations for outstanding service.

Each Trawniki student got a rifle for use on training assignments, but their superior officers took the guns back at night. Just because the SS needed POW guards didn't mean they trusted them. Platoon commanders, usually ethnic Germans, carried pistols.

An important part of Trawniki training included fieldwork during which students were evaluated. Trainees guarded local concentration and work camps for Jews. They went on Jew-hunting raids in local villages under the supervision of the German police. If they were sent on a shooting operation rather than a roundup, they were expected to fire and kill. Between three and four hundred Trawniki men, for example, took part in the liquidation of the Warsaw Ghetto from June to September 1942. And in August 1942 in Lomazy, Poland, fifty Trawniki men working with the German police were ordered to kill seventeen hundred Jews. With a vodka bottle in one hand and a gun in the other, they shot them all.

In some instances, individual trainees were ordered to shoot a Jew eyeball to eyeball as a test of grit and loyalty. "A German officer led our platoon into the woods," a former Trawniki man explained after the war. "We were sent in groups of ten to stand next to groups of ten Jews. The Jews stood in a single line. We were then ordered to shoot a Jew." There is no evidence to suggest, however, that each trainee *had* to execute a Jew as his final "exam."

If Trawniki trainees needed Jews to practice on, they didn't have far to go. Trawniki was a multi-use facility that included the guard training school, a concentration-work camp for Jews, and an F. W. Schultz and Company factory that made mattresses and furs, and repaired boots and uniforms for the German army. Each day, the SS rented out to the Schultz factory four to six thousand Jewish workers, at five zlotys a head for men and four for women. That was enough money to pay the salaries of the Trawniki men who guarded them.

Maintaining discipline in the ranks of the Trawniki men was a constant, vexing problem and grew worse as the Soviets began to defeat the Germans and push them west toward Poland. Between 1942 and 1945, at least one thousand (20 percent) Trawniki men deserted or tried to desert. Those who were caught were punished. If they offered armed resistance, they were court-martialed and executed. If they didn't resist, they got a few weeks in the brig before rejoining their platoons. There were several guard mutinies at the camps. Stealing Jewish valuables from the storage bins was a common crime. So were curfew violations and AWOLs to local villages for vodka and women. Like typhus, drunkenness and theft were epidemic.

Most of the desertions occurred once it became clear that the Red Army was winning its war with Germany. The motives for fleeing were far from noble. Some feared being executed by the Germans as war crimes eyewitnesses or by the Soviets as traitors; for others, the dwindling number of new Jewish prisoners presented fewer opportunities to steal and simple boredom.

Although Trawniki men were called SS guards and were subject to court-martial for major infractions like deserting with armed resistance, or stealing gold and jewels from the storage rooms, or telling villagers what was going on inside the death camps, they were not members of the SS and, therefore, were *not Nazis* in even the broadest use of the word. They worked *for* and collaborated *with* the SS as prisoners of war or as civilians without being members of that racially pure organization. They belonged to a category called "German SS soldiers," received the same pay and food rationing as a regular German soldier, and were buried with honors if they were killed in the line of duty. The Germans no longer considered them POWs. Compared with life in a POW camp, life as a Trawniki man was a gift from Himmler. He received warm clothes and plenty of food, as promised. Far from the front lines, he was as safe as one can be during a war. He got regular days off, two weeks paid vacation, and a monthly salary of fifteen to forty-five reichmarks

($75 to $225) for tobacco, vodka, movies, and women. And he received free medical care in a German military hospital.

Although the SS executed guards who dipped into the heaps of cash and jewels stolen from the Jews, they closed their eyes to minor pilfering and trading food for valuables with the prisoners, thereby providing the Trawniki men additional sources of spending money. Families of the civilian Trawniki volunteers from Poland, Belorussia, and Ukraine could even apply for support benefits.

There was no graduation ceremony for the Trawniki men. When the SS thought a trainee was ready and needed, they posted him out as a private or *Wachmann*. His assignment was entered onto an index card and into his personnel record, then filed in the Trawniki administrative office.

A Trawniki man could be assigned a cushy security job guarding an estate housing SS brass, an airplane factory, a bridge, or a warehouse filled with stolen Jewish property. He could be posted to any of the hundreds of local concentration or labor camps without gas chambers, or to a camp with gas chambers, like Majdanek. He could be assigned to ride shotgun on transport trains carrying Jews to Belzec, Sobibor, or Treblinka, or to help the SS process and gas the Jews taken there. Each death camp employed between ninety and 180 Trawniki men at any given time.

Once posted, the Trawniki man retained organizational ties to his alma mater, which had the authority to recall, retrain, and repost him as needed.

• • •

In late October 1943, Himmler got a bad case of jitters. The uprisings in Treblinka (August) and Sobibor (October) stunned him. Jews actually fighting back? He ordered both camps razed, all documents destroyed, and all buried corpses dug up and burned. Then, under the cynical name Operation Harvest Festival, Himmler ordered the SS in the Lublin district to exterminate every Jew still in a work camp and to ferret out those who were hiding and shoot them. The order included an estimated six thousand Jews at the Trawniki concentration-work camp.

The following summer, 1944, the German police and SS staff at Trawniki fled west in advance of the Red Army. The approximately eight hundred Trawniki men stationed at the camp at the time had a choice.

They could either desert or follow the SS and regroup. To remain in the camp would be suicide. The Red Army would execute them before they could say "Joseph Stalin."

A few Trawniki guards disappeared into the woods, but the vast majority followed their SS bosses and were reassigned to guard camps and facilities in the west, primarily at Flossenbürg and Sachsenhausen. By the time the Red Army got to Trawniki in July 1944, the camp complex was a ghost town of barbed wire and empty barracks and offices. All the file cards with names, identity numbers, and postings had been destroyed by order of Commandant Streibel. Approximately twelve hundred (around 20 percent) of the personnel files survived the war.

· · ·

The Trawniki story had a mixed ending. The British captured Major General Globocnik, but he crunched a cyanide capsule before they could jail him. In 1970, Karl Streibel and five other Trawniki SS officers went on trial in Hamburg. All were acquitted, claiming they were just following orders, had never killed or brutalized any civilian, and didn't know what was going on down the tracks at Belzec, Sobibor, and Treblinka, even though transports crammed with Jews on the way to the death camps rolled by the camp nearly every day.

For their part, the Soviets tried and convicted as many as one thousand Trawniki men well into the 1960s. Some were executed. Others, like Ignat Danilchenko, were sentenced to twenty-five years of hard labor in a Siberian gulag.

In the final analysis, the Trawniki men had been indispensable to Operation Reinhard and its extermination processes and machinery. For the most part, they were good at their jobs. Supervised by fewer than two hundred SS officers, they helped rob and kill 1.7 million Polish Jews in less than three years (approximately two thousand a day).

In his letter recommending SS Captain Karl Streibel for a promotion to major, General Globocnik wrote: "These units have proved themselves in the best way . . . especially in the framework of the resettlement of the Jew."

CHAPTER NINETEEN

Egg on the Face

In 1979, the Department of Justice (DOJ) decided that it wanted Walter Rockler to be the first director of its new Office of Special Investigations (OSI). Rockler, who was working as a tax attorney in Washington, didn't want the job. He had served as an intelligence officer during World War II. Afterward, he prosecuted German bankers for the Nuremberg Military Tribunal. Like other veterans, he had tried his best to put the war behind him, and he didn't relish the thought of revisiting it.

Rockler explained to Justice that, although he had experience prosecuting Nazi bankers, he knew little about Nazi SS camps and SS guards. Besides, his wife was a former Estonian slave laborer and he didn't want to bring SS camp atrocities into his home. Furthermore, he had college-age kids. How could he support them on a paltry government salary? Finally, he was involved in several tax cases against the Internal Revenue Service. Working for the government while prosecuting the government would be a conflict of interest.

Rockler's arguments did not dampen the Justice Department's enthusiasm. OSI needed someone with Rockler's credentials to guide its baby steps. As a former Nuremberg prosecutor, he would send a message to the world—OSI was not going to be another Washington eunuch. It would be aggressive in finding and expelling Nazis and Nazi collaborators in the United States.

DOJ worked out a compromise. Rockler would take command of OSI for six to eight months as a part-time contract employee on an hourly basis. He could still work part-time at his law firm, Arnold & Porter. The department would sign a conflict-of-interest waiver and Arnold & Porter would continue to pay his full partnership draw, less his government fee.

Martin Mendelsohn, a career Justice Department attorney, would be Rockler's deputy director. A protégé of Elizabeth Holtzman, Mendelsohn had been the director of OSI's predecessor, the Special Litigation Unit (SLU). As Rockler's assistant, Mendelsohn would now direct OSI litigation, supervise prosecutors, prioritize cases, and assign personnel to work on them.

When Walter Rockler agreed to helm the new OSI, he brought with him his own agenda. Besides finding Nazis and European Nazi collaborators, he wanted to hunt American Nazi collaborators who were not part of OSI's mission. While investigating German financiers, Rockler had stumbled on a list of thirteen Wall Street banks that had collaborated with German banks in laundering the stolen property and dirty money that helped finance the Holocaust and made Wall Street richer. Back in the United States after the Nuremberg Tribunal was dissolved, Rockler refused to do business with any of the banks on the list. Although he never went public with the list, he shared the names with John Loftus, a new OSI attorney.

A graduate of Suffolk University Law School, Loftus joined the U.S. attorney general's honors program for newly minted lawyers for one year with the blessing of the Boston law firm that had hired him. A young attorney with contacts in the Justice Department could be useful to the firm.

"Welcome to the Justice Department," Loftus's new boss had told him. "You now represent the most corrupt client in the world—the United States government."

Loftus thought he was joking.

One day in 1979, Loftus had spotted a memo on the bulletin board. A new DOJ Office of Special Investigations was looking for volunteers to hunt, prosecute, and deport former Nazis and Nazi collaborators. Loftus applied and got a job on the OSI team. The Nazi investigation Rockler assigned him to was the Belarus Project, which—along with its high-level security clearance—came with unprecedented access to secret State Department, Defense Department, CIA, and FBI intelligence records. Rockler asked Loftus to keep his eyes open for any documents relating to the thirteen banks while he was rummaging through highly classified government documents.

In the eighteen months he spent on the Belarus Project, Loftus didn't find much about Wall Street banks, but he uncovered a government secret that would soon make him the whipping boy of the CIA, the Department of State, and the Justice Department.*

Soon after he had agreed to direct OSI, Rockler told his superiors at Justice that he wanted to replace Martin Mendelsohn, who he believed was withholding materials from him. Mendelsohn denied the charges, but under the circumstances it would be difficult for the two men to work together. The Justice Department chose Allan J. Ryan Jr. for the deputy spot. Mendelsohn stayed on as an OSI prosecutor.

Ryan had stumbled into his new job. Like John Loftus, he was Catholic. And like everyone already on the OSI team, he was young—early thirties—and well credentialed with degrees from Dartmouth College and the University of Minnesota Law School, and a clerking stint for Supreme Court justice Byron White. What made Ryan stand out in the search for a new OSI deputy director was his courtroom experience on cases ranging from veterans' rights to the law of the sea.

Ryan had been serving as assistant U.S. solicitor general when his boss put the Feodor Fedorenko appeal on his desk. After studying Judge Roettger's opinion and the government's brief, Ryan didn't think the botched case was winnable on appeal. But after reading the trial transcripts, he changed his mind. What swayed him most was one simple fact. Fedorenko admitted he had been an armed guard at Treblinka. Like Roettger, Ryan found the survivor stories of Fedorenko's alleged brutality bone-chilling. But unlike Roettger, he found the eyewitnesses both credible and irrelevant. As Ryan understood it, immigration law did not require the government to prove Fedorenko committed atrocities against private citizens. U.S. v. Fedorenko was a denaturalization case, not a war crimes trial.

Ryan won the appeal but, like DeVito with Dachau and Private Galione with Dora, he couldn't push the case out of his mind. Although he was savvy and skeptical, he was shocked to learn that Nazi collaborators were actually hiding in America. So, when Philip Heymann, as-

---

* Members of Walter Rockler's family do not recall him talking about a specific list of thirteen American banks that allegedly had collaborated with the Nazis. And a search of his papers failed to turn up such a list. Walter Rockler died in 2002.

sistant attorney general in charge of the Criminal Division at Justice, asked Ryan if he would join OSI as Rockler's deputy director, Ryan was intrigued. True, the future of OSI was uncertain and the task impossible given the ages of the alleged Nazis and eyewitnesses, but the job sounded exciting.

Ryan talked over the tempting offer with his wife. "Forget [job] security," she told him. "What do you really want to do?" Ryan took the job.

• • •

Walter Rockler left OSI after a year of service, much longer than he and his law firm had agreed to when he signed up. He wouldn't miss the Justice Department job. Rockler hated political arm-wrestles and thought public relations work was a waste of his time. And he certainly could do without the death threats from Eastern Europeans who believed he was operating a Jewish witch hunt.

Ryan stepped into Rockler's shoes. As OSI's first full-time director, he had a critical decision to make. Should he try John Demjanjuk for lying on his U.S. visa application about being a guard at Treblinka, or for being a guard at Sobibor? It wasn't an easy call, and it had caused a rift on the OSI team even before Rockler left and while Ryan was still deputy director.

The major sliver under Ryan's skin was George Parker. The Justice Department attorney had been assigned to investigate the Demjanjuk case when OSI was still just a gleam in Elizabeth Holtzman's eye. No one knew the shoals and eddies of the Demjanjuk case better than Parker. And Parker was deeply troubled.

Soon after its first organizational meeting in the summer of 1979, OSI had asked Moscow for a certified copy of the alleged Trawniki card and any information it might have on Demjanjuk. A package from Moscow arrived in Washington several months later, in January 1980. It contained a sworn statement from Ignat Danilchenko, the former Trawniki man who said Demjanjuk had served with him at Sobibor; two certified photos of Iwan Demjanjuk's Trawniki card (front and back); and statements from two former Treblinka guards.

Ryan looked at the photos of the ID card placing Demjanjuk at Sobibor and said to himself: "Gotcha, you son-of-a-bitch." To Ryan, the Trawniki card complemented the government's complaint that Demjanjuk was Treblinka's Ivan the Terrible.

George Parker looked at the photos, read the three statements, and was worried. Both former Treblinka guards swore they had never heard of Iwan Demjanjuk and neither one recognized his photo. Parker feared that Demjanjuk was turning into another Frank Walus. And the last thing OSI needed, while it stretched its legal wings, was another Walus.

• • •

Frank (Franciszek) Walus was a fifty-five-year-old immigrant and retired factory worker from southwest Chicago who didn't smoke or drink and rarely left Little Poland except to go fishing and pick wild mushrooms. In January 1977, around the time the government filed charges against Fedorenko, it also filed a complaint against Walus, alleging he had been a member of the Nazi Gestapo, had committed atrocities against Jews in the Polish towns of Kielce and Czestochowa, and during his naturalization hearing had failed to report his membership in a Nazi organization.

Nazi hunter Simon Wiesenthal triggered the investigation into Walus's background with a letter to the INS outlining the Gestapo allegations and furnishing the names of several eyewitnesses. That Walus was born in Germany and was a citizen of Poland and could speak both Polish and German did not help his case.

Waving his U.S. citizenship papers over his head and close to tears, Walus shouted to the reporters who had gathered outside his home minutes after the government served him a copy of the charges: "It's a dirty, dirty, dirty trick. . . . The Jews are making a lot of trouble for me." The cry echoed across Chicago for months before, during, and after the Walus trial as Poles, Jews, and neo-Nazis drew lines in the sand. Media coverage was heavy. Emotions seethed, then boiled over.

In an assault that came to symbolize Chicago's polarization, a man with an aerosol can attacked Walus in the Loop and sprayed his face and eyes with a chemical. When police caught the attacker running down LaSalle Street and asked him why he did it, he said: "Because I'm a Jew and he's a Nazi."

Walus was taken to a hospital, where doctors cleaned and bathed his eyes. He suffered no permanent injury and the Jewish community issued a public apology. But emotions continued to run at such fever pitch that authorities requested extra marshals in the courtroom and the hallway outside and ordered security guards to search all spectators before they passed through a metal detector. The threat of violence was so real that

Walus's defense attorney refused to appear for the court's reading of its finding, fearing for his personal safety.

If he had enemies, Walus had supporters, too. A neo-Nazi group publicly offered to hire an attorney to represent him and to help foot his legal bills, no strings attached. Calling the trial "a Jewish witch hunt and mockery of justice," the group threatened to march through predominantly Jewish Skokie, a Chicago suburb. Walus declined the neo-Nazi offer until unpaid invoices mounted on his desk.

"If the devil would give me money," he said, "I would take it."

Presiding over the three-and-a-half-week bench trial was eighty-two-year-old Julius Hoffman, known to Chicagoans as the crotchety, cantankerous judge who steered the post–Democratic National Convention trial of the "Chicago Seven" ten years earlier, in 1969. Judge Hoffman had been the star of that raucous show. The drama climaxed when he ordered U.S. marshals to bind, gag, and chain defendant Bobby Seale to his chair. Hoffman didn't like being insulted in Yiddish and called "pig . . . fascist . . . racist . . . dinosaur . . . Julius Hitler . . . a disgrace to Jews." And worse.

Although Hoffman was a media sweetheart who provided good copy, the "sadistic old bastard" was disliked by attorneys who had the misfortune to face him. Nothing illustrated their contempt for the judge better than a survey conducted by the Chicago Council of Lawyers long before the Chicago Seven trial.

When asked, "Viewed over-all, do you favor his [Hoffman's] continued service in his present post?" only 25 percent of the lawyers who responded to the survey said yes.

When asked, "Does he demonstrate patience and a willingness to listen to all sides?" 78 percent said no.

When asked, "Is he impartially courteous towards lawyers and litigants?" 79 percent said no.

With numbers like those, the judge was sure to turn the Walus trial into another Julius Hoffman Show.

As with Fedorenko, the government's case against Walus was built entirely on eyewitness identification and testimony. Eleven men and women identified Walus as the brutal Gestapo agent they remembered, first from a photo spread, then in person in the courtroom. One eyewitness described how she saw Walus shoot a woman as she left a hospital. "Her daughter came running out and bent down over her mother," the witness said weeping. "He shot her, too."

Another witness testified that a superior officer ordered Walus to "dispose" of two sick, crippled men. "Walus motioned with his hand for them to walk ahead," the witness said. "I saw [him] take out his pistol and shoot the two men in the back."

A third eyewitness said that he saw Walus stop a Jewish woman and her two young daughters during the liquidation of the Czestochowa ghetto. He ordered her to undress. When she refused, he shot her dead.

Yet another eyewitness testified that she saw Walus separate a group of children from their parents. "He took them to a near-by building," she said. "I heard horrible cries and screams." Then she heard gunshots. Then silence. Pointing to Walus seated in the courtroom less than six feet from her, she cried, "Here is the murderer!"

Anticipating a defense argument that it was unlikely that eyewitnesses could positively identify Walus after nearly forty years, Judge Hoffman studied old photos of himself as a young lawyer before he went bald. "It is remarkable how I look today much as I did then—even though the curl is now out of my hair," he told the defense attorney from the bench.

The packed courtroom burst into laughter, including five neo-Nazis sitting in a pew dressed in Nazi uniforms. Hoffman grinned from his perch.

In his defense, Walus argued that the Reich had taken him to Germany as a forced laborer in 1941, when he was seventeen years old, and that he worked on farms until the end of the war. Unlike the prosecution, however, the defense presented both eyewitness testimony and documentary evidence to substantiate the alibi. Among the documents were health insurance records that listed employer payments to the government for Walus's service (similar to U.S. Social Security payments). The records placed Walus on farms as he had testified. And five German farm wives testified that Walus was working for their husbands during the time when the prosecution said he was beating and killing Jews in Poland.

The government brushed all the evidence and testimony aside. It argued that the health records could be forgeries, part of a Nazi plot to provide cover for their Gestapo agents, or they could have been forged by Walus after the war. And it tried to impugn the testimony of the defense eyewitnesses, arguing that they were all friends of Walus, and that their husbands were former members of the Nazi Party and, therefore, were merely trying to protect one of their own.

In the end, Judge Hoffman ruled against Walus and ordered him to surrender his certificate of citizenship. "In the face of the case presented by the United States," Hoffman wrote, "the court (simply) cannot accept what was essentially an alibi defense by Frank Walus."

Totally convinced that he would be acquitted, Walus was stunned and embittered by Hoffman's decision. "It's a terrible conspiracy," he told the media outside his home on South Kilborn Avenue. "Eleven Jewish witnesses lying like hell."

Chicago Tribune columnist Mark E. Chapman nicked a raw nerve when he argued that it was time for Americans to finally lay World War II to rest and begin living in peace and harmony. "Are the atrocities charged against this one man any worse than the atrocities committed by American soldiers on the defenseless [citizens] of Nuremberg, Dresden, Hiroshima, Nagasaki, or even as recently as Viet Nam?" he wrote. "Is there anyone who is not a criminal who participates in a war? . . . The trial of Frank Walus, regardless of its outcome, is an anachronism that should never have happened."

But Walus hadn't survived World War II as a slave laborer only to let a legal battle sink him. He hired investigators and attorneys to unearth even more evidence to prove the government had the wrong guy, including statements from historians that the Reich did not admit Poles into the ranks of the Gestapo. Three Europeans who had read about the Walus conviction in newspapers came forward to "prevent a miscarriage of justice." A Frenchman and a Pole swore in affidavits that they had worked with Walus in Germany, and a German Catholic priest swore he knew Walus in Germany as a regular parishioner.

Walus presented the new evidence to Judge Hoffman and asked for a new trial. When Hoffman denied the motion, Walus appealed, arguing that Hoffman had placed too heavy a burden of proof on him and had ruled in favor of the government on each and every question of evidence and procedure. He accused Hoffman of making "inflammatory" in-court statements and showing bias throughout the trial. He further argued that the new evidence proved he was innocent. Walus asked the appeals court to reverse Hoffman's decision.

The appeals court stopped just short of ruling judicial bias, one of the most serious charges a plaintiff can level against a sitting judge. In its twenty-nine-page opinion, it called Hoffman's in-court rulings and his weighing of evidence "disturbing . . . troubling . . . troublesome" at least seven times.

The court was troubled by how Hoffman and the government had handled eyewitness testimony. Like Judge Roettger in the Fedorenko case, the appeals court called the Walus photo spread and identification procedure deeply flawed. It pointed out that Walus's picture was taken in 1959, when he was thirty-seven years old, almost twenty years after he had allegedly committed war crimes. Furthermore, the photograph (an enlargement) was light, grainy, and out of focus, which made identifying facial features nearly impossible.

The court found even more troubling the fact that Israeli police and investigators told at least some, if not all, of the witnesses that Frank Walus was under investigation for war crimes committed in Kielce and Czestochowa before showing them the photo spread. And when one witness said she could not identify anyone, the investigator pointed to Walus's picture and asked if she recognized him.

Given the poor quality of the Walus photo spread and the attempts to influence and prompt witnesses, the appeals court accused both Judge Hoffman and the government of giving too much uncritical weight to photo identification. The court further faulted Hoffman because he repeatedly "frustrated" defense attempts to cross-examine prosecution witnesses. Quoting trial transcripts at length, the court pointed out that when the defense asked a prosecution witness if he recalled seeing any scars or other identifying marks on Walus, Hoffman blocked the line of questioning.

"Let's not waste our time," he told the defense attorney.

The appeals court called the government's attempt to impugn Walus's documentary evidence "weak" because it failed to craft a coherent, credible theory to "sweep it away." Instead, the government nitpicked the "inconsequential inconsistencies" in the array of documents, then tried to explain the evidence away with "troublesome" forgery theories that strained credulity. And instead of thoroughly investigating Walus's alibi during the pretrial discovery period, as was its obligation, the court said, the government relied on yet another unsupported Nazi conspiracy theory.

The appeals court concluded that the instances of Judge Hoffman's troubling in-court decisions, rulings, and interferences did not "support the defendant's extraordinary charge of bias." It therefore declined to reverse Hoffman, but it was a close call. The court found Walus's new evidence so convincing that to affirm Judge Hoffman would be an "intolerable injustice." The court ordered a new trial—to be presided over by a judge other than Julius Hoffman.

The problem of whether to retry fell into Allan Ryan's lap. Like the appeals court, he had serious doubts about the guilt of Frank Walus and was not about to leap into the fire with his eyes closed. He sent two investigators to Europe to examine the evidence for and against Walus "down to its floor nails."

The OSI investigators interviewed farmers, farmworkers, and German health insurance officials. They examined whatever insurance records they could. Their seven months of digging either supported Walus's alibi or led to dead ends. OSI concluded: "There is no question of retrying the case. The only issue we face is how to back away from it."

Ryan dropped the case with an apology to Walus. OSI offered to pay his out-of-pocket expenses but not his legal expenses, which amounted to $60,000. A district court judge eventually ordered the government to pay Walus $31,000 in court costs.

Everyone lost.

The Israeli police, who had found and interviewed the witnesses for the Walus trial, as well as the witnesses themselves, were devastated by Ryan's decision not to retry. To them, Walus was a Gestapo murderer. They saw. They knew. No one or nothing could ever change their minds.

Menachem Russek, chief of the Israeli Nazi war crimes investigation unit, voiced the feelings of all in a moving letter to Ryan:

> It's 3:00 a.m. on Thanksgiving morning, and my ears still echo from the hard words of your telephone call. Your expression "this is my decision" hangs heavy on my heart and prevents me from sleeping. I suddenly remember that terrible day when I arrived at the Auschwitz death camp and saw the long line of elder men and women and mothers with their children in their arms, surrounded by S.S. troops, marching to their deaths. . . . I saw the flames and smoke from those innocent victims rise to the sky. I raised my eyes to the heavens in search of a miracle, but none came. A terrible feeling of helplessness overcame me. . . .
>
> This evening when I heard your decision regarding the Frank Walus trial, I lowered my eyes as, again, a feeling of helplessness overcame me. This time with shame . . . I saw the [witnesses] spiritually broken, tears in their eyes, as though blood was still running from their wounds, not believing their own ears that a decision had been taken not to renew the Walus case. I felt them losing their faith in the world's greatest democracy. They feel they have been deceived, in that the trial in Chicago was no more than a well directed show. . . .
>
> Your decision has left me in shock. . . . It hurts that I must say these strong words, but please understand and accept them as words of pain coming from a man who lost most of his family in the Nazi concentration camps. A man who has seen the terrible atrocities of the Holocaust and the destruction of his people in Europe.'

Walus was in pain as well. "It was a terrible nightmare," he said after the appeals court decision. "I feel happy because. . . this darkness is over. . . . I will never get back my reputation."

Walus never did. Jews still believed he was a convicted Nazi, and Chicago's southwest side Poles, who had no love for the Gestapo, shunned him.

Judge Hoffman didn't fare well, either. In 1982, the Executive Committee of the U.S. District Court rapped his knuckles. It ordered that he be given no new cases because of "his age and complaints that he was acting erratically and abusively from the bench." He died in 1983 at the age of eighty-seven.

Indeed, the last thing OSI needed was another Walus case.

• • •

George Parker was aware of the pressure OSI was under from Congress, the Justice Department, and the Jewish community. He knew that the Walus and Fedorenko defeats—the Supreme Court had not yet ruled on Fedorenko—fueled suspicions in the émigré communities that Justice was fronting a Jewish conspiracy of revenge. Convinced that OSI was blindly walking into another wrong-man fiasco, Parker wasn't sure what he should or could do to prevent OSI from making a legal and ethical blunder. He discussed his concerns with a colleague. She suggested that he write a memo to Rockler and Ryan, presenting a point-by-point analysis of the case against Demjanjuk and spelling out OSI's options.

CHAPTER TWENTY

The Doubt Memo

When we filed our case against John Demjanjuk in 1977, Parker began his memo, we had no evidence that Demjanjuk was a Trawniki man who had served as a guard at Sobibor.* All we had were references and unsubstantiated quotes in a communist newspaper.

New information in the communiqué from Moscow contradicts our current pleading that Demjanjuk is Ivan the Terrible—two certified photos of a Trawniki-issued ID card and Soviet-provided statements from Danilchenko and two former Treblinka guards. The Trawniki card and Danilchenko's statement place Demjanjuk at Sobibor. The two Treblinka guards said he was not at Treblinka. This as yet unproven evidence warrants a reevaluation of our pleading.

In support of the Ivan the Terrible theory:

We have eyewitness evidence from the Israeli police positively identifying Demjanjuk as Ivan the Terrible. And when Israeli investigator Miriam Radiwker pointed to Demjanjuk's photo and told two witnesses that she had evidence that the man in the photo was a guard at Sobibor, both witnesses insisted he was at Treblinka. In fact, all the Israeli witnesses appear to be unshakable in their identification of Demjanjuk as Iwan Grozny.

* George Parker's memo is paraphrased here for readability and clarity. In no way does this rendering alter the meaning or emphasis of the original document.

Against the Ivan the Terrible theory:

Both Poland and the Soviet Union conducted war crimes investigations of atrocities at Treblinka. Each compiled a list of guards who had served there. Iwan Demjanjuk's name did not appear on either list. Furthermore, the picture of Demjanjuk in the photo spread that the INS sent to Israeli police was that of a man ten years older than the "Ivan the Terrible" whom the witnesses knew from Treblinka. That age difference could have led to misidentifications based on facial features. Furthermore, former Treblinka guards claim that Ivan of Treblinka "rarely if ever" left Treblinka. That casts doubts on any theory that Demjanjuk served in both camps at different times. Finally, all the eyewitnesses describe Ivan the Terrible as about five feet, ten inches tall. Demjanjuk was six feet, one inch.

The evidence that Demjanjuk served at Sobibor is also flawed. We haven't found a single witness—a German or a Trawniki man—who can testify that he saw Trawniki cards similar to the one ascribed to Demjanjuk. Under that circumstance, the trial judge may well refuse to allow the card to be entered as evidence. And Danilchenko's statement about serving with Demjanjuk at Sobibor has inconsistencies that might destroy or damage his credibility. Since we haven't interviewed him, his statements have little value except to raise more doubts.

We are trapped. We have little admissible evidence that the defendant was at Sobibor, yet serious doubts as to whether he was at Treblinka. Even if we are comforted by the conviction that we have the right man but for the wrong act, ethical canons probably require us to alter our current position.

Given our dilemma, we have two basic options and two realistic choices.

Option A: Maintain the Status Quo

The trial will begin soon and it's too late to change direction because we will appear weak and indecisive. Why should we change anyway? We all believe that the seven eyewitnesses who have seen the photo spread to date are sincere and will appear credible on the stand. And even though Demjanjuk was at Sobibor, it is still possible he was also at Treblinka.

On the other hand, we have good reason to believe that Demjanjuk was at Sobibor and never at Treblinka. The American Bar Association Code of Professional Responsibility cautions against a prosecutor trying a criminal case if he has serious doubts. Even though the John Demjanjuk denaturalization case is *not* a criminal case, the damage to the defendant, if found guilty of immigration fraud, requires us to adopt a strict interpretation of the code.

Based on my knowledge of the case, I strongly recommend against this first option.

Option B: Amend the Pleading

Strike Treblinka and Ivan the Terrible . . . Substitute Sobibor and Trawniki

We have statements from Danilchenko and two other former Sobibor guards placing Demjanjuk at the camp in March 1943. As a Sobibor guard, Danilchenko tells us, Demjanjuk assisted directly in the prosecution of civilians. The information from the three guards dovetails with the Trawniki card. Furthermore, Demjanjuk said in his visa application form that he was a farmer in the village of Sobibor from 1937 to 1943.

On the other hand, since the three statements supplied by the Soviet Union are inadmissible as evidence in their present form, our entire case will rest on the weight the judge places on the Trawniki card. Without other supporting documentation, we cannot expect more from him than finding Demjanjuk culpable of being an involuntary trainee at Trawniki.

I consider this option tactical suicide and a legal blunder. That leaves us with only two ethical choices.

Choice One: Dismiss the Case

If we do not believe Demjanjuk was at Treblinka and cannot prove at this time that he was a guard at Sobibor, we should drop the case—at least until the Soviets make Danilchenko available for a deposition. If we adopt this choice, however, there will be political fallout, and the judge may not be willing to allow us to refile at a later date when we are fully prepared.

Choice Two: Expand the Pleading

Remove the Ivan the Terrible charge...Keep the Treblinka guard charge...
Add Sobibor and Trawniki

This option focuses on what we believe to be true—that Demjanjuk was an extermination camp guard. It eliminates what we doubt to be true—that he was Ivan the Terrible. This option will not destroy the denaturalization case against Demjanjuk because he was an armed guard at a death camp and lied about it to the vice consul.

On the other hand, since we cannot now prove with clear and convincing evidence that Demjanjuk was at Sobibor, and we do not believe he was at Treblinka, this choice is a simple ruse to skirt the ethical problems of Option A.

In the past, I opposed amending the pleading to include a reference to Sobibor and Trawniki because I believed that Demjanjuk could not have been both Ivan the Terrible and the Sobibor guard described by Danilchenko. And in the past, OSI has opposed the dismissal of the case despite gnawing doubts about its veracity.

I recommend we perform radical surgery on our pleading. And I recommend that we make a decision about which path to follow within the next couple of weeks.

• • •

OSI director Walter Rockler called a meeting two weeks after he got George Parker's memo. Besides himself and Parker, present at the meeting were his deputy Allan Ryan and Norman Moscowitz, an OSI attorney helping to prepare the Demjanjuk case for trial. Rockler got right to the point.

"If he [Demjanjuk] was at Sobibor, is he still subject to denaturalization under the law?" he asked. Ryan, Parker, and Moscowitz all concluded that he was.

Rockler then asked Moscowitz whether he agreed with Parker that Sobibor and Treblinka were "irreconcilable." Moscowitz said he didn't see the two as "contradictory." The SS could have rotated Demjanjuk from one camp to the other as needed.

During that short meeting of ten to twenty-five minutes, the four attorneys did not discuss the ethical issue Parker had raised in his memo, and Parker did not bring it up. Rockler leaned toward dropping the case. His experience as a Nuremberg prosecutor had taught him not to give too much weight to eyewitness accounts without documentation to support them. Since the Ivan the Terrible case was based on eyewitness testimony without documentation, it should not go to trial. And to try Demjanjuk as a Sobibor guard instead of as Ivan the Terrible of Treblinka wasn't worth OSI's time and effort. There were other more important and better-documented cases waiting to be investigated. If Demjanjuk belonged anywhere, it would be close to the bottom of OSI's list of alleged Nazi collaborators.

When Rockler returned to his law practice at Arnold & Porter, he left the final decision about the Demjanjuk case to his successor, Allan Ryan. Rejecting Parker's recommendation to delay the trial, Ryan chose the status quo option—try John Demjanjuk as Ivan the Terrible.

Ryan's decision fed Parker's dissatisfaction. He had been upset when

the Justice Department fired Martin Mendelsohn as OSI deputy director and hired Ryan over the "intense opposition" of Elizabeth Holtzman
and others. Parker had been part of Mendelsohn's inner circle, where his
opinion was sought and respected. Once Ryan took over the reins, Parker felt left out. The meeting over his memo only served to strengthen
that feeling. Besides, Parker never intended to make government service
his life's work. Ryan's decision to take OSI down what Parker considered
an unethical path gave him the nudge he needed.

Parker quit.

There is no evidence to suggest that Ryan was miffed or upset by Parker's decision to return to a poorly paid job in legal services. He pressed
forward on the theory that Demjanjuk served as a guard at both camps.

Danilchenko's alleged statement, which OSI had, was part of his 1949
war crimes trial testimony. It was useful as a lead but worthless as evidence and certainly inadmissible in court for a number of reasons. Even
though Danilchenko may have sworn to tell the truth, it was possible
that the KGB tortured or threatened to torture him if he didn't say what
it wanted to hear. The KGB could have prepared his "testimony" and
ordered him to sign it, or else. Or he could have lied hoping to get a better deal. The fact that his twenty-five-year sentence was commuted to
eight years for no apparent reason tended to support the perjury theory.

Natalia Kolesnikova, who had prosecuted Danilchenko and others
in the 1949 Kiev trial, admitted as much. "All the men had invariably
done worse things than they would admit," she said. "And they tried to
protect themselves—sometimes by accusing others to reduce the risk to
themselves."

If Danilchenko was to be of any use in the Demjanjuk trial, OSI
would have to depose him as well as videotape his testimony in case he
couldn't or wouldn't testify in America. As a first step in its promised
cooperation with OSI, the Procuracy of the USSR—equivalent to the
U.S. Department of Justice—assigned Kolesnikova to take Danilchenko's sworn statement to assist OSI in its investigation and prosecution of
John Demjanjuk. A certified copy of Danilchenko's testimony, as well as
statements from several other witnesses, arrived in Washington in January 1981, just weeks before the Demjanjuk trial was scheduled to open.
The Danilchenko Protocol, as it was called, made the government's case
stronger.

But which case? And could it be trusted?

CHAPTER TWENTY-ONE

The Voice from Siberia

A s the prosecutor who tried Danilchenko in 1949, Natalia Kolesnikova knew a lot about Sobibor. Part of her interview strategy
with him was to look for contradictions between what he said at
his trial in Kiev and what he would tell her now. She was also hoping to
hear more details about who Iwan Demjanjuk was, what he looked like,
and what he did at Sobibor. Anything to help the Americans.

Kolesnikova would later tell writer Gitta Sereny that the Procuracy
of the USSR was no longer interested in Danilchenko. "We only wanted
to question him as a courtesy to the American prosecutors who wanted
to know more about his connection to Demjanjuk and Sobibor."

Before beginning her interview in Tyumen, Siberia, in November
1979, Kolesnikova explained to Danilchenko the responsibility of a witness under the Soviet Criminal Code and the penalty for making false
statements, refusing to give a statement, or being evasive. Danilchenko
signed a statement that he understood and accepted this responsibility.

The interview began.*

• • •

The gas chamber at Sobibor in camp three was camouflaged, secret,
and guarded by a special detachment of SS guards. During the first six

* What follows is not a literal transcription or translation.

months of my service at the death camp, one or two trainloads of Jews arrived daily. Each train had approximately twenty-five cars with fifty to sixty Jewish men, women, and children in each. Sobibor also had a fleet of five or six trucks that it used to transport Jews from neighboring ghettos.

As a rule, all the Jews were killed on the day they arrived. That made Sobibor nothing more than a factory for mass murder. During the six months I worked there, it gassed fifteen hundred Jews a day until fall 1943, when fewer and fewer trains arrived.

The Germans organized the company of Sobibor guards into four platoons with approximately thirty men in each. The platoons were based on height. A German officer was in charge of the company. A *Volksdeutsche* led each platoon. Since I was just over six feet tall, I ended up in the First Platoon—the tall man platoon.

Demjanjuk was already at Sobibor and in the First Platoon when I arrived. I don't know when he came there or from where. But I did know he trained at Trawniki because he told me.

Demjanjuk was taller than me. He had gray eyes, light brown hair, a receding hairline, and was stocky. He wore a black uniform with a gray collar and always carried a loaded rifle except when he guarded the outside perimeter of the camp. Then he carried a submachine gun to shoot any prisoner who tried to escape and to prevent unauthorized personnel from entering the camp.

Like all guards at Sobibor, including me, Demjanjuk took part in the mass killing process—from unloading the boxcars, to marching the new arrivals to the gas chamber, to forcing them inside. I don't know if Demjanjuk ever killed anyone for resisting.

Unlike the healthy arrivals, the sick were immediately taken to camp three under the pretext of going to an infirmary for medical help. When they got there, they were shot. It is possible that some guards did the shooting on orders from the Germans. If so, I couldn't say if Demjanjuk was among them because I was never present.

I saw Demjanjuk hit and rifle-butt prisoners at the unloading dock like all the other guards, including me. But from what I observed, he did not stand out as especially cruel.

The Germans considered Demjanjuk an experienced and efficient guard, and they repeatedly assigned him to round up Jews from the neighboring ghettos and villages and bring them back to die. For conscientiously following orders, the Germans rewarded him with extra leave. I am not sure if he also got a promotion.

Just before the Soviet army crossed into Poland, the Germans posted me and Demjanjuk to Flossenbürg, Germany, to guard an aircraft factory and a concentration camp there. Each guard at Flossenbürg, including Demjanjuk and me, was tattooed on the inside of the left arm with his blood type in case he was ever wounded. I still have my tattoo—the letter *B*.

In April 1945, as the Russian army began pushing across Germany, the Germans evacuated the entire camp of Regensburg, where Demjanjuk and I now worked, and assigned us to guard the prisoners on their march to another camp in Nuremberg. I escaped. I suggested that Demjanjuk come with me, but he refused. I never saw Demjanjuk again, and I have no idea what happened to him.

• • •

Danilchenko read the transcribed deposition without requesting any corrections or changes. Before signing it, he swore that the statement was correct. Either Kolesnikova or an assistant prosecutor showed Danilchenko three photo spreads with three pictures each, one of which was Demjanjuk. The three men in the first spread were soldiers in Soviet uniforms. Danilchenko correctly identified Demjanjuk. The men in the second set of photos wore Trawniki-type uniforms. Danilchenko correctly identified Demjanjuk. And the men in the third spread wore suits and ties. Once again, Danilchenko correctly identified Demjanjuk.

Two other former Sobibor guards also signed sworn statements that they knew Demjanjuk from Sobibor. One picked him out from the photo spread. The other did not, but recognized his name.

Kolesnikova was convinced that Danilchenko was telling the truth. None of what he said contradicted what he had testified to in his Kiev trial or what she knew about Sobibor and the mass murders that took place there. Most important, Danilchenko understood the penalty for perjury. And since Danilchenko had already served time for his crime, there was no advantage for him to lie.

• • •

OSI chose to view Danilchenko's sworn statement as supportive of its Ivan the Terrible theory rather than a contradiction to it. Buttressed by the statement, Ryan decided to amend OSI's complaint. Service at

Trawniki and Sobibor was added to the Ivan the Terrible allegation. Although the court most probably would have accepted Danilchenko's sworn statement into evidence, Ryan chose not to offer it.

Ryan also declined Moscow's invitation to OSI investigators to depose, cross-examine, and videotape Danilchenko for themselves, instead of relying on Kolesnikova's interrogation. The denaturalization trial of John Demjanjuk that was about to open would focus totally on Treblinka and Ivan the Terrible, not on Sobibor. The ghost of that decision would eventually come back to haunt OSI. When it needed Danilchenko, it would be too late. He would be dead. On February 10, 1981, the day before the trial opened, Judge Frank J. Battisti granted OSI's motion to add Trawniki and Sobibor to the government's complaint. Demjanjuk's attorney, John W. Martin, was not dancing for joy. Even though he had known about the alleged Demjanjuk-Trawniki connection for more than a year because he had a copy of the Trawniki card photos, he felt the need for more time to prepare a defense against the new amendment.

Martin asked Judge Battisti for a sixty-day delay of trial. Battisti said no. Martin filed a motion for a jury trial. Battisti denied the motion.

Part One: Epilogue

In 1980, Bishop Valerian Trifa agreed to voluntary deportation rather than face trial for concealing his collaboration with the Nazis as the Romanian Iron Guard leader who instigated the 1941 pogrom against the Jews of Bucharest. He said that continued court proceedings placed a great financial strain on his Romanian Orthodox Church. Portugal agreed to accept him in 1982, then changed its mind two years later when it learned of his fascist sympathies. Before Portugal could expel him, Bishop Trifa died of a heart attack at the age of seventy-two.

In 1981, the Justice Department cut a deal with an ailing Otto von Bolschwing. If he voluntarily gave up his U.S. citizenship rather than face a long denaturalization process for collaborating with the Iron Guard in Romania, the government would allow him to remain in the United States. The deal was apparently a reward for his years of government service as an OSS-CIA operative. Baron von Bolschwing died in Sacramento, California, from a rare brain disease in 1982 at the age of seventy-two.

Also in 1981, the Justice Department filed charges of immigration fraud against Tscherim Soobzokov, who was then embroiled in a lawsuit with Anthony DeVito, Howard Blum (who had written a book about DeVito called *Wanted!*), CBS, and the *New York Times*. Soobzokov argued that he had fully disclosed his wartime activity to the CIA before the agency hired him. Since OSI did not have enough clear, unequivocal and convincing evidence against Soobzokov, it lost the case.

In 1983, a district court in New York stripped Boleslavs Maikovskis of his U.S. citizenship. The court ruled that he had concealed his collaboration with the Nazis in the murder of the entire population of the Latvian town of Audrini, among other war crimes. Fearing he would be executed if extradited to Latvia, Maikovskis fled in 1987 to Germany, where he was tried for war crimes. Before his trial was over, the court ruled he was too frail to continue. He died in 1992 at the age of ninety-two.

In 1986, after a protracted legal battle, a district court in California finally stripped Andrija Artukovic of his citizenship. He was found guilty of concealing his membership in the Croatian Ustasha and for ordering the deaths of hundreds of thousands of Orthodox Christian Serbs, Jews, and Gypsies. He was extradited to Zagreb, Yugoslavia, where a court sentenced him to death for war crimes. He was never executed because the court later ruled he was too ill with dementia. Artukovic died in a prison hospital at the age of eighty-eight.

In 1985, vigilantes assassinated Tscherim Soobzokov in Paterson, New Jersey. His murder in Paterson—home to 2,500 American Circassians—was described in over one thousand pages of reports released to me by the FBI under an FOIA request. These FBI reports shed light on a little-known chapter in America's relationship with former Nazis.

• • •

Soobzokov's next-door neighbor was startled from her sleep at 4:20 A.M. on August 15, 1985, by the incessant barking of her dog and someone banging on her front door. She jumped out of bed and ran to the window to see who was there. Soobzokov's new Buick Riviera, parked at the curb, was on fire.

The woman rushed downstairs and opened the door for the caller, whom she knew. While he was dialing 911, she ran next door to Soobzokov's house, her black and white terrier barking at her heels. The house was dark. She rang the bell and banged on the window. A light flipped on and the sixty-one-year-old Soobzokov appeared in the hallway.

"Your car!" the woman shouted, turning her face away from the house and pointing to the flames.

Soobzokov opened the front door, then the screen door. There was a ten-second delay before an explosion blew him back into the hallway and knocked the woman and her dog to the ground. When he opened the screen door, Soobzokov had tripped a wire that detonated an eight-inch-long, booby-trapped, galvanized pipe bomb filled with smokeless rifle powder. A second shorter but wider pipe bomb failed to detonate.

The woman struggled to stand and managed to drag herself home. Her dog followed. When they reached the front door, the dog lay down and died. The passerby called an ambulance for the woman, then went to check on Soobzokov. He was alive and conscious but in a state of shock. His wife, daughter, and grandson were all injured when they ran barefoot over broken window glass to help him.

A truck parked across the street quietly pulled away.

Doctors at St. Joseph's hospital worked on Soobzokov for eight hours. They amputated his right leg above the knee and removed bomb fragments. During the operation, he suffered cardiac arrest. (He had a serious heart condition.) Doctors resuscitated him. Although he was in critical condition, they believed he would live if his damaged heart could stand the stress to his shattered body. Soobzokov's Good Samaritan neighbor was only slightly injured.

A phone caller identifying himself as a member of the Jewish Defense League (JDL) took credit for the bombing, uttering the JDL slogan, "Never again."

The FBI assigned the Soobzokov case to its Domestic Terrorism Unit, a task force that most Americans didn't even know existed. As the FBI saw it, the attempt on Soobzokov's life was just one in a string of assassination attempts that began eight years earlier, in 1977. It was just one act of terrorism in a spree that both puzzled and worried the bureau. But unless one were a Jew, an Arab, a neo-Nazi, or an alleged Nazi collaborator, the series of intimidations, assaults, murders, and attempted murders mostly passed under American radar.

• • •

It all began with the publication of Howard Blum's *Wanted! The Hunt for Nazis in America.*

Wanted! told the story of INS investigator Anthony DeVito, who had discovered Soobzokov living in Paterson and working as the chief purchasing agent for Passaic County. Not only did Soobzokov not like the book, but he filed an $11 million slander suit against the publishers and distributors of the book, the author Blum, De Vito, who was featured in it, and nine other named individuals.

The lawsuit created even more adverse publicity for Soobzokov, who was also on the Karbach list published in the *New York Times*. He began to receive a steady stream of threatening phone calls and hate mail, some sent to his office and some to his home. Cars followed him and crept by his house late at night with their lights out.

Given the public outrage over a Nazi hiding in America, New York prosecutors opened a grand jury investigation in 1978 into Soobzokov's alleged war crimes as a Waffen SS officer and a policeman who collaborated with the Nazis. That same year, under the prodding of Elizabeth Holtzman, the Justice Department had created OSI, which immediately assigned teams of historians, researchers, and attorneys to investigate more than five hundred cases of alleged Nazi collaborators living in the United States. One of them was Tscherim Soobzokov.

In May 1979, a grand jury failed to hand down an indictment against Soobzokov because: prosecutors had not provided eyewitnesses to his alleged war crimes; Soobzokov kept invoking the Fifth Amendment; and the CIA refused to release his file, which detailed his work for the agency in Jordan and which also contained lie detector reports detailing his wartime activity.

A few days after the federal grand jury folded without an indictment, Soobzokov returned home from work to find a package sitting on his dining room table. It was the size of a cigar box, wrapped in brown paper. Soobzokov noticed what looked like wires at two corners of the package and called the police. Explosives experts detonated the powerful and potentially deadly bomb without injury.

The next day, the Associated Press and other media outlets received the same anonymous phone call. "You better write this down because I'm only going to say this once," the caller said, speaking rapidly. "Parcel bombs have been sent to Nazi war criminals across the United States.... This is from the International Committee Against Nazism."

The caller wasn't lying. Five package bombs had been mailed from a New York post office on Seventh Avenue and Thirty-Fourth Street. Four bombs were sent to offices of the American Nazi party in Lincoln, Nebraska; Chicago; and Alexandria, Virginia. No one was injured because either the recipients handed the packages over to the police unopened or alert postal clerks blocked their delivery.

Five deadly bombs in one day was a new record for the FBI. The bureau's terrorism unit took the threats seriously and opened an investigation, code name ICANBOM. Agents soon learned that the International

Committee Against Nazism (ICAN), an organization the bureau had never heard of, was a nonviolent group dedicated to bringing Nazi war criminals around the world to justice. The FBI concluded that the caller who took credit for the package bombs was using ICAN for cover. The real perpetrator, the FBI believed, was a virulent, armed, and dangerous cell inside the Jewish Defense League.

Founded by right-wing extremist Rabbi Meir Kahane in 1968, the JDL started out as a neighborhood patrol group that protected Brooklyn merchants and Hasidic Jews from a surge of anti-Semitic threats, robberies, and assaults.

The JDL soon broadened its goals, according to the FBI, to include intimidating anti-Semitic enemies of Israel; harassing the Soviet Union and its satellites because of their anti-Semitic policies; and expelling all Arabs from Israel. The JDL symbol was a clenched fist inside a Star of David. Its slogan: "Every Jew a .22."

The FBI believed that the JDL was a loosely organized paramilitary group of more than six thousand young Jews covertly trained in terrorist tactics at Camp Jedel in Sullivan County, New York. The bureau also believed that Jedel JDL recruits received instruction in karate, rifle and pistol marksmanship, and the making and planting of bombs.

Rabbi Kahane didn't try to hide JDL's objectives. "If we see guns being used openly by certain groups," he said, "we will tell the police, 'either you people stop it, or we will have to use them also.'"

In 1974, the year Elizabeth Holtzman first read the INS files in New York, Kahane left Brooklyn for Jerusalem, where he formed the Kach Party, a militant, anti-Arab group of terrorists. Hundreds of young JDL Jews from the United States followed him. The FBI believed that Kahane continued to direct violent American JDL cells from Israel.

After the 1977 publication of Blum's book, the JDL added a new goal, according to the FBI—exposing and harassing Nazi collaborators. The bureau was so concerned about potential violence that it notified each alleged Nazi collaborator on OSI's active investigation list about the package bombs. It asked them to report to local bureau offices any suspicious or threatening activity, from heavy-breathing phone calls in the middle of the night to hate mail, death threats, and assaults.

Six months after the five parcel bombs were mailed from New York, OSI filed charges against Soobzokov for lying on his visa application about his wartime activities. OSI was forced to drop the charges, however, when the CIA furnished a document showing that Soobzokov had disclosed his membership in the Waffen SS during his visa application interview. Although voluntary membership in the Waffen SS made an applicant automatically ineligible for a U.S. visa, the CIA had managed to get Soobzokov into the country with the understanding that he would spy on the Circassian community for the agency and the FBI.

With the 1979 dismissal of criminal charges by a federal grand jury and immigration fraud charges by OSI, Soobzokov became a target. Violence against him and other alleged enemies of Israel began to escalate across the country:

- JDL members regularly picketed Soobzokov's home, carrying signs that read: "Death to Soobzokov—JDL . . . Nazi Murderers Have No Rights." Members of the local Circassian community pelted the demonstrators with stones under the watchful eyes of the Paterson police.

- Soobzokov received anonymous threatening letters. "Soobzokov—you are a Nazi butcher of men, women and infants," one said. "You will die and when you are dead, you will eternally suffer for the crimes you have committed." The handwritten letter was signed, "A child of a survivor." Another letter read: "Unless you drop your court suits, we will kidnap your [three] children one by one. Then we will assassinate you, you pig. . . . Okay?"

- The FBI received a warning letter: "What happened [package bombs] is nothing like what is going to happen. And although we're sure every Nazi headquarters is being watched, we possess now the membership records of every Nazi group in the country. Every Nazi is a target. The only rights Nazis have is [sic] for burial. Never Again!"

- A twenty-year-old member of the JDL infiltrated Nazi and white supremacy groups in New Jersey and Delaware. She supplied the JDL with membership lists—names, addresses, telephone numbers, photos, places of work—as well as organization plans. But she got caught. The head of the New Jersey KKK and a leader in the Delaware National Socialist Liberation Front lured her to a motel in Vineland, New Jersey, on the pretext of holding a meeting. They cuffed her hands behind her back and repeatedly raped her as punishment. In the process, they broke her right wrist.

- The house of a Forest Hills, Queens, businessman who sold Nazi books and paraphernalia was firebombed with a Molotov cocktail.

- A man representing himself as a reporter stabbed a guest in the home of Boleslavs Maikovskis in Mineola, Long Island, then fled. The assailant later identified himself to the media as a member of Jewish Executioners With Silence (JEWS). He said that Maikovskis had been his target. After that incident, vigilantes lobbed Molotov cocktails at Maikovskis's house several times. A year earlier, in 1978, several shots had been fired into his home, seriously injuring him.

- In the Venice section of Los Angeles, a vigilante planted a bomb at the Fox Theatre, which was featuring a series of Russian films. The bomb was discovered and no one was injured.

- Three months before the Soobzokov bombing, a pipe bomb exploded at the front door of George Ashley's home in Los Angeles. Ashley, a nationally known Holocaust denier, was sleeping at the time and no one was injured. The letters "JDL" were spray-painted in dark blue on the walkway leading to his house. The JDL denied responsibility for the bombing.

- A week before the Soobzokov bombing, twenty-five young Jews gathered in a Paterson area synagogue to hear Mordechai Levi speak. Levi was the leader of the Jewish Defense Organization, a radical JDL splinter group. During his high-octane speech, Levi singled out Soobzokov as an enemy of Israel. "One doesn't ignore Nazis," he railed. "One doesn't debate Nazis. One destroys Nazis."

- Two days before the Soobzokov bombing, a tan station wagon tried to run him over as he crossed a street near his home.

- The day after the Soobzokov bombing, a Boston police officer was disarming a twelve-inch pipe bomb discovered in front of the building that housed the Massachusetts chapter of the American-Arab Anti-Discrimination Committee. The bomb accidentally detonated. Two officers were injured.

- A week after the Soobzokov bombing, a Paterson police officer working on the case received an anonymous letter. "You better not mix up in our case into Mr. Soobzokov," the handwritten note said. "You are a Nazi. . . . We will get you."

- A few days later, the Passaic County sheriff received an anonymous, typewritten letter. "You are barking up the wrong tree in the Soobzokov case," it said. "One of his own committed this crime. Many of his friends hated him with a passion. Others were deeply jealous of him. As having Circassian-Jordan (ARAB) background, these people may relegate [sic] to murder for revenge. He was not a 'highly respected leader' as stated. Soobzokov was wealthy and loaned money out as a Shylock. Maybe a debtor tried to do him in. Who but this circle of 'friends' had knowledge of his new car? His arrogance and superior attitude among his following is not tolerated by all. This group of pesty [sic] Jews are not the ones your [sic] looking for."

• • •

A week after the Paterson bombing, doctors gave the police permission to interview Soobzokov if they promised to ask only yes-and-no questions. Soobzokov had agreed to answer with a nod of his head.

Did you see or hear anything during the night prior to the explosion, investigators asked.

Yes, Soobzokov nodded.

Was the JDL responsible for the bombing?

Yes!

Do you know who was directly responsible for placing the bomb at your doorstep?

Yes!

Do you have any additional information for us?

Yes!

Before he was strong enough to actually speak to the police, Soobzokov died of a massive heart attack. The medical examiner ruled his death a homicide. The violence didn't stop with the last beat of Soobzokov's heart.

At 4:30 A.M. on September 6, 1985, a man walking down a street in Brentwood, Long Island, saw flames leaping up the right side of the home of Elmars Sprogis. The passerby ran to the front door to warn the family.

Sprogis was a seventy-year-old former Latvian policeman accused of arresting Jews, transporting them to killing sites, guarding them until they were shot, and then looting their homes. OSI had filed immigration fraud charges against him but couldn't make them stick because all eyewitnesses were dead. A federal judge found Sprogis not guilty of lying on his visa application, and dropped the charges.

The man trying to warn the Sprogis family triggered a pipe bomb. He suffered severe burns and his right leg had to be amputated. "Listen, carefully," an anonymous caller told *Newsday* the next day. "Jewish Defense League. Nazi war criminal. Bomb. Never again."

A month later, Alex Odeh, the West Coast regional director of the American-Arab Anti-Discrimination Committee, was assassinated by a pipe bomb planted outside his office door in Santa Ana, California. The night before his assassination, Odeh had appeared on television defending Palestine Liberation Organization leader Yasser Arafat.

During a press conference shortly after the Odeh murder, the FBI announced that the bombings of Soobzokov, Sprogis, and Odeh were related, and it attributed the terrorist acts to the JDL. The announcement provoked an angry response from Irv Rubin, who had succeeded Rabbi Kahane as JDL leader.

"It's absolutely absurd, obscene, and outrageous that the FBI would release to the media a statement saying there may be a link between the death of Odeh and the league," Rubin said. "It's now time to put up or shut up. Instead of making libelous and slanderous statements, the FBI should make an arrest." Rubin himself had been acquitted of solicitation-to-murder charges after he allegedly offered to pay anyone who killed or maimed American Nazi Party members in Chicago.

There were no FBI arrests. After more than ten years of forensic examination of the bombs and bomb fragments, bomb parts manufacturers, fingerprint analyses, phone call and car rental traces, and hundreds of interviews, the FBI closed its parcel bomb and pipe bomb investigations. The bureau was unable to find enough evidence to file charges against any members of the JDL, which every major U.S. Jewish organization condemned.

The JDL got a bitter taste of its own medicine when its founder, Rabbi Meir Kahane, was shot at close range in the neck and chest in 1990 while delivering a speech to Zionists in a Manhattan hotel near Grand Central Terminal. He died at Bellevue Hospital an hour later. The shooter was an Arab-American man. In 1994 a JDL member went on a shooting binge inside the Cave of the Patriarchs in Hebron, the birthplace of Abraham. The cave is sacred to Jews, Muslims, and Christians. After the gunman killed thirty Muslim worshippers, Kahane's Kach Party was declared a criminal organization and outlawed in Israel.

In 1992, Irv Rubin slit his throat with a razor blade while waiting in prison for his attempted-murder trial to begin. He had been charged with planting bombs at a Los Angeles mosque and at the office of California congressman Darrell Issa, a Lebanese American Christian.

The JDL still exists but the FBI no longer considers it a terrorist organization.

PART TWO

Facing the Judge

CHAPTER TWENTY-TWO

A Hornet's Nest in Cleveland

If the Walus and Fedorenko losses rattled OSI as it waited for the opening rap of the gavel in *United States of America v. John Demjanjuk*, it didn't show. Neither did OSI allow those earlier losses to slow its dizzying momentum. For one thing, Walus and Fedorenko were not OSI cases. The unit didn't exist when the two were tried. For another thing, OSI had twenty-one other cases besides Demjanjuk either awaiting trial, already in the courtroom, or under appeal. By comparison, in the thirty-six years between the end of World War II and 1981, when the Supreme Court stripped Fedorenko of his U.S. citizenship, the Justice Department had tried only *one* case—Hermine Braunsteiner.

All but four of OSI's twenty-one active cases involved Eastern Europeans: One Estonian, four Lithuanians, six Latvians, and six Ukrainians. They lived in communities across the country ranging from New York, Philadelphia, Baltimore, St. Petersburg, and Miami on the East Coast; Sacramento and Los Angeles on the West Coast; and Chicago and Cleveland in the Midwest.

With Congress, the Department of Justice, Demjanjuk sympathizers, and the Jewish community closely watching from the sidelines, OSI was caught in a squeeze. A failure to convict John Demjanjuk could mean a "short life span" for OSI. But a conviction might only prove that the United States had become the willing dupe of Moscow and the KGB.

Given the high stakes, defendants and their lawyers and sympathizers subjected OSI to "unrelenting attack."

Émigrés from Soviet-bloc countries had reason to be both frightened and concerned. Beginning with the surfacing of Demjanjuk's name in 1975, the KGB had been targeting them through a disinformation program directed at OSI. Herbert Romerstein, former chief of the U.S. Information Agency's Office to Counter Soviet Disinformation, attempted to put that Soviet program in perspective in an article published in the *Ukrainian Quarterly* in 2004.

• • •

As Romerstein explained, the Soviet Union had a public relations problem in 1975 when the first article about Demjanjuk appeared in a communist newspaper. Moscow wanted the West to see the USSR as a peaceful state, eager to punish those who committed crimes against humanity. But Moscow couldn't escape the fact that it was at the same time persecuting Ukrainians and Jews who protested against Soviet repression, and it was refusing to allow Jews to freely emigrate to the West. Even more troubling to Moscow was a growing movement, both in the Soviet Union and in North America: Ukrainians and Jews uniting to show the world that the USSR was still a brutal, totalitarian state.

Watching from the secure shores of America and Canada, émigré communities with emotional, historical, and family ties to their home countries saw the sudden Soviet willingness to help America find, prosecute, and deport or extradite alleged Nazi collaborators as a diversion to draw attention away from its own historical and current crimes against humanity.

The Soviet Politburo saw America's sudden interest in Nazi collaborators as an opportunity and quickly seized it. It ordered the KGB to blitz the West with phony documents like Michael Hanusiak's Ukrainian list and propaganda like *Lest We Forget*, Hanusiak's exposé on alleged Ukrainian collaboration with the Nazis that featured more than 150 pages of reports and photos.

A Soviet propaganda brochure aimed at the West clearly spelled out the KGB storyline. The fragile but growing bond between Ukrainians and Jews was, it said, "a wicked marriage . . . a sinister alliance between Zionists and Ukrainian bourgeois . . . a malignant partnership of the

Magen David [Star of David] and the nationalist trident [Ukrainian national emblem] fostered by the CIA."

The United States was the KGB's primary Cold War target because of its large Baltic and Ukrainian population. Its objectives in the United States were carefully formulated: Destroy the bond between Jews and Ukrainians, depict émigré communities as nests of Nazi collaborators, and discredit the Ukrainian nationalism movement. One way to accomplish those objectives was to help OSI collect "evidence" against its growing list of alleged Nazi collaborators.

One KGB technique to trick American prosecutors was to manufacture witnesses. In 1980, the year George Parker wrote his OSI ethics memo about prosecuting the Demjanjuk case, Colonel V. Medvedev, a high-ranking KGB official, published an article in *Sbornik KGB*, a secret internal magazine. He noted that OSI was eager to try anyone who had collaborated with the Nazis, regardless of nationality and no matter how long it took. Medvedev observed that the KGB had quickly learned how to please U.S. prosecutors—give them witnesses. "Practice shows," Medvedev wrote, "that concrete evidence from [a] witness thoroughly interrogated on a high professional level appears to be very important proof in Nazi . . . cases."

To accomplish its goal of conning OSI, the KGB either "coached" witnesses or "fixed" the sworn statements of witnesses to make the subject look like a Nazi collaborator.

An anonymous Soviet official, at the risk of his life, confirmed Medvedev's admission. He told an American diplomat in Moscow in 1981 that Soviet witnesses were being coached for days before being allowed to give depositions to OSI prosecutors, in order to make their testimony more incriminating. The allegation was brought to the attention of OSI, which dismissed it as the grumble of a "disgruntled" official.

• • •

Congressman John Ashbrook of Ohio agreed with the émigré community, which saw the KGB-furnished documents as a ruse, and publicly espoused the doctrine of *Presumption of Forgery*. "Evidence from Soviet sources is tainted by the communist history of lies and forgeries," Ashbrook said in a speech on the floor of the House of Representatives. "It should not be utilized in American courts."

A member of the House Permanent Subcommittee on Intelligence, Ashbrook was deeply influenced by the subcommittee's hearings in 1980, *Soviet Covert Action—The Forgery Offensive*. For two days, Ladislav Bittman, aka Brychta, former chief of the Disinformation Department of Czechoslovak Intelligence Services who defected to the United States in 1968, and six CIA officials recited chapter and verse on a wide variety of Soviet forgeries ranging from a U.S. Army field manual and personal letters, to documents involving every major U.S.-Soviet concern from NATO to SALT II.

"We are facing an enemy who has the advantage of a gigantic, well-orchestrated, secret apparatus around the world," said Bittman, who directed Czechoslovakia's dirty tricks against the United States from 1954 to 1968. "The basic principle of the communist espionage imperium is to use and abuse every weakness of the opponent."

John McMahon, CIA deputy director for operations, testified that forgery was one of the Soviet's "major weapons" in its propaganda arsenal. The KGB office responsible for deploying that arsenal, he pointed out, was Service A of the First Chief Directorate, a bureau high on the Soviet organizational chart. Service A specialized in forgeries, the planting of press articles and rumors, disinformation, and media control.

McMahon noted that not only had the number of forgeries increased in recent years, but they also had become technically more sophisticated. "Forgeries are a preferred weapon," he said, "because they do not involve a high degree of political risk . . . or high operational risk." The hearing report contained an appendix of more than fifty pages of what the CIA classified as Soviet forgeries.

The Soviet forgery hearing reflected Ukrainian mistrust of the Soviet Union and its fear and hatred of the KGB. The Ukrainian community believed that Moscow was dangling John Demjanjuk as bait, and OSI had swallowed it. For Ukrainian Americans, the Nazi hunt in America had become an OSI-Jewish conspiracy with the KGB pulling the strings.

Given the émigré suspicion and hatred of the KGB, the Demjanjuk case stirred deep emotions in greater Cleveland's thirty thousand Ukrainians. On Sunday, February 9—two days before the Demjanjuk trial opened—St. Vladimir's Ukrainian Orthodox Church held a standing-room-only service on behalf of Demjanjuk and his family. Conducted by four priests, it was a traditional old-world service with men on one side of the church and women on the other.

After the service, 450 people gathered in the church hall for a political rally and traditional Ukrainian music and dancing. The keynote speaker was Valentyn Moroz, a professor of history and a leader of the Committee Against the Use of Soviet Evidence (CAUSE). Moroz was a Ukrainian hero. A former dissident and member of the Ukrainian national movement, he had been arrested in Ukraine, tried, convicted on trumped-up KGB charges, and sentenced to hard labor in Siberia. After fourteen years in a gulag, Moroz was released in a U.S.-Soviet prisoner swap in 1979.

"Soviet evidence and witnesses are bluffs," Moroz said. "The Soviets don't need Demjanjuk. He is not a political force. But what they are looking for is a precedent. If it works, they will try again and again. The Soviets are doing their work with American hands."

As Demjanjuk supporters left St. Vladimir's social hall, they dropped bills into cardboard boxes sitting at the doors. Demjanjuk's trial had not yet begun, and his legal fees were already more than $112,000. CAUSE was a major contributor to the Demjanjuk Defense Fund, along with the neo-Nazis.

On February 10, 1981, the eve of Demjanjuk's trial, seventy-five Ukrainians gathered in front of Cleveland's old Federal Building on Public Square to hold a vigil. Most, if not all, were members of St. Vladimir's parish. A nun with a large cross dangling from her neck waved a burning Soviet flag. Nearby, a group of Jewish students standing under a Star of David flag shouted, "All Ukrainians are Nazis! All Ukrainians kill Jews!" while U.S. marshals and mounted police stood guard around the perimeter of the square.

The next morning, an estimated 150 Ukrainian protesters marched in front of the Federal Building. Cleveland was in the middle of the biggest snowstorm of the season, and the demonstrators walked in freezing rain. Some carried signs demanding a ban on the use of Soviet-supplied information.

"We are protesting against a *Soviet trial* in American courts," Moroz told reporters. Others held up yellowed copies of old newspapers featuring stories about Ukrainian peasants starving to death during Stalin's forced famine. An elderly Ukrainian woman in a babushka held a poster that said, "Russia murdered 7,000,000 Ukrainians in the artificial famine in 1933 alone."

That sign triggered another deep emotion running through the heart of the Ukrainian community—resentment against Jews, rarely talked about publicly for fear of being labeled anti-Semitic, but deeply felt.

• • •

In their unrelenting emphasis on the murder of six million Jews during the Holocaust, Jews and most of the rest of the world paid scant attention to the estimated three to four million Ukrainians Stalin starved to death in the genocidal famine of 1932–33. Some Ukrainian scholars refer to it as the Ukrainian Holocaust. Add to that figure the estimated three to four million Ukrainian civilians killed during World War II and the resulting six to eight million Ukrainians murdered is staggering.

Why should six million Jews get all the attention and sympathy?

Then there was the Ukrainian community's anger at the media. A few alleged Ukrainian Nazi collaborators got the spotlight, the rest stood in the shadows of suspicion. The media made it look as if the majority of Ukrainians were Jew-haters and murderers. What about the two million hardworking Ukrainians in America and Canada, their staunch anticommunism, and their refusal to forget their countrymen suffering behind the Iron Curtain?

Why did the media portray the North American Ukrainian community as a hiding place for Nazi collaborators? The simple fact was, if all of the 260 alleged Nazi collaborators on the OSI target list were Ukrainian, it would amount to only one one-thousandth of 1 percent of the total Ukrainian population in America and Canada.

Why did the media overlook the role Ukrainian nationalists played in World War II? Twenty percent of the Red Army that fought the Nazis were Ukrainians. Thousands of Ukrainians dogged the Nazis in partisan units. Some Ukrainians were even imprisoned in concentration camps for helping Jews. And the Ukrainian Catholic metropolitan, Andrei Sheptytsky, was one of the few high-ranking Catholic Church leaders who spoke out specifically against Hitler and the systematic murder of Jews—unlike Pope Pius XII, who never condemned Hitler or Nazism by name, and Archbishop Stepinac, who supported the Nazis and the Ustasha in Croatia.

Why couldn't the media understand the difference between a Ukrainian and a *Volksdeutsche* living in Ukraine? It was true that some Ukrainians collaborated with the Nazis as Einsatzkommandos. Historians placed the number at an estimated one thousand out of a population of forty million. But historians failed to point out that the majority of those Einsatzkommandos were *Volksdeutsche*, not real Ukrainians. Didn't every other country in Europe, from France to Lithuania, have its share of Nazi collaborators? What about Japan? Why pick on Ukrainians, the strongest anticommunist community in America?

Finally, Ukrainian Americans were deeply upset at the inherent bias of the denaturalization process. It denied the defendant a jury trial because the issue at stake was *civil*, not criminal. But if an American citizen was entitled to a jury trial over a leg splintered in a car accident, why wasn't he entitled to a jury when the "precious gift" of U.S. citizenship was at stake? And why didn't Jewish judges and prosecutors disqualify themselves from OSI cases?

Didn't OSI and the American legal system understand that a guilty verdict in a denaturalization trial did more than reduce the defendant to a man without a country? It might be a death sentence. Could there be any doubt that if John Demjanjuk were deported to the Soviet Union, as OSI wanted, he would be executed based on the verdict of a single American judge, perhaps a biased Jew like Julius Hoffman? What would have happened to Frank Walus if he had not gone to expensive lengths to prove the government had the wrong man?

With these emotions and doubts about the integrity of OSI and the American system of justice swirling inside and outside his courtroom, Judge Frank Battisti donned his robes to decide the life and death of John Demjanjuk.

CHAPTER TWENTY-THREE

The Opening Salvo

Frank Battisti was no Julius Hoffman, but he was just as controversial. As chief judge in the Northern District of Ohio, he had presided over the trial in 1974 during which eight Ohio National Guardsmen were accused of violating the civil rights of the four Kent State University students whom they had shot and killed during the campus rampage in May 1970. Battisti found the Guardsmen not guilty. His decision angered the Kent State student body and civil rights leaders alike.

To some, Battisti looked like a right-wing bigot.

Two years later, in 1976, Battisti ruled that Cleveland's public school system was guilty of racial discrimination and ordered school busing. His decision angered the Board of Education and most of the city. Death threats followed.

A fellow judge observed: "He withstood much of the hostility and acrimony, bitterness and ostracism of the community, in order to be true to his oath and the Constitution."

To some, Battisti looked like a civil rights hero.

Battisti wasn't controversial just for his legal decisions. To some of his peers, he was an independent judge known for compassion. To others he was a courtroom dictator. Demjanjuk's defense attorney got a taste of the dictator when Battisti dismissed his motion for a jury trial, approved the government's amended pleading on the eve of the trial, and refused to grant a sixty-day extension.

Facing Battisti for the government were Assistant U.S. Attorney John Horrigan and OSI attorney Norman Moscowitz. The Justice Department had assigned Horrigan to the Demjanjuk case long before OSI was created, and OSI was not happy that Horrigan was still attached. It blamed him for delaying the trial by one year, either because he wasn't committed or because he shoved the Demjanjuk case to the bottom of his priority list. To forestall further delays, OSI wanted total control. Given the ages of the defendant and witnesses, one year was a long time.

The Justice Department compromised. It kept Horrigan on the case but appointed Moscowitz lead counsel.

Moscowitz complemented Horrigan. He was a sharp, clear thinker, a good legal strategist, and he knew the jots and tittles of the case from Demjanjuk's capture by the German army in 1942 to his surrender to the Allies in 1945. If Horrigan and Moscowitz had serious differences about how to try the case, they wouldn't show up in the courtroom.

Compared to Horrigan, however, Moscowitz had little courtroom experience and even less in dealing with the most crucial issue in all Nazi collaborator cases—elderly and emotional survivors who positively identify a Nazi collaborator after thirty or more years.

John W. Martin, an African American, led the defense team. As a former prosecutor for Cuyahoga County, which includes Cleveland, Martin knew his way around the courtroom, and Judge Battisti was no stranger to him. A legal aid volunteer, Martin was known in Cleveland for his big heart and fierce dedication. Once on a case, he worked seven days a week, sometimes for nothing or nearly nothing. Martin took the Demjanjuk case when no one else would touch it.

Martin and his defense co-counsel, Spiros Gonakis, were at an extreme disadvantage. Because Demjanjuk didn't have deep pockets, their pretrial investigation and travel were limited. How could they afford to go to Israel to depose Miriam Radiwker? Or to the Soviet Union to seek permission to take videotaped depositions of witnesses willing to testify that Demjanjuk was not Ivan the Terrible? How could they hire expensive document examiners to test the Trawniki card photos? Or pay an expert witness to testify in court?

In spite of that handicap, the defense had an important edge over the prosecution. The government carried the heavy burden of truth. *The defense didn't have to prove a thing.* Its job was to make the government's evidence appear unconvincing and to raise as many doubts about it as possible. And there was the rub. There was no jury. It was much easier to sow doubt in a panel of impressionable men and women than to sway a single judge who knew all the lawyerly tricks of the courtroom game.

Based on its pleading, the government had to prove in a clear, unequivocal, and convincing way that John Demjanjuk:

- Was trained at Trawniki.
- Was Ivan the Terrible.
- *Could* have been a guard both at Sobibor and at Treblinka.
- Committed specific crimes that made him morally unacceptable for U.S. citizenship.
- Lied on his visa application in a material way.
- Would have been denied a U.S. visa and citizenship if he had revealed his wartime activities.

• • •

Forty U.S. marshals guarded the courtroom on the morning of the first day of the trial. They lifted a knife from a man trying to enter and they arrested a woman causing a disturbance in the hall outside the courtroom. But for the most part, the atmosphere in the court building was serious and calm.

Dressed in a dark blue suit and light blue shirt, John Demjanjuk sat on a pew inside the elegant courtroom with its green-gold marble walls and vaulted ceilings. Hands folded in his lap, he sat straight and appeared serene. Sitting in the pew behind him were his wife, Vera, and their children—Lydia, Irene, and teenager John Jr. In the stenographer's office at the rear of the courtroom was a red and tan tote bag with coffee and the Demjanjuk family's lunch.

The courtroom and gallery were packed with Ukrainians and Jews waiting in almost reverential silence for Battisti to enter. Sprinkled throughout the courtroom were Ukrainian men and women wearing traditional blouses and skirts. They added a splash of color.

Judge Battisti entered. The prosecution asked prospective witnesses to leave the courtroom, as was customary. Battisti intervened. Vera was a prospective defense witness. He told her she could stay. As it turned out, she would not take the stand in her husband's behalf. She was too emotionally distraught.

The prosecution called its first witness to the stand, Earl F. Ziemke.

Before he began his direct examination of Ziemke, Horrigan told Battisti that he should feel free to interrupt him to ask the witness questions.

"Oh, I will feel free," Battisti replied.

The courtroom broke out in laughter. Demjanjuk smiled.

Earl Ziemke was the first indication that OSI had learned a lesson or two from the Frank Walus fiasco. To win denaturalization cases would demand a stable of historians to find documentary evidence, evaluate it, and testify to its authenticity. A marine during the war, Ziemke had fought in the Pacific battles of the Caroline Islands and Okinawa. He was a professor of history at the University of Georgia and a specialist in World War II and the eastern front. He was a perfect prosecution witness—clear, authoritative, with documentation to support his every historical argument.

Demjanjuk had sworn in a pretrial deposition that the Germans had captured him in Kerch, sent him to a POW camp in Rovno in western Ukraine for a few weeks, then transferred him to another POW camp in Poland whose name he could not remember. With that testimony as a foundation, Ziemke's single task was to show that Demjanjuk could have arrived at Trawniki by July 1942. If he failed, much of the government's case would crumble.

Guided by Horrigan's methodical questioning, Ziemke constructed a historical framework and time line from Demjanjuk's capture during the battle of Kerch sometime between May 8 and May 19, 1942, based on German and Soviet war records, to his brief incarceration in the Rovno POW camp in western Ukraine in May–June, to his arrival at Trawniki in July. To support that time line, Horrigan sought to determine how Demjanjuk got to Rovno.

"Were there any Soviet prisoners of war taken by the Germans during the battle of Kerch?" Horrigan asked Ziemke.

"Yes . . . The figure varies," Ziemke testified. "The most conservative figure is 125,000."

"What did the Germans do with the POWs they captured at Kerch?" Horrigan asked.

"They gathered them together in the assembly area on the Crimean Peninsula or the Crimea itself, and then, as fast as . . . transportation was available, they would move them further west away from the front."

"What type of transportation?"

"Railroad," Ziemke said.

The answer was important to the prosecution case. Most of the early POW camps like Rovno were in western Ukraine. If Demjanjuk had been marched the more than one thousand miles from Kerch in the south to Rovno in the west, for him to have gotten to Trawniki by July would have been impossible.

"Is there a particular reason," Horrigan asked, "why the Germans brought the POWs all the way to western Ukraine?"

"The Germans didn't want to have large numbers of Soviet prisoners of war . . . right behind their front," Ziemke said.

In his history lesson from the stand, Ziemke had constructed an unbreakable historical chain of events—Demjanjuk's capture in Kerch in May, his imprisonment in Rovno in June, and his arrival at Trawniki in July. That chain led straight to the Trawniki card, where the prosecution case against Demjanjuk really began.

Next, the government called Wolfgang Schefler to the strand.

• • •

Like Earl Ziemke, Schefler was a historian and researcher who specialized in the study of Nazism. A professor at the Free University of Berlin, he was an old hand at playing expert witness in war crimes trials. And as a historical researcher, he had the opportunity to rummage through World War II archival files all over Europe.

Schefler had three jobs to perform for the prosecution. First, he had to establish that Trawniki men routinely committed crimes against humanity while working for the SS. Second, he had to prove that Trawniki men were routinely shuffled back and forth between Treblinka and Sobibor without the knowledge of Trawniki headquarters. And finally, he had to verify the historical authenticity of the Trawniki card, which he was predisposed to find real. After examining thousands of original and photocopied World War II documents—many supplied by the Soviet Union—Schefler had never found a single forgery.

The government began its direct examination of Schefler by establishing the importance of the Trawniki men in the Nazi extermination program.

"Did Trawniki play a role in any aspects of Action Reinhard?" government prosecutor Norman Moscowitz asked.

"Trawniki units were involved in many ghetto cleanup operations," Schefler said. "They moved out those deemed transportable. The others were killed on the spot—people in hospitals or orphanages or in old folks' homes. . . . Because of the lack of [German] manpower, they were an essential part of Action Reinhard."

"What kinds of duties did they have at the extermination camps?"

"Guarding the camp and supervising the deportees as they came from the train," Schefler said. "That includes the supervision of the people being herded into the gas chamber."

The Supreme Court had ruled in the Fedorenko case that the mere wearing of a uniform and the carrying of a gun at a Nazi camp constituted assistance to the enemy in the persecution of civilians.

"Did they receive uniforms?" Moscowitz asked.

"Former SS uniforms and, to some extent, former Belgian army uniforms," Schefler said. "The majority were black. Later on they were replaced by . . . earth-brown uniforms."

"Were the Trawniki men armed?"

"In varying degrees."

Next, to strengthen his case against Demjanjuk as a Nazi collaborator, Moscowitz used Schefler to explain how the Trawniki men had been contractually employed by the SS, an organization defined as criminal by the International Military Tribunal at Nuremberg.

"Did they take an oath or pledge of any sort?" Moscowitz asked.

"To perform and obey the service orders of the SS and the police," Schefler said.

"They were legally subject to court-martial . . . and therefore accepted the discipline and regulation of the SS?"

"Yes, that's what it means," Schefler said.

The prosecution had scored its first major point. If it could later prove that Demjanjuk was trained at Trawniki and/or served at Sobibor or Treblinka and lied about it on his visa application, he could be stripped of his U.S. citizenship and deported as a Nazi collaborator. The government did not have to prove that Demjanjuk had personally beaten, shot, or killed anyone. If it did offer credible evidence of war crimes, the evidence would serve to strengthen its argument that Demjanjuk was *morally unacceptable* for U.S. citizenship.

Having made that point clearly and with historical precision, Moscowitz quickly moved to a critical issue in the prosecution case: How was it possible that the Trawniki card listed Sobibor as a Demjanjuk posting, but not Treblinka? Ivan the Terrible and Treblinka were the heart of the prosecution case. Sobibor was just a sidebar.

"Is it fair to say," Moscowitz asked, "that Trawniki men were assigned to varying locations [as] needed?"

"That is completely correct," Schefler said.

"In the transfers between camps and other places, was the Trawniki administration involved?"

"Normally no," Schefler said. "Trawniki had no jurisdiction over exchanging back and forth."

"To your knowledge would Trawniki maintain *records* concerning such transfers?"

"We don't know of any."

Moscowitz felt he had scored his point and moved on to the Trawniki card itself, the prosecution's only piece of documentary evidence. He handed Schefler the Soviet-certified photos of the front and the back of the card.

"Dr. Schefler," he asked, "would you look at Government Exhibit No. 5 and tell the court what this appears to be?"

"A Service ID with a specific number."

"Is there any indication on the card where this service record ID is from?"

"The document was issued by the representative of the SS Reichsfuehrer and the chief of police," Schefler said. He went on to testify that all the organizational details on the card were appropriate and historically accurate, including the three official seals. The defense would later insinuate that they were forged.

There was no date on the Trawniki card and the defense would also later argue that the card was a forgery because it was undated. The Germans would never issue a document without a date. In his questioning of Schefler, Moscowitz used the military rank of Ernst Teufel, the supply clerk who cosigned the card, to determine a probable issue date for the card. Teufel had signed the card as *Rottenführer*, or corporal.

Schefler testified that German records showed that on July 19, 1942, Teufel was promoted to *Unterscharführer*, or sergeant. Schefler told the court that it would be a breach of German military protocol for Teufel to sign an official document with his previous lower rank.

According to Ziemke's and Schefler's combined testimony, therefore,

Demjanjuk arrived at Trawniki sometime between July 1 and July 18, 1942. The prosecution failed, however, to explain why the card was undated.

Moscowitz had one final question before he moved on to another topic. As a historian, did Schefler consider the Trawniki card a forgery?

"[The forger] would have to have supernatural powers," Schefler said.

In his pretrial deposition, Demjanjuk had admitted openly and candidly that the Germans tattooed him with his blood type.

"Are you familiar with the practice of the German forces . . . of tattooing the blood-type group on the body of the troops?" Moscowitz asked Schefler.

"Yes . . . On the inside of the left arm."

"Was this practice . . . followed by *all* the German forces?"

"No," Schefler said. "I only know of the practice in the SS."

"What would that indicate?"

"That he belonged to some sort of unit which required it," Schefler said.

"What kind of unit would that be?"

"Guard units at extermination camps, or any number of other SS units."

"To your knowledge, was there ever any practice of tattooing prisoners of war with such blood groups who *were not* in the service of the SS?"

"No," Schefler said.

• • •

In his cross-examination of Schefler, defense attorney John Martin tried to raise doubts about the authenticity of the Trawniki card, as he would throughout the rest of the trial.

"Dr. Schefler," Martin began, "you testified that the Soviets captured certain documents in the Lublin district . . . when they were sweeping westward, is that correct?"

"Yes, not just there but from all over," Schefler said.

"Certainly it is not inconceivable that they could have captured SS *stamps and seals*, is it not?"

"I don't know," Schefler said.

"Have you ever seen a card *exactly like this*?"

"I have never seen an identical card," Schefler said.

Next, Martin moved on to Schefler's credibility as an expert witness.

"Is it fair, sir, to assume that you are not an expert on the questioned documents?" Martin asked.

"I do consider myself an expert—as an historian—in the examination of historical details contained in the documents."

"But surely, you do not consider yourself *so expert* that you could give testimony as to their authenticity or genuineness?" Martin pressed.

"Objection," Moscowitz said. "It's been asked and answered."

"I'm going to sustain it because I think we've gone far enough," Battisti ruled.

Finally, Martin challenged a critical point the government needed to establish—that Treblinka was not listed as a posting on the alleged Demjanjuk Service ID card because Trawniki approval was not required in order to shuffle guards between death camps.

"Do you have *any documents* of these so called transfers amongst the camps?" Martin asked.

"My testimony is based on the statements of different individuals in different trials," Schefler said.

Martin chose not to ask Schefler whether it was historically accurate to have an *undated* Trawniki-issued ID card. Perhaps Martin knew, or suspected, what Schefler would answer: Undated Trawniki ID cards were common.

• • •

The prosecution scored several major points in its powerful opening double-barreled salvo: Trawniki men were integral to Himmler's plan to murder all the Jews of Europe; they collaborated directly with the SS, a criminal Nazi organization; because they were armed and wore special uniforms, they were ineligible for a U.S. visa; and the Trawniki card was historically accurate in every detail.

In response, the defense attempted to raise two doubts in the mind of Judge Battisti about the authenticity of the Trawniki card: As a unique, one-of-a-kind document, it must have been forged; and the card was undated and, therefore, could not be authentic.

To complement the testimony of Schefler about the *historical* authenticity of the Trawniki card, the prosecution called document examiner Gideon Epstein to the stand to testify about the *forensic* authenticity of the card.

CHAPTER TWENTY-FOUR

Under the Microscope

Gideon F. Epstein was a forensic document examiner with more than twenty years experience hunting forgeries, first for the army, then for the INS. With extensive training in handwriting comparison, he was one of a small pool of sixty-seven certified document examiners in the United States. His job as a prosecution witness was as complex as it was critical—to determine if the Trawniki card was authentic or a KGB forgery.

OSI was unable to provide Epstein with the original card for examination because Moscow had failed to deliver it before the trial as promised. All Epstein had to work with were the Soviet-certified photos of the front and back of the card, and for comparison purposes, two known or proven signature samples of Trawniki commandant Karl Streibel, and two of Trawniki supply officer Ernst Teufel.

Epstein studied the writing on the card under a powerful stereoscopic microscope using various degrees of magnification in order to analyze, measure, and compare the characteristics of the handwriting. He began with the speed the author used to sign his name and whether he wrote with "careless abandon."

Speed is important because it determines whether the handwriting was produced naturally and without conscious control over the writing process. The strokes of a forger would be slower and more deliberate, no matter how many times he practiced.

Next, Epstein studied the pressure the signer used to produce the writing and the degree of smoothness in forming characters, and the up and down strokes of the writing, which produce areas of lightness and darkness. Important for his analysis were the patterns and variations that are so subtle, they are nearly impossible to reproduce.

Finally, since the body and the hand shake ever so slightly when someone writes, Epstein analyzed the tremor pattern in the sample writing. And since the stroke of the pen does not stop on a dime, Epstein examined and compared the feather, or trailing, at the end of each word. Like snowflakes, no two tremor and feather patterns are alike.

These characteristics—speed, abandon, naturalness, and the variations and patterns of pressure and smoothness, tremor and feathering—would help Epstein determine whether the writing was traced or forged. He would depend on no single writing characteristic to reach a conclusion about the authenticity of Streibel's and Teufel's signatures.

"After examining and performing these tests . . . on the *questioned* and the *known* signature of Streibel," Horrigan asked, "did you come to any conclusions?"

"Yes I did."

"What were those conclusions?"

"The person who made the known signatures," Epstein said, "also made the signature . . . in the questioned German identification card."

Next, Epstein concluded that the two known signatures of Teufel also matched the signature on the photograph of the Trawniki card. To illustrate how he arrived at his conclusions, Epstein presented the court with a letter-by-letter analysis of blowups of all the signatures he had compared.

"There were no differences found in any of the characteristics," Epstein concluded.

Epstein went on to explain how he had used a low-power stereoscopic microscope to study the background tone of the Trawniki card photos to determine if there were any erasures, or if any of the cardboard fibers were disturbed. He further explained how he had used a variety of filters, films, and lighting to see if touching up, whiting out, or substitutions were present on the card.

Substitution was an important prosecution concern. Demjanjuk supporters alleged that the KGB stripped in Streibel's and/or Demjanjuk's name. To perform that kind of fraud, the forger would have to remove the old signature from the card. In so doing, he or she would disturb the paper in some detectable way.

Epstein testified that the only disturbance he found in the background of the card was the *N* in *Nikolai*, Demjanjuk's father's first name. Someone had erased the letter and corrected it. "This I assume was done by the typist when the document was made," Epstein said, adding that the *N* in *Nikolai*, was identical to all the other N's on the card.

Finally, Epstein examined the photo on the card. Did someone remove the original picture and substitute Demjanjuk's, as his supporters alleged? Again, if a substitution were made, the seal and/or the official German stamp on the photo would have been disturbed.

"This was studied microscopically," Epstein said, "and it was determined to be one and the same seal. . . . My conclusion, after completing the tests on this document, was there are no alterations, substitutions, or inter-lineations."

Horrigan knew that the defense would try to debunk Epstein's conclusion because the document examiner had looked at two photos of the card rather than the original card.

"The fact that the government's Exhibits 5 and 6 were photographs, did that hamper your investigation in any way?" Horrigan asked.

"It would have been preferable to have the original documents," Epstein said. "As far as the examination was concerned, I felt that I was not restricted by the use of photographs."

"It affected your opinion in no way?"

"It did not."

• • •

John Martin was ready for Epstein. His job was to cast serious doubt about the validity of Epstein's conclusions. He began by alleging bias.

"What is your religion?"

"I am Jewish," Epstein said.

Martin made his point and moved on.

"Mr. Epstein, the tests or the conclusions that you reached here are *not conclusive*, are they?"

"They are as conclusive as I can render them," Epstein said.

"Experts do differ in their conclusions," Martin said. "Do you agree with *that*?"

"Yes, I would agree to that."

"Often time *[sic]* conclusiveness to one expert might not be conclusiveness to another expert. Would you agree to *that*?"

"I am assuming," Epstein clarified, "that you are talking about two people who are completely qualified and who have both received the *same material* to examine. In a case such as this, they should both reach the same conclusion."

Martin changed his tack. "The conclusions . . . are not on an equal par with fingerprints, are they?" he asked.

"That is incorrect, sir," Epstein said. "Handwriting identification is a positive identification, and it is considered along the same line as voice prints [and] fingerprints."

"Are you testifying here that your tests . . . .and conclusions are on an *equal* footing . . . with a fingerprint conclusion?"

"Yes."

"Mr. Epstein, certainly the expert . . . say you, for example . . . is not infallible?"

"I know of nothing that is really in that category other than mathematics," Epstein said. "I think we are all fallible."

Next, Martin challenged Epstein by pointing out differences in strokes, spacing, loops, and letters on the blowup photo signatures Epstein showed the court. Epstein explained how each variation was consistent with his findings.

"If a person had your background and knowledge and was attempting . . . to fabricate or forge a signature," Martin asked, "would he not be aware of the spacing habits and all these things you told us about?"

"The person may be *aware* of something but *unable* to duplicate it," Epstein said. "I have tried many times . . . and found that I am a total failure at it."

"But do you not deny that one trained in fabricating documents would have a greater success than you?"

"Yes."

Martin had found one major weakness in Epstein's analysis of the Trawniki card and he waited until the end of his cross-examination to exploit it. The flaw: There were critical standard tests that Epstein did not do.

"You have not performed any tests that would reflect or indicate to you when these signatures were written, have you?" Martin asked.

"This has to be done only from the originals."

"So that it is fair for us to assume then that we have no idea when . . . that signature was written?"

"Not from my examinations, no."

"Then you cannot say whether or not . . . it is a genuine document that was prepared in 1950, 1960, or 1970, can you?"

"No."

"Is it possible to ascertain the source of the printed material?"

"If you had the original document."

"Is it possible to ascertain . . . *the model* of the typewriter used to produce the specimen?"

"Again having the ability to examine the original document."

"Are there any techniques that exist to determine the *kind of ink* that is used on the document?"

"Yes, there are several," Epstein said. "But again you would need the original document."

"Mr. Epstein, there are persons who, if trained properly, could forge documents such as these. Is that right?"

"I can only say that I have never seen any."

• • •

Next, the government called Heinrich Schaefer and Otto Horn to the stand by way of videotaped testimonies taken in Frankfurt and Berlin, Germany, a year earlier.

CHAPTER TWENTY-FIVE

From the Horse's Mouth

As a *Volksdeutsche* who had worked in the Trawniki office with Ernst Teufel, Heinrich Schaefer was a valuable witness. Unlike Ziemke, Schefler, and Gideon Epstein, Schaefer was actually at Trawniki. As an eyewitness, he had three jobs to accomplish for the prosecution: Establish a date when the Trawniki school opened, confirm Schefler's academic description of the school, and reinforce Epstein's conclusion that Streibel's and Teufel's signatures were authentic.

Like Demjanjuk, Schaefer was a former Red Army soldier, captured by the Germans, and sent to a POW camp in western Ukraine. At the end of August 1941, German police arrived at the camp with several empty transport trucks. At the time, Iwan Demjanjuk was recovering from shrapnel injuries in a Soviet hospital. The police selected Schaefer and fifty or sixty other *Volksdeutsche* and ordered them into the trucks. Then they drove the POWs for about five hours to Trawniki.

On the videotape, Horrigan began his examination of Schaefer by establishing a timeline for Demjanjuk's transfer to Trawniki, a point the government would return to time and again.

"Were there any other Soviet army prisoners of war . . . there when you first arrived?" Horrigan asked.

"We were the first."

"What, if anything, did you do there?"

"For the first two weeks, nothing at all," Schaefer said. "Then we were divided into military . . . groups. And then we received light training."

"How long were you so trained?"

"Until the middle of December."

"Were there any further POWs that arrived after you?"

"Soon," Schaefer said. "Every week . . . people would come from the prison camps."

"Were all these ethnic Germans?"

"Usually Ukrainians."

"You indicated that at this time you were given a uniform," Horrigan said. "Would you describe that uniform, please?"

"Black . . . without any insignia. . . . The German troops did not wear this uniform."

"Did you always have the same uniform?"

"No."

"Would you describe your second uniform?"

"This also was a uniform which German troops did not wear," Schaefer said. "The color was a so-called earth brown."

"Was your picture ever taken at Trawniki?" Horrigan asked.

"Yes."

"Were other people's picture[s] taken?"

"To the best of my recollection, everybody," Schaefer said.

"Were you assigned a number?"

"Everybody got an official number."

After his training was over in December 1941, the SS assigned Schaefer to the Trawniki administrative office because he was fluent in German. His job was to pay the salaries of the trainees and the nearly two hundred Trawniki graduates who worked at the complex. One of the men Schaefer worked with was Ernst Teufel, who issued clothing and uniforms to the guards and trainees. Teufel was a hard name to forget. It means "devil" in German.

Horrigan showed Schaefer the photos of the Trawniki card.

"Calling your attention to the area right of center, at the bottom . . . can you identify the writing there?"

"It's Mr. Teufel's signature."

"How do you know?"

"I saw the signature frequently," Schaefer said. "In particular, the way he started . . . the first letter. It's like a big 7."

"On what kind of documents?"

"Various."

The video showed Horrigan handing Schaefer the two photos of the Trawniki card.

"Can you identify the card?" Horrigan asked.

"An official ID card like the people who received training in Trawniki had," Schaefer said.

"Did you have one?"

"Yes."

"Do you see what appears to be a signature?"

"That's Streibel's signature and he was commander of the camp."

"Do you recognize the writing as Streibel's?"

"I remember the writing as such because I often had leave passes signed by him," Schaefer said.

By the end of the videotaped testimony, Schaefer had scored two strong points and one weak one. He had established that every Trawniki man had his picture taken and every Trawniki man received an ID card. And he had supported Epstein's conclusion that the signatures of Streibel and Teufel were authentic.

In his cross-examination, Martin scored a big point. Although Schaefer was working in the Trawniki office as paymaster when Iwan Demjanjuk allegedly enrolled in the school, he could not remember an SS guard by the name of Demjanjuk, nor could he identify his photo.

If Martin scored a big point, he also made a huge mistake. He failed to ask Schaefer a critical question. Although Schaefer testified that he was issued a card similar to but not identical to the alleged Demjanjuk card, Martin chose not to ask him how his card differed from Demjanjuk's or whether he had ever seen a Trawniki card exactly like Demjanjuk's. More important, he never asked Schaefer if he thought the Demjanjuk card was authentic. Had he done so, his answers would have shocked the court:

- The Trawniki card listed the items of clothing given to Iwan Demjanjuk. Schaefer would later say in a sworn affidavit, "There never was issued an identification paper to a guard, which at the same time contained a list of objects which were received by him. The list of equipment was a special document, which was kept at the camp administrative office where I worked."
- The equipment list on the Demjanjuk Trawniki card did not include a rifle. Schaefer would later swear: "It is completely unimaginable that there was no carbine given to a guard. That was, to a certain

extent, his right arm, without which he could not perform his duty."

- The name Demjanjuk appeared on the Trawniki card *twice*. Schaefer would later swear: "Every guard in Trawniki, including myself, had an identification paper on which his name appeared only once. A card such as the one which was shown to me and which shows the name Iwan Demjanjuk twice, was never issued by me. I know of no such cards."

- The Demjanjuk Trawniki card stated that Iwan Demjanjuk was posted to Okszow and Sobibor. Schaefer would later swear: "This document could not have been issued at Trawniki. Official transfers were never recorded on identification documents."

- The Demjanjuk Trawniki card was not dated. Schaefer would later swear: "The date of issuance had to be on *every* identification card. Otherwise, such a paper was automatically invalid."

. . .

During the war, Otto Horn was a male nurse in the German army's Medical Services Company. After a serious battle injury, he landed a desk job at Trawniki for a few months, before being transferred to Treblinka in the fall of 1942. He was a reluctant but important witness because he was a German, not an emotional Jewish survivor whose memory might be clouded by a forty-year hunger for revenge.

Moscowitz took Horn's sworn videotaped testimony at the U.S. consulate in West Berlin in 1980, the year before the trial opened. He began the direct examination by asking Horn if he could remember any of the guards at Treblinka. Horn said he recalled two Ukrainians. One was Iwan. He couldn't remember the name of the other.

Next, Moscowitz questioned Horn about the two photo spreads he had viewed in the small living room of his Berlin apartment prior to his videotaped testimony. Both Moscowitz and his boss, Allan Ryan, were aware of the criticism leveled at the photo spreads and identification procedures used in the Walus and Fedorenko cases, and they were determined not to make the same mistakes. Ryan had insisted that the pictures for the Ivan the Terrible spreads conform to the stipulations of the U.S. Supreme Court. Under his instructions, OSI prepared two spreads with eight clear pictures in each. One spread contained Demjanjuk's visa application photo, the other the Demjanjuk Trawniki card photo. Ryan had also insisted that two OSI team members be present at every showing of the photos, and that afterward, each write up a separate report stating who said what to whom, and who did what and how.

Moscowitz's job was to establish that OSI followed the book when it showed Horn the two sets of photos. But before the videotape could show Horn answering the first photo spread question, Martin's co-counsel, Spiros Gonakis, objected. The courtroom technician stopped the video. Gonakis complained that neither he nor Martin had been present when OSI showed Horn the photos, which, he argued, was a violation of his client's Fourteenth Amendment right to due process. He asked the court to rule Horn's photo identification inadmissible.

Battisti overruled the objection and the videotaped testimony continued.

Moscowitz began with the first photo spread.

"When you were looking at these photos, was anyone holding them?" he asked Horn.

"They were on my table in front of me."

"Were you in control of them?"

"Yes."

"Did anyone suggest to you that you pick out a particular photo in any way?"

"No," Horn said.

"Did you in fact identify or recognize someone in those photographs?"

"Iwan."

"Were you shown another set of photographs?"

"Yes."

"When you looked at those photographs . . . where was the first [set]?"

"They had been removed," Horn said.

"How many photos were in that set?"

"Also about eight."

"Did anyone suggest to you that you identify or pick a particular photograph?" Moscowitz asked.

"No."

"In this group, did you recognize the photograph of any person?"

"Yes. The one I found out on the first set," Horn said.

"And what was his name?"

"Iwan."

"The Iwan whom you stated was at the gas chamber?"

"Yes."

"Where *was he* at the gas chambers," Moscowitz asked. "Outside or inside?"

"Inside."

"What was he doing?"

"He directed, or he co-directed, the prisoners into the chambers," Horn said.

"Did there come a time when you saw him at any other part of the gas chamber?"

"At the place where the engines were."

"These are the engines of the gas chamber?"

"Yes."

"Did you see Iwan go into this room where the motors were?"

"Yes."

"What if anything did you see him do there?"

"I didn't go in there," Horn said. "I only saw him *going in.*"

Moscowitz then approached the issue in another way.

"What would happen in the gas chambers after . . . Iwan entered that motor room?" he asked.

"Objection."

The answer called for speculation. How could Horn possibly know what happened inside the motor building if he wasn't present?

"Overruled."

"They certainly turned on the engines and gassed the people," Horn said.

"How long would the process of gassing last?"

"Perhaps an hour."

"And what if anything happened after that hour was over?"

"The chambers were opened," Horn said.

"And what happened then?"

"The corpses were carried away into the pit . . . for burning."

Anticipating that the defense would attempt to characterize Horn as an unsavory war criminal, Moscowitz asked: "Mr. Horn, were you tried in court for your activities at Treblinka?"

"At Düsseldorf . . . 1964–1965," Horn admitted.

"And what was the verdict?"

"I was acquitted."

"Completely?"

"Entirely," Horn said.

Horn was the only German found not guilty in the Treblinka war crimes trial in Düsseldorf. The court did not believe that supervising the burying of the corpses of Jews murdered in gas chambers, while he stood by and watched, was a crime against humanity.

Moscowitz scored two big points. Horn had identified Iwan as the Ukrainian guard who herded victims into the gas chambers and who was inside the motor room when the gassing took place. He had not actually seen Iwan start the motor, however, or direct the gas to the chambers. Second, he had positively identified John Demjanjuk as Iwan from two photos in two correctly presented spreads.

However valuable Horn was to the prosecution, he was far from a sympathetic witness. He had described the killing process at Treblinka in cold, unemotional terms as if he were describing cattle rather than people. And he tried to portray himself as innocent of all wrongdoing as a euthanasia project worker and as a Treblinka guard who supervised the gruesome burying and burning of hundreds of thousands of corpses of men, women, and children.

• • •

Martin's job was to destroy Horn's credibility by characterizing him as a war criminal and, therefore, not trustworthy. As a nurse, Horn had worked in T-4, Himmler's secret euthanasia program, designed to rid Germany of the elderly, chronically sick, and mentally handicapped. Himmler didn't consider them good Aryan specimens and their care cost too much. Its name was an abbreviation for Tiergartenstrasse 4, the address of the project headquarters in Berlin.s T-4 murdered more than two hundred thousand people before religious and public pressure forced the Nazis to discontinue the program.

"Were you part of the T-4 organization?" Martin asked.

"No."

"Yet you worked in their offices in Berlin?"

"Yes."

"And you worked at their euthanasia *locations* doing clearance work?"

"Yes."

"You had to take charge of urns?"

"Yes."

"Were these the remains of the children that were gassed and burned?"

"There were no children gassed there," Horn said. "These were adults, mentally ill adults. . . . The urns were empty."

Horn went on to claim that the SS was no longer euthanizing people when it drafted him. The claim sounded self-serving and Martin ended his T-4 cross-examination on that note. He asked Horn what he did at Treblinka.

Horn said he supervised Jewish workers.

"What were your duties in supervising the Jews?" Martin asked.

"They were burning corpses and shoveling earth into pits," Horn said.

"Did you ever see this person you describe as Iwan commit any atrocities, do anything other than hang around the gas chamber?" Martin asked.

"No, I didn't."

Once again, the answer did not appear honest. Every witness to follow Horn would describe the atrocities Iwan committed right under Horn's nose.

"How old was this man that you remember as being Iwan?"

"About twenty-four, twenty-five."

"What color was his hair?"

"Dark to black."

"How tall was he?"

"Approximately 180 centimeters [about six feet]."

"How much did this person weigh?"

"Seventy-five to eighty kilograms [about 165–75 pounds]."

"What kind of uniform did he have?"

"I think a black one."

Martin scored three solid points. First, Horn was more than a simple bystander to Nazi atrocities and, therefore, his testimony was tainted. Second, if Horn could be believed, Iwan was not a monster as the Treblinka survivors would later describe him, casting some doubt on their credibility. And third, the Iwan whom Horn knew at Treblinka had dark hair, not blond, as the Trawniki card described Demjanjuk's hair.

• • •

Next, the government called five Treblinka survivors in a row to testify that John Demjanjuk was the Ivan the Terrible they saw and feared. For spectators, it was the high point of the trial and they flocked to the courthouse door.

CHAPTER TWENTY-SIX

Without a Doubt

The crowd in the courthouse lobby on the morning the first Treblinka survivor was scheduled to testify was unruly. There was pushing and shoving as spectators jostled to get closer to the metal detector, the gateway to a seat in the courtroom or gallery. Under these conditions, it was impossible for the marshals to create anything that resembled an orderly line. A news release issued by a Ukrainian group suggesting that Holocaust survivors had become "psychotic with revenge and hate" did not help to defuse a potentially explosive situation.

• • •

The prosecution called Chiel Rajchman to the stand. Then living in Montevideo, Uruguay, Rajchman was born in Poland, captured by the Nazis in 1942, and sent to Treblinka along with his sister. The SS selected him to sort clothes. They sent her to the gas chamber. On his second day in the camp, Rajchman found her dress in the pile of clothes he was sorting. He cut a piece of it when no one was looking and treasured it like a photograph until the day he escaped.

The SS took Rajchman off the sorting line after a few days and made him a "barber." His new job was to cut off the hair of naked women and girls, their last stop before being driven down the camouflaged path that the SS called the "Road to Heaven." It was a wrenching, stressful job. He had to remove a woman's hair in five quick cuts and drop the locks into a valise. Six cuts and he would join her in the gas chamber.

Next, Rajchman worked for Otto Horn in camp two. He pulled bodies from the gas chambers, loaded them onto large wheelbarrows without sides, and raced them to the pits. If he didn't move fast enough, the Germans or Trawniki men who worked around the gas chambers would beat him, like the guards beat the slave miners in Camp Dora.

When Rajchman arrived at the long, deep pit, he would slide the corpse(s) off the wheelbarrow into the hole, where groups of Jews waited to stack them head to toe. When the pit was filled, they covered the bodies with sand and chlorine. In February 1943, as the Red Army pushed west, Himmler ordered the bodies to be dug up and burned to destroy the evidence.

Toting corpses was so traumatic that many prisoners assigned to the gruesome task hung themselves by their belts. Rajchman told the court that he wanted to hang himself, too, but he couldn't do it. Instead, he asked the chief dentist, who pulled gold teeth from the dead, for some poison. The dentist got him a job as his assistant.

Pulling teeth was a lot easier than carting victims, some of whom were still breathing. When there were no transports, Rajchman cleaned blood, flesh, and bone from the teeth. Then he separated the gold teeth from those with other metals and polished them until they gleamed.

Long before the trial began, Rajchman had identified Demjanjuk as Ivan the Terrible from the two legally correct OSI photo spreads. Since he worked next to the gas chambers, Rajchman had had a chance to observe Ivan at work. He recalled him as armed with a both a rifle and a pistol. For a Trawniki man who was not a *Volksdeutsche* to be given a pistol was a sign of prestige and trust.

Horrigan conducted the direct examination of Rajchman. His job was to get the witness to identify Iwan as an exceptionally cruel guard, and then identify Demjanjuk as Iwan.

"Do you recall the names of any Ukrainians in camp two?" Horrigan asked.

"I remember them well," Rajchman said. "The biggest devil, who engraved himself in my memory . . . was called Iwan. His assistant was called Nikolai."

After he testified that he saw Iwan herd victims into the gas chamber buildings before Iwan himself entered, Rajchman went on to describe some of the atrocities he saw Iwan commit. One day, Iwan picked up an auger and walked over to a Jew. He ordered the man to bend over, Rajchman testified, then he began drilling into the prisoner's buttocks. When the man began crying from pain, Iwan laughed and said if he screamed, he'd kill him.

Soon after escaping from Treblinka and while in hiding, Rajchman began a diary. Horrigan asked him to read out loud what he had written in it about Iwan thirty-eight years earlier. The courtroom listened in stunned silence.

"He gets a sharp knife. When a worker runs by, he cuts off an ear. Blood spurts out but he had to run on with the carrier (litter for corpses). Iwan waits until he runs back then tells him to get into the pit where he (Iwan) shoots him."

Horrigan showed Rajchman the two OSI photo spreads. From both the visa photo and the Trawniki card photo, he identified Demjanjuk as Ivan the Terrible of Treblinka. Vera collapsed. An ambulance took her to St. Vincent Charity Hospital, where she was treated for hysteria. She would not return to the courtroom for a week.

Martin's job was to cast doubt that the man Rajchman positively identified as Ivan the Terrible was the John Demjanjuk sitting a few feet from him. Martin couldn't attack the OSI photo spreads, since they were legally correct. But he could zero in on two physical characteristics in Rajchman's description of Ivan the Terrible that did not match Demjanjuk—height and hair color. Rajchman's answers were cagey.

"How tall was he?" Martin asked.

Rajchman pointed to Martin and said to Judge Battisti, "Taller than him."

"About how much did he weigh?"

"I never weighed him."

The courtroom burst into laughter.

"Could you give us your best estimate?"

"How can I know what he weighed?" Rajchman said. "I know he was strong like a horse. He carried a long pipe and he split people's heads with it. That I know."

"What color was his hair?"

"Not light."

"Was it dark or black?"

"Possibly dark," Rajchman said.

"What were his facial features?"

"I don't know how to explain it."

"Let me help you," Battisti said. "Elongated? Was it elongated or long?"

"It's possible sort of elongated."

Demjanjuk's face was oval.

The prosecution called Eliyahu Rosenberg to the stand.

• • •

Like Rajchman, Rosenberg was born in Poland, rounded up in the Warsaw Ghetto by German soldiers and Trawniki men, and taken to Treblinka. Like Rajchman, he carted dead bodies to the pit for several weeks. Like Rajchman, he testified against Otto Horn at the Düsseldorf Treblinka trial. And like Rajchman, he lost relatives at Treblinka. His mother and father were gassed there, and on the very day he arrived at the camp, he pulled a cousin out of the gas chamber with his own hands.

Rosenberg had identified Demjanjuk, but not positively, as Ivan the Terrible from the photo spread Miriam Radiwker had shown him in Israel, the spread that Judge Roettger had called so badly flawed that it could not "pass muster."

There were two buildings at Treblinka that housed gas chambers, Rosenberg told the court. The smaller of the two had three chambers, which were antiquated and no longer in use. The larger had ten, two rows with five chambers in each with hermetically sealed doors. Each chamber was about eighteen feet long and about fifteen feet high. The walls were cement with white tile up to a point to make the chamber look like a shower room. There was a fake electric light dangling from the ceiling and "shower pipes" through which the gas was delivered. Each chamber held as many as five hundred men, women, and children. A diesel engine supplied the carbon monoxide. On a good killing day, Treblinka could gas five thousand Jews.

At the entrance to the gas chamber buildings, which was stuccoed and whitewashed to look like a bathhouse, was a sign with a quotation from the Old Testament: "This is the gate of the Lord. The righteous shall enter through it." Along the walls were flower boxes watered and tended by several of the Jews who worked in camp two.

"Who operated the gas chamber?" Horrigan asked.

"Two Ukrainians," Rosenberg said.

"Do you know their names?"

"Iwan and Nikolai."

"Did you see them . . . at the gas chambers?"

"Every day, whenever there were transports."

"Would you describe this Iwan?"

"He was a tall man about 23, 22, 24 [years old]. He was broad shouldered, round face. He had gray eyes. His ears stuck out a little. Short hair, not especially light."

The description closely matched the picture on the Trawniki card.

"What do you recall Iwan and Nikolai doing at the time the transports came?"

"They beat people. . . . Iwan had a . . . pipe, sword, a whip, and he tortured the victims with them before they entered the gas chambers, especially the women," Rosenberg said. "He cut pieces between their legs. I saw this with my very eyes."

Rosenberg testified that he not only saw Iwan drive victims into the gas chamber buildings, but he also saw him enter it, presumably to force them into the chambers.

"Now after they entered the gas chamber, what, if anything did Iwan and Nikolai do?"

"They returned to the room where the motor was, and they activated the motor."

"Mr. Rosenberg, were you ever present at the gas chambers while they were in operation?" Horrigan asked.

"Yes."

"Would you describe what you would see at such a time?"

"The outside doors of the gas chambers were closed," Rosenberg said. "I stood on the ramp, and we waited until the victims had been choked. I heard and saw how they entered the gas chambers. I heard the screams, the crying of the children, 'Mama, Daddy . . . Hear, Oh Israel.' After a short period, about a half an hour, everything was quiet."

"And then what happened?"

"A German went up, he put his ear to the door, and he said in German, 'They are all asleep. Open the door,'" Rosenberg said. "We opened the door and . . . started to remove the corpses. . . . Practically everyone still groaned."

Even though Horrigan knew Miriam Radiwker's photo spread was flawed, he showed it to Rosenberg anyway. Once again Rosenberg picked out Demjanjuk's photo (no. 16) as Iwan of Treblinka. And from the OSI spread, he picked out the photo on the Trawniki card as that of Iwan.

• • •

The next witness was Georg Rajgrodzki, a retired architect who was born in Poland and currently lived in West Germany. Like Rajchman and Rosenberg, Rajgrodzki had carried corpses to the burial pit under the supervision of Otto Horn. Unlike the other witnesses, Rajgrodzki got a personal taste of Ivan the Terrible. Iwan had given him twenty lashes that nearly killed him. Although he recovered, Rajgrodzki knew his days were numbered. A violin saved his life.

One of the Germans found a violin that had belonged to a dead Jew and asked if anyone could play it.

"I can," Rajgrodzki volunteered.

"Okay, play."

That day the supervisor of the camp kitchen, an Austrian, happened to be in the small group of Treblinka personnel who had gathered to hear the Jew play. He asked Rajgrodzki to play some Viennese music. The waltz Rajgrodzki selected landed him a cushy job in the kitchen, where he stayed . . . and played . . . until the uprising.

Rajgrodzki recalled playing for Iwan and Nikolai one day in the summer of 1943. By that time, the transports to Treblinka were reduced to a trickle and the guards were bored. Himmler had already liquidated Belzec, and it was just a matter of time before he would close Treblinka as well. Rajgrodzki had put together a trio—violin, harmonica, and clarinet. By the time the group finished its first piece, Ivan the Terrible was in tears.

Like the witnesses before him, Rajgrodzki testified that he frequently saw Iwan and Nikolai drive Jews into the larger gas chamber building, enter it, and then, after everyone was locked in one of the ten gas chambers, enter the building that housed the motor.

• • •

The next witness was Pinchas Epstein, who was born in Poland and currently lived in Israel. He had positively identified Demjanjuk as Ivan the Terrible from the photo spread Miriam Radiwker showed him. The government was fortunate to have Epstein. He was one of the six witnesses who had testified at Fedorenko's trial three years earlier. Judge Roettger had verbally abused and "attacked" those witnesses so "roughly" that they felt like they, not Fedorenko, were on trial. No one was eager to testify in America again. Epstein lost his whole family at Treblinka—his father and mother, two brothers, and two sisters. That may have been the reason he agreed to sit in the witness chair one more time. For them.

Like the three witnesses before him, Epstein had carried corpses to the pit under the supervision of Otto Horn. He recalled how the Germans had accused a group of Jews of planning an escape. Iwan ordered the men to lie facedown on the ground.

"He split one skull after another . . . with an iron pipe," Epstein said.

Epstein also testified about three Jews who *did* escape. Germans and guards tracked them in the snow and dragged them back to the camp. "Iwan tortured them all day with his metal pipe," Epstein said. "He broke their hands and feet."

The SS hanged them during the evening roll call.

"Have you ever had occasion to be present when the motors to the gas chamber were turned on?" Horrigan asked Epstein.

"Yes, sir."

"Were you able to see this area closely, the area where the chambers were?"

"Yes, sir."

"And do you know who operated the motors?"

"Two Ukrainians. One was Iwan and the second was Nikolai."

Epstein described how he sat down to rest one day near the gas chamber building while he waited for Fritz Schmidt, the German officer in charge of camp two and the gassing, to say, "They are all asleep. . . open the doors." From his vantage point, Epstein could actually see inside the engine building. He watched Iwan and Nikolai turn on the motor and direct the gas into the chambers.

• • •

The final witness was Sonia Lewkowicz from Israel. She had worked in the Treblinka laundry in camp two until the uprising. For the most part, she said the same things the previous four witnesses had testified to. Iwan was cruel. He herded victims into gas chambers and worked in the building with the motor. Demjanjuk was Iwan.

• • •

George Parker had been right in his doubt memo. He predicted that the witnesses would strike the court as sincere and unshakable in their conviction that John Demjanjuk was Ivan the Terrible. Through accumulation and repetition, the government scored huge points during its witness examinations. Each one had identified Demjanjuk as Iwan from photo spreads offered to them in the courtroom. Each gave a description of the Iwan they knew that was close to Demjanjuk's description on the Trawniki card. Each saw Iwan herding Jews into the gas chamber building and entering the motor building. One actually saw Iwan turn the motor on. Each graphically described the cruelty of Iwan.

Given the strength of the combined testimony of five survivors who worked near the gas chambers, the prosecution decided not to call any of the other four survivors waiting in the witness room. Why risk angering Battisti by presenting more of the same?

• • •

In the face of such emotionally powerful and convincing evidence, Martin had an impossible job trying to mount any kind of defense. He used a two-point strategy to create as much doubt as he could. First, he attacked the identification process. Then he challenged the witnesses' physical description of Demjanjuk as Iwan.

Martin pointed out that Miriam Radiwker's photo spread was seriously flawed. And he insinuated that the witnesses might have been coached or might have talked about the photo spread among themselves, in effect ganging up on Demjanjuk. But try as he might, Martin couldn't question his way around the dramatic *in-court* identifications of John Demjanjuk as Iwan from both the Radiwker and OSI photo spreads.

Martin methodically asked each witness to describe Iwan's height and the color of his eyes and hair so that he could later argue that their descriptions did not match Demjanjuk, and therefore, that the government had got the wrong man, as it did in its Walus case.

• • •

Before it rested, the government called four witnesses in a row to prove the last point of its trial strategy: If U.S. immigration examiners had known the truth about Demjanjuk's wartime activities, they would not have recommended him for a U.S. visa, granted him one, or awarded him U.S. citizenship.

CHAPTER TWENTY-SEVEN

A Question of Eligibility

D aniel Segat was a U.S. Army intelligence interrogator during the war. After the war, he helped the International Refugee Organization (IRO) resettle the thousands of refugees under its care. Segat was so good at his job that the IRO quickly promoted him first to chief eligibility officer, then to a seat on its review board, which settled tricky cases.

Moscowitz took Segat's videotaped testimony in New York. His job was to establish Segat as highly credible, then get him to testify that the IRO would not have recommended Demjanjuk for a U.S. visa if it had known about his wartime activities.

"Would you briefly describe what your duties were as a field eligibility officer?" Moscowitz asked.

"To determine the eligibility of all applicants for IRO assistance in my area," Segat said.

"What were the consequences to an applicant of a determination that he was *eligible* for IRO assistance?"

"He acquired a legal document which entitled him to—it's like a passport almost—to all the services that IRO was able to render, including care, maintenance, and immigration."

"What were the consequences to the applicant if he were found *ineligible*?" Moscowitz asked.

"He was deprived of all the things I mentioned before," Segat said. "Deprived of the possibility to emigrate."

Moscowitz handed Segat a copy of the IRO eligibility manual and asked him to find and read to the court the criteria of ineligibility.

"[Any persons] who can be shown to have assisted the enemy in persecuting civilian population . . . of countries [that were] members of the United Nations," Segat read. "[Any others who] have voluntarily assisted the enemy forces since the outbreak of the Second World War."

"If the IRO discovered that an applicant had lied or made misrepresentations . . . did that have any effect on the processing of his application?"

"He would be prima facie *ineligible*," Segat said.

Moscowitz knew the defense would argue that it was common for immigration personnel to encourage applicants from the Soviet Union to lie about their countries of origin so they would not be forcibly repatriated.

"Did you, or *any* members or employees of IRO *ever* encourage or instruct an applicant to give incorrect information?" Moscowitz asked.

"To the contrary," Segat said. "Our job was to elicit the truth."

"If an applicant . . . was a citizen of the Soviet Union, would that fact . . . have any impact or effect on finding that he be eligible or ineligible?"

"No," Segat said. "Not in itself."

"If the applicant . . . became a German prisoner of war, would [that] have any impact on the applicant's eligibility?"

"No bearing on his eligibility," Segat said.

In a pretrial deposition, Demjanjuk admitted to being a soldier in General Vlasov's liberation army. Moscowitz asked if membership in Vlasov's army made him ineligible for a U.S. visa.

"It would make him prima facie *ineligible*," Segat said. "The burden of proof shifts to him. . . . We would listen to their appeal, and if we are satisfied that they are *not volunteers*, they are eligible."

"What if . . . an applicant were a former Soviet soldier taken prisoner by the Germans who was later trained by the Germans at a training camp for concentration camp guards?" Moscowitz asked, referring to Trawniki. "What impact, if any, would that have on that applicant's eligibility?"

"He would be declared prima facie *ineligible*," Segat said.

"If an applicant were a Soviet soldier, taken prisoner by the Germans, who served as a guard in a Nazi concentration camp or . . . extermination camp, what impact if any would that have on that applicant's eligibility for IRO assistance?"

"He would be declared *ineligible*."

Segat's damaging testimony presented Martin with a huge challenge in his defense of Demjanjuk, whose main argument was that he had lied out of fear of repatriation to the Soviet Union, where he would have been executed for serving in Vlasov's army.

"Were you aware," Martin asked Segat, "that Russian repatriation officials visited DP camps in the American zone, and that there was a time when they forcibly repatriated USSR citizens found in these camps?"

"I am aware that they were visiting camps," Segat said. "But I am *not aware* of a Russian repatriation official forcibly taking anybody out of the camp."

"Did you ever gain any knowledge of an executive order issued by President Truman putting a halt to forcible repatriation?"

"No, sir," Segat said. He couldn't have because Truman never issued such an order.

Since the refugees spoke more than a dozen different languages, the IRO hired hundreds of interpreters to interview them and record their answers. Martin tried to establish that refugees paid interpreters to falsify their applications by saying they were born in a country other than the Soviet Union, usually Poland, because they were afraid of being forcibly repatriated.

Did Segat know about any cases where interpreters forged applications for refugees?

"I know of many cases where that occurred, yes. . . . If [we] found out that there was some forgery or something, we simply got rid of them."

The government called Leo B. Curry Jr. to the stand.

• • •

Like Judge Battisti, Leo Curry had landed on the beaches of Normandy. After the war, he served as an investigator for the war crimes trials tribunal in Manila. From 1948 to 1952, he worked with the U.S. Displaced Persons Commission, which reviewed the reports of the IRO and passed further judgment on the eligibility of applicants for U.S. visas. Curry's job as a prosecution witness was to complement and reinforce Segat's testimony. He had personally approved Demjanjuk for a U.S. visa in 1950.

"Mr. Curry, would you describe how an application arrived at your desk at the Commission?"

"The file or case history was prepared for the most part by the IRO and handed to the Commission," Curry explained.

"Once the file reached the Commission, were there any other checks or inquiries made?"

"A great number of checks . . . to determine [the applicant's] character, his history," Curry said.

"What would you consider to be the *major* source of information about each applicant?"

"Affidavits, sworn statements."

"Was the applicant interviewed?"

"In an instance where there may be an apparent conflict in time and place," Curry said.

"Once the determination to immigrate under the Displaced Persons Act was made, would a report or recommendation of some sort be issued by the Commission?" Moscowitz asked.

"A final report of approval."

"Who would make that report?"

"I, for one, as a case analyst."

"What would be the next step?"

"The entire dossier would be forwarded to the U.S. Consular Service for their consideration of a visa."

"What were the consequences to an applicant if he were found ineligible by the Commission?"

"He would be refused admission to the United States."

As he did with Segat, Moscowitz went on to establish that being trained at Trawniki, serving in Vlasov's army, and working as a death camp guard would each render an applicant ineligible according to the Displaced Persons Act, while merely being a Soviet POW would not.

Moscowitz asked: "Take the case of a Red Army [POW] who, at some point, served in a *German-organized* unit for Ukrainians for the purpose of fighting against the Soviets?"

"The Commission would want to know whether, in fact, this service was forced or whether it was voluntary."

"Who would bear the burden of proving . . . this service was forced or voluntary?"

"The applicant."

"How difficult . . . would it be for such an applicant to demonstrate involuntary service?"

"In my experience, highly unlikely," Curry said.

"Why is that?"

"I have yet to recall *anyone* having stated that they *voluntarily* served."

"Everyone claimed he had served involuntarily?"

"Everyone did."

• • •

Martin began his cross-examination of Curry with the same line of questioning he had used on Daniel Segat.

"During your tenure with the Displaced Persons Commission, were you ever aware of any forced repatriations—prior to your arrival there or subsequent to your arrival there—of Soviet citizens by Russian officials?" Martin asked.

Curry had joined the commission in 1948.

"Prior to my arrival, yes."

"Did you, or would you have had, access to a Presidential order . . . from President Truman regarding forceful repatriation?"

"If any such proclamation was made . . . during the time I was there, I would have been aware of it," Curry said. Of course he wasn't aware of it, because President Truman never issued such a proclamation.

"If in a concentration camp, there were Jewish inmates who were forced . . . by the Germans to guard prisoners . . . would they be eligible for immigration to the United States?"

Martin was referring to the SS practice of appointing Jewish Kapos to help supervise Jewish workers. Sometimes, they were ordered to lash fellow prisoners with a whip. It was a delicate line of questioning. The Jewish community greeted any attempt to compare Jewish Kapos to Trawniki men with outrage.

"My interpretation would be no," Curry said.

The 1948 Displaced Persons Act did not distinguish between voluntary and involuntary persecution of civilians, as the Supreme Court had pointed out in its Fedorenko decision. The Displaced Persons Commission had come to that same conclusion in 1945.

Demjanjuk said on his visa application that he was born in Poland, not in Ukraine. Martin knew that the prosecution would try to turn that misrepresentation into another argument for why Demjanjuk should be stripped of his citizenship. Martin hoped to weaken that argument.

"If an applicant . . . concealed his place of birth solely out of fear of repatriation back to Russia, would that exclude him?" Martin asked.

The question was a tactical error.

"I would not have considered it reason for the misrepresentation of place of birth," Curry said.

• • •

Moscowitz had the option to make a re-direct examination of Curry. He took it.

"Mr. Curry, you indicated that a lot of the information which the Commission relied upon came from the applicant," Moscowitz said. "Could *all* of that information . . . have been checked out?"

"No."

Moscowitz was making a vital prosecution point here. The defense had argued, and would continue to argue, that the IRO and the Displaced Persons Commission had thoroughly checked Demjanjuk's background and failed to find his name on any list of Nazi collaborators, weakly suggesting that he could not have been a collaborator if he was not on a list of suspects. Moscowitz destroyed the argument.

"You indicated . . . that you were aware that at some point prior to your service with the Commission, there was forcible repatriation of Soviet citizens. Do you know when that was?" Moscowitz asked.

"It would be the summer of 1945."

"To your knowledge did it continue beyond that?"

"No."

Demjanjuk began his U.S. visa application process in 1950, when, according to Curry, there were no more forced repatriations.

• • •

The prosecution presented two more witnesses to hammer home its ineligibility argument.

Harold Henrikson was the vice consul who had granted Demjanjuk a visa to the United States in 1952. Like Segat and Curry, he testified that if he had known Demjanjuk was a Trawniki man, or served as a death camp guard, or was a soldier in Vlasov's army, he would have found him ineligible for a U.S. visa. And if he had known that an applicant was a Soviet citizen, a soldier in the Soviet army, or a Soviet POW, those facts would *not* render him ineligible.

Donald Pritchard was the naturalization examiner in Cleveland who had interviewed John Demjanjuk when he applied for U.S. citizenship in 1956. Pritchard testified that if he knew an applicant for citizenship assisted the Nazis in the persecution of civilians, he would have recommended denial of U.S. citizenship.

Pritchard closed the prosecution's circle of interlocking testimony. Each of the four former immigration and naturalization officials—three of whom had personally reviewed Demjanjuk's applications and had interviewed him—testified that if he had known that Demjanjuk had graduated from Trawniki, or served at a death camp, or had been a member of Vlasov's army, or misrepresented his country of origin for whatever reason, he would have either denied Demjanjuk a visa or recommended against naturalization. Each testified that fear of repatriation was not a valid extenuating circumstance. Taken as a whole, the testimony was about as unassailable as testimony can get.

Before resting its case as planned, the prosecution requested the court's permission to recall Gideon Epstein, the prosecution's forgery expert. Epstein had just returned from Washington, D.C., where he had examined the original Trawniki card, which the Soviets had made available at its embassy there.

"After comparing the *original* document with the government Exhibits 5 and 6," Horrigan asked Epstein, "what conclusions, if any, did you come to?"

"Government's Exhibits 5 and 6 are photographic copies of that original document I examined at the Soviet embassy," Epstein said. He went on to say that nothing he saw on the original Trawniki card changed his opinion about its authenticity.

As part of his examination of the original card, Epstein compared Demjanjuk's Cyrillic signature on the original and two other Demjanjuk *non-Cyrillic* signatures—one from his visa application and one from a postal change-of-address card filed in a Cleveland post office. It was an apples-and-oranges comparison and Epstein was forced to conclude: "I was unable to reach a *definitive* conclusion as to the common authorship . . . due to the absence of sufficient individual handwriting characteristics between the questioned and the known."

Epstein also admitted that he still had not conducted any ink, paper, or typeface analysis of the card. Neither the prosecution nor the defense asked him why.

Epstein's final testimony was a disappointing conclusion to a strong government case. Demjanjuk's signature on the Trawniki card was the most important element in determining authenticity or fraud.

On that somewhat disheartening note, the prosecution rested.

CHAPTER TWENTY-EIGHT

Fear's the Thing

I n quick succession, the defense called Michael Pap, Jerome Brentar, and Edward O'Connor to the stand. The three expert witnesses would constitute the core of the Demjanjuk defense. Martin gave them two tasks—suggest that the Trawniki card was a KGB forgery, and firmly establish the fact that Demjanjuk hid his true wartime activity from immigration officials because he was afraid of being forcibly deported to the Soviet Union and executed as a deserter.

Michael S. Pap, a Ukrainian American, was a professor of history at John Carroll University, outside Cleveland. He lectured across the country on the evils of communism, wrote extensively on the history of Ukraine, and directed John Carroll's Institute for Soviet and East European Studies. He was bitterly anticommunist and anti-Soviet, and a national promoter of the Independent Ukraine movement.

"Pap" is a relatively common ethnic German name in *Volksdeutsche* communities in Bohemia, Slovakia, Poland, Yugoslavia, and Hungary. OSI deposed him in 1980 in preparation for Demjanjuk's denaturalization trial. During the deposition, Pap made a distinction between his nationality (Ukrainian) and his citizenship (Czech). He argued that because he was born in Czechoslovakia, he was a citizen of that country and not a citizen of the Soviet Union. The distinction was important because as a Czech citizen he could not be forcibly repatriated to the Soviet Union after the war.

Pap testified that he was a student at the State College of Czechoslovakia when the war started. When the Reich invaded Czechoslovakia in 1941, the Germans deported him to Austria as a forced laborer. He worked in a factory outside Vienna until Austria was liberated by the Allies.

If Pap was an ethnic German (*Volksdeutsche*), he was a lucky one. The Reich had passed a law requiring all ethnic Germans living in the territories it occupied to enlist in the Waffen SS. The Displaced Persons Commission defined the Waffen SS as inimical to the United States. Therefore, its members were ineligible for a U.S. visa. (Members of the Waffen SS Baltic Legions were an exception.)

After the war, Pap studied at the University of Heidelberg. After receiving his doctorate in political science in 1948, he worked briefly for the International Refugee Organization as a counselor. More than likely he knew Edward O'Connor, who was the European director for the war relief services of the U.S. Catholic Church. Pap entered the United States in 1949 and became a U.S. citizen in 1952. He taught at the University of Notre Dame before joining the history faculty of John Carroll University in 1958.

By any definition, Jerome Brentar was a controversial figure. He was either a Good Samaritan trying to save the life of an innocent man, or an intellectual who honestly questioned the "absurdities and contradictions in the Holocaust story," or an anti-Semitic Holocaust denier and neo-Nazi revisionist.

Because he was a player in Republican Party politics, Brentar tried to hide whatever his true feelings were about Jews and the Holocaust. But he let his guard down during a live radio interview after the Demjanjuk trial. On the John McCulloch show at WJW in Cleveland he compared John Demjanjuk standing before American judges to Jesus Christ standing before Pontius Pilate.

Asked if he meant that Jews today wanted to frame Demjanjuk as they had framed Christ, Brentar said: "Who else? Who else? . . . Here was the poor innocent man, standing there like Christ before Pilate. And [the Jews] had witnesses who were not telling the truth . . . yelling 'Let his blood be upon us and our children.'"

Brentar went on in the interview to call all Jewish Holocaust survivors Nazi collaborators "because they cooperated with the Germans" to stay alive. Asked if he thought of himself as an anti-Semite, he replied: "Absolutely not! Look, I'm a Catholic. I pray to a Jew every day, and to his Jew-mother."

Edward O'Connor, a right-wing Catholic, had graduated from the University of Notre Dame and the Jesuit-staffed Niagara University in Buffalo, New York. Immediately after the war, O'Connor headed the War Relief Services of the U.S. National Catholic Welfare Conference in Europe. He fully supported his church's unspoken anticommunist platform—Catholic fugitives from communist countries would be sponsored by the American Catholic Church and once in America, they would be helped even if they had collaborated with the Nazis.

O'Connor's actions and decisions clearly demonstrated his Catholic and pro-Nazi bias. As a member of the Displaced Persons Commission, O'Connor "forced through" the DPC decision to make members of the Baltic Legions eligible for U.S. visas. It was a position strongly supported by the American Catholic Church because so many former legionnaires were Latvian Catholics.

Also as a member of the DPC, O'Connor supported another controversial commission decision. In 1950, the CIA began asking refugee organizations for the names and addresses of all displaced persons in the United States. Some groups balked at the request because it was not clear whether the information the CIA wanted was "confidential." DPC agreed to nudge the organizations that were refusing to cooperate. "It is altogether desirable," the DPC advised, "that local representatives of the voluntary agencies and State Commissions and Committees make available to fully identified CIA agents the addresses of displaced persons."

Two years later, O'Connor also championed the 1952 Immigration and Naturalization Act (Public Law 414), which opened America's door to Nazi war criminals who had never been convicted. And as chairman of the National Security Council's psychology and strategy board, O'Connor fully endorsed and participated in planning Cold War covert actions that depended on former Nazi collaborators.

O'Connor was "the single most important activist" in the Anti-Bolshevik Bloc of Nations (ABN), a neo-Nazi group, according to Christopher Simpson, author of the 1988 groundbreaking book *Blowback*. Dominated by members of Ukrainian organizations defined as inimical to the United States by the Displaced Persons Commission, ABN had at least half a dozen well-known Nazi collaborators on its board of directors. Most notorious among them were Alfreds Berzins and Radoslaw Ostrowsky (in Belorussian, Radaslau Astrouski). Berzins was an anti-Semitic Latvian lieutenant in the Waffen SS accused of torturing, killing, and deporting two thousand Jews. He was on

CROWCASS Wanted List Number 14. Ostrowsky was the former pup-pet president of Nazi-occupied Belorussia and president of Belorussia's government-in-exile until his death in 1979. The Nuremberg tribunal defined Nazi quislings like Ostrowsky as criminals.

Funded by the CIA and billed as patriotic, pro-American, and an-ticommunist, ABN attracted right-wing Republicans, neo-Nazis, anti-Semites, and Holocaust deniers like Jerome Brentar and Austin App, author of *The Six Million Swindle* and the reputed father of Holocaust revisionism. ABN was so convincingly apple-pie American that it per-suaded the U.S. Congress to pass unanimously a "Captive Nation Week" resolution in 1959.

O'Connor was no fan of OSI, whom he would later call a KGB col-laborator, in a lengthy article in the *Ukrainian quarterly*.

• • •

On the morning Michael Pap took the stand to defend John Demjan-juk, two hundred Ukrainians peacefully demonstrated in the square out-side the court building in support of his testimony. They were waving the blue and yellow flag adopted in 1918 as the national symbol of the short-lived Ukrainian People's Republic.

John Martin began his direct examination of Pap by noting that Moscow kept lists of Soviet citizens who had been forced laborers and POWs. Moscow considered *both groups* Nazi collaborators and traitors.

Martin needed to establish that refugees knew about the lists and feared the Soviet repatriation teams that visited DP camps. "Were you familiar with the list of collaborators that was passed around?" he asked Pap.

"Yes. Up until about 1947—and even into 1948," Pap said, "Soviet authorities were permitted to provide [to the IRO] a list of names of those people whom they suspected to have been Nazi collaborators."

"Did you ever see such a list?"

"Yes."

"And if a person's name was on this list . . . what, if anything, would happen to him?"

"He would be deported," Pap said. "From 1948 . . . the deportation was not enforced. But still the people were very much afraid."

"Are there any figures available as to how many . . . Soviet [civilians] were repatriated forcibly between the end of the war and 1948?" Martin asked.

"Over two million."

"Were you familiar with the policy whereby an applicant might give a place of birth as a small town somewhere in Poland?"

"It was basic knowledge."

"Do you have an opinion why this was done?"

"Because they were afraid that if they would identify themselves as former citizens of the Soviet Union, they would be simply deported to the Soviet Union," Pap said. "The Soviet Constitution reads: 'desertion to the enemy . . . shall be punishable with all the severity of law as the most heinous of crimes.'"

"What would happen to a . . . *prisoner of war* if he was returned to the Soviet Union?"

"Two and a half million were deported," Pap explained. "About a million were executed immediately and the rest were sentenced to fifteen years of hard labor."

Pap turned to Judge Battisti: "In 1957, Your Honor, an amnesty was offered by Khrushchev. Only twenty percent of those [deported] were still alive."

"Twenty percent of what figure?" Battisti asked.

"Of the two and a half million."

Pardon for political prisoners, including former POWs and their families, was part of Khrushchev's de-Stalinization program. He issued the decree in September 1955, not in 1957.

"Based on your research and studies of the Soviet Union, did it ever come to your attention where the Soviet Union . . . participated in forged documents?" Martin asked.

"Yes. From the inception of the Soviet government, the basic preoccupation was to forge evidence," Pap said.

"Do you have an opinion as to *why* the Soviet government . . . would be interested in presenting or providing some type of discord between the Ukraine and Jewish people?"

"Objection, Your Honor."

"Sustained."

The question was speculative and Pap was not an expert on Soviet internal politics. Battisti's ruling was a temporary setback for the defense.

• • •

Moscowitz conducted the cross-examination of Professor Pap. He began with an attempt to taint his testimony as totally biased. "I take it that you consider yourself an opponent of the Soviet government, is that correct?"

"Based on the research and documents I have examined," Pap said.

"For example, you're in favor of an independent Ukraine?"

"Categorically."

"That's a matter of personal belief, is that correct?"

"No!" Pap said. "It's a matter of the right of nations to self-determination—a concept which was born in the United States."

Next, Moscowitz began to question Pap's credibility on the subject of Soviet-forged documents.

"Have *you yourself* examined any documents which you allege the Soviets produced?"

"I read an article."

"You yourself have not examined any documents in this case—documents that you made claim had been falsified by the Soviet Union—is that correct?" Moscowitz pressed.

"No, I didn't."

"Have you *ever* examined documents obtained from the Soviet Union that you believe were falsified?"

"Yes."

"You yourself had seen falsified documents?"

"I saw them in printed books," Pap conceded.

"In other words, you read accounts of *other peopl*e who claimed that there were falsified documents?"

"Yes."

"You are not a documents examiner, are you?"

"No, I am not."

"Are you aware, sir, that there are captured German documents in the possession of the Soviet government?" Moscowitz asked.

"Yes."

"Isn't it possible that if they had such documents—which implicated a former Soviet citizen in collaboration with the Germans—that they would make such documents available?"

"I think they would, yes."

"How would you satisfy yourself that the document was authentic?"

"I would want to have the examination of those documents by specialists," Pap said.

"And would you be satisfied as to its genuineness if the Soviet government made available the *original document* itself for inspection?"

"Experts again."

Pap knew he was in trouble as a defense witness and he attempted to change the topic. "Your Honor," he said, "I know for sure the Soviet Union has a division in the KGB which is producing forged documents on the order of the government."

Pap was probably referring to Service A of the KGB's First Chief Directorate, which John McMahon, CIA deputy director for operations, had described during a hearing by the House Select Committee on Intelligence the previous year.

"Have you been over to *see* this division at the KGB?" Moscowitz asked.

"No."

Moscowitz returned to the issue of the validity of documents supplied by the Soviets in denaturalization cases. He called Pap's attention to the case of Wladymir Osidach, who was then on trial in Philadelphia for collaborating with the Nazis as a policeman and lying about it on his visa application. As part of its case, the government accused him of rounding up and exterminating Jews in Rawa-Ruska, Ukraine. The federal district court in Philadelphia would eventually strip Osidach of his U.S. citizenship, but he would die before he could be deported to the Soviet Union, where most likely he would have been tried and executed.

"Mr. Osidach admitted that the Soviet documents implicating him as a Ukrainian policeman were *valid and true*," Moscowitz said. "Wouldn't that have a bearing on your opinion as to whether such documents could be given credence?"

"If the accused *admits* that the document is real, well, then there is no problem. . . . It is interesting, Your Honor," Pap said. "The timing is interesting."

Pap's observation gave Martin an opening for his re-direct examination. He jumped on it.

"Would you care to explain about the timing?" Martin asked.

"To me, it is very interesting that these various cases of collaboration are brought after thirty-five years," Pap said. "It is happening because the Soviet Union is . . . very much afraid of the collaboration between Jewish and Ukrainian communities. . . . They want to initiate a kind of situation where the Jews and the Ukrainians will fight each other and, therefore, divert attention from what they are doing in the Soviet Union."

• • •

Jerome A. Brentar, the son of Croatian immigrants, was the owner of the Europa Travel Service in Cleveland and the major organizer of the Demjanjuk legal defense fund. Like the prosecution's expert witness Daniel Segat, he had worked as an eligibility officer for the IRO after the war. Brentar was especially useful to the IRO because he spoke fluent German, Russian, Ukrainian, Polish, and Czech.

Apparently, the prosecution did not know at the time of the trial that Brentar was a Holocaust denier, and as such, a totally compromised defense witness.

Defense co-counsel Spiros Gonakis conducted the direct examination of Brentar because Martin was in Florida taking the deposition of Feodor Fedorenko with permission of the court. Gonakis needed Brentar to support the testimony of Professor Pap—that Demjanjuk had lied on his various applications because he was afraid of being forcibly taken back to the Soviet Union. Both Segat and Leo Curry had testified that there was no reason to fear forced repatriation in 1950, the year Demjanjuk applied to the IRO for refugee status, because forced repatriation ended sometime between 1945 and 1948.

"Are you familiar with the term 'forced repatriation'?" Gonakis asked.

"Absolutely."

"Would you tell us what that means to you?"

"This is one of the blunders that we Americans had made," Brentar said. He went on to explain that the Allied Military Command in postwar Germany assigned American and British soldiers to round up Soviet POWs and civilians who refused to leave West Germany, and then to hand them over to Soviet authorities.

"[American soldiers] behaved just like the SS," Brentar said. "They would bayonet them, shoving these people mercilessly into the trains, which [would take them to Soviet] death camps. . . . And there were people who had to be carried because they were already beside themselves. Some were even committing suicide. . . . About two and a half million good, solid citizens were deported to the Soviet Union from Germany as well as Austria."

"When you were affiliated with the IRO [in 1947] was there any forced repatriation?"

"Thank God that after three years," Brentar was forced to admit, "America came to its senses and they stopped it."

"What kind of involvement did you have with the refugees, above and beyond your routine of interviewing the applicants?"

"I went to every camp I knew where refugees were and from whom I could get some information," Brentar said.

"What fears, if any, did these Soviet people tell you about in the camp?"

"Objection, Your Honor . . . Hearsay."

"Overruled."

It *was* hearsay, but Battisti was interested in the issue so he cut the defense some slack.

"The KGB was all over," Brentar continued. "There was open season on these Soviets. They would disappear overnight. There were bombs sent through the mail to these refugees. There was poison put in their food . . . so the people were living in an atmosphere of fear and tension."

"Would you run into any difficulties with people that you thought were Soviet citizens on their application?"

"Many of them did not want to divulge their true names, or their nationality or place of birth. Had them changed," Brentar said. "Or they just didn't give me the truth. After the letdown of the Americans and the British, they didn't trust any one of us."

"If you had a Soviet POW who was involuntarily conscripted into a Ukrainian unit which saw *no action* against the Allies, what would his eligibility status be?" Gonakis asked.

"They would be considered for eligibility under the mandate of the IRO constitution."

Prosecution witnesses Segat, Curry, and former vice consul Henrikson had each testified that they would have considered such persons *ineligible*.

"Upon whom was the burden of proof?"

"On him. But in most cases," Brentar said, "I gave them the benefit of the doubt."

"Why?"

"A person is not guilty . . . until he's *proven* guilty."

"Is there anything in the IRO manual that said you should give the applicant the benefit of the doubt?" Gonakis asked.

"Absolutely."

Brentar asked for a copy of the IRO manual, the same book Daniel Segat had quoted from earlier. Brentar read: "If an applicant has no documents, then he should make an attempt to get them. If he has done so, or if it is impossible to do so, and if his story is otherwise credible, he should be given the *benefit of the doubt*."

• • •

Horrigan began his cross-examination of Brentar where Gonakis had left off.

"Would you turn to page eight of the IRO manual, please?" Horrigan said. "Do you see number thirteen?"

"Should I read it out loud?"

"Yes."

Brentar read: "Most stories that are inconsistent seem to refer to wartime activities. But this often arouses a presumption of *voluntary* assistance to the enemy."

Having made his point, Horrigan tried to impugn Brentar's credibility as an expert witness.

"During the time you were in the IRO you saw [Soviet] repatriation teams, did you not?"

"Yes . . . escorted by MPs."

Soviet repatriation agents were neither welcome nor safe in DP camps.

"And these individuals were allowed to visit DP camps only with the *permission* of the United States government. Isn't that correct?"

"Yes."

"No one could be *forced* to speak to Russian officials about going back home. Isn't that correct?"

"Not in 1948."

"Isn't it true that on some occasions American government officials refused to allow Russian teams to come in and even speak to these individuals?"

"They were afraid there would be an uprising," Brentar said. "And they couldn't guarantee the safety of the Soviet repatriation team."

"So it was *voluntary* repatriation?"

"Yes."

"And you *never saw* any forcible repatriation any time you were over there, did you?"

"No I didn't."

• • •

Edward M. O'Connor, who held advanced degrees in political science and sociology and who had been awarded an honorary doctorate from the University of Heidelberg, had served as a refugee relief leader immediately after the war. The U.S. Army considered O'Connor's work so important that it gave him the temporary rank of major general and a hassle-free travel pass signed by General Dwight D. Eisenhower.

As a hands-on expert on displaced persons, O'Connor had testified before Congress and the United Nations, and President Truman appointed him to the Displaced Persons Commission when it was created. Given his experience, O'Connor's credentials as an expert witness on the plight of European refugees were impeccable. If the prosecution knew anything about his Catholic bias and his ties to the CIA and neo-Nazi organizations, it did not use the information to impugn his testimony in support of John Demjanjuk.

• • •

O'Connor's only job as a defense witness was to establish beyond doubt that refugees were *still* deathly afraid of Soviet agents and repatriation in 1950.

"You testified that you had occasion to visit the [IRO] camps during your tenure as a commissioner between 1948 and 1952," Martin said. "During that span of time, did you yourself experience *any fear* from the people who were in these camps?"

"Oh, yes," O'Connor said. "And, more particularly, these kinds of matters were brought to my attention by the various chaplains of all faiths that were serving in these camps, who were very close to these political refugees. . . . I would try to persuade [them] that no one could be forcibly repatriated against their will. But those fears remained."

O'Connor further testified that if a refugee lied about his past *out of fear*, the Displaced Persons Commission would show mercy, and the refugee would be given a chance to correct the lie. If he did, he would be eligible.

"Were you familiar with a Soviet list containing names of alleged Nazi collaborators?" Martin asked.

"There was no *one* list. There were many lists that the Russian repatriation teams had developed," O'Connor pointed out. "U.S. military authorities would take it, call the people out and interview them, investigate them. . . . If they were found to be collaborators or having participated voluntarily in any activity with the Nazis, they would be turned over."

• • •

Like that of the prosecution, the defense's opening salvo was strong. All three of its expert witnesses presented clear and compelling arguments that Soviet citizens were afraid of forced repatriation well after 1948, the year the prosecution argued the practice had ended. The problem for the defense was—its strong argument was irrelevant. The Supreme Court had ruled in its precedent-setting Fedorenko decision that extenuating circumstances, like fear and voluntariness, could not be used in determining eligibility for a U.S. visa. The defense also failed to suggest with any degree of credibility that the Trawniki card was a forgery. Up to this point, the defense of John Demjanjuk was a hopeless nondefense.

Before the defense called its most important witness to the stand, it presented five reputation and character witnesses—the lay president of St. Vladimir's Orthodox Church, the president of the church council, a fellow worker at the Ford plant, a neighbor, and the Reverend Stephen Hankevich, who had served at St. Vladimir's for twenty years. Father Hankevich's testimony was typical.

"How do you know Mr. Demjanjuk?" Gonakis asked the priest.

"He's been a member of my parish since I arrived in Cleveland," Father Hankevich said. "I see him at church practically every Sunday. The [Demjanjuks] are practical Christians, receive the sacraments of our church. Their children attend our school. He was on our board of auditors of our church, elected by the body of our congregation. He was a member of our Ukrainian school PTA."

"Do you have an opinion as to Mr. Demjanjuk's reputation for truthfulness and honesty?" Gonakis asked.

"Yes."

"What is it?"

"I think he's an honest man, a devoted man, a family man, a practical Christian," Father Hankevich said.

The defense called John Demjanjuk to the stand.

CHAPTER TWENTY-NINE

His Day in Court

The courtroom was packed on the morning of March 4, 1981, when Demjanjuk took the stand, and U.S. marshals were turning people away at the courthouse door. In an attempt to maintain order and control, they had resorted to issuing tickets to the trial. Inside the second-floor courtroom, more marshals walked up and down the aisles collecting tickets and escorting out anyone who had managed to sneak in.

From the witness chair, John Demjanjuk radiated the same calm and confidence he had from his pew in the front row facing Judge Battisti and the Treblinka survivor-witnesses. Other than leaning closer to his interpreter to ask a question, he sat still and not even a ripple of emotion clouded his face. He had waited six years for this moment and the chance to defend himself.

• • •

The Demjanjuk family's ordeal began in 1975 with three mysterious phone calls in a row from a man claiming to be an officer at the West German consulate in Detroit. Vera took the calls. Each time she told the man, who refused to say why he was calling, that her husband was at work. A week later, the man appeared on her doorstep on Meadow Lane in Seven Hills. This time her husband was home.

The man identified himself by name and produced his diplomatic identification badge. West German prosecutors wanted Mr. Demjanjuk to testify at a war crimes trial, the diplomat explained. They believed he had useful information about Sobibor and Treblinka.

Soon after that strange and troubling encounter, friends and neighbors began telling the Demjanjuks about being interviewed by INS investigators who wanted to know if Mr. Demjanjuk had ever talked about what he did during the war.

John Demjanjuk knew for sure he was a target in 1976, when the INS summoned him to its Cleveland office for questioning. And he knew the investigation was official when he opened a certified envelope from the Department of Justice on August 25, 1977. Inside the envelope was the government's complaint, *United States of America v. John Demjanjuk, a/k/a, Iwan Demjanjuk, a/k/a, Ivan Grozny (Ivan the Terrible)*.

Vera fainted. An ambulance took her to a hospital.

• • •

Like Frank Walus's attorney, John Martin chose an alibi defense. Demjanjuk could not have been at Trawniki, Sobibor, and Treblinka when the government alleged he was, because he was a POW in a labor camp in Poland at the time. And later, he couldn't have been a guard at any other camp or Nazi institution because the Germans had first sent him to Graz, Austria, to be inducted into an all-Ukrainian unit of the German army, then to a place called Oelberg, Austria, to be inducted into Vlasov's liberation army.

Martin began the serious questioning of his client with the blood-type tattoo, which, the prosecution had argued, was proof that Demjanjuk worked for the SS. Since Demjanjuk's command of English was minimal, the court provided an interpreter.

"While you were at Graz, did you have occasion to receive a blood-grouping type tattoo?" Martin asked.

"Yes."

"Would you point to where this was placed on your body?"

Demjanjuk pointed to the inside of his upper left arm.

"This was done at Graz by whom?"

"A doctor."

"Did the other POWs taken to Graz receive this tattoo also?"

"Everyone," Demjanjuk said.

Danilchenko had sworn in his statement taken by Soviet prosecutor

Natalia Kolesnikova that he and Demjanjuk were tattooed while doing guard duty in Flossenbürg, Germany. Martin's argument: Yes, my client had the tattoo—not because he was an SS guard, but because he was an involuntary soldier in Vlasov's liberation army.

"After Graz, could you tell us where you were taken?"

"We were loaded onto railroad cars and shipped to Oelberg," Demjanjuk said.

"When you arrived at Oelberg, what was there?"

"The Russian army had been organized there."

"What if anything did you do there?"

"We didn't do anything there," Demjanjuk said. "We were waiting for uniforms and shoes which we never got. . . . Those soldiers who had uniforms were sent to Bohemia, and the rest of us—who had only the old Italian uniforms—were sent with one officer to Bischofshofen [Austria]."

"Do you recall when?"

"This was 1945."

"And from Bischofshofen where were you taken or where did you go?"

"We stayed there at a prisoner of war camp which had been vacated," Demjanjuk said. "And then the Americans came and took us to Munich."

Martin established two major defense points in that exchange with his client. First, if Demjanjuk was at Graz and Oelberg, he could not have been at Flossenbürg and Regensburg as Danilchenko alleged. And second, he never *actually fought* against the United States or against any of its allies. Membership in Vlasov's army did not, in and of itself, make Demjanjuk ineligible for a U.S. visa.

Next, Martin began discrediting previous witness testimony that John Demjanjuk was Ivan the Terrible.

"Presently, how tall are you?" Martin asked.

"Six feet, one inch."

Most of the witnesses had testified that Ivan the Terrible was shorter. And the Trawniki card described Iwan Demjanjuk as around five feet, eight inches tall.

"Calling your attention to 1942, 1943, were you the same height?" Martin asked.

"Possibly."

"What color were your eyes in 1942, 1943?"

"Blue."

The Trawniki card, and each witness who was asked that question, said Ivan the Terrible's eyes were gray.

"What color was your hair?"

"Light blond."

Each witness had described Ivan the Terrible's hair as dark to black.

"Was your hair long or short?"

"Long," Demjanjuk said.

Each witness had described Ivan the Terrible's hair as short.

"During the time you were a prisoner of war . . . to the end of the war, were you ever given a haircut?" Martin asked.

"No."

"At any time during the war years, were you in any concentration camp where civilian population were kept?"

"No," Demjanjuk said, in effect denying that he was ever a guard at any German-run camp.

Martin showed Demjanjuk the two certified photos of the Trawniki card.

"Have you ever during the war years been issued documents similar to this?" he asked.

"Never."

"Is that a photograph of you?"

"I cannot say. Possibly it is me."

"Why can't you be sure?"

"Because I never had such hair as the man in the photograph except in the Russian army," Demjanjuk said.

"The uniform in this photograph . . . Did you have such a uniform at any time that you were a POW?"

"No."

"The Italian uniform that you were given, what color was that?"

"Green."

Martin couldn't prove that the photo on the Trawniki card came from the files of the KGB. The best he could do was to suggest it.

"Did you learn after arriving in the United States that your mother was receiving a pension from the army?" he asked.

"Yes."

"Why?"

"Because they told her that I was missing in action and gave her a pension," Demjanjuk said.

"Did there come a time that your mother had the pension stopped?"

"When my mother learned that I was still alive, she went and turned down the pension."

Martin showed Demjanjuk a copy of the article, "Punishment Will Come," published in *News from Ukraine* in September 1977. The paper featured two photos of the Trawniki card with the alleged picture of Demjanjuk.

"Have you seen this before?"

"Yes."

"At your home?"

"Someone sent it to us . . . in the mail."

"Was this the first time you had seen photos of this kind?"

"Yes."

"Do you know where that paper is from?"

"From Ukraine."

Martin moved on to the reason why Demjanjuk did not reveal to the IRO, the Displaced Persons Commission, and the U.S. vice consul that he had been a POW and a soldier in Vlasov's army.

"During the times you were in the camps . . . did you have a fear of being forcibly repatriated to the Soviet Union?"

"Yes—'45, '46, '47 were the most terrible years," Demjanjuk said.

"*After* '47 did you fear being repatriated to the Soviet Union?"

"There was fear, but it wasn't as bad as before," Demjanjuk admitted. "Soviet officers weren't going around anymore."

"Would you tell us why you were afraid of being repatriated to the Soviet Union?"

"Because I had been a soldier of the Red Army and there was a regulation that if you were going to be taken prisoner of war, you had to shoot yourself, and I hadn't done so," Demjanjuk said.

"Was it out of this fear that you made certain misrepresentations on your IRO application and visa application?"

"Yes."

• • •

Horrigan conducted the cross-examination of Demjanjuk. The prosecutor showed him a copy of his original 1951 visa application. Demjanjuk said he didn't recognize it. Horrigan began to review some of the information on the form.

"Were you in Sobibor, Poland, from 1934 to 1943?" Horrigan asked.

"No."

"And [the application] also indicates that from 1943 to 1944 you were in Pilau, Danzig. You were not in Pilau, Danzig, during that period of time?"

"No."

"This application, Mr. Demjanjuk, is under oath, is it not?"

"I don't remember whether it was under oath," Demjanjuk said.

Horrigan handed Demjanjuk the visa application.

"Mr. Interpreter, would you stand, please, and read the fourth line from the top?" Horrigan asked.

"'I, the undersigned applicant for immigration visa and alien registration, being duly sworn, state the following facts regarding myself.'"

"That must be true then," Demjanjuk said.

"Is that your signature?"

"Yes."

Horrigan went on to establish the years when Demjanjuk applied for IRO refugee status (1950) and for a visa (1951), in order to refute the claim that he lied because he was afraid of being forcibly repatriated.

"Mr. Demjanjuk, isn't it a fact that by 1947, you were no longer afraid of repatriation?" Horrigan asked.

"We were afraid even longer. We didn't know who would be taken, and what would happen," Demjanjuk said.

"Do you recall the Germans asking the Russian prisoners of war . . . to volunteer for work outside the camp?"

"There was no question of a German *asking* someone if you wanted to do a job," Demjanjuk said. "He told you to do a job, and if you didn't, he would hit you with a pole or a whip, and you had to do it."

"Did you ever hear the Germans asking for volunteers?"

"I did not."

Horrigan began to probe Demjanjuk's testimony that he was in Oelberg from late 1944 to May 1945 as a soldier in Vlasov's army.

"What were your duties? What did you do?" Horrigan asked.

"We had no duties because we had no uniforms. We were waiting for uniforms and we were being fed, brought back to health," Demjanjuk said.

"Did you indicate in your deposition that at Oelberg you guarded a Ukrainian general or Russian general?"

Horrigan was referring to a pretrial deposition taken the previous year, in February 1980.

"I didn't guard him," Demjanjuk said. "I was *assigned* to guard him."
"I call defense counsel's attention to the deposition of Mr. Demjanjuk."
Horrigan read from the transcripts.

Q. What were you doing in Oelberg?
A. I was like a soldier but a guard.
Q. What were you guarding?
A. A general.
Q. American general?
A. A Russian general.
Q. Who was a prisoner of war?
A. Yes.

Horrigan asked: "Do you remember those questions and answers?"
"I remember," Demjanjuk said.
"Did you have a gun while you were at Oelberg?"
"No."
"What were you guarding this general with, a pipe?"
"Your Honor," Martin interrupted. "I'm going to object to the remark of the government's lawyer. I think this witness ought to be treated with dignity."
"Answer the question," Battisti ordered.
"I have already replied that I did not *guard* the general," Demjanjuk said. "I was only assigned to the unit which was to guard him, and there were seventy to one hundred people in this unit."
"When did you tell the American authorities about your service with the Germans in this Russian military unit?" Horrigan asked.
"When my deposition was taken."
"And why didn't you tell them earlier than this?"
"Because no one asked me."
"Mr. Demjanjuk, you indicated that you had a tattoo and you received this from the Germans, is that correct?"
"Yes."
"And is that tattoo still there?"
"No."
"What happened to it?"
"When I was in Graz, everyone had a tattoo, but in the Russian national army [at Oelberg], tattoos weren't given and I took it off," Demjanjuk said.

"You no longer had a tattoo there. You have a scar. Is that correct?

"Yes."

"And you took it off because you were in the *Russian* unit. Is that correct?"

"Yes."

"You wanted to be like the rest of the boys, is that right?" Horrigan said.

"Objection."

"Overruled."

"So you maimed yourself. Is that right?"

"So it appears," Demjanjuk said.

Horrigan showed Demjanjuk the photo exhibits of the Trawniki card once again.

"Is that you?"

"Looks like me, but I am not one hundred percent certain," Demjanjuk said. "I have never seen such a photo taken of me, and so I am not certain."

"But it looks like you, doesn't it?"

"Possibly."

"Very similar to you, isn't it?"

"Yes, possibly."

"You indicated to your attorney that you have always had blue eyes, is that correct?"

Once again, Horrigan showed Demjanjuk the copy of his visa application form.

"Would you tell us the color of the eyes [given] in this visa application?"

"Gray."

"When did your eyes change color?"

"Objection."

"Overruled."

"I don't know when this changed," Demjanjuk said.

"You indicated to your attorney that your hair was light blond?"

"My hair was blond, yes."

"And this . . . visa application of Iwan Demjanjuk, do you see the color of that man's hair?"

"Brown."

"Was the color of your hair ever dark blond?"

"My hair was always its normal color. I never dyed it," Demjanjuk said.

"Which was?"

"Light blond."

"Yet in 1951, this application says your hair was brown. Is that correct?"

"I didn't write that myself," Demjanjuk said, indicating that the interpreter filled out the application form.

Once again, Horrigan called Demjanjuk's attention to the Trawniki card.

"Government's Exhibit 6 indicates this Iwan Demjanjuk, who was trained at Trawniki, has a scar on his back," Horrigan said. "Do you have a scar on your back?"

"Yes."

"It indicates that this Iwan's father's name was Nikolai. Was your father's name Nikolai?"

"In Russian, and Mikolai in Ukrainian."

"This Trawniki training card indicates that this Iwan Demjanjuk was born in April . . . April 3, 1920. When were you born?"

"The same."

"And this indicates that this Iwan Demjanjuk was born in Dubmacharenzi."

"In Dubovi Marcharentzi [Makharintsi]," Demjanjuk corrected.

"Do you see a signature there?"

"Yes."

"In what language is the signature?"

"Ukrainian," Demjanjuk said.

"That would be in the Cyrillic alphabet, would it not?"

"Yes."

"What does it say?"

"Demjanjuk."

"Is this your signature?"

"I don't think so," Demjanjuk said. "I never wrote the [JA and JU] the way it is written here."

"The man in the picture there, is he in a Russian uniform?" Horrigan asked.

"I don't know what kind of uniform this is."

"It's not a Russian uniform, though, is it?"

"I cannot say because it is dark and it isn't clear," Demjanjuk said.

"You remember wearing such a uniform?"

"Never," Demjanjuk said.

. . .

Martin used his re-direct to try to repair some of the damage Horrigan had inflicted. He began with Vlasov's army.

"Did you at any time, or did the unit at any time . . . do any fighting at all?"

"None."

"Had you *volunteered* to join these units or were you just taken there by Germans forcibly and involuntarily?"

"The Germans sent me," Demjanjuk said.

"Would you tell us what year it was when you were at Oelberg and you had the tattoo removed?"

"Nineteen forty-five."

"Had you at that time, any plans of coming to the United States?"

"At that time, no one considered such a possibility," Demjanjuk said. "No one knew anything about immigration then."

"At that time, had you ever heard of the IRO or Displaced Persons Commission?"

"We didn't hear anything."

Martin showed Demjanjuk the photo exhibit of the Trawniki card once again.

"Is that your signature?"

"It is *not* my signature."

Martin held up the exhibit for Battisti to see.

"There should also be an apostrophe after the *m* and following the letter *j*," Demjanjuk said. "Rules require that."

. . .

Demjanjuk's testimony contained one important and unexpected piece of new information. After claiming for five years in pretrial depositions and interrogatories that he could not remember the name of the Polish POW camp where he had been incarcerated from July 1942 *to October 1944*, Demjanjuk testified that the name of the camp was Chelm.

Chelm was the heart of his alibi. How could he have been at Trawniki, Treblinka, and Sobibor if he was penned behind barbed wire in the Chelm POW camp? The admission caught the government by surprise. Moscowitz recalled historian Earl Ziemke as a rebuttal witness.

Ziemke testified that there was a POW camp in Chelm, Poland, in 1942.

"Is it possible for the defendant, or any other prisoner of war of the Germans, to have been in a prisoner of war camp in Chelm, Poland, in *October 1944*?" Moscowitz asked Ziemke.

"No."

"Why is that *not* possible, sir?"

"Because Chelm, Poland, was at that time in Soviet hands," Ziemke said.

"When did the Soviets . . . push the Germans out of Chelm?"

"Probably on the twentieth of July, 1944."

It was the defense's turn to be caught by surprise. It had no one prepared and ready to refute Ziemke.

Before closing the defense's case, Martin addressed the court in obvious embarrassment. He had failed to find a single defense expert to study and test the Trawniki card. Theoretically, the defense did not have to prove that the card was a forgery. All it had to do was create reasonable doubt that the card was a fake. Practically, however, given the strong prosecution testimony of Gideon Epstein, the only effective way to create that doubt was to have a second expert witness refute Epstein's findings.

The defense had had ample time to find its own experts. The prosecution had made photos of the card available to the defense months before the trial opened. During the trial, the Soviet embassy in Washington had offered the prosecution and the defense an opportunity to examine the *original* card at the embassy. The prosecution did; the defense did not. To further accommodate the defense, the embassy brought the card to Cleveland for one day, and only one day, so the defense could study it. Again, the defense failed to have a document expert present. Finally, the Soviets gave the defense one last chance. It kept the card in Washington over the following weekend for the defense experts. Once again, Martin failed to get a document examiner to test the original card before it was returned to the Soviet archives in Moscow.

"I would like to say [this] for the record, lest the court feel we were not there in good faith," Martin said. "I contacted experts. The one in New York wanted the document flown to New York to the Russian embassy there. The one in Washington . . . wanted the document at least two days in order to examine it. And [a third one] works for the

CIA, and because the government was part of this lawsuit could not become involved. . . . For those reasons, I wanted the court to know we did go and make a conscientious attempt."

Unfortunately for John Demjanjuk, the defense was forced to close without ever having its own expert refute the conclusion of the prosecution's expert, Gideon Epstein, that the Trawniki card was authentic.

• • •

The following Sunday, the Ukrainian community celebrated with the Demjanjuk family at St. Vladimir's. They celebrated because they believed that John Demjanjuk would win. And they celebrated their homeland.

After the church service, 450 well-wishers filled the social hall and opened their pocketbooks wider. They rocked the hall with "Nimohay-alita," the traditional Ukrainian song of cheer:

Many years, many years, many
To life and health
Many years, many years, years!

A Ukrainian folk choir sang golden oldies, bringing back memories of a better time and hope for a future independent Ukraine. A Parma high school student played the bandura—a lute-like folk instrument. A young girl dressed in a traditional Ukrainian blouse and skirt presented John and Vera Demjanjuk with a bouquet of roses, and gave corsages to daughters Lydia and Irene.

The Demjanjuk family wept.

CHAPTER THIRTY

Wrapping It Up

In closing, Moscowitz summarized the case against Demjanjuk, arguing that the government had met its burden of proof with convincing and unequivocal evidence.

The German army took Demjanjuk prisoner during the battle of Kerch in May 1942 and sent him to a prisoner of war camp in Rovno, Ukraine, Moscowitz began. A few weeks later, in early June, the Germans transferred him to another POW camp in Chelm, Poland. Soon after his arrival there, around mid-July 1942, he either volunteered or was selected to be trained as an SS guard at Trawniki, where he received military training. After graduation, he took an oath of loyalty to the SS and agreed to submit to them. From Trawniki, he went to Treblinka, where eight hundred thousand men, women, and children were murdered, and where he operated the diesel motor that delivered gas to the chambers. For a period of time in 1943, he also served at Sobibor. Toward the end of the war, he served in a division of Vlasov's army, recruited by the Germans to fight against the Soviet army. Finally, he admitted in court that he lied on his visa application about where he was during the war, claiming he had been a farmer in Poland, then a forced laborer in Germany.

Next, Moscowitz began to pick the defense apart, piece by piece.

Martin wanted the court to exclude the Trawniki card simply because it was supplied by the Soviet Union and, therefore, was somehow tainted. But Schefler proved that each detail on the card was historically accurate. And Epstein proved the card was neither forged nor tampered with.

Moscowitz argued that all five Treblinka survivor-witnesses had positively identified Demjanjuk as Ivan the Terrible from either the Israeli photo spread or a second double photo spread prepared by the prosecution, or from both.

Moscowitz reminded the court that Demjanjuk was, by his own admission, both a driver and a mechanic. Then he quoted from Otto Horn's testimony to suggest that those two unusual POW skills confirmed that Demjanjuk was Iwan of Treblinka:

"Moscowitz: This Iwan whom you picked out, is there anything else that distinguished him from the other Ukrainians?"

"Horn: Yes, he could drive. He could work the engines."

Moscowitz reminded the court that Demjanjuk could not have been in Chelm—the core of his alibi—when he said he was because, as historian Ziemke proved, Chelm was in Soviet hands when Demjanjuk testified he was still a German prisoner there.

Ziemke also testified that the Germans only drafted into Vlasov's army men who were *already* collaborating with them, not POWs whom they did not trust.

Finally, Moscowitz argued that four former American immigration officials testified that if Demjanjuk had revealed that he had been trained at Trawniki, had served as a guard in a death camp, had received the SS blood-type tattoo, or had been a soldier in Vlasov's army, he would have been denied a visa to the United States as well as U.S. citizenship.

• • •

Martin's closing was more complex, his job more subtle. Since he didn't have the burden of proof, his task was to cloud the government's case with so much doubt that Judge Battisti would have to rule in Demjanjuk's favor.

"It is our contention that the *sole issue* in this case, after hearing all the testimony, has to be whether or not this gentleman seated here—Mr. Demjanjuk—was indeed the Iwan who served at Treblinka," Martin began. "For sure, there has been no . . . credible testimony or evidence in reference to Mr. Demjanjuk . . . serving at *Sobibor*."

Martin went on to argue that whether Demjanjuk was in a Ukrainian unit of Vlasov's liberation army had no bearing in this lawsuit because it was not a charge in the government's original pleading. Then he mounted his attack on the Trawniki card, beginning with Schefler, who testified that he had never seen a Trawniki ID card identical to the one attributed to Demjanjuk.

"Are we to assume then, that the government's Exhibit 6 was the *only* type of card ever prepared like that?" Martin asked. "Is that what the government wants us to believe?"

The card should not have been admitted in the first place, Martin argued, because it was not a public document like a birth certificate. Once it was admitted over the strong objection of the defense, however, Gideon Epstein failed to test the ink, paper, and typewriter type on the original.

"He gave us no reason why," Martin reminded the court. "This spurious document [is] untrustworthy on its face."

Battisti stopped Martin cold.

"I have no recollection of any testimony that *in any way* indicates that these documents were spurious," Battisti scolded. "[You can't] simply come in and say, 'this is a spurious document' and sit down, or 'that is a false document' and sit down. Do you think the court can adopt a finding with that sort of evidence?"

Duly chastised, Martin continued to attack the card. Epstein was nothing more than a hired gun, he argued, and everyone knows you can find an expert to give an opinion on just about anything.

"The government did not have to use *opinion testimony* in regards to Exhibits 5 and 6, Your Honor," Martin argued. "Karl Streibel was alive and supposedly, according to [the government], ready to be a witness in this lawsuit in May of 1980, less than a year ago. Indeed, the government arranged to transport defense counsel and themselves to Hamburg to this man's deposition."

Moscowitz objected. "Counsel is testifying to matters that are completely outside the record at this point."

Battisti overruled him.

Martin went on to explain that the former Trawniki commandant had agreed to be deposed. But on the very morning of the deposition, the interview was canceled. Martin told Battisti that he called Streibel and asked him why he declined to testify at the last minute. Streibel said he didn't cancel the interview. Someone called him and told him not to come to the U.S. embassy for the videotaping. No explanation was given. Streibel said he had not seen the card, but he knew it was a forgery.

He would never have signed a document that did not have a date on it.

More than likely, the government probably decided not to depose Streibel because they found his answers to predeposition questions self-serving like Fedorenko's and his memory unreliable. Be that as it may, there was no legal reason why Martin could not have deposed Streibel himself, as he had Fedorenko.

Martin went on to score a series of smaller points, like so many jabs. None of them was a knockout punch:

- Prosecution witness Heinrich Schaefer could not establish that all Trawniki men received a tattoo.
- Fedorenko had said in a sworn deposition that he was never issued a Trawniki card or any similar document.
- Fedorenko also swore he never got a tattoo.
- The Soviets knew about the scar on Demjanjuk's back because he was confined to several Soviet hospitals for four months. There were medical records.
- Otto Horn never saw Iwan commit atrocities even though he worked right next to him at Treblinka.
- After the war, the U.S Army hired Demjanjuk as a truck driver. Surely it would have done a security check. And if they found out that he had collaborated with the Nazis, they would not have hired him.
- There was witness coaching, prompting, improper showing of the photo spreads, and exchange of information among the prosecution survivor-eyewitnesses. There were major discrepancies in the witnesses' descriptions of Iwan, proving that Demjanjuk could not have been Ivan the Terrible.

"No one has come into this courtroom, took that witness stand, looked this man in his eyes and said, 'You are the one,'" Martin said.

"Why didn't you ask?" Battisti said.

"Your Honor, this gentleman does not have to *prove* he is innocent here. The burden of proof is on the government."

"Do you believe there was an Iwan at Treblinka?" Battisti asked.

"I do, Your Honor. I certainly do. And I believe that people have suffered as a consequence of this Iwan."

Battisti then asked Martin to read Pinchas Epstein's description of Ivan the Terrible from the trial transcripts.

Martin recited: "Twenty-two to twenty-five, tall, broad shouldered, short neck, a round face, ears protruded slightly, high forehead, with an athletic build."

"Do you think this is a fair description of the defendant, a fairly good description?" Battisti asked.

"I didn't know the defendant in 1942, but based upon what he testified as to how he looked, I would say no," Martin said, "because he testified that in 1942 he was half-starved, and he looked gaunt, more or less, or skinny. . . . Sure it's a good description of him *now*. It might very well resemble him. He might look like that, but are we going to speculate and base this decision on the fact that Mr. Demjanjuk might *look similar* to someone?"

Martin then went on to accuse the government of hiding the details of its investigation from the defense.

"We were never told in this courtroom how the lawsuit got started, who the investigators were, whether they conducted themselves properly and afforded the usual safeguards to the defendant. . . . Wouldn't the court be at least in a better position to judge the fairness of these photo spreads if, in fact, you had the persons who conducted the photo spreads to come here into this courtroom before you, take the stand, and testify to you so that you would know that there was nothing suggestive about the photo display? . . . You cannot revoke this man's citizenship—the most priceless possession in the world—on the basis of closed-door investigations on the other side of the world."

"You're not suggesting the *Soviets* are conducting this trial, are you?" Battisti asked.

"No," Martin said. Then he started to enumerate Judge Roettger's problems with Miriam Radiwker's photo spread at the Fedorenko trial.

"Objection." Moscowitz argued that what Roettger thought about the photo spread was not relevant in this trial.

Battisti agreed, then tried to clear up a point in the defense testimony. Demjanjuk said that the Germans sent him to the town of Oelberg, Austria, toward the end of the war in 1945.

"Does such a place exist?" Battisti asked.

"I believe Dr. Schefler testified that he wasn't able to find it, or had not heard of it," Moscowitz said.

"Well, *you* tell me," Battisti said to Martin. "The defendant . . . said he was a prisoner of war there for four to six months, and he was assigned to a unit to guard a general. Now, the professor says he never heard of the place, doesn't know *about* it, doesn't know *of* it. I'm asking you whether such a place exists and, if so, where is it?"

Martin held up a map. "It's not on this map," he said.

"What you are really saying is—you don't know where it is, either, is that correct?"

"No, I couldn't find it on this map."

"The defendant said he was there as a prisoner of war about four to six months . . . and you don't know where that is! None of us know where it is!"

No one could find the city on a map because they had misspelled it. The correct spelling was *Heuberg,* and it was in Germany, not Austria.

Martin continued his closing argument.

"If indeed this man had been a guard at Sobibor," he said, "he would not have put Sobibor down [on his visa application] and put himself right next to this place."

"You mean he made a mistake," Battisti said.

"And certainly, if he had . . . committed all these crimes," Martin argued, "he could have changed his name . . . a common practice."

Finally, Martin made the same observation Judge Roettger had made in the Fedorenko case. One lone man had to defend himself against the combined resources of the USSR, the Israeli police, West German investigators, and the United States government.

"All these countries, these superpowers, have been brought together against this one man," Martin argued.

• • •

Moscowitz answered the allegation.

"Your Honor, Mr. Martin is, indeed, correct that the government has expended many resources in this case, sought the help of many foreign governments. . . . The reason for this is, Your Honor, that thirty-five years ago, when this defendant sought the privilege of immigrating to this country, he lied about where he was during the war. If he told the truth then—even told what he tells today—this inquiry would have taken place thirty-five years ago . . . in Europe . . . when memories were fresher, when more people were alive."

Why Fedorenko had no tattoo is open to speculation, Moscowitz argued. And his deposition contradicted his court trial testimony. Fedorenko swore in his deposition that he never saw a Kapo beat a Jew.

He never saw an SS guard beat a Jew. He never even *heard* of an Iwan who ran the gas chambers.

"Mr. Fedorenko didn't know much about anything," Moscowitz said. "He saw no evil and heard no evil at Treblinka, and at this deposition, he would speak no evil of another Ukrainian."

Moscowitz further argued that the origin and pursuit of the case against Demjanjuk was hardly secretive. The pretrial discovery period lasted *at least two years*, he pointed out. The defense had the names of the Demjanjuk investigators in the United States and in Israel. Mr. Martin could have deposed them at any time, or he could have submitted interrogatories.

Continuing the argument, Moscowitz returned to the Trawniki card.

"[Mr. Martin] mentions by the way, Your Honor, that it is easy to get an expert to come into the court to give an opinion about anything you want," Moscowitz reminded Battisti. "It is easy apparently for anyone *except* Mr. Martin, who could get no expert that he was satisfied with, apparently, to come into court. . . . .He never asked Mr. Epstein why he didn't do the other tests. . . . The answer would have been: 'They weren't necessary.' . . . The defense has put on *no evidence* about the credibility of these cards. All he asks are further questions about them."

Next, Moscowitz attempted to prove to the court why the Trawniki card could not have been a forgery.

"There are only two ways, Your Honor, this card can be phony," he explained. "One is to make up the card from fresh in this KGB forgery factory, some place in Moscow that Pap was testifying about. Mr. Epstein indicated that is not possible. The signatures of Streibel and Teufel are genuine.

"The only other possibility is that you take a genuine card with Streibel's and Teufel's signature and you cross out all the information on someone else, and you stick in information about John Demjanjuk.... That is not possible because Mr. Epstein testified there was no tampering with the surface of the card."

Moscowitz next addressed the height discrepancy issue. He pointed out that Demjanjuk testified that he was six feet, one inch tall. On his petition for naturalization, he said he was six feet even. The card says he was five feet, ten inches tall.

"A two-inch difference is hardly significant," Moscowitz concluded.

Actually, the Trawniki card said Demjanjuk was five feet, eight inches tall, a four- to five-inch difference.

Finally, Moscowitz tried to buttress the prosecution's weakest point—Demjanjuk's service as an SS guard at Sobibor.

"Evidence strongly suggests that for some period of time—we can't say how long or how short—he was at Sobibor," Moscowitz argued.

He pointed out that Heinrich Schaefer testified that it was a common practice to transfer guards between death camps after they left Trawniki. Then he all but admitted that the government did not prove that Demjanjuk served at Sobibor. "To some extent, Your Honor, this is speculative . . . but it all fits together."

Finally, Moscowitz tried to make the most of Demjanjuk's claim on his visa application that he was a farmer in the village of Sobibor during the early war years.

"The defendant still hasn't explained the odd coincidence—the extraordinary coincidence—that out of the thousands of hamlets, towns, big cities in Poland to hide," Moscowitz argued, "he put down the poor, small, insignificant farming village of Sobibor—a place [near the death camp] where he contends he never was."

The next but far from final word was Judge Frank Battisti's. It would be a three-month wait.

CHAPTER THIRTY-ONE

The Grinding Wheels of Justice

The defense had tried to argue that the Trawniki card was tainted, tampered with, and forged. In his twenty-five-page ruling, issued on June 23, 1981, Judge Battisti dismissed that attempt in one sentence. "At no time during the entire course of the trial," he ruled, "was *any evidence* introduced to substantiate these speculations." Battisti then went on to analyze the government's evidence for the authenticity of the card.

Battisti ruled that Wolfgang Schefler had proved without a doubt that the Trawniki card was historically accurate. Schefler's testimony was corroborated by Heinrich Schaefer, the paymaster at Trawniki, who testified that the school issued ID cards to all its trainees, and that each trainee had had his photo taken in the summer of 1942, the year Demjanjuk arrived at the camp. Schaefer further identified as authentic the signatures of Karl Streibel, the camp commandant, and Ernst Teufel, the supply officer.

Battisti ruled that Gideon Epstein had proved without a doubt that the Trawniki card was authentic. Battisti pointed out that Epstein had performed a series of scientific tests both on the two photos of the card and on the original. Based on those tests, Epstein concluded that the signatures of Streibel and Teufel were authentic and that the card had not been tampered with and was not a forgery.

Battisti duly noted, but was not swayed by, the weaknesses in the government's case for authenticity: The card lacked a date; both Schefler and Schaefer admitted they had never seen an ID card exactly like the one attributed to Demjanjuk; Epstein did not analyze the ink, paper, or typewriter type on the card; Epstein's analysis of Demjanjuk's signature was inconclusive; and Demjanjuk's categorical denial that the signature on the card was his because two apostrophes were missing in the Cyrillic script, making the signature grammatically incorrect. None of these weaknesses, singly or taken as a group, created a serious doubt in Battisti's mind.

Finally, Battisti found that the photograph on the Trawniki card "clearly reflects the facial features of the defendant." He emphasized that Demjanjuk did not deny the picture was a photograph of him.

"Possibly it is me," Demjanjuk had admitted.

"On the basis of *all the evidence*," Battisti ruled, "the Court concludes that the Government's exhibits 5 and 6 are authentic and clearly show that the defendant was at the German SS training camp of Trawniki."

• • •

Next, Battisti turned his attention to the six Treblinka witnesses—five Jewish survivors and Otto Horn, the German guard who supervised the burning of the corpses. Battisti pointed out that each witness worked near the gas chamber buildings and the building housing the motor that produced the lethal carbon monoxide gas. That placed them in a position to see Iwan on an almost daily basis.

Battisti noted that each witness had identified Demjanjuk as Iwan from at least one of several photo spreads. The defense sought to exclude that evidence on two grounds. First, it argued that the identification processes in Israel, West Germany, and elsewhere were conducted outside the presence of the defense counsel, violating the Fourteenth Amendment guarantee of due process. Battisti ruled that the *mere absence* of the defense at the showing did not deny the defendant due process.

"Our legal system has always placed *primary reliance* for the ascertainment of truth on the test of cross-examination," the judge said. "Effective cross-examination can be utilized to reveal any deficiencies in photographic identification procedures."

Battisti pointed out that the defense had, in fact, conducted rigorous cross-examination of all six witnesses. The opportunity to do that "adequately compensated for the absence of the defense counsel at the pretrial identification proceedings."

Second, the defense argued for the exclusion of the pretrial identification testimony of four of the five witnesses from Israel—Rosenberg, Lewkowicz, Epstein, and Rajgrodzki—because they had identified Demjanjuk as Ivan the Terrible from the deeply flawed photo spread offered by Miriam Radiwker. The defense argued that pretrial identifications of these four witnesses were "conducive to mistaken identification."

Unlike Judge Roettger in the Fedorenko case, Battisti gave little weight to the flaws in the Radiwker photo spread. He ruled that "thorough cross-examination of each witness failed to depreciate, in any way, the certainty of the identifications made by each witness."

Battisti went on to say: "Each witness identified defendant as Iwan, known from Treblinka, on the basis of the defendant's visa photograph. In addition, four of the five witnesses shown defendant's picture on the Trawniki card identified him. The fifth, Rajchman, who failed to select the card photograph at a pretrial session did so in open court. There is no indication that the investigators conducting the identification procedures, in any way, suggested the identification of the defendant's photographs."

Battisti concluded: "An examination of the *totality of circumstances* in this case reveals the reliability of the identification of . . . the witnesses."

Finally, Battisti turned his attention to the witnesses' physical description of the Iwan they remembered at Treblinka. "It may be fairly said," the judge observed, "that the following general description was offered by all the witnesses: young man, twenty-two to twenty-five years of age, tall, strong physique, dark or dark brown hair."

After giving no weight to height or hair-color discrepancies, Battisti noted that the defense offered the deposition testimony of Feodor Fedorenko. Defense counsel Martin had interviewed Fedorenko a few days before the end of the trial, with Battisti's permission. The convicted former Treblinka guard swore he did not recognize the man in either the Trawniki card photo or in the visa application photo. And he swore he did not know a Treblinka guard named Iwan who operated the gas chambers.

"The Court finds that the testimony of Fedorenko is not credible," Battisti ruled. He then concluded: "Since the Court finds both the pretrial and trial photographic identification to be reliable, it must be concluded that defendant was present at Treblinka in 1942–1943. . . . Since the Court has found that defendant was present both at Trawniki and Treblinka, it is not necessary to determine whether defendant was *ever* present at the concentration camp Sobibor."

• • •

Next, Battisti went on to review Demjanjuk's testimony, which raised several serious doubts in his mind. Most important, he found that the authenticity of the Trawniki card "undercut" Demjanjuk's credibility and most of his testimony. He noted that Earl Ziemke showed that it was unlikely that Demjanjuk was a POW at Chelm in the fall of 1944, as Demjanjuk claimed, because the Soviets occupied the camp by that time. Battisti pointed out that Demjanjuk's admission that he had a blood-type tattoo "raised serious questions" about his whereabouts during the war and the veracity of his testimony. And he noted that Schefler had testified that only persons affiliated with the German SS were given such tattoos, and that it was unlikely that any ordinary Russian POWs would be so marked.

The core of the defense's case was that Demjanjuk lied on his visa application because he was afraid of repatriation to the Soviet Union, where he would be executed as a deserter. Battisti found that fear specious and he gave it no weight or serious consideration. (As the Supreme Court had ruled in the Fedorenko appeal, the Displaced Persons Act of 1948 did not make a provision for extenuating circumstances.) Battisti further found that Demjanjuk's membership in Vlasov's liberation army was, like his service at Sobibor, irrelevant in and of itself, given that the government had proven without a doubt that Demjanjuk was at Trawniki and Treblinka.

Finally, Battisti reviewed the testimony of immigration officers Daniel Segat, Leo Curry, and Harold Henrikson. He concluded that "the government has shown by clear and convincing evidence that the defendant . . . willfully misrepresented [his service at Trawniki and Treblinka] on his visa application."

Battisti concluded: "The Court finds that the November 14, 1958, order of the United States Court for the Northern District of Ohio, admitting the defendant, John Demjanjuk, to citizenship of the United States of America, is hereby revoked and vacated, and his Certificate of Naturalization, Number 7997497, is canceled on the grounds that such order and Certificate were illegally procured, and were procured by willful misrepresentation of material facts."

• • •

The Demjanjuk family drew their drapes and went into seclusion while reporters and TV crews waited patiently outside their home on Meadow Lane for a statement that would never come. One reporter lost his cool and began banging on the door. The Demjanjuks called the police.

In a weak attempt to heal the distrust and bitterness between Jews and Ukrainians stirred up by Demjanjuk's trial and Battisti's ruling, the Jewish and Ukrainian communities issued a joint statement: "We categorically reject the concept of guilt by association employed so frequently against Jews and Ukrainians in an attempt to blame all the members of a group for the actions of individuals."

John Demjanjuk appealed Judge Battisti's decision to the United States Court of Appeals for the Sixth Circuit. While he was waiting for a decision, the government ordered him to appear for a deportation hearing (order to show cause) at a U.S. immigration court in Cleveland. His attorney, John Martin, advised him not to go. His case was still under appeal, Martin argued, and the government had no right to proceed with deportation until the appeals court ruled.

U.S. marshals arrested and cuffed Demjanjuk when he didn't show up for the hearing.

Part Two: Epilogue

While John Demjanjuk was waiting for the appeals court decision on his denaturalization, OSI was chasing thirty more cases through the courts and investigating another five hundred. Almost all were alleged Nazi collaborators. One of them was Karl Linnas. Like John Demjanjuk, Linnas was important to the survival of OSI. Moscow was beginning to cooperate with OSI researchers and prosecutors and OSI needed to keep Moscow satisfied, if not happy.

Like other former Nazi collaborators living in the United States, INS investigators had found Karl Linnas enjoying a quiet life as a retired land surveyor in Greenlawn, New York, on Long Island. He was on the original Karbach list. A grizzled man with a huge white Santa Claus beard, he was spending his retirement writing music for children's bands.

Linnas's past was not so philanthropic.

Before the German occupation of the Baltic countries, Linnas was a member of Estonia's anticommunist Home Guard, the Omakaitse. The Nazis recruited him to be commandant of a concentration-work camp in Tartu, Estonia's second largest city. Under his three-year watch, camp guards—mostly Estonian volunteers—murdered between 3,500 (U.S. estimate) and 12,000 (Soviet estimate) Estonian Jews and Gypsies, Soviet POWs, and Jews transported to Estonia from Germany, Poland, and Czechoslovakia.

The Tartu guards were systematic. They loaded prisoners into a small red bus and drove them to an antitank trench outside the city. On their way to execution, the guards beat the men and raped the women and girls. According to eyewitnesses and a U.S. Department of State cable from Moscow, Linnas was a brutal camp commandant who personally supervised mass executions.

"Linnas frequently travelled to execution site, where he directed shooting of people and personally gave coups de grace with pistol to those who remained alive," the U.S. embassy in Moscow cabled Washington. "He maintained brutal regime in camp, beat those under arrest, and mocked them."

When the Red Army reoccupied Estonia in 1944, Linnas joined the 38th Estonian Police Battalion and fought with Germany against the Soviet Union in a Baltic Legion. Like Demjanjuk, he received a severe shrapnel wound. He was taken to a German hospital for treatment. After his release, he remained in Germany until the end of the war.

Linnas swore on his visa application to the United States that he had been a student and draftsman in Estonia until May 1943, when he was conscripted into the Estonian army. It sounded plausible, except that there was no Estonian army. Linnas immigrated to the United States in 1951, the year before Demjanjuk did.

To date, there is no evidence that any U.S. intelligence officer, army official, or State Department employee helped Linnas enter America or that he had ever worked for the CIA. However, several "restricted" pages have been removed from his declassified CIA file, which may indicate a Linnas-CIA relationship. The government refused my Freedom of Information request to declassify those pages.

In 1962, the Soviet Union tried Linnas, Juhan Jüriste, and Ervin Viks as "murderers" and "German Fascist handymen" and sentenced all three in absentia to death, based on eyewitness testimony from both former Estonian guards and victims alike. Jüriste pleaded guilty. Viks was living in Sydney, Australia, which declined to deport him to Estonia to stand trial. And twenty years after Estonia had formally requested Linnas's deportation, a U.S. federal court in New York stripped him of his U.S. citizenship based on witnesses and documents supplied by the Soviet Union.

Meanwhile, Johannes Soodla, another Estonian who allegedly had served as a guard at the infamous Tartu concentration camp, was living quietly in California. A decorated hero in the Estonian War of Independence, Soodla had been a ranking officer in the Estonian Home Guard before serving as a brigadier general in an Estonian battalion of the Waffen SS. For his dedicated service, the Germans awarded him the Iron Cross second class. After the war, Soodla worked for the CIA in Trieste, Italy.

In 1961, Moscow asked the United States to deport Soodla to stand trial for war crimes. The Soviets even gave the State Department Soodla's home address in Glendale, California. State declined to hand him over, however, and the INS failed to investigate Soodla for probable visa fraud. When OSI was finally up and running, Soodla—born in 1897—was already dead.

Finally, in 1984, an immigration court ordered Linnas deported to Estonia for retrial. The deportation order, once again, pitted Jews against émigrés. The fight was more than another Washington teapot tempest. The Linnas deportation issue divided Congress and the White House, the Department of State and the Department of Justice. Former White House communications director Pat Buchanan, for example, was a staunch supporter of Linnas and an avowed enemy of OSI. He received fifteen thousand cards, letters, and phone calls against deporting Linnas to Estonia.

At stake were three political issues. If deported to Estonia, Karl Linnas would set a new precedent. The United States did not recognize the communist satellite states of Estonia, Latvia, and Lithuania as legitimate governments. Therefore, Baltic Americans argued, to deport Linnas to Estonia would be the equivalent of legitimizing Moscow's illegal incorporation of the Baltic countries.

Furthermore, Baltic Americans pointed out that Linnas had been tried and convicted in a Soviet kangaroo court. To deport him back to Estonia would be to *sanction* Soviet-style evidence such as forged documents and eyewitness testimony extracted through blackmail and torture.

OSI argued that the Soviet Union was eagerly awaiting Linnas's return to Estonia. Not to deport him would jeopardize the cooperation of Moscow, which had already supplied evidence to OSI for the Fedorenko, Demjanjuk, and other trials. Without Moscow's continued help, OSI would be unable to make its cases and would slowly starve to death, a point that did not go unnoticed by OSI's enemies.

OSI further argued with a clear conscience that the evidence it had received from the Soviets and that it used to denaturalize Linnas was reliable. Historians had examined the documents and attorneys had grilled witnesses. OSI was convinced not only that Linnas had lied on his visa application, but also that he was guilty of major war crimes. Furthermore, the Soviet Union promised to retry Linnas if he were deported either to Estonia or the USSR. OSI believed the Soviet promise.

The White House opposed deporting Linnas to Estonia. How would it look to the world if President Ronald Reagan, the archenemy of Moscow, caved in to Jewish pressure and delivered Linnas to the Soviets on a platter? The State Department and George Shultz supported their boss. The Justice Department didn't. Attorney General Edwin Meese backed OSI and supported the immigration court's deportation decision.

Instead of succumbing to gridlock, Washington quickly hammered out a face-saving compromise. If no other country in the world was willing to take Karl Linnas, he would be deported to Estonia. The international search for a taker began. The State Department asked West Germany if it wanted to extradite Linnas. Germany said no, he wasn't a German. Next, State asked Israel if it wanted to extradite him. Israel said no. All the evidence against Linnas was in the Soviet Union, which Israel trusted about as much as it trusted the Palestinians. Finally, State sent out an SOS to seventeen countries, from the Philippines to Venezuela.

No one wanted Karl Linnas.

When the Supreme Court decided not to review the Linnas case in December 1986, four years after he had been stripped of his U.S. citizenship, the State Department began making plans for Linnas's deportation to Estonia. It wasn't simple. The transatlantic flight from New York to a far corner of Eastern Europe required refueling. But where? Afraid that Linnas supporters might attempt to kidnap him while the plane sat on a runway, the State Department chose Czechoslovakia for the refueling layover. The communist country promised tight airport security.

What happened next played like a scene from a Washington soap opera.

Without warning, Panama offered Linnas asylum on humanitarian grounds. Washington heaved a heavy sigh of relief and accepted the generous offer. Now all it had to do was dodge the Jewish flak that was sure to explode over the capital. Attorney General Meese agreed to be the fall guy for the White House.

On Passover 1987, Elizabeth Holtzman got a call from Eli Rosenbaum, a former OSI prosecutor who would soon return to that office. Rosenbaum was upset. The Justice Department had secretly made a deal, he told Holtzman, to deport Linnas to Panama instead of to Estonia. Since the Central American country did not have an extradition treaty with the Soviet Union, America was, in effect, providing a safe haven for Linnas. The deal was a political pitch to the hearts and wallets of voters.

Holtzman was steaming.

It was no accident that the Justice Department chose to smuggle Linnas into Panama during Passover, when Jewish offices were closed and most Jews were home observing the holy day with their families. Holtzman was angry at the cynical attempt to use the Jewish holiday as cover to sneak a murderer of Jews out of the country. And she was seething at the thought that a war criminal like Linnas would, in her words, "live out his life peacefully, resting on a beach under a palm tree."

There was no time to be religious or philosophical on that Passover day. Holtzman huddled with her top aide, Ed O'Malley; Rosenbaum, who would one day head OSI; and Menachem Rosensaft, a lawyer and Jewish leader. The four came up with an end-around play. They would notify the press that Panama was about to grant sanctuary to a Nazi collaborator and that Jewish groups were poised to rise up in protest. O'Malley and Rosenbaum would then separately call the Panamanian embassy to express indignation and to issue a warning about the next-day tidal wave of protest. Jews would march on Washington, they assured the embassy, and demonstrate outside Panamanian offices from the United Nations to Panama City.

The sucker-play worked.

Panamanian embassy officials in Washington agreed to a three o'clock meeting that Passover afternoon. Holtzman and her team rode the shuttle from New York to Washington, where the embarrassed Panamanian ambassador to the United States told them that Panama had withdrawn its offer to accept Karl Linnas. Not since the debate over the fate of the Panama Canal, the ambassador said, had there been so much media attention. Then he startled Holtzman and her group by stating that Panama's acting president, Eric Arturo Delvalle, was Jewish, a fact not widely known.

That night, an exhausted Eli Rosenbaum sat in an uncomfortable hot seat facing Patrick Buchanan and Robert Novak on CNN's *Crossfire*. Buchanan argued that Linnas was not responsible for the deaths of twelve thousand Jews and that to deport him to Estonia would be to lynch him. The number of alleged victims, Buchanan argued, was Soviet-supplied disinformation. At most, Linnas was responsible for the deaths of four or five hundred men, women, and children, Buchanan conceded.

"How many Jewish bodies are enough to meet the quota?" Rosenbaum shot back. Buchanan didn't respond.

The United States eventually deported Linnas to Estonia. But before the Soviets could make good on their promise to retry him, Linnas died from heart and kidney failure. His deportation and death only served to further enrage Baltic, Ukrainian, and Belorussian émigré communities and convince them that OSI and the Jews were out to get them. Émigré publications warned their readers not to cooperate with OSI investigators. They could be next.

But Moscow was happy. And that made OSI happy.

THE BUTCHER OF LYON

In January 1983, while Demjanjuk was waiting for his deportation hearing to open, another ticking bomb plopped into the lap of political Washington. His name was Klaus Barbie, the Butcher of Lyon. Like offal rising from a river bottom, new evidence suggested that the United States was hiding another dirty secret. The media were on it like flies on rotting beef. If the new evidence was correct, Barbie was a Jekyll and Hyde story. Jekyll (Uncle Sam) hunting Nazi war criminals for prosecution at Nuremberg by day. Hyde (Uncle Sam) hiring the best of the lot by night.

OSI director Allan Ryan followed the unfolding Barbie story with alarm. He knew that some Barbie dirt was sure to smudge OSI and challenge, if not cripple, its shaky credibility. To protect OSI from allegations of hiding the truth from the American people, Ryan asked the Justice Department for permission to open an immediate in-depth and fully-funded investigation of the U.S. role in *l'affaire Barbie*. If the Justice Department didn't pull the story together, Ryan argued, "every network, newspaper and self-styled Nazi hunter would."

After sitting on the fence for nearly three months, U.S. attorney general William French Smith, Meese's predecessor, caved in to the mounting media pressure for answers and gave Ryan the nod. Over the next six months, Ryan rummaged through a roomful of government documents and conducted hundreds of interviews. What he found confirmed his worst nightmare.

• • •

Berlin had a problem in Lyon, France, in 1942. Resistance fighters (Maquis, from the French word for underbrush) were blowing up bridges and supply trains, hiding Allied airmen shot down over France and Belgium, and assassinating German officers. Berlin sent SS Captain Klaus Barbie to Lyon to clean up the mess. As Lyon's new Gestapo chief, Barbie's job was to capture Resistance leader Jean Moulin, crack the spine of the movement, and ferret out every Jew within reach. Barbie was somewhat successful.

On a tip from a Resistance snitch, Barbie captured Moulin during a clandestine meeting and tortured him. Moulin died without revealing the names of his fellow Maquis. Because he failed to break Moulin, Barbie managed only to cripple the Resistance. With the help of French collaborators, he murdered up to four thousand Frenchmen, sent hundreds more to Camp Dora, and rounded up approximately fourteen thousand Jews, including orphans, for transport to Auschwitz.

Unlike Ustashi Andrija Artukovic and Iron Guardist Viorel Trifa, Barbie was not satisfied watching his men torture suspects inside his Gestapo headquarters in Montluc prison, dubbed Hôtel Terminus. Barbie was a hands-on kind of Nazi who rolled up his sleeves and personally beat men and women with enthusiasm. From time to time, he played God with an acetylene torch. For the most part, however, he left the really nasty torture to his goons.

U.S. intelligence officers loved him.

In 1972, French Nazi hunter Beate Klarsfeld found Barbie hiding in La Paz, Bolivia, under the name Klaus Altmann. West Germany immediately asked Bolivia to extradite him so it could try him for crimes against humanity. But the Supreme Court of Bolivia's right-wing military dictator and drug czar, General Hugo Banzer, refused the extradition request.

Barbie lived in La Paz for eleven more years under the protection of his boss, General Banzer, until a new Bolivian government was formed in 1983. The new government decided to get rid of Barbie along with the general. It arrested him on minor fraud charges, ordered his expulsion, and put him on a flight to Frankfurt, where he was welcomed with shudders of shock. Not sure what to do with him on such short legal notice, Germany put him on a Lufthansa flight back to La Paz. The Bolivians, in turn, flew him to French Guiana, just north of Brazil, where a French military jet was waiting to fly him to Lyon and a room in Hôtel Terminus.

Not only did Barbie's arrest make international headlines; it smoked out from retirement a former U.S. Army Counter Intelligence Corps (CIC) officer with a problem of conscience. The officer told NBC's *Today* show that he had hired Barbie in 1947 to inform on Soviet activities in Europe. More international headlines. The *New York Times*, among others, wondered out loud how Klaus Barbie ended up in Bolivia with a new identity. If he had worked for CIC in Germany, could it be that the United States had helped the Butcher of Lyon escape to South America?

• • •

Soon after World War II had ended, CIC learned that an organization of former SS officers was planning to infiltrate and take over the political administration of the American and British zones in West Germany. A former Nazi on CIC's payroll infiltrated the group and gave CIC a list of its members. Sitting near the top of that list was Klaus Barbie. Fearing a rebirth of Nazism, CIC set up Operation Selection Board to sweep through West Germany and arrest members of the neo-Nazi group. Selection Board operatives would neutralize known and suspected war criminals by delivering them to Nuremberg for further investigation and prosecution.

Barbie escaped Operation Selection Board's dragnet by jumping out of a window during a raid. He made his way to Memmingen, a small town sixty-five miles west of Munich. Robert S. Taylor, a CIC agent working in Memmingen, got a tip from one of his Nazi informants that Barbie was in town and would make an excellent CIC asset.

Taylor knew that Barbie was a major target of Operation Selection Board. What should he do? Hand him over to Nuremberg or hire him? Taylor took the dilemma to his superior. Although both men knew that Barbie had headed the Gestapo in Lyon, they decided that he would be more valuable as a full-time, well-paid informant than as a convicted war criminal. So they hired him and gave him a highly sensitive assignment. Spy on French and British intelligence operations and provide a list of communists who had infiltrated them.

Barbie was so good at his job that Taylor and his boss informed CIC headquarters that Barbie was working for them and producing a stream of valuable information. The news tied both the tongue and the hands of CIC headquarters. Barbie had become the proverbial man who knew too much. If CIC handed him over to Nuremberg for prosecution, he could severely damage its clandestine operations and compromise its spy network of former Nazis. Imagine what would happen if the British and French learned that their American ally had infiltrated their intelligence operations.

Meanwhile, former French Resistance fighters were coming out of the shadows and describing to the French media how Klaus Barbie had tortured them and their colleagues in Hôtel Terminus. What followed was a Keystone Kops chase across Western Europe. German and French police began knocking on doors and plying their informants for information about Barbie. The French government asked the U.S. government to help find the infamous Butcher of Lyon. And unaware that the military already *had* Barbie, the State Department issued an order to find and arrest him for extradition to France.

CIC watched the chase from the sidelines.

In January 1950, three years after Barbie began working full-time for CIC, the French press reported that the Butcher of Lyon was living openly in Munich in the American zone. An embarrassed and nervous CIC quickly hid him, like Otto von Bolschwing hid Viorel Trifa after the failed coup in Romania, until it could sneak him out of Germany.

Soon after the war—perhaps even before the war officially ended— British and American intelligence agents were running a "ratline," or underground railroad, from Austria to Italy, and from Italy to Central and South America. They used the ratline to plant spies around the world. Father Krunoslav Draganovic, a Croatian Ustashi colonel working out of a Croatian seminary in the shadow of the Vatican, handled the ratline paperwork for the Allies.

CIC paid Father Draganovic, a Franciscan friar, fourteen hundred dollars to provide a set of documents for Barbie, his wife, and two children. They included travel papers from Vienna to Genoa, Red Cross passports, and visas to Bolivia, all under the name of Altmann. Draganovic did a steady business with the British and Americans—no one knows how many hundreds of former Nazis he helped escape—and he used the profits to fund his own "Vatican Ratline," which specialized in finding safe havens in South America and the Middle East for his fellow Ustashi war criminals.

Draganovic completed the Barbie paperwork in ten weeks and Klaus Altmann and his family sailed from Genoa in March 1951. Case closed. Barbie was free and on his own. Only a couple of CIC officers and Father Draganovic knew where he was.

Allan Ryan finished his OSI report in August 1983. He managed to convince Attorney General William French Smith to release the report, *Klaus Barbie and the United States Government*, to the media, arguing that it was important for the integrity of OSI investigations that its boss, the Department of Justice, be open and honest.

Secretary of State George Shultz invited the chargé d'affaires of the French embassy to his office, where he presented the diplomat with a copy of the Ryan report and a note expressing "deep regrets to the government of France."

Ryan's strategy worked. When the *New York Times* received a copy of the Klaus Barbie report a few days later, its editorial page was bursting with national pride. "How rare it is for a proud and powerful nation to admit shabby behavior," it said. "The admission of blame the United States made . . . first to itself and then to France, goes far to redeem national honor."

Ryan quit OSI soon after the release of his report to teach, practice law, and write a book, *Quiet Neighbors*, which described his work with OSI, including a chapter summarizing his Barbie investigation. Missing from Ryan's book was any mention of George Parker and his memo expressing doubt about the wisdom of prosecuting John Demjanjuk as Ivan the Terrible.

PART THREE

To Deport or Not to Deport

CHAPTER THIRTY-TWO

Fighting for His Life

While sitting in a jail in Missouri, John Demjanjuk, along with his children, who were holding vigil outside the jail, staged a hunger strike. The government unlocked his cell after eleven days. Martin had been right. The immigration court had no authority to open a deportation case against Demjanjuk while the denaturalization order was under appeal.

The Demjanjuk family decided to replace John Martin. Were they unhappy with the nondefense he had mounted before Judge Battisti? Did Martin ask to be replaced? If so, perhaps he was tired. He had worked on the Demjanjuk case for two years. Perhaps he wisely concluded that immigration law is tricky and he lacked the experience to navigate it.

The Demjanjuks asked their friend and financial supporter Jerome Brentar for advice on whom to hire. Brentar, the probable anti-Semite and Holocaust denier, who had testified in Demjanjuk's behalf before Judge Battisti, turned for advice to his friend Edward O'Connor, the former deeply compromised DPC commissioner who had also testified for Demjanjuk. O'Connor volunteered his son Mark.

Like John Martin before him, Mark O'Connor was a fiercely dedicated lawyer who didn't trust any document supplied by the Soviet Union. If he had any neo-Nazi or anti-Semitic leanings, they would not show up in the courtroom or during media interviews. Unlike Martin, who

had been a county prosecutor, O'Connor had limited courtroom experience—he called himself just a country lawyer—and less than a nodding
acquaintance with the complexities of immigration law. And like Martin,
he wasn't eager to take on the controversial case. A tearful phone call
from Demjanjuk's older daughter, Lydia, made him think it over.

"It took me almost six months to decide," he later recalled. "I visited
John and his family. I talked it over with my family and I finally made my
judgement: 'In my mind, this is not the man.'"

O'Connor chose attorney John Gill, an amateur graphologist, as
his co-counsel. Both lawyers had represented Frank Walus in his legal
fracas with Simon Wiesenthal. Walus sued the Nazi hunter for allegedly forging incriminating documents and orchestrating false testimony
against him as a Gestapo agent. Wiesenthal countersued for libel. Walus
settled out of court with an apology and an offer to pay Wiesenthal's attorney fees and court costs.

• • •

Demjanjuk's final deportation hearing began in April 1983, eight years
after his name first surfaced on the Ukrainian list and two years after his
denaturalization trial. After a series of delays, it ended a year later. The
deportation issue was not complicated. Should John Demjanjuk, no longer a citizen of the United States, be allowed to remain in the country as
a permanent resident or should he be compelled to leave because he had
allegedly violated seven U.S. immigration law statutes?

Demjanjuk's job was to argue that even though he had lied on his
visa application and had been stripped of his U.S. citizenship, he should
not be deported. For its part, the government chose to argue its case
negatively—destroy Demjanjuk's arguments through cross-examination
of the defense witnesses without offering witnesses of its own. In lieu of
witnesses, the government placed into evidence the entire denaturalization case of more than two thousand pages of transcripts and a mountain of exhibits and documents.

Administrative Judge Adolph Angelilli didn't make it easy for Demjanjuk. He ruled that the denaturalization decision of Judge Battisti was
final (collateral estoppel), meaning that the defense was not allowed to
challenge either Judge Battisti's ruling or his courtroom conduct. In effect, John Demjanjuk stood before the court irrevocably stripped of his
U.S. citizenship.

U.S. immigration law allows a respondent in a deportation hearing to choose the country he would like to be deported to should he lose his case. If a respondent declines to pick a country, the government selects one for him. When Demjanjuk waived his right to choose, the government requested his deportation to the Soviet Union, should the court find Demjanjuk deportable. Judge Angelilli granted the government's request.

The thought of a war crime trial in the Soviet Union was sobering and chilling. To avoid facing a judge in a communist country, Demjanjuk took the only avenue left open. He pleaded for asylum under the Refugee Act of 1980 for religious, political, and security reasons. The only place in the world where he would be safe from the vindictive arm of the KGB, he argued, was the United States of America. The plea was a gamble and the stakes couldn't have been higher.

For John Demjanjuk, it would either be life in the United States or death in the Soviet Union.

• • •

Mark O'Connor opened the defense with a humanitarian argument that bordered on a deliberate lie. He argued that Demjanjuk was too sick to be deported. In response, the government subpoenaed Demjanjuk's medications and sent them to a pharmacologist for a certified analysis. There were only two prescriptions. The pharmacologist certified that one was for mild pain, and the other was for moderate colitis. As a result, Judge Angelilli ruled that Demjanjuk was healthy enough to face the court and, if found deportable, healthy enough to be deported.

Having lost the red-herring argument, O'Connor wove a seamless defense around the concept of Demjanjuk's fear. He argued:

- Demjanjuk had lied on his 1951 visa application out of real and justifiable fear either that the United States would deliver him to Soviet agents if they knew he had been a POW and a soldier in Vlasov's army, or that the Soviets would get a copy of his U.S. visa application and kidnap him. Soviet spies were everywhere in Western Europe after the war, especially among the interpreters hired to process refugees. Interpreters could be bought or black-mailed into providing the names and camp locations of Soviet citizens.

- Unable to find Demjanjuk in a DP camp, Moscow assumed he was dead until Danilchenko swore in 1949 that Iwan Demjanjuk served with him at Sobibor. The KGB immediately placed him on a secret most-wanted list of one hundred Trawniki men.
- Sometime during the 1950s, the KGB learned from Demjanjuk's letters to his mother that he was living in Cleveland.
- In 1975, the KGB began to frame Demjanjuk with the forged Trawniki card in order to trick the United States into deporting him to the Soviet Union.
- To send Demjanjuk back to the Soviet Union would be a death sentence. The communists would execute him for any one of three reasons—he had been a POW (desertion), a soldier in Vlasov's army (treason), and a truck driver for the U.S. Army after the war (collaborating with the new Cold War enemy).
- The KGB had a long history of assassinating former Red Army soldiers whom they considered traitors. The only country safe from Moscow was the United States of America.

There was a major flaw in O'Connor's argument. Feodor Fedorenko chose to be deported to the Soviet Union so that he could be reunited with his first wife and son. When he arrived in Ukraine, Moscow didn't arrest and execute him for being a former POW and a self-admitted Nazi collaborator at Treblinka. He was alive and free, even as O'Connor argued his case.

To get around that fact, O'Connor reasoned that the KGB was too smart to arrest Fedorenko while Demjanjuk was still free. Trying and executing him before Demjanjuk's deportation to the Soviet Union might bias Judge Angelilli in Demjanjuk's favor. Why take a chance? Once Demjanjuk arrived safely in Ukraine, O'Connor argued, the Soviet Union would shoot or hang both him and Fedorenko with a double drumroll.

O'Connor called his first witness—John Demjanjuk.

• • •

Unlike Judge Hoffman in the Frank Walus trial and Judge Battisti in the Demjanjuk trial, Judge Angelilli gave O'Connor, an aggressive attorney, wide latitude to explore and develop the tightly woven arguments of fear and frame-up. But Angelilli made it clear from the opening rap of his gavel that he was no pushover.

"Don't tell me *my* job," he scolded O'Connor during an early bench argument. "You do *yours*."

And when O'Connor moved from his designated place in the courtroom, Angelilli stopped him cold. "This is *my* courtroom and I'll tell you where you can and cannot stand," he scolded again. "If you want to move, ask!"

O'Connor began his brief direct examination of Demjanjuk, whom he planned to recall later, by dragging out an old argument—that Demjanjuk had lied on his visa application out of fear. But O'Connor pushed the issue further than John Martin had during the denaturalization trial. He argued that Demjanjuk's fear of forcible repatriation was both *real* and *justified*.

"At the time you were still residing in Germany," O'Connor began, "what made you believe that these repatriations were happening—that people were being sent back to the USSR for trial?"

It was a question John Martin did not ask during the denaturalization trial.

"The Soviet mission was traveling from one camp to another to enlist people," Demjanjuk said through an interpreter. "At night [they were kidnaping] people for deportation."

"Were you aware of this *directly* . . . or did you hear about it?" O'Connor asked.

It was another question Martin hadn't posed.

"We were afraid even to *sleep* in the camps. We used to leave . . . at night and sleep outside."

On his visa application, Demjanjuk swore that he was born in Poland, not in the Soviet Union. O'Connor needed to establish that emigration personnel had encouraged Demjanjuk to lie to avoid being forcibly repatriated.

"When you [said] you were a resident of Poland," O'Connor asked, "had you been told by anyone—your comrades or someone helping you from IRO—that that would be enough to stop forced deportation?"

"The answer is yes."

"Do you feel [now that] you would be assassinated if you were in any other country but the United States?"

"Yes," Demjanjuk said.

• • •

OSI attorney Bruce Einhorn wasted no time challenging Demjanjuk in his cross-examination. He began by reading Demjanjuk's written responses to a list of asylum questions posed earlier by the court.

> Question: Is the United States protecting you from something?
> Demjanjuk: From the Soviet Union.
> Question: What will happen if you get to that country?
> Demjanjuk: Either hanging or execution.
> Question: If Judge Angelilli orders you deported to the Russians, do you feel you will be persecuted?
> Demjanjuk: You should know that he would deport an innocent person directly to his execution.
> Question: In your understanding of Russian law or Soviet law, are you a traitor to the motherland?
> Demjanjuk: Yes.

Einhorn asked Demjanjuk if he wanted to change any of those answers. When Demjanjuk said he did not, Einhorn began to challenge them.

"Do you know," he asked, "whether Ukrainians have been assassinated by Soviet agents in any other democracy other than the United States?"

"Stepan Bandera was killed by Soviet agents," Demjanjuk said.

"Where?"

"In Germany."

"Other than this *alleged* Stepan Bandera?"

"At the moment, I am not able to spell their names," Demjanjuk said.

In questioning Demjanjuk about assassinations, Einhorn showed his historical ignorance and lack of trial preparation. Bandera was a famous Ukrainian hero who fought for independence both before and during World War II as a leader of a Ukrainian guerilla army. After the war he was an international leader in the Ukraine independence movement. His assassination by cyanide in Munich on October 15, 1959, by Soviet agent Bohdan Stashynsky made headlines around the world. If Einhorn had done his homework, he could have argued that to compare Demjanjuk to Bandera would be like comparing a Virginia tobacco farmer to George Washington. Bandera posed a threat to Moscow. Demjanjuk did not. Einhorn moved on to another topic.

"Can you tell us what provision of Soviet law . . . required all Soviet prisoners of war . . . to commit suicide?"

"There was a regulation—and we were told about it—that we have no right to be taken prisoner of war. That we have to commit suicide."

"How was the law described to you? Was it cited to you?"

"It was given through an officer," Demjanjuk said.

"Do you remember the name of the law?"

"All I know is that there was a regulation."

(Historian Matityahu Meisel, a specialist in World War II Russian military history, would later testify in another Demjanjuk trial: "There was no such order . . . to commit suicide rather than being taken captive.")

"Do you know for certain that *every* Soviet prisoner of war who returned to the Soviet Union . . . was executed by Soviet authorities?" Einhorn asked Demjanjuk.

"Yes."

"Since you know it for a fact, can you tell us how many executions there were?"

"I cannot give you an exact number," Demjanjuk said. "One was spared, ten were executed."

"How do you know this?"

"It was in the press."

"Are you aware of the general Soviet amnesty after World War II with regard to Soviet prisoners of war?"

"I've never heard of such an amnesty," Demjanjuk said.

"Would it refresh your recollection to know that the proclamation was issued by Nikita Khrushchev . . . in the 1960s?"

Again, Einhorn didn't bother to check his historical facts. The Khrushchev pardon was granted in 1955. It freed only those POWs who had not been charged with war crimes, not Trawniki men like Danilchenko, Fedorenko, and Ivan the Terrible, who, in effect, had been charged.

"I was never aware of it, and I never tried to find out about it," Demjanjuk said. "I was already living in a free country which I love, and that's all I have to say in this matter."

On his application for a suspension of deportation, Demjanjuk had written: "I have been sentenced to death in Russian occupied Ukraine for assisting the American forces in Germany after WW II, for deserting the Red Army, for refusing forced repatriation, and for service in the Vlasov Army."

Einhorn pressed Demjanjuk on the claims.

"Do you continue to swear that the answer you gave . . . to be the truth and the whole truth?"

"Yes."

"Could you refer me to the *specific provision* in the Soviet law which provides a criminal sentence for assisting American forces by driving a truck after the conclusion of the Second World War?"

"There is no question about it," Demjanjuk said.

"Could you tell me the name of the law . . . that makes 'there is no question about it'?"

"How can you expect me to know a paragraph of the law," Demjanjuk complained. "There is just a general law that you cannot serve in another army."

"Were you *in* the United States Army, or were you simply *working* for the United States Army?"

"We had black uniforms, but we were considered as working *for* the American army."

"So you were never in the United States Army as an enlisted man with a rank, grade, and green army uniform, were you?"

"No."

"Do you deny the fact that forcible repatriation to the Soviet Union ended in 1947, four years before you applied for a visa?"

"I cannot tell you whether it was '47 or '48 or '46. I don't think that's relevant," Demjanjuk said. "I was under *constant fear* that I may be forcibly returned."

"I'm not interested in your fear. I'm interested in the *fact*. Do you think that your witness, Mr. Jerome Brentar, lied under oath when he told us . . . that forcible repatriation to the Soviet Union ended in 1947?"

Einhorn was referring to Brentar's testimony at the denaturalization trial.

"I don't think Mr. Brentar would be lying," Demjanjuk said.

"You wouldn't contradict him, would you?"

"No, I would not."

"Do you believe that the dangers you would face in being returned is [*sic*] a *shared danger* of your fellow Ukrainians living in this country or the west?"

"Yes. We are all considered collaborators by the communists."

"Do you believe that the United States court system is a fair and free one?"

"I do believe in American justice," Demjanjuk said, "but I want to tell you that I personally did not get justice."

"Do you believe that the United States court system is fair to everybody but you?"

"I don't know about other cases."

Einhorn asked Demjanjuk if he believed that fellow Ukrainians had ever collaborated with the Nazis as death camp guards during the war.

"Now that I am involved in this case," Demjanjuk said, "I have read many books in which they state that there were Ukrainians employed in this capacity. If the books are making such a statement, who am I to deny it?"

"Do you think that such persons . . . should remain citizens and residents of the United States of America?"

"It all depends under what conditions these people were in that job. If they were *forced* to do it, is one thing," Demjanjuk said. "If they voluntarily went to it, it's another thing."

Demjanjuk had a book giving statistics about KGB assassinations in the West. He asked Angelilli's permission to have the clerk read the statistics into the record. Angelilli compromised.

"Make a copy," he said. "I'll read it, and place it into the record, and take it into account when I make my decision."

The defense also had a copy of a National Archives film showing American soldiers in Plattling, Bavaria, in February 1946, forcibly rounding up Russian soldiers who had been German POWs for repatriation to the Soviet Union. Shot in black-and-white without sound by the U.S. Army Signal Corps, the eight-minute film was drenched in despair. Hundreds of frightened Soviet soldiers, not a single smile among them. Waiting for their names to be called by a Russian official. Climbing into trucks with armed American escorts. The trucks backing up to empty boxcars. Being searched for weapons by American soldiers. Filing into the cars. A train engine billowing smoke that refuses to rise. A string of boxcars stuffed with Soviet soldiers heading east through a flat, bleak landscape.

One frame graphically portrays POW despair. A young soldier's bare chest is crisscrossed with razor cuts. The cameraman had documented for posterity at least one symbolic instance of what was *really* happening at Plattling in 1946.

Angelilli refused to enter the film into evidence.

Before Demjanjuk stood down, Angelilli wanted to make sure that he understood what he had to prove to win his asylum plea. "You must base your claim on . . . what the foreign government would do to threaten your life, or your freedom," Angelilli explained. "Or to persecute you on account of five elements—race, religion, nationality, political opinion, and social group."

Angelilli then gave Demjanjuk a chance to plead for his life without the threat of cross-examination. Demjanjuk thanked him.

"First of all, I'm a deeply religious person, a Christian," he began. "I believe in God . . . I give this as my first reason why I cannot go back to the Soviet Union. Most of the churches are closed . . . converted into warehouses, social clubs with dances going on, or warehouses for military ammunition. A large number of priests and bishops were murdered, and there is no religious freedom in that country.

"Second point. As a Ukrainian national, I cannot go back to the USSR because Ukraine, my fatherland, does not exist. . . . My country is an occupied country, and there is absolutely no freedom. . . . I would be persecuted in that place, not only as a politically guilty person, but simply as a Ukrainian national. . . .

"I would also like to say that, should I be deported to the Soviet Union as a former member of the Soviet army, I'm pretty sure they would drag me from one locality to another simply to show that, even after forty years, they were able to succeed to get a person . . . back . . . for punishment."

Next, Mark O'Connor called three Demjanjuk supporters to the stand—Michael Pap, Frank Walus, and Jerome Brentar. Both Pap and Brentar had testified at his 1981 denaturalization trial.

CHAPTER THIRTY-THREE

Never Heard of Him

O'Connor needed historian Michael Pap to bolster Demjanjuk's plea for asylum based on fear of execution or assassination. Pap treated the court to a brief but important history lesson.

The Germans captured four million Soviet soldiers during the war, he testified. Hitler deliberately starved, executed, or worked to death half of them, and the Soviets forcibly repatriated most of the rest. Stalin was tough on his returning soldiers.

"They were all given fifteen years of hard labor with an indication that none of them should be alive at the end of fifteen years," Pap said. "Stalin *could* have given them the death sentence, but he needed manpower. [When] Khrushchev offered amnesty . . . there were very few alive."

"Dr. Pap, what would [happen] if John Demjanjuk was deported back to the Soviet Union by order of this court?" O'Connor asked.

"There is no doubt in my mind that the Soviets would apply Article 133 of the Constitution . . . desertion to the enemy. He was a deserter from the Red Army, and therefore he would be punished. Severely punished. He might get the death penalty."

"What advantage would there be [in] persecuting a simple factory worker?"

"It would show to the people—to the oppressed nations in Eastern Europe—that they have no alternative but to cooperate with the system," Pap said. "'Look what happened to this individual! That's what will happen to you.'"

Demjanjuk had also argued that the KGB would assassinate him if he were deported to any country outside the Soviet Union, but for the most part he had failed to document his fear during Einhorn's cross-examination. O'Connor used Pap to provide evidence of continued KGB assassinations of former Soviet citizens living in the West.

"Since the Second World War we have evidence of *at least* twelve cases where assassinations took place," Pap testified. "At first the Soviet government denied it. In one case an Austrian court, and in one case a French court proved beyond a doubt the involvement of the KGB. The [KGB] admitted it."

• • •

O'Connor's next witness would be Frank Walus, who was testifying at the request of Jerome Brentar.

Brentar was working closely with O'Connor, who called him a "key figure" in the defense of Demjanjuk. The Cleveland travel agent was out to prove that the Ivan the Terrible charge was a lie concocted by OSI and the international Jewish cabal. In preparation for the deportation hearing, Brentar made more than twenty trips to Europe and two to Israel to expose the fraud.

He visited former SS officer Kurt Franz, the last commander of Treblinka, in a prison just outside Düsseldorf, where he was serving a life sentence. Franz told Brentar: "Several years ago, six of you people were here. . . . And I told them [Demjanjuk] is not Ivan the Terrible. Ivan the Terrible was much older, had dark hair, and was taller. He had to stoop because he was so tall. So why do you come here again and ask the same questions?"

Brentar tried to get an interview with German chancellor Helmut Kohl. Kohl's adjutant told him: "If you want any help from us, you have to ask the Israelis for permission."

Brentar interviewed Menachem Russek, head of the Israeli police investigation unit on Nazi crimes. He told Russek: "You're being misled by the OSI. This is an innocent man." Brentar concluded that Russek was as eager as OSI to frame Demjanjuk as he had framed Frank Walus.

Brentar visited Treblinka and its neighboring villages. He knocked on doors and showed residents a photo of Demjanjuk. No one had ever seen the man in the picture before. He located three former inmates of Treblinka who remembered a guard called Iwan and who agreed to testify at the deportation hearing that Demjanjuk was not the Iwan they knew. Brentar learned that someone at OSI had warned Polish authorities not to issue visas to these witnesses because Jerome Brentar was a rich Holocaust revisionist who had bought their testimony with American dollars. Brentar also discovered that the same person had called the U.S. consulate in Warsaw and said, "Don't let the witnesses come. The [deportation] hearing is over."

But the hearing wasn't over, leading Brentar to conclude that OSI's case against John Demjanjuk was built on lies, exaggerations, distortions, fabrications, innuendos, and dirty tricks.

In Frank Walus, Brentar had found a dedicated collaborator who spoke fluent German and Polish. Walus was a bitter man. He never forgave the U.S. government and the Jews for conspiring to have him executed as a former Gestapo agent. His trial before Judge Julius Hoffman in Chicago had ruined his reputation and forced him to live in isolation, like a moral leper in a legal limbo.

Julius Hoffman convicted him. The appeals court declined to overturn the conviction. Instead, it granted him a new trial. But OSI refused to retry him. Where did that leave him? In the eyes of Chicago's Jews and Poles alike, Frank Walus was a convicted war criminal who got off the hook.

Walus believed that if it hadn't been for Jerome Brentar, who dug up the evidence that won him a new trial, he would be a dead man like Demjanjuk would be if he were deported to the Soviet Union.

There was one incident that came to symbolize Walus's life after Julius Hoffman. He was standing in line at a neighborhood market in Chicago's Little Poland to buy kielbasa. A non-Jewish, Polish woman cut in front of him. "I don't have to wait behind a Nazi," she said. "Nazis have no rights."

Fueled by comments like that of the Polish woman, Walus's rage was so consuming that whenever he heard a priest say the word *Israel* during Mass, he would get up and walk out. When Brentar invited Walus to visit Poland with him, all expenses paid, to prove that Ivan the Terrible was a hoax, Walus pounced on the offer. And when O'Connor asked him to be a witness at Demjanjuk's deportation hearing, he gladly agreed.

Walus testified that he had visited the villages around Treblinka and interviewed a string of older residents. Most remembered several Ukrainian guards called Iwan. (If the villagers didn't know the real name of a Ukrainian guard, they simply called him "Iwan.") The guards came to town to drink and cavort with women—pros as well as wives and single women willing to exchange favors for food, warm clothes, shoes, or money. Not a single villager had ever heard of a Ukrainian guard called Iwan Grozny, Walus testified. He even furnished the court with sworn statements from two of the residents.

When he stepped down from the stand after his brief testimony, Walus was convinced that his "evidence" proved without a doubt that there never was an Ivan the Terrible at Treblinka, and that the government and the Jews were framing John Demjanjuk just as they had framed and destroyed him.

O'Connor then called Jerome Brentar to the stand.

• • •

Brentar's job was to support the testimony of Walus and to prove that Demjanjuk's fear of forced repatriation was justified.

"They laughed at me," Brentar testified about his visit to the village of Treblinka. "And I felt a little self-conscious because there just isn't any Ivan Grozny."

"Why did you go over there?" O'Connor asked.

"I was interested in learning the truth of Treblinka. . . . .And I think I found the truth. There *was no* Ivan the Terrible. This is just sheer Hollywood sensationalism to give more emphasis on this man's deportation."

"What makes you think he's innocent?"

"OSI . . . couldn't find anything in Washington to nail him with," Brentar said. "They went to Germany. They couldn't find anything in Germany to nail him with. They couldn't find anything in Poland to nail him with. So they went to the Soviet Union, where you can get tailor-made, custom-made, whatever you want—especially to incriminate people who are from the Soviet Union."

"That's your opinion?" Judge Angelilli asked.

"That's the God's truth."

Because Brentar had screened refugees for the IRO after the war, O'Connor used him to prove that refugee personnel had encouraged Demjanjuk to lie on his visa application to save his life.

"Were you ever aware of any false statements that were made by displaced persons?" O'Connor asked.

"Especially by the Ukrainians and Russians," Brentar said. "[They] would try to conceal their place of birth and their residence . . . saying they came from the Polish part of what was Ukraine. . . . People disappeared overnight, would be kidnapped, and would be sent back to the Soviet Union. . . . The Soviets had their spies—people who were paid. . . . Some even had access to files."

Brentar quickly qualified his testimony, however, by saying he and his staff had no proof the applicants were lying.

"We were not interested in detecting the lies because we knew *why* the people were lying. . . . It was not by choice, but by sheer compulsion to save themselves from a fate that [we] would not like to think about. . . . We gave them the benefit of the doubt."

"Were you aware of your subordinates putting the wrong place of birth . . . or encouraging the displaced person to put the wrong place of birth?" O'Connor asked.

"Some were even *coaching* the person saying 'it's better for you to say this or that,'" Brentar said. "The Max Kolbe Foundation, with whom I worked very closely, admitted there were over fifty thousand people who went through the foundation with false names and false histories out of sheer fear of repatriation."

The Kolbe Foundation was named after Maximilian Kolbe, a Polish priest who died at Auschwitz in August 1941.

"Repatriation by whom?"

"By the gutless allies—the English, the Americans—who sold these people down the river, and sent them forcibly back to the Soviet Union."

"Was this a *reasonable fear* or just a paranoia?"

"Reasonable fear," Brentar said. "There were times I came to the camp to work and there was a lot of commotion, and I asked what happened, and they said this person was here last night but they are not here now, and we don't know what happened to them. They are from Eastern Europe."

"Over what period of time?"

It was important for O'Connor to establish that refugees were afraid of repatriation as late as 1951, the year Demjanjuk applied for a U.S. visa.

"Basically '47, '48, and '49 . . . even some in 1950," Brentar said. "There are people *still* living in a subconscious fear of being forcefully repatriated. . . . I know a dozen people [in America] who are living under false names."

"Wasn't there some concern about the humanitarian issue here, or the moral issue?"

"It was just stupid, selfish indifference on the part of our authorities," Brentar said. "They couldn't care less what happened to the people once they left the American [sector]. . . . And some of these people were skin and bones. They . . . just threw them in [the trains], and their bones hit the wooden floors and would—oh, you could hear the bones on the floor. . . . And some of these poor people were starting to fight, resist. And there were all kinds of battles going on to get these people back into the cars, lock the doors, and go. Many people committed suicide even before the trains left the camps."

CHAPTER THIRTY-FOUR

Blackmailed and Betrayed

On the stand, Demjanjuk had testified that immigration officials encouraged him to lie on his visa application to save himself from forced repatriation to the Soviet Union, where he would be executed as a POW deserter, a Vlasov's army traitor, and an employee of the U.S. Army. The government, under the pretext of ascertaining facts and only facts, had belittled and challenged that fear, suggesting that Demjanjuk was lying when he testified that he was still afraid in 1951, when he applied for a U.S. visa. The government's distorted cross-examination—either through historical ignorance, deception, or trickery—left critical questions twisting in the careless breeze of courtroom argument.

Was there an official decree, presidential or otherwise, ending forced repatriation in 1948 as the government contended? If so, who issued it and when? Did forced repatriation actually end after that "decree" was promulgated? If not, were Soviet citizens still afraid after 1950, as Demjanjuk alleged, or was he lying, as the government suggested? If Demjanjuk had reason to fear, was that fear a fact to be considered in deciding whether he was deportable, or was it irrelevant, as the government claimed?

Given that Demjanjuk was pleading for his life, and that both the prosecution and the defense distorted or fabricated historical facts, it is important to dissect the forced repatriation issue with the scalpel of historical hindsight.

It is a painful operation.

In staggering round numbers:

- 8.35 million Soviet POWs and forced laborers were taken prisoner by the Germans.
- One third of them (2.78 million) were either executed or died from starvation, disease, and overwork by the end of the war.
- About 5.6 million survived the war.
- Of those, 3.4 million ended up in the Soviet zone and were immediately transported back to the Soviet Union, whether they wanted to go or not.
- The rest (2.2 million) ended up in DP camps in Germany and Austria under the care of America and Great Britain.

What happened to those 2.2 million and why is a complicated story of cowardice and profound inhumanity.

• • •

Soon after the Normandy invasion in June 1944, American soldiers stumbled on a surprise package—enemy soldiers in German uniforms who couldn't speak German. Who were they? And what was the U.S. Army supposed to do with them?

Privy to intelligence reports, the War Department and its upper military echelons were far from surprised. They had known for some time about the deployment of Soviet POWs in the Waffen SS, Ukrainian and Vlasov's army divisions, and in the regular German army (Wehrmacht). Combined, these deployments totaled nearly *one million* non-German men in German uniforms, fighting the Soviets in the east and the Americans and British in the west. It was the largest military defection in history. Why these men chose to collaborate with the Germans was sometimes simple, sometimes as complex as the war itself.

Some volunteered in order to save themselves from death by starvation and overwork. Most Ukrainians, Balts, Belorussians, and Cossacks collaborated out of hatred for communism and a false hope of establishing independent states after the war. Loyal communists like General Vlasov fought against their own Red Army because they believed that Stalin was destroying their homeland. Some were conscripted into the SS Waffen and the regular German army.

What choice did Stalin leave his POWs? When he vowed to punish them as traitors, he betrayed them all.

The capture of these SS Waffen and Wehrmacht Soviet soldiers presented Washington with a pounding migraine. Simply put, the Soviet Union demanded its traitors back. If the United States refused to return them, then the Red Army might not hand over the more than sixty thousand American and British servicemen and women it was about to liberate from German stalags in the east.

It was pure blackmail.

For Great Britain, it was a quick, easy decision. Long before Britain signed a Yalta repatriation agreement, Prime Minister Anthony Eden announced an unequivocal repatriation policy—return all Soviet POWs captured in German uniforms. No exceptions. If they refuse or resist, force them at bayonet point or shoot them. England wants its boys back home safely at any cost.

Washington waffled for seven months. Contributing to its indecision was a fear that if the United States caved in to Moscow's demand to hand over all Soviets captured in German uniforms, Germany might retaliate against the American POWs it was holding in the stalags still under its control in the west.

For Washington, it was a lose-lose situation.

For the most part, the U.S. departments of State, War, and Justice all opposed forced repatriation on either legal or humanitarian grounds. Legal . . . because the 1929 Geneva Convention made it clear that captured soldiers were to be treated as citizens of the country whose uniforms they were wearing at the time of capture. They were not required to divulge their true nationality. Although the convention did not *explicitly* condemn forced repatriation, the practice ran contrary to international legal tradition and the spirit of the convention.

Humanitarian . . . because the State Department knew what would happen to repatriated German collaborators once the Red Army and the KGB got their hands on them. The U.S. embassy in Moscow sent Washington daily reports about Soviet policies and the proclamations of Joseph Stalin. And Stalin's public position was as clear as it was unforgiving.

"In Hitler's camps there are no prisoners of war, only Russian traitors," Stalin told the international press, "and we shall do away with them when the war is over."

On the other hand, General George C. Marshall and General Dwight

D. Eisenhower and most of their high-level brass favored caving in to the blackmail. The United States was at war, and war was an exercise in pragmatism. The definition of morality belonged to the victor. The task at hand was to get some sixty thousand American and British men and women back home safely. If the price was a million Soviets POW traitors, so be it. There was no room for compassion. Wouldn't the United States demand the return of all American POWs captured in battle wearing *German* uniforms?

Besides the fate of American POWs, there was a second issue at stake, and it was just as chilling. Marshall and Eisenhower both saw a humanitarian problem looming large on the horizon the likes of which the world had never seen—millions of sick and starving refugees who were bound to end up in American hands after the war. The immediate return of the Soviet POWs among them would ease the problem. As Eisenhower advised Washington: "Russians [are] a considerable charge against the resources of this theater. The only complete solution to this problem, from all points of view, is the early repatriation of these Russians."

The U.S. military knew that the Soviet Union would never be satisfied with the return of a few hundred thousand Soviet POWs captured in German uniforms. Like a good blackmailer, it would always demand more. And more meant *all* Soviet POWs, whether they wore a German uniform or not. Didn't Stalin call them all traitors? And when the Soviets demanded the return of all Soviet POWs whether they collaborated or not, wore German uniforms or not, the U.S. military was prepared to round them up. For the Americans, compliance would mean a million fewer postwar mouths to feed, families to house, bodies to heal, background checks to make, and papers to shuffle.

It was a win-win.

By early December 1944, six months after the Normandy invasion, two things had become clear. Germany was caught in a death squeeze—the Americans pressing from the west, the Soviets from the east. The Reich had only months to live. That made the threat of German retaliation against Allied POWs unlikely. Secondly, as the German threat of retaliation faded, the Soviet threat grew stronger. The Red Army had already liberated the stalags in Poland that were holding Americans and was on the verge of doing the same in Hungary. In a matter of months, the Red Army would further liberate Yugoslavia, Czechoslovakia, and Romania, each of which was known to hold Allied POWs.

It was time to toss the Soviets a bone.

The United States was holding nearly half a million German prisoners of war in America. Of those, between four and ten thousand turned out to be Soviet citizens captured in German uniforms. They were imprisoned in stockades on military bases in New Jersey, Pennsylvania, Virginia, Idaho, Alabama, and Arkansas. Most did not want to return to the Soviet Union.

The bone? Those POWs who had *voluntarily admitted* that they were Soviet citizens.

It was a safe decision. Since those POWs were "all claimants to Soviet nationality," they probably wouldn't resist repatriation. They might even welcome it. If they refused to return to the Soviet Union, however, U.S. soldiers would force them with fixed bayonets.

The pressure on Washington was mounting by the day. Moscow's ambassador to the United States was breathing heavily on the White House, and the Red Army representatives who regularly visited U.S. stockades holding the Soviet POWs were growling like a Russian bear. Besides, Washington reasoned, when the POWs freely admitted being Soviet citizens, didn't they give up their right to be treated as German POWs under the Geneva Convention?

Early in December 1944, the War Department ordered the military to sift from the POW population held in the United States those Soviets captured in German uniforms and to segregate them at Camp Rupert, Idaho. The War Department then ordered the military to winnow out from the Camp Rupert group those POWs who had admitted to Soviet citizenship. Of those, the military selected an initial group of eleven hundred to be escorted from Camp Rupert to Portland, Oregon, and placed on a Soviet ship anchored in the harbor.

Seventy POWs of that initial group refused to leave Camp Rupert. Three attempted suicide—one by hanging, one by stabbing, and the third by beating his head against a barracks beam. U.S. soldiers easily crushed the rebellion. The POW convoy arrived in Portland at the end of December 1944 and the prisoners were loaded onto the Soviet ship. In a last spasm of despair, at least three attempted suicide by jumping overboard into the winter sea before the ship set sail for the Siberian port of Vladivostok. Two drowned. One was forcibly rescued.

Judging from firsthand accounts of similar Soviet POW voyages, the "liberated" prisoners from America who claimed Soviet citizenship were received amicably by captain and crew in the hopes of avoiding a bloody mutiny. The POWs sang Russian folk songs, drank Russian vodka, and seemed truly happy to be returning home. Once they reached Soviet ports, however, the Red Army and the KGB greeted them with contempt, hostility, and brutality.

Two months after the first shipment of eleven hundred Soviet POWs had left America, and just days before the Yalta Conference in Crimea, the United States handed over to the Soviets another fifteen hundred Camp Rupert Soviet prisoners.

Upon disembarkation in Siberia, those Soviet POWs were immediately imprisoned, interrogated, and screened. Stalin temporarily tabled his vow to "do away with them" because he needed more soldiers on the western front. He redrafted them into the Red Army and they went on to help liberate Berlin. When Stalin no longer needed them, he sentenced the enlisted men among them to fifteen to twenty-five years of hard labor and executed their commanding officers.

Moscow, of course, wasn't satisfied with just twenty-six hundred repatriated POWs. The bone from Washington had only served to sharpen its teeth and whet its appetite. When Stalin came to Yalta in February 1945 to meet with Winston Churchill and Franklin Delano Roosevelt, he brought a unilateral repatriation agreement and a new fountain pen. In that agreement, he demanded the return of:

- All Soviet volunteers and conscripts in the Waffen SS. Of the thirty-eight Waffen SS divisions fighting mainly in the east, twenty-five (60 percent) were made up of non-Germans, including *Volksdeutsche*.
- All Soviet volunteers and conscripts in the Wehrmacht (*Osttruppen*). After the invasion of Normandy, the German army had deployed one hundred *Osttruppen* battalions (one thousand to twelve hundred men each) from Norway to France, from Yugoslavia to Crete, from Germany to Italy.
- All soldiers in the Vlasov and Ukrainian divisions.
- All Soviet POWs liberated from work camps and concentration camps.
- All Soviet civilian forced laborers (*Ostarbeiter*).

In a word, Stalin wanted all 2.2 million Soviet citizens—soldiers and civilians—back in the communist fold. There were three reasons for his uncompromising greed. He wanted to punish all of them as deserters and traitors. At the same time, he wanted to make sure there would be no sizable anticommunist bloc outside the Soviet Union to challenge his authority or plot against him. And he wanted to con the West into believing that all Soviets citizens were eager to go home.

As a pragmatist, however, Stalin really didn't want every single Soviet back. He was too wily for that. He needed a manageable number of former Soviet citizens sprinkled across the West whom he could later recruit or blackmail into spying for the Soviet Union in the new Cold War.

Stalin was also too cagey to raise a delicate repatriation issue with Churchill and Roosevelt at Yalta: how to handle Soviet citizens who refused to go back. Stalin had a very good reason for his silence on the issue. He didn't want even to acknowledge to Churchill or Roosevelt that there were Soviet citizens who did not want to return to the motherland. And he knew that if he didn't bring up the issue, London and Washington wouldn't have the guts to voice it, either.

As the Americans and British would soon find out, Stalin's threat to imprison liberated Allied POWs if Washington and London didn't give him what he demanded was a bluff. The Soviet leader had no intention of wasting time and squandering resources in a game of POW poker. To the contrary, all across Eastern Europe, the Red Army was opening the gates of POW camps, if they weren't already open, and moving on. True, some Allied POWs ended up in gulags, more by accident than policy, but the vast majority were left to fend for themselves. They could head east to Moscow and knock on embassy doors. Or trail at a safe distance behind the Red Army until it bumped into Allied forces. Or head west on their own, dodging German units as Private Galione had done when searching for Camp Dora. Or wait for a U.S.-Soviet prisoner exchange of some kind.

For his part, Roosevelt was both uninterested and ignorant about the repatriation issue. It was no secret that he favored the military over the State Department. And repatriation was a military problem, not a diplomatic one. Let General John Deane, head of the U.S. military mission in Moscow, handle it.

General Deane's hope was that Stalin would agree to a U.S. airlift to rescue the freed American servicemen and women behind the Soviet front line. When Stalin refused and wouldn't budge on his own demands, Deane went ahead and signed a repatriation agreement at Yalta. So did the British and the French.

By May 1945, three months after General Deane signed the Yalta agreement, the new policy had made its way into the *Guide to the Care of Displaced Persons in Germany*, the official manual of the Supreme Headquarters of the Allied Expeditionary Force. "After identification by Soviet representatives," the guide said, "Soviet displaced persons will be repatriated regardless of their individual wishes."

No one doubts today that parts of the Yalta repatriation agreement were a violation of the Geneva Convention and international law. Nor would anyone deny that the United States and Great Britain—and France, to a much lesser degree—handed over Soviet citizens to the Red Army knowing full well that there would be no warm bear hug on the other side of the border. Some would even label the forced return of Soviet civilians and POWs who did *not* collaborate with the Germans as a crime against humanity.

How many Soviet citizens returned willingly? How many felt they had no realistic choice but to go back? How many were duped or blackmailed into returning? How many resisted with two-by-fours and bare knuckles? How many committed suicide?

No one on either side of the Red divide kept tally, and most historians would consider any estimates little more than guesses. A few examples, however, illustrate the fear and hatred, hope and despair, cruelty and deception that consumed more than 2.2 million Soviet citizens in the early years after World War II.

CHAPTER THIRTY-FIVE

Into the Valley of Tears

At nine o'clock in the morning on June 29, 1945, Lieutenant Colonel G. M. Treisch, commandant of the Fort Dix, New Jersey, stockade, ordered the 154 Vlasovites imprisoned on the post to gather in the yard outside their barracks. Treisch had received orders from Washington to escort them to an American ship anchored in New York harbor. The ship would take them to Germany, where they would be handed over to the Soviets.

The Fort Dix Vlasovites were the remnant of the American-held Soviet POWs captured in German uniforms. They were a tough, resourceful group who knew that either death or a gulag awaited them in the Soviet Union. Months before, U.S. Military Police had tried to deliver them to a Soviet ship anchored at Seattle. Prodded on board by bayonets and gun butts, they bided their time with patience and cunning.

When the Americans left the ship, the POWs attacked the Soviet sailors with bare fists and teeth and with such determination—one account said they also damaged the ship's engines so badly that it couldn't set sail—that the War Department called off the operation and escorted the jubilant POWs all the way across the country to New Jersey.

Colonel Treisch made a foolish mistake that pleasant June morning. He told the POWs that they were going home. Instead of cheering, they refused to budge. Angry and feeling betrayed by false promises, they demanded to be treated as German POWs under the Geneva Convention. They had good reason to feel betrayed.

Toward the end of the war, U.S. bombers dropped millions of leaflets across Europe from the shores of Brittany to the eastern front, promising Soviet POWs fighting with the Germans good treatment in accordance with the Hague and Geneva conventions if they surrendered. The leaflets also denounced as a lie German counter-leaflets stating that the Americans would forcibly repatriate those soldiers naïve enough to believe their promises.

As they stood their ground at Fort Dix surrounded by rifles and machine guns, the POWs taunted their guards, trying to provoke them into opening fire. When the soldiers refused to shoot, the POWs rushed back into their barracks on the command of their senior officer and set the building on fire. Better to quickly burn to death with honor in the shadow of Lady Liberty than to die a slow, shameful death under the Soviet hammer and sickle.

In response to the rebellion, Colonel Treisch ordered his men to lob tear gas grenades into the barracks. The rear door suddenly flew open and choking Soviet POWs charged out waving table legs and knives crafted from aluminum mess kits. They attacked the first guards they met, injuring three. Soldiers fired back, wounding seven. Two POWs tried to scale the barbed-wire fence. Soldiers pulled them down, lacerating their hands.

After thirty minutes of knives, clubs, and fists, Treisch's men restored order. While one group guarded the POWs, another donned gas masks and entered the barracks. They found three Vlasovites hanging from the rafters by their belts and fifteen empty belts dangling next to them.

Early the next day, June 30, a convoy of trucks, each carrying four POWs and five MPs, and a cortege of eight ambulances with the wounded, arrived at Pier 51 in New York harbor. Waiting to welcome them were the media, three hundred spectators, eighty heavily armed MPs, and the U.S. Navy transport *Monticello*, the former Italian luxury liner *Conte Grande*.

The Vlasovites never got the chance to fight back this time. Like the ending of a Hollywood B movie, the escort commander received a last-minute reprieve order from Washington. The riot at Fort Dix the previous day had earned international headlines, and an embarrassed Moscow wasted no time responding. It accused the United States of trying to forcibly prevent eager Soviet prisoners from returning to their motherland. In response, Washington did what it does best. It ordered an official investigation.

Meanwhile, U.S. soldiers escorted the Soviet POWs back to Fort Dix, took away their belts and shoestrings, and imprisoned them in a barracks without a stick of furniture. They slept on bare mattresses on the wooden floor under a twenty-four-hour suicide watch.

When the official investigation concluded that the POWs had resisted out of fear of repatriation, the military took no chances. It doped the prisoners' coffee on the morning of August 31, 1945, then transported them back to Pier 51 and a waiting ship that set sail for Germany under a cloak of such secrecy that even the media missed the bon voyage. The United States buried the three Soviet soldiers who had hanged themselves in the national cemetery on the left bank of the Delaware River near Fort Mott State Park, New Jersey.

As historian Mark Elliott put it: "Three tombstones there . . . constitute the sum total of physical evidence that the United States forcibly repatriated at least four thousand Soviet citizens from American soil."

. . .

In yet another twist of post–World War II irony, the U.S. military in Germany designated Dachau as a holding pen for Vlasovites and former SS officers waiting denazification. Dachau . . . where the SS murdered more than forty thousand prisoners of all European nationalities and where Himmler had established an SS training school for new recruits. Where Dr. Sigmund Rascher and his fellow Nazi scientists conducted hypothermia, high-altitude, and saltwater experiments on humans. Where Iron Guardist war criminal Viorel Trifa enjoyed Nazi protection and hospitality after the failed coup he had instigated in Bucharest.

On January 19, 1946, American soldiers ordered 399 Soviet POWs imprisoned in Dachau to climb into trucks parked inside the camp. Like their fellow Vlasovites at Fort Dix, the Soviets refused. Baffled and confused, the guards marched the men back into the barracks and waited for further orders.

Two days later, a reinforcement of five hundred soldiers, mostly Americans, arrived at Dachau. Once again they ordered the POWs out of the barracks. Once again the POWs refused. In a replay of Fort Dix, soldiers lobbed tear gas grenades into the building, stormed the barracks in gas masks, and drove the men into the prison yard, where many stood naked and shivering in protest. Others, suffering from self-inflicted razor cuts and stab wounds, fell bleeding into the snow.

"The scene inside [the barracks] was one of human carnage," an observer later reported. Men dangling from rafters in the throes of death, two disemboweled men, a man who had smashed his head through a window pane and ran his neck over the sharp edge. Men begging to be shot.

All in all, thirty-one Soviet POWs had attempted suicide. Eleven succeeded. Twenty were hospitalized with deep gashes, and many suffered cracked skulls. A soldier who cut the men down from the gallows observed: "It just wasn't human."

U.S. soldiers herded the remaining 368 Soviet POWs into a train waiting on the tracks. The convoy was destined for a holding pen in Plattling, Bavaria, near the Czech border. There the Dachau POWs would join the rest of the tattered Vlasovites (about sixteen hundred) still left in Germany. In spite of a "shoot to kill" order, six men escaped on the way to Plattling, which was the subject of the brief U.S. Army Signal Corps film that Demjanjuk's defense had tried and failed to get entered into evidence at his deportation hearing.

In the predawn darkness on February 24, 1946, while the Soviet POWs were still asleep, a ghostlike column of U.S. tanks, leading a contingent of soldiers wearing rubber-soled shoes and armed with guns and riot clubs, crept down the road to the Plattling camp.

A whistle shrieked. Floodlights switched on. U.S. soldiers broke into the barracks. They beat and dragged the POWs into the prison yard, some clothed only in underwear. Soldiers searched them, tossing whatever they found into the snow and mud—watches, razor blades, crusts of bread, pencils. Then they ordered the POWs to lie facedown in trucks. If a prisoner dared to move, soldiers beat him with clubs.

Armored reconnaissance cars accompanied the convoy from the camp to the Plattling railroad station, where a chain of cattle cars stood empty. Once loaded and under heavy U.S. guard, the train took the POWs to a wooded rendezvous point just across the border in Soviet-occupied Czechoslovakia, where they were handed over to Soviet soldiers. The Americans left their cargo standing in groups along the tracks, half-naked in the February morning. Dangling from tree branches behind them were hundreds of bodies, the remains of previous batches of POWs executed by the Soviets.

"What happened at Plattling," one historian wrote, "was repeated in almost every other camp. There was no reason and no mercy."

An American artillery officer in the 102nd Infantry Division described his role in the massive repatriation operation. "For about two weeks day and night," he wrote in a letter, "I led about seventeen trucks on shuttle service all over Germany and France on this mission [of rounding up Soviet POWs for repatriation]. There were thousands of other trucks doing the same."

The fate of the POWs captured in German uniforms or liberated from work camps was dire. Most officers were executed, some on the spot by angry Red Army soldiers. Since Stalin badly needed workers to rebuild Russia, the rest were sentenced to between fifteen and twenty-five years of hard labor in factories, construction sites, and gulags. The stiffer sentences went to those who had resisted repatriation. Most died before Nikita Khrushchev's amnesty ten years later.

• • •

If the fate of the Soviet POWs was tragic, what can be said about the 1.5 million Soviet civilians whom the Germans uprooted from their homes and forced to work for the Reich in the West? Now they languished in American and British POW camps throughout Europe, their future uncertain. Under the terms of the Yalta agreement, they too had to be forcibly repatriated if they resisted. Their only hope was luck and compassion.

Some got lucky. Few found compassion.

The Soviets mounted a massive propaganda campaign aimed at convincing its citizens to return home voluntarily. Leaflets, pamphlets, newspaper articles, films. Promises of warm welcomes. Old homes returned. Good jobs. Education opportunities. Above all, the comforting love of mother Russia. The campaign worked. Thousands streamed east to transfer points, mostly on foot, sometimes in trucks or carts or by ferry. The elderly and sick, women and children, mothers pushing baby carriages. They carried the tatters of their lives in boxes, suitcases, and canvas bags.

Mandolins, accordions, and folk singers waited for them at the transfer points. There were bright garlands, pictures of a beaming Joseph Stalin, and huge streamers bearing slogans like "Long live the Motherland" affixed to waiting railcars pointing east. It was all staged to keep the thousands calm and to provide footage for reporters from the West.

Most returning civilians entered the Soviet Union smiling. Some were truly happy to be going home, eager to rejoin what was left of their families. Others returned with frozen smiles, the only possible response to being abandoned and betrayed by both the Americans and the British to the terror of a vindictive regime.

All were duped.

There were no cushy jobs waiting. Only hard menial work without the possibility of promotion. There were no open classroom doors, no return to ancestral homes. Only stigma and isolation on the fringes of Soviet society, where they could not infect "good Russians" with poison from the West.

As historian Mark Elliott concluded in his aptly titled book, *Pawns of Yalta*: "The toll of human destruction from Russia's boundless vindictiveness toward returners must encompass not only those killed outright and those who languished or perished in camps. It must also encompass the remainder of returner-pariahs, crippled physically and spiritually by malevolent, security-obsessed figures ensconced behind the Kremlin's ornate facade."

Not all Soviet civilians returned. Some hid. Many lied on visa applications, saying they were born in Poland. Some attacked the Soviet repatriation teams who had the right to visit the DP camps under the terms of the Yalta agreement. A DP mob killed at least one. Some fought U.S. military police with sticks, stones, and fists. Whole groups refused to get into trucks. Two examples illustrate their despair.

. . .

On July 12, 1945, U.S. military police broke into a makeshift DP church, a former gymnasium, in Kempten, Bavaria. Huddled around the altar seeking sanctuary were four hundred Soviet civilians, weeping and begging for mercy. The American soldiers rushed at them with clubs, knocking some senseless, dragging the rest outside praying and screaming. The soldiers left behind smashed icons, torn sacred vestments, and pools of blood.

A team of Soviet soldiers was waiting outside the church to take them home. The Soviets smiled in amusement at the brutal scene—Americans beating helpless people about to be deported east, like the SS and Gestapo rounding up Jews for the extermination camps. The Soviets loaded the group into trucks and drove them to a nearby train station, where they spent the night. Some managed to escape before morning. The rest left for the Soviet Union the next day.

. . .

On the morning of June 1, 1945, several thousand Cossack civilians—mostly old men, women, and children—stood in frightened silence outside their transit-camp barracks near Lienz, Austria, a sleepy picture-postcard village in a mountain valley. Even the babies didn't cry. They had good reason to be scared. Surrounded by British tanks, they were about to be pushed across a wooden bridge spanning the Draga River into Soviet-occupied Yugoslavia. From there, Red Army soldiers would escort them home to the Soviet Union.

A little to the east, closer to the Draga, the British were rounding up several thousand Cossack fighters whose families were waiting back at the Lienz camp. The Cossack soldiers were part of the 25th SS Cavalry Corps, a bitterly anticommunist force—forty to fifty thousand strong—made up of former POWs, Red Army defectors, and civilian volunteers from Cossack communities across Eastern Europe.

The Cossacks had begun collaborating with Germany as soon as it invaded the Soviet Union in 1941, naïvely hoping, like the Ukrainians, to topple Stalin and establish an independent state. Given the Cossacks' historical reputation as fierce fighters, the Germans used them mainly to hunt partisans in the mountains of Eastern Europe.

The 25th Cavalry had surrendered to the British several weeks before that June morning believing that they could help the Allies fight communism in the new Cold War. The British detained them and their families, who had fled the Soviet Union with them, as well as other civilian refugees in transit camps in Austria and Italy. The Lienz compound was one of the largest. Like the Americans, the British promised the Cossacks that they would not be forcibly repatriated to the Soviet Union.

Like the Americans, the British lied.

All during the night of May 31 and well into the early morning hours of June 1, priests in the Lienz transit camp had heard the confessions of those who wanted to make peace with their God before the British or the Soviets murdered them. Hundreds begged God's forgiveness for the terrible sin they were about to commit. Standing in that frightened, silent crowd was Eugenia Borisovna Polskaya, a former Cossack refugee camp nurse and a journalist who would later describe what she witnessed on that spring morning in a picturesque Alpine valley.

As they stood waiting, the crowd heard gunshots up ahead, near the Draga. Older children climbed on the shoulders of adults to look east, toward the wooden bridge and Yugoslavia on the other side. They called out what they saw: British soldiers throwing unarmed 25th Cavalry Cossack soldiers into trucks, beating them with iron clubs, shooting those who fought back with their fists, men trying to run across fields to safety, more gunshots, dead bodies strewn in the fields, mounted Cossack cavalrymen streaming across the bridge.

Soon the British tanks began to push the Cossack civilians gathered in the camp square toward the river. Priests led them in song, as if the combined sound of their voices raised in a last hopeful prayer would soften the hearts of the British soldiers, who seemed to be everywhere. As they pushed forward, the tanks crushed makeshift pulpit-altars erected in the square, grinding icons into the dirt. Soldiers beat the heads of resisters and laggards with riot clubs.

"The soldiers scurried," Polskaya wrote, "taking away dead bodies on stretchers. [They] were like wolves: they caught, caught, caught—and beat."

As she got closer to the bridge, Polskaya saw men and women ahead of her pulling off their boots and leaping into the water. "Oh, my god, the river was full of splashes, rising hands, and heads, and bodies swirling in whirlpools," she wrote. "They were dragged down stream. . . . Women jumping down with their children, having tied themselves [together] with horse reins."

A medical doctor strapped her child to her body, wrote another survivor, and injected it, along with her mother, sister, and herself, with morphine. They all leaped from the bridge to "freedom" below.

On the Yugoslavian side of the river, along the edge of the forest, Cossack cavalrymen were hanging from trees by bridle reins, some still twitching in the last throes of suicide. Their riderless horses raced through the woods neighing, spooked by the cries and screams, the gunshots, the wailed prayers, and the smell of fear and death. British soldiers were cutting down the bodies.

Polskaya was lucky. She survived the trip back to the Soviet Union in a boxcar and was sentenced to only six years in prison for resisting repatriation.

• • •

The United States backed out of forced repatriation just as it had backed in. By November 1945—nine short months after America, Great Britain, and France had signed repatriation agreements—2 million out of 2.25 million Soviet citizens in the West had been repatriated. Because of bloody roundups like the one in Kempten, Bavaria, General Eisenhower, who had once supported forced repatriation, banned the practice in all areas under his command until Washington could review its policy. Military historians now doubt that he had the authority to make that decision.

A month later, in December 1945, Washington forbade the use of force in repatriating civilians who had not collaborated with the enemy. But it still sanctioned force in returning Soviet POWs. Other than the one civilian exemption, there was no decree, presidential or otherwise, formally ending forced repatriation. By then, of course, except for about 250,000 hard-core resisters who managed to escape the Soviet dragnet by luck, cunning, and deception, there was no one left to repatriate.

The last Soviet repatriation team left Germany for Moscow in March 1949, when it was clear that they couldn't persuade the remaining hard core to go home and that the United States would never hand them over. Those left behind in the West were a small price to pay. With the help of America, Great Britain, and France, the Soviets had succeeded beyond their wildest dreams. They had repatriated *ninety percent* of the Soviet civilians and former Red Army POWs who ended up in the West after the war.

Also they left behind a legacy of fear. Would Soviet agents hunt down and kidnap or murder those Soviet civilians and former POWs who managed to elude the Americans and the British?

For years after it forced the last Soviet citizen to return to the communist Soviet Union, the United States denied it had ever sanctioned force. "To force those people to go back to a life of terror and persecution," President Eisenhower proclaimed in a speech in May 1953, "is something that would violate every moral standard by which America lives. Therefore, it would be unacceptable in the American code, and it cannot be done."

Eisenhower's newfound sense of morality and fair play came nine years too late.

In 1977, a U.S. Army veteran who had been ordered to forcibly repatriate POWs during those baffling and hectic nine months in 1945 was still troubled. He asked a question President Eisenhower had artfully dodged.

"Who's going to have to answer for all this suffering?"

If Soviet POWs suffered, so did American soldiers. Compliance with the dictates of the Yalta agreement took its toll on those men who, like the 102nd artillery officer, were ordered to do the dirty work. Some bent the rules. Others disobeyed orders at the risk of court-martial. Some helped POWs escape. Others looked the other way as POWs ran into the woods. On one occasion, twenty-one of the twenty-five soldiers assigned to deliver POWs to the Soviets reported sick.

Long after the war, U.S. veterans were still suffering from post-traumatic stress nightmares, anxieties, and even nervous breakdowns. "My part in the Plattling operation," social activist William Sloane Coffin wrote in his memoir, "left me with a burden of guilt I am sure to carry for the rest of my life."

Brigadier General Frank L. Howley echoed Coffin's feeling. "The cries of these men, their attempt to escape, even kill themselves," he wrote, "still plague my memory."

• • •

The historical facts of forced repatriation impinge directly on the deportation hearing of John Demjanjuk, one of the hard core who managed to hide from the Soviets.

Did President Truman issue a presidential decree ending forced repatriation in 1948, as the government argued in both the denaturalization trial and the deportation hearing of Demjanjuk?

No.

Were displaced persons still afraid of forced repatriation as late as 1950, as Demjanjuk and his witnesses, Edward O'Connor, Michael Pap, and Jerome Brentar, argued?

Yes. The Soviets kidnapped and assassinated former citizens well into the 1970s.

Did Soviet citizens routinely lie about their country of origin to avoid forced repatriation?

Yes.

Did refugee agency employees routinely advise their clients to lie about their country of origin to avoid forced repatriation?

Yes.

Were eight out of ten POWs who returned to the Soviet Union, willingly or unwillingly, executed, as Demjanjuk argued?

No. For the most part, just officers and some Trawniki men were executed. Others like Danilchenko were sentenced to hard labor in Siberia.

CHAPTER THIRTY-SIX

A House Built on Sand

OSI attorney Bruce Einhorn couldn't wait to flay Jerome Brentar under cross-examination. By this time, the government knew that the Cleveland travel agent and Demjanjuk financial supporter was a Holocaust denier.

"Mr. Brentar," he began, "you don't consider yourself, do you, an expert on post-World War Two repatriation?"

"I don't want to be an expert."

"But do you *consider yourself* an expert?"

"Well, I know there was repatriation."

"Mr. Brentar, do you consider yourself an expert on the subject?"

"Expert in what capacity? I know that it happened."

"Did you do *firsthand* scholarly research on the subject?"

"Well, I read quite a bit about it. I read about the Yalta agreement and the—"

"Mr. Brentar, do you have firsthand knowledge on the subject of repatriation," Einhorn pressed, "or is your knowledge *secondhand*?"

"They didn't sell, or give out ringside seats, to the forceful repatriation."

Judge Angelilli intervened. "Please answer the question," he said. "I don't want arguments."

"No," Brentar admitted. He was not an expert on repatriation.

"Thank you," Einhorn said.

Next, Einhorn read quotations from Brentar's court testimony at

Demjanjuk's denaturalization trial, during which he admitted that he was not an expert on either the IRO or the KGB.

Having established that Brentar wasn't an expert on *any* issue relevant to the deportation hearing, Einhorn tried to prove that Brentar was biased, suggesting that he was both an anti-Semite and a Holocaust denier. Einhorn read a transcript of Brentar's recent trial testimony in another OSI case:

Q: There was mass murder at the concentration camps, wasn't there?
A: Well, this is what some say.
Q: You are not convinced though?
A: Well . . .
Q: You shrugged your shoulders. What does that mean?
A: Well, there were people who were killed, yes.
Q: Was there no mass murder at concentration camps?
A: That is . . .
Q: Open to question?
A: Yes.

Einhorn put the trial transcripts down. "Is that the colloquy, Mr. Brentar?"

"I wasn't there [in Treblinka]," Brentar said in his defense. "Were *you* there?"

"Your Honor, I have to object," O'Connor finally said. "I just want to know what the relevancy is."

"I think interest in *bias* would be a clear, relevant factor in cross-examination," Einhorn parried. "Don't you, sir?"

O'Connor didn't press the objection any further, and Einhorn returned to Brentar.

"With all your world travels on this case," Einhorn asked, "have you gone to Israel to interview any of the *witnesses* in the Demjanjuk case who survived Treblinka, and Iwan Grozny?"

"No, sir."

Next, Einhorn tried to trap Brentar in a deception.

"Is it not a fact, sir," he asked, "that the rules and regulations under which you operated as an IRO officer excluded from . . . eligibility individuals who . . . had participated in Nazi and SS-controlled organizations hostile to Allied forces?"

Einhorn, of course, was referring to Vlasov's Liberation Army, which was dedicated to fighting the Soviet Union, a U.S. ally during the war.

"Well, I would have to check my manual," Brentar said. "I have it at home."

"So you don't know offhand?"

"I could look it up and I can tell you," Brentar said.

"As long as you don't remember, sir, that pretty much answers my question."

Judge Angelilli took over the cross-examination of Brentar from Einhorn, and he didn't tap-dance around the issue. "Do you believe there were people gassed in some chambers in Germany somewhere, or Poland, or one of these places? *Any one of them?*"

"I don't know, Your Honor," Brentar said. "I wish I *could* believe."

"Did it happen or not?"

"People did die in the concentration camps."

"From gassing?"

"Well, I guess it did happen," Brentar said.

"To a few people or to a lot of people?"

"I would say more people died of starvation and typhus and overexertion in work than maybe of gassing."

"I heard you say you were in Dachau," the judge said, recalling earlier testimony.

"Yes, I was."

"You said you don't believe anybody was gassed in Dachau?"

"Because it's proven there were *no gasses* [sic] at Dachau, Your Honor," Brentar said. "They had phony caps—shower caps."

"You don't believe anybody died in Dachau?"

"Not in Germany. There were *no* gas chambers in Germany or Austria," Brentar said.

"Now, you have made an exhaustive study of Treblinka," Angelilli pressed. "Did they gas people at Treblinka?"

"They had gas chambers in Treblinka, yes."

"How many did they kill there?"

O'Connor was so upset at the judge's line of questioning that he interrupted. "Why are you subjecting the witness to these questions?" he demanded.

"I have a duty to find out what this witness believes," Angelilli said, "because he has been accused of bias by the government."

"Now, do you believe *nobody* died there?" Angelilli continued.

"I was *told* that people were gassed in Treblinka."

"Did they tell you how many? Did they say boxcars? Boxcars full of people? What did they say?"

"They said boxcars were brought in to Treblinka," Brentar admitted.

"Did they say anybody ever left there *alive*?"

"That was never discussed."

"Didn't you ask them if it was true people died there and never got out?" Angelilli pressed harder.

"Well, there were people who died there. Yes."

"You didn't have the curiosity to know—to know for sure if they died? I have no further questions," Judge Angelilli said.

• • •

In his re-direct, Mark O'Connor tried to repair the damage inflicted by Einhorn and Angelilli. "You want the *whole* story?" O'Connor asked.

"Right. And this is the way the Holocaust should be presented to the world," Brentar said. "And [not] just saying we Jews were the victims. *Everybody* was a victim."

"You are not biased against the Jewish people?"

"Absolutely not. I helped when . . . the Jews came with these phony documents [after the war]. I did not reject *one person*, because I knew they suffered."

O'Connor offered into evidence a book about Treblinka written by Jean-François Steiner. The book described how Ivan the Terrible was killed during the August 1943 uprising at the camp. If Ivan the Terrible was already dead, how could Demjanjuk be Iwan Grozny? In anticipation of Brentar's testimony, OSI attorney Michael Wolf had interviewed Steiner by phone before the hearing. Wolf told the court that Steiner had admitted to him that the story of Iwan Grozny's death during the insurrection was fiction. Steiner then went on to say that he did not have any information or evidence that the real Ivan the Terrible was dead. He agreed to sign a sworn affidavit to that effect.

O'Connor next called for the videotaped testimony of Rudolf Reiss to be presented to the court.

• • •

O'Connor offered Reiss, a former Waffen SS sergeant and a Trawniki administrator, as an expert on the structure of the German army, conditions during World War II, and the administrative structure of Trawniki. O'Connor's co-counsel John Gill had questioned Reiss under oath in Hamburg, where he lived.

The court watched Reiss claim in broken English that he had never volunteered to serve in the Waffen SS. He was conscripted, entered the corps as a private, worked his way up to *Unterscharführer* (sergeant), then went to officers' training school. After he was badly wounded on the Russian front, the SS sent him to Trawniki, where he joined Ernst Teufel, who had also been seriously injured in battle. Like Teufel, Reiss served at Trawniki while Demjanjuk allegedly trained there.

Trawniki had three supply administrations—one for cash, one for clothes and weapons, and one for food. Teufel worked for the clothes and weapons administration. Reiss was a cashier in the paymaster's office along with Heinrich Schaefer, who had testified for the prosecution at Demjanjuk's denaturalization trial.

In his direct examination of Reiss, Gill focused on the Trawniki card in an attempt to prove it was a forgery. Like Heinrich Schaefer before Judge Battisti, Reiss testified that he did not recall a Ukrainian named Iwan Demjanjuk at Trawniki and that he never saw an ID card identical to the one allegedly issued to Demjanjuk.

Gill handed Reiss photographs of the front and back of the card. Reiss studied them under a handheld magnifying glass for a few moments, then testified that one of the seals on the card had a light-to-dark shading. That flaw indicated that something was either blocked out or erased. Furthermore, Reiss said, the inscription on the seal was historically incorrect. And there was a grammatical error in the German word *Fest-nehmen* (arrest or seize). The word should not be hyphenated. And there appeared to be two different capital A's and T's in the printed text on the card, suggesting that two different documents were merged. And there were irregularities with the borders and . . .

Einhorn lost his patience. He objected to Reiss's video testimony because neither O'Connor nor Gill had presented Reiss as a document expert and, therefore, the court had never approved of him as an expert graphologist.

"I'm going to have to support the objection," Judge Angelilli ruled. "This man—not having been qualified to be an expert—can make *no finding* as to what the document says or doesn't say, or whether the printing is correct or incorrect."

Angelilli's decision was a serious blow to the Demjanjuk defense.

Reiss was its only "document expert." Denied expert status, Reiss could add little except to deny that Trawniki ever issued ID cards to its Trawniki men. As a cashier, Reiss testified, he checked "dog tags" for identification before paying salaries, not a card of any kind, once again suggesting that the Trawniki card allegedly issued to Demjanjuk was a forgery.

• • •

Like Gill, Einhorn had gone to Hamburg to cross-examine Reiss. The court now watched that segment of the videotape. Einhorn's strategy was to completely destroy Reiss's credibility as an expert witness and to portray him as biased.

"Are you a professionally trained or licensed document examiner?" Einhorn asked.

"No."

"Have you done any postgraduate work in history?"

"I did not study history at a university," Reiss said.

"Are you a professional printer?"

"No."

"Do you read or speak Russian fluently?" Einhorn asked.

"No."

"Ukrainian?"

"No."

Einhorn pointed to the two photos of the card. "Would your opinion [of the card] change," he asked, "if you knew that a West German historian and an American document examiner had reviewed these copies, and the originals, and determined them to be authentic?"

"No."

Einhorn then got Reiss to admit that he had been a member of a Death's Head (Totenkopf) unit of the Waffen SS, whose insignia was a skull superimposed on crossbones. The Order of the Death's Head was responsible for the administration of the death camps and its members had been defined as inimical to the United States.

"During your participation in the German invasion of the Soviet Union, isn't it true that SS Einsatzkommandos followed your unit into the Soviet Union and engaged in the wholesale killing of unarmed Jews?" Einhorn asked.

"I don't know whether that actually happened," Reiss said.

"Did you pass through a town [in Latvia] called Daugavpils?"

"We went through the city to get to the front."

"Then you are aware, are you not, that the SS executed en masse the unarmed Jews of that city?"

"I don't know that," Reiss said.

"Do you know that in the official report of an SS Brigadefuehrer [brigadier general] [Jürgen] Stroop, it was reported that Trawniki men were used to suppress the Jewish uprising of Warsaw between April and May 1943?"

"I don't know because I have not seen it," Reiss said.

"Do you know this information from any other source?"

"No."

"Are you aware that Trawniki men guarded prisoners—people, human beings—in the work camp of Trawniki?"

"No."

"Are you aware that guards . . . trained at Trawniki, were sent to work at the SS death camps of Treblinka, Auschwitz, Sobibor, and Belzec?"

"I know that *Wachmänner* went to these places, but without knowing what they were."

"When you joined the Death's Head organization—the Totenkopf Division—were you given training?"

"Yes, of course."

"Are you aware of the SS training manual [that states] that the German nation, led by the Fuehrer and his SS, would not regard the Jewish danger lightly, nor rest as long as a Jew lived in the world?"

"Never."

After a break in the videotape, Michael Wolf took over the cross-examination.

"Do you know what occurred at the Treblinka camp?" Wolf asked.

"Later, I heard of it."

"How much later?"

"After the end of the war," Reiss said.

"Is it true that Trawniki men were assigned to work at the Treblinka camp?"

"Yes."

"Did you ever hear who worked as guards at the camp?"

"No."

Like Fedorenko before him, Reiss apparently heard little and saw nothing.

• • •

The defense was having a rotten day. The government had virtually destroyed its witnesses during cross-examination. O'Connor had planned to call three more to the stand to help repair some of the damage. But because none of them knew anything directly or personally about Demjanjuk, their testimony would be hearsay evidence. Judge Angelilli refused to admit them. That left O'Connor little choice. He called John Demjanjuk back to the stand.

CHAPTER THIRTY-SEVEN

The KGB Did It

O'Connor handed Demjanjuk a photograph of the Trawniki card. "Mr. Demjanjuk, would you take a look at this KGB *document*, please."

"I object to the characterization," Einhorn said.

"Overruled."

"In the upper . . . left-hand portion at the top, there is a photograph *alleged* to have been on a card that exists someplace in Russia. Have you ever seen the original card? Ever?"

"Never," Demjanjuk said.

O'Connor continued. "Looking at this KGB evidence—"

"Same objection, Your Honor."

"Mr. O'Connor, please!" Angelilli chided. "I expect that you act professional. You will identify it as 'my exhibit No. 6' hereafter. And to the recorder, I want you to strike, in *every* instance, any remark about Exhibit 6. . . . Now proceed."

"May the record now reflect," O'Connor said, "that the judge has given the *court recorder* the responsibility to decide what is derogatory."

Angelilli let the comment pass. It was obvious that O'Connor was already preparing his appeal.

"Mr. Demjanjuk, is that your picture?" O'Connor asked, as John Martin had asked during the denaturalization trial.

"I don't know," Demjanjuk said, repeating what he had said during the trial.

"Either it is your picture or it's *not* your picture."

"Objection, Your Honor," Einhorn interrupted. "Counsel is abusing his own witness."

"Sustained."

"Could that picture of you have been taken when you were in the Soviet army?" O'Connor continued, suggesting that the KGB had removed an original photo from the Trawniki card and substituted an old army picture of Iwan Demjanjuk.

"I'm not able to tell," Demjanjuk said. The man on the card had hair. The Red Army shaved the heads of its recruits. "I don't even remember whether a picture *was* taken at the time of induction into the Red Army."

"May the record reflect I'm now showing the witness a photo album that the Russians presented to the respondent's attorney, Mr. Martin, after the denaturalization hearing. . . . Three photographs of individuals in *military* uniforms with caps."

Soviet prosecutors had shown those same three photos to Danilchenko and other former Trawniki men to see if they could identify Demjanjuk. There is no doubt the pictures came from a KGB file.

"Do you recognize any of those three men?" O'Connor asked.

"One is a picture of me. Two are my friends."

"Friends from when?"

"From the time when we all were inducted," Demjanjuk said.

"Where is your picture?"

"In the middle."

"Do you remember when that picture was taken?"

"In 1941. I went to a photographer," Demjanjuk said. "All three of us went together."

"Did your military unit request you to get that photograph?"

"No. We had the pictures taken so that we could send them to our parents."

"Did you send that picture to your parents?"

"Yes. All three of us," Demjanjuk said. "We wrote letters together and we mailed the letters together."

"How many positive prints?"

"More than four."

"Did you at any time turn over to the Soviet army, or any representative of the government . . . any of those photographs?"

"Never."

O'Connor's questions about the chain of events were meant to suggest that the KGB had either rifled through the mail or searched the home of Demjanjuk's mother.

O'Connor next showed Demjanjuk a single photo. It was the same image as the middle picture of him on the triple photo display.

"And who is that?"

"That's me."

"When did you *get* that photograph?"

"My wife . . . brought the picture back to me from my mother."

"Do you have *any idea*, Mr. Demjanjuk, how the Russians got that [same] picture?"

Angelilli cut O'Connor off. "I don't want to hear that. . . . Please continue," the judge said, indicating that he got the point the defense was trying to make and didn't want to waste court time with repetition.

O'Connor showed Demjanjuk a second set of pictures that Martin had received from the Soviets after the denaturalization trial—three older men, each in civilian shirt and tie.

"Do you recognize any of those three men?"

"I can recognize my own picture," Demjanjuk said.

"When was this picture taken?"

"At the time when I needed a picture for American citizenship."

"Were you in the Soviet Union when you applied for American citizenship?"

"I was right here in Cleveland."

"Did you mail a copy of that photograph to the Russians . . . or the KGB?"

"Never."

"How did they get a picture of you from the United States?"

"Objection!" Einhorn said. "Calls for speculation."

"I'm going to let him answer," Angelilli ruled.

"I have no idea," Demjanjuk said.

O'Connor next showed Demjanjuk a third set of photos the Soviets gave Martin—three men wearing Russian clothes.

"Have you ever seen any of those three . . . photographs before?"

"No," Demjanjuk answered. "The middle picture is the same picture that is shown on the [Trawniki card] from the Soviet Union."

"The men . . . on either side of that middle photograph—do you recognize any one of them?"

"No."

"Would you have any idea how—for the judge, please—how the Russians would have gotten *any* of those three pictures?"

"I'm going to object, Your Honor," Einhorn said.

"I'm going to allow the question," Angelilli ruled.

"I don't know anything," Demjanjuk said.

The Soviets had also given Martin copies of two letters Demjanjuk had written in Cyrillic script, one to his mother and the other to his niece living in Ukraine. O'Connor asked Demjanjuk if he knew how the Soviets got copies of those two letters.

"I am aware that these documents came from the Soviet Union, but who made them?" Demjanjuk said in complete frustration. "I'm amazed that the court does not allow the use of the expression *KGB* when we're all aware that it's . . . the KGB who is behind making those documents."

Next, O'Connor showed Demjanjuk an enlarged photo of the Trawniki card.

"There is writing on the left-hand portion of this photographic copy," O'Connor said. "Would you look at this writing and indicate whether that's in Cyrillic characters?"

O'Connor was referring to three letters of the alphabet written on the card in purple ink.

"Cyrillic," Demjanjuk said.

"In the Russian language?"

"Yes."

"I'm pointing now to three Cyrillic letters. Can you tell me what those letters are?"

"MVD," Demjanjuk said.

"Do you have any idea . . . what those three letters stand for?"

"Objection, Your Honor," Einhorn said. "I don't see the relevance of this line of inquiry."

"I'm going to let him answer," Angelilli replied.

"This is the same as KGB," Demjanjuk said.

The initials MVD stand for the Ministry of Internal Affairs, a forerunner of the KGB, which was created in 1954.

"Is that Cyrillic writing in the center of this photograph?" O'Connor continued.

"Yes."

"Can you read what that word is?"

"'Demjanjuk.'"

"Is that your signature?"

"No."

One of the government's charges against Demjanjuk was that he was a member of Vlasov's army recruited to fight against the Soviet army. The Soviets were U.S. allies at the time. O'Connor wanted to establish that even though Demjanjuk was in Vlasov's army, he never fought the Russians.

"At the time you were in Oelberg [Heuberg], were you ever given a gun?" O'Connor asked.

"Twice," Demjanjuk said.

Demjanjuk testified at the denaturalization trial that he was never issued a weapon at Heuberg.

"Did they ever give you ammunition for the gun?"

"Yes."

"Did they indicate to you that you were going to get orders to go into battle?"

"Yes."

"Do you know who you were going to be fighting against?"

"The Russians," Demjanjuk said.

"Did they ever tell you that you were going to be fighting the Americans or the British?"

"Only against the Russians."

"Did you ever fire the weapon?"

"No, never."

• • •

Finally, O'Connor called Demjanjuk's son, John Jr., to the stand. The job of the eighteen-year-old college student was to argue hardship for himself and his mother if his father were deported to the Soviet Union.

"I know my father is an innocent man, an innocent victim of the KGB," John Jr. began. "There is no other alternative [but] to continue our support. . . . If my father goes, I go. . . . I can't just sit down, and let them take him away, and forget about it. . . . I am an anti-communist. . . my mother is an anti-communist. And I don't trust the Russians. And I think that's reason enough to consider it a hardship for me to go to the Soviet Union."

The defense rested.

Once again, the life of John Demjanjuk was in the hands of a single American judge. Demjanjuk's plea for asylum posed a tough question for

Judge Angelilli, one that invited judicial bias. To the court, Demjanjuk was Ivan the Terrible as determined by Judge Battisti and upheld by the Sixth Circuit Court of Appeals. Assuming that Demjanjuk's argument for asylum was cogent and persuasive, would Judge Angelilli offer the protection of the United States to a man whom the world considered inhumane and evil? Or would he conclude that John Demjanjuk must be deported to the Soviet Union to face possible criminal charges and possible execution if found guilty?

. . .

Demjanjuk had rolled the dice on asylum. They came up snake eyes. In his May 1984 decision, Judge Adolph Angelilli delivered fifteen pages of bad news to John Demjanjuk and his family. The entire deportation hearing, Angelilli began his ruling, centered around two interlocking questions. Is John Demjanjuk deportable? And if so, should the court grant him asylum?

Like Judge Battisti, Angelilli found the defense of John Demjanjuk to be a nondefense. "The Court considers that the crucial issues in these proceedings," he wrote, "are the respondent's behavior and activity . . . between 1941 and 1952 before he entered the United States. *None* of the witnesses was able to address those issues [or] could testify that they knew the respondent during the crucial years mentioned. . . . *None* of the witnesses satisfied this Court that they had anything to offer."

On the other hand, Angelilli wrote, the evidence of record—the denaturalization trial and appeals court records—"satisfies this court that the respondent is deportable by evidence that is clear, convincing, and unequivocal."

As if that weren't bad enough, Angelilli did not find John Demjanjuk's testimony to be convincing even in the best light. Demjanjuk had admitted that he had served in Vlasov's army, an organization defined as inimical to the United States. He had also conceded that he lied in his visa application about where he had been during the war years, and that he had received and subsequently removed the blood-type tattoo from his left arm.

Angelilli went on to deny Demjanjuk relief as an asylee under the Refugee Act of 1980 because he had failed to prove that the Soviets treated *all POWs* as deserters, or that those who were found to be deserters had *all* been executed.

Angelilli concluded: "It is ... ordered that the respondent's application for asylum . . . be and is hereby denied. It is further ordered that the application for suspension of deportation . . . be and is hereby denied."

As harsh as the rulings were, Angelilli offered John Demjanjuk a kind and merciful—some would argue too kind and too merciful—way out of the United States. He ruled: "It is further ordered that in lieu of an order of deportation respondent be granted *voluntary departure* without expense to the Government on or before 30 days from the date of this decision or any extension as may be granted by the Immigration and Naturalization Service. [Otherwise] respondent shall be deported from the United States to the Union of Soviet Socialist Republics (Russia)."

The choice to leave the United States voluntarily was a realistic one. Canada had accepted other alleged former Nazi collaborators who had been ordered or were about to be ordered to leave America. More likely than not, Canada would have accepted Demjanjuk as well. But he chose not to leave the country voluntarily.

Before the United States could send him back to the Soviet Union, the State of Israel requested his extradition to stand trial there as Ivan the Terrible of Treblinka. On January 27, 1986, nine years after OSI filed its initial complaint against him, John Demjanjuk was escorted in handcuffs by U.S. marshals from a federal penitentiary in Springfield, Missouri, where he had been waiting for the outcome of his last failed appeal, to JFK International Airport in New York and onto El Al flight 004 to Tel Aviv.

Like the Soviet Union, Israel had the death penalty.

Part Three: Epilogue

John Loftus blew a whistle on *60 Minutes*. In "The Nazi Connection," a May 1982 segment of the CBS News show, Loftus, a former OSI prosecutor who had never prosecuted a Nazi case, accused the State Department of smuggling more than three hundred Belorussian Nazi collaborators into the United States, helping them become U.S. citizens, using them as spies, training them as guerilla fighters, and hiring them as propagandists for CIA front organizations like Radio Free Europe and Radio Liberation, which became Radio Liberty in 1956.

The group included the entire Nazi puppet government of Belorussia (modern Belarus), Loftus told *60 Minutes*, from its president to its chiefs of police. Loftus went on to accuse the U.S. government of hiding sensitive Nazi files from Congress, GAO investigators, INS, and the courts. He told *60 Minutes* that he had found the missing files buried in U.S. Army vaults and that many had tabs that said, "Do not disclose to GAO unless authorized."

Loftus accused the Justice Department of ordering the tabs.

The *60 Minutes* story made headlines across the country and Washington was swift to react. Loftus's former boss, Allan Ryan, wrote a letter to CBS assuring the nation that the Justice Department was continuing its investigation of alleged Belorussian Nazi collaborators and that charges would be brought against them, if warranted. Two weeks after its original broadcast, *60 Minutes* aired excerpts from Ryan's letter in which he called Loftus's allegation irresponsible.

"Mr. Loftus persistently made such claims while he was employed by this office," Ryan wrote, "but he was unable to document them satisfactorily and eventually left the office. The investigation has continued quite thoroughly without him."

An outraged House Judiciary Committee, which reviewed some of Loftus's classified documents, which he had copied illegally, asked the GAO to have a second look at America's use and protection of former Nazi collaborators. Once again, the committee posed a carefully worded question to the GAO: Were there any government programs to help Nazi war criminals and Nazi collaborators emigrate to the United States and to conceal their backgrounds? Three years later, in 1985, the GAO issued its second report.

After stating that the FBI and the CIA had delivered all the files it had asked for, the GAO said that it found no specific programs to help former Nazis and Nazi collaborators emigrate to the United States other than the two already known—Operation Paperclip, which brought nearly one thousand German and Austrian scientists to America, some of whom may have been members of the Nazi Party and lesser war criminals; and the CIA program (established under Section Eight of the CIA Act of 1949) to bring to America each year up to one hundred former Nazis and Nazi collaborators—war criminals or not—as long as they were of either intelligence or scientific value.

For a second time, the FBI and the CIA had duped the GAO, according to Loftus. They hid incriminating files on the 114 alleged Nazi collaborators whom the GAO had singled out by name for scrutiny. The resulting GAO report was little more than a tease. Because of its tiny sample, GAO said, it could not determine the scope of American use and protection of former Nazis and Nazi collaborators. Neither could it extrapolate the number of war criminals involved. Then, after praising the government agencies for delivering the files it had requested, the GAO covered itself by saying that "intelligence agencies often assigned projects with innocuous names which do not reflect the projects' purposes and, therefore, GAO cannot assure that it requested *all* relevant project files."

Among the relevant project files the GAO didn't get were those with innocent-sounding names like Aerodynamic, Bloodstone, Circle, Hagberry, Headache, Odeum, Ohio, QRPlumb, Redcap, Redsox, Rusty, Tobacco, and Zipper, to name a few.

Although the GAO went on to summarize in some detail twelve cases of American use and support of former Nazis and Nazi collaborators, it did not identify the twelve by name.* Liberal congressmen like Barney Frank of Massachusetts were more than miffed. Calling the GAO report "totally inadequate," Frank went on to say during a congressional hearing on the report, "I have never been more disappointed in a GAO work than I am today." And former congresswoman Elizabeth Holtzman was characteristically blunt: "The action of U.S. intelligence agencies and officers documented in the GAO report—working with suspected war criminals and mass murderers, following a morally bankrupt policy, and deliberately deceiving other government agencies—took place without public disclosure."

John Loftus had created a public relations nightmare, and he quickly became a Washington pariah.

• • •

For eighteen months, while Loftus was still at OSI, he had sifted through reports about Belorussia and Belorussians, hunting for who, what, when, where, why, how, and how many. Some of the documents he found were written in Cyrillic Russian and had never been translated. Most were stored in underground vaults like the ones he found in the U.S. archives complex in Suitland, Maryland, just outside Washington. Each vault was crammed floor to ceiling with classified files.

"No one had the faintest idea what's down there," Loftus would later write.

The documents in the vaults would remain secret and unorganized until President Obama's 2009 directive to streamline the declassification process of 400 million pages. As a result, government agencies have sent—and continue to send—millions of secret and top-secret pages to the National Archives for declassification review.

Allan Ryan had already replaced Walter Rockler as OSI director when Loftus handed in the first draft of the "Belarus Project"—a report containing a list of forty suspected Belorussian Nazi collaborators living in the United States. Ryan greeted it with a great deal of enthusiasm and

---

* In response to an FOIA request by the author for the names of the twelve former Nazis and Nazi collaborators described in its report, the GAO responded that the names were no longer available. It said they were part of the accompanying its report and, by internal regulation, all documentation is destroyed after five years. An FOIA request for a copy of Loftus's first Belarus report is still pending.

told Attorney General Benjamin Civiletti that the report was the "single most important matter in which OSI was engaged." Civiletti, who had successfully argued the government's Supreme Court appeal against Feodor Fedorenko, authorized an expansion of the Belarus investigation. More researchers were added.

The deeper Loftus dug, the more he discovered that files were missing, deliberately misplaced, or sanitized by a secret Special Operations Division (SOD) stationed at the U.S. intelligence center in Fort Meade, Maryland, about twenty miles from Washington. Based on what he learned from interviews with SOD staff, Loftus claimed that Nazi files were hidden from the GAO and OSI investigators on orders from the Justice Department itself. One example was a note attached to a U.S. Army intelligence file on Emanuel Jasiuk, a Belorussian Nazi collaborator whom the CIA had recruited after the war. It read: "Defense material NOT cleared for review by GAO. DO NOT disclose to GAO until notified to do so. . . . General Counsel, Washington, D.C."

If such orders were issued, *who* at Justice had issued them, and *why?* Loftus asked Ryan and Ryan's superior, Richard Sullivan, for permission to follow the trail. Permission was denied.

There was more to the decision to limit the Belarus investigation than met the eye. In the course of his research, Loftus had stumbled on a top-secret CIA program involving assassins, saboteurs, guerillas, and propagandists, most of whom were former Nazi collaborators. The program was aimed at Belarus's next-door neighbor, Ukraine, and its discovery was nitro in a jar. When Loftus first learned of it in 1980, the Ukrainian operation was still alive and thriving with New York City as its base. It was the biggest and most successful CIA espionage program of the entire Cold War. The departments of State and Justice and the CIA guarded the identity of its chief Ukrainian asset like an atomic secret.

Loftus learned the asset's real name.

Based on his continuing research, Loftus expanded his original list of confirmed and suspected Belorussian Nazi collaborators. He concluded that they were part of an ambitious State Department plan to recruit and illegally sneak into America the potential leaders of future independent states and to use them as domestic and international Cold War operatives.

Loftus learned that many of the Belorussians he was looking for were either living in South River, New Jersey, or buried in the cemetery of South River's St. Euphrosynia Orthodox Church. Loftus and several coworkers, accompanied by a New Jersey state trooper for protection, visited the small graveyard one night in 1981. The cemetery's iron gate was chained and locked. They climbed over the wall.

Flashlight in hand, Loftus walked through rows of tombstones, jotting down the names engraved on them. He would later compare them to the names on his master list. Dominating the graveyard was a stone pillar atop a mound. Etched on its base were the words GLORY TO THOSE WHO FOUGHT FOR THE FREEDOM AND INDEPENDENCE OF BYELORUSSIA. Affixed to the column was a picture of Radaslau Astrouski (Polish spelling Radoslaw Ostrowsky), the former president of Belorussia's Nazi puppet government, former puppet mayor of Minsk, an independence guerilla fighter, a national hero, and one of the highest-ranking known Nazi collaborators to hit the shores of America.

Ostrowsky had been living in South River and working for the State Department since 1956, according to Loftus. He died in 1979, the year OSI was established. Surrounding Ostrowsky's final resting place behind the church where he had worshipped for more than twenty years, as if to pay homage and keep him company, were the graves of the Nazi collaborators who had been under his command as the puppet president of Belorussia.

They were "mayors, governors, and other officials," Loftus later wrote, "men who had ruled the Nazi puppet state of Byelorussia; who had guided the Einsatzgruppen—the mobile killing squads—across a good part of Eastern Europe; who had assisted in the mass murder of thousands of Jews."

The 1948 Displaced Persons Act defined "quislings"—those who served as puppets of an occupying enemy force—as Nazi collaborators. As such, they were ineligible for a U.S. visa. In so ruling, the United States was following the lead of the Nuremberg Military Tribunal, which defined as war criminals those who had collaborated with the Nazis by "participating in a common design." The 1952 immigration law, which replaced the Displaced Persons Act of 1948, however, ruled that quislings were eligible for U.S. visas.

. . .

John Loftus made his allegations and spun out his theories in *The Belarus Secret*, a book he wrote after leaving OSI and published in 1982. According to Loftus, Nazi planners screened leaders in the Belorussian government-in-exile living in Western Europe and selected twenty, two-man teams to administer the major cities of Belorussia. Each team member had earned his loyalty stripe by working with an Einsatzgruppe. The Germans appointed Radoslaw Ostrowsky mayor of Minsk and puppet president of Belorussia. As a reward for his collaboration, the SS promised to make him mayor of Moscow one day soon.

Ostrowsky and his fellow Belorussian collaborators were so successful that by the time the German army retreated west in 1944, eight hundred thousand Belorussian Jews—90 percent of the country's Jewish population—had been murdered. The number did not include the thousands of other Jews who were transported to Minsk for execution. Anti-German Belorussians would eventually take credit for saving the lives of approximately eighty thousand Jews who survived the Nazi extermination program by hiding them in barns and forests.

How these Belorussian collaborators ended up living as free men in South River, New Jersey, according to Loftus, is a Cold War tale of State Department, military, CIA, and FBI duplicity, lawbreaking, obstruction of justice, perjury, and cynical disregard for human life. Although the Nazi collaborators entered the United States in a variety of ways, Loftus noted a discernible pattern. To illustrate that pattern, he cited the case of Emanuel Jasiuk.

• • •

The Nazis recruited Belorussian Emanuel Jasiuk, along with Ostrowsky, in Warsaw in June 1941, just a few weeks before Germany invaded the Soviet Union in Operation Barbarossa. They made Jasiuk the mayor of Kletsk, a medium-size town with a large Jewish population near Belorussia's border with Poland. As a Nazi puppet mayor, Jasiuk also had jurisdiction over the territory surrounding Kletsk. His job was twofold. He would provide Einsatzgruppe B with the names of communists, communist sympathizers, and Polish intellectuals and troublemakers for execution. (Once part of Poland, western Belorussia had a large Polish population.) And he would organize the local police to help identify, round up, rob, and murder the Jews in his jurisdiction.

Under Jasiuk's supervision, the Kletsk police uprooted an estimated four thousand Jewish men, women and children and imprisoned them in a ghetto in the center of the town. The police then supervised the digging of a long trench behind a local church within walking distance of the ghetto. When the ditch was completed, Jasiuk ordered his men to march the Jews—men first, followed by women and children—to the trench where German soldiers and Belorussian volunteers shot them. Four thousand in one eight-hour day. Five hundred an hour.

Jasiuk and other Nazi collaborators fled with the German army just before the Soviets reoccupied Kletsk in July 1944, the same month the Red Army liberated Chelm and took possession of Trawniki. Working for the Nazi regime in Berlin, Jasiuk organized the Waffen SS Belarus Brigade, made up of Belorussian volunteers, many of whom were fellow war criminals.

As a gifted organizer with contacts throughout the Belorussian community living in DP camps, Jasiuk was of great potential value to the United States when the war ended in Europe. He could help America solve its daunting espionage problems and realize its "impossible dream" to recruit, train, arm, and unleash against the Soviet Union—when needed—a mighty guerilla army of Eastern Europeans passionate about liberating their home countries. Guerillas would be trained in secret military camps in the United States and West Germany and would be ready and waiting for Washington's call to arms.

Frank Wisner wasted no time. A former State Department employee who had joined the newly created CIA, Wisner immediately set up shop in Germany to recruit potential guerilla army organizers. He hired Emanuel Jasiuk and others to organize and unite the Belorussians in the DP camps, especially former members of the Waffen SS Belarus Brigade. With unrestricted travel papers from the State Department, Jasiuk moved with ease from one camp to another dressed in a U.S. Air Force uniform. He quickly set up a CIA-funded Belorussian spy network, united the old Belarus Brigade, and helped Wisner spirit future national leaders and warriors to America.

After Wisner completed his work in Germany, he returned to Washington, where he became chief of the CIA's new department of clandestine operations. Wisner wanted Jasiuk to continue working for him in the United States, but that posed a problem. As a quisling Nazi collaborator and war criminal, Jasiuk was not eligible at that time for a U.S. visa.

Wisner found an easy fix.

During Jasiuk's expedited visa hearing in Germany, two State Department officials vouched for him and argued that he should be granted a fast-track visa because he was providing invaluable services "of a highly confidential nature." The State Department officials went on to corroborate Jasiuk's fictitious cover story that he had worked as a slave laborer on a farm in Bavaria during the war.

CIC investigators responsible for screening visa applications didn't buy the alibi and dug deeper. They learned that Jasiuk was "the central figure in a Nazi underground railroad" that helped Belorussian war criminals find a home in the United States. When CIC informed the State Department that it was going to arrest Jasiuk, Washington ordered the corps to drop its investigation. It did, but not before leaving an incriminating file behind. John Loftus claimed he had found the file and freely quoted from it.

Jasiuk went to work for Wisner and the CIA in South River, New Jersey, in 1951. He soon became head of the South River Chapter of the Belorussian Central Council, the equivalent of the country's government-in-exile. His credentials, identifying him as an official representative of "the Belorussian Democratic Republic in the United States of America," were signed by Ostrowsky, the former quisling president of Nazi-occupied Belorussia and the then president of the Belorussian government-in-exile.

Jasiuk's job was to continue to recruit Belorussians for the CIA's planned guerilla army and to heal the rift between the two fractious Belorussian communities of South River and Brooklyn. To fund Jasiuk's operations, Wisner laundered money through Radio Free Europe, Radio Liberty/Radio Liberation, and CIA-funded émigré research institutes.

Jasiuk wrote to both Truman and General Eisenhower that he would supply troops to invade the Soviet Union when America was ready to launch an attack. That was music to the ears of J. Edgar Hoover. The FBI chief sent agents to visit Jasiuk, who was then working for the Thomas Electronics Corporation in Passaic, New Jersey. Their mission was not to arrest Jasiuk, but to recruit him into Hoover's ever-growing domestic spy network. In exchange for information, the FBI would label all complaints about Jasiuk being a Nazi collaborator and a war criminal as "false claims," one of several word tricks the FBI used to protect its friends and informants.

• • •

Washington viciously attacked *The Belarus Secret*. Because Loftus had signed a confidentiality agreement as a condition for reviewing classified CIA documents, he had to submit his book to the agency for publication approval. The agency heavily censored the manuscript, Loftus says, cutting any references to the role the Vatican played in smuggling former Nazis out of Europe as well as the names of every Nazi collaborator *still alive*—especially the director of the CIA's top-secret espionage program, QRPlumb.

The CIA took Loftus's frontal assault on its integrity and credibility very seriously. It denied his allegation that the agency either censored parts of *The Belarus Secret* because they contained classified information or that it recommended changes in the text. It also denied that it had hidden files from the GAO and OSI or had allowed any other government agency to do so. The CIA did admit, however, that it had "sanitized" nine of the files Loftus requested.

Suspicious by nature, the CIA didn't trust Loftus, and for good reasons. Midway through his Belarus investigation, the agency noted, Loftus began requesting information on subjects not relevant to OSI's mission, which was to find alleged Nazi collaborators living in the United States, to build cases against them, to charge them with visa fraud, and to expel them. Instead, Loftus was asking for files on subjects like NTS (an anti-communist émigré organization of Russians known as Solidarists), Radio Liberty, and Radio Free Europe, all of which the CIA had funded at one time or another. Furthermore, the agency argued that Loftus's requests were unreasonable. It had 3,500 separate files on RL and RFE *alone*.

The CIA concluded that Loftus was on a fishing expedition in CIA waters, motivated by a "personal agenda." Although it was worried that Loftus might go public and jeopardize some of its ongoing projects, the CIA chose not to attack him publicly.

The Justice Department was equally spooked by what Loftus knew. It threatened him with disbarment if he revealed the name of any living Nazi collaborator, and with prison if he revealed the contents of classified documents. For the record, OSI debunked everything Loftus wrote. In its 2006 draft internal history, *The Office of Special Investigations: Striving for Accountability in the Aftermath of the Holocaust*, OSI devoted an entire chapter to trying to prove that John Loftus's work was distorted and factually incorrect. At the same time, it devoted only one sentence to George Parker, without even mentioning his highly critical doubt memo about the prosecution of John Demjanjuk. Knuckles bared, OSI accused Loftus of sensationalism, faulty research, exaggerated claims, historical errors, and speculative conclusions based on incomplete and inaccurate sources. And OSI implied that Loftus had abused his top-security clearances by collecting data for a book on government time, instead of investigating alleged Belorussian Nazi collaborators still alive in America, not sleeping in a cemetery behind a church in South River, New Jersey.

OSI historian David Marwell, for example, called *The Belarus Secret*, published by Alfred A. Knopf, the worst kind of amateur history. "It is *bad* history because it is poorly written, poorly researched, and poorly documented," he said in a memo to his boss, Allan Ryan. "It is *fraudulent* history because it mangles facts, distorts events, and misrepresents major themes."

In effect, OSI was calling John Loftus either a liar, a conspiracy fruit-cake, a greedy headline chaser, or an incompetent investigative attorney—the very same charges INS had leveled at its investigator Anthony DeVito and its prosecutor Vincent Schiano.

American Jewish Nazi hunter Charles R. Allen Jr. joined in the Loftus-bashing frenzy. A respected author who had written extensively about Nazis in America in the monthly magazine *Jewish Currents*, Allen totally shredded *The Belarus Secret* in a review article, calling Loftus, in effect, both a fraud and a liar.

The Loftus brouhaha was about more than some faulty footnotes and historical errors. Unlike Nazi hunters Simon Wiesenthal, Charles Allen, OSI, and others, Loftus attempted to look beyond the trees in order to see the forest. He didn't ask: Is this particular man or woman a former Nazi collaborator? Instead he asked: Did the United States have a *policy* to recruit Nazi collaborators and bring them to America? If so, who was responsible for the policy? Who was responsible for its implementation? And how widespread was it?

Loftus answered those overlapping questions in *The Belarus Secret* as follows: Yes, there was an open-door policy for Nazi war criminals. The State Department was the major bad guy. And the policy was so broad that it included "nearly all the puppet regimes established by the Third Reich from the Baltic to the Black Sea."

Loftus's conclusions were roundly denounced as either false or unsupported. But the intensity of the brawl over his serious allegations raised two cynical questions. Did Washington go after John Loftus, not because he was wrong, but because it wanted to protect a secret? And was OSI publicly rejecting Loftus's work in the hope that the CIA would not use his exposé, which was based on classified documents, as an excuse not to cooperate in ongoing and future OSI investigations?

• • •

Since the publication of Loftus's decidedly flawed *The Belarus Secret* thirty years ago, the government has declassified millions of pages of secret and top-secret military, White House, CIA, State Department, and FBI documents; historian John Lewis Gaddis published his much-anticipated biography, *George F. Kennan: An American Life*; Belorussian historian Leonid Rein published *The Kings and the Pawns*, a critical analysis of Belorussia's collaboration with the Nazis; World War II historian Timothy Snyder published *The Reconstruction of Nations: Poland, Ukraine, Lithuania, Belarus*; and historical journalist Christopher Simpson published *Blowback*, a groundbreaking book on America's use of former Nazis and Nazi collaborators.

These new documents and books show that what Loftus wrote about Emanuel Jasiuk was accurate. They also shed critical light on Loftus's allegations against the State Department and clarify the lines of responsibility for America's open-door policy for Nazi war criminals. In sum, they prove that Loftus was much more right than wrong.

THE BELORUSSIAN QUISLINGS

Loftus alleged that the Germans prepared for the invasion of Belorussia by recruiting teams of exiled Belorussians to become the backbone of the new Belorussian Nazi puppet government. The allegation is important because it is the foundation for Loftus's specific charge that the United States brought at least three hundred Belorussian quisling war criminals into the country.

Books devoted specifically to the collaboration of Belorussians with their Nazi occupiers during World War II are rare in the West. Historian Leonid Rein's 2011 work, *The Kings and the Pawns*, is a welcome exception. A Belorussian who received his doctorate at the University of Haifa, Rein is a research fellow at the Yad Vashem Holocaust center in Jerusalem. His highly documented, award-winning work supports Lotfus's first Belarus allegation.

According to Rein, Belorussian exiles living in Germany and Poland prepared for the Reich's invasion of the Soviet Union in June 1941. Those living in Berlin formed a group called "The Center," whose members were selected to form the leadership of the quisling government after Operation Barbarossa. At the same time, exiles living in Poland helped German military intelligence establish a saboteur training center outside Warsaw. Shaped into teams of up to fifty men, the Belorussian saboteurs were parachuted behind the Soviet lines with instructions to blow up strategic railroads and bridges in preparation for the German invasion.

Also with the help of Belorussian exiles in Germany and Poland, the leaders of Einsatzgruppe B selected Belorussian volunteers to help their 655 Einsatzkommandos identify, round up, rob, and kill Jews. The Germans called their volunteers "trusted people" (*Vertrauensmänner*, or *V-Leute*).

After the invasion, the Germans formed an estimated thirty thousand, two-men teams (German estimate) and appointed them to the two key positions in local governments throughout Belorussia—mayor and police chief. The teams and their minions made the execution of eight hundred thousand Jews in eighteen months possible. Public support for the genocide was, for the most part, largely irrelevant to the success of the operation.

Belorussian Boris Grushevsky witnessed the brutality of the police in the town of Stolpce: "The policemen were sitting on the top of this pit. They had submachine guns. There were also several Germans. It was the policemen who shot. The Jews were standing in columns in front of the pit. . . . The Jews were made to take off their clothes and approach the pit, a few at a time, and enter it. They lay down and were shot. . . . Some of the Jews were only wounded and tried to get up. Blood was gushing from their wounds."

In screening potential team members, the Germans looked for volunteers who were anticommunist, not Jewish, and preferably not Polish. Administrative skills or experience were not factors. The tasks assigned to the teams were to control the local population, keep peace and order, supply the Germans with food and goods on demand, and help exterminate Jews. As Rein concluded, the quisling mayors and police chiefs played "a prominent role in the persecution of Belorussian Jews—especially their ghettoization—and in the requisition and disposal of murdered Jews' property."

The Germans eventually installed a mostly symbolic national puppet government with a president and cabinet. "The Germans made it clear," Rein wrote, "[that] their duty was solely to help weed out 'the enemies of the state.'"

Loftus had reached a broad, sweeping conclusion about Belorussian collaboration in the Holocaust: that no other country in Eastern Europe matched Belorussia in its willingness to assist the Nazis in exterminating Jews and in the barbarity of its collaborators. Rein agrees with part of Loftus's conclusion. "In most cases," he wrote, "local [Belorussian] policemen participated enthusiastically in the massacres, displaying a measure of cruelty that the Germans themselves often found repulsive." But he rejects the rest of Loftus's conclusion that Belorussia stood out as the worst Holocaust collaborator in Eastern Europe. Rein suggests that Latvia, Estonia, Lithuania, Russia, and Ukraine were just as enthusiastic and cruel as Belorussia in helping Nazi Einsatzgruppen identify, ghettoize, rob, and murder Jews—a charge even more damning than Loftus's.

THE OPEN-DOOR POLICY

The most important allegation Loftus made was that the United States had formally adopted an open-door policy for former Nazi war criminals and that the Department of State was mostly responsible for the policy. Military, State Department, and National Security Council documents declassified since the publication of *The Belarus Secret* prove that indeed there was an open-door policy by virtue of nonexclusion—that is, the U.S government *did not explicitly forbid* its agencies from using Nazi war criminals. The declassified documents spell out in detail who crafted the incremental policy and when. It began with a very long telegram.

In February 1946, less than a year after the war in Europe was over, Washington posed a question to the U.S. embassy in Moscow—what the hell are the Russkies up to? U.S. ambassador Averell Harriman chose George Kennan, a bored and brooding junior foreign service officer with a keen mind, a degree from Princeton, and a flair for writing, to craft an intelligent response to that rather embarrassing question. Kennan was a logical embassy choice. He spoke Russian fluently and, like his father, had traveled to all corners of the country, including Siberia and its gulags. A serious student of Russian history, politics, and literature, Kennan understood the "Russian soul" better than any foreign service officer, including Harriman.

From his sickbed, Kennan dictated an answer to a stenographer in what is known as the Long Telegram, a six-thousand-word cable that suggested—for the first time—a clear and coherent U.S. policy toward the Soviet Union. The Long Telegram also became the first link in a chain of decisions leading to a U.S. open-door policy for former Nazi war criminals and established Kennan as America's top Kremlinologist, ensuring him a primary role in formulating that policy.

After treating Washington to a much-needed lesson on the nature and character of the Russian people, Kennan offered two reasoned and sobering conclusions about how to deal with the Soviet Union. First, there could be "no permanent peaceful coexistence" with the USSR because the Kremlin never compromised by signing treaties and pacts. The Soviets were so insecure that they could only maintain power by ruthlessly destroying rivals. Second, "military intervention [was] . . . sheerest nonsense [and] should be forestalled at all cost."

By eliminating the two options of peaceful coexistence and war, Kennan left Washington with only one choice—containment. The United States, he argued, could ultimately defeat communism if it prevented the cancer from spreading to the non-Soviet nations of Western Europe, and if it developed strategies and programs that fractured the Soviet empire in so many places that it would slowly crumble.

Kennan planted several seeds in the Long Telegram that would bear fruit in the next four years. First, the best way to contain the Soviets was to help rebuild the nations of Western Europe (and Japan) so that they would have the will, strength, and resources to fight and defeat Soviet influences in their homelands. That seed would soon flower into the five-year Marshall Plan.

To *outsmart* the Soviets, the United States must understand Russia and its aims because "there is nothing as dangerous or as terrifying as the unknown." That seed would flower into the hiring of hundreds of Eastern European scholars to help America collect and analyze intelligence about the Soviet Union.

To *defeat* the Soviets, the United States must encourage and support the growth of nationalism in the communist satellite countries until the Soviet Union lost control and collapsed. That seed would flower into covert propaganda and espionage operations aimed at destabilizing the Soviet world.

The State Department considered the 1946 Long Telegram so important that it shared the cable with every high-placed bureaucrat in Washington who could read. Secretary of State George C. Marshall offered Kennan the job of directing State's new and powerful Policy Planning Staff. The PPS mandate was to think long-term, paint large canvases, and write top-secret policy papers for consideration by the National Security Council (NSC) and ultimately by the president.

How could Kennan say no?

"Over the next two years," Kennan's official biographer John Lewis Gaddis observed, "the PPS became the principal source of ideas for the NSC." Papers prepared by PPS were routinely relabeled as NSC documents with few changes. If approved by President Truman—as they were in most cases—they became national policy.

Recognizing that it needed someone with espionage experience to help develop PPS intelligence-related policy papers, the State Department hired Frank Wisner as deputy assistant secretary for occupied countries. Wisner was an interesting choice for the job. Unlike Kennan, he was neither a deep thinker nor a brilliant analyst. During the war, he had gotten his feet wet as an OSS covert operative in Cairo and Amman. From the Middle East, OSS sent him to Bucharest, where he set up a network of spies, code name Hammerhead, that included Nazi collaborator Nicolae Malaxa and other Romanian Iron Guard war criminals.

History is ambivalent about Wisner. To some, he was an espionage rogue elephant; to others, a sincere, dedicated, competent spy, and a good administrator. To still others, he was a gullible dreamer full of contradictions. Charming, warm, funny, and gregarious, he loved to dance, sing, and drink into the wee hours. At the same time he was as secretive and illusive as the spy world he lived in.

As enigmatic as Wisner was, however, friends and critics alike agreed on one thing—his burning intensity and hatred of communism bordered on clinically obsessive. And without doubt, he was one of the most important of the Cold War strategists responsible for opening the U.S. door to former Nazi war criminals.

• • •

Frank Gardiner Wisner was born into privilege in Laurel, Mississippi, a town his family owned, from the local bank to the sawmill that made the Wisners rich. He grew up in a world that was, as one writer put it, "secretive, insular, elitist, and secure in the rectitude of its purposes." Maids dressed him. He had little contact with the outside world. His only playmates were his cousins. He was driven and competitive, traits he learned from playing parlor games with his mother, a woman who hated to lose, even to her son. Sickly as a child, Wisner built up muscles by pumping iron. He never walked. He ran.

Unlike so many of the Cold War warriors and armchair generals he would later hire, Wisner did not attend an Ivy League school. He went to the University of Virginia, which was at the time more like a private institution than a public university. Besides being a driven student, he was such a good athlete that the U.S. Olympic Committee invited him to attend the 1936 Olympic trials as a sprinter and hurdler. His father said no.

After college and law school, Wisner ended up at the Wall Street firm of Carter, Ledyard & Milburn. Life as a corporate attorney was so boring that he joined the navy six months before the Japanese attack on Pearl Harbor. The navy assigned him to a desk shuffling papers. With the help of a former UVa law professor who had contacts in Washington, Wisner got himself transferred to the Office of Strategic Services (OSS), the forerunner of the CIA, which would soon become his home.

With the code name Typhus, Wisner arrived in Soviet-occupied Bucharest in August 1944. Besides spying on the Romanian Communist Party, his job as OSS station chief in the Romanian capital was to negotiate the safe return of eighteen hundred American fliers shot down over that nation's oil fields, which he did to the complete satisfaction of Washington.

In Bucharest Wisner rented a mansion, threw lavish parties for the Romanian elite, and became an informal advisor to King Michael and the queen mother. All the while he fed Washington a steady stream of accurate information, filled with dire warnings about an impending communist takeover. Washington read his communiqués with interest, but did nothing. In January 1945, Wisner watched helplessly as the Soviets rounded up eighty thousand ethnic German men (*Volksdeutsche*), ages seventeen to forty-five, and ethnic German women, ages eighteen to thirty, and forced them into boxcars bound for slow death in the work camps and mines of the Soviet Union. His helplessness soon turned to despair as he saw King Michael driven into exile and his Romanian friends disappear into the night, never to be heard from again. Washington still read his communiqués with interest, and still did nothing.

Unable to watch Romania turn into another communist satellite, Wisner quit OSS in late 1946 in complete disgust and returned to Wall Street. But baptized in the blood of Bucharest, he had become a born-again crusader with a mission to fight the evils of communism. How could he sit in a law office writing briefs while the Soviets were taking over the world?

In the summer of 1947, a year after he returned to Wall Street, Wisner went to work at the State Department. A former client of his law firm got him the job and became his boss. One of the first things Wisner did as deputy assistant secretary was to tour the displaced persons camps in Western Europe. Most DP camp visitors saw a mob of poor, frightened, squalid, and disoriented refugees. Wisner saw seven hundred thousand potential Cold War recruits. As soon as he returned to Washington, he established a study group at the State Department to prepare a policy paper on why and how to mine the mother lode of Eastern European refugees, thousands of whom had military training and experience in guerilla units, Vlasov's army, and Waffen SS battalions.

. . .

Between 1947 and 1950, the newly created National Security Council formulated America's open-door policy for Nazi war criminals based, for the most part, on secret and top-secret policy papers prepared by George Kennan's Policy Planning Staff and by the NSC's interim advisory group—the State–Army–Navy–Air Force Coordinating Committee (SANACC). The chairman of SANACC was the State Department's committee member.

December 1947. Ten months after Kennan's Long Telegram from Moscow, the NSC fired its first salvo in the Cold War. Based on the Long Telegram, it authorized the newly formed CIA "to initiate and conduct . . . covert psychological operations designed to counteract Soviet and Soviet-inspired activities."

March 1948. Three months later, SANACC expanded the NSC's December directive. It proposed that both the NSC and the CIA "promptly begin in Free Europe and Asia a systematic and combined program of screening refugees from the Soviet world" to be used for covert operations. SANACC also recommended the creation of a psychological warfare advisory group within the NSC. Edward O'Connor, who would later testify on John Demjanjuk's behalf at the latter's 1981 denaturalization trial, soon became chairman of the new psychological warfare group.

As a first step in America's psych warfare effort, SANACC recommended that the departments of the Army, Navy, and Air Force should each be authorized to bring into the United States, with visa status, "fifty aliens . . . [and that] the Department of State should be authorized to bring in one hundred." Fifty of State's one hundred were to be deployed at the Voice of America (VOA), which had been transferred to State Department jurisdiction in 1946. SANACC chose "Bloodstone" as a code name for the covert warfare program and recommended that "the word itself be handled as Top Secret."

June 1948. For its second Cold War salvo, the NSC charged the CIA with "conducting espionage and counter espionage operations" outside the United States using Eastern European recruits. Furthermore, the operations should be planned and executed in such a way "that any U.S. government responsibility for them is not evident and that, if uncovered, the U.S. government can plausibly disclaim any responsibility for them."

Significantly, the NSC included the following in its definition of espionage: covert propaganda, economic warfare, sabotage, subversion against hostile states, and assistance to underground resistance movements and anticommunist guerilla and liberation groups.

Also in its June 1948 policy paper, the NSC authorized the CIA to develop clandestine programs in partnership with the military so as to be ready in the event of war with the Soviet Union. To avoid overlap in espionage operations and to ensure at least some accountability, the NSC took Kennan's suggestion and created the Office of Special Projects. A covert activity umbrella organization, its name would soon be changed to the nondescript Office of Policy Coordination (OPC) to disguise its true purpose.

The creation of OPC ignited a spirited and protracted turf war. Ever distrustful of the military establishment, the State Department wanted both control over OPC's covert operations and deniability in case they were revealed. As Kennan saw it, political warfare activity was "an instrument of U.S. policy and [he] hoped to man the controls." Although he favored placing OPC in the CIA for cover, Kennan wanted it to "operate independently," with the State Department pulling the strings. The CIA would have none of it.

In the end, State, Defense, and the CIA reached what would turn out to be an unworkable compromise. OPC would belong to the CIA, whose director would be responsible for ensuring that OPC's covert activities "were consistent with U.S. foreign and military policy." The CIA director would be guided by representatives from the departments of State and Defense. Secretary of State George C. Marshall appointed

Kennan to be the State Department's representative on the OPC panel and Kennan would soon become deeply involved in Project Umpire, an early OPC psych war operation in Germany.

August 1948. The Joint Chiefs of Staff called for the creation of a Guerilla Warfare School and a Guerilla Warfare Corps. Trained by the U.S. Army and the CIA and composed mostly of Eastern Europeans, the corps would conduct covert operations for the CIA with guidance from the military. The original proposal for the guerilla school and corps came from the Department of State.

March 1950. The NSC authorized the FBI and the CIA to work together to exploit the knowledge, experience, and talents of the Eastern European refugees living in the United States and to protect them from retaliation by the Soviets. To avoid future legal challenges in the use of war criminals, the NSC charged the Justice Department with finding ways within and around the law to bring them to America.

Finally, the NSC commissioned the Department of State to appoint OPC's director. It was only fair. OPC was State's baby. At the recommendation of George Kennan, Marshall chose Kennan's Sunday night drinking buddy, Frank Wisner.

None of the declassified documents from 1947–50 that created Cold War policies and strategies prohibit the use of former Nazis and Nazi collaborators in the three broad U.S. covert programs—psychological, political, and guerilla warfare. The closest any document came to addressing the issue is a delicately worded statement in a May 1948 top-secret SANACC report: "In the case of those who are *excludible* under the law, the Attorney General should authorize temporary entry under [his] discretionary authority."

The fact that the NSC and the White House did not exclude former Nazis and Nazi collaborators from its proposed covert programs was an endorsement to use them. There is a legal precedent to support this argument. The U.S. Supreme Court based its 1981 decision in the Feodor Fedorenko case on policy formulation by nonexclusion. The High Court argued in that case that Congress could have stipulated that assistance to the enemy had to be voluntary to warrant exclusion from the United States, but it deliberately chose not to. Therefore, Congress established a policy to exclude both those who voluntarily and involuntarily assisted the enemy. Conversely, the NSC and the White House could have stipulated that former Nazis and Nazi collaborators should be barred from participation in U.S. covert activity programs, but they deliberately chose not to. Therefore, it is logical to conclude that the intention of the NSC and the White House was to include former Nazis and Nazi collaborators in covert programs if they were useful enemies.

The endorsement of using war criminals in U.S. covert operations by nonexclusion should come as no surprise. Military intelligence was already employing them extensively in Europe and would continue to do so until the mid-1950s (see epilogue to part 4). And the two men most responsible for formulating the Cold War policies (George Kennan) and their execution (Frank Wisner) had no scruples about using war criminals as propagandists, espionage agents, and guerillas. Wisner had already hired Iron Guardists in Romania during and after the war. And Kennan had opposed the Allied denazification plan after the war. If the Allies imprisoned Nazi leaders, he reasoned, they would be denying Germany the brains it needed to rebuild itself into a strong and viable anticommunist force in Western Europe. Furthermore, Kennan voiced no objections to the "extralegal character" of OPC's ambitious covert plans.

Working under leadership that favored the use of former Nazis and Nazi collaborators and without a policy banning their use, CIA station chiefs and case officers and agents did not hesitate to hire them. In a 1950 report advocating concealment of the Nazi backgrounds of CIA recruits, Peter Sichel, the agency's top man in Berlin, told the head of the CIA in Germany: "Membership in the SS, or the SD, or the *Volksdeutsche* [German intelligence] no longer is regarded as a strike against any personality." In fact, SS, SD, and Abwehr experience was viewed as an asset, not a liability.

"We would have slept with the devil to obtain information on communists," a former CIA agent confessed to a GAO investigator.

By the early 1950s, with Kennan back at the U.S. embassy in Moscow, the containment policy had morphed into liberation policy. Top-secret NSC directive No. 86 provided the initial impetus for a concerted propaganda campaign to encourage the citizens of Soviet bloc nations to rebel against the Soviets and to defect to the West. OPC espionage programs soon began to multiply like paramecia in a petri dish. By 1952, Wisner, "who had a new idea every ten minutes," was running hundreds of covert projects simultaneously under a mind-boggling number of code names. OPC was managing seventeen overseas stations and employing twenty times more people than it had in 1949. As Burton Hersh put it in his book *Old Boys*: "Wisner pragmatically overloaded the books with paramilitary and political action projects, often at the expense of analysis or disinterested intelligence gathering."

In 1952, OPC merged with the CIA's Office of Special Operations to form the Office of Clandestine Services, with Wisner at the helm. All espionage activity was finally under one roof at CIA headquarters in Langley, Virginia, and would remain there.

• • •

If John Loftus erred by naming the Department of State as the ultimate bad guy in crafting and supporting America's open-door policy for Nazi war criminals, it was because he failed to clearly distinguish between the policy designer, the policy authorizer, the policy implementer, and the policy facilitator.

The policy *designer* was indeed the State Department and George Kennan, who, according to his official biographer, "was so influential that the government had agreed to almost everything he had recommended." The policy *authorizer* was the NSC, with the approval of President Truman. The policy *implementer* was the CIA, through OPC and Frank Wisner, with some oversight by the departments of State and Defense, which were also policy facilitators. The State Department did conduct some limited covert operations on its own (BLOODSTONE and the Grumbach Organization) and in collaboration with the Department of Defense (Project Solarium).

BLOODSTONE

As the first major planned, coordinated, and serious U.S. covert program, Bloodstone was the fuse that ignited the Cold War. Begun in 1948, it had three objectives, each of which required extensive use of former Nazis and Nazi collaborators: 1) recruit European scholars and experts to collect and analyze intelligence on the Soviet Union; 2) recruit displaced persons and émigrés to help train Americans in foreign languages, propaganda techniques, and intelligence gathering; and 3) screen and recruit DPs and émigrés for clandestine warfare that included extraction of political defectors from the Soviet Union and its satellites, sabotage, and assassination. To guide Bloodstone, the NSC and

SANACC created a board of representatives from the departments of Justice, State, and War. Sitting on the panel was Robert C. Alexander, a high-level bureaucrat in the State Department's visa office. His job was to see to it that Bloodstone recruits received visas, one way or another.

Bloodstone's experts would serve as consultants to the State Department and OPC and as scholars-in-residence at major universities such as Harvard and Johns Hopkins. The propagandists, trained by State and the CIA, would disseminate misinformation about communism, keep the dreams of independent homelands alive, encourage a dozen or so governments-in-exile, and win the trust of Europeans trapped behind the Iron Curtain. The Voice of America, Radio Free Europe (RFE), and Radio Liberation/Liberty (RL) would become their homes.

Funded, equipped, and managed by the CIA, RFE beamed broadcasts to Russia; RL broadcast to the Soviet satellite countries. Cofounded by Wisner, the two stations would become, as he fondly put it, his "mighty Wurlitzer" organ on which he could play any political tune he wanted.

Wisner secured $5 million from the U.S. Treasury as Bloodstone seed money. With it, he recruited an initial 250 Nazi collaborators from communist-bloc countries, gave them a soundproof recording booth and a microphone, and put them to work for VOA, RFE, and RL, according to Christopher Simpson, who first exposed Bloodstone in his book *Blowback*. At the same time, the three stations became conduits for covert payments to national and international émigré organizations and research institutes, and to governments-in-exile.

Bloodstone experts, scholars, and propagandists were not Einsatzkommandos or fascist ethnic cleansers in blood-splattered boots. "They were the cream of Nazi collaborators," Simpson observed, "the leaders, the intelligence specialists and scholars who had put their skills to work for the Nazi cause." To illustrate his point, Simpson singled out two experts on the Soviet Union—Nikolai Poppe, a Russian *Volksdeutsche*, and Gustav Hilger, a German. Both men "played leading roles in Nazi Germany," according to CIA historian Kevin Conley Ruffner.

Nikolai Poppe was the world's greatest authority on Soviet Siberia and Outer Mongolia. During the war, he served as a translator for the Nazis in both of those German-occupied countries. Although Einsatzkommandos were busy killing Soviet Jews, Poppe steadfastly denied that he helped them in any way.

When the Germans retreated, they took Poppe with them and put him to work as a researcher at the Wannsee Institute in Berlin and at the German East Asian Institute in Czechoslovakia. The think tanks did research on "the Jewish problem."

Both the Soviets and OPC lusted after Poppe. Moscow wanted so badly to try and to execute Poppe as a traitor and war criminal that it attempted to kidnap him. And the CIA put out an APB on him. The agency eventually found him hiding in the British zone of postwar Germany and contemplating suicide. Poppe was afraid that the Soviets might snatch his daughter or his semi-invalid wife and blackmail him into returning to Russia. Suicide would solve the problem. His two sons had managed to make it to England, where they were living safely under aliases. That Poppe was wanted by the Soviets made him even more desirable to the Americans.

Although U.S. officials at the State Department and OPC knew about Poppe's Nazi collaboration, the United States asked Great Britain if it could have him. The British sighed in relief and said good riddance. Moscow had been pestering Britain to hand over Poppe under the Yalta repatriation agreement but it had refused on principle. According to recently declassified intelligence files, the CIA secretly moved Poppe from the British zone to the American zone in operation "Father Christmas," and from there to the United States. He arrived at Westover Field, Massachusetts, on a U.S. Air Force transport in May 1949 and went to work for Bloodstone as a consultant to the State Department's Policy Planning Staff.

Gustav Hilger was a German citizen who had been born in Russia. His father was German, his mother Russian. As a former diplomat at the German embassy in Moscow, Hilger was another huge catch. His firsthand experience with both Soviet officials and anticommunist groups made Hilger OPC's most prized trophy.

Hilger's hands were hardly clean. During the German-Soviet war, he recruited men for the Waffen SS and helped the Wehrmacht organize Vlasov's army. There is also evidence to suggest that he actively assisted Einsatzkommandos in rounding up Jews. After retreating to Germany with the German army, Hilger continued to work for the Nazi foreign ministry and served as personal secretary to Joachim von Ribbentrop, Germany's foreign minister. (Ribbentrop was convicted and executed at Nuremberg.) Hilger also is credited with helping to round up Italian Jews and to arrange asylum in Germany for Hungarian soldiers implicated in the murder and deportation of thousands of Hungarian Jews.

After the war, Hilger spied for the United States as a member of the Gehlen Org. The CIA was so impressed with his credentials that it promised U.S. citizenship for him and his family if he agreed to work for the State Department in America. With the backing of George Kennan, the CIA asked the INS to waive its required examination of Hilger at his port of entry, and requested that his case be handled "on a classified basis." Hilger went to work as a consultant for State and the CIA. As promised, he eventually received U.S. citizenship under the CIA's one-hundred rule exception.

"The fact that the Office of Policy Coordination wanted Nicholas [*sic*] Poppe and Gustave [*sic*] Hilger as consultants and brought them to the United States for permanent residence is a significant step," CIA historian Ruffner reasoned. "German diplomats and Russian social scientists with Nazi records, in addition to German wartime intelligence officers and agents, were now regarded as valuable assets in the struggle against the Soviet Union."

Although many of the Soviet Union experts, scholars, and propagandists employed by Bloodstone in America and in Western Europe were "gentleman" Nazis and collaborators, the same cannot be said of Bloodstone's Eastern European covert operatives. By way of example, Simpson cites three Albanian pro-Nazi fascists admitted to the United States under the Bloodstone program—Midhat Frasheri, Xhafer Deva, and Hasan Dosti.

Frasheri was the head of Balli Kombetar, a pro-Nazi fascist group in Albania. Deva was Albania's former quisling foreign minister. Dosti was its former quisling minister of justice. All three Nazi collaborators were directly involved in the deportation of Jews to Sobibor, Belzec, and Treblinka. (At the time Bloodstone recruited Deva and Dosti, quislings were barred from entry into the United States under the Displaced Persons Act of 1948.)

Bloodstone was absorbed into other CIA clandestine programs in the early 1950s. By the time OSI was formed in 1979, Hilger, Frasheri, and Deva were already dead. Poppe and Dosti were still alive, but were never prosecuted for visa fraud.

THE GUERILLA ARMY

The Lodge Act, described in chapter 3, provided the legal justification for a "guerilla army." The act authorized the armed services to enlist up to 12,500 "aliens," specifying that the recruits must be single men, eighteen to thirty-five years old, who were willing to serve in the U.S. Army for five years. The volunteers would have to agree to remain single until they completed basic training as "Regular Army Unassigned" privates, with commensurate pay. As an inducement to enlist, the United States guaranteed recruits permanent U.S. residency at the end of their service as long as they were honorably discharged. The volunteers who passed a series of tests administered by the U.S. Army in Germany would be trained by the army and the CIA at Camp King, West Germany, and in military schools and camps in the United States.

Barred from service in the new guerilla army were German nationals and citizens of NATO nations. This ensured that virtually all enlistees would be Eastern Europeans. Also excluded as unacceptable were anarchists, communists, convicted criminals, alcoholics, drug addicts, and sex offenders unless granted a waiver from the army's adjutant general. There was no directive prohibiting the recruitment of *non-German* Nazi collaborators.

According to a 1951 top-secret, sixteen-page report, "special consideration" would be given to qualified applicants who had experience in guerilla and mountain warfare, police and security work, and military intelligence and counterintelligence. In other words, the army was looking for former Vlasov army soldiers, Waffen SS volunteers, and freedom fighters. The army estimated its guerilla requirements as: 7,400 men between September 1951 and July 1952; 6,100 men between July 1952 and July 1954; and 2,400 yearly thereafter.

By 1950, when the Lodge Act was passed, it was well-known that freedom-fighting guerillas had frequently engaged in the ethnic cleansing of Jews, Gypsies, Poles, Ukrainians, Orthodox Serbians, and Russian POWs, among others. It was also known that local police and security units in countries occupied by the Nazis were organizations that had been designated as criminal by the Nuremberg Tribunal and defined as inimical to the United States by the Displaced Persons Commission.

The army determined that there were thousands of middle and Eastern Europeans fit for guerilla army service and provided the following estimates: Estonians (5,850); Latvians (16,925); Lithuanians (12,625); Poles (209,725); and Czechoslovakians (1,025).

As envisioned by the Joint Chiefs of Staff (JCS) and the CIA, the guerilla army-in-waiting would be specially trained and ready to respond to a Soviet nuclear attack in Europe. Donning protective gear, troops would file into five B-23 bombers specifically designated for a nuclear counterattack and they would parachute behind the Iron Curtain, according to Simpson. Once on the ground, their task would be to crush any remaining communist resistance and to prevent the Red Army from regrouping.

Frank Wisner played a major role in recruiting the best and most experienced Eastern Europeans for the guerilla army, but he faced what seemed like an insurmountable problem. The best and most experienced were former Nazi collaborators. How would he sneak them into the United States for training?

Wisner wasn't bashful. In a closed-door session with the heads of congressional committees, he asked for authorization to bring fifteen thousand émigrés of his choice into the United States. Congress laughed, then authorized the CIA to open the door for five hundred—no questions asked—over a three-year period under a little-noticed law, the Displaced Persons National Interest Case.

Not satisfied with congressional orts, Wisner took his plea directly to the White House. Based on information he supplied, the NSC issued—in addition to directive No. 86—intelligence directives No. 13 and No. 14, which were declassified in 2011 under my Freedom of Information Act request. Unobtrusively tucked in those directives was a provision authorizing the CIA to recruit guerillas through private émigré groups that helped displaced persons and defectors secure U.S. visas.

It was a devilishly simple scheme probably suggested by the Department of Justice, which the NSC had commissioned to work on the visa issues. Wallet in hand, the CIA would approach a private refugee organization such as the Committee for a Free Latvia. It would tell committee leaders the kinds of émigrés it wanted, emphasizing former Vlasov army soldiers, Waffen SS volunteers, and freedom fighters, all of whom already had some military training and experience. When the committee presented the CIA with a list of candidates, agents would screen them and select the most promising. The refugee organization committee, which more often than not had former Nazi collaborators as members, would then sponsor each selected émigré for a U.S. visa and the CIA wallet would open wide.

Convinced that World War III could begin as early as 1952, the military, for planning purposes, designated July 1 of that year as the date of the Soviet invasion of Western Europe. Over a ten-year period (1950–60), the CIA poured at least $100 million into the NSC-sponsored recruitment programs, according to Simpson. The precise number of guerillas trained at Camp King and in the United States is not known because many documents dealing with the guerilla army are still classified, if not destroyed. Authors like Christopher Simpson and Evan Thomas place the number at five thousand.

THE GUERILLA CORPS

In addition to the guerilla army, the Joint Chiefs of Staff and the CIA envisioned a small, flexible, and highly trained guerilla corps, which it renamed Special Forces. (They were the prototype for the Green Berets.) Once trained, the corps would become the "organizers, fomenters, and operational nuclei of guerilla units."

Guerilla corps volunteers were rigorously screened and tested in Germany. In the beginning, most failed the required English Knowledge Evaluation Test. In June 1951, for example, the European Command lamented the fact that only 8 percent of the 1,004 applicants who took the exam passed. Army evaluators then recommended that, if an applicant passed all other screening tests and evaluations, he should be enlisted and given special English classes.

After the initial screening in Germany, the enlistees were shipped to Camp Kilmer, New Jersey, for further evaluation. Of vital importance to the military and CIA were their language skills, training in police work, experience in guerilla and resistance warfare, skill in signal corps operations and clandestine radio communication, and their willingness to be air-dropped behind enemy lines.

Camp Kilmer used a standard form to assist evaluating each enlistee. The entry for Liber Pokorny, for example, said: RA 10-812-811 . . . speaks, reads, and writes Slovak, Czech, German, and Russian . . . desires airborne training . . . Gestapo background . . . did not participate in guerilla warfare or resistance movements . . . radio operator . . . former member of the Czech army.

The volunteers selected to be guerillas would be trained at established army schools, supplemented by courses at navy and air force schools, the National War College, and the State Department.

The JCS was clear on who would employ the newly trained guerillas.

"The primary interest in guerilla warfare during peacetime," the Joint Chiefs said, "should be that of the Central Intelligence Agency and during wartime . . . the National Military Establishment."

Once trained, the guerillas would be deployed to rescue VIP fugitives and defectors from behind the Iron Curtain, kidnap high-ranking communists, sabotage industries and communications, assassinate double agents and communist political leaders, and train and lead indigenous armies of freedom fighters in the Soviet Union and its satellites.

It is unknown how many guerillas the military and the CIA ultimately trained and deployed and how many were former Nazi collaborators. A series of declassified, top-secret records from the Camp Kilmer processing center list the names of 279 men screened and selected for service in Special Forces units. Fifteen percent of those voluntarily reported that they had former police affiliations.

Well into the 1950s, the CIA kept Special Forces assassination teams on call at U.S. air bases around the world, according to Simpson. And they were good. According to one high-level military officer, "Some of these guys were the best commercial hit men you have ever heard of."

• • •

George Kennan went on to become U.S. ambassador to the Soviet Union. He would later say that proposing covert action was the biggest mistake he ever made. "It didn't work out at all the way I had conceived it," he admitted in 1975. "We had thought that [covert action] would be used when and if an occasion arose when it might be needed. There might be years when we wouldn't have to do anything like this."

For Frank Wisner, the conclusions were even gloomier. The failed Hungarian revolution probably contributed to his depression, because most of the insurgents killed in that 1956 uprising had been trained in Operation Redsox, Wisner's pride and joy. He had promised the insurgents that the United States would provide help if they stood up to the communist regime. "Help" never arrived and Wisner never fully recovered from feelings of failure and guilt.

Two years after the Hungarian fiasco, Wisner was committed to a mental institution with manic-depressive psychosis. He killed himself with a shotgun in 1965.

PART FOUR

Hunting for Ivan the Terrible

CHAPTER THIRTY-EIGHT

They Don't Understand

On February 28, 1986, El Al flight 004 landed in a remote corner of Tel Aviv's Ben Gurion International Airport. Waiting on the tarmac to welcome John Demjanjuk to Israel after his eleven-hour flight was Alex Ish-Shalom, chief of the special investigation team assigned to the Demjanjuk case.

Dressed in a brown suit, open-neck shirt, and dark-rimmed glasses, and appearing calm and alert, Demjanjuk picked his way down the plane's portable staircase. When he reached the tarmac, Ish-Shalom read Demjanjuk his rights. A U.S. marshal unlocked his handcuffs. An Israeli policeman recuffed him.

Demjanjuk asked a marshal who had accompanied him on the flight if he could "kiss the ground of the Holy Land." The marshal said no. Then he turned to Ish-Shalom and told the police investigator something that Demjanjuk had said at a reflective moment during the trip.

"They don't understand," Demjanjuk had complained to the marshal. "There was a *war* on." Prosecutors and judges would later interpret Demjanjuk's remark as an indirect admission of guilt.

Demjanjuk walked a few yards down the runway, past reporters screaming questions, and stepped into a Brinks armored car. Escorted by a string of police cars, the rented Brinks took him to Ayalon Prison, a maximum-security penitentiary in Ramla, ten minutes from the airport. It was the prison where Adolf Eichmann was held and where he was executed by hanging in 1962 for his role as architect of the Final Solution. Eichmann was the last Nazi to be tried, and the only criminal to be executed, in Israel.

For Demjanjuk's own safety, Ayalon isolated him from the general prison population of five hundred in a cheerful yellow-walled but windowless cell, twelve feet by twelve feet. Three guards watched over him during the day, two at night. A closed-circuit TV camera recorded his every move, except when he exercised in a private, concrete-walled courtyard.

Outside the prison fences, most Israelis supported the Demjanjuk trial but without a show of enthusiasm. "A dust of indifference has settled over Israel," as one writer put it. "A creeping oblivion." Or as another Israeli observed, "Enough! We know it already." Demjanjuk had nothing to add.

But he did have something to add after all, as Israel was soon to find out.

John Demjanjuk was certainly no Adolf Eichmann, who boasted that he never killed a Jew. Demjanjuk was an alleged death camp guard who sat at the bottom of the Treblinka organizational chart. As Ivan the Terrible, however, he was hardly a cookie-cutter Trawniki man. He was an amalgam of the worst features of death camp guards. A Frankenstein of Eichmann's creation. A people-janitor responsible for the last cleanup. The effect of Eichmann's cause. An evil but necessary cog in the wheel of extermination. A monster of unimaginable cruelty who pulled girls from death lines and raped them before driving them into gas chambers. A butcher who sliced off ears. A swordsman who cut and stabbed those who didn't move deeper into the gas chamber to make room for more victims.

And he enjoyed it all.

The inhumanity of Ivan the Terrible forced Israel to face the horns of a painful dilemma. As a nation, it didn't want to rip off the scabs of its Holocaust history. Germany should be trying Demjanjuk, not Israel. But Germany was even less eager than Israel to revisit its past, and it didn't ask for Demjanjuk's extradition. In effect, it was pushing Israel into a war crimes trial role that posed serious consequences.

If Israel did try Demjanjuk, what about the hundreds of other alleged Nazi collaborators whom the United States was trying for visa fraud, stripping of U.S. citizenship, and deporting? Would Israel have to extradite them, too? Must it become the world's dumping ground? A graveyard for World War II war criminals?

But the specter of Bohdan Koziy still haunted the conscience of Israeli decision makers.

• • •

Bohdan Koziy had been a policeman and Nazi collaborator during the 1941–44 German occupation of Ukraine. OSI tried him in Fort Lauderdale in 1981, two years after Fedorenko faced Judge Roettger and while Demjanjuk was standing before Judge Battisti in Cleveland. Eyewitnesses, supported by some documentation, accused Koziy of murdering Jews in the Stanislau region of Ukraine. One execution stood out from the hundreds of others.

Four witnesses testified at the Fort Lauderdale trial that they had watched in horror as Koziy snatched the preschool daughter of a Jewish doctor from her home. As he dragged the child down the street to the local police station, she cried, "Mother, he's going to shoot me!" The mother followed behind, begging Koziy to let her daughter go. Koziy took out his pistol. The mother turned her back, unable to watch. He stood the girl at a wall, turned, took three paces, turned again, and shot her.

Koziy lied on his U.S. visa application, saying that he was a tailor's apprentice and farmer during the war. He entered the United States in 1949 and, after doing menial jobs, saved enough money to buy a motel in Clinton, New York. He later moved to Fort Lauderdale, where he bought another motel.

Unlike Demjanjuk, who pleaded for asylum without choosing a deportation country in case he lost, Koziy wisely chose Costa Rica, which, like Panama, did not have extradition treaties with Germany or Israel. So while Demjanjuk was sitting in an Israeli jail waiting for his war crimes trial to begin, Koziy was a free man sipping rum and Coke in the warm sunshine of Central America.

How many more Koziys would there be if Israel did not take the heavy and unwanted responsibility to act when no one else would?

• • •

For Israeli decision makers, to extradite or not to extradite wasn't just a matter of long-delayed justice for Ivan the Terrible or an opportunity for a momentary catharsis. It was a matter of Holocaust education.

The new generation of Israeli youth, like young Jews everywhere, grew up in the shadow of the Holocaust, a sad but embarrassing piece of history that barely touched their lives and dreams. They needed to pierce the fog of that embarrassment before they could see what had happened to their ancestors and why, and how those events helped create and shape the nation of Israel. Ivan the Terrible offered an educational and emotional experience that a Nazi technocrat like Eichmann did not.

The Eichmann trial was about a cold, bloodless man, a plan, and numbers. For the most part, it was an intellectual process. The Ivan the Terrible trial would be about a brutal mass murderer of men, women, and children—the tangible reality behind the cold numbers. It promised to be an intensely emotional ordeal. The question was: As an educational tool, would the trial of Ivan the Terrible be worth all the tears and rage it was bound to evoke? Why not let the Soviets try him and execute him?

For two good reasons:

Hidden behind an iron curtain, a Soviet trial would have no educational value whatsoever for Israelis or anyone else. Nor would it necessarily serve the demands of justice. A communist war crimes trial would always be viewed with skepticism as a KGB-sanctioned sham.

Justice must be done. If not in Germany, then in Israel. Ivan the Terrible must pay and, while paying, educate Israel and the world about what happened in a little-known death camp called Treblinka, where more than eight hundred thousand Jews were murdered, and where a sadistic guard stuffed them into gas chambers and turned on a diesel motor.

Yitzhak Shamir, Israel's foreign minister, spoke for the majority when he argued that the State of Israel was the refuge for tens of thousands of Holocaust survivors. It was a matter of "historic justice" to try John Demjanjuk.

There were contrary voices. Some argued that Demjanjuk was a small fish. If Germany didn't want to bother with him, why should Israel? To try him would not only set a dangerous precedent; it would also send a message to the world. Israelis are out for revenge. Got more war criminals? Send them to us. Israelis know how to take care of them. The nooses are already tied and swinging.

Others saw a trial of John Demjanjuk as a political liability. It would increase border tension with Lebanon and fuel the hatred of Israel's enemies. And a dramatic trial might inflame ultratraditionalist emotions that could further divide the nation and adversely affect world opinion.

Still others argued that the trial would be another unnecessary journey into the heart of darkness. What damage might it do to the psyches of the children and grandchildren of survivors? Hadn't they suffered enough? What good could it possibly do to lead them there again? Wouldn't it just feed Israel's self-perception as "victim"? A belief that the world owed it something? "That Israel does not have to feel accountable for its actions as other countries do, because of what was done to Jews in World War II?"

Finally, a Demjanjuk trial would go down forever in the annals of Israeli history as a mini-Eichmann trial and, as such, would reduce the significance of that important 1962 event. As one observer explained, it would be like "restaging a funeral in order to add importance to the deceased."

• • •

The day after he arrived in Israel, John Demjanjuk stood in court and listened to a judge read the charges against him under the 1950 Israeli "Nazi and Nazi Collaborator Punishment Law." The charges went far beyond the generic and impersonal "crimes against humanity."

"These Nazi crimes were committed against *Jews* as Jews," the judge told Demjanjuk. "Therefore Israel, as the Jewish state, has the right to punish these crimes."

"I'm completely innocent," Demjanjuk said in his defense. "I was never in that place what everyone tells me—Treblinka—or a Nazi collaborator. I was myself in a prison camp. How you can transform a POW into a gas chamber operator is beyond me."

The judge went on to explain that Israeli law prescribes a maximum penalty of death by hanging, but that death wasn't mandatory.

"It seems to me that you've already determined my guilt," Demjanjuk told the court, "and that my punishment is certain to be death."

Anticipating a large number of spectators and reporters, the government decided to conduct the trial in the Hall of the People, an auditorium with banked rows of old, red movie theater seats inside Jerusalem's convention center. Adjacent to the Hall of the People was a room wired for live, closed-circuit TV coverage of the trial. Two signs at the entrance to the center, used mostly for community entertainment, foreshadowed the legal proceedings.

One read: "Box Office for Performances." The other read: "Deposit Weapons Here."

• • •

The State of Israel versus John Demjanjuk opened on February 15, 1987, almost a full year after Demjanjuk stepped off the Boeing 747 at Ben Gurion Airport and asked to kiss the ground. The trial would revolve around four identity questions, the answers to which would determine whether Demjanjuk would live or die:

- Was the *photo identification* procedure used by Miriam Radiwker valid? If not, witness identifications of Demjanjuk as Ivan the Terrible would be cast into doubt or ruled invalid.
- Were the *witnesses* who identified Demjanjuk as Ivan the Terrible credible under cross-examination? If not, there could be a reasonable doubt that Demjanjuk was Iwan Grozny.
- Was the *Trawniki card* valid? If not, there would be no documentary evidence that Demjanjuk was trained at Trawniki and served as a guard at any death camp.
- Was John Demjanjuk's *alibi* credible? If not, he would fail to prove without a reasonable doubt that he was elsewhere when the government alleged he was at Treblinka.

The evidence offered by both the prosecution and the defense in answer to those four questions would go far beyond what had been offered at Demjanjuk's denaturalization trial and deportation hearing, both in terms of the number of witnesses and the scope and depth of their testimony.

Like defendants at Nuremberg, John Demjanjuk would face not a jury but a tribunal of three judges. Israeli law required the Supreme Court of Israel to select the president of the panel. It chose one of its own, Justice Dov Levin, a recent appointee. Levin had the reputation of being accommodating in the courtroom but tough on sentencing in his chambers. A whip-cracking courtroom manager, he brought an important skill to a trial that was bound to generate heat at the bench and emotion in the audience.

The two teams of attorneys in black robes took their places shortly before 8:30 A.M. on Monday, February 15. The defense team—Mark O'Connor and his two co-counsels, John Gill and Yoram Sheftel—sat to the left of the auditorium stage where the judges would preside. The prosecution team sat on the right—state attorney Yonah Blatman, lead attorney Michael Shaked, and attorneys Michael Horovitz and Dennis Gouldman.

While the lawyers were shuffling papers at twin curved tables, a smiling John Demjanjuk entered the courtroom dressed in a brown sport coat and open shirt. "Boker Tov," he called to the thin crowd of mostly elderly survivors and religious Jews quietly sitting on benches. Good morning! Then to the TV cameras, "Hello, Cleveland."

Unlike Eichmann, who was locked in a glass booth, Demjanjuk took his place in a dock directly behind his legal team, a translator next to him. Police officers sat on either side, more to protect than to guard.

The panel of judges entered at 8:30 sharp dressed in white shirts and black ties. Justice Levin took the middle seat on the stage under the seal of the State of Israel and next to the blue and white Israeli flag. District court judge Zvi Tal took the seat on Levin's left, district court judge Dalia Dorner on his right.

Mark O'Connor was the first to address the court. "John Demjanjuk," he said in his opening statement, "was never in a death camp....He was conscripted and served in combat against the Third Reich. He..."

So began the much-anticipated trial of John Demjanjuk, aka Ivan the Terrible. The ordeal for him and his family and the trauma for Israel would last a year.

Chief Defense Attorney Mark O'Connor (standing) addresses a question to Demjanjuk

CHAPTER THIRTY-NINE

Memory on Trial

The first critical witness to take the stand was Israeli police investigator Miriam Radiwker. She would spend three days there, caught in a good-guy, bad-guy tug of war, with Judge Dov Levin as the referee. Both the prosecution and the defense wanted to pull her to their side of the guilty-or-innocent line. To a great degree, the validity of the photo identifications of John Demjanjuk as Ivan the Terrible rested on her testimony.

The prosecution questioned Radiwker first, gently and surely guiding her through her photo identification process with Treblinka survivors. Who created the photo album. How she found the witnesses and arranged for interviews. How she presented the photos. What questions she asked and how she asked them. How and when she handwrote the deposition reports signed by the witnesses.

Radiwker came across as professional and thorough. That left the defense team with the task of rattling her into inconsistencies, breaking her self-confidence, and destroying her credibility.

The problem was, there was no defense team. There was an uneasy shotgun marriage between Cleveland and Jerusalem, with Mark O'Connor as the autocratic lead attorney and Yoram Sheftel as his flamboyant co-counsel. They would take turns cross-examining Radiwker.

O'Connor was out to get first blood. His job was daunting. Prove that Radiwker had a faulty memory and, therefore, was an unreliable witness, and convince the panel of judges, especially Levin, that she was biased and unprofessional. The 1950 Israeli "Nazi and Nazi Collaborator Punishment Law" acknowledged the pitfalls of relying on witness identification years after an event. The law sought to protect defendants in Nazi and Nazi collaboration cases from misidentification, as happened in the Frank Walus case. The defense was encouraged to use extensive "memory tests" in its cross-examination of witnesses like Radiwker, who was testifying about what she did and said twelve years earlier, and Treblinka survivors, who would be describing what they saw more than forty years ago.

O'Connor planned to use the memory test as the major weapon in his attack on Radiwker, hoping to hear her say, "I don't remember . . . I'm sorry but I don't remember." He had an advantage over her in the cat-and-mouse game about to begin. She was eighty years old. How hard could it be to break an old lady alone and vulnerable on the witness stand?

But Radiwker had an advantage over O'Connor. As a hunted Jew, she had survived World War II. If she could outwit the Nazis and the Soviets, how hard would it be to outfox a country lawyer from Buffalo?

• • •

"Shalom! Boker Tov!" O'Connor began. "Mrs. Radiwker, you indicated that your date of birth was 1906. Is that correct, ma'am?"

When Radiwker didn't respond, O'Connor said: "That's very impolite for me to ask that as the first question. I understand."

"Not at that age, Mr. O'Connor," Judge Levin said. "At that age, we already know the truth."

The courtroom grinned.

O'Connor questioned Radiwker American-style. Unlike the Israeli attorneys, who stood behind their court-appointed tables, he paced the floor, tossing out questions over his shoulder, spinning to face the witness, approaching the stand, looking the witness in the eye as if searching for the hint of a lie. Israeli schoolchildren loved him, even though they shouldn't have. Wasn't he defending a Nazi collaborator? Wasn't he the dude in the *black* hat? But O'Connor was such a good imitation of the lawyers they watched in American gangster movies and on American TV shows that they began to imitate his walk and his American-accented Hebrew—"boker tov . . . tada raba."

"Mrs. Radiwker, you indicated that you were born in . . . Poland," O'Connor continued. "Is that correct?"

"I was born when it was still Austria. Later it became Poland. And now it's Russia."

"What you are saying now is that your place of birth was in the former Austro-Hungarian Empire?"

"Yes."

"But you indicated that, in fact, it was Galicia. Is that true?"

"I was born in the Galicia *region*," Radiwker clarified.

"But the place of your birth, ma'am, was that in the Ukraine?"

"A Ukrainian village."

"Do you remember the name of the village?"

"Laski."

"Can you tell me those schools or institutions that you studied in?"

"At the time of the First World War, my parents fled from the Russians and moved to Vienna. I had my primary schooling in Vienna. My secondary schooling was in Stanislawow [near Laski]. . . . University studies at the school at Yagalonite University in Krakow. And I hold the degree of master of jurisprudence."

"Can you tell me when you graduated with your master's degree?"

"In 1930."

"What languages do you speak?"

"Polish, Russian, Yiddish, German, and Hebrew, of course. Not brilliant Hebrew—but still . . . Once upon a time I had full command of Ukrainian, but I haven't used it in so many years."

At this early point in his cross-examination, O'Connor realized he was in trouble. Radiwker was a seasoned attorney with more court-room experience than he had. Aware of what he was trying to do in his cross and why, she made it a point to be clear, precise, and specific. And she answered his questions without hesitation and with great self-confidence, leaving O'Connor in a bind. He had committed the defense to memory-testing. His best hope was to continue the test, rattle her, wear her down, find a weakness, or create an opening he could exploit.

Radiwker testified that, after receiving her master's degree, she practiced law in Poland until the German occupation in September 1939. It was an opening. Was it possible that she collaborated with the Germans as an attorney? If so, it would be an interesting twist. A Nazi collaborator testifying against an alleged Nazi collaborator.

O'Connor went fishing. He asked Radiwker to describe her legal career in Poland. She quickly and decisively dashed his hope. Before the invasion, she told the court, Poland severely limited her employment options as a Jew. Although she could practice law, she could not become a judge unless she converted to Christianity. And when the Germans occupied Poland, she couldn't practice law at all.

"Can you indicate to us, ma'am, what you were doing then?" O'Connor asked in frustration.

"I sat at home until the seventh of November, 1939, [when] I crossed into the Russian occupied zone."

Radiwker went on to explain how she and her husband fled farther east into Belorussia in front of the advancing German army in an attempt to stay three steps ahead of the Einsatzkommandos who were killing Jews with the help of Belorussian collaborators like Radoslaw Ostrowsky and Emanuel Jasiuk. The Soviets eventually drafted her husband into the Red Army and he ended up defending Stalingrad under the command of General Vlasov. For some reason, possibly because he was a Jew, Moscow ordered him to fill out a background questionnaire. When he naïvely reported that he had once served as an officer in the Austrian army and the Polish reserves, Moscow sent him to Siberia.

"When did he come back?" O'Connor asked.

"He didn't return, he didn't return," Radiwker said, close to tears. "He died there."

Judge Levin interrupted. "You are questioning on a subject which is sensitive," he chided O'Connor. "Would you kindly be as delicate as possible?"

O'Connor went fishing in another pond.

"Did you at any time make contact with *any officials* of the Soviet government?"

"No!"

"And at the time of the Russo-German war, what did you do?"

"I was accepted into a lawyer's association," Radiwker said.

Radiwker explained that the association was a legal cooperative in which an administrator found the clients, parceled out the work, collected the fees, and paid the lawyers.

"You were practicing law in an area controlled by Soviet forces, is that true?"

"Until 1957. Then we were permitted to move to Poland."

"Can you indicate the type of law that you were practicing?"

"Whatever was available. Criminal cases. Civil cases," Radiwker said. "My first case was to defend a Jew who had sold chickens. He bought the chickens for twelve and he sold them for sixty. He told the court frankly that he made a good profit. . . . .He got five years in prison."

Having failed to show that Radiwker had a weak memory, collaborated with the Nazis, or worked in an official capacity for a communist government, O'Connor once again changed his tack. He tried to establish that as a lawyer in the Soviet Union, Radiwker had willingly participated in a corrupt legal system that deprived citizens of their human rights.

"As a defense attorney, ma'am, under the Russian rule," O'Connor asked, "do you feel that you had the *full opportunity* to represent your client?"

"I always had the courage to defend my client."

"Do you feel there was justice in those courts?"

"I couldn't say there was *not* justice."

"In order to practice law before Russian judges, did you have to go to Moscow at any time? Or did you have to receive any special training?"

"No, I did not go to Moscow," Radiwker said in response to the first part of O'Connor's double question. To the second part: "I simply read their codex. It's not a very large one."

"You never practiced any law [dealing with] crimes against the state or anything to do with the military code of justice. Is that true?"

"There were special lawyers . . . authorized to deal with cases such as these," Radiwker said. "It wasn't for me to do it. Nor did I want to."

O'Connor failed to tire Radiwker, break her, fault her memory, or implicate her in any compromising activity. To make matters worse,

Judge Levin was losing patience with the endless stream of biographical questions, some of which were so meandering that Radiwker forgot the question by the time O'Connor finished asking it. Levin kept interrupting O'Connor to say that this question was irrelevant, that question unclear.

Radiwker immigrated to Israel in 1964. O'Connor asked her about her subsequent career. "Mrs. Radiwker," he said, "when you came to Israel, ma'am, you indicated within a fairly short period of time you obtained employment. How did you get that job?"

"I took my daughter and my [second] husband to Auschwitz, just as one goes to visit a grave ... to achieve separation from relatives," Radiwker said. "Having seen what went on there, I decided that if I have the opportunity, I will devote my life to work that deals with the crimes of Nazis."

Both Radiwker and her second husband had lost relatives during the Holocaust. The Nazis killed his first wife and only child. While still in Poland, she had heard about an Israeli police unit investigating Nazi war crimes and learned that they needed jurists and investigators fluent in German. Once settled in Israel, she applied for a job and, given her legal background, the police hired her immediately.

Radiwker's testimony about Auschwitz evoked memories of lost family and images of gas chambers and ovens. It brought tears to her eyes. O'Connor asked for a break.

"I do not see a need," Judge Levin said.

"I can see the witness in *tears*," O'Connor objected.

"She isn't quite as tearful as she may appear to you," Levin replied. "Auschwitz is not something that a Jew can mention with joy, to say the least. Only with deepest sadness. . . . But she can respond. She will respond. She's prepared to respond."

It was as if Levin were telling O'Connor, "You may need a break. She doesn't."

Radiwker retired from the Nazi investigation unit in 1976 at the age of seventy, as Israeli labor law required, but she stayed on as a special contract employee, working four days a week instead of six. The Nazi unit assigned her to investigate the nine Ukrainian suspects on the American INS list.

Radiwker had testified earlier under direct examination that she didn't know anyone on the list, including Demjanjuk and Fedorenko, and that her superior gave her three "ready-made" pieces of cardboard with a total of seventeen photos pasted on them. During her testimony at the Fedorenko trial eight years earlier, however, she had said through an interpreter that *she herself* arranged and pasted the photos.

O'Connor was eager to exploit the contradiction. But Radiwker stopped him cold. "That was *not true*," she snapped back. "It was my job to show the witnesses these photographs. That's what I did." The interpreter had mistranslated, she said.

Radiwker's explanation was more than plausible. Simultaneous courtroom translations were always a problem, as the Jerusalem trial itself illustrated. The proceedings were conducted in Hebrew with witnesses testifying in Hebrew, German, English, Dutch, and Ukrainian. Levin was constantly telling attorneys and witnesses alike to slow down, to wait for the translation. And witnesses were frequently confused by imprecisely translated questions.

O'Connor next questioned Radiwker about who had supplied the background information on each of the names the INS sent the Israeli police for investigation. It was an obvious gimmick to sneak the KGB into the courtroom.

"Do you know what the origin of that information was?" O'Connor asked. "Did it come from sources in the United States or did it come from sources in the Soviet Union?"

"I don't know," Radiwker said. "I don't know *where* the Americans got their information."

"At any time in 1976, or subsequent to 1976, did it come to your attention, ma'am, that the charges related to [Demjanjuk] came from the Soviet Union?"

"I had no information about *any* connection with Russia or *any* information that might have come from Russia."

The mouse had the cat in a corner. O'Connor had failed to prove that Radiwker arranged the faulty photo spread, was biased because she knew about Demjanjuk before she got the assignment to investigate the nine alleged Nazi collaborators on the INS list, or heard about the Soviet-supplied Trawniki card. He didn't have many moves left.

"When you took [their statements]," he asked, "they were not taken down by means of an electronic device such as a tape recorder?"

"We were not so sophisticated yet."

O'Connor had finally scored a point. In 1976, the tape recorder was a common tool in criminal investigations around the world. By failing to use one in their investigation of alleged war criminals who might stand trial one day, the Israeli police showed themselves to be either amateurs, careless, or penny pinchers.

O'Connor moved on to the list of names corresponding to the numbers under each picture in the photo spread. He was hoping to establish that Radiwker had made it easy for the witnesses to identify Demjanjuk as Iwan of Treblinka because they could see the list. If they could, the identification process would be compromised. Once again, Radiwker dashed his hope.

"There *was* such a list," she admitted. "But it was [hidden] so that the witness could not possibly see it."

O'Connor returned to the Fedorenko trial. Radiwker stayed in the same Florida motel as the Treblinka witnesses and dined with them. Thus she had had an opportunity to coach the witnesses. O'Connor suggested that she must have chatted with them about the trial and Judge Roettger. Radiwker vehemently denied fraternizing. O'Connor then tried to show that she had a *motive* for coaching them. Knowing that she had been upset at the way Judge Roettger treated the witnesses during the trial, he asked her about Roettger's bench examination of the Treblinka survivors.

"I cannot describe for you the kind of treatment they received," Radiwker said with a passion bordering on anger. "Every witness a liar, a deceitful person."

O'Connor went in for the kill. "Is it not true, ma'am, that there was some indication by this judge that, in fact, the witnesses you had examined were coached?"

"My witnesses don't *need* coaching," Radiwker replied.

O'Connor had nothing more to add and no new lines of questioning to open. He ended his half of the cross-examination of Miriam Radiwker with what amounted to an admission of defeat.

"I would like to take this opportunity, Your Honor," he said, "to thank this witness for tolerating all these hours of questioning, her patience, her unbelievable intellect, her absolutely unbelievable physical stamina and strength. . . . I have nothing but admiration for her."

"Thank you very much," Radiwker said. "I am not feeling well."

Sheftel relieved O'Connor.

CHAPTER FORTY

The Mouse Who Ate the Cat

Yoram Sheftel felt at home in the Hall of the People. As a defense attorney in high-profile drug, murder, robbery, and rape cases—he once defended Miami mob boss Meyer Lansky, who had sought refuge in Israel—he was no stranger to the judges sitting before him. Iconoclastic, cocky, and smart, he wasn't afraid to brawl with the bench. And from the very first legal argument the defense lost, he knew without a doubt that John Demjanjuk would never get a fair trial in Dov Levin's courtroom.

Shefy, as Sheftel liked to be called, had understood when he accepted, over the fears of his own family, O'Connor's invitation to codefend John Demjanjuk that he would become the hate object of survivors and religious extremists alike. Shefy didn't care. If there was anyone he held in contempt it was the cowards and hypocrites who avoided doing what was right out of fear of public opinion. Shefy refused to be one of them.

Before he agreed to join the defense team, Sheftel had interviewed John Demjanjuk in his prison cell. He found the American to be a very simple man—like the Ukrainian peasants his grandmother had told him about—with a poor memory, easily confused, and emotionally dependent on Mark O'Connor. At the end of the two-hour interview, Demjanjuk had passed the Shefy smell test—an intuition that the accused wasn't lying.

Besides believing that John Demjanjuk was innocent, Sheftel was convinced that Mark O'Connor could never win without him. For one thing, O'Connor was sure to drown in the sea of Israeli law. But more important, Sheftel believed the American was simply incompetent. After hearing O'Connor's opening statement on the first day of the trial, Sheftel concluded that the guy didn't know what he was talking about. And after O'Connor's cross-examination of Miriam Radiwker, which Sheftel considered senseless, embarrassing, and ultimately damaging, he discovered that O'Connor didn't even prepare for his witness examinations. Even worse, he refused to listen to advice on which points to raise.

In sum, Sheftel believed that the entire Demjanjuk case would rest on his shoulders.

Besides knowledge of Israeli law, Sheftel brought to the defense another valuable skill. His father was from Caucasia and his mother was a Ukrainian Jew from Rovno, the site of the POW transit camp where Demjanjuk was briefly imprisoned after his May 1942 capture in Kerch. Having learned Russian from his parents, Sheftel was able to speak directly to Demjanjuk, who also spoke Russian, without the filter of a translator.

Sheftel also brought a major bias to the defense team. He viewed the trial as a theatrical event and the courtroom as a Holocaust classroom designed to educate Israelis at Demjanjuk's expense. He believed that Judge Levin's first major courtroom decision proved his point.

Demjanjuk had admitted to all the facts about the Holocaust contained in the indictment save one—he was not Ivan the Terrible. Sheftel argued that, in accord with Israeli law concerning stipulations, the prosecution should be barred from presenting testimony about the history and nature of the Holocaust.

Judge Levin dismissed his opening-session objection and ruled: "We allow the prosecution to act as it sees fit and put forward evidence as it requires with respect to facts which are not in dispute."

Translated: The fix was in. Demjanjuk's goose was on the spit and the coals were red hot. No argument, no matter how cogent and convincing, could possibly stop his trip to the gallows because Israel would be "educated" *only* if Demjanjuk swung by a rope. The trial was bound to become a Roman arena "with everyone baying for the blood of Demjanjuk."

The spectators got the message from the bench. At the close of the first session, after guards hustled Demjanjuk out of the courtroom amid screams of "murderer," the audience turned on Sheftel like a pack of hyenas. "Kapo," they yelled at him. "Nazi . . . Piece of filth . . . They should kill *you* . . . It's a shame you are alive . . . Shameless bastard."

The catcalling grew to a thunderous crescendo with angry, threatening gestures. Guards rushed to protect Sheftel, but he brushed them off. There was no way he would let a lynch mob intimidate him. He felt that his entire professional life had been a preparation for this trial. It was a watershed in his career, and no one was going to take away his opportunity and duty to defend John Demjanjuk.

Sheftel calmly walked down the aisle and out of the courtroom.

Sheftel even had the chutzpah to call the proceedings a "show trial" during an open court session, which earned him a contempt-of-court threat from Judge Levin. Sheftel apologized, but only after he had made his point. Totally humiliated by having to grovel before the court, he vowed to make the judges and prosecutors rue the day they got involved in the lynching of John Demjanjuk.

Like defense attorneys everywhere, Sheftel had a basic distrust of the police, especially their sneaky habit of showing photo spreads without a defense attorney present. That was precisely what Miriam Radiwker had done in the Demjanjuk case. Sheftel's distrust was based on personal experience. He had never found a single instance where the Israeli police had conducted a proper photo spread in the absence of a defense attorney, and he was eager to flay police investigator Miriam Radiwker during his cross-examination of her photo identification procedures.

• • •

Sheftel began with the handwritten depositions she had taken from Treblinka survivors Avraham Goldfarb and Eugen Turowsky. Both men had testified at the Fedorenko trial in Fort Lauderdale. Both were now dead.

In an attempt to establish professional incompetence and bias, Sheftel challenged Radiwker about what she *did not say* in her written reports, but should have. Shades of defense attorney John Martin in Cleveland, who challenged document examiner Gideon Epstein on the tests he *had not* performed on the Trawniki card.

In accordance with memory-test guidelines, Sheftel would not allow Radiwker to consult her own original reports. Like O'Connor before him, his plan was to trap her in inconsistencies, then rattle her into self-doubt and frustration. Several times, he thought, he had confused her. But before he could go in for the kill, Judge Levin interrupted the flow of his cross-examination. It was almost as if Levin was trying to protect Radiwker, give her a rest, let her compose herself.

Under direct examination, Radiwker had testified from memory that she had shown Goldfarb three cardboard pages with a total of seventeen photos pasted on them. Sheftel held up a copy of the deposition that Radiwker had prepared and Goldfarb had signed. "It doesn't say *anywhere*—'pictures one to seventeen,'" Sheftel said.

Any attorney would see this as a trick question designed to confuse the witness. To a layman, however, it was a simple lie. Goldfarb had said in his sworn deposition: "I was shown seventeen photographs of Ukrainians on three brown cardboard sheets."

Although Radiwker suspected Sheftel's question was a trap, she insisted that she had shown Goldfarb all seventeen pictures and she did not ask Judge Levin for permission to review what she had written in the Goldfarb deposition eight years earlier. She'd catch Sheftel next time he tried to use the dirty trick.

The next time came when Sheftel questioned Radiwker about Goldfarb's identification of Demjanjuk as Iwan Grozny. He was hoping to confuse her into admitting that she planted the name "Iwan" in his mind. That would be witness prompting and would invalidate the identification.

"Is it true," Sheftel asked, "that when [Goldfarb] pointed to sixteen [Demjanjuk's photo] and said 'it looks familiar to me,' he did *not add* the name Iwan?"

"Yes."

"And a half hour later, you questioned him again?"

"Yes."

"He refers to picture number sixteen . . . and he uses the name *Iwan*. . . .Did you mention the name Iwan?"

"I request permission to see the record."

"What you are saying is: 'I don't remember?'"

"I am not saying I don't remember. I am saying that because of the fact that I am not sure, I want to see the deposition."

"You can't remember without looking at your deposition?" Sheftel repeated, waving the papers in front of her.

"I don't say I can't," Radiwker said. "I *don't believe* your description of the content of my deposition."

Sheftel did not appreciate the jab. "I would like to tell the bench," he whined, "that it is not *for her* to give grades or marks to counsel."

Judge Levin gave Radiwker permission to review her report. She read it, then answered Sheftel's question: "I asked [Goldfarb] whether he remembered a Ukrainian by the name of *Demjanjuk*. He answered,

'I do not remember the names of [the guards], but I do remember a Ukrainian by the name of Iwan.'"

Having lost that skirmish, Sheftel didn't give up. He kept challenging Radiwker's reports. Why didn't you say this? Why did you say that? Didn't you lead the witness here, suggest something there? Didn't you send clues that Iwan Demjanjuk's and Feodor Fedorenko's photos were in the spread? Why did you interview witnesses twice? And when you did, why didn't you write two separate reports?

Radiwker answered each question patiently, specifically, and clearly.

Sheftel called her attention to the photo spread. Radiwker admitted that the spread was far from perfect and that, at one point, she added three more pages of pictures to the three pages her supervisor had given her. She also admitted that she was inconsistent in presenting photos to the witnesses, sometimes showing the entire three pages, sometimes just page three, containing the photos of Demjanjuk and Fedorenko. On one occasion, she showed a witness only three photos. "I acted upon the guidelines [from INS]," Radiwker said in her defense.

"The guidelines said at least three," Sheftel pointed out. "Why did you [sometimes] put thirty or forty in front of them?"

"I wanted to do it as well as I could. . . . I had more photos so I simply put more before the witnesses."

"What's the biggest picture on this page?" Sheftel asked, showing her page three of the photo spread.

"Demjanjuk."

"What is the second biggest picture?"

Judge Levin interrupted. Since Radiwker didn't paste the pictures on the cardboard pages, he ruled, the question was irrelevant.

"The witness is not a *robot*," Sheftel said in frustration. Levin had just killed his cross-examination. "She's an attorney. She's a police worker. If she hadn't liked them, she could have told her supervisor."

The defense had run out of line-of-questioning options. Radiwker had proven that her memory was excellent. She clearly explained from memory what she had done, why, and how. And she candidly admitted that the photo spread, which she did not compose, was flawed. She became emotional to the point of tears once and cried on the stand once. But with the help of Judge Levin, or so Sheftel thought, she didn't crack. She didn't break. She outlasted two cross-examiners for two days with feistiness and aplomb.

CHAPTER FORTY-ONE

The Last Survivors

The Demjanjuk trial crept up on Israelis like a morning mist, taking them by surprise, turning Treblinka into a national obsession, albeit briefly. At first, spectators trickled into the gallery of the Hall of the People. Survivors and the merely curious soon became bored with the history lessons, legal games, and incessant bickering at the bench, which they may or may not have been able to hear or follow. But as soon as they learned that survivors would be taking the stand, they came to the convention center in droves, arriving at five o'clock in the morning and standing outside for hours, hoping to get a seat in the gallery or in the adjacent hall with television monitors. All wanted to witness and be part of history. Teachers and their classes. Survivors and their children. Yeshiva students in black. Teenagers in tight jeans.

The Treblinka witnesses might be the last survivors to publicly bear witness in a court of law to the atrocities the Nazis and their collaborators visited on the Jews of Europe. Their testimony would be a parting gift to Israelis, most of whom had either forgotten—or never really learned—the horrendous details of what had happened during the Holocaust, a seminal event in Jewish history.

"This is probably the last time we will bring to trial a major Nazi," commented a high school teacher attending the trial with his class. "Our generation bears the responsibility to go and listen to this, because from here on in it is only going to be textbook."

A government official took his eleven-year-old daughter to the trial. "I want her to hear something that she'll never forget for the rest of her life," he said, "so that thirty or forty years from now when her children come to her and ask what happened, she'll have an answer."

Those who managed to get a seat inside the center were not disappointed. They were swept up in the testimony of the seven men and one woman who wept on the stand, stammered and slumped, and writhed in pain for twelve traumatizing days.

Overcome with grief and anger, an elderly Polish Jew popped up from his bench. "You're a liar!" he shouted at Demjanjuk. "You murdered my father. You're a murderer." If the spectators around him hadn't restrained the old man, he would have attacked Demjanjuk. Policemen escorted him out of the convention center past hundreds of people pushing and shoving to get inside.

"Order in the court" became an exercise in judicial futility.

The courtroom wept and raged. So did the nation of Israel. Men, women, and children listened to live broadcasts on Channel One radio. At home and at work. On radios in taxicabs and buses. On transistors glued to ears. In cafés and bars. They listened to incomprehensible horror stories about Ivan the Terrible of Treblinka, where more than eight hundred thousand Jews were murdered. *Treblinka*. It was a word tucked in Israel's distant memory, but little understood.

Until now.

• • •

Each witness repeated the testimony he or she had given in Cleveland six years earlier, adding new details about the twisted, sadistic mind of Ivan the Terrible.

Yosef Cherney, who carried corpses from the gas chambers to the burial pits, was so emotionally distraught that Judge Levin asked him to please control himself. "I am trying," he said through tears. "I am now experiencing Treblinka, Honorable Judges. I am *now in* Treblinka."

Cherney spoke in Hebrew in a high, almost feminine voice as he digressed momentarily from his Iwan Grozny testimony. The court was indulgent.

"There was another murderer in Treblinka, not a human being," he said. "It was a dog. It's name was Bari. . . . It was tall with brown spots all over, floppy ears, and big jowls.

"I remember, Your Honors. I remember. . . . " Cherney broke down, then described how one of the guards decided to have a little pre-gas-chamber fun. The guard pointed to a naked man and ordered Bari:

"Mensch, fass den Hunt. [Man, grab the dog]," Cherney said, visibly shaking at the witness stand. "The dog tore the prisoner's genitals off. And the blood! He cried to us, 'Save me!' But how could we? And he walked like that with blood streaming between his legs.

"Can history understand such a thing? Is there a historian who can understand such a thing? Where *is* he?"

After he finished the story, Cherney seemed to be in a daze, suffering in some secret place. "What am I doing here?" he finally said. "I'm humiliating myself. They don't know anything. My children. They didn't know."

Cherney paused and turned to look at the audience sitting in stunned silence. "Where is my daughter?" he asked in tears. His eyes pleaded for forgiveness. "What should I do? I didn't want to tell you."

. . .

Eighty-six-year-old Gustav Boreks, the oldest Treblinka survivor to testify, was a barber at Treblinka. He told the court: "The women didn't want to come in. They were afraid to come in. But Ivan would take his bayonet and force them in with it. He stuck them with his bayonet.... Whole pieces of flesh were hanging from them. The blood was dripping."

Boreks's wife and two children were murdered at Treblinka. At times during his testimony, he seemed disoriented, as if trapped somewhere between Treblinka and Jerusalem. He became so confused that when O'Connor asked him how he had traveled from Israel to the United States, he said "by train." At one point, he simply bowed his head and wept. Bailiffs had to help him off the stand. Judge Levin wished him a long life.

Avraham Lindwasser, who also helped remove bodies from the gas chambers, testified next. "Many of the corpses had cutting and stabbing wounds," he said. "Wounding and stabbing the victims before killing them with gas in order to fill the gas chambers faster—this was his own personal sadism. It was not for nothing that they called him Ivan the Terrible. . . . I am *now sitting there* in Treblinka."

Yechiel Reichman, who worked near the gas chambers, testified: "I carry this demon within me. I see him everywhere. I see him day and night. I see him in everything with his vicious deeds. I never thought that, in my lifetime, I would have the opportunity to stand and accuse this devil. . . . In my eyes he was a devil just like other devils. . . . Sometimes I don't sleep. And I wake up screaming. . . . *I cannot free myself* of this Treblinka."

The two most important witnesses were Pinchas Epstein and Eliyahu Rosenberg. Unlike Boreks, who was old and confused, they were both in their sixties and had sharp memories.

• • •

Choking back tears, Pinchas Epstein, who was seventeen years old when the Nazis took him to Treblinka, told the court about his arrival at the camp in a train filled with Jews driven mad by thirst. The guards had a game waiting for them. A bathtub filled with water.

"Anyone who got near it was terribly beaten by the [guards]," Epstein said. "I saw bodies with their heads split open."

Epstein paused, unable to continue.

"I know it's hard for you," Judge Levin said. "But please go on."

"It was horrible to look at the corpses that were removed from the chambers," Epstein said. "People with crushed faces. People with stab wounds. Pregnant women stabbed in their bellies. Women with their fetuses hanging half out. Young girls with stab wounds on the breasts, with eyes gouged out."

One of Epstein's memories was especially painful. He recalled how Jewish workers pulled a twelve- or fourteen-year-old girl out of the gas chamber. By some miracle, she was still alive and breathing. They sat her down.

"Her words are still ringing in my ears," Epstein said. "Ya chze Mamusy [I want my Mommy]."

The convention center sobbed.

Epstein paused and took a drink of water. "I have a granddaughter her age," he said. Then he removed his glasses and dried his eyes.

Iwan was amused by the scene, Epstein continued. He singled out a young Jew named Djoubas and began whipping him without mercy.

"Iwan ordered him: 'Take down your pants,'" Epstein said. "I am ashamed to repeat before this Honorable Court the word that Iwan said."

Epstein paused, once again biting back tears.

"'Come fuck!' And Djoubas mounted this child," Epstein said. "They took the girl to where they took all the corpses and shot her. I would find difficulty in comparing Iwan even to an animal, because I know that an animal, if sated, does not attack. . . . Iwan was never sated. He would prey every day, every moment . . . a monster from another planet."

Epstein went on to describe how the gruesome work of taking corpses from the gas chambers affected the Jews forced to do it. "There wasn't a night that someone didn't hang himself," he told the court. "It was mostly people who the day before had recognized a wife, father, or relative among the dead they cleared out of the gas chamber."

Epstein pointed at Demjanjuk sitting barely seventy feet away. "He's sitting here!" he cried, pounding the podium with his fists to applause from the gallery. "I dream about him every single night. . . . *He is etched in me.* In my memory. Every night. I cannot free myself. . . . This is the man. . . . I remember him. I see him, I see him, I see him!"

Epstein apologized to the court for his outburst.

• • •

Eliyahu Rosenberg, who had carried corpses to the burying pits, testified: "There was a thick, viscous material, almost like lava from a volcano, which bubbled on the top of the pits. The earth would rise and then subside. As it fell, we would be ordered to throw in another layer of bodies."

He described how a group of Jewish children ran naked into a gas chamber one winter day to escape the subzero weather. "They saw a door and ran in just to get out of the cold."

He recalled how an SS guard saved his life. Iwan had ordered him to have intercourse with a dead woman. In panic, he ran toward Iwan's boss, SS Sergeant Fritz Schmidt, and told him what Iwan said. Rosenberg couldn't do it. He'd rather die. "I'll deal with Iwan," Schmidt said. And he did. Rosenberg lived. Saved by a Nazi.

He told the court how Iwan once gave him thirty lashes for stealing bread and made him count the lashes out loud. After each, he had to say "thank you."

He told the court that the designer of the gas chamber placed a window in the door so an observer could watch the Jews die. The window was useless because the breaths of the dying fogged it up.

He described what death sounded like outside the chambers: "Suddenly the engine began making a loud noise and terrible screams were emitted from the gas chambers. 'Mama, Tatta, Shma Israel [Hear, Oh Israel], Ruchaleh, Moshe.' And the walls trembled. And we outside trembled, too. At long last, it subsided, and I could hear the moaning of the people, and then slowly—ever so slowly—it died out."

Rosenberg used Yiddish when he recalled what Schmidt said: "Ale shluft." They're all asleep.

The courtroom grew quiet and tense when a prosecutor showed Miriam Radiwker's photo spread to Rosenberg. He identified photo sixteen as that of Iwan Grozny. "You told Mrs. Radiwker if you saw Iwan alive," the prosecutor reminded him, "you would recognize him."

"I request that the honorable court order him to take off his glasses," Rosenberg said.

"His glasses," Judge Levin said. "Why?"

"I want to see his eyes."

O'Connor objected, then he approached the bench. After a brief word with Judge Levin, O'Connor agreed to Rosenberg's request. "My client has nothing to hide."

Demjanjuk took off his glasses and stood. Pointing to a spot right in front of him, Demjanjuk said: "Mr. Rosenberg, would you please approach? Right here."

Rosenberg left the witness stand and quickly walked over to Demjanjuk, never taking his eyes off him, while spectators shouted, "Murderer... to the gallows!"

Six feet tall and standing on a platform, Demjanjuk towered over Rosenberg.

"Look at me!" Rosenberg demanded.

The courtroom was quiet now as spectators watched, frozen in anticipation and shock. No one coughed or stirred.

Demjanjuk smiled and met Rosenberg's stare. Then he offered Rosenberg his hand and said, "Shalom!"

Rosenberg stumbled backward into the arms of the guards. "Murderer!" he cried out with clenched fists. "How dare you put your hand out to me!"

Rosenberg's wife, who was seated in the third row, screamed and fainted into the arms of her daughter. The police carried her out while bailiffs led Rosenberg back to the witness stand, where he rested his head on the podium. There was so much shouting and screaming in the courtroom that it looked as if the session was over. After repeated tries, Judge Levin restored order.

"You were asked to come close," Judge Levin said to Rosenberg. "You stopped and looked. What is your answer?"

Rosenberg gripped the witness stand and yelled:

"This is Iwan. I say so without hesitation and without a shadow of a doubt. It is Iwan from the gas chambers, the man I am looking at now. I saw his eyes. I saw those *merderische oygen!*" Those murderous eyes!

After he calmed down, Rosenberg said in a philosophical tone, "He who has been in Treblinka will never get out. He who has not been there will never get there."

$\cdot$ $\cdot$ $\cdot$

Mark O'Connor and John Gill got stuck with the delicate and thankless job of questioning the Treblinka survivors. Sheftel didn't have the stomach for it. "No way will I cross-examine survivors of Treblinka," he had told O'Connor before he agreed to serve as co-counsel. "I can't." Eventually, he agreed to question them only on police procedures used in the identification process.

O'Connor and Gill believed the survivors' stories about Ivan the Terrible and were deeply moved by their suffering. But both attorneys were convinced that the survivors were pointing their collective finger at the wrong man. The defense's job was to cast doubt on the reliability of their memories. Unlike Judge Roettger's examination, O'Connor and Gill were gentle but grueling.

At one point during his questioning of Sonia Lewkowicz, who did the laundry in a building near the gas chambers, in order to test her memory Gill asked where she hung up the guards' shirts and socks to dry.

Judge Levin lost his cool. "Is it important to know where they hung up the laundry?" he asked. "There is a limit to what you can ask. What is the difference where the laundry was hung when 850,000 human beings were killed at Treblinka?"

At another point, O'Connor asked Rosenberg: "Wasn't there anything you could have done?" suggesting that he was himself collaborating with the Nazis.

"How could I have helped them?" Rosenberg said. "By screaming?

They would have shoved me straight into the pit of blood. Don't ask me questions like that, I beg you. You weren't there. . . . I've never been asked such a terrible question. Not even by the worst anti-Semites."

Rosenberg then pointed at Demjanjuk. "Ask *him* what would have happened to me!"

Judge Levin noticed that Demjanjuk had muttered something in response to Rosenberg's outburst. He asked O'Connor what his client had said. O'Connor huddled with Demjanjuk.

"He said," O'Connor replied, "'You're a liar.'"

Rosenberg had written in his 1945 diary, two years after his escape from Treblinka, that Iwan Grozny died during the August uprising.

"How can you possibly come to this court," O'Connor demanded none too gently, "and point the finger at this gentleman when you wrote in 1945 that he was killed? He didn't come back from the dead, Mr. Rosenberg."

Even Demjanjuk laughed.

Rosenberg sat in a chair behind the witness stand with his arms defiantly crossed in front of his chest.

"I didn't *see* him dead," he said. "Others told me."

• • •

Sheftel thought O'Connor's cross-examination of the Treblinka witnesses was pathetic. Instead of testing their memories on nonemotional issues, he spent too much time grilling them about the shocking details of what they said they saw and experienced. In the end, O'Connor accomplished nothing but to upset the witnesses, further inflame the emotions of the spectators, and try the patience of the judges. No matter how gently or firmly he questioned the Treblinka survivors in his hunt for inconsistencies and memory lapses, he could not shake them from their conviction: John Demjanjuk, sitting seventy feet away from them, was Ivan the Terrible of their nightmares. Just as George Parker had predicted in his doubt memo, they were totally convinced and totally convincing.

• • •

If the testimony of the Treblinka survivors united Israel, however briefly, it reopened the wounds of suspicion and racial hatred on both sides of the Cuyahoga River in Cleveland. For the seventy thousand Jews living along the east bank of the river, the trial evoked memories of pogroms and Ukrainian militiamen helping the Nazis round up, rob, and murder Jews.

"Every nation has its heroes and collaborators," said one elderly émigré from Odessa who survived by fleeing before the advancing German army, like Miriam Radiwker and her husband. "And it is true that *some* Ukrainians hid Jews. Unfortunately, however, most of them worked for the Nazis."

West of the river, Ukrainians blamed the Jews for their own holocaust. "People talk about how we Ukrainians waved flags to greet the Germans when they invaded Ukraine," the owner of a popular Ukrainian tavern said. "But nobody mentions the way Jews popped up in good positions when the Communists came. They suddenly appeared, running around in red armbands."

The president of the Cleveland branch of the Ukrainian Congress, which represented most of the 1.5 million Ukrainian Americans, sadly observed: "This case has created exactly what the Jews want to prevent—more anti-Semitism."

A Ukrainian professor of history observed: "My concern is that when they get done with us, we'll look like barbarians." The recent telecast of the docudrama *Escape from Sobibor* fed into that fear. The three-hour Sunday night movie depicted all the guards at Sobibor as Ukrainians. As Father Stephen Hankevich, the pastor of Demjanjuk's St. Vladimir's Ukrainian Orthodox Church, put it: "It is not only John on trial. It is the Ukrainian nation that's on trial."

CHAPTER FORTY-TWO

The Battle of the Experts

Each side called five expert witnesses to pass judgment on the authenticity of the Trawniki card. As a group, they reviewed every feature of the document—signatures, photograph, printing, typewriter, ink, paper, seals, and blotches. They defended their conclusions for days on end through in-court demonstrations using diagrams, charts, photo overlays and montages, and probability projections. The pendulum of their testimony swung from fascinating to boring. Most of the time it was stuck on boring, which encouraged so much spectator chatter that Judge Levin had to repeatedly call for order because it was hard to hear the testimony.

It was up to the judges to decide who was more expert.

The prosecution opened the face-off with Amnon Bezaleli, chief document examiner of the Israeli police department and head of its identification laboratory. Bezaleli specialized in handwriting analysis, and in particular, in forged drivers' licenses—three thousand per year—working in a laboratory equipped with state-of-the-art optical tools including comparison microscopes, stereoscopes, infrared and ultraviolet ray scanners, and wavelength gauges.

Bezaleli's primary task for the prosecution was to authenticate the three signatures on the Trawniki card—SS Major Karl Streibel, supply officer Ernst Teufel, and Iwan Demjanjuk. His secondary task was to examine the printing, ink, and major blemishes on the card. Projecting enlarged photos on a courtroom screen, Bezaleli walked the judges through his analyses for two full days. His conclusions were crisp, clear, and confident:

- The signatures of Streibel and Teufel were authentic with certainty, but the signature of Iwan Demjanjuk was problematic and, thus, only probably authentic.
- Only one typewriter was used for the card—an Olympia model 23 manufactured in 1930. Everything about the typewriter was consistent with a card dating to 1941. There were no discrepancies.
- The stiff green paper used for the card was composed of rag, textiles, and bits of garments. It was a low-quality paper consistent with wartime scarcities, and it dated to the early 1940s.
- Only one kind of ink was used to create the official stamp, which was partly on the photo and partly on the card. The stamp was, therefore, not forged.
- The picture on the card had been reglued at some point. It could not be determined, however, whether the picture had accidentally fallen off the card or had been deliberately removed and replaced.
- Based on all the tests and observations, the card was not *doctored* in any way, and it was not a forgery, with some degree of certainty.

As decisive and confident as he was, Bezaleli left two big issues dangling: Demjanjuk's signature *could* have been forged; and the original card photo *could* have been removed and replaced with a photo of Iwan Demjanjuk.

The second prosecution witness was Gideon Epstein, who had testified six years earlier as the government's only expert document examiner at the 1981 Demjanjuk deportation trial in Cleveland. Epstein reached the same conclusions in Jerusalem that he had in Cleveland. They were identical to those of Bezaleli: The signatures of Streibel and Teufel were authentic, and the signature of Demjanjuk was only probably authentic.

In preparation for the Jerusalem trial, Epstein conducted a series of advanced tests he had not had time to perform in 1981. He examined the different color inks on the card, studied the large yellow-orange stains under ultraviolet light, and examined the perforations on the Trawniki card photo that did not appear on the paper it was glued to.

Epstein concluded:

- The writing on the card was done with both a fountain pen and pencils ranging in color from aqua blue to purple-black. Because the use of different colored pencils and ink was common on World War II documents, the color variations were of little significance.
- The yellow-orange stains were probably dried glue. It would take an evaluation by a certified chemist to determine with absolute certainty whether the substance was glue or a solvent. The latter would suggest card tampering and possible forgery.
- In all likelihood, the perforations on the picture were staple holes. It was common to find such holes on the photo but not on the document to which it was attached. Photographs were frequently stapled to a temporary document so they wouldn't be lost in a paper shuffle.
- There were different typeface and font designs on the Trawniki card. Such variations in the printing or typesetting were normal on World War II documents.
- The half of the official seal on the photograph and the half of the seal on the page matched perfectly. This proved that only one stamp was used.

Like Bezaleli, Epstein concluded that the card was not forged. And like Bezaleli, he left the same two issues dangling—the authenticity of Demjanjuk's signature and the possible substitution of card photos.

The third prosecution expert witness was Reinhardt Altman, a photo identification expert from Wiesbaden, Germany. Altman had worked for the German police for nearly thirty years, starting as a criminal investigator and ending up as a photo identification instructor. His job was to compare the photo on the Trawniki card to proven photos of John Demjanjuk—including two contemporary video frames of him entering the Jerusalem courtroom—to determine if the picture on the card was his.

A pioneer in the field of photo identification, Altman chose twenty-four predictive facial features for comparison, including jaw, hairline, eyes, nose, and especially the distinct configuration of the ear and the delicate line patterns of the inner lip. Then he conducted three tests. First, he compared the Trawniki photo with proven Demjanjuk photos, feature by feature. Next, he cut reproductions of the photos in half, placing the left half of the Trawniki photo next to the right half of known photos. Finally, he superimposed a proven photo over the Trawniki photo and concluded: "There is not the slightest doubt that these photographs are of one and the same person."

The fourth prosecution expert witness was Patricia Smith. She held a degree in dental surgery from the London Hospital Medical College, had studied physical anthropology at the University of Chicago—one of the world's leading schools in that discipline—and was professor of dental morphology at Hebrew University in Jerusalem. Unlike Altman, she not only compared facial harmony and disharmony, she *measured* them—the length of eyebrows, the distance between the eyes, the length of the bridge of the nose.

Step by step, Smith took the court through a fourteen-feature comparison of the 1942 Trawniki photo and a current video-derived photo of Demjanjuk entering the courtroom. To demonstrate "concordance" or matching, Smith used an overlay of each of the fourteen enlarged features from the two photos, projected on a courtroom screen.

Like Altman, Smith concluded that the 1942 photo on the Trawniki card was without a shadow of doubt that of John Demjanjuk.

The final prosecution expert witness was Tony Cantu, a paper and ink specialist with a doctorate in chemical physics from the University of Texas. Cantu's U.S. government career was as colorful as it was checkered. He began as a forensic scientist at the Justice Department, advanced to a document-dating specialist at the Bureau of Alcohol, Tobacco and Firearms, and ended up paper-chasing forgers for the FBI and the Treasury Department. In all, Cantu had conducted more than ten thousand investigations involving paper and ink.

Cantu tested the six different inks used to make the card signatures, translator notes, typewriter letter impressions, and seal impressions. Employing a hypodermic needle with the tip converted into a boring tool, Cantu extracted two or three samples from each of the six inks and subjected them to chemical analysis. Cantu also analyzed the Trawniki card paper fibers, looking for two ingredients that would definitively date the paper after World War II—glass, which was introduced around 1950, and synthetic fibers, first introduced around 1953.

Cantu concluded:

- None of the inks on the card was manufactured after 1941.
- The unbleached pulp and groundwood in the card fibers were consistent with paper available in 1942. None of the fibers con-

tained any materials that suggested the paper was manufactured after 1942.

- The purple ink that the Russian translator used to write his translation of the card was available from 1941 up to 1948.

There was little that defense attorneys O'Connor and Gill could do in their cross-examination of the prosecution's five expert witnesses except challenge their credentials in an attempt to destroy their credibility; argue that their conclusions were subjective and, therefore, unscientific and suspect; and label their conclusions invalid because their analyses were superficial:

- Amnon Bezaleli had no academic or technical training in forgery identification. Most of his work dealt with alleged forged contemporary drivers' licenses. His experience, therefore, was narrow, limited, and irrelevant to the examination of the Trawniki card. And because there were several key tests Bezaleli did not perform, his conclusion that the card was authentic was invalid.
- Gideon Epstein's analysis was so superficial that he didn't bother to analyze the three numerals Teufel had allegedly written on the card. Nor did he bother to count the number of ink colors or the number of Germans who wrote on the card. Nor did he analyze the ink found in the perforation holes. Nor did he measure and compare the signature strokes on the card with the strokes of Streibel and Teufel in the proven signatures. Epstein's conclusion that the card was authentic, therefore, was based on a sloppy and incomplete examination.
- Reinhardt Altman's analysis was based on the science of anthropology, but the technician had no training in the field. His conclusions were nothing more than voodoo conjury; his montages were merely optical illusions and "trix-mixes." Every conclusion Altman drew was unscientific and completely subjective.
- Patricia Smith admitted that there were differences in the facial features she compared. Those differences invalidated her conclusions about authenticity.

O'Connor and Gill couldn't touch Tony Cantu. The prosecution rested.

• • •

At this point in the trial, the Demjanjuk family knew that the defense was in deep trouble. Historians seemingly had proved that John Demjanjuk could not have been in Chelm when he said he was because the Germans had long since evacuated the camp; and they seemingly had proved also that Demjanjuk could not have been part of Vlasov's army when he said he was because the army didn't exist at that time. The Treblinka survivors were unflinching in their identification of John Demjanjuk as Ivan the Terrible. And the prosecution's argument favoring the authenticity of the Trawniki card was formidable and almost overwhelming.

But the prosecution had a weakness that did not go unnoticed. The Treblinka survivors were old and too sure of themselves. Israelis were beginning to doubt. Amir Shaviv, the legal correspondent for Israeli television, who kept his fingers on the pulse of the trial, voiced that doubt with precision and eloquence.

"It is very frustrating that after five months of hard work by the prosecution," he said in a telecast, "we still cannot stand up and say, without a shred of doubt: 'John Demjanjuk, you are Ivan the Terrible.' What is even more frustrating is that I would like to be able to hate John Demjanjuk, but I can't, because I am not certain that he is Ivan. And I would like to be able to pity John Demjanjuk—this old man all alone in a cell, far from home, away from his family—but I can't, because I am not sure that he is *not* Ivan."

Unfortunately for the Demjanjuk family, Amir Shaviv would not decide the fate of John Demjanjuk. Judges Dorner, Tal, and Levin would. And as the family saw it, the defense had failed to sow a doubt in the bench. Someone was to blame, and that someone was Mark O'Connor.

The family decided to pressure Demjanjuk into firing O'Connor. But that would leave the defense leaderless and in the lurch just days before it must mount its counterattack.

CHAPTER FORTY-THREE

Now What?

M ark O'Connor was more than a lawyer whom the Demjanjuk family hired to defend their husband and father. He was a supportive and understanding friend who had hung in there with them for five turbulent, frightening years. But the list of gripes against O'Connor was long and growing, and sacking him was no spur-of-the-moment decision. It was months in the making.

At the end of April 1987, more than two months after the trial had begun and just before the prosecution was about to present its five expert witnesses, John Demjanjuk Jr., or "Johnnie," as everyone called him, returned to Jerusalem from an extended visit in Cleveland with his mother, his sisters, Lydia and Irene, and Irene's husband, Ed Nishnic, who controlled the Demjanjuk Defense Fund purse strings. Johnnie immediately called Yoram Sheftel and asked him to come to his hotel. It was urgent.

Johnnie got right to the point. "Ed and I spent a lot of time in Cleveland discussing what's going on," he told Sheftel. "And we reached the conclusion that O'Connor is not living up to our expectation. His performance is flawed, and as a result, the defense is in a very bad position."

It was much worse than flawed. According to Sheftel, the defense *had* no defense. Three days before Johnnie returned to Jerusalem, O'Connor had let it slip during a discussion with Sheftel that he didn't have a single defense witness lined up, except John Demjanjuk. And he hadn't even begun to prepare Demjanjuk for his make-or-break testimony.

The admission shocked Sheftel. The defense was coming down to the wire and it had no strategy or counterattack. Realizing he had said too much, O'Connor asked Sheftel not to tell the family. Sheftel agreed. Johnnie's message from Cleveland changed his mind.

When Sheftel told Johnnie what O'Connor had admitted, Johnnie wasn't surprised. He had attended much of the trial and saw for himself how O'Connor's cross-examinations seemed rambling and pointless. Johnnie told Sheftel that his brother-in-law Ed would be calling the next day, and he wanted Sheftel to level with Ed, to tell it like it was, to hold nothing back. This was no time to be kind or forgiving.

The next day, Sheftel laid it out for Ed, chapter and verse:

O'Connor was so autocratic that Sheftel and Gill would only learn about defense motions and concessions when Judge Levin announced his rulings on them in the courtroom.

O'Connor never presented his co-counsels with an overall defense strategy because he didn't have one. He bumbled his way along, scoring an inconsequential point here and a dubious point there. He completely missed prosecution weaknesses.

O'Connor came to his cross-examinations totally unprepared and without a plan. And he refused to listen to the advice of his co-counsels on which points to make and which pitfalls to avoid.

O'Connor's questions were so convoluted and meandering that Judge Levin frequently had to ask him to rephrase them so the witness—and the court—could understand them.

O'Connor constantly lied to Demjanjuk about what was really happening in the trial. He took credit for every success and blamed Sheftel and Gill for every failure. And he conspired to undermine Demjanjuk's confidence in his co-counsels.

Sheftel thought that O'Connor was more interested in Mark O'Connor than in his client. He was always giving interviews to the press and smiling into TV cameras instead of preparing his cross-examinations. He was so vain that he once asked Sheftel to request the court to install a TV monitor at the defense table so he could watch himself in real time. And he was so insensitive that he asked Sheftel to petition the court for permission to allow O'Connor's wife to sit at the defense table as a paralegal, which she was not.

In sum, Sheftel told Ed Nishnic that the defense was losing the case now, and would most certainly lose it in the end, if O'Connor stayed on.

Sheftel had two private issues with O'Connor that he didn't share with Ed. One was philosophical and the other was deeply personal.

O'Connor believed that the Demjanjuk case could be won, and that he was indeed winning it. Sheftel believed that the court had already made up its mind. John Demjanjuk is Ivan the Terrible and must die in the gallows like Eichmann. Sheftel believed that the defense was certain to win, not in Dov Levin's court, but on appeal in Israel's Supreme Court. The defense strategy, therefore, should be to build a strong case for an appeal.

Sheftel had already put both courts on notice. Two weeks before his conversation with Johnnie, he had filed a motion requesting the three judges to resign because of their hostility toward Demjanjuk. When they refused, he appealed to the Supreme Court and lost.

Sheftel also had a deeply personal motive for exposing the failures of Mark O'Connor. It was almost a vendetta. O'Connor had not stood up for Sheftel when Judge Levin dressed him down in his chambers during a recess after he had called Levin's proceedings a "show trial." All three judges were furious at the insult, which, of course, had been caught on camera.

"I don't understand why the court is treating the defense so harshly," O'Connor complained to Judge Levin during the in camera scolding.

"The court is treating the defense with great respect," Levin said. "The problem is not the defense. The problem is *Mr. Sheftel*, who does not know how to behave and who dares accuse the court of conducting a show trial. . . . Sheftel, you will apologize straight away and beg the court's pardon."

Then Levin softened. "This is the trial of your life. Don't ruin yourself," he advised Sheftel. "Listen to what I am saying and apologize."

Sheftel didn't mind apologizing. It was the begging he found humiliating. But beg he did, and most eloquently. He never forgave Mark O'Connor.

Back in Cleveland, the Demjanjuk family decided on a compromise without informing their husband and father. With his critical testimony looming larger and ever more important, John Demjanjuk had enough to worry about. The family told O'Connor that they expected the defense to finally start working together like a team. Autocracy was out. Democracy was in. From now on, each defense decision would be decided by vote. The majority wins.

It didn't work. O'Connor, Sheftel, and Gill soon dragged their differences into the courtroom. They bickered loudly and publicly before spectators, TV cameras, and the bench. At one point, O'Connor bluntly told the media, "I would never buy a used car from Sheftel." It was clear to everyone who watched and listened that the defense was falling apart.

It was O'Connor who drove the final nail into his own coffin. He and Sheftel got into a heated argument over the cross-examination of prosecution witness Otto Horn, who had supervised the burying of corpses at Treblinka and had, more or less, identified Demjanjuk's photo as that of Ivan the Terrible. The argument quickly grew angry and accusatory.

"You're fired," said O'Connor, who was known for his explosive temper.

"You're hired," said Johnnie, who viewed the argument as the final straw. And with that, Sheftel became the Demjanjuk family's personal attorney and trial advisor.

The next step in the Demjanjuk family drama was obvious. Fire O'Connor. The problem was—the Demjanjuk *family* couldn't sack him. The family wasn't on trial, John Demjanjuk was. Court rules stipulated that the accused had to decide whom he wanted to represent him. And the problem was, John Demjanjuk didn't seem to understand how badly his case was faring. Could his wife and children convince him to cut his emotional ties to O'Connor?

• • •

Demjanjuk's behavior before and during the trial had been very erratic. One moment he was extending a hand to Treblinka survivor Eliyahu Rosenberg and saying, "Shalom!" The next moment he was calling the man a liar. One moment he was sitting passively in his dock listening to the trial over headphones, serene and seemingly uninterested, as if someone he didn't know was on trial for his life. The next moment he seemed irritated. One moment he would ignore the taunting spectators. The next, he would clasp his hands in the air like a boxer who had just scored a KO and blow kisses to the gallery.

At one point, Demjanjuk shocked the entire courtroom—spectators, bench, prosecutors, and his own defense. He raised his hand at the end of the cross-examination of Professor Wolfgang Schefler. Judge Levin recognized him. Demjanjuk told Levin that he had some questions he wanted to ask the professor.

"These questions are very important to me," Demjanjuk said. "I am a long time in jail now and I don't know what the future may hold for me."

O'Connor apologized to the court for the interruption. The prosecution objected. Levin granted the request. "This is a most important trial," Levin said, ordering a microphone for Demjanjuk. "It is very important to the accused to ask one or two questions. The same questions—it appears to the accused—that the defense doesn't manage to formulate properly."

Historian Wolfgang Schefler, who had testified at the Cleveland denaturalization trial, was a prosecution expert witness on Trawniki. He had just finished answering cross-examination questions about the two kinds of uniforms—black and khaki—that he claimed the Trawniki men wore. And he had testified that the man in the picture on the Trawniki card appeared to be wearing the black uniform of a Trawniki man.

"Professor Schefler!" Demjanjuk began. His "cross-examination" would last forty-five minutes. "You said that black uniforms were introduced into Trawniki later, and at first there were some sort of yellowish uniform. I have heard that is not true, and I would like you to clarify this."

Schefler told Demjanjuk that he didn't say yellowish uniforms but khaki. When Demjanjuk kept pressing, Schefler lost his composure. "Maybe *you* tell us what happened," he said.

Even Judge Levin seemed stunned by Schefler's response. "This last offer is not acceptable," Levin said. And O'Connor muttered loud enough for the bench to hear, "Impartial, huh?"

Demjanjuk next questioned Schefler about the alleged photograph of himself on the Trawniki card. "I saw it first eight years ago, and I've seen a great many, many things that apparently would show that this is a forgery."

Demjanjuk then said something that stung the defense table. "For example," he said, "I was also wearing a pullover."

The defense almost cheered when Demjanjuk finally sat down. He had practically admitted being a Trawniki man . . . unless, of course, Demjanjuk had been mistranslated.

Demjanjuk exhibited the same mood swings in his Ayalon prison cell. At one point, he tried to push visiting police investigator Alex Ish-Shalom out the door. On other occasions, he chatted with him as if he were a friend instead of a cop on a fishing expedition. Demjanjuk remained so distant from the trial that he didn't want to discuss it, even with his family. And when his daughter Irene came to visit, all he wanted to do was sing Ukrainian folk songs. It was as if he was living in a state of shock—this can't be happening to me. Hadn't the court, and Israel, already found him guilty? So why be concerned if things weren't going well? At times, he seemed depressed. At times, as happy as a child with a new toy.

Most of the time, Demjanjuk lived in an optimistic world of his own creation. He decorated his cell walls with hundreds of letters, Christmas and Easter cards, pictures of Christ and the Virgin Mary, as if to insulate himself from the bad news of the courtroom.

Demjanjuk's mood swings aside, the family had one thing going for it in its determination to get rid of John O'Connor. John Demjanjuk had never been an assertive man. He had always relied on his wife, Vera, to make the big decisions, and sometimes the small ones as well. Because he was passive by nature—not exactly the image of Ivan the Terrible— he had allowed his family to pick both lead attorneys, John Martin for the denaturalization trial and Mark O'Connor for the deportation hearing and the Jerusalem trial. If the family ganged up on him now, he would listen.

John Demjanjuk signed two blank pieces of paper the family gave him, either suspecting or knowing why. With the help of Sheftel, the family then drafted a letter above each signature. In one, Demjanjuk notified the court that he intended to fire O'Connor, asking for a trial extension to prepare for his defense with his new lead attorney. In the other, he told O'Connor he was finished.

"I am totally dissatisfied with your conduct of my defense, your conduct with my family, and your conduct with defense funds," Demjanjuk wrote O'Connor. "These concerns of mine have been stated to you once and again previously. . . . Consequently, this is to notify you that you are being discharged immediately."

• • •

Mark O'Connor was not happy about being sacked. His list of gripes against Sheftel sounded like Sheftel's own list against O'Connor: not preparing for cross-examinations, trying to poison the Demjanjuk family against him, posing as the "savior" of John Demjanjuk, hogging media attention, making legal moves behind his back, and using the trial to boost his legal career.

O'Connor added three more gripes that were not on his co-counsel's list. Sheftel was burned out and no longer capable of defending Demjanjuk because the rejection he experienced from his fellow countrymen had broken him. Furthermore, Sheftel was conspiring with the enemy—the prosecution—to get rid of O'Connor. And finally, Sheftel was a closet hypocrite, telling the Demjanjuk family that he supported them and would fight for them while in his heart he considered them to be anti-Semitic goyim.

O'Connor wrote Judge Levin a three-page letter accusing Sheftel of brainwashing the Demjanjuk family into getting him fired. "Mr. Sheftel convinced them to pressure the accused into signing two letters, backdated to June 30, 1987, removing his lead counsel from the case," O'Connor wrote. "Mr. Demjanjuk had confided in me in prison that, although he desires my representation in the case, he must follow the direction of the family."

O'Connor went on to warn the court of impending disaster if it accepted Sheftel as the new lead defense counsel. "Since Mr. Sheftel has refused for weeks to coordinate any trial preparation with me and visited the defense office in Jerusalem solely for the purpose of removing additional defense documents, he is *totally unprepared* to proceed."

Then O'Connor tendered his resignation.

But it wasn't quite that simple. "The decision to release the counsel is in our hands," Judge Levin said in a special hearing on who would be in and who would be out. "We can accept it, and we can refuse to accept it, *especially if it is contingent on postponing the rest of the trial.*"

The court needed to hear John Demjanjuk say that he wished to replace his lead counsel. Demjanjuk began his plea: "My family has decided to discharge O'Connor because he continued to work from my detriment—"

"And what is *your* decision?" Judge Levin interrupted. "What is your decision?"

"I have decided to accept my family's decision. I am in a cage, I am in jail. So I am *forced* to accept my family's decision."

"I can accept that answer except for the word 'forced,'" Judge Levin said. "No one is forcing you. The decision has to be yours."

"I told you that my family's decision is *my* decision," Demjanjuk replied forcefully.

That settled, the court needed to know whom Demjanjuk chose to replace O'Connor. Sheftel offered the court a signed power-of-attorney. Given all the sneaky moves he had witnessed so far in the O'Connor firing fiasco, Judge Levin didn't trust anyone.

"Does the defendant request that Mr. Sheftel be his defense attorney in the trial before us?" Levin asked Demjanjuk.

"Yes."

"Did you sign the document Mr. Sheftel is holding in his hands?"

"Yes."

"Do my colleagues and I understand correctly, that the defendant intends to tell us that from this moment on he will be represented by attorneys John Gill and Yoram Sheftel? Yes or no."

"Yes."

Demjanjuk then said in a strong, clear voice, "From everything that has been said here now, it seems to me that you are trying to scare me."

Like Sheftel's show trial comment, Demjanjuk's accusation stung. "What kind of language is that?" Levin asked.

"Your Honor, I apologize for having used a word that wasn't so appropriate," Demjanjuk said. "But I've only got four years of education."

The final issue to be settled was a possible delay of the trial because of a change of counsel. Levin made it clear that if Demjanjuk insisted on a postponement, it would be a deal breaker. No delay of trial was the condition allowing Demjanjuk to change his legal representation—a simple case of courtroom blackmail. Judge Levin had Demjanjuk by the throat and was squeezing. Demjanjuk gave in to the pressure and agreed not to ask for a delay.

"Does the defendant stand by his decision even if there is no postponement of the trial? Is that the defendant's position?"

Demjanjuk said yes.

Mark O'Connor was out. According to the Demjanjuk family, he had been paid six hundred thousand dollars over the five years he served as Demjanjuk's attorney. Yoram Sheftel was in, and he was bound to receive even more hate mail and death threats.

O'Connor returned to his law practice in suburban Buffalo. He would eventually be disbarred for one year by the Supreme Court of New York for, among other charges, "engaging in conduct involving dishonesty, fraud, deceit or manipulation . . . and comingling client funds with personal funds." O'Connor would not seek readmission to the bar after the one-year penalty ended.

The O'Connor affair would have been little more than a sad and grubby struggle of attorneys over power and purse if the life of John Demjanjuk did not depend on the outcome. Was the Demjanjuk family's decision to fire O'Connor and hire Sheftel a wise one? They didn't have long to wait for an answer. Sheftel opened the defense of John Demjanjuk on July 27, 1987, one week after the court had accepted him as Demjanjuk's new lead attorney.

CHAPTER FORTY-FOUR

The Ship That Almost Sank

L ike the prosecution, the defense presented five expert witnesses
to testify about the authenticity of the Trawniki card. As a group,
they had two jobs: discredit the findings of the prosecution's five
expert witnesses and prove the card was a forgery.

The first defense expert was Edna Robertson, the defense's answer to
prosecution handwriting experts Amnon Bezaleli and Gideon Epstein.
She looked promising on paper. An American psychologist from Panama City, Florida, with a master's degree in graphology, she had made
more than ten thousand signature comparisons, testified as an expert
witness in more than fifty U.S. trials, and was the president of the World
Association of Document Examiners (WADE).

Robertson's testimony got off to a bad start. Prior to the trial, she
had examined the original Trawniki card in the Israeli police laboratory
in Jerusalem. However, her analysis had been conducted in her Florida
laboratory using not original documents but enlarged photos of the card
and proven signatures. Analysis from photos cast an immediate doubt
on her conclusions. And unlike Bezaleli and Epstein, whose opinions
were strong and conclusive, all of Robertson's were qualified, and therefore highly vulnerable to cross-examination.

Robertson's first two conclusions surprised Sheftel and the defense.
First, both Bezaleli and Epstein had concluded that the signature of

Trawniki commandant Karl Streibel was authentic *without a doubt*. Robertson appeared to support them when she concluded that the signature was *possibly authentic*. Second, both Bezaleli and Epstein had testified that the signature of supply officer Ernst Teufel was *probably authentic*. Sheftel expected Robertson to testify that the signature was forged. Instead, she concluded that it was fraught with so many problems that *no firm conclusion* could be reached about it genuineness.

However tentative she was on her first two conclusions, Robertson was far from a total disappointment. Her next set of conclusions delivered exactly what Sheftel had hoped for:

- The signature of Iwan Demjanjuk was a fake. Bezaleli and Epstein had concluded that the Demjanjuk signature on the card was probably authentic.
- The yellow-orange spot on the card was a solvent used to loosen the photo so that it could be removed. Epstein had testified that the blotch was probably dried glue, but he couldn't be sure because he wasn't a chemist. Neither was Robertson.
- Two different kinds of inks were used to impress the seal on the Trawniki card, strongly suggesting forgery. Both Bezaleli and Epstein testified that only *one* ink was used.
- The original photograph on the card was removed and replaced. Both Bezaleli and Epstein agreed that the photo on the Trawniki card had either fallen off or had been removed. Because they couldn't tell which, neither could say whether the photo on the card was the original photo or not.
- The stamp impression on the photo was made with *two different* stamps to give the impression that one stamp had been used. Epstein had concluded that only one stamp had been used.
- The various ink and pencil colors on the Trawniki card were highly suspicious, suggesting forgery. Epstein found them to be normal on a World War II document.

The differences between the prosecution and defense testimony up to this point were as stark as they could be. Robertson's string of observations and conclusions added up to forgery: Two different stamps and inks were used to make the phony seal on the picture; a solvent was used to deliberately remove the photo, which was then replaced by a different photo; and the Demjanjuk signature on the card was a fake.

Bezaleli and Epstein had concluded that the Trawniki card was authentic.

Michael Shaked conducted the cross-examination of Edna Robertson. He wore the white hat in the courtroom and, as far as survivors and their families were concerned, Mickey Shaked, as he liked to be called, was a hero. Born in Israel, he had graduated from Hebrew University's school of law. As an assistant DA, he was a dangerously modest and unassuming man with a soft-spoken voice. Friends and foes alike agreed that he came to a cross-examination with a sharp scalpel and better prepared than the witnesses themselves. His treatment of those unfortunate enough to face him often bordered on brutal.

Given Robertson's attack on the conclusions of Bezaleli and Epstein, Shaked had no choice but to crush her at the stand. He systematically went about shredding her credibility and destroying her self-confidence.

"What do they call you," he began in a condescending tone. "Doctor Robertson or Professor Robertson?"

Sheftel was on his feet in a flash. "I think that the question is insulting," he said. "It is absolutely clear . . . that Ms. Robertson is neither a doctor nor a professor. The purpose of the question is to insult her, and I do not think that such questions have a place here. I—"

The interpreter signaled Sheftel that his microphone was not turned on.

"Better there be no microphone," Judge Levin said. "The comment is not fit for a microphone. Please sit down."

A few minutes later, Sheftel objected again, this time to a line of cross-examination that he felt was out of place.

"You have apparently come here today in a very aggressive mood," Judge Levin said, "and it would be worth your while to cool down. . . . From this point forward, objections, if there are any objections, may be made only by Mr. Gill."

The grounds for appeal were growing by the day.

Shaked got Robertson to admit that she did not qualify for membership in the prestigious American Society of Document Examiners, and that forensic document examiners did not respect her organization, WADE. In fact, U.S. courts disallowed WADE members from testifying as expert witnesses because, among other things, the organization did not require forensic document experience as a condition for membership.

Shaked noted that Robertson's conclusion that a solvent had caused the large yellow-orange stain on the Trawniki card was based on a purely visual inspection. He asked Robertson: "You did not conduct any further tests or examination—chemical analysis or whatever—in order to make sure that it was *in fact* a solvent?"

"That is correct," Robertson said. "I am not a chemist."

By this time, Shaked had Robertson exactly where he wanted her—on the defensive—and he kept pushing her to the edge of an emotional cliff. He got her to admit that her conclusion about the two inks used in stamping the seal over the Trawniki card photo was based on a *visual* inspection, and that she had taken neither ink nor paper samples.

"How [could you give] an expert opinion in court about the subject of ink," Shaked demanded, "when you don't know anything, and *have no idea* either about paper or about ink?"

"I didn't say I didn't know *anything* about ink. I have a general knowledge," Robertson said lamely. "I would add that the tests that I have performed on the inks are accepted tests in *my profession*."

Picking up on Robertson's "I have a general knowledge" statement, Shaked asked: "In chemistry, what does 'Ca' stand for?"

"I'm not a chemist."

Ca, of course, is the chemical symbol for common calcium.

"If you look at a molecular chart, do you know what it is about?"

"No!"

"How do you testify in court about ink, if you don't know its chemical composition," Shaked pressed. His voice had a hard edge.

"There is no need to be so abrasive," Judge Levin scolded.

"Do you know what paper that is," Shaked asked more gently, referring to the Trawniki card.

"I don't test paper. I am an *observer*," Robertson said. "I look for differences."

Next, Shaked baited a trap. Robertson had not taken the time to stop in Germany to view the *original* proven signatures of Karl Streibel and Ernst Teufel. She based her conclusions about their authenticity on a visual analysis of enlarged *photos* of the original signatures.

"How, as a self-respecting expert, could you base your opinion on blown-up photographs," Shaked asked.

"It was a provisional and qualified opinion," Robertson said in her defense.

"Provisional in what sense?"

"I never, never give an [unqualified] opinion based on copies."

Having elicited that strong denial, Shaked sprung the trap. He reminded Robertson about another signature comparison case in which she gave an *unqualified* opinion based on a photograph of a signature.

"I should have been more careful and qualified my statement," Robertson said, clearly embarrassed.

"You acted against a basic principle of your profession?"

"Yes," Robertson said, quickly adding, "in this *one* example."

Shaked saved the best until last. Robertson testified that she found two different inks in the seal over the Trawniki card photo, which led her to conclude that there were two different seals, suggesting forgery. Her conclusions were based on her analysis of the seal ink on a sophisticated visual spectral comparator (VSC) provided by the Israeli police laboratory. It was the same instrument Bezaleli had used to prove that there was only *one* ink present in the stamp on the photo.

Under cross-examination, Robertson admitted that she had had problems operating the VSC. She could manipulate a few of the controls but could not manage the scanner's critical color filter system, which was necessary to accurately measure the luminescence contained in the ink. One kind of luminescence meant one ink. Two kinds meant two inks.

Shaked called for another VSC analysis of the seal, this time in court. Bezaleli operated the scanner, projecting images onto the courtroom screen. With the proper use of the filters, it became clear that there was only one kind of luminescence . . . one ink.

Visibly shaken and emotionally exhausted, Edna Robertson stepped off the witness stand. The next day, she told the press: "They have humiliated me in front of the whole world. My career has been destroyed. From now on they will laugh at me in every court."

The second defense witness was William A. Flynn, chief document examiner in the Arizona Department of Public Safety Crime Laboratory. Trained both by the Pennsylvania State Police and the FBI, he was a certified forensics document examiner and forgery expert like Gideon Epstein. And although he had only an associate's degree, he made up for his lack of academic credentials with experience. Over his twenty years as a "questioned document" examiner, he had analyzed more than fifteen thousand alleged forgeries.

Flynn had a bias that he honestly admitted to the court. The discoveries of the Mormon Salamander Letters in the United States and the "Hitler Diaries" in Germany in the early 1980s had turned Flynn into a cautious and conservative document examiner. Initially, both documents were declared authentic by handwriting experts, only to be declared forgeries later by forensic scientists who had analyzed the ink and paper the forger used to create his documents. It was Flynn himself who had proven conclusively that the Mormon letters were forged, based on a sophisticated ink comparison analysis.

Before Salamander and the Hitler Diaries, Flynn had been willing to pronounce a document definitely genuine or definitely not genuine. After Salamander and the Diaries, Flynn added a third category—*cannot tell.* Flynn's cautious distinction did not make the defense clap for joy. What it needed at this point were definitive, not tentative, conclusions from Flynn, whose testimony was supposed to be the defense's answer to Amnon Bezaleli's and Gideon Epstein's conclusions about the authenticity of the three Trawniki card signatures.

Flynn cautiously concluded:

- Streibel's signature fell in the *cannot tell* category.
- Teufel's signature was only *possibly* genuine because his handwriting was "erratic" and, therefore, easy to forge.
- Even John Demjanjuk himself probably would be unable to say with certainty that the signature made forty years ago was *his own.* Therefore, it was *highly unlikely* that Demjanjuk's name appearing on the card was executed by John Demjanjuk.

Judge Levin observed that the expert witnesses the court had heard so far seemed to agree on facts, but disagreed on what to make of them. "Is it possible," Levin asked Flynn, "that there might be a difference of opinion . . . with regard to the *interpretation* attached to these findings?"

"Yes," Flynn said, sounding like a witness for the prosecution.

In preparation for his testimony, Flynn had personally forged Streibel's and Teufel's signatures to demonstrate to the court how easy it was to re-create them. He also produced a very clever photomontage of himself in an SS uniform.

Shaked objected. Flynn's forgery skills were not on trial; the Trawniki signatures were, he argued.

"Objection sustained," Levin ruled. "The entire matter is irrelevant to this trial."

Sheftel was disappointed and angry. He thought that Flynn was going to declare Demjanjuk's signature a forgery and the Trawniki card a fake. Flynn did neither. And now his nemesis, Judge Levin, had tossed out Flynn's important demonstration, blocking a major line of defense questioning. Sheftel would have none of it.

"Under these circumstances," Sheftel told Levin, "we waive [Flynn's] testimony and request that it be struck in its entirety from the record."

Both the court and the prosecution were momentarily stunned by the totally unexpected response to Levin's ruling.

"What's *your* position," Levin asked Shaked.

"We definitely have much to question [the witness] about in cross-examination," Shaked said, "and we insist on our right to do so."

Flynn had his own surprise waiting for the court. He refused to submit to a cross-examination, because, he told the court, Nishnic, who had hired him to testify for the defense, forbade him to do so. Nishnic had threatened to sue him if he submitted to a cross-examination.

At this point, Judge Levin was more than irritated. He didn't relish being challenged by an American moneybag. Ruling that Nishnic's threat was witness intimidation, he ordered the police to investigate Nishnic for possible criminal obstruction of justice. Then he ordered Flynn to answer Shaked's cross-examination questions under penalty of contempt of court.

Shaked conducted a clever and devastating bait-and-trap cross-examination. Although Flynn never really called the Trawniki card a forgery as the defense had expected and paid him to do, he had cautiously implied it. To make his trap work, Shaked had to do what Sheftel couldn't do—get Flynn to commit to a forgery conclusion.

"How can you come to the *inference* that it must have been forged?" Shaked innocently asked Flynn.

"My position is," Flynn explained, "we cannot tell positively if Teufel and Streibel are genuine or not, and the Demjanjuk signature—in my opinion—is *forged*. . . . And since [the Trawniki card] was in the hands of the KGB, they would be a likely candidate."

Flynn had finally used the F-word. Shaked was now ready to bait the trap. A few weeks before the trial, and after he had studied the original Trawniki card, Flynn talked about the Demjanjuk case at a forensic document seminar in Palm Springs, California. Shaked had obtained a transcript of Flynn's comments and read aloud from it:

"I have examined the card firsthand for three days . . . microscopically, and there's nothing about the card that I can see that *would not* have passed muster."

"I don't remember my exact words," Flynn said. "I don't think I said that."

Shaked then sprung the trap. He played a tape recording of Flynn's seminar remarks. The click of the machine at the end of the recording echoed through the courtroom with dramatic finality.

William Flynn's own words had just made his entire direct testimony worthless.

• • •

The third defense witness was Yasser Iscan, the defense's answer to Patricia Smith, who had made morphological comparisons based on photomontages of facial features such as nose, ears, and chin. A professor of forensic anthropology and a consultant to medical examiners in Florida, Iscan out-credentialed Patricia Smith, who did not have a degree in anthropology. His job as an expert defense witness was to either destroy Smith's credibility or to cast serious doubts about her final conclusion: The photo on the Trawniki card was *definitely* that of John Demjanjuk.

Like Flynn, Iscan had a bias. He told the court that the photo superimposition technique used by Smith was "essentially worthless," and he set out to prove his point by replaying and reanalyzing Smith's seven-minute video demonstration for the bench.

As the video played, Iscan pointed out what he considered to be imperfect photo matchings, or areas where two images did not appear to coincide. Iscan also pointed out to the court where Smith's photomontages appeared to be too dark or too fuzzy to warrant a positive conclusion.

Iscan then explained to the court that he had done his own comparison of the Trawniki card photo and the proven photos of Demjanjuk in his own laboratory. Based on that examination, he concluded:

- Comparing proven photos with the Trawniki card photo was like comparing apples and oranges. Therefore, it is not possible to say whether the Trawniki card photo was that of John Demjanjuk or not.
- Smith's conclusions were based on optical illusions created in a laboratory.

As a defense witness, Iscan had a major weakness—his credibility as an expert witness on the subject of photo identification. In his cross-examination, Shaked attacked that weakness without wasting a moment of court time.

First, Shaked got Iscan to admit that his principal work centered on identifying for medical examiners the age and sex of skeletons, not real people. Then Shaked got Iscan to admit that in determining the age and sex, he did not study the skull or what was left of the face. He only examined the thorax, pelvis, and femur of the skeleton. The face was the issue in the trial, not a leg bone. Finally, Shaked got Iscan to admit that photo identification was outside the area of his expertise.

In sum, although Iscan was indeed an expert, he was not an expert on the subject he had just testified about. His photo analysis and conclusions were, therefore, that of a nonexpert and useless.

• • •

The fourth expert defense witness was Anita Pritchard, a doctoral candidate in psychology at Columbia Pacific University in Marin County, California, across the Bay Bridge from San Francisco. She was the defense's answer to photo analysts Reinhardt Altman, who cut Demjanjuk photos in half and reassembled them, and Patricia Smith, who superimposed one Demjanjuk image on top of another creating a montage. Like Robertson, Pritchard was a certified graphologist. Her specialty was physiognomy, the art of appraising character or personality from facial features. As a practitioner, she did photo comparisons of faces without using gimmicks like montages, video projectors, scanners, or multiple cameras. Pritchard's only analytical instrument was her naked eye.

John Gill had found Pritchard in Houston in his last-minute rush to recruit expert witnesses. There had been little time to prepare her for her testimony until she arrived in Jerusalem a few days before she was scheduled to testify. When the two defense attorneys questioned her in her hotel room, they learned that she had served as an expert witness in only *one* trial, and that her academic and research credentials were worse than weak. At that late date, however, the defense had little choice but to put her on the stand and pray. She was all they had at the moment. She was their Hail Mary pass.

Pritchard testified that both Altman and Smith used photo comparison techniques that were untested and not accepted in the scientific community. Echoing the conclusion of Iscan, Pritchard explained that the images they created were so suggestive to the human eye as to be little more than optical illusions. And conclusions based on optical illusions were themselves illusions.

Pritchard concentrated on Altman. She studied photos of Altman's cut-and-match display provided by Gill and testified that Altman had altered the photographs when he cut and sized them for the comparison. His matches were fake. In effect, Pritchard was calling Altman a forensic fraud. A snake-oil salesman.

To prove her point, Pritchard randomly selected photos of twelve male models from magazines. Then she cut each picture in half and reassembled them, randomly placing half of one model's picture next to half of another model, just like Altman had done with his Trawniki card photo and his proven photos of John Demjanjuk. Ten out of twelve of Pritchard's randomly selected and matched photo halves appeared to be just as correlated as Altman's Demjanjuk photo halves. The pieces reasonably matched.

Pritchard smiled at the court as if she had just scored a first-round knockout. The bench did not smile back. It was not impressed with her theories or her unscientific demonstration. If Shaked had been rough on Edna Robertson, he showed no mercy with Anita Pritchard, who had just called one of his expert witnesses a fraud. Shaked's plan was not to humiliate her on the stand as he had Edna Robertson, but to completely break her.

Shaked began the destruction of Anita Pritchard by challenging her credentials as an expert witness. Was she an anthropologist?

No.

Was she an anthromorphologist?

No.

Was she a morphologist?

No.

Did she have any specialized knowledge of morphology of the face?

No.

Had she published any articles in professional journals dealing with the psychology of visual perception, her specialty?

No.

Did she read—or even know—the professional journals relevant to her field?

Only a few.

How much did she know about neurology?

A little.

Physiology?

A little.

Optics of the eye?

A little.

"Since you don't know these disciplines, how can you talk about visual perception?" Shaked demanded. He moved on to her in-court, photo-halves demonstration.

Was her sliced-photo demonstration based on scientific criteria?

No.

She said she *randomly* selected the photos used in the demonstration. Did she even know the rules for random selection?

No.

Did she analyze Altman's work from his *original* display or from photos of his display?

Photos.

From photos? How can you call yourself an expert?

Shaked wasn't finished with Pritchard just yet. He got her to admit that the only book she had authored was self-published; that Columbia Pacific University was not an accredited school; that her master's in psychology from the University of Oklahoma was granted by the department of human relations, not the department of psychology; and that most of her education in graphology was through correspondence courses.

"You're creating an *illusion* that you're an expert," Shaked hammered. "Maybe you should take back what you told the court earlier. . . . Tell the court you're not an expert."

In the end, Pritchard, who had finally reviewed Altman's original photos and montages between court sessions, recanted her earlier testimony. "My *entire* qualified opinion must be removed from my testimony. . . . There were no alterations in the Altman composites. If offense was taken, I apologize."

As Pritchard left the stand, Shaked offered his hand as if to say, "I'm sorry. I was just doing my job."

The defense of John Demjanjuk had just turned from disaster to catastrophe.

Pritchard locked herself in her hotel room that evening. When she didn't appear for dinner, Sheftel thought he better check to see if she was okay. He called her room. She didn't pick up. He knocked on the door and called her name. She didn't answer.

Sheftel found the hotel manager and told him that something was wrong with his guest, Ms. Anita Pritchard. She didn't answer the phone or the door. Sheftel and the manager rushed to her room and unlocked the door with a master key. They found Pritchard in her pajamas spread-eagled on the bed and unconscious. She had swallowed a bottle of pills.

Sheftel rushed Pritchard to the emergency room, where a doctor pumped her stomach. When she became aware that she had failed to kill herself, she ripped out the intravenous tubes. Nurses reattached them and watched over her. Pritchard returned to Houston a few days later.

At this critical point in the trial, the defense was frustrated, humiliated, and desperate. Shaked had crushed Edna Robertson. He had turned William Flynn into a prosecution witness. He had dismissed Yasser Iscan as irrelevant. And he had completely destroyed Anita Pritchard.

If that wasn't enough grief for the embattled defense, time was fast running out. It needed a big gun, an expert among experts, a forensic scientist with impeccable credentials. Sheftel asked Ed Nishnic to find such a person and fast. He would be the defense's last hope. The redeemer.

Nishnic found Julius Grant.

• • •

Eighty-six-year-old Julius Grant was a British chemist with a doctorate in toxic metals from the University of London; an internationally recognized expert in handwriting, paper, and ink analysis; and a highly sought-after freelance expert on dating documents and paintings. He had more experience as a historic document examiner than all the prosecution experts combined, and he had served as an expert witness in more than seventy countries around the world, a record no expert witness before him could even come close to matching.

It was Julius Grant who had conclusively proven for the *London Sunday Times* that the Hitler Diaries were fake. He reached his unqualified and undisputed conclusion in just five hours by chemically determining that the ink used in making the diaries was recent ink, not ink from the 1940s. Grant had also proven that the "Mussolini Diaries" were forgeries and that the mummy of Egyptian pharaoh King Tutankhamen, discovered in 1922, was authentic.

Grant's task as a defense witness was huge—prove that *all five* prosecution expert witnesses—Bezaleli, Epstein, Altman, Robertson, and Smith—were wrong in one way or another, by showing that *at least one* important element on the Trawniki card had been forged. As Grant took the stand, his boney hands and slight frame belied his physical strength and inner resolve. But he quickly showed the court just how tough he was when he declined the chair Judge Levin offered him and remained standing for the entire three days of his testimony, which was articulate, reasoned, precise, clear, and cautiously wise.

Grant made it clear to the court that he based his analysis of the Trawniki card signatures on two graphology principles. First: "Handwriting comparison is not an exact science. . . . You cannot identify a person with certainty from handwriting. . . . There are times when the forger is more clever than the handwriting expert, as in the *Hitler Diaries*."

Second: "When a person signs his name—whether he does it once, twice, or a thousand times—he never does it twice exactly the same."

With those two conditions in mind, Grant analyzed the original Trawniki card, the original and proven signatures of Karl Streibel, *photos of*—but not the original proven signatures of—Ernst Teufel, the card paper and ink, the questioned Demjanjuk photo, the perforations on the card, and the ink in the perforation holes.

Grant concluded:

- It was *highly probable* that Streibel's signature was authentic. He added, however, that it was possible the signature had been written by a very sophisticated forger.
- Teufel's signature was convincing but only *possibly authentic* because he (Grant) had not examined the original signatures.
- The Demjanjuk signature was *forged.*
- The ink in the perforations on the card photo was identical to the ink the Russian translator had used for his writing on the card. The ink got into the holes *after* they were made, leading him to doubt the authenticity of the photograph.
- Based on his chemical analysis of the age of the glue used to fix the photo to the card, the photo was replaced in the Soviet Union, not at Trawniki.
- It was unlikely that the paper was made during World War II because of the heavy rag content of the card. Rags were so precious during the war, they were "hoarded like gold."

Putting all the pieces together, Grant concluded: "Indications are that the identification card is not authentic. In this evaluation, I am greatly influenced by the accused's signature on it, which I find not to be his."

The redeemer had done what Sheftel hoped he would. The internationally famous and highly respected Julius Grant had declared the Trawniki card a fake. All Shaked could do during his cross-examination was to rub some of the luster off Grant's clear and reasoned conclusions.

In effect, Grant had cast a gray shadow of doubt over the whole Trawniki card. His testimony was so authoritative that the court could neither dismiss it nor treat it lightly. The question was: What weight would the judges give his opinions in their deliberations?

Convinced that Grant had changed the whole course of the trial, the defense presented its next witness with less panic and more confidence. His task was huge—convince the court that he was never trained at Trawniki and that he was not Ivan the Terrible. Rather, he was a Russian POW imprisoned in a camp in Poland and a newly inducted soldier in General Vlasov's army.

CHAPTER FORTY-FIVE

Victim or Liar?

I f it please the court," the accused said to a packed Hall of the People. "I am John Demjanjuk."

Thus began the swan-song defense of "Ivan the Terrible." More than three hundred spectators had gathered in the courtroom to hear him lie and, if they were lucky, to be treated to another emotional drama. To those who had been following the trial, Demjanjuk was already half-guilty even before he answered the first question. To the survivors and their families, his testimony was a waste of time. On to the gallows!

John Gill conducted the direct examination. As seasoned defense attorneys, both he and Sheftel knew it was always risky to place a defendant on the stand. But what choice did they have? If Demjanjuk did not testify, it would be interpreted as an admission of guilt.

Gill's job was to show that Demjanjuk was a simple, honest man with nothing to hide, change Demjanjuk's image from perpetrator to victim, and make his wartime alibi sound believable. Gill began with Demjanjuk's childhood. The court was both patient and indulgent.

Demjanjuk testified that it had taken him eight years to complete four grades of school, and not because he was slow. "My parents were very poor, and we had nothing to wear. No shoes to put on," he explained. "If my father had any job whatsoever, I had to stay home. . . . Except for the third grade, I spent two years in each grade. When I was in fifth grade, and asked to repeat it for a third time, they would not let me do it. I received what was called a *disqualification* report card."

After being expelled from school, Demjanjuk joined a Komsomol, a communist youth organization, and plowed fields on a collective farm (*kolkhoz*). A dependable worker, he was eventually promoted to labor team organizer.

Like everyone in their village, the Demjanjuk family suffered terribly during Stalin's forced famine (the Holodomor) of 1932–33. "It was so horrible it goes beyond anything that humanity had known up to then," Demjanjuk testified. "Our entire family—my mother, my sister, myself—were swollen from hunger. . . . We ate rats, our cat, and our bird. People were lying dead in their homes, in their yards, on the roads, exposed to sunlight. No one buried them."

As soon as it became clear that they would starve to death like their neighbors, the family sold all their belongings for food. When they had nothing left, they sold their home for eight loaves of bread and headed east for another *kolkhoz*, where a relative lived and worked. She had food.

The Demjanjuk family returned to their village the following year when the famine was officially over. "We didn't find anyone alive," he testified. The family moved into the abandoned house of a relative, and Iwan returned to his old job on the *kolkhoz*.

Russia's war with Finland in the winter of 1939–40 changed his life. All the *kolkhoz* tractor drivers were drafted into the army, and young Iwan was given their job. When none returned after the war, Iwan's temporary job became permanent, until late 1940, when he received a draft notice ordering him to report to an induction center with a plate, spoon, and two pairs of underwear.

When Iwan showed up without the underwear because he couldn't afford any, the army sent him back home. But when Germany invaded the Soviet Union the following summer, the army quickly recalled him—it didn't much care whether he brought extra underwear or not—and sent him to artillery training school. From there, he joined the front line at the Dnieper River, where he was seriously wounded.

"I couldn't move. I couldn't budge. I couldn't walk," Demjanjuk testified. "I shouted. I was screaming with pain."

Comrades took Demjanjuk to a house where there were other wounded soldiers. The next day, the army sent him to the first of four hospitals in four different cities. After doctors finished patching him up, leaving a piece of shrapnel in his back close to his spine, the Red Army sent him to defend Kerch, on the Crimean peninsula. The German army captured him there.

"The Germans had bombed us," he recalled for the court. "And there was no place to hide. We were sitting in our trenches, and the Germans just came up and took us prisoner."

The Germans put Demjanjuk and seventy other Soviet POWs to work widening the railroad tracks to accommodate German railcars and repairing the sections of track damaged by bombs. They got bread and coffee three times a day and slept in a railroad car. Six to eight weeks later, Demjanjuk was sent to a transit POW camp in Rovno, Ukraine.

"It was very small," Demjanjuk testified. "We could barely stand.... So during the day we were taken outside the camp into a clearing in the forest where we could either lie down or sit down. We were fed once a day. A pot of some kind of porridge. Just water ... At night we could only stand."

After a week or two at Rovno, the Germans sent Demjanjuk to Chelm, Poland.

Up to this point in his direct examination, John Gill had shown John Demjanjuk to be an ordinary victim of Joseph Stalin and the German army. But as soon as Demjanjuk told the court that the SS had sent him to the POW camp in Chelm, his defense alibi began.

When he arrived at Chelm, Demjanjuk testified, there were no barracks. Prisoners slept on the ground. His first job was to help assemble prefab barracks on railroad tie foundations. He also helped unload coal, potatoes, and turnips at the nearby railroad station.

"Conditions were atrocious," he said. "All we thought about was *food*. . . I would have given my life for a loaf of bread."

Then Demjanjuk got lucky. The Germans gave him a bare bunk inside a barracks during the 1942–43 winter. The unlucky slept in the cold and snow. Most did not make it through the winter. Beginning in the spring of 1943—when the Trawniki card indicated he was serving at Sobibor—Demjanjuk testified that he began digging and cutting peat outside the Chelm camp with about seventy other POWs until winter, when the ground froze.

The SS built a Trawniki subcamp outside the tiny village of Dorohucza, not far from Chelm, Trawniki, and Sobibor. A mixture of Dutch and Polish Jews worked in the peat fields along the Wieprz River together with Soviet POWs from the Chelm camp. Trawniki men guarded them.

Either the following fall or early winter of 1944, Demjanjuk told the court, the Germans gave him and three to four hundred other Ukrainian POWs Italian uniforms and loaded them onto trains destined for Graz, Austria. They were told they were going to join a German army all-Ukrainian division that was about to be formed. They would fight the Soviets, not the Americans, French, or British.

"We were put into stables," Demjanjuk testified. "We didn't have anything to do. We sat around and played cards. Then doctors called us in."

A doctor drew blood from Demjanjuk's finger and typed the blood. A machine stamped a blood-type tattoo on his arm. He began removing the tattoo, he testified, when he learned that the Waffen SS divisions were also tattooed. Not wanting to be associated with the SS, he used a sharp stone to scrape the mark off his arm. It took a long time. Scrape, heal . . . scrape, heal . . . until all that remained was a scar.

Demjanjuk said that after the war he took a driver training course offered by the U.S. Army at the POW camp in Landshut, Germany. After he passed his driver's test and received a license, he worked for the Americans as a truck driver for two and a half to three years. He wore a black uniform and was paid a carton of cigarettes a week.

Have you ever been enlisted in the SS? Gill asked at the end of his direct examination of Demjanjuk. Have you ever served in a death camp?

"Honorable Judges, I am not the hangman or henchman you are after," Demjanjuk pleaded. "I was never at Trawniki, Sobibor, or Treblinka. . . . My heart aches, and I grieve deeply for what was done to your people by the Nazis . . . because you were Jews. I wish to be believed. Please do not put the noose around my neck for the things that were done by others."

State attorney Yonah Blatman began the cross-examination of John Demjanjuk. Like Michael Shaked, whom he had hired to lead the prosecution team, Blatman was meticulously prepared. How could he not be? He had three young attorneys trained in American law schools to do the team's nonlegal research. (A second team handled the legal research.) As a group, they were fluent in Hebrew, English, German, Yiddish, and Russian.

Like Shaked, Blatman was systematic. For weeks before his cross-examination, he had studied and analyzed every sworn statement Demjanjuk had made, from his pretrial deposition and interrogatories in Cleveland in 1977 to his pretrial interviews with the Israeli police in Jerusalem. Besides finding inconsistencies and contradictions in the statements, Blatman discovered what he believed was a revealing pattern: John Demjanjuk's alibi kept growing more specific over the years, with more and more detail added to make his story sound real and credible.

Blatman believed that Demjanjuk, like a spider, had spun a web of lies to explain why he could not have been at the Trawniki training school in 1942 and later at Treblinka. Blatman's cross-examination plan was to expose the tissue of lies and destroy the web. He took five days to do it.

The cross-examination quickly turned into a game of courtroom dodgeball. Whenever Blatman pointed out a contradiction, Demjanjuk would say "bad translation" or "what do you expect, it happened forty years ago?" or "I was under pressure and got confused" or "you're just trying to trick me."

Blatman began with a string of small contradictions—here you say in the fall, there you say in the winter; here you say 200, there you say 300. Then he moved on to larger issues.

In Cleveland, Demjanjuk testified that Vlasov army soldiers did not have a blood-type tattoo. He removed his because he wanted "to be like the other boys." In Jerusalem, he testified that he removed the tattoo when he learned that Waffen SS soldiers had them because he didn't want to be associated with the SS.

In Cleveland, Demjanjuk testified that he had guarded a Russian general as a member of Vlasov's army. In Jerusalem, he testified that he was *supposed* to guard the general but never did because he did not have a proper uniform and was too weak and emaciated for guard duty.

In Cleveland, Demjanjuk testified that as a soldier in Vlasov's army, he was going to be sent to the front. In Jerusalem, he testified that he was skin and bones. If he was too weak and emaciated to simply guard an unarmed Soviet general, how could he fight at the front?

In Cleveland, Demjanjuk swore that he had been captured in Kerch by the German army in late 1942 or early 1943, the exact time when the U.S. government argued during the denaturalization trial that he was being trained at Trawniki and posted to Treblinka. Several historians had testified that the battle of Kerch took place in May 1942.

In Cleveland, Demjanjuk testified that when he arrived at Chelm, there were a few barracks. In Jerusalem, he said that were no barracks when he arrived at the camp.

In Cleveland, Demjanjuk testified that he built and cleaned barracks at Chelm. He added no more details. In Jerusalem, he said that besides assembling the barracks, which took a few months, he unloaded food and supplies from trains and he dug peat for nine or ten months with about seventy fellow Ukrainian POWs. "I can still see them before my eyes," he said. But he couldn't remember a single name.

In Cleveland, Demjanjuk testified that there were only Russian POWs at Chelm. In Jerusalem, he said there were also some Italians.

In Cleveland, Demjanjuk testified that he had written to his niece in Ukraine for copies of his birth certificate and military records, and that his wife Vera had visited his and her own mother in Ukraine. If he was so afraid of the Soviets, why did he endanger the lives of his niece and his wife?

In Cleveland, Demjanjuk testified that the KGB frame-up began in the mid-1950s when he wrote to his mother and Vera sent her packages. Later he said the frame-up began when Vera visited Ukraine in 1964 and 1966.

In both Cleveland and Jerusalem, Demjanjuk testified that he had completed only four years of school. If so, how could he have been admitted into the Komsomol, a communist leadership incubator, when he was so uneducated?

In Cleveland, Demjanjuk testified that he worked as a driver for an international relief organization right after the war, in 1945. In Jerusalem, he said he first drove a truck for the U.S. Army in 1947, after he got a driver's license. If he drove a truck in 1945 immediately after the war, he must have known how to drive one *during* the war, like Ivan the Terrible.

In Cleveland, Demjanjuk claimed his eyes were blue. On his visa application, he wrote that his eyes were gray—the same color mentioned on the Trawniki card.

In Cleveland, Demjanjuk testified that he went to school for four years. In Jerusalem, he said he attended school for eight years, and that the only grade he did not repeat was third.

• • •

Under the pressure of Blatman's relentless cross-examination, Demjanjuk appeared calm most of the time. On occasion his face turned red, either in anger or embarrassment at being caught in a contradiction he couldn't talk his way out of.

Judge Levin, for one, was visibly disturbed by what appeared to be Demjanjuk's evasions. "You have a talent for not answering questions," he lectured. "You are the *accused* in this case. You must be believed. You can't say things that run counter to your testimony in the United States and expect to be believed."

"My tragic mistake," Demjanjuk said, "is that I can't think properly. I can't answer properly."

The cross-examination got deadly serious when Blatman began to attack the heart of Demjanjuk's alibi—the eighteen months he said he had spent in the POW camp in Chelm. Prior to Demjanjuk's testimony, a historian had argued for the prosecution that the accused could not have been at Chelm in the fall of 1944 when he said he was because authenticated records showed that the camp was evacuated in April 1944 in anticipation of an invasion by the Red Army.

Blatman began simply enough by asking Demjanjuk to describe his work as a peat digger. The attorney then worked his way up to a Clarence Darrow crescendo.

"Every day . . . our entire barrack set out to dig," Demjanjuk said. "It wasn't far from Chelm. . . . Sometimes they would transport us. Other times we would walk."

"How long did you work at it?"

"For a long time, maybe nine or ten months. That is all we did."

Nine or ten months neatly covered an as yet unaccounted for period in Demjanjuk's alibi.

"Were you fed?"

"Not enough."

"What was your physical condition?"

"Fairly good, but I was losing weight for lack of food."

"Were there people in the camp who died of starvation?"

"Many."

"Did you see this?"

"In our barrack. People died. Especially those who smoked."

Demjanjuk didn't smoke.

Blatman demanded to know why it took Demjanjuk five years to remember the name Chelm when he had suffered so much there. How could he *not* remember?

Demjanjuk turned to the judges. "Have you ever forgotten anything in your lives?" he asked.

"You remembered the [four] hospitals you were in," Blatman pointed out. "The whole history of it. The *only thing* you forgot was Chelm, where you underwent the most horrendous experience of the war."

"That was *my country*," Demjanjuk explained. "I couldn't forget those places so easily. . . . Everything that happened in the Soviet Union I could remember."

Blatman picked up on "that was my country." Demjanjuk remembered the names of the cities that he had lived in after the war. They were all in Germany and Austria, not in the Soviet Union.

"The city of Landshut, is that in the Soviet Union?"

"In Landshut, I lived for a long time. Almost two years."

"And the city of Regensburg? Is it in the Soviet Union?"

"I lived in Regensburg for a long time too."

"And the city of Ulm, is that in the Soviet Union?"

"I lived in Ulm a long time too."

"How long did you live in Ulm?"

"I can't say exactly. About six months, maybe more."

"And how long did you live in Chelm, as you contend?"

"About eighteen months . . . Why I forgot, I can't say."

"Well, maybe all this question of recollection and memory has a different reason. You simply *weren't* at Chelm."

"It is *you* who are saying that," Demjanjuk complained.

"You are claiming that you were made to work at hard labor without food, without decent living conditions, with people dying nearby?"

"Yes."

"And that you came out of this camp skin and bones?"

"Yes. And it was an atrocity."

"That you cannot forget? Neither the horror of it nor the camp itself?"

"I want to forget. But one never forgets them," Demjanjuk said. "Just like anyone who survived the Holocaust can't forget them."

Shaked took over the cross-examination from Blatman. Relaxed and intimate, he reminded Demjanjuk that he had testified in Cleveland that the Cyrillic signature on the Trawniki card was not his because it lacked apostrophes that he always inserted after the *m* and *n* in his name. Shaked then produced several Cyrillic signatures that Demjanjuk had provided to the Israeli police. None of them had the apostrophes.

Shaked moved on to Demjanjuk's truck driving skills. His claim that he didn't know how to drive a truck during the war was a critical point in his defense. SS officer Otto Horn had testified at the Cleveland denaturalization trial that Iwan of Treblinka not only drove a truck, which was unusual for a Ukrainian, but spent off hours in the garage tinkering with motors. Because Iwan knew about engines, Horn testified, the SS assigned him to operate the diesel motor that supplied the gas for the Treblinka chambers. Furthermore, Fedorenko had testified in Fort Lauderdale that the Germans were looking for POWs with driving skill for training at Trawniki. Shaked quoted Fedorenko's testimony: "We were lined up, and the Germans picked out those who could be useful—drivers and technicians."

Demjanjuk claimed that he did not know how to drive a truck in 1947 when he applied for a truck driving job for the U.S. Army in Landshut. He had to take a monthlong driving course. Yet in a pretrial interrogation about fighting the Germans in a battle at the Dnieper River, he said that when his unit ran out of ammunition, his commanding officer told him to jump in a truck and go get more.

Demjanjuk told the court that he had been mistranslated. To become a driver in the Soviet Union, he testified, one needed several years of education in a technical school. He only completed fourth grade.

Shaked reminded Demjanjuk that he had testified earlier that he would have died for a loaf of bread, suggesting that if he could get better food by volunteering to collaborate with the Nazis, he would have.

"If they were asking about drivers . . . you could have said, 'Yes. I am a tractor driver. I can drive a vehicle.'"

"You are mixing up a tractor driver with a car driver," Demjanjuk said like a good attorney. "All I knew was how to open a cap and fill [the tank] with kerosene. And then of course you had to use the starter. And if that didn't get the thing moving, you have to call the foreman."

"You are in a great plight, in a very difficult situation, at Chelm, isn't that true?"

"Yes."

"And you were in fact going hungry?"

"Yes."

"And you are forced to work very, very hard?"

"Yes . . . Nobody asked whether anyone knew how to drive a tractor. So I couldn't get out."

Shaked asked Demjanjuk whether, if the Germans had asked him to collaborate, he would have done so.

"I don't know whether I would have agreed to work or would have preferred to die," he said.

Shaked next pointed out a contradiction on Demjanjuk's visa application, where he claimed he was a "driver" in the town of Sobibor.

"I never said such a thing," Demjanjuk claimed. "What I said at the time, what I wrote, is that I'd been on a *farm*. That I'd been working for a farm. . . . The clerk wrote down 'a driver in Sobibor.'"

Shaked then probed the strange coincidence that had puzzled every prosecutor and judge involved in Demjanjuk's circuitous journey through the courts. Of all the Polish towns and villages to select as his wartime residence, why did he select *Sobibor*?

Demjanjuk had a ready explanation. He told the court that he never intended to write Sobibor on the application. He wanted to put down *Sambor*, another village in eastern Poland. But the clerk told him to put down Sobibor.

"The person who helped me had a small map," Demjanjuk explained. "On the atlas, he found this place. He said: 'This is the best place because that's where there is the highest concentration of Ukrainians.... Mention it.' Do you think that if I *had been* in Sobibor, I would have given that name?"

"In other words, you are saying now that whoever had been to [the death camp of] Sobibor must be out of his mind to put down Sobibor. That's what you are saying, isn't it?"

"Yes."

Demjanjuk also swore on his visa application to the United States that he had worked as a laborer at Pilau, a fishing village near Danzig, after the war. Pilau was also the site of a camp guarded by Trawniki men and where Jews were executed. The coincidences were stacking up. Demjanjuk was a farmer in Sobibor before and during part of the war; briefly worked at Pilau, the site of a Nazi camp; was imprisoned in Chelm, close to Trawniki; and dug peat outside a Trawniki subcamp. To the court, it looked as if Demjanjuk had crafted an alibi around places he would have known had he trained at Trawniki and served at Sobibor.

Judge Levin pressed Demjanjuk even harder than Shaked had. "Would you have gone to work for them as a driver or mechanic?" he asked.

"Had I been a driver," Demjanjuk said, "possibly yes. No one asked me to do it."

"But if you *had* been asked," Levin pressed harder, "you definitely would have gone to work for them?"

"I think so," Demjanjuk said. "I felt that if I was selected, I might be able to run away. The second reason—you couldn't turn them down because you would have been shot."

Shaked had the next to final word.

"As the question looks now, after all the testimony has been heard, there is no way to avoid concluding you are in fact Ivan the Terrible from Treblinka."

The spectators murmured their approval.

"That is not a question," Shaked added, "and I don't expect a response from you."

Demjanjuk had the final word.

"That's a lie," he said.

The defense called Willem Wagenaar to the stand. Next to Julius Grant, he would be its most important witness.

CHAPTER FORTY-SIX

The Last Hope

Willem Wagenaar was a professor of experimental psychology (EP) and dean of the Faculty of Social Science at the University of Leyden in the Netherlands. A prolific writer, he had authored an impressive string of articles and books on the workings of memory in general, and the problems inherent in eyewitness photo identification and court testimony in particular. As a memory expert he asked: Under which conditions was the memory reliable?

Wagenaar was the first experimental psychologist to testify in an Israeli trial. EP was a relatively new science, and neither the judges, nor the media, nor the sparse crowd of one hundred spectators who gathered in the courtroom to hear his testimony seemed to know why he was there. The Israelis had long since become bored with the trial and Israeli newspapers no longer gave it front-page coverage. Israeli youth in particular seemed to have lost interest after the emotional and riveting testimony of the Treblinka survivors.

Actually, Wagenaar was not the defense's first choice. Elizabeth Loftus was. The dean of American experimental psychologists, she was a strong and vocal critic of the indiscriminate use of eyewitness testimony in court trials and the reliability of eyewitness accounts, which cannot be verified. But Loftus was also Jewish, and some members of her family objected to her testifying on Demjanjuk's behalf. She listened to her relatives, said no, and recommended Wagenaar. The most she could offer was to come to Jerusalem to help prepare Wagenaar's testimony.

Wagenaar, who testified in English, made it perfectly clear to the court what he would and would not do as an expert witness. To the disappointment of the gallery, he said he would not evaluate the memory of each Treblinka witness who had testified and pronounce it "reliable" or "not reliable." He *would* provide the court with a set of research-tested guidelines it could use in evaluating the reliability of those witnesses.

"The expert can *only assist* the court," Wagenaar said, "by explaining which conditions favor the correct identification of guilty suspects, and which favor the mistaken identification of innocent suspects."

Wagenaar went on to further clarify his role: "My task is limited to commenting on the quality of the tests. . . . Whether the tests prove that the memories are reliable is something for the *court* to decide."

Wagenaar explained that he would evaluate both the memory test (Radiwker's photo spread) and how it had been administered to the Treblinka survivors. In so doing, he picked up where Sheftel had left off in his cross-examination of Radiwker after Judge Levin ruled that his line of questioning was irrelevant because Radiwker had not chosen the photos for the spread.

Before he began the substance of his testimony, Wagenaar stole some of the thunder from the prosecution. The Treblinka survivors presented a unique situation to experimental psychologists, Wagenaar confessed. The survivors had known Ivan the Terrible nearly forty years ago, and they had seen him daily for as long as a year or more. Most studies of witness memory dealt with robbery or rape victims who had seen the perpetrator *briefly and recently*. As a result, he and the court would be sailing together through uncharted waters without a body of research to guide them.

The prosecution tried to block Wagenaar's entire testimony, which went to the very heart of the Demjanjuk trial because it challenged the memories of the Treblinka survivors by asking: Did they point to the wrong man? In response, Michael Shaked argued that the evaluation of the photo spread was the task of the court, not the domain of an expert witness.

Judge Levin rejected Shaked's argument but expressed a concern of his own. Would Professor Wagenaar merely lecture the court on theory? The question signaled to Shaked the strategy he should use to win over the bench against this witness—label Wagenaar's testimony as theoretical and, therefore, irrelevant.

Like a good debater, Wagenaar defined his terms so there would be no confusion about his testimony. "The objective of the identification test [photo spread] is to prove that the witness's memory is *so accurate* that confusion with another person is very unlikely."

The identification of a face from memory is a tricky feat, Wagenaar told the court. One hundred percent accuracy, especially after a long time, is rare, and consequently there are no absolutes, only *likely* and *unlikely*. The critical question, therefore, was this: Were the memories of the Treblinka survivors accurate enough that confusing Iwan Demjanjuk with Ivan the Terrible was very unlikely?

Having set the stage for the critical part of his testimony, Wagenaar began an in-depth and critical evaluation of Miriam Radiwker's photo spread, how the Treblinka survivors responded to Demjanjuk's photo number sixteen, and how they described the Iwan they knew. His testimony was devastating, and there was nothing Mickey Shaked could do to stop him.

Wagenaar began with a contradiction that troubled him deeply but didn't seem to bother the court. "It is clear," he testified, referring to the 1975 photo spread, "that not *all* the witnesses, at *all* instances, were *perfectly certain*. Nor were they at *all* times perfectly accurate." Yet each witness had identified the Demjanjuk photo and the man himself in the courtroom more than ten years later with *absolute certainty*.

Wagenaar then pointed out another issue that did not seem to trouble the court, but should have. A significant number of Treblinka survivors interviewed by Radiwker and her successor, Martin Kolar, *could not* identify Demjanjuk as Ivan the Terrible from the photo spread. This was so underreported by the Israeli police and so totally dismissed by the prosecution as irrelevant, Wagenaar pointed out, that no one had even bothered to tally how many survivors were *not* able to identify Demjanjuk.

By Wagenaar's count, the number ranged from twenty to thirty-two, or at least twice as many as those who *did* identify Demjanjuk. It was true that some of those survivors who failed to identify Demjanjuk as Ivan the Terrible did not work near the gas chamber. But that was clearly not the case with Schlomo Helman, who helped build the new gas chamber at Treblinka under the watchful eye of Iwan Grozny and who was at the camp longer than any other survivor.

Next, Wagenaar went on to present a list of factors, which he called "response bias," that could *predispose* a witness to select a certain photo in the spread. He then applied each factor to the Radiwker photo spread and the identification process to determine if the memory test was valid. The most relevant factors were:

The witness attaches great importance to the punishment of the perpetrators, which motivated him to select someone from the spread.

There can be no doubt that the Treblinka survivors wanted their torturers as well as the murderers of their families to pay for their crimes.

All the photos in the spread are pictures of a suspected criminal.

All the photos in the Radiwker spread were of suspected war criminals. If a witness realized that fact, he could point to *any picture* with the assurance that he was not condemning an innocent person. In effect, the witness was motivated to select someone—*anyone*—and could rest assured that even if he was wrong, justice would be done.

OSI's George Parker had presented this same hypothetical argument in his doubt memo. Even if John Demjanjuk *was not* Ivan the Terrible, Parker had said, playing devil's advocate, he was still a war criminal who lied on his visa application and, therefore, should be stripped of his citizenship. It was why Parker had rejected trying John Demjanjuk as Ivan the Terrible as unethical.

The witness has a strong reason to believe that the picture of the perpetrator is in the photo spread.

The Treblinka witnesses had good reason to believe that a war criminal from Treblinka was in the photo spread Miriam Radiwker presented to them. Why else would she interview them about what they saw at *Treblinka*? Furthermore, the investigation process itself linked Treblinka to the photo spread, even though Radiwker had not actually said: "There is a Treblinka guard among the photos. Can you identify him?" It was implied.

If a Treblinka survivor had seen the ad Radiwker placed in Israeli newspapers, he would know whom to look for in the photo spread. The ad read: "The Nazi Crime Investigating Division is conducting an investigation against the Ukrainians Iwan Demjanjuk and Feodor Fedorenko. Survivors of the death camps Sobibor and Treblinka are requested to report to the Israel police headquarters."

The witness believes he will never forget the face of the perpetrator as long as he lives.

Down to a person, the Treblinka witnesses had all stated in depositions or had testified in trials that they could never forget Ivan the Terrible or his face. They lived with him day and night. That conviction gave a witness confidence in selecting a photo that might not have been a picture of the real perpetrator.

The witness knows that previous witnesses also made positive identifications.

Miriam Radiwker testified that she did not tell the witnesses about the other Treblinka survivors she had already interviewed, or would interview, or what they had said. But she didn't have to. All the Treblinka survivors knew one another. They had the opportunity to discuss Radiwker's investigation among themselves, and may indeed have done so.

Only one picture in the photo spread fits the general description of the perpetrator.

Each Treblinka witness came to his interview with an image of Ivan the Terrible locked in his memory. Although there was some disagreement about Iwan's height and the color of his hair, all witnesses agreed on three physical characteristics: round face, short neck, incipient baldness. Out of the seventeen photos in the spread only *one* matched those three characteristics.

To prove the point, Wagenaar had conducted a simple test on twenty-five of his psychology students. He gave each a copy of the Radiwker seventeen-picture photo spread and asked them to identify every photo, if any, matching a man with a round face, short neck, and premature baldness. Every student selected one photo and the same photo: number sixteen, John Demjanjuk.

Next, Wagenaar gave each student a second photo spread with eight pictures, one of which was the Demjanjuk photo. The other seven reasonably resembled him. Only 8 percent of the students selected Demjanjuk.

One photo calls attention to itself because it is markedly different from the others and thus predisposes the witness to subconsciously select it.

Demjanjuk's photo number sixteen was by far the largest photo in the entire spread. It leapt off the page.

The number of people in the spread is small, five or six.

INS had asked Radiwker to show the witnesses at least three photos. Experts agreed that three pictures are not sufficient for a valid memory test. Israeli law agreed. It required at least eight. Some Treblinka survivors, however, had viewed only three photos, thus satisfying INS requirements, but not meeting Israeli and U.S. standards.

The interrogator makes conscious or unconscious suggestions, calling attention to one particular picture, or makes specific reference to someone in a picture.

Radiwker testified that she did not coach any witness or suggest anything, directly or indirectly. She merely placed the photo album before the witness and asked him to look at the pictures and tell her if he recognized anyone. Her testimony was not quite accurate.

During at least one interview, Radiwker pointed at Fedorenko's photo number seventeen and said: "Look carefully."

The witness is asked to look again to see if he recognizes anyone else in the photo spread, suggesting that there is someone the interviewer is hoping the witness will identify.

After Goldfarb and Eliyahu Rosenberg, among others, had identified Demjanjuk as Ivan the Terrible, Radiwker asked them to look at the pictures a second time to see if they recognized anyone else.

The witness is exposed to an identity parade containing the same suspect.

The Israeli police showed several Treblinka survivors more than one photo spread. The repetition reinforced the witness's conviction that he had made the right choice the first time and encouraged him to stand by his identification.

Like Judge Roettger in the Fedorenko case, Wagenaar went on to further criticize the photo spread. Demjanjuk's photo number sixteen and Fedorenko's photo number seventeen were not only the largest on page three of the spread, they were also the clearest, making them stand out even more. The other six pictures on page three were blurred, especially numbers fourteen and fifteen. Furthermore, the black/white contrast was very low in all seventeen photos, washing out facial details. And photos ten and thirteen were so out of focus that they were useless. Those vague pictures, Wagenaar argued, sent viewers a subtle message: These pictures could not possibly be important, so why should we bother to study them?

If all the photos, save one, failed to come *even close* to looking like Demjanjuk, Wagenaar concluded, what difference did it make how many pictures the police presented to witnesses? They would still have only one choice. In effect, the Israeli police photo spread or memory test set the witnesses up to select photo sixteen.

Finally, Wagenaar was highly critical of Israeli police procedures themselves. He pointed out that the police did not provide or require specialized training for its investigators as most police forces do. Being a lawyer like Miriam Radiwker was not in and of itself a qualification for police work.

Nor did Israeli law require that defense counsel be present at a lineup or photo spread interview.

Nor did it require that the witness be told: "A person you know may or *may not* be in the lineup." Radiwker's introduction, "Look and see if there is someone you know," was not an acceptable photo identification introduction.

Nor did the Israeli police require transcripts of the recorded photo spread interviews and identifications. That omission raised a critical legal question. Should the court even allow Radiwker's depositions into evidence? Was it fair to make Demjanjuk the victim of such a lack of professionalism?

Considering the flaws in the design and presentation of the photo spreads, Wagenaar concluded that the memory tests performed by the Israeli police did not "constitute valid tests of memory."

Sheftel sat down with a smile on his face. Wagenaar had boxed Dov Levin into a tight corner. But Sheftel was certain that Levin would find a way to dismiss Wagenaar's entire compelling testimony as "theoretical." More grounds for appeal.

• • •

Like Julius Grant, Willem Wagenaar left Shaked few openings for his cross-examination. He began by challenging Wagenaar's credentials and relevance as an expert witness. He tried to get Wagenaar to admit that his testimony was based not on his own work, but on the research and writings of other experimental psychologists. In fact, he had not written even a single article about the subject of his testimony, identity parades or photo spreads. It was all *theory*.

Shaked got Wagenaar to admit that his list of response biases was indeed based on experimental studies, but all the studies were *theoretical*. They may have been tested on students, but they had never been tested on actual police lineups or on the equivalent of death camp survivors.

Shaked also got Wagenaar to admit that although he had testified as an experimental psychologist in forty court cases, only one dealt with photo spreads or police lineups.

Shaked argued that Wagenaar's testimony was not the testimony of an expert witness, but that of a biased "partisan" because the use of experimental psychologists in courts was hotly contested in the United States, the only country in the world where experimental psychologists were admitted as expert witnesses. Why hadn't he told the court that?

Shaked further argued that the very tenets of experimental psychology relating to witness identification were not accepted by the international scientific community. Why hadn't he pointed that out to the court? In fact, experimental psychologists themselves disagreed about whether they should be admitted by the court as expert witnesses. Why hadn't Wagenaar told the court that?

Because it wasn't true, Wagenaar said.

A *minority* of experimental psychologists believed that it was not appropriate to testify as experts in *every single* case, but none believed that experimental psychologists should *never* testify about identification.

Shaked argued that the classroom experiment with Radiwker's photo spread was worthless. There was a huge difference between a psychology student who had never seen Ivan the Terrible and a Treblinka survivor who had. The test, therefore, was no test at all. It was all *theoretical*.

Finally, Shaked tried to turn Wagenaar into a prosecution witness, as he had done with the defense's document expert William Flynn.

"Would you agree that it is correct to say that your opinion is: It would be very inaccurate to say that one *cannot* accurately recognize a face of someone whom that person knew well forty years ago?"

"The general statement is," Wagenaar said, "a ridiculous statement."

Wagenaar testified that memory discrepancies are *normal* because, although the details of a face or an event are locked in the memory, the keys to unlock those details are missing. For example, a person might not remember a fishing trip he had taken many years ago. But if someone showed him a photo of himself sitting in a boat holding up a string of fish, lost details will flood his memory. So when Demjanjuk said, "I can't remember . . . it was more than forty years ago" he had no cue to help him retrieve the memory. And when he said, "I just remembered while I was in jail," a cue had reminded him of the lost memory.

"As long as discrepancies are part of the norm," Shaked said, "then it is reasonable to assume that it is the sort of forgetfulness that could happen to any one of us. If, however, it goes *beyond* what is normal, then there is the possibility that we are dealing with deliberate lies?"

"Yes," Wagenaar said.

• • •

Later that night, Sheftel celebrated at the Notre Dame Hotel with Ed Nishnic, Wagenaar and his wife, and Elizabeth Loftus. They all believed that Wagenaar had proven that the photo spread had no evidentiary value, and that Wagenaar had created much more than a reasonable doubt about the Treblinka survivors' identification of John Demjanjuk as Ivan the Terrible. Not that it made any difference. Sheftel believed Dov Levin had his mind made up from the moment he tapped his gavel. The testimony of Willem Wagenaar would never make him doubt that John Demjanjuk was Ivan the Terrible. In that, he was like the Treblinka survivors. Because they wanted Demjanjuk to be Iwan Grozny, he was.

That was understandable for a survivor. But for a judge?

CHAPTER FORTY-SEVEN

To Doubt or Not to Doubt

Y our verdict must not only be founded on the *evidence*," the defense warned the court in its closing argument. "But it must also withstand the test of time so that in five or ten or fifty years it shall be said, 'Justice was done in Jerusalem—Demjanjuk was acquitted according to the law.'"

Survivors and their families burst into tears. "Liars!" they shouted.

The prosecution pleaded with the court to convict John Demjanjuk of being Ivan the Terrible based on the evidence, and only the evidence, it had presented.

Vera Demjanjuk burst into tears. "You're all liars!" she shouted.

Who was lying? Who was telling the truth?

The court convened on April 18, 1988, just over a year after the trial had begun, to answer those questions in its four-hundred-page opinion. The reading took all day. Judge Levin began at just past 8:30 A.M. Judge Zvi Tal took over at 1 P.M. And Judge Dalia Dorner relieved Tal at 3 P.M.

The night before the reading of the verdict, hundreds of Jews from the United States, Europe, and Israel held vigil on the vast, empty field that was once the death camp of Treblinka. They gathered in the center around a monument resembling a tombstone. They wept, rocked, and prayed in a Babel of tongues.

Carved into the memorial column in six languages were the words "Never Again." One mourner waved the blue and white flag of Israel. Another wept for his parents, sister, brother, aunt, and uncle, whom Ivan the Terrible had murdered there. Another wore the black and white striped cap of a Treblinka survivor. He said: "All I know is that if I had a gun, I would shoot him with my own hands." He was a harbinger of the emotion that would grip the Hall of the People the following morning.

. . .

Complaining of a back problem, John Demjanjuk chose to watch and listen to the verdict on a closed-circuit TV monitor in a prison cell erected inside the convention center. Vera, John Jr., Irene, and her husband, Ed Nishnic, sat in the third row. Behind them, the courtroom was packed with survivors and their families.

"We have before us an indictment, wide-ranging, saddening and shocking in content," Judge Dov Levin began. Twenty television cameras watched. "Its words sear. Its events horrify. It seems as if the facts which constitute the foundation of the charge have been set down on the pages of the indictment with repressed pain, tearful eyes, and a trembling hand. . . ."

MIRIAM RADIWKER AND WILLEM WAGENAAR

The court had fallen in love with Miriam Radiwker.

"We hold that Mrs. Radiwker's testimony is *totally credible*," the court ruled. "We were deeply impressed by her honesty and sincerity, and by her incredible memory. . . . We accept her explanation. We absolutely reject the suspicion, implicit in the defense's censure, that Mrs. Radiwker is testifying in order to advance the conviction of the accused."

The court dismissed Willem Wagenaar and his two days of testimony in one sentence: "We shall not rely on Professor Wagenaar's opinions, as expressed before us."

Although the court recognized some, but not all, of the facts Wagenaar cited during his testimony, it rejected each and every conclusion Wagenaar had drawn from those facts. It also discarded the list of response biases he had offered the court to guide the judges in their deliberations about the reliability of the identifications made by Treblinka survivors. The court seemed to be scolding Professor Wagenaar: How *dare you* come to Israel from the Netherlands and criticize the Israeli police and its procedures as defective and unprofessional!

The court was especially hostile toward Wagenaar's criticism of Radiwker's qualifications for her job as a police investigator. "We absolutely reject," the court ruled, "that she is unqualified in investigation procedures or that she made leading suggestions to witnesses interrogated. As a rule, Mrs. Radiwker acted precisely according to the directives of the United States immigration authorities."

The court also rejected Wagenaar's testimony that Radiwker's introduction to the showing of the photo spread—"Look at the photographs in the album, and see if you recognize anyone"—was not acceptable because it was misleading and suggestive.

In effect, the court voided Wagenaar's two damning conclusions: The photo spread was not a valid test of memory; and the photo identification procedures were so inconsistent, flawed, and unprofessional that they invalidated the Treblinka witnesses' identification of John Demjanjuk as Ivan the Terrible.

"We do not believe that the time has arrived for experimental psychology to enter fully into the confines of the court," the court ruled. "As in regard to Professor Wagenaar's testimony on the subject of identification parades, we do not find it possible to rely on his evidence."

THE TREBLINKA SURVIVORS

Recognizing that the identification of John Demjanjuk as Ivan the Terrible by Treblinka survivors was the "heart of the case," the court had posed three questions before the trial began. It answered each during the course of its written opinion:

Q. Was it possible to remember and faithfully describe events which occurred forty-five or more years ago?

A. It was indeed possible to remember and describe what had happened.

Q. Could people who had survived the valley of slaughter and experienced its horrors forget what they had seen every day?

A. It was impossible to forget the scenes of horror, the atmosphere of terror, and all that occurred in the extermination camp.

Q. Was it possible that someone who had experienced the horrible reality described in the indictment could remember the events in detail while forgetting the image and facial features of the perpetrator to such an extent that they would not be able to identify them?

A. It was impossible to forget Ivan the Terrible and his facial features.

With these clearly articulated biases as guides, the court evaluated the reliability of each Treblinka witness individually and assigned his or her testimony a weight. Then it studied the cumulative identification evidence in toto and ruled:

- No witness was completely unreliable.
- Four witnesses gave "firm and impressive testimonies"—Eliyahu Rosenberg, Yosef Cherney, Gustav Boreks, and Pinchas Epstein. Each could be relied on with "almost absolute certainty."
- Other witnesses corroborated and supported their positive identifications.

"The accumulative weight of these identifications," the court ruled, "creates a totality which may be safely relied upon as the basis for an incriminating finding. . . . After all the evidence, we have reached the clear conclusion that the possibility of the identifiers having substituted the defendant for Iwan Grozny, because of an amazing similarity between them, is far-fetched and beyond the limits of a reasonable doubt."

At this point in the reading, the Demjanjuk family knew what the court's verdict would be. To avoid the pain of hearing the judge pronounce their husband and father guilty of crimes against humanity and the Jewish people, they fled the courtroom and did not return.

THE TRAWNIKI CARD

The defense had argued that the Trawniki card was a forgery because it was a unique, one-of-a-kind document. Given the three new samples of Trawniki ID cards supplied by the Soviet Union during the trial, the court ruled that the Demjanjuk Trawniki card was "not a unique solitary document," and that certificates of that type were routinely processed at Trawniki.

The defense had argued that the Trawniki card was supplied by the Soviet Union and should not be admitted as evidence. The defense further argued that the KGB had both the skill and opportunity to forge the Trawniki card and, therefore, the court should presume that it had.

The court rejected the "presumption of forgery" argument as unfounded and wishful thinking. It further ruled that Trawniki card errors, such as spelling mistakes and the Demjanjuk height discrepancy, could be convincingly attributed to the Trawniki clerk who recorded the data.

"There is *nothing* in these errors," the court ruled, "and it is possible to hold that the identifying details recorded in the certificate are those of the defendant."

The court ruled that the Trawniki card photo was indeed a photo of John Demjanjuk. It based its conclusion not on the testimony of expert witnesses, but on two other factors—Demjanjuk's testimony in which he admitted, "It looks like me but I am not one hundred percent certain," and the court's own naked-eye comparison of the card photo with the face of John Demjanjuk sitting in the dock before it. Based on that visual inspection, the court concluded that, because the photo looked like John Demjanjuk to the court, it *was* John Demjanjuk.

"A positive determination by an expert as to the identity of the photograph is not required," the court ruled. In one sentence, the court dismissed as irrelevant the photo comparison testimony of Reinhardt Altman, Patricia Smith, Anita Pritchard, and Yasser Iscan. Their combined testimony had spanned eight days.

The court's personal and positive identification of the Trawniki card photo as that of John Demjanjuk left open the question of whether the card photograph was part of an overall card forgery. The defense had argued that a true photograph of Iwan Demjanjuk had been fraudulently attached to the card. The KGB had taken an old army photo of Iwan Demjanjuk, superimposed a black Trawniki uniform over it, removed the original photo from the card, and attached the doctored picture.

In reaching its conclusion about the authenticity of the card photo, the court relied exclusively on the testimony of Amnon Bezaleli, the Israeli police laboratory director. It found his testimony so totally convincing that it did not need a confirming opinion and ruled that the "photograph is authentic."

The court also ruled that the Trawniki card ink, paper, typeface, and seals were authentic, as were the signatures of Karl Streibel, Ernst Teufel, and Iwan Demjanjuk. The court based its findings on its conviction that the testimony of the prosecution witnesses was more expert and convincing than the testimony of the defense witnesses.

On the broader question of whether the Trawniki card itself was authentic or forged, the court rejected the considered opinion of Julius Grant, who had declared the card a forgery. It found that in making such a judgment, Grant had stepped beyond the scope of his expertise.

Grant was a chemist and an expert on ink and paper, the court noted. However, his determination that the card was a forgery was based almost exclusively on his analysis of the signature of Iwan Demjanjuk. He had arrived at the forgery determination not by analyzing ink and paper, his area of expertise, but by analyzing the characteristics of handwriting.

Grant was not an expert on handwriting analysis.

Having eliminated Grant's testimony, the court ruled that the Trawniki card was authentic, based on the testimony of prosecution experts Amnon Bezaleli, Gideon Epstein, and, ironically, on the Palm Springs seminar statement of defense expert witness William Flynn, who had said: "I have examined the card firsthand for three days. I have examined the thing microscopically, and there's *nothing* about the card that I can see that would not have passed muster."

The court was not disturbed by the fact that Treblinka was not listed as a posting on the Demjanjuk ID card. The court argued that the Trawniki card was merely supporting evidence in the case against Demjanjuk. The court, therefore, ruled: "There is nothing in the absence of the entry itself to negate the possibility that the defendant was in Treblinka, and there is certainly nothing in that omission to damage the certificate's authenticity."

In the end, the court ruled that the Trawniki card and each element in it were authentic.

THE ALIBI

The court noted that an alibi defense like John Demjanjuk's is a two-edged sword. When it is established, there is nothing better because it proves that the prosecution witnesses are either lying or mistaken. But when the alibi is not convincingly established or fails, it serves to reinforce the prosecution's evidence, giving it "credibility and weight."

The court ruled that Demjanjuk's alibi failed. His explanation that for five years he had simply forgotten the name of the POW camp (Chelm) where he had been imprisoned, and then suddenly remembered it, was preposterous. In reaching that decision, the court was influenced by the fact that Demjanjuk couldn't describe the camp he said he lived in for eighteen months.

"It is inconceivable that a person who spent eighteen months in one place would not be able to answer and give details of the place and the people with whom he came in daily contact. . . . This one-dimensional paucity of detail, and the absence of nuances, show that this version is fabricated."

The court drew the same conclusion about Demjanjuk's alleged work as a peat digger and for the same reason—the paucity of detail.

In making its determination that Chelm and the peat-digging assignment were lies, the court rejected each and every alternative explanation offered by Professor Wagenaar under direct examination by defense counsel Yoram Sheftel: Demjanjuk never knew the name of the camp; Chelm was so similar to the other camps that Demjanjuk had been in that it was not especially important to remember it; Demjanjuk simply forgot to mention it; difficult childhood and terrible war experiences had hardened his feelings to such an extent that Chelm did not stand out in his mind.

Instead, the court accepted the prosecution's theory that Demjanjuk had fleshed out his alibi over time to make it sound more realistic and credible.

Just days before the end of the trial, the Demjanjuk family had received under an FOIA request a copy of the Danilchenko Protocol, which the Soviet Union had given to OSI in 1978—eight years before the Jerusalem trial. The court had entered the former Sobibor guard's deposition into evidence under Israel's 1950 Nazi and Nazi Collaboration Punishment Law after the prosecution and defense summations.

Noting that Danilchenko swore that both he and Demjanjuk had served in a Waffen SS unit in Flossenbürg, Germany, where they received the blood-type tattoo, the court ruled that Demjanjuk's removing of his tattoo was incriminating evidence.

"The removal of the tattoo—a lengthy and painful process—has no reasonable explanation," the court reasoned, "other than disguising the clear evidence connecting the defendant with the SS forces."

In the end, the court ruled that John Demjanjuk lied when he testified that he was imprisoned at Chelm. And he lied when he testified that he later went to Graz, Austria, and Heuberg, Germany, first to join an all-Ukrainian division and later to join Vlasov's army. Three historians—Drs. Matityahu Meisel, Shmuel Spector, and Shmuel Krakowsky—had testified that Demjanjuk could not have been in Graz and Heuberg when he claimed he was.

Finally, the court listed what it considered to be incriminating statements by Demjanjuk:

"You are pushing me to Treblinka."

"Why are you making such a fuss of my matter. Like with Eichmann? Eichmann was big, while Ivan is a little."

"The Germans come and tell you . . . 'You must be with us' . . . who are you to refuse? . . . Can you imagine that someone was able to refuse? . . . This they don't understand. . . . So why trials? To try for what?"

"When the Germans would offer collaboration, who could have refused? Isn't that clear? There was a war. *Germans* were in the SS. Why aren't they asking *them*? Why aren't *they* tried? [Why] only Ukrainians?"

The court ruled:

"We, therefore, view these expressions—even in the qualified manner in which they are stated—as the beginning of a confession."

After the three judges read the court's opinion, Judge Dov Levin read the verdict.

CHAPTER FORTY-EIGHT

To Hang or Not to Hang

T he verdict in this trial is based, first and foremost, on the testimony and statements of the identifying witnesses," an exhausted Judge Levin began. "We are aware of human weakness and the failings of human memory. But we have also learned how powerful are the torments imprinted on the souls of the survivors who were snatched like burning brands from that inferno. How fresh is their wound which has not yet healed! Their memory is a living memory. Their testimony is a truthful testimony."

The court went on to reject Demjanjuk's insinuations that Ivan the Terrible was just a little fish and should not be compared with Adolf Eichmann. The court also rejected the argument that death camp guards obeyed an order against their will. They served the Nazis in uniform while armed, Judge Dorner had pointed out, receiving a salary and enjoying freedom of movement.

"We find that the defendant *is* Ivan the Terrible," Judge Levin concluded. "The deeds of that Ivan, as specified in the indictment, have been proved before us. . . . We convict the defendant of:

"Crimes against the Jewish people.

"Crimes against humanity.

"War crimes.

"Crimes against persecuted people.

"Given on this day: 18 April, 1988."

• • •

The court reconvened a week later to pronounce the sentence. Demjanjuk sat in the courtroom in a wheelchair, allegedly in pain. He had no choice. Israeli law required the accused to be present when the sentence was read. Demjanjuk didn't even try to stand up when the judges entered. His back was too sore.

Once again, the courtroom was packed. Would John Demjanjuk hang or spend the rest of his life in Ayalon Prison? State attorney Yonah Blatman asked for the noose. He argued: "Demjanjuk stood at the entrance to hell and was zealous in the extreme. He was one of the greatest oppressors the Jewish people ever had. With every fresh transport, Demjanjuk committed premeditated murder 100,000 times over."

Demjanjuk repeatedly crossed himself during Blatman's plea.

Defense counsel John Gill reminded the court of the Frank Walus case in Chicago, where eleven survivor eyewitnesses had been wrong. He further argued that the death penalty was morally unacceptable. "Tendencies in enlightened countries has [sic] been away from it," Gill pleaded. "Don't commit a second horrendous crime."

After the prosecution and defense completed their arguments for and against the death penalty, Judge Dov Levin gave the floor to John Demjanjuk.

"The convicted man has the last word," he said.

Demjanjuk pleaded: "It has been very painful for me to listen to reports of the tragedy that befell your people during the Nazi period. Six million died a terrible death, and I hope they reached the kingdom of heaven. I believe there *was* an Ivan the Terrible, but I was not that man. Last week you convicted me. And you made a big mistake, and God will be my witness."

The court recessed for three hours. When the judges returned to the courtroom, Demjanjuk shouted in Hebrew, "I am innocent!"

Judge Zvi Tal then read the sentence in a flat voice devoid of all emotion: "Most things can be forgiven, but in this case there is no forgiving, not in law and not in feeling. Demjanjuk's crimes stand above time. It is as if Treblinka still existed, Iwan were still swinging his sword or his iron pipe, cutting into live flesh, causing streams of blood. . . . There is no name to describe these crimes and there is no adequate punishment.

"We decree the death penalty."

The courtroom erupted in joy. Spectators applauded and danced.

They chanted "Death, death, death!" They sang folk songs. "Death to Iwan!" They wept and hugged. "Death to all Ukrainians!" They hurled threats at Yoram Sheftel. A group of school kids sang *Am Israel Hai*— The Jewish People Live! "Death! Death! Death!"

One lone survivor's voice rose above the din: "May his name and memory be erased and forgotten!"

Demjanjuk crosses his heart upon hearing the pronouncement of his death sentence.

• • •

Ukrainian communities across the United States and Canada were shocked and angry.

"It's a travesty of justice," the Reverend John Bruchok, pastor of St. Mary's Ukrainian Orthodox Church in Lorain, Ohio, said. "I saw his face. I saw the face of a gentle man."

In Demjanjuk's hometown of Parma, Ukrainians spoke out with bitterness:

"He was just a man, not a monster . . . "

"This is all a terrible mistake . . ."

"It stinks. They just needed a scapegoat . . ."

"It's been so many years. And he doesn't bother anybody. Why stir things up?"

"It's like everyone's saying the *Ukrainians* are the evil ones . . ."

As if to prove the point, vandals spray-painted St. Vladimir's Orthodox Church, where the Demjanjuk family worshipped, with purple circles like targets.

For its part, the Jewish community hunkered down until the storm blew over. Cleveland rabbis reported threats to their synagogues. Akron Jews suffered such a barrage of threats that they asked for special police protection.

Editorials around the world called for a commutation to a life sentence both because there was a reasonable doubt about the validity of the evidence against Demjanjuk, and because to hang a man was barbaric.

The *London Times* spoke for many countries when it editorialized: "If Israeli authorities could see their way to commuting the death sentence, this would further mark the emergence of Israel as the civilized state it aspires to be."

• • •

It was now up to the Supreme Court of Israel, which was required under Israeli law to review all death sentences. As final arbiter, it had the authority to commute Demjanjuk's sentence to life in prison. Or it could uphold the defense appeal arguing judicial bias and vacate the verdict of Judge Levin's court. All John Demjanjuk could do in his cell on death row was pray . . . and wait.

It would be a five-year wait.

Part Four: Epilogue

While John Demjanjuk was on trial for his life in Israel, four noteworthy events were occurring elsewhere. If three of the events brought some measure of justice—or the promise of it—the fourth raised questions about the very existence of justice.

First, Klaus Barbie, the Butcher of Lyon, was sentenced to life in prison. Unlike Israel, France did not have the death penalty. Barbie died of leukemia four years later at the age of seventy-seven while Demjanjuk was sitting on death row.

Second, based on eyewitness testimony, the Soviets executed Feodor Fedorenko by firing squad for serving the Nazis as a guard at Treblinka and for beating and driving Jews into the gas chambers. The Soviets had waited until John Demjanjuk was safely locked in an Israeli prison, facing a hangman's noose, before they executed Fedorenko. His death supported Demjanjuk's argument that deporting him to the Soviet Union would have been a death sentence.

Third, the Soviet Union and the U.S. Holocaust Memorial Museum Council issued a joint statement that had implications for Demjanjuk's future appeal before the Israeli Supreme Court. The Soviets agreed to open their archives on Nazi genocide to American historians and archivists. The agreement included an invitation to the U.S. Holocaust Memorial Museum, which had not yet opened, to microfilm or microfiche Soviet Holocaust-related documents, millions of which were haphazardly filed in a string of archives across the Soviet Union. The documents included records on Nazi executions of Jews, young communists, and Gypsies, as well as captured German documents like the three Trawniki ID cards that the Soviets had provided to Israeli prosecutors during the Demjanjuk trial.

The U.S.-Soviet agreement offered new hope to the Demjanjuk defense. Perhaps Moscow would grant Demjanjuk investigators permission to search for archival evidence proving that the testimony of Treblinka survivors had pushed the wrong man to the foot of the gallows.

Fourth, OSI released a lengthy report on Robert Jan Verbelen, a convicted Belgian Nazi collaborator who had worked for and was protected by the United States after the war. Reinforced by newly declassified government documents, the publication offered a glimpse into the inner sanctum of U.S. espionage in the "Dodge City" days just after World War II. During that time, America, England, and France were scrambling to gather information about the new threat to their national security—their former ally Joseph Stalin and the Soviet Union. As illustrated by the following three accounts, the story the Verbelen report told was not a pretty one.

THE SPY NETS

While the Justice Department was stalking John Demjanjuk as Nazi collaborator Ivan the Terrible of Treblinka, the CIA and the Justice Department were trying to protect the identity of a major convicted Nazi war criminal. His name was Robert Jan Verbelen. To the embarrassment of the intelligence establishment, however, Nazi hunters uncovered evidence that Verbelen had worked for the U.S. Army Counter Intelligence Corps (CIC) in Austria immediately after the war.

The Department of Justice handled the Verbelen leak the way it had dealt with the Klaus Barbie scandal. It commissioned OSI to unravel the story, and for the same reasons. The Justice Department didn't want to be accused of a cover-up that could cripple or destroy the credibility of an already beleaguered OSI. And Justice wanted to manage the spin on the story to control the damage.

OSI issued its internal Verbelen report in 1988 while John Demjanjuk was waiting for the Israeli Supreme Court to decide whether he should ascend the gallows, spend the rest of his days in prison, face another trial as Iwan of Sobibor, or go free. For national security reasons, the report "could not make public" every detail of the U.S.-Verbelen connection. In spite of that limitation, the document sketched a clear picture of America's postwar espionage operations in Austria. And more important, it illustrated the total dependence of U.S. intelligence agencies on the services of former Nazi SS and SD officers, Gestapo chiefs, Einsatzkommando leaders, German army intelligence officers (Abwehr), and a string of vicious Nazi collaborators stretching from Croatia to Latvia.

• • •

Robert Jan Verbelen was a decorated officer in the Flemish SS and a leader of DeVlag, a pro-Nazi organization of young Flemish fascists who considered Hitler their führer. As a lieutenant in the Flemish SS, Verbelen recruited fellow SS men and members of DeVlag into terror teams and death squads that worked closely with the Nazi SD security detail in Belgium to help keep the country safe for its German occupiers.

Like Gestapo chief Klaus Barbie in Lyon, Verbelen's mission as security corps leader was to crush the Belgian resistance. And like Barbie, he failed. The best he could do during his two-year reign of terror was to arrest, imprison, torture, and murder hundreds of resistance fighters, some of whom ended up in Camp Dora excavating tunnels in the Harz Mountains. To punish the resistance and to deter others from joining it, Verbelen's terror squads attacked and assassinated Belgian politicians and judges who refused to support the Nazis. They gunned down policemen sympathetic to the Belgian resistance. And they tossed grenades into taverns, pubs, and cafés frequented by Belgian anti-occupation nationalists.

As a reward for his dedication, the SS promoted Verbelen to captain and awarded him the German War Meritorious Cross. When the Allies liberated Belgium in September 1944, three months after the Normandy invasion, Verbelen fled to Germany with the retreating German army, leaving his wife and two children behind. Unable to punish Captain Verbelen personally for his crimes, Belgian resistance fighters murdered his family instead.

Not long after the war ended, a Belgian military war crimes court tried sixty-two members of DeVlag and convicted fifty-nine, among them SS Captain Verbelen, who was sentenced in absentia to death. Unlike France, which asked the United States to help locate and extradite Klaus Barbie, Belgium did not seek U.S. assistance in finding and extraditing Verbelen. If it had, the United States would not have had far to look. Like Barbie in Munich, which was the heart of U.S. espionage in Germany, Verbelen was working for the CIC in Vienna, the center of U.S. espionage in Austria.

When Verbelen arrived in Vienna in 1947 with false papers identifying him as Peter Mayer, a Czech displaced *Volksdeutsche* with no military history, the CIC was no longer in charge of searching for Nazis to prosecute at Nuremberg. Instead, untrained and inexperienced CIC agents were hiring them under a new mandate to gather intelligence about the Soviet Union, Eastern Europe, and communists living in the Allied zones. Although Congress created the CIA in 1947, it was not yet up and running and OSS had been disbanded. That left an intelligence-gathering vacuum. The U.S. military filled it.

As one would expect from a military detachment, CIC's covert espionage program was highly organized. It divided the American zone in Austria into subdetachments centered in Salzburg, Linz, Gmunden, and Vienna. Each subdetachment set up a string of fifteen to twenty field offices. Each field office, in turn, ran nets (networks) of sources, sub-sources, informants, and stringers. Because CIC didn't have any spies of its own under deep cover in the Soviet Union or its satellites, it was forced to rely completely on the services of former Nazis and Nazi collaborators eager to walk through the open door and work for the United States in order to avoid arrest, trial, and punishment.

Without digging very deeply, OSI investigators identified thirteen Nazi war criminals who had held key positions in CIC's Austrian spy web. Although OSI declined to reveal their names in its 1988 report for national security reasons, they included: a Yugoslavian general who was on a British-American list of Nazi collaborators to be "handed over to Yugoslavian authorities immediately" after they were arrested . . . the chief of Security Services in a Nazi puppet state and a Balkan Gestapo agent, both wanted by their native countries for ordering the burning of villages and the massacre of their inhabitants . . . a Nazi collaborator wanted in his native country for torturing and murdering two Catholic priests and an unspecified number of Jews as chief of a Jewish ghetto that was eventually liquidated . . . a Romanian Iron Guardist who played a role in Viorel Trifa's January 1941 uprising and massacre of Jews in Bucharest... and an SS lieutenant colonel responsible for the torture of resistance fighters and POWs, and the extermination of Jews in several countries.

CIC had both eyes open when it hired those war criminals and others like them to form the spine of American espionage operations in

Austria. Corps guidelines cautioned its agents against hiring known or convicted Nazi war criminals, but did not preclude them from hiring *unconvicted* members of Nazi organizations that the Nuremberg Military Tribunal defined as criminal—SS, SD, Gestapo, and Secret Police, among others. As a result, the CIC's hiring of war criminals was, to a great extent, an application of the "don't ask, don't tell" rule. As OSI explained in its 1988 Verbelen report: "Nearly all the former CIC agents interviewed acknowledged that membership in the SS or participation in questionable wartime activities *did not disqualify* a person from use as a CIC informant. Indeed, Verbelen's first CIC control agent maintained that it was *advantageous* to use such persons, not only because of their knowledge and experience, but also because their dependence upon the United States for protection ensured their reliability."

In other words, war criminals were useful to the United States because they could be blackmailed.

Verbelen took the usual path to employment by the United States. A friend and former SS officer working for the 430th CIC in Vienna introduced "Peter Mayer" to Captain Frank Hastings, head of the Vienna espionage office. Hastings rightly assumed that Mayer was also a former SS officer, and didn't bother to investigate his background. Why should he? Mayer came highly recommended by one of CIC's top SS sources and, as far as Hastings knew, he wasn't a known or convicted war criminal and, therefore, was eligible to work for the United States.

At the time he hired Verbelen, Hastings was running three nets of spies in Vienna, headed by agents code-named Bobi, Nick, and Hermann. Bobi and Nick were ethnic German Nazi collaborators from a Baltic country. Hermann was a former Austrian Nazi SS officer. The nets were filled with suspected war criminals. Hermann, for example, had "succeeded in developing a large net of informants who were, for the most part, former members of the Nazi party, SS, or SD."

Hastings assigned Verbelen, aka Peter Mayer, code name Herbert, to Project Newton, which was tasked with collecting intelligence on the Austrian Communist Party. As the head of one of three nets embedded in Newton, Herbert quickly recruited a string of more than twenty Nazi subsources, and he would later brag that his net of spies, sources, and informants actually numbered 130.

• • •

The CIC wasn't just running spy nets in the American zone of Austria. From its field office in Gmunden, it supervised three other espionage projects—Mount Vernon, Montgomery, and Los Angeles. According to recently declassified CIA files, SS Major Wilhelm "Willi" Hoettl, aka Goldberg, former deputy head of the SD in Budapest and later the head of the SD in Vienna, ran two of the nets for the CIC under the title of "control chief." One of Austria's seven hundred thousand Nazis, Hoettl in turn hired former detention camp mates to work for him. Among them were Erich Kernmayer, a Nazi propagandist and the Nazi press chief in Vienna; SS officer Karl Kowarik, the director of the Austrian Hitler Youth organization; former SD officer Werner Moser; and former SD Major Karl Haas, who, according to a top-secret CIA report, "utilizes the services of former Abwehr colleagues."

Hoettl and his boys all came from U.S. Detention Camp Marcus W. Orr, near Salzburg. With twelve thousand Nazi detainees, it was the largest pen in Austria. While detained in Camp Orr, Hoettl and his friends became members of the Spinne (Spider), a political organization created in the camp to plan the resurrection of the Austrian Nazi party and the second *Anschluss* or annexation to Germany.

Project Mount Vernon ran nets in the Soviet-occupied zone of Austria. Project Montgomery ran a net of Hungarians and Hungarian refugees, especially *Volksdeutsche*. Its mission was to penetrate the Hungarian army and Soviet occupying forces and to supply CIC with information on their leaders, plans, and operations.

Project Los Angeles's mission was to penetrate and collect information on the Italian Communist Party and to compile a list of high-level communists targeted for assassination. The chief source of the Los Angeles net was Karl Haas. Two other top sources, according to the secret report, were Monsignor Federico Fioretti, a Vatican official and director of the Vatican press bureau, and Bishop Alois Hudal, pastor of German Catholics living in Italy and a key player in the Vatican ratline that found safe havens for former Nazis and Nazi collaborators in the Middle East and South America.

• • •

In 1956, nine years after it had hired him, the CIC learned that Verbelen was a convicted war criminal. At this point, the CIC was winding down its espionage operations in Austria because the Allied occupation was over and Austria was once again a fully independent country. To the U.S. Army, Verbelen was no longer a useful enemy. Not only was he unreliable because he had lied about his wartime activity; he was also suspected of double dipping—working for the Americans and the British or French at the same time. More important, he was hopelessly compromised. The Soviets had uncovered him and tried to blackmail him into becoming a double agent.

The CIC decided not to tell Belgium where Verbelen was hiding. Since Belgium had not requested his extradition, the United States was under no legal obligation to deliver him. Like Klaus Barbie, Verbelen had become a dangerous liability as a man who knew too much. It was in the interests of the United States to protect him because his exposure would also reveal the scope of U.S. covert operations in Austria.

The United States had little choice but to cut Verbelen loose "without prejudice . . . suitable for intelligence re-employment." The Austrian state police immediately hired him as a paid informant, probably at the recommendation of the CIC. Verbelen went on to become an Austrian citizen under his real name.

In 1962, fifteen years after Belgium had convicted him, the Austrian department of justice learned from former resistance fighters that Belgium had sentenced Robert Jan Verbelen in absentia to death for crimes committed as a captain in the Flemish SS. Austrian prosecutors tried him for the murder of seven named Belgian resistance fighters and asked for a life sentence. In turn, Belgium asked for his extradition. Both lost.

A Viennese court acquitted Verbelen of war crimes because, it said, he had just followed orders when he executed the seven civilians. The Austrian Supreme Court disagreed. Concurring with the Nuremberg Military Tribunal that obedience to a superior does not justify the commission of a crime and may only serve to mitigate punishment, it overturned the lower court decision, recommending a retrial.

In the end, the Austrian justice department declined to retry Verbelen. And without a conviction, his Austrian citizenship remained valid since he had not acquired it fraudulently. That left Belgium with empty hands because Austrian law prohibited the extradition of Austrian citizens.

Verbelen went on to write a string of espionage novels and to serve as a spokesman and publicist for neo-Nazi organizations. He died a free man in 1991, while John Demjanjuk was still sitting on death row. One hundred former SS men and neo-Nazis attended his funeral.

The Verbelen story is important for two reasons. It demonstrates that America's use of former Nazis and Nazi collaborators was extensive. And it shows clearly that their employment and subsequent protection was no bureaucratic accident. It was a U.S. Army open-door policy.

QRPLUMB

Mykola Lebed was one of America's most sensitive Nazi secrets. The State Department, the Pentagon, and the CIA not only protected him for decades; they guarded his deeply buried file like junkyard dogs. John Loftus stumbled across Lebed's records in U.S. Army intelligence vault number six at the National Archives in Suitland, Maryland, in 1980 while working on the Belarus Project for OSI director Walter Rockler. Loftus's discovery so unnerved the Justice Department and the CIA that both threatened him with criminal prosecution if he ever revealed Lebed's name.

What was so special about Mykola Lebed that Washington went to such lengths to keep his story locked in a basement vault?

Lebed was a fiercely passionate and ruthless leader in the Organization of Ukrainian Nationalists (OUN) from 1931, when western Ukraine was part of Poland, to 1991, when the Soviet Union dissolved. OUN's primary enemy was Poland.

To most Ukrainian dreamers of and plotters for an independent republic, Lebed was a national hero like his superior, Stepan Bandera, whom the CIA considered "dangerous" and whom the KGB assassinated in Munich in 1959. But to Moscow and his Ukrainian political enemies, Lebed was a Gestapo-trained terrorist, Nazi collaborator, and sadistic war criminal who had murdered thousands of Poles, communists, Jews, and Ukrainian rivals.

On the eve of the German invasion of the Soviet Union, OUN was bitterly divided between two opposing political factions. OUN-M was led by Andriy Melnyk, an elderly moderate and conciliatory nationalist. The larger OUN-B was led by Stepan Bandera, a much younger, radical, and ambitious politician. According to recently declassified intelligence files, Mykola Lebed was Bandera's number-two man and chief of the SB (Sluzhba Bezpeky), the underground terror arm of OUN-B. Both factions had planned and participated in the assassination of Polish officials before the war and conducted a "reign of terror" against Polish civilians. "The mere mention of the name 'Bandera,'" the OSS reported a few months after the war, "invariably brings curses and imprecations among Polish refugees."*

Divided or not, OUN's hatred of Stalin and the communists presented Germany with a unique opportunity. Why not recruit both factions and their combined army of thousands of freedom fighters to help Germany conquer the Soviet Union? Didn't the Reich, Melnyk, Bandera, and Lebed have the same enemies—Poles, Soviets, and Jews?

To attract OUN and its resistance fighters, Germany offered a deal. It promised the organization an independent Ukraine in exchange for its help in defeating the Red Army and making Eastern Europe *Judenrein*. Germany failed to explain, however, how or when the independent state would be created and which OUN faction would lead it. Unaware that Berlin considered Slavs less than human (*untermenschen*) and that it planned to use them as slaves after Germany conquered Europe, both OUN factions swallowed the bait.

While the SS was recruiting and training the Belorussian exiles, who would soon form the core of the Nazi puppet government in their homeland, the Gestapo was training Lebed and his fellow Banderist terrorists as guerillas, saboteurs, and assassins at its center in Zakopane, near Krakow. According to one of the Gestapo trainees, Lebed personally supervised the torture and execution of Jews to "harden" his men.

At the same time, Bandera was helping the Germans assemble and train two Ukrainian brigades of mostly OUN members, code names Nightingale and Roland, to fight the Soviet army and help Einsatzkommandos round up and execute Jews, according to recently declassified CIA documents. Roland and Nightingale did their jobs well. A high German source later reported that OUN had "rendered valuable services . . . in the war against the U.S.S.R."

On June 30, 1941, nine days after Germany invaded the Soviet Union and without German approval, the Banderists hastily convened a National Assembly in L'vov, the capital of western Ukraine, proclaimed an independent country, and created a new government made up exclusively of OUN-B members. The assembly appointed Lebed security minister and national police chief.

"By the will of the Ukrainian people," the Banderists announced over

---

*The Displaced Persons Commission ruled that the leadership and officers of both OUN factions were inimical to the United States.

a radio station they had seized, "the Organization of Ukrainian Nationalists under the direction of Stepan Bandera proclaim the renewal of the Ukrainian state. . . .

"Long live the Sovereign Ukrainian State!

"Long live the Organization of Ukrainian Nationalists!

"Long live . . . Stepan Bandera."

What followed next was a drunken orgy of violence. Banderists began assassinating angry OUN-M rivals who had been outfoxed by Bandera in his political power grab. (The total number of rivalry murders is unknown.) And Lebed organized mass roundups, torture, public hangings, and executions under the popular slogan "Death to Jews and Communists." According to historian Yehuda Bauer, the Banderists "killed all the Jews they could find . . . many thousands."

Taken by surprise, Germany was not pleased with Bandera's swift and unapproved proclamation of an independent state, and it blamed him for driving the final wedge between OUN-M and OUN-B, the two factions Germany was courting. In response, the Gestapo rounded up Bandera and most of his leaders and placed them under house arrest in Germany. The Reich then dissolved the six-week-old Independent Ukraine.

Bandera's arrest left Lebed, who had escaped the Gestapo dragnet, in charge of OUN-B. Angry and vindictive, he established two secret training camps in western Ukraine, regrouped the Banderist arm of the Ukrainian Insurgent Army (UPA), declared a guerilla war against the Germans occupying his homeland, and issued a blunt manifesto to the Gestapo who had trained him:

"Long live greater Independent Ukraine without Jews, Poles, and Germans. Poles behind the San [River]! Germans to Berlin! Jews to the gallows!"

Lebed was an ambitious killer. He proposed to "cleanse the entire revolutionary territory of the Polish population" as an act of revenge against Polish partisans who had been crossing the San and preying on Ukrainian civilians, burning down their villages and executing their residents. Eyewitness Moshe Maltz, a Jew hiding in the woods, reported in 1943: "Bandera men . . . are not discriminating about who they kill; they are gunning down entire villages. Since there are hardly any Jews left to kill, the Bandera gangs have turned on the Poles, literally hacking Poles to pieces. Every day . . . you can see the bodies of the Poles . . . floating down the Bug [River]." On one day alone in July 1943, Lebed's Banderists raided as many as eighty villages, killing up to ten thousand Poles.

Scholars estimate that Ukrainian militia slaughtered 90,000 Polish men, women, and children, and that Polish militia butchered 20,000 Ukrainian civilians, including women and children.

Lebed's UPA became more than a gadfly to the German and Soviet armies. It was a well-trained, highly disciplined, and elusive guerilla army. It blew up troop and supply trains, destroyed arms depots, attacked military installations, and disrupted military campaigns. It posed such a threat to the German occupation of the Soviet Union that the Gestapo declared Lebed public enemy number one and distributed posters announcing he was sought dead or alive.

When it became clear that the tide of war had changed and that the German army was beginning to lose, the SS released Bandera and his men and promised, once again, an independent Ukraine after it defeated the Soviets—if UPA stopped killing Germans. The Banderists played along. They would help the Germans get rid of the communists. Then they would get rid of the Germans.

Lebed and most of his UPA guerillas began collaborating with the Nazis, until the summer of 1944, when the Red Army recaptured Ukraine and drove the Germans into Poland, signaling the beginning of the end of the war. Lebed and many of his fellow terrorists followed the German army west in Operation Sunflower (Sonnenblume).

Thousands of resistance fighters, however, did not follow Lebed. Some returned to their villages ready and willing to take up arms again if needed. Others holed up in the Carpathian Mountains and reassembled. From their craggy retreats, the Banderist guerillas preyed on western Ukrainian civilians. They looted and raped and destroyed villages that refused to feed and supply them. And they robbed and killed Jews who had managed to survive Einsatzgruppen raids.

After the war, Bandera made his way to Germany, where the CIC seriously considered hiring him to help unite the various Ukrainian political factions. In the end, however, the CIC decided not to use Bandera because he was "extremely dangerous" and deeply hated by a substantial number of the Ukrainian refugees. British intelligence hired him instead.

Because his face was well-known in Eastern Europe after the war, Lebed made his way to Rome and offered his services to the CIC. Like Nazi rocket scientist Wernher von Braun with his thousands of pages of ballistic missile designs for trade, Lebed brought his own chip to the American bargaining table. He had a treasure trove of names and lists—nationalists still inside Ukraine whom the United States could recruit; communist agents in Ukraine whom the United States could assassinate; experienced and skilled killers whom the United States could hire; and thousands of OUN members with compromising war histories living in DP camps whom the United States could recruit with promises of steady employment and protection. *

The CIC knew that Lebed's hands were bloody. From interviews with Ukrainian DPs, it concluded that Lebed was "ruthless . . . cunning . . . [with] Gestapo training . . . a well-known sadist and collaborator of the Germans" who had been a co-conspirator in the assassination of Polish interior minister Bronislaw Pieracki in 1934.

For its role in that murder, the League of Nations had condemned OUN as a terrorist group, and Poland had sentenced Lebed to life in prison. He was either freed from jail by the Germans when they invaded Poland in 1939 or escaped during the confusion after a bombing raid.

War criminal or not, CIC deemed Lebed vital to U.S. interests and hired him in 1947, the same year it hired Klaus Barbie and Robert Jan Verbelen. The main concern of CIC immediately after the war was Soviet infiltration into the Allied sectors of partitioned Germany and Austria, especially the American zone. With help from Ukrainian contacts in DP camps, Lebed supplied CIC with accurate and vital information about Soviet espionage in Western Europe.

Within months of hiring Lebed, however, CIC developed a severe case of the jitters. Soviet bloodhounds and Ukrainian assassins, bent on revenge for Lebed's execution of their compatriots, were hot on his heels. With agents, spies, and informants in all Allied sectors of Western Europe, it would be only a matter of time before the Soviets or Lebed's Ukrainian enemies learned that he was in Rome working for America.

The CIC moved Lebed, aka "Roman Turan," to Munich, where Frank Wisner snapped him up. With Lebed's help Wisner created the sprawling Operation QR Plumb, which, among other projects, em-

---

* The Lebed list can no longer be accessed at the National Archives. Either it was destroyed, lost, or is still classified. John Loftus uncovered more than eleven volumes of handwritten names and descriptions of Banderists and UPA members in Lebed's CIC files at Archives. The U.S. Army had translated the documents from Cyrillic to Roman script and computerized the names. Loftus showed the list to his superiors at the Department of Justice. Some of the men on the Lebed list were also OSI targets.

ployed teams of assassins and saboteurs made up of UPA war criminals and former Waffen SS men, especially from the German-trained Nightingale and Roland brigades. The men were assigned to hit squads with code names like Operation Ohio, Operation Hagberry, and Operation Lithia. In Operation Ohio, for example, Lebed (code name P/2) recruited a squad of Ukrainian ex-Nazi collaborators who were credited with assassinating at least twenty suspected double agents and Soviet spies in an American DP camp near Munich.

Lebed also supervised espionage operations inside Ukraine as part of the larger Operation Redsox, a joint American and British venture. Under subproject Aerodynamic, Lebed organized parachute drops of men (Apostles) and supplies to the UPA hiding in the Carpathian Mountains. Supply bundles included grenades, guns and ammo, radio sets, maps and money, wristwatches, collapsible shovels for trenching, compasses, canteens, and flashlights. He also created a safe courier route between Germany and Ukraine through Czechoslovakia. With the help of British intelligence officer and Soviet mole Kim Philby, the KGB eventually captured and executed up to 75 percent of the agents air-dropped into Ukraine.

Within two short years under Lebed's grassroots leadership and with eager help from the Ukrainian Supreme Liberation Council (UHVR), a major Ukrainian liberation group that the CIA financed, Wisner had "established a secure underground movement" in Ukraine made up mostly of former Nazi collaborators and war criminals.

Like the CIC in Rome, the CIA in Munich soon got the jitters. With Soviet kidnappings and assassinations routine, and Lebed's Ukrainian enemies still hunting for him, "Roman Turan" was no longer safe in Europe. Wisner and the CIA smuggled Lebed and his wife and daughter into the United States in 1949, the same year a former U.S. covert agent helped Romanian war criminal Nikolae Malaxa procure a visa to the United States.

New York City became Lebed's new base of espionage operations. He wasn't alone. In 1951, the CIA admitted to the INS: "There are at least twenty former or active members of the Security Branch (SB) of OUN-B in the United States at the present time."

Unaware that Lebed was a top CIA operative, INS began investigating him for visa fraud, probably based on a tip from one of Lebed's Ukrainian political enemies. As part of its background investigation, INS interviewed Ukrainian Americans and learned what the CIC had discovered four years earlier—that Lebed was "one of the most important Bandera terrorists . . . [responsible] for wholesale murders of Ukrainians, Poles, and Jewish [*sic*]. . . . In all these actions, Lebed was one of the most important leaders."

Noting the CIA's interest in Lebed, INS debriefed the agency on its findings with a warning that its star agent was a prime candidate for deportation. In response, CIA deputy director Allen Dulles made a strong case for a cover-up. The charges against Lebed were false, Dulles argued. Lebed had fought with equal zeal against the Nazis and Bolsheviks. Furthermore, Lebed and his contacts had been of "inestimable value" to the CIA and its operations, and he was "urgently needed." Finally, Dulles argued that to deport Lebed would "severely damage national security" and "create serious repercussions among the anti-Soviet Ukrainian groups all over the world."

Dulles wasn't necessarily lying. The Wisner clique inside the CIA knew about Lebed's war criminal background, but the agency as a whole probably did not. Confronted with Dulles's cogent arguments to protect Lebed and his identity, the INS reluctantly caved in.

"We have always cooperated with the Central Intelligence Agency within the permissible limits of the law," INS commissioner Argyle Mackey told the CIA, "and have in this case suspended further investigation of what appears to be a clear-cut deportation case." According to newly declassified documents, Mackey went on to ask the CIA to inform INS when Lebed was no longer useful.

In spite of the INS promise to drop its investigation of Lebed, the CIA was not about to take any chances. To secure his continued services, the agency played its trump card. Invoking the "one hundred rule" recently approved by Congress, it asked the attorney general to grant Lebed U.S. citizenship and to make it retroactive. Then the CIA offered to share Lebed with the FBI.

Director J. Edgar Hoover instructed a team of agents to interview Lebed as a possible FBI source and to conduct a background check on his wartime activity. The agents learned about Lebed's alleged UPA war crimes from Ukrainian Americans. They also obtained captured German documents from the British intelligence agency MI5 that "expressed German appreciation of, and favor towards, bands of Ukrainian insurgents who apparently fought guerilla warfare against the Soviets. In one Lebed was described as the political leader of the Ukrainian Rebellion Army [*sic*], a valuable aid for the German High Command."

The CIA put Lebed in charge of a massive psych warfare program in New York, code name QRDynamic, under a front organization called the Prolog Research and Publishing Association, with sister offices in Munich, Paris, and London. Dynamic's objective was "to produce and infiltrate into the Soviet Union material aimed at keeping alive the Ukrainian national spirit while exploiting the vulnerabilities of the Soviet system." Lebed—still known as P/2—and a handful of his most trusted men, including Dynamic's vice president, Myroslav Prokop, and its operations officer, Anatol Kaminsky, hired Ukrainian authors, scholars, journalists, radio broadcasters, and poets to deluge Ukrainians on both sides of the Iron Curtain with propaganda calling for an independent Ukraine. Dynamic's Ukrainian hires were not told they were working for the CIA.

Dynamic's Munich office published a steady stream of books and articles through the Ukrainian Society for Studies Abroad; beamed thousands of Nova Ukraina radio broadcasts each year into Ukraine from Athens and Munich; dropped millions of leaflets on the Ukrainian countryside; and published its own newspaper, *Suchasna Ukriana* (*Ukraine Today*) to counter Soviet-backed Ukrainian papers like Michael Hanusiak's *News from Ukraine*, which had featured the photos of John Demjanjuk's alleged Trawniki card.

Working out of his New York publishing company office, Lebed traveled around the United States and Canada preaching the Gospel of Independent Ukraine, attempted to unite the Ukrainian émigré communities behind him, and undertook information gathering and dissemination missions to Europe. He retired from Prolog in 1975, the same year in which Hanusiak sent his Ukrainian list containing Iwan Demjanjuk's name to Senator Jacob Javits and Elizabeth Holtzman was badgering Henry Kissinger to seek help from West Germany, Austria, Israel, Poland, and the Soviet Union for archival documents on former Nazis and Nazi collaborators.

Ten years later, in 1985, a bureaucrat at the State Department or the Justice Department goofed. He inadvertently handed over a top-secret Lebed file to GAO investigators. Without mentioning Lebed by name, the subsequent GAO report to Congress did summarize his Nazi collaboration, war crimes, and CIA connection.

Under pressure from Holtzman, Peter Rodino, the chairman of the House Judiciary Committee, threatened to hold public hearings on the unnamed Nazis and Nazi collaborators listed in the GAO report. At the same time, the CIA heard rumors that OSI was investigating Lebed's wartime activity.

The CIA panicked. If the GAO report, which already had been made public, was not officially "corrected," if Rodino held hearings, and if OSI aggressively pursued its investigation of the former Banderist leader, Lebed's name was bound to be made public and Operation QRPlumb and its subgroup QRDynamic would be compromised. The CIA couldn't risk it. As the agency put it in a secret synopsis of Plumb operations: "QRPLUMB is one of the oldest, and most effective CA [covert action] operations targeted on the Soviet Union and is the only project conducting CA operations inside the Soviet Ukraine."

The CIA went to the plate and struck out. The GAO refused to amend its report. Then the CIA hit two home runs. It was told by OSI director Neal Sher that "his office does not have a file on Mr. Lebed and, at the moment, has no basis for initiating an investigation of him. If such investigation is warranted in the future, he will inform the Agency of his action. . . . He recommended that we inform our Congressional oversight committee and Congressman Rodino of the case and our security concerns, especially since he had indications that Congressman Rodino was under pressure from certain quarters to hold hearings on the GAO report."

Rodino caved in to CIA pressure and canceled the hearings on the twelve nameless Nazi collaborators in the GAO report. The Lebed issue made a media splash, left no ripples, and quietly disappeared.

In the end, Lebed admitted he was a terrorist. He told OSI investigators that he had been "indirectly involved in the planning of the political assassination" of Polish interior minister Pieracki before the war, but he denied that he had ever collaborated with the Germans. And he refused to answer further OSI questions about his activity as a Banderist because "he was protecting live persons."

When the Soviet Union dissolved in 1991, the CIA dissolved Plumb and severed its ties to Prolog with a final payout of $1.75 million that would, according to QRPlumb CIA files, "provide for a more natural, and thus, less risky—from a security standpoint—transition to private support. Upon receipt of the termination payment, the relationship between the CIA and the project will end."

Lebed died a free man in 1998. To most Ukrainians, he is still a national hero who risked his life to fight for an independent homeland. As one Ukrainian historian put it, the allegations of war crimes against

Lebed and other Ukrainian freedom fighters were nothing more than "typical KGB-sponsored disinformation about the Ukrainian struggle."

• • •

The Lebed story is a case study of how the CIA recruited a major war criminal and why it protected him. At the same time it raises a troubling question. INS commissioner Mackey told the CIA that Lebed was a clear-cut deportation case and that the service had "always cooperated with the Central Intelligence Agency."

How many other clear-cut Nazi deportation cases did INS try to bury at the request of the CIA? Andrija Artukovic? Otto von Bolschwing? Hermine Braunsteiner? Wernher von Braun? Nicolae Malaxa? Boleslavs Maikovskis? Arthur Rudolph? Tscherim Soobzokov? Hubertus Strughold? Viorel Trifa?

RUSTY AND ZIPPER

Brigadier General Reinhard Gehlen was one of the biggest, best known, and most politically dangerous and controversial Cold War spies of the postwar era. Books have been written about him and his espionage work for the United States from 1946 to 1956. His spy network, which the United States called the Gehlen Org, worked first for the CIC under code name Rusty, then for the CIA under code name Zipper.

Gehlen moved in and out of the shadow world of smoke and mirrors, asset theft and double-agent perfidy, blackmail and assassinations, and top-secret communiqués. As a result, much of what has been written about him and his organization is riddled with gaps, weak links, and blurred connections. Newly declassified documents have filled in some holes and clarified some issues.

General Gehlen was the Reich's chief of the Foreign Army–East (FHO), an intelligence-gathering organization with two missions. The first was to collect military information about the Soviet Union. The second was to pinpoint the location of Jews, communists, Gypsies, and other enemies of the Reich so that Einsatzkommandos, with the aid of local police and militia volunteers, could arrest, rob, and murder them. Given the critical postwar intelligence role that Gehlen played, first for the United States, then for West Germany, it is important to ask whether he was a war criminal. The answer is as murky as Gehlen's own spy world.

Reinhard Gehlen was a soldier in the German regular army. He was not a member of the Nazi Party nor did he belong to any Nazi criminal organization such as the SS, SD, or Gestapo. Like Holocaust architect Adolf Eichmann, General Gehlen was a desk man. As such, it is unlikely that he got his gloves bloody rounding up and shooting the more than 1.5 million Jews, Gypsies, and communists who were executed in the forests of the Soviet Union, Gehlen's territory of expertise. What is clear, however, is that his agents did his dirty work.

To supply Gehlen with the intelligence information he demanded, his men interrogated, then approved or supervised the torture and the starvation and/or execution of three to four million captured Soviet soldiers in POW camps like Rovno and Chelm. The number is equivalent to the entire population of Los Angeles. Like the Dora Nazis who knew about and approved the use of slave laborers to excavate tunnels, Gehlen knew how his agents extracted the intelligence information they fed him. There is no evidence to suggest that he objected to their methods.

The CIC never placed Gehlen's name on—and in fact they more likely scratched it from—the Central Registry of War Criminal and Security Suspects (CROWCASS). If General Gehlen had been tried for war crimes, however, he undoubtedly would have been as slippery as a double agent, arguing like Eichmann in Israel and Romanian Iron Guardist Bishop Valerian Trifa in America that he never killed or tortured anyone. Whether he ever pulled the trigger, personally ordered the execution of POWs, or was present when they were tortured and murdered will probably never be known. Be that as it may, the Displaced Persons Commission defined high-level intelligence officers (*Abwehrmänner*) like Gehlen inimical to the United States.

Anticipating the defeat of Germany, Gehlen, like von Braun and Lebed, feathered a warm nest for himself. He microfilmed FHO's extensive files on the Soviet Union and buried them in the Alps in airtight, rustproof canisters. Among the documents were Soviet five-year plans; analyses of Soviet defense production capabilities; the sites of Soviet research centers and critical oil and mineral deposits; and the names of Communist Party officials.

When Gehlen surrendered to the U.S. Army just before the end of the war, he offered CIC the microfilm and his entire anti-Soviet espionage network, most of which was still in place. Frank Wisner interviewed him in Germany and the CIC debriefed him for months at

Fort Hunt, Virginia, a suburban Washington POW interrogation center, code name "Box 1142." Once again following the principle of "don't ask, don't tell," the interrogators never seriously investigated Gehlen for suspected war crimes. They asked "Is he useful," not "What war crimes did he commit?"

The CIC was impressed with Gehlen's cache of microfilm, his Soviet intelligence experience, and his pool of intelligence officers, agents, and informants. It was also desperate. The United States didn't even know where to find the major bridges in the Soviet Union, much less have any reliable information about its new enemy's troop strength, weapons deployment, long-range-missile capabilities, and nuclear research.

For the CIC, and soon for the CIA, Gehlen was a gift from Ares, the god of war.

In late 1946, a year and a half after the war ended, the CIC hired Gehlen, code name Utility, and his entire network and set him up at a secret location in Pullach, a small town south of Munich and the site of a former Waffen SS training camp. At the insistence of the United States, Gehlen promised not to employ SS, SD, or Gestapo men. But sensing that Washington was just trying to cover its backside, Gehlen stuffed the upper echelons of the Org with war criminals, using phony papers and false names to avoid detection and prosecution at Nuremberg. How many? Historian Timothy Naftali, a specialist on Gehlen, cautiously concluded: "At least one hundred of Gehlen's officers and agents had served with the SD or Gestapo, and the number may in effect be significantly higher."

Naftali and journalist Christopher Simpson have compiled a partial list of the major Nazi war criminals who ran the Gehlen Org. Besides Klaus Barbie, the Butcher of Lyon, there are four especially vicious Nazis on their list—Alois Brunner, Franz Six, Emil Augsburg, and Erich Deppner. The crimes against humanity of these former Nazis are important because they illustrate the kind of murderers the United States either approved for employment in Operations Rusty and Zipper or indirectly hired by looking the other way.

• • •

SS Major Alois Brunner was one of the first former Nazi colleagues Gehlen hired. Brunner's credentials were impeccable. According to recently declassified CIA files, he was the architect of the Nazi extermination system, which began with penning Jews in ghettos so they could be easily located when the time came to load them into wagons, vans, and trains for transport to death camps. Eichmann considered Brunner "his best man."

Unlike Eichmann, however, Brunner was more than just a genocide planner. He trained cadres of Gestapo, German police, SS officers, and Nazi collaborators, like Trawniki men, in the art of exterminating Jews with speed and efficiency. And he practiced what he preached.

Brunner had rounded up and sent an estimated forty-seven thousand Austrian Jews for deportation, personally leading one transport to an SS camp outside Riga, Latvia, before the death camps were up and running. From Vienna, Brunner went to Berlin, where he helped deport German Jews. He was then posted to Greece, where he sent an estimated forty-three thousand Salonika Jews to Auschwitz and Treblinka. After Greece, he was posted to France, where he took over the bustling Drancy transit camp outside Paris. As Drancy commandant, he sent another estimated twenty-five thousand men, women, and children directly to the gas chambers. From France, Brunner went to Slovakia to mop up the last remaining Jews.

France never forgave Brunner. In 1954, it convicted him in absentia and sentenced him to death. At the time, he was working for the United States in the Gehlen Org under the name Alois Schmaldienst. Fearing for his life, he fled to Syria, probably on the Vatican ratline, under the name Dr. Georg Fischer.

Syria welcomed Brunner, granted him asylum, and hired him to create a state security organization. Not long after he settled in Damascus, the CIA hired him through the Gehlen Org to help Egypt develop its brutal security police force. Brunner's presence in the Middle East did not go unnoticed. The Israeli Mossad sent him a special greeting, but he survived. The letter bomb merely blinded him in one eye and tore off several fingers of his left hand.

When France and Germany learned that Brunner was living comfortably in a Damascus hotel, they requested his extradition. Syria refused to give him up. In 1987, Brunner granted the *Chicago Sun-Times* an interview during which he was as candid as a protected Nazi war criminal could be. "The Jews deserved to die. I have no regrets," he said. "If I had the chance, I would do it again." Brunner is probably dead now. If not, he would be over one hundred years old.

• • •

Dr. Franz Six was a prewar college professor with degrees in law and political science and dean of the faculty of the prestigious University of Berlin. During the war, SS Brigadier General Six was an intelligence officer like Gehlen, a protégé of Heinrich Himmler, and an Einsatzgruppe leader responsible for the murder of thousands of Jews and other civilians in the Soviet Union, according to recently declassified CIA files. Eichmann called him *Streiber* (eager beaver).

After the war, one United States, so to speak, used the CIC to find and punish Dr. Six for war crimes. He avoided detection and arrest by joining the other United States, which used the CIC to help staff the Gehlen Org. Unaware that Dr. Six was working for the United States, however, an ambitious CIC investigator discovered him and turned him over to the U.S. military tribunal at Nuremberg before the United States could rescue him.

Nuremberg convicted Dr. Six of murder and sentenced him to twenty years in prison. An attorney on the team that prosecuted Einsatzgruppen criminals at Nuremberg called Dr. Six "one of the biggest swine" of them all. After Dr. Six served four years in prison, America granted him clemency as part of its generous program to free Nazi war criminals convicted by the United States. A week later, Dr. Six was back at work for the United States in the Gehlen Org. He died a free man in Germany.

Dr. Emil Augsburg was a Polish-born colleague of Dr. Six with a doctorate in Soviet studies. In 1941, he joined the SD. His assignment was to carry out "special duties" in Poland, a euphemism for killing Polish Jews, according to recently declassified CIA files. Like Dr. Six, Augsburg also led an Einsatzkommando unit in the Crimea region of Russia, where the German army had captured Iwan Demjanjuk in May 1942. Augsburg's personnel records show that he had achieved "extraordinary results . . . in special tasks," another euphemism for the murder of Jews. The extraordinary results earned him a promotion to major.

Around the same time the German army took Demjanjuk prisoner during the battle of Kerch, Augsburg was seriously wounded in an air attack and evacuated to Berlin. After his recuperation, the SS assigned him to create an index of Soviet leaders to be targeted for behind-the-lines assassination. After the war, Augsburg hid in a Benedictine monastery in East Germany and eventually made his way to the Vatican, where he found a safe haven.

His creation of the Soviet name index made Augsburg, aka Althaus and Alberti, extremely valuable to the Org. Gehlen hired his former colleague and gave him two critical espionage assignments—to supervise the agent net that interrogated émigrés and defectors from the East, and to create airtight cover stories for Org agents scheduled to cross into the Soviet Union on espionage assignments. Gehlen considered him "a shining star . . . a godsend."

Poland convicted Augsburg in absentia, but Germany declined to hand him over for punishment. Instead it hired him to work for Gehlen, who was now employed by the new West German intelligence service. Germany eventually fired Augsburg on suspicion of working for communist East Germany. Like Dr. Six, Emil Augsburg died a free man.

SS Major Erich Deppner was to Holland what Klaus Barbie was to France and Robert Jan Verbelen was to Belgium. His assignment from Berlin was to crush the virulent Dutch resistance. As the head of a security team, Deppner is credited with torturing and murdering approximately 450 Dutch resistance fighters, according to Dutch sources. He also is credited with killing the last remaining Soviet POWs held in Holland's Kamp Amersfoort.

Deppner commands a highly emotional place in the memory of Holland's Jewish community. He was the first commandant of the Dutch transit camp of Westerbork, from which more than one hundred thousand Jews, including Anne Frank, were transported to death camps—at first to Auschwitz, and later to Sobibor during the time John Demjanjuk was allegedly serving as an SS guard there.

The United States hired Deppner, aka Egon Dietrich and Ernst Borchert, through the Gehlen Org. Precisely what he did for Rusty and Zipper is not fully known. The Dutch repeatedly asked Germany to extradite him, but Germany always refused. Finally, in 1964, almost twenty years after the war and perhaps under pressure from Holland, West Germany tried Deppner for murdering more than sixty Soviet POWs. Germany acquitted him for the same reason Austria had acquitted Robert Jan Verbelen—he had just been following orders.

Like Franz Six and Emil Augsburg, Erich Deppner died a free man, in 2005.

• • •

Based on newly declassified documents, it is possible to draw several conclusions about the Gehlen Organization. First, when the CIA took over "control" of the Gehlen Org from the CIC in 1949, shortly after Congress had approved the CIA's new espionage charter, the agency's employment policy was simple and clear. As historian Naftali put it: "There was no internal CIA policy against hiring Nazi war criminals."

Second, Operation Zipper grew like a tumor as long as the CIA nourished it with cash. The Gehlen Org was so bloated that, at its peak, it was running up to four thousand agents and informants for the United States.

Third, the CIA never lost control of the Org because it never had control. And it certainly didn't know how many Nazi war criminals it was employing through Gehlen. Nor did it care.

Fourth, the Gehlen Org was corrupt from top to bottom. Besides the usual internal power struggles and competition for talent and money, the Org was infested with double agents, double and triple dipping, Soviet moles, and fraudulent reporting. Much, if not most, of the information the Gehlen Org provided the United States was based on rumor, faulty sources, and outright lies.

Finally, under the guise of national security protection and perhaps as a final World War II irony, the Gehlen Org turned out to be a danger to U.S. national security. As a rogue espionage program, it opened a back door into U.S. intelligence operations in Europe for communist moles. And it deliberately planted or cultivated a false notion in the minds of Washington decision makers and eager spooks like Frank Wisner. That false notion cost the United States billions of dollars, created unrealistic expectations in émigré communities, and cost the lives of thousands of covert operatives and underground insurgent soldiers who believed in America.

Reinhard Gehlen had convinced the United States that Stalin was about to attack West Germany and start World War III. He spoon-fed the United States the lie because he thought—and rightly so—that the lie was what the budget-hungry Pentagon and CIA wanted to hear. The Allen Dulleses, the Frank Wisners, the J. Edgar Hoovers, and the Joe McCarthys of America were all ears.

Victor Marchetti, a former Soviet military analyst for the CIA and a vocal critic of the agency's failed policies, summarized the value of the Org in sobering terms.

"The Gehlen organization provided nothing worthwhile in understanding or estimating Soviet military or political capability in Eastern Europe or elsewhere," Marchetti wrote. "The agency loved Gehlen because he fed us what we wanted to hear. We used his stuff constantly, and we fed it to everybody else: the Pentagon, the White House, the newspapers. They loved it, too. But it was hyped up Russian Boogeyman junk, and it did a lot of damage to this country."

Whether or not one agrees with Marchetti's harsh assessment, the conclusion to America's ten-year espionage waltz with Reinhard Gehlen is as inescapable as it is damning. Under the guise of national security, and based on false assumptions and misguided Cold War pragmatism, the United States allowed itself to be duped into becoming an international employment agency for Nazi war criminals and terrorists.

Finally, as symbols of corruption and cover-up, Robert Jan Verbelen, Mykola Lebed, and Reinhard Gehlen add perspective and context to the John Demjanjuk story. By all Holocaust standards, Demjanjuk was a minor war criminal, a colorless death camp guard whom no one seems to remember. As a Trawniki man, he had no intelligence value to the United States. After the war, he didn't work for the CIC, the CIA, the Gehlen Org, or the FBI. He tested diesel motors for the Ford Motor Company in Ohio and was not privy to embarrassing U.S. secrets.

That made John Demjanjuk a perfect diversion for the American intelligence establishment with secrets to hide, and perfect fodder for the American justice system and its courts.

PART FIVE

Justice on Trial

CHAPTER FORTY-NINE

Death to the Nazi Lawyer

John Gill went home to Chicago leaving Yoram Sheftel without a co-counsel for the Demjanjuk appeal at the Israeli Supreme Court. Sheftel was not disappointed. Since Gill didn't know Israeli law, to keep him on the defense team would have been unfair to John Demjanjuk, who needed wily Israeli attorneys to argue his case before the High Court.

Sheftel began searching for an Israeli lawyer of stature willing to defend a convicted Nazi collaborator. And there was the rub. It was easy to find attorneys of stature, but nearly impossible to find one willing to suffer the hatred of his countrymen and to risk his life and career for a legal principle.

There was an exception. His name was Dov Eitan, and Sheftel was lucky to get him.

Eitan had been an Israeli judge for seventeen years. In 1983, Eitan was pressured to resign from the bench for engaging in politics as a judge. He had signed a left-wing petition condemning the Israeli invasion of Lebanon and calling for an immediate withdrawal of Israeli troops.

Now in private practice, Eitan watched much of the Demjanjuk trial on television and was deeply troubled by what he heard and saw. Judge Levin was so biased that he was "disgracing Israeli justice." So when Sheftel invited him to join the Demjanjuk appeal, Eitan accepted, but only if Demjanjuk could convince him face-to-face that he was not Ivan the Terrible.

After interviewing Demjanjuk for hours at Ayalon Prison, Eitan concluded that Demjanjuk was never at Treblinka, and he agreed to argue in his behalf before the Supreme Court. "I want to tell you as clearly as possible," Eitan told Demjanjuk, "you did not receive a fair trial." Demjanjuk wept and the death threats against Eitan began. They never let up.

The Demjanjuk appeal was scheduled for early December 1988, eight months after the Levin court sentenced Demjanjuk to death. Eitan would argue the jurisdictional issues—about one-third of the case—and Sheftel would argue both the evidentiary issues and the alleged bias of Judge Levin and his court. A week before the appeal hearing, however, Sheftel got a hysterical phone call from his assistant at eight thirty in the morning. Dov Eitan was dead, she said.

Eitan had arrived at his office in the heart of downtown Jerusalem just after eight, the police reported. No one was there. He left his briefcase on his desk and apparently walked to the eighteen-story City Towers office complex one block away. He entered the building, stepped into an elevator, and pressed the button for the eighteenth floor. When the light didn't go on, he asked the only other passenger how he could get to the top. The passenger told him that this particular elevator only went to the fifteenth floor. The passenger got off at the seventh floor; Eitan exited at the fifteenth. He walked to a window, opened it, and jumped, landing on the pavement outside a dress shop. There were no eyewitnesses on the fifteenth floor. He did not leave a suicide note.

Sheftel was shocked, then baffled. Suicide? How was it possible? He had chatted with Eitan the previous day and made an appointment to meet with him to discuss the appeal. Eitan had shown no signs of stress. To the contrary, he seemed to be looking forward to his argument before the bench.

Sheftel rushed to Eitan's home, where he found Eitan's wife, Miriam, just as baffled. "They say he committed suicide," she said through her shock and grief. "That can't be. I don't believe it. . . . We ate breakfast together. He told me he was going to his office, and we made an appointment to meet at eleven to buy a new suit for the appeal."

Could Eitan have been murdered? Did he go to the City Towers to meet someone? Did someone knock him out and shove him out the window? Did someone threaten to kill his wife and family if he didn't leap? His body was so badly smashed that, if someone had beaten him and tossed his unconscious body out of the fifteenth-floor window, the injury would never be detected.

Just days before Eitan's death, Yisrael Yehezkeli, a regular spectator at the trial who was frequently heard shouting at Sheftel from his seat, paid a visit to Sheftel's mother under an assumed name. Yehezkeli was a seventy-year-old Holocaust survivor whose entire family—parents, brothers and sisters, aunts, uncles, and cousins—were murdered at Treblinka by Ivan the Terrible.

"How can you allow your son to defend a Nazi murderer?" Yehezkeli asked.

She told him she had cried when she heard that Yoram was defending Demjanjuk.

You better see to it that your son quits the Demjanjuk case, Yehezkeli warned her. If he doesn't, he will be killed. So will Eitan.

Yehezkeli had made a similar threat to Eitan and his wife, Miriam.

Mrs. Sheftel took the warning seriously. Her son did not. Why should he? It was just one more threat in a long list. Besides, didn't the Israeli police and the medical examiner rule Eitan's death a suicide? Eitan had felt trapped, Sheftel reasoned. Frightened by the death threats, he wanted to drop the case. But he couldn't because he felt morally obligated to represent his client. Suicide must have been his only way out.

John Demjanjuk and his family were certain that Eitan's death was no suicide. Right-wing extremists had promised to kill their new defense attorney and they did. In the wake of Eitan's death, the family was deeply worried about Sheftel, who didn't seem to take Yehezkeli's warning seriously. Maybe Sheftel was in denial, talking himself into believing the death of his colleague and friend was suicide because he needed to. Maybe he couldn't admit that he might be next.

Soon after the memorial service for Eitan ended, Sheftel was heading for the front door of the Sanhedria Funeral Parlor to join the cortege to the cemetery. He stopped to chat with Edna Shabtai, the widow of a famous Israeli writer. Yehezkeli, who was waiting in the lobby, began screaming.

"His face looked like that of a man in a trance," recalled a journalist covering the funeral. "It wasn't possible to understand exactly what he was saying, but the general message was: 'Finally I caught up with you....Now I'm going to do to you what [the Nazis] did to us.'"

Yehezkeli then tossed liquid from one of two small bottles into Sheftel's face. Some hit Shabtai as well. Fortunately, most of it landed on the wall behind them.

Sheftel felt a burning pain in his eyes, ran to a nearby sink, and began splashing water on his face. "I went into shock," he recalled later. "The voice was still shouting, but I could not grasp what it meant. . . . The pain in my eyes was growing worse. My sight was blurring. . . . I was terrified I was going blind."

A mourner hustled Sheftel into his car and rushed him to the Bikur Cholim Hospital emergency room ten minutes away. Doctors washed and flushed his eyes, then gave him the news. It was a hydrochloric acid solution. His right eye was slightly injured and would probably fully recover. His left eye probably would not.

The Israeli police arrested Yehezkeli. Although he pleaded guilty to the assault on Sheftel, he denied having anything to do with the death of Dov Eitan. "All the Jews are happy for what I did," he bragged. "Let Sheftel be wiped off the face of this earth. I wish that both his eyes would have fallen out. . . . He poured salt on the wounds of all survivors."

The maximum sentence for aggravated assault under Israeli law is twenty years. The court sentenced Yehezkeli to three and ordered him to pay Sheftel eleven thousand dollars for the physical injuries he sustained.

As Sheftel was recovering from his eye injury, the pressure from his family, especially his mother, to quit the Demjanjuk case became intense. For two years, he had received death threats almost daily. He soon became inured to them, treating them as emotional bluster and brushing them away like houseflies. Now, because of the publicity and newspaper photos, everyone in Israel who could read knew who he was. And the big white bandage over his left eye made him hard to miss as he walked down the street. Perhaps it was his imagination, but Sheftel swore he could feel hatred burning through his suit.

Sheftel knew he had gotten off easy. Maybe blinded in one eye. Maybe scars like the Phantom of the Opera. But what about next time? And what about John Demjanjuk? How could he "send a man to the gallows just to satisfy Holocaust survivors"?

After giving serious thought to quitting the case, Sheftel refused to give in to fear and pressure. He was a born iconoclast, driven by a desire "to disturb, disrupt, spoil, and explode into fragments, all provocation by the establishment, and the Demjanjuk case was provocation from the beginning." And now, blind in one eye, he had a "physical bond uniting" him to John Demjanjuk.

Because of the death of Eitan and the serious injury to Sheftel, the

Supreme Court delayed the Demjanjuk appeal for eighteen months. Meanwhile, Sheftel flew to Boston to undergo new, radical eye surgery. The Demjanjuk defense fund offered to pay his medical bills and expenses. The operation was a success. In time, doctors told him, his vision would be fully restored. His face would not be disfigured. The only scars would be internal.

• • •

While Sheftel was crafting his Supreme Court appeal argument, the Demjanjuk defense got its first big break. A former Polish prostitute who had lived in a village near Treblinka during World War II told all to *60 Minutes*.

CHAPTER FIFTY

Tick Tock

Her name was Maria (Marianna) Dudek and she lived in Volka Okgrolnik, a tiny Polish village that hadn't changed much since 1942. The wood houses were mostly in need of paint and repair. The main street was not paved. There was no running water. Horses pulled hay wagons. Cows grazed in backyards. Chickens scratched in the dirt out front. The only concession to the twentieth century was electricity.

Beginning in mid-1942 and ending in August 1943, when Treblinka was liquidated, Iwan Grozny was a frequent guest at Dudek's house. Demjanjuk supporter Jerome Brentar had visited her five years earlier on his trip to Poland with Frank Walus to prove that John Demjanjuk was not Iwan Grozny. Brentar had testified at Demjanjuk's deportation hearing that Dudek told him she knew a Ukrainian guard called Iwan. When Brentar showed her a photo of Demjanjuk, she said the man in the picture was not the Iwan she knew. Brentar then asked her if she had ever heard of a Treblinka guard called Iwan Grozny. Dudek slammed the door in his face.

Maria Dudek did not slam the door on *60 Minutes* interviewer Ed Bradley. Although she spoke freely about her relationship with the Iwan she knew in 1942–43, Dudek declined to appear on camera because she did not want to be seen or remembered as a former prostitute who serviced death camp guards. The *60 Minutes* cameraman managed to get a shot of her wearing a white babushka and peering out her front window.

Dudek told *60 Minutes* that whenever Iwan came to visit her, he brought a bottle of vodka he purchased at the village shop run by her husband. She said she was absolutely certain that Iwan's last name was Marchenko, not Demjanjuk, whom she did not know and whose face she did not recognize.

Both Sheftel and Nishnic were excited by the CBS interview with Dudek, hoping that she would be the big break they needed to save John Demjanjuk from the gallows. In March 1990, two weeks after *60 Minutes* aired the Dudek story, the two men paid Maria Dudek a surprise visit. There were two items on their wish list: Find Dudek credible, and convince her either to give videotaped testimony or sign a sworn statement. As insurance, they recruited Dudek's local priest to help.

Dudek was a small woman, just over five feet tall with white hair, friendly and polite, honored to have the priest in her home, but not pleased to see the American and the Israeli. She served tea under a single, bare lightbulb that dangled from the ceiling. There were no outlets or electric appliances.

After Dudek repeated what she had told *60 Minutes*, Sheftel showed her a photo spread that contained a picture of Iwan Demjanjuk. Once again, she failed to identify him. Sheftel then selected the Demjanjuk photo from the spread and gave it to her saying that it was a picture of Iwan Demjanjuk who had just been convicted in Israel of being Iwan Grozny. He would be hung soon if Sheftel could not prove he was the wrong man.

Once again, Dudek said she did not recognize the name Demjanjuk or the man in the picture. But as cooperative and as decisive as she was, Dudek refused to give videotaped testimony or sign a statement. Her priest pleaded with her. It was her duty as a Christian to save the life of an innocent man, he argued. Dudek still refused. If the bishop ordered her to testify, would she do it? the priest asked. Only if Lech Walesa or the pope ordered her to, Dudek said. "I made a big mistake when I agreed to talk to the American television. There are lots of other people who knew Iwan Marchenko. Why are you hounding me?"

Sheftel and Nishnic left Volka Okgrolnik both pleased and disappointed. Maria Dudek had convinced Sheftel, once and for all, that Iwan Demjanjuk was not Iwan Grozny. But without sworn testimony, her positive identification of Iwan Marchenko was at best legally interesting and supportive.

Before returning to Jerusalem, Sheftel and Nishnic stopped in Warsaw to visit the Commission for the Investigation of Nazi Crimes Committed on Polish Territory—the Glovna Komisia, for short. Two commissioners welcomed them. Sheftel asked for any archival documents they had containing the name Iwan Marchenko. There were two. In them, a former Treblinka guard identified Iwan Marchenko as a fellow guard, but he did not name Marchenko as the operator of the gas chambers or as Iwan Grozny. Like Dudek's interview, the two documents were merely supportive evidence.

What the defense needed was a smoking gun.

Just before they left the Komisia office and to their complete surprise, one of the commissioners told Nishnic and Sheftel that if they wanted to know who Iwan Grozny was, they would have to visit the Ukrainian district court in Simferopol, Crimea, where Feodor Fedorenko had been tried four years earlier, in 1986.

"There in the [Fedorenko] case file," he said, "you will discover all the material you need about the real identity of the two gas chamber operators at Treblinka."

As soon as he got back to Jerusalem, Sheftel submitted a motion to the Supreme Court to delay the upcoming appeal arguments once again, so that he could visit the court in Crimea and hunt for an alleged Fedorenko case file. During the hearing on the postponement request, the High Court trumped Sheftel. It had a transcript of the *60 Minutes* show and a copy of a 1986 recorded statement made by Maria Dudek's late husband, Kazhimezh. In the statement, Mr. Dudek not only confirmed what his wife had told *60 Minutes*, he went beyond it. He said that Iwan Marchenko, who frequently came to his shop to buy vodka, had confessed "without shame" that he and Nikolai Shelaiev operated the gas chambers at Treblinka.

The court was smitten. The tide was changing.

Both documents were a blow to the prosecution, whose entire trial case had been built around a single charge—Iwan Demjanjuk was Ivan the Terrible. To refute the new evidence, Michael Shaked offered the court a copy of Demjanjuk's 1948 application to the International Refugee Organization (IRO) for refugee status. On the form, Demjanjuk had listed his mother's maiden name as Marchenko. Based on that document, Shaked argued that Demjanjuk and Marchenko were the same person.

OSI had toyed with the same theory in an attempt to reconcile guard service at Treblinka with guard service at Sobibor. Perhaps OSI had shared its reasoning with Shaked.

Like good lawyers, Shaked and Sheftel struck a deal after the postponement hearing. If Sheftel dropped his request for a delay of the appeal argument, Shaked would agree to enter into evidence both the *60 Minutes* transcript and the statement of Kazhimezh Dudek.

The marathon to save John Demjanjuk from the gallows was on. The clock was ticking.

At this point in the pre-appeal stage of the Demjanjuk drama, two things were clear. Although the Supreme Court had postponed the appeal hearing for eighteen months after the death of Dov Eitan and the acid attack on Sheftel, it was not about to postpone it again. And once the defense and prosecution finished their appeal arguments before the bench, the High Court would not indefinitely delay its decision just to give Sheftel time to hunt for the ghost of Iwan Marchenko.

Sheftel's mission was clear: Go to Ukraine. Get a Soviet document proving that Demjanjuk's mother's maiden name was not Marchenko. And find the Fedorenko case file. Unfortunately, there was a problem with the Don Quixote mission.

Yoram Sheftel was Jewish.

Because it was difficult for a Jew to get a visa to the Soviet Union in 1990 despite the glasnost thaw, the Demjanjuk family called on Ohio congressman James Traficant for help. A Demjanjuk supporter who had been useful in the past, Traficant agreed to pester the Soviet embassy in Washington to grant visas to Sheftel, Johnnie Demjanjuk, and an American Ukrainian lawyer fluent in Ukrainian who had agreed to travel with them. All three applied separately. All three lied. They said they were going to the Soviet Union to visit relatives.

While he was waiting for the Soviets to grant or deny him a visa, Sheftel argued the Demjanjuk appeal before the Israeli Supreme Court.

• • •

It was May 1990, two years after the Levin court had sentenced John Demjanjuk to the gallows. Sheftel stood alone, wearing dark glasses, before the panel of five Supreme Court justices. It was payback time. Yoram Sheftel was putting Judge Levin on trial and, by extension, the Israeli justice system. And for once, Levin could not object, snarl, insult, bully, or overrule.

Even though his left eye had not completely healed, Sheftel didn't have to wear dark glasses indoors. He used them merely for dramatic effect, to remind the High Court and the media of how the Demjanjuk show trial had turned into a deadly circus with justice playing the role of ringmaster.

The courtroom chosen for the appeal hearing was the antithesis of the Hall of the People. It was "a chamber of genteel seediness," not a renovated movie theater. It held only eighty spectators, not three hundred. Television cameras were forbidden. Photographers were excluded during the hearing.

John Demjanjuk sat in a specially constructed wooden cell flanked by policemen. Two interpreters perched behind him. Shaked and four government attorneys sat at the prosecution table for a replay of the David and Goliath battles in Fort Lauderdale, Chicago, and Cleveland. Money versus small pocketbooks. Legal wolves stalking a lone man.

Although the tiny courtroom was filled for the opening session, it would remain nearly empty for the rest of the appeal hearing. It was as if the once-riveting trial of Ivan the Terrible had never happened. As if John Demjanjuk no longer existed. As if Israel was poised to pause from its daily business only on the day when the gallows trapdoor swung open.

The stakes were high for Satan's attorney, as Sheftel's enemies called him. If he lost the appeal and Demjanjuk were hanged, what was left of his reputation would be shattered, his legal career would be finished, and his life would be in even greater jeopardy.

The five justices entered the courtroom at precisely 9 A.M. and took their seats on hard wooden chairs behind an unimpressive dark wood bench. "Are you John Demjanjuk?" Chief Justice Meir Shamgar asked?

"Yes," Demjanjuk said in a loud, clear voice.

"Mr. Sheftel, you may begin."

Sheftel's appeal would take ten days. Five of his arguments were familiar ones from the trial: the Trawniki card (forged); Danilchenko's sworn statement that Demjanjuk was at Sobibor (mistaken identity); the Trawniki photo (doctored); and Demjanjuk's alibi (sound).

Sheftel's plan was to restate, redocument, and refocus the same arguments the defense had mounted in the Levin court, but without interruptions from the bench and objections from the prosecution. His goal was to do what the defense had failed to do earlier—establish reasonable doubt.

Two other arguments were fresh and formed the heart of the appeal case: Israel's lack of jurisdiction to try Demjanjuk for genocide, and Judge Levin's deep-seated bias against the defense.

Sheftel argued that Israel legally could not try Demjanjuk for genocide under the terms of its extradition request and treaty with the United States. The only jurisdiction Israel had was to try Demjanjuk for the murder of civilians. The hairsplitting was critical. Genocide carried the possibility of a death penalty under Israeli law, while the maximum sentence for "regular" murder was life in prison.

Unlike the textbook jurisdiction issue, the bias charge was subjective and transparently personal. Sheftel's beef with Judge Dov Levin went back fourteen years, to 1976, the first time the young lawyer appeared in Levin's district court, and it continued unabated until the last Demjanjuk defense argument.

The friction between the two men had erupted during a criminal conspiracy trial in 1979. Sheftel's clients were on trial for allegedly bombing a building, though fortunately no one was injured in the blast. In the middle of the trial, Judge Levin decided to take a fourteen-week vacation. That meant that Sheftel's clients, charged but still innocent, would have to sit in jail for more than three months, waiting for Levin to reconvene the court. Sheftel objected to the extended leave, arguing that if Levin insisted on absenting himself for fourteen weeks, his clients should be freed. Levin disagreed.

While Levin was traveling abroad, Sheftel filed an appeal to the Supreme Court and won half a victory. The High Court chided Levin, its favored candidate for an upcoming seat on the bench, for abandoning a trial in progress. Given the violent nature of the alleged crime, however, the court declined to order the release of the accused.

Sheftel sensed that his career as a lawyer in Israel was dead. Dov Levin would never forgive him for the public embarrassment and for jeopardizing his appointment to the Supreme Court. The Demjanjuk case was proof that Levin was out to get even. Sheftel felt that, throughout the trial, Levin had "never stopped snarling . . . harassing . . . insulting . . . and humiliating him." And now as he stood before the bench, armed with trial transcripts, Sheftel was ready to prove it. His attack took seven hours. None of the justices interrupted him as he quoted and argued from the more than eight thousand pages of the trial record. Among the perceived insults and humiliations were bench statements made by Levin, such as "The public is also beginning to be bored by the argument . . . Completely unethical defense attorneys . . . This is an unfit and unseemly defense team . . . The consequence of defense scheming . . . The defense is throwing sand in our eyes . . . Whining defense attorneys . . . You're giving us a headache."

Sheftel went on to argue that Levin had misused private meetings in chambers without a court recorder present to make rulings, in effect turning a public trial into a private one with no written record to prove his abuse of judicial authority.

Sheftel accused Levin of applying a double standard. For example, he had allowed the prosecution to probe the political leanings of witnesses while blocking the defense from doing the same. And he had demanded a schedule of witnesses and a rigid timetable from the defense, but not from the prosecution.

Sheftel further argued that Levin was competing with the Klaus Barbie trial in progress in Lyon, France, to see which court would reach a verdict first, thus limiting and crippling the defense. The refusal to postpone the trial after Demjanjuk fired his lead counsel, Mark O'Connor, was one example. The introduction of the Danilchenko Protocol during closing arguments was another. Both the prosecution and the defense requested time to go to the Soviet Union to study and verify the statement of Danilchenko, who had died the year before the trial opened, that Demjanjuk was a guard at Sobibor. Judge Levin refused to delay the court's verdict. Even so, Klaus Barbie won the race.

To some extent, one could attribute Sheftel's attack on the credibility of Judge Levin and his court to a case of sour grapes. Losing attorneys love to blame judges for their defeats. But Sheftel presented one highly documented bias argument that did not smack of distortion or self-serving interpretation.

Before the trial opened in Jerusalem, the Levin court hired a clipping service to prepare a daily album of what the media had reported about the trial. The court asked the service to present three copies to the court clerk each morning. Then the court instructed the clerk to deliver the albums to the judges before the court convened. Sheftel learned about the clippings by accident, and he personally saw the judges reading them in their chambers before the morning sessions.

Like a jury, sitting judges were required by law to isolate themselves from media reports that might influence or sway them. Sheftel felt that the court's breach of that ruling invalidated the entire Demjanjuk trial. He confronted Judge Levin, who admitted that he and the other judges had received the daily clippings and read them.

Sheftel felt that if the public learned about the clipping service, it would be outraged and demand a mistrial. With that in mind, he asked the court's permission to call the manager of the service to the stand.

Judge Levin refused. He had already admitted to the facts, he pointed out. Therefore, court testimony about them and the public's so-called need to know were irrelevant. Sheftel was free, of course, to argue his point during an appeal, Levin said, but the clipping service issue would not be raised in his courtroom.

Twenty-four of the newspaper articles in the clipping albums, written by a Holocaust survivor for a popular Israeli daily newspaper, were clearly inflammatory and an apparent criminal infraction of Israel's *sub judice* (under a judge) rule, which forbade the publication of anything liable to affect the outcome of a trial. A court would eventually find the author of the articles, the newspaper, and its editor guilty of a violation of the *sub judice* law.

"At its own instigation," Sheftel told the High Court justices, "the [Levin] court was exposed to wild accusations and aspersions against the defense, the defense counsel, and the Ukrainian people."

How could the Levin court reach an unbiased judgment, Sheftel argued, when it deliberately exposed itself to inflammatory writings? As a consequence, the lower court trial was "a travesty."

Sheftel concluded his ten-day appeal with a condemnation of the Demjanjuk trial: "A trial in which all these things—or even ten percent of them—happened, was not due process but a perversion of justice."

The end of the appeal hearing left the defense with two troubling questions. How long would it take the Supreme Court to rule on the appeal? And would Sheftel have enough time to prove that John Demjanjuk was not Ivan the Terrible before it did?

CHAPTER FIFTY-ONE

How Sweet It Is

In early September 1990, almost two years after the Jerusalem trial ended and some four months after Sheftel's argument before the Supreme Court, Johnnie Demjanjuk and his American lawyer left for Ukraine. Sheftel followed three days later. They all met in Simferopol, Crimea. Johnnie had no trouble getting a copy of the marriage certificate of his grandparents. On it, his grandmother's maiden name was listed as Juliana Tabachuk, not Marchenko as Shaked had argued. John Demjanjuk had written Marchenko, a common Ukrainian name, on his IPO application because he couldn't remember the name Tabachuk. So much for the prosecution theory that John Demjanjuk was *both* Iwan Demjanjuk and Iwan Marchenko because he gave Marchenko as his mother's maiden name!

While in Simferopol, where the Feodor Fedorenko case file was supposedly kept, the Demjanjuk team went to see Oleg Tatunik, the judge who had tried Fedorenko four years earlier. In his mid-forties and young by Western standards for a seat on the bench in a criminal court, Judge Tatunik was surprisingly open and friendly for a Soviet official. His meeting with the three men was private.

Judge Tatunik readily confirmed what the Polish commissioner had told Sheftel. In preparation for the Fedorenko trial, he explained, the court had collected all the statements that former Treblinka guards had given to the KGB prior to their war crimes trials. "In many of the statements attached to the file," the judge said, "there is mention of the two criminals who operated the gas chambers. If I am not mistaken, the statements gave their names as Iwan Marchenko and Nikolai Shelaiev."

The good news, however, came with bad. Although the Fedorenko file was archived in the KGB headquarters down the street, it could not be released without permission from the KGB main office in Kiev, the Ukrainian capital. That could take weeks, if not months, and there was nothing Judge Tatunik could do to help them.

The defense team was elated. So close! And disappointed. So far! The best it could do under the circumstances was to find a well-placed Ukrainian to pry the file loose from the tight fist of the KGB. They recruited Aleksandr Yemets, chairman of the Human Rights Commission of the Ukrainian Supreme Soviet and a leader in the independent Ukraine movement. Then the team returned home to beg and bargain. How much muscle did Yemets have? If he got the file, would it be in time to save the neck of John Demjanjuk?

• • •

Back in Jerusalem, Sheftel managed to wring two concessions from the Supreme Court. First, it agreed not to announce its final ruling before January 1, 1991. Then it scheduled an eleventh-hour hearing on the new Marchenko developments for December 31, the day before its announcement deadline. That gave Sheftel six short weeks to make his final pitch to the court, with or without the Fedorenko file.

While he waited for word from Yemets, Sheftel knew that John Demjanjuk's life would only be spared in one of two ways. Either Sheftel had to prove that Marchenko was Ivan Grozny, or Demjanjuk would have to admit to the charge that he had served as a guard at the Sobibor death camp. Guard service under the Israeli 1950 Nazi and Nazi Collaborator Prosecution Act was not a capital crime allowing for a death sentence. If Demjanjuk would admit to Sobibor, Shaked had agreed to concede that Demjanjuk was not Ivan the Terrible. But John Demjanjuk refused to admit to a crime that he swore he never committed, even if it would save his life. That made the Fedorenko file his only lifesaver.

The willingness of the government to drop the Ivan the Terrible charge if Demjanjuk admitted to Sobibor was, in Sheftel's mind, a face-saving and hypocritical stance. Israel had not requested the extradition of Ukrainian policeman and Nazi collaborator Bohdan Koziy, whose U.S. citizenship had been revoked for lying on his visa application and who was now living freely in Costa Rica. Nor had it sought to extradite Feodor Fedorenko, who had admitted being a guard at Treblinka. So why would it want to try John Demjanjuk for serving at Sobibor based on a single piece of so-called evidence—the Trawniki card? Demjanjuk was only of interest to Israel as Ivan the Terrible.

On December 11, three weeks before the Supreme Court was due to announce its appeal ruling, Yemets faxed a report from Kiev. The KGB office there had allowed him to review the Fedorenko case file. He found no mention of Iwan Demjanjuk in the documents. Iwan Marchenko was everywhere. By way of example, Yemets quoted the statement of former Treblinka guard Piotr given on March 6, 1951, before his execution for war crimes:

"He [Iwan Marchenko] was Ukrainian. I don't know where he was born. He served in the Red Army and was taken prisoner by the Germans and then went to the Trawniki training camp. From there he was sent to Treblinka where he served as operator of the diesel engine that sent the gas into the gas chambers, and also took part in tormenting and shooting Jews. He was tall, solidly built, broad-shouldered, with a dark complexion, round face, and long nose."

Yemets promised to return to the KGB office as soon as he could to copy the entire file and mail it to the defense. Sheftel was not about to take any chances that the package might "disappear." Demjanjuk haters were everywhere. If they were willing to blind Sheftel with acid, they certainly wouldn't hesitate to steal a file.

For protection, Sheftel leaked the gist of the Fedorenko file to the media. Although the planted news item went mostly unnoticed, there was now a record of the file's existence. Then, Sheftel instructed Yemets to mail the documents to a safe house in Holland where Sheftel would be waiting.

The Fedorenko file never arrived.

Before Yemets could copy the documents, the KGB sent the file to Moscow, where an official Israeli delegation was reviewing it. The Israeli delegation was, of course, Shaked and his staff. That meant that the prosecution would get the file and have total control over it, not Sheftel, who had discovered it and disclosed its existence, contents, and whereabouts to the Supreme Court and, thus, to the prosecution.

The question now was: How long would the prosecution sit on the Fedorenko documents before releasing them to the defense? And would they be released in time to save John Demjanjuk?

In spite of the uncertainty, two things were clear. The prosecution would delay releasing the file as along as it could while it scrambled to build a case against Iwan Demjanjuk as a guard at Sobibor. And it was going to be a nasty race to the wire.

• • •

The Supreme Court convened on December 31, 1990, to hear an update on the unfolding Ivan the Terrible drama. The High Court could announce its appeal decision as early as the following day. If it did, John Demjanjuk would most likely be executed. Deep down, even Sheftel did not believe the court would grant the appeal and free Demjanjuk based on the appeal arguments alone. Only the Marchenko evidence could save him.

Before the eleventh-hour hearing, Sheftel laid a legal trap that fooled no one. He requested that the High Court release John Demjanjuk immediately based on new Marchenko information. Sheftel knew, of course, that the High Court was not about to free Demjanjuk based on alleged documents it had not reviewed. But the petition gave Sheftel a legal opening to explore at the hearing the contents of the file and to quote from the statements of former Treblinka guards like Piotr in the hope that the court would delay its appeal decision.

Besides statements that the operator of the Treblinka gas chamber was Iwan Marchenko, the file contained another important piece of evidence—a photo of Iwan Marchenko. During the discussion of the file contents at the hearing, Shaked had to admit that the photo, identified by former Treblinka guards as that of Marchenko, did not resemble Demjanjuk in any major way. Marchenko was eleven years older, much taller, with a scar on his face, and features that did not match Demjanjuk's.

It was clear from the questions the judges asked that they were more than curious about the Fedorenko file. Doubt was finally beginning to gnaw at them, and they gave Sheftel a decisive victory. They would not rule on the appeal until after they had received and reviewed the entire Fedorenko file.

By June 1991, however, six months after the prosecution had reviewed the Fedorenko file in Moscow and three months after it had received the file from the Soviet Union, the prosecution was still refusing to release the documents to Sheftel and the Supreme Court.

It was time to play a trump card.

Sheftel told a sympathetic reporter that Demjanjuk was planning to stage a hunger strike if the prosecution did not release the Fedorenko file to the defense within three weeks. The reporter called Shaked for a comment. A few days later, Sheftel got a letter from the prosecution office. "The translation and typing have been completed," Shaked wrote, "and I am making available to you copies of the Russian and Hebrew version of the statements from the Fedorenko file."

As he tore open the brown envelope addressed to him, Sheftel knew that if the file contained the documents he believed it should, he had won his case. "I was trembling with emotion," he later wrote. "In my wildest dreams, I had never imagined that there would be so much material and that it would offer such firm proof. . . . In all my years of legal practice, I had never been so happy and so satisfied as in those precious moments."

The most important statement in the file was that of Nikolai Shelaiev, who operated the Treblinka gas chamber with Iwan Marchenko and who was executed in 1952. Shelaiev said: "Iwan Marchenko—I do not know his father's [first] name—was born in 1911 in Dnepropetrovsk, not a party member, married. Among his children, there was one son who was, at that time, 1943, nine years old. He was conscripted into the Red Army at the beginning of the war for the motherland, and served in the army as a private.

"Description: tall, black hair, brown eyes, thin face, large, narrow nose; an inconspicuous diagonal scar on his cheek; solidly built, square shoulders, erect gait. I first met him in September 1942, and worked with him as operator of the motor that emitted exhaust gas and transferred it to the gas chambers where the people were killed."

The Supreme Court accepted all the statements from the Fedorenko file as appeal evidence but it declined to immediately set Demjanjuk free as Sheftel had requested. The court said it needed time to study the contents of the file which contained eighty statements made by thirty-seven former Treblinka guards, all of whom were dead. Each of the statements named Iwan Marchenko as the operator of the gas chamber.

The hunt for the real Ivan the Terrible was over. It was now just a matter of waiting on the court.

• • •

The Supreme Court convened in late July 1993 to render its life-or-death decision. It had been more than seven years since John Demjanjuk stepped off a 747 at Ben Gurion Airport and was denied permission to kiss the ground of the Holy Land. And it had been sixteen years since the U.S. Department of Justice filed charges of immigration fraud against him.

Rumors that Demjanjuk would be acquitted had been flying for weeks and security was especially tight inside the courtroom, in the adjacent room with closed-circuit television, and on the street outside. Both rooms were packed with the media, survivors, and their families. Demjanjuk sat impassively in the wooden cell with his guards and interpreters. His son and son-in-law sat in the second row. His wife, Vera, was back home in Ohio.

The High Court had five choices:

- Uphold the conviction and the death sentence of the Levin court.
- Uphold the conviction but commute the death sentence to life in prison.
- Reverse the decision of the Levin court because Demjanjuk had not received a fair trial.
- Acquit Demjanjuk because of a reasonable doubt that he was Ivan the Terrible.
- Find Demjanjuk not guilty of serving at Treblinka, but guilty of serving at Sobibor.

The appeal ruling was over four hundred pages. Chief Justice Shamgar read a summary that took two hours. The five justices ganged up on Sheftel.

The Supreme Court upheld every major lower court ruling from the authenticity of the Trawniki card to the false alibi. It further found that the State of Israel had the jurisdiction to try Demjanjuk for genocide because genocide was a legitimate expansion of the crime of murder. The court also found as totally reliable: the photo identifications by Treblinka survivors; the identification procedures of Miriam Radiwker; and the survivors' court testimony. And like the lower court, it dismissed as baseless assumptions Professor Wagenaar's testimony that Miriam Radiwker's photo spread and photo identification interviews were invalid. Finally, and the deepest cut of all, the High Court failed to find Judge Levin and his court guilty of bias. Based on these findings, Demjanjuk's neck was already in the noose.

With the courthouse full of emotional survivors and their families and the nation of Israel curiously or anxiously waiting, the Supreme

Court then committed an act of courage that echoed around the world.

"The main issue of the indictment sheet filed against the appellant was his identification as Ivan the Terrible," Judge Shamgar reasoned. "A substantial number of survivors of the Treblinka inferno identified the appellant as Ivan the Terrible....He was convicted in the district court....

"Before us, after the hearing of the appeal ended, there were submitted statements of various [former Treblinka guards], which spoke of someone else as Ivan the Terrible. We do not know how these statements came into the world and who gave birth to them. . . . When they came before us, doubt began to gnaw away at our judicial conscience. Perhaps the appellant was not Ivan the Terrible of Treblinka. . . . By virtue of this gnawing, we restrained ourselves from convicting the appellant of the horrors of Treblinka. . . .

"Iwan Demjanjuk has been acquitted by us, because of doubt, of the terrible charges attributed to Ivan the Terrible. . . . Our verdict is unanimous."

The courthouse erupted into screams and tears and death threats. Bystanders stoned the car carrying Sheftel, Nishnic, and Johnnie Demjanjuk away from the courthouse. "Nazi, Nazi, Nazi!" they shouted.

Like the Polish survivors who had testified against Frank Walus, the Treblinka survivors remained totally convinced that Iwan Demjanjuk was, and always would be, the real Ivan the Terrible. "Had I known that such a thing would happen," Yosef Cherney said, voicing the feelings of all the Treblinka survivors, "I wouldn't have taken it upon myself and stood up in court. . . . It's very painful. You have no idea how painful. . . . I am in shock, great shock. The justices made a mistake. They have done an injustice to millions because he is the criminal [Iwan Grozny], the Nazi criminal. Not in my worst dreams did I think something like this could happen in a Jewish state. . . . The Nazis can now celebrate."

Then Cherney got carried away and began to scream: "I . . . I . . . Cherney Yosef. Am I not authentic? Am I not authentic? Am I not authentic? I *am authentic*! . . . Don't let us be forgotten."

"I lost my whole family, two hundred people. . . . All killed in Treblinka!" shouted another angry Holocaust survivor outside the courtroom. He waved an album of yellowing photos at passersby. "Look at them!" he cried.

"Why should a survivor come forward after this?" said stunned Auschwitz survivor Noah Klieger, a member of Rabbi Kahane's right-wing Kach Party. "Let's say you catch another Demjanjuk. Nobody's going to put him on trial. This was the *last* fight. We are all dying—those of us who saw what happened."

The reaction of other Israelis ran the gamut from stunned to proud. Most were simply relieved that *l'affaire Demjanjuk* was over except for the tears and rage. "It's a great day for the system," said Israeli journalist and author Tom Segev. "Yet at the same time, a man who had been declared a war criminal goes free, and that makes everyone uneasy. . . . The great drama developed into an embarrassing farce."

"I am not looking for justice," shouted angry Kach Party spokesman Noam Federman. "I am looking for revenge!"

"In retrospect," said a relieved member of the Israeli parliament, "perhaps it would have been better had this event not occurred at all."

The *Jerusalem Post* editorialized: "That Demjanjuk is now a free man is nothing less than devastating to those who believe no Nazi war criminal should be allowed to get away with genocidal crimes. But it is for the sake of democratic justice, not revenge, that the war against such criminals has been waged."

Other editorials from around the world were genuinely complimentary. The *New York Times* and the *Cleveland Plain Dealer* echoed the sentiments of most of the international press, including the Jewish press.

"The Israeli Supreme Court," the *Times* said, "showed extraordinary wisdom and courage in acquitting John Demjanjuk of charges that he was Ivan the Terrible. The decision, an emotionally charged issue for Holocaust survivors, was a stirring affirmation of the integrity and fairness of Israel's judicial system."

And the *Plain Dealer* wrote: "The decision was impressive in its reasoning and candor, a tribute to the integrity of the Israeli justice system."

While Demjanjuk supporters cried and prayed in Cleveland in the mistaken belief that the ordeal was over for their persecuted son, Jews across the country wailed and raged with blind hatred. "His nationality is enough to make him guilty," said one Detroit Jew. "Maybe he wasn't Ivan, but he was Ukrainian, and he had a lot of Jewish blood on his hands," said another. "If Demjanjuk would stand in front of me now," said a Cleveland Jew, "I am not responsible for what I would do."

Amid the anger and hatred, there were calming voices of cold reason. "The rule of law has to govern," said Zev Harel, president of Kol Israel, a Cleveland organization of approximately 350 Holocaust survivors. Kol Israel was not a lone voice crying in the wilderness of pain. Jewish organizations across the country supported the decision of the Israeli Supreme Court, but with a profound sadness.

There was more pain to come.

• • •

The double irony of the Demjanjuk acquittal was not lost on trial observers and pundits. If Yisrael Yehezkeli had not tossed acid in Sheftel's eyes, the Demjanjuk appeal would not have been delayed for almost two years, the new Marchenko evidence would not have been discovered, and John Demjanjuk would have been hanged. And after the Demjanjuk family and its attorneys had argued for sixteen years that Soviet-supplied documents should not be admitted in court as evidence because they were tainted and not to be trusted, it was Soviet-supplied evidence that saved Demjanjuk's life.

Although the acquittal in Jerusalem was a moment of relief and joy for John Demjanjuk, his family, and his supporters, it was only half a victory. The High Court noted that the Israeli bill of indictment also charged Iwan Demjanjuk with being a guard at Sobibor, and that there was credible evidence that indeed he had served at that death camp. But the court declined to find him guilty of the charge because the government had chosen to build its entire case around Ivan the Terrible. As a result, John Demjanjuk had been denied a reasonable opportunity to defend himself against the Sobibor charge.

"We saw no room to hold him for another crime," Chief Judge Shamgar concluded. "The matter is done, but not completed."

The Supreme Court seemed to be saying, Enough is enough. We legally acquitted John Demjanjuk, but we morally convicted him.

For Holocaust survivors and their families, the acquittal was a betrayal of their suffering and losses, and the deaths of six million Jews. To protect Demjanjuk from rampant assassination threats, the Israeli Department of Justice immediately ordered him to be deported to any country that would take him. Then it did the safest thing it could think of while it waited for a taker.

It arrested John Demjanjuk and sent him back to his cell in Ayalon Prison.

The pot of bitterness boiled for days. U.S. attorney general Janet Reno made it clear that the United States would not let Demjanjuk back into the country. She stood firmly by OSI, which argued that Israel had acquitted Demjanjuk "on a technicality." The Trawniki card proved that Demjanjuk had been trained at Trawniki and had served as a guard at Sobibor. Either fact made him inadmissible to the United States.

There was one show of generosity. The day after the acquittal, the newly minted Republic of Ukraine extended a warm invitation to John Demjanjuk to come home and stay as long as he liked, no questions asked. Demjanjuk accepted. His life was in constant danger in Israel and he had no idea how many more days or weeks or months he would have to sit in prison, a freed but fettered man.

Three days after he was acquitted, John Demjanjuk was packed, with visa and ticket in hand. He was about to leave Ayalon Prison under heavy guard for Ben Gurion Airport and an afternoon flight on Air Ukraine bound for Kiev when the Israeli Supreme Court ordered his departure to be delayed for ten days. It needed time, the court said, to consider a citizen petition to try Demjanjuk as a guard at Sobibor. The petition was submitted by Kach Party member Noah Federman and Yisrael Yehezkeli, who had been released from prison after serving two years of a three-year sentence for the acid attack on Sheftel.

Demjanjuk asked for a tranquilizer and unpacked his bags.

Two weeks after the acquittal, Israel's attorney general announced that he would not try John Demjanjuk for allegedly serving as a Trawniki-trained guard at Sobibor, Flossenbürg, and Regensburg. He cited three reasons for his decision. If Israel tried Demjanjuk, it could be a violation of double jeopardy protection guaranteed by Israeli law. Furthermore, there wasn't enough evidence to convict Demjanjuk at the present time, and it was doubtful that the prosecution would ever be able to find enough for conviction. Finally, after seven years of legal proceedings, it would be unreasonable to drag the case out any further.

Three weeks after the acquittal, the Supreme Court convened a public hearing to announce its decision on the petition to retry John Demjanjuk. Given the emotion and death threats, security was extremely tight. Before the court opened for business, Israeli police brought a bomb-sniffing dog into the courthouse to hunt for explosives. During the hearing, armed policemen ringed the courtroom.

Three of the court's five justices ruled on the appeal. They independently and unanimously upheld the decision of the attorney general. Stressing that "reasonable is not the same as correct," the judges concurred that it would be unreasonable to retry Demjanjuk, and that the State of Israel would, therefore, not reopen the case.

"We have no choice but to let him go," Judge Gabriel Bach said.

Reaction to the final decision of the Supreme Court of Israel was immediate, emotional, relieved, reasoned, and hateful. "You bring shame to the Jewish people!" a woman shouted from the rear of the courtroom. "Shame on you!"

"I had two acids. Thirty-two percent and one hundred percent," Yehezkeli said. "I'm sorry I didn't use the one hundred percent." He then tore his shirt as a sign of mourning and, with outstretched arms, shouted at the journalists: "I want to die. Kill me!" Then he collapsed.

"We will make justice," vowed Kach leader Baruch Marzel. "Demjanjuk will one day be killed by good Jews and not by corrupt Jews like we have in the High Court. . . . If not in Israel, then somewhere else."

"As far as I am concerned, the question is not whether John Demjanjuk is an innocent person," said Efraim Zuroff, director of the Simon Wiesenthal Center in Israel. "But is John Demjanjuk Ivan the Terrible, or another terrible Ivan?"

"I am very sad," said a Sobibor survivor. "How can he leave alive from the Jewish state that grew from the mourning of the children of the Shoah [Holocaust]?"

"[Israelis] are fed up with the case," said Auschwitz survivor Noah Klieger. "A Jewish State can be fed up with a Nazi murderer? How is such a thing possible?"

"Preposterous," said Rabbi Marvin Hier, founder of the Simon Wiesenthal Center in Los Angeles. "We may be losing sight of who the real victims are in this case. They are not John Demjanjuks."

Meanwhile, in Cleveland, the U.S. Sixth Circuit Court of Appeals, which had upheld the lower court's decision both to strip Demjanjuk of his U.S. citizenship and to extradite him to Israel, ruled that Demjanjuk could return to the United States. The court argued that he had been tried in the United States and extradited to Israel as Ivan the Terrible, not as a guard at Sobibor. Furthermore, the Justice Department's prosecution of Demjanjuk had been careless and sloppy. And finally, given that Demjanjuk's life was in danger, the humanitarian thing to do was to allow him to come back to the United States, where he would be "safe."

John Demjanjuk was finally free to come home.

Wearing bulletproof vests under their sweaters and jackets, Johnnie Demjanjuk, his brother-in-law Ed Nishnic, Ohio congressman James Traficant, and two burly off-duty police officers flew to Israel to escort John Demjanjuk back to Cleveland. The vests were not a grandstand play for media attention. Jewish extremists had repeatedly threatened to assassinate "Ivan the Terrible," and the Demjanjuk family didn't want to take any chances, especially after the suspicious death of Dov Eitan and the acid attack on Yoram Sheftel.

When El Al commercial flight 001 landed at New York's JFK Airport on September 22, 1991, a crowd of reporters shouting questions and demonstrators burning effigies of John Demjanjuk were waiting. Wearing a natty white Panama hat, striped shirt, and blue jacket, John Demjanjuk greeted the crowd with raised fists, as he had often done in the Jerusalem courtroom. Then his security team hustled him into a Cessna turbojet paid for by Demjanjuk supporter Jerome Brentar.

The Cessna wasted no time taking off for Cleveland's Hopkins International Airport, where a crowd of protesters and friends eagerly waited. At the same time, protesters led by Rabbi Avi Weiss were holding vigil outside Demjanjuk's home in Seven Hills. Cluttering the lawn next to them were TV cameras and booms, walkie-talkies, Nikons, and reporters chatting on mobile phones.

Demjanjuk fooled them all. Just as the Cessna was approaching Hopkins Airport, the pilot radioed the tower with a new flight plan. He was going to land at the small Medina Municipal Airport a few miles south, he said. And when the plane taxied to a stop on the Medina runway, Demjanjuk's escorts hurried him into a Lincoln Continental, which whisked him away to an undisclosed location for an undisclosed period of time to keep him safe.

It was not the welcome home that John Demjanjuk had dreamed about for eight years in his small cell in an Israeli prison.

• • •

The U.S. Sixth Circuit Court of Appeals had been following the unfolding Marchenko drama in Jerusalem with great interest and concern. Did OSI know or suspect, the court asked itself, that Iwan Marchenko was Iwan Grozny when it tried John Demjanjuk on immigration fraud charges as Ivan the Terrible?

To get to the bottom of its own question, the appeals court, like the Israeli Supreme Court, committed an act of courage. It reopened the denaturalization issue and appointed an independent judge (special master) to investigate OSI on the court's behalf. What did OSI know? When did OSI know it? Did OSI commit prosecutorial misconduct? Did OSI perpetrate fraud on the court?

The answers were sitting inside a Dumpster.

CHAPTER FIFTY-TWO

The Dumpster Tales

Ever since Judge Battisti had stripped John Demjanjuk of his U.S. citizenship in 1981, the Demjanjuk family and its attorneys suspected that OSI was withholding documents they were entitled to under the law. OSI had written to Moscow, Berlin, Jerusalem, and Warsaw asking for any and all documents relating to Iwan Demjanjuk. And OSI investigators had traveled to the Soviet Union, Israel, Germany, and Poland looking for and interviewing potential witnesses. As a result, OSI received several information packets from overseas. But in spite of all the international traffic and investigative flurry, OSI had given the Demjanjuk defense team very few documents and only a handful of names of potential witnesses who might clear Demjanjuk's name or strengthen his defense.

OSI confirmed defense suspicions when it deliberately withheld Soviet-provided statements from five former Trawniki men until *after* Judge Battisti found Demjanjuk guilty of lying on his visa application. The statements were a mixed bag. None of the witnesses recognized the name Iwan Demjanjuk, and four of the five witnesses did not recognize photographs of him. Those four Trawniki men supported the defense. The fifth witness swore that he had trained at Trawniki with the man in the photos. He supported the prosecution.

Feigning outrage, Demjanjuk's defense attorney John Martin accused the government of prosecutorial misconduct because it failed to inform the defense of potential new witnesses *before* the trial, as required by the U.S. Code of Criminal Procedure. It was a sneaky attempt to withhold evidence from the defense, Martin argued. The government knew that the five reports would have "an impact on the Judge's decision." He asked Battisti to declare a mistrial.

Martin was half right. Judge Battisti found that the government was indeed at fault when it failed to disclose in a timely manner the identity of one witness who had positively identified Demjanjuk's photo. On the other hand, he found that the government did not breach any rule when it withheld the identities of the other four Soviet witnesses, because they had denied knowing Demjanjuk at Trawniki and failed to identify the photos.

Battisti concluded that the sworn statements of the five witnesses, either as individuals or as a group, would not have changed his decision in the case in any way. Therefore, Demjanjuk was not entitled to a new trial.

The five-document flap was not a futile and meaningless legal maneuver because it raised a critical question. If OSI had withheld one set of documents that the defense was entitled to, how many more documents was it hiding from the defense?

Immediately after Battisti's ruling, Martin demanded that OSI deliver all its Demjanjuk-related documents, including those it had received from West Germany, Poland, Israel, and the Soviet Union. He needed them, Martin argued, to prepare the defense's denaturalization appeal.

OSI responded: "All relevant and discoverable documents in the Government's possession have already been part of the records of these proceedings."

That wasn't true.

Denied the undisclosed documentary evidence buried in OSI files, John Martin had lost the denaturalization appeal, Mark O'Connor had lost the asylum plea, Judge Angelilli had ordered Demjanjuk to be deported to the Soviet Union, the Sixth Circuit Court of Appeals in Cleveland had approved Demjanjuk's extradition to Israel, and Judge Levin had condemned Demjanjuk to death by hanging.

All through these legal battles, the Demjanjuk family and its attorneys never gave up searching for the exculpatory evidence it was convinced OSI was hiding. They got a bizarre break in the early 1980s, while Demjanjuk was waiting for the appeals court to review Judge Battisti's denaturalization order. Two enterprising Estonian supporters of John Demjanjuk began collecting OSI's garbage each day from a Dumpster behind the Hamilton Building on K Street in Washington, D.C., where OSI rented office space. Then they packaged the papers they found mixed in with Styrofoam coffee cups and apple cores and sent them to the Demjanjuk family. Some of the papers were stamped CLASSIFIED.

The first two garbage nuggets were a pair of reports describing in detail OSI's photo identification interview with Otto Horn at his home in Berlin in 1979. Horn was the Treblinka SS officer in charge of burying the corpses taken from the gas chambers. His photo identification of Demjanjuk as Iwan Grozny who operated the gas chamber at Treblinka was especially important because he was a German officer, not a Jewish survivor, and because he had worked side by side with Iwan the Terrible for more than a year. If anyone could identify him, it would be Otto Horn.

One Dumpster report was written by investigator Bernard J. Dougherty Jr., the other by historian George W. Garland. The reports, which complemented each other, proved that Horn's identification of Demjanjuk as Ivan the Terrible was compromised and suggested that he had committed perjury.

In effect, the two reports completely undermined the credibility of Horn's entire testimony.

. . .

In preparation for the denaturalization trial in Cleveland, Dougherty and Garland had shown two legally correct photo spreads to Otto Horn. Each spread contained eight photos. The Trawniki card photo was in the first batch; Demjanjuk's visa application photo was in the second. Following OSI rules, both investigators wrote independent reports after the interview.

OSI prosecutor Norman Moscowitz had questioned Otto Horn about the first photo spread during his videotaped testimony for the 1981 denaturalization trial in Cleveland.

"Did you in fact identify or recognize anyone in those photographs?" Moscowitz asked Horn.

"Iwan," Horn testified without hesitation.

That is not what Dougherty recalled. "Horn studied each of the photographs at length," Dougherty wrote, "but was unable to positively identify any of the pictures."

Next, Moscowitz questioned Horn about the second photo spread. "When you looked at those photographs . . . where was the first [set]?"

Whether Horn could or could not see the first photo of Demjanjuk while he studied the second set of photos was a critical point. If Horn could see the first picture, his identification of the second picture would be inadmissible.

"They were put away," Horn testified without hesitation.

That's not what Dougherty recalled. "The first series of photographs," Dougherty wrote, "was then gathered and placed in a stack, off to the side of the table—with that of Demjanjuk lying face up on top of the pile." Horn studied both photos, then said they were pictures of the same person. "After a few more moments of careful study," Dougherty wrote, "Horn positively identified the photographs of Iwan Demjanjuk as being the Iwan he knew at the gas chamber in Treblinka."

It is not clear how Demjanjuk's photo ended up on top of the first photo spread pile. Or whether it was placed there accidentally or deliberately.

But because the defense didn't have a copy of the Dougherty-Garland reports and was not present at the Berlin photo identification session that Dougherty and Garland had conducted with Otto Horn, Martin had been unable to challenge Horn during his cross-examination. As a result, Judge Battisti was impressed with Horn's pivotal testimony.

"The court finds no aberration in the conduct of these [Horn] identifications," Battisti had ruled. "Since the Court finds both the pretrial and trial photographic identifications to be reliable, it must conclude that defendant was present at Treblinka in 1942–1943."

If OSI had not been able to offer Otto Horn's sworn testimony in court because it was not credible, or if defense attorney John Martin had confronted Horn with the contradictions during his cross-examination, would Judge Battisti have been so sure of himself? And if Martin had received a copy of the two OSI reports in time to submit them to the appeals court as new evidence, would the appeals court have declared a mistrial or ordered a new trial, as it did in the case of Frank Walus?

• • •

Not long after uncovering the Horn photo identification reports, the Demjanjuk family discovered two more nuggets in the Dumpster papers. The first was a cable about Feodor Fedorenko sent by the American embassy in Moscow to the State Department in August 1978, while the Justice Department was preparing for both the Demjanjuk denaturalization trial in Cleveland and the Fedorenko denaturalization trial in Fort Lauderdale. OSI had failed to share the cable with the defense.

The cable identified by name six former Treblinka guards who had been interviewed by the KGB. The defense felt that OSI had the legal obligation to reveal the statements of the six Trawniki men because they were potential defense witnesses.

The second nugget was a cable from the Justice Department to the Polish Glovna Komisia (Main Commission) dated July 29, 1981, a month after Judge Battisti had stripped Demjanjuk of his citizenship. OSI already had Soviet-supplied excerpts from eighteen statements by former Trawniki men about Fedorenko and Treblinka. In the cable OSI asked the Polish Main Commission to request the complete statements from Soviet officials.

The defense felt that it was entitled to the eighteen excerpts because it was possible that one or more of the Trawniki men knew the identity of the real Ivan the Terrible. The defense felt it was entitled to interview them as possible witnesses.

• • •

If the Demjanjuk family had been suspicious of OSI before it retrieved the Dumpster papers, it was now totally convinced that OSI was deliberately withholding exculpatory reports vital to the defense. The family engaged Washington attorney John H. Broadley and Ohio representative James Traficant to apply to the Department of State and the Department of Justice, under the Freedom of Information Act, for all Demjanjuk-related letters, cables, memos, and reports. If State and Justice refused to release the documents, or if the documents they did release were so heavily redacted as to make them useless, the family authorized the attorneys to take the government to court.

It was a two-year tug of war that took place while John Demjanjuk was on trial in Jerusalem. The Demjanjuk family was forced to sue. It won.

Among the documents the court ordered the Justice Department to release, over the strong objections of OSI, were two items pointing to Iwan Marchenko as Ivan the Terrible. The first item was an article about Treblinka guards written by a member of the Polish Main Commission. The article in the *Commission Bulletin* contained a list of seventy former Treblinka guards gathered from Polish and Soviet documents and war crimes testimony. Iwan Demjanjuk was not on the Polish list. Iwan Marchenko was.

The second item was a file known as the Fedorenko Protocol. It contained two red-hot, smoking guns. The first was Nikolai Petrovich Malagon, a former Treblinka guard. In a sworn statement dated March 18, 1978, three years before the Demjanjuk denaturalization trial as Ivan the Terrible, Malagon said: "While at the Treblinka death camp, I met the guard Nikolai [*sic*] *Marchenko*, who drove a gas chamber [motor]. I do not know where he is at the present."

A Soviet prosecutor then showed Malagon three cards with three photos pasted on each. Each card contained a picture of Iwan Demjanjuk. Marchenko's photo was not among the nine. Malagon failed to identify anyone in the pictures as Marchenko, and he failed to recognize the photo of Iwan Demjanjuk as someone he knew either at Treblinka or at Trawniki.

The second smoking gun was Pavel Vladimirovich Leleko, another Treblinka guard. In a sworn statement also dated March 1978, Leleko said: "When the procession of doomed people approached the gas chamber building Marchenko and Nikolai, the motorists [operators] of the gas chambers shouted: 'Walk faster or the water will become cold!' . . . The Germans and the motor operators then competed as to atrocities with regard to the people to be killed.

"Marchenko, for instance, had a sword with which he mutilated people. He cut off the breasts of women....When the loading of the chambers was completed, they were sealed off by hermetically closing doors. Motorists Marchenko and Nikolai started the motors. The gas produced went through pipes in the chambers. The process of suffocation began."

The defense concluded that OSI had deliberately concealed the Malagon and Leleko sworn statements because it was committed to trying John Demjanjuk as Ivan the Terrible even if he wasn't.

• • •

To conduct its investigation, the U.S. Sixth Circuit Court of Appeals appointed a special master—Thomas A. Wiseman Jr., a senior district court judge in Nashville, Tennessee. Judge Battisti would have been the logical choice for the job because he knew the Demjanjuk case well and sat on the bench in Cleveland, the home base of the Sixth Circuit. But Demjanjuk attorneys would most certainly have filed a motion to remove Battisti from the case had he been chosen. Whether or not to appoint Battisti, however, turned out to be moot. A tick bit the judge while he was hiking, and he subsequently died of Rocky Mountain spotted fever at the age of seventy-two.

Judge Wiseman spent three months reviewing all the withheld documents and deposing all the OSI attorneys involved in the Demjanjuk case. Among others were former OSI director Walter Rockler, the recipient of the doubt memo that questioned the ethics of prosecuting Demjanjuk as Ivan the Terrible; his successor Allan Ryan; George Parker, who wrote the doubt memo; Martin Mendelsohn, who led the early investigation of Demjanjuk; and Norman Moscowitz, the lead prosecutor in Demjanjuk's Ivan the Terrible denaturalization case.

The government presented to the special master two arguments in defense of the OSI attorneys. First, it argued that there were so many overlapping OSI investigations going on at the time that not every OSI prosecutor knew what was in every other prosecutor's file. The government conceded, however, that some OSI attorneys and investigators did know about the existence of the documents in question. Moscowitz, for example, had read the Polish commission's list of former Treblinka guards and the Fedorenko Protocol, in which two former Treblinka guards identified Iwan Marchenko as Ivan the Terrible. But Moscowitz did not know, the government argued, about Parker's doubt memo and the Otto Horn photo identification reports written by OSI investigators.

Second, the government argued that OSI was not required by law to release the documents in question. True, the 1963 Supreme Court decision in *Brady v. Maryland* had found that the "suppression by the prosecution of evidence favorable to the accused upon request violates due process." But *Brady* was a criminal case. Demjanjuk was a *civil* case. Therefore, the government argued, the *Brady* decision did not apply to Demjanjuk.

• • •

Special Master Wiseman's conclusions and recommendations to the Sixth Circuit Court of Appeals shocked and disappointed the Demjanjuk family, which was totally convinced that OSI had framed their father and husband. Judge Wiseman quickly dispatched the charge of prosecutorial misconduct by agreeing with the government's interpretation of *Brady*. The charge of fraud on the court was a more complicated issue.

To prove fraud on the court, Wiseman argued, Demjanjuk would have to clearly show that an officer of the court had deceived the court by being intentionally false, willfully blind to the truth, or in reckless disregard of the truth by positively concealing something the officer had the duty to disclose.

Wiseman conceded that OSI had played "hardball" with the Demjanjuk defense by not fully cooperating as it had promised. He faulted OSI attorneys for "failing to ask questions regarding the evidence they possessed, and this error prevented them from asking questions designed to obtain additional evidence." Their failure to challenge the evidence they possessed, Wiseman wrote, "led them to abandon leads which contradicted their interpretation of the evidence." Wiseman dismissed George Parker's doubt memo, saying that it was not a "smoking gun" nor was it evidence of a "breach of any ethical duty."

In his special master's report to the Sixth Circuit court, Wiseman concluded that OSI attorneys had acted in good faith. "They did not intend to violate the Rules of their ethical obligations. They were not reckless; they did not misstate the facts or the law as they understood them, and did not make statements in ignorance while aware of their ignorance or behave with *willful blindness*. . . . My recommendation to the Court is that . . . no action be taken against any of the government attorneys who prosecuted Mr. Demjanjuk."

• • •

In November 1993, two months after Demjanjuk returned to the United States from Israel, the Sixth Circuit Court of Appeals ruled on his denaturalization appeal and his allegations of prosecutorial misconduct and fraud upon the court. After reviewing Special Master Wiseman's 240-page report, the Sixth Circuit accepted some of his analysis of the evidence but none of his conclusions.

The court found that Judge Wiseman erred when he ruled that *Brady* did not apply to Demjanjuk's civil trial. In the denaturalization trial of John Demjanjuk, the appeals court pointed out, the government charged that "Demjanjuk was guilty of mass murder" as the cruel and brutal Ivan the Terrible. In effect, the appeals court ruled, the Demjanjuk case was a criminal case by intent. Thus *Brady* applied.

Having clarified that legal issue, the Sixth Circuit went on to rule on the interrelated issues of prosecutorial misconduct and fraud on the court. It was not as generous or forgiving as consulting Judge Thomas Wiseman. Unlike the special master, who concluded that OSI did not prosecute Demjanjuk for political reasons, the Sixth Circuit accused OSI of placing politics and a "win at any cost" attitude above the dictates of justice. In effect, the court was saying that OSI had been committed for political reasons to seeing John Demjanjuk die for a crime he did not commit.

"It is obvious from the record," the appeals court further ruled, "that the prevailing mind set of OSI was that the office must try to please and maintain very close relationships with various interest groups because their [OSI's] continued existence depended on it."

Unlike the special master's finding, the final conclusion of the appeals court was as strong and as accusatory as the law allowed: "We hold that the OSI attorneys acted with *reckless disregard* for the truth and for the government's obligation to take no steps that prevent an adversary from presenting his case fully and fairly. This was *fraud on the court* . . . whereby recklessly assuming Demjanjuk's guilt, they failed to observe their obligation to produce exculpatory materials requested by Demjanjuk. . . .

"We vacate the judgment of the district court and the judgment of this court in the extradition proceedings on the ground that the judgments were wrongly procured as a result of prosecutorial misconduct that constituted *fraud on the court*."

The Demjanjuk family felt both vindicated and angry. OSI had framed their husband and father. Like the emotional Holocaust survivors, they thirsted for revenge. Surely the American system of justice would punish the guilty attorneys.

What they didn't understand during their short-lived victory celebrations was that the 1993 Sixth Circuit Court of Appeals finding of prosecutorial misconduct and fraud on the court was little more than a censure. Prosecutorial misconduct by an attorney is not a crime punishable under the Federal Criminal Code. At best, it is punishable by disbarment by the appropriate state supreme court, and/or dismissal from the Justice Department. Unlike prosecutorial obstruction of justice, which is prosecutable, fraud on the court is too broad a legal term to be useful.

Playing the role of a "supreme court," the American Bar Association (ABA) reviewed the unanimous decision of the three appeals court judges and overturned it, clearing all the OSI attorneys involved in the Demjanjuk case. The Justice Department referred the allegations against its OSI attorneys to an internal watchdog unit, the Office of Professional Responsibility (OPR). Like the ABA, OPR overturned the findings of the Sixth Circuit Court of Appeals as unfounded. It ruled that none of its prosecuting attorneys in the Demjanjuk case had committed prosecutorial misconduct, and that the facts in the case did not support a finding of fraud on the court.

John Demjanjuk had gone through three emotionally grueling and frightening trials in Cleveland and Jerusalem as Ivan the Terrible. The verdict of death by a noose hung over his head for five years as he sat in a jail cell on death row waiting for the Israeli Supreme Court's life-or-death decision. His family suffered emotional trauma and financial loss for more than twelve years. And the men who framed him got off free.

Was that justice? the family asked.

• • •

The decisions of the Israeli Supreme Court and the U.S. Sixth Circuit Court of Appeals raise a deeply cynical question. Was there an international conspiracy involving the United States, the Soviet Union, Poland, and Israel to try and to convict John Demjanjuk as Ivan the Terrible when they knew he was not?

As early as 1978, three years before the Demjanjuk denaturalization trial, both Moscow and the Polish Main Commission knew from the sworn statements of several Treblinka SS guards that the real Iwan Grozny was Iwan Marchenko. Before the Demjanjuk trial in Jerusalem even opened, the 1986 Fedorenko trial in Crimea had left no doubt that Iwan Marchenko was Iwan Grozny. But as far as the record shows, neither Poland nor the Soviet Union explicitly told OSI that they had the wrong man. Nor did they volunteer the Crimean documents that proved Iwan Marchenko was Iwan Grozny.

If nothing else, Moscow and Warsaw were embroiled in a conspiracy of silence. Both wanted or were willing to see John Demjanjuk hang for crimes he did not commit.

The unanswered question: Did the Israelis also know, or suspect, that Demjanjuk was not Ivan the Terrible before the Jerusalem trial? If not, did the Israelis conclude, or suspect, that Demjanjuk was not Ivan the Terrible during the trial? A United States appeals court accused

OSI of being willing to see an innocent man hang so it could stay alive. Did Judge Levin's court unjustly convict an innocent man to teach the nation of Israel a lesson in Holocaust justice?

Conspiracy or not, the Demjanjuk case was not over, as the Israeli Supreme Court had pointed out in its acquittal decision. There was still the matter of Sobibor, and OSI was not finished with John Demjanjuk.

CHAPTER FIFTY-THREE

Trial by Archive

O SI finally got around to following George Parker's advice. In his 1981 doubt memo, just weeks before the denaturalization trial of John Demjanjuk was about to open, Parker had recommended "radical surgery": Drop the Iwan Grozny charge and build a case against John Demjanjuk as Iwan of Sobibor. Since there wasn't enough evidence in 1981 to try Demjanjuk as a Sobibor guard, other than a disputed Trawniki card and an unchallenged statement by former Sobibor guard Ignat Danilchenko, OSI would in effect have to start over.

After the U.S. Sixth Circuit Court of Appeals reinstated John Demjanjuk as a lawful American citizen in 1993, OSI took Parker's advice. Eight years later and twenty-three years after the government first filed charges against Demjanjuk, OSI was ready. It still did not have a single live witness who could place Demjanjuk at Sobibor. What it did have, however, was a string of new documents found in Soviet and German archives.

John Demjanjuk didn't stand a chance. The archives were stacked against him.

• • •

The denaturalization trial in the case of *United States of America v. John Demjanjuk a/k/a Iwan Demjanjuk* opened in Cleveland at the end of May 2001. As expected, the government presented an impressive array of historical and technical document experts to testify about the authenticity of the Trawniki card as a whole and the validity of each element on it, from signatures to photo and seals, from typefaces to paper and ink. This time, however, they had four new Trawniki identity cards to use for comparison. The new documents came from archives in a number of countries and, like the Demjanjuk card, had spelling mistakes. One of the new cards was a service pass issued to Ignat Danilchenko.

Prosecution historians and document examiners authenticated each new card, including the signatures of Trawniki commander Karl Streibel and supply officer Ernst Teufel, which matched their signatures on the Demjanjuk card. The four new ID cards destroyed the defense argument that Trawniki *did not issue* service passes, as some of its witnesses had testified at the first denaturalization trial and in Israel. And since none of the new cards was exactly alike, they also refuted the argument that the Demjanjuk card was unique, and therefore it must have been forged.

Demjanjuk's new defense attorneys were John Broadley, who had helped the Demjanjuk family retrieve OSI documents through FOIA requests and lawsuits, and Michael Tigar. In the face of the new evidence, they mounted a well-prepared and aggressive defense. In fact, it was the best defense John Demjanjuk had received to date. But no matter how clearly, cogently, and fiercely they fought, they could not tumble the array of government expert witnesses.

In lieu of its own experts, the defense had to rely on an old strategy—pounce on what the prosecution experts had not done. They had not dusted the Demjanjuk Trawniki card for fingerprints—which would have proven that Iwan Demjanjuk had never touched the document—when the technology to do so was available. They failed to follow the archival trails of the new documents, which would have led them to evidence favorable to the defense. They also failed to establish a proper chain of evidence, which allowed for forgery and cast serious doubt on the authenticity of the new documents.

Given the embarrassing acquittal of John Demjanjuk as Ivan the Terrible by the Israeli Supreme Court and the finding of OSI prosecutorial misconduct by the U.S. Sixth Circuit Court of Appeals, Judge Paul Matia took extra care to be fair, reasoned, and precise in his analysis of the evidence presented by both sides. To make sure that it was clear at all times where the court stood on each piece of evidence, Matia wrote a ninety-three-page supplemental court paper, *Findings of Fact*, to serve as a foundation for his rulings.

In his analysis of the authenticity of the Demjanjuk Trawniki card,

Judge Matia noted that there were spelling mistakes on the document. (The defense argued that the errors proved forgery.) After ruling that the mistakes were minor and inconsequential, Matia attributed them not to sloppy forgers but to uneducated ethnic German interrogators who entered the data on personnel forms.

Matia also noted discrepancies in the descriptions of the height of Iwan Demjanjuk as reported by Treblinka survivors and various documents. The numbers ranged from five feet, eight inches, to six feet, one inch. (The defense argued that the height discrepancy proved forgery.) Given the consistency in the descriptions of *other* physical characteristics of Iwan Demjanjuk, Matia ruled that the height discrepancy was not critical.

In making his ruling, Matia took into account the fact that the height of both Demjanjuk and Danilchenko had been underreported on their individual ID cards. A comparison of the data showed that Demjanjuk had been described as two centimeters taller than Danilchenko. The height difference between the two men was consistent with what Danilchenko had reported in his 1979 sworn statement to a Soviet prosecutor. (At the Israeli trial, Judge Dorner had observed from the bench that tallness was a prized Aryan physical feature. The ethnic German interviewers at Trawniki, she pointed out, may have consciously or subconsciously made tall Soviet POWs appear shorter as a matter of ethnic pride.)

Like Judge Battisti in his analysis of the evidence presented at Demjanjuk's first denaturalization trial, Judge Matia accused the defense of arguing Trawniki-card forgery without offering any credible evidence. The defense had submitted into evidence the Israeli trial testimony of document examiner Julius Grant, in which he concluded that the Cyrillic signature of Iwan Demjanjuk on the Trawniki card was a forgery. To rebut Grant's testimony, the prosecution put document examiner Gideon Epstein on the stand. (Epstein had also testified for the prosecution at the 1981 denaturalization trial and at the Israeli trial.) Judge Matia, like Judge Levin's court in Jerusalem, did not find Grant's testimony reliable or credible. However, Matia did find Gideon Epstein's rebuttal testimony persuasive.

Finally, Judge Matia found that the "defendant has attacked the authenticity of the [document] on various grounds, but the expert testimony of the [prosecution's] document examiners is *devastating* to the defendant's contentions."

Like Judge Battisti in 1981 and the Israeli court in 1988, Judge Matia ruled that the Trawniki card was "an authentic German wartime document issued to the defendant." Because the card was authentic, it proved three of the prosecution's charges: Iwan Demjanjuk had graduated from Trawniki, had served as an SS guard at Sobibor, and had lied about his wartime activity on his visa application to the United States.

• • •

The government also offered into evidence six new documents supporting the authenticity of the Trawniki card. The first document was found in the Lithuanian Central State Archives in Vilnius. The other five came from the German Federal Archives in Berlin. Prosecution historians and document examiners had studied and tested each piece of new evidence for historical consistency and authenticity as thoroughly as they had the Trawniki card. They concluded that all six documents were authentic.

Document one was a disciplinary report issued at Majdanek on January 20, 1943. The Majdanek concentration-work camp was suffering from a typhus epidemic that month and the camp commandant imposed a quarantine on all camp personnel, from SS officers to SS guards.

Four guards violated the quarantine on January 18 to go shopping in Lublin. They got caught. On the order of SS Sergeant Hermann Erlinger, they each received twenty-five lashes "with a stick" as punishment. One of the punished guards was *Deminjuk 1393*.

Serving with "Deminjuk" at Majdanek, with its gas chambers and ovens, was Hermine Braunsteiner, the Mare of Majdanek, who was later tried and convicted of stomping to death hundreds of women and children. Besides Jews and Poles, there were Soviet POWs imprisoned in the camp as well, creating another World War II irony. A Soviet POW was paid by the Nazis to prevent fellow Soviet POWs from escaping almost certain death by overwork, typhus, starvation, a bullet, or gas.

Document two, issued on or about March 26, 1943, was a roster of eighty-four Trawniki men who were assigned to be transferred from Trawniki to Sobibor. "Effective today," the roster said, "the following guards will be brought from Trawniki Training camp to the above place of duty."

Number thirty on the list was *Demianiuk 1393*. The transfer roster gave his rank as *Wachmann* (private), and his date and place of birth. Except for the spelling of Demjanjuk's name, the information on the roster was consistent with the information on the Trawniki card. A notation at the top of the roster indicated that only eighty of the eighty-four men listed had actually been transferred to Sobibor as part of an "SS Special Detachment." Number thirty was one of the transfers. Danilchenko, who was also on the list, was transferred to Sobibor as well.

Document three was another transfer roster, dated October 1, 1943, two weeks before the prisoner uprising at Sobibor, the death knell of that death camp. The 140 men on the transfer roster were being sent from Trawniki to a concentration camp in Flossenbürg, Bavaria, near the Czech border, not far from Plattling, where the Soviet POW revolt against forced repatriation took place.

Early on, Flossenbürg employed prisoners to work in nearby limestone quarries. In 1943, however, there was a more urgent need. The Messerschmitt Aircraft Corporation had built an assembly plant a mile from Flossenbürg and needed workers. So while Operation Reinhard was winding down in eastern Poland, where Belzec, Sobibor, and Treblinka had already been liquidated, Flossenbürg was "bursting at the seams." More prisoners required more SS guards.

Entry number fifty on the Flossenbürg transfer roster was *Demianjuk 1393*. Once again, his name was misspelled. Once again, the roster listed his date and place of birth and gave his rank as *Wachmann*, indicating that he had not received a promotion in the two years he had served as a Trawniki man. The personal data were consistent with the entries on the Demjanjuk ID card.

Historical documents indicate that an SS Death Head's battalion ran the Flossenbürg camp, where thousands of Jews, Gypsies, Jehovah's Witnesses, and other civilians were held. The Trawniki men assigned to Flossenbürg were, therefore, inducted into the Death's Head battalion as auxiliary soldiers and received the SS blood-type tattoo.

Documents four, five, and *six* were a Flossenbürg weapons log, a roster of guards, and a work order report. The weapons log indicated that *Wachmann Demianiuk 1393* had received a rifle and bayonet on October 8, 1943, a week after his transfer from Trawniki.

The undated roster of 117 Death's Head guards listed *Demenjuk 1393* as entry number 44. Based on notations on the documents, the list had been created between December 10, 1944, and January 15, 1945, when John Demjanjuk testified he had been at Graz, Austria, and Heuberg, Germany, as an inductee into Vlasov's army.

The work order report issued on October 4, 1944, a year after Demjanjuk arrived at Flossenbürg, noted that he had been assigned to guard a prison detail constructing a bunker in the main camp.

The new documents bolstered the credibility of Danilchenko's 1979 sworn statement. In it, he said he served at Sobibor. The Trawniki transfer roster listed him as a transferee to Sobibor. In it, he said Iwan Demjanjuk was already at Sobibor when he arrived. The transfer roster indicated that not all of the transferees left Trawniki for Sobibor on the same day. In it, he said that he and Iwan Demjanjuk were transferred to Flossenbürg. The Trawniki transfer roster listed him as a transferee to that camp along with Iwan Demjanjuk.

The new documents also solved a problem. Danilchenko said in his sworn statement that he had met Iwan Demjanjuk at Sobibor in March 1942, a year earlier than the transfer roster claimed. Given the accuracy of the rest of Danilchenko's sworn testimony, Judge Matia accepted the incorrect year as a simple memory lapse.

Judge Matia ruled that the six supporting documents were "authentic German wartime documents." Realizing that his decision would be highly scrutinized around the world, Matia explained his reasoning. He argued: "The randomness and relative rarity of the documents actually supports their authenticity. If the Soviets had set out to create *false* documents, they would not have allowed the omissions and minor inaccuracies that occur in the trail of documents in this case.

"The location of these documents in the archives of several different countries also buttresses their authenticity, as their dispersal at the chaotic end of World War II does not seem at all unusual.

"The various spellings of the defendant's last name in the documents actually lends further credence to them, since the conversion from the Cyrillic alphabet to the western alphabet produces such variations, and a counterfeiter would have used *one spelling consistently*."

Besides the new documents listed above, prosecution historians introduced new evidence that Iwan Demjanjuk could not have been in the Chelm camp in the fall of 1944 because the last 444 prisoners held there had been transferred to Skierniewice, a city in central Poland, in the spring of 1944. The Soviets found a ghost camp when they entered Chelm in July.

Prosecution historians also produced German army troop movement charts showing that Iwan Demjanjuk could not have been a soldier in Vlasov's army where and when he said he was, because either Vlasov's army did not exist at the time or its divisions were deployed elsewhere.

• • •

The Demjanjuk defense team added a new argument to its old arsenal of KGB forgery and mistaken identity. The photo of Iwan Demjanjuk on the Trawniki card, the defense argued, was not the photo of John Demjanjuk but that of his cousin with the same name. This was no rabbit in the hat. John Demjanjuk actually had a cousin named Iwan Andreevich Demjanjuk, born on February 22, 1921, in the same village where Iwan Nikolai Demjanjuk had lived. Like the government's case against Demjanjuk, the cousin argument was not based on eyewitness testimony, but on two archival documents found in the Soviet Union.

The first document was an undated index card containing a series of unconnected notes: "Iwan Dem'yanyuk . . . Andreevich . . . 1920 [*sic*] born . . . resident of the village of Dubovye Makharintsky [*sic*] . . . Trawniki, Lyublin, L'vov." The entry stated that the source of the information was Vasilij Litvinenko, a former Trawniki man whom the Soviets had tried and convicted of war crimes along with Danilchenko.

The second archival document was a copy of Litvinenko's statement given to Soviet interrogators in June 1949. Litvinenko swore in the statement that he knew a Trawniki man named Iwan Andreevich Dem'janjuk who had two false white metal teeth in his upper jaw. Litvinenko said he trained with Iwan Andreevich at Trawniki and later served with him at a concentration camp in Lublin.

As supportive evidence, the defense offered the court the sworn statement of Mariya Demjanjuk, another cousin. "As far as I know," Mariya said, "I. A. [Iwan Andreevich] Demjanjuk was called up for military service before the war, in about 1940."

Judge Matia didn't buy any of it.

Before the trial opened, the prosecution had asked Ukraine to provide the military service record of Iwan Andreevich Demjanjuk. The Ukraine government replied that, after "extensive searches," it was unable to find any official record that Iwan Andreevich Demjanjuk had ever entered, served in, or was demobilized from the Soviet army during World War II.

Furthermore, Matia pointed out, the defense did not produce a picture of Iwan Andreevich to compare with the photo on the Trawniki card. Nor did the defense produce any evidence that this Iwan Andreevich had an identifying scar on his back. All it had was a statement from John Demjanjuk saying that the photo on the Trawniki card looked like his cousin.

That left the sworn statement of Litvinenko. Was he credible?

Judge Matia didn't think so. He pointed out that nine of the twenty-three Trawniki men Litvinenko named during his Soviet interrogation had false white metal teeth, a highly "curious" observation. "If such false teeth were that common, how would he be able to remember which trainees had them?" Matia asked. "And why would he know who had metal teeth in their upper jaw unless they were all in the front?"

Furthermore, Litvinenko claimed that he had served with Demjanjuk at a Lublin camp. The defense failed to provide any documentary evidence that a Trawniki man named Demjanjuk had ever served in a Lublin detachment, while the prosecution presented documentary evidence that he could not have.

Even Litvinenko's Soviet interrogators didn't think he was a reliable witness. They noted that he said he suffered from such an alcohol problem that he once sold his pants for a bottle of vodka. Is memory seen through an alcoholic haze a memory to be trusted?

Finally, Judge Matia asked a cogent question. If John Demjanjuk believed that the Trawniki card photo was that of his cousin Iwan Andreevich, why did he wait twenty years to bring it up?

The defense also presented a series of statements from former Trawniki men who did not recall being trained at Trawniki with a guard named Demjanjuk. And those who saw a photo of him did not recognize him. If so many Trawniki men could not identify Iwan Demjanjuk as a fellow trainee and SS guard, the defense argued, as it had in Jerusalem, it was reasonable to doubt that he had ever been a Trawniki graduate and a Sobibor guard.

Just as Judge Levin's court had done, Judge Matia dismissed the argument as specious. There were more than five thousand Trawniki men. It is reasonable to assume that not every one of them had trained with, worked with, or even met Iwan Demjanjuk.

• • •

During the trial, the defense offered three more Soviet documents as evidence. The first was a top-secret most-wanted list containing approximately one hundred names. Labeled "Announced as a Subject of an All-Union Search," the all-points bulletin was issued by the 4th Directorate of the MGB, Ministry of State Security (a forerunner of the KGB), and was dated August 31, 1948. Entry number twenty on the most-wanted list was Iwan Nikolai Demjanjuk.

The second Soviet document was an updated MGB most-wanted list issued four years later, on July 29, 1952. Also on that list was Iwan Nikolai

Demjanjuk. This time, however, the MGB added *1393* to his name and provided a copy of his Trawniki card photo. The new additions to the Soviet most-wanted list indicated that sometime between August 1948 and July 1952, the Soviets had either located the original Demjanjuk Trawniki card (the prosecution's claim) or had forged it (the defense's claim) in an attempt to build a war crimes case against Iwan Demjanjuk.

A third KGB document dated March 17, 1969, stated that "the following persons have not been located after searches were done to their former places of residence." On the list was Iwan Nikolai Demjanjuk 1393. His cousin Iwan Andreevich, however, was living in the village when the KGB made its search. If the real Iwan Demjanjuk was Iwan Andreevich—not Iwan Nikolai—wouldn't the KGB have arrested him?

During the course of the trial, the defense had inadvertently created a new definition of the terms *forged* document and *authentic* document. A forged document was a Soviet document provided to the prosecution. An authentic document was a Soviet document provided to the defense.

• • •

In May 2002, citing the U.S. Supreme Court's Fedorenko decision that *involuntary* persecution of civilians is not a mitigating circumstance, Judge Matia ruled:

"The Government has proven by clear, convincing, and unequivocal evidence that the defendant assisted in the persecution of civilian populations during World War II. . . . His entry to the United States in 1952 was therefore unlawful and his naturalization as a United States citizen was illegally procured and must be revoked. . . .

"Defendant shall surrender and deliver to the Attorney General of the United States (or his designee) within ten days of the date of this order, his Certificate of Naturalization, No. 7997497, and any United States passport or other documentary evidence of the U.S. citizenship he may have.

"Defendant is forever restrained and enjoined from claiming any rights, privileges or advantages under any document evidencing U.S. citizenship."

For the second time in twenty years, John Demjanjuk was a man without a country. But before the United States could deport him to a country of his choice, Germany requested his extradition to stand trial in Munich as Iwan of Sobibor. After all appeals were exhausted, John Demjanjuk left for Munich in May 2009 on a stretcher.

CHAPTER FIFTY-FOUR

Germany on Trial

If Israel had greeted its trial of Ivan the Terrible with indifference and addiction, fascination and pain, Germany greeted its trial of Sobibor guard John Demjanjuk with stoic resignation, seasoned with a dash of skepticism. If Germany was responsible for the Holocaust, Germany must face it. Let's get it over with and move on.

But why *John Demjanjuk?*

That Israel chose to try Ivan the Terrible as a major Nazi collaborator was understandable. He was a monster who tortured and killed hundreds of thousands of Jews. But John Demjanjuk? Why would Germany want to try an alleged SS guard who sat on the bottom rung of the Nazi ladder? Besides, Demjanjuk wasn't even German. He was born in Ukraine and committed his alleged crimes in Poland. Let Ukraine or Poland suffer the trauma.

And why now?

Some would argue that the decision of the United States to pursue John Demjanjuk as Ivan the Terrible was political. Score a big one for OSI and save it from extinction.

Some would argue that the decision of Israel to try John Demjanjuk as Ivan the Terrible was also political. Use the trial to educate young Israelis about the reality of Treblinka and the painful details of the Holocaust upon which the Jewish state was founded.

Wasn't Germany's decision to try ninety-year-old John Demjanjuk as Iwan of Sobibor political as well?

In 1958, Germany had created and funded a special office for the prosecution of Nazi war criminals. Although the office had conducted hundreds of recent investigations, it hadn't tried a single Nazi or Nazi collaborator for nearly twenty years. Between 1979, when OSI was created, and 2009, when the German trial opened, OSI had stripped more than three hundred Nazi collaborators of their U.S. citizenship and deported or extradited most of them before they died. During that same time period, Germany had tried just a handful of Nazi criminals. The German Nazi war crimes office appeared to be doing nothing but spending money and blowing smoke. It needed to justify its existence.

The United States came to the rescue.

OSI gave Germany John Demjanjuk, gift-wrapped and tied with a bow. If his trial was meant to be a German Nazi-era coda, it was far from a dramatic Beethovenesque flourish. It was more burp than bang.

Furthermore, hadn't Germany done enough?

At least the country had the courage to face the war crimes of its leaders. What about the rest of the world, especially the United States and Great Britain, which were so eager to try and to convict Nazi war criminals at Nuremberg? How many public war crimes trials had the United States and Great Britain initiated to prosecute and sentence their *own* World War II war criminals?

What about the American and British soldiers who had brutally rounded up Soviet civilians and POWs, herded them into cattle cars at bayonet point, and shipped them east to face execution, slow death in a labor camp, or virtual slavery in a factory?

If it was a crime for the SS, Gestapo, and Trawniki men to round up Jews for the camps, why wasn't it a crime for American and British soldiers to round up Soviet citizens for the gulags? And what about the political and military architects of the forced-repatriation reign of terror? Weren't they guilty of the crimes against humanity that they had ordered their foot soldiers to commit?

Unlike the United States, Germany had held Treblinka trials in Düsseldorf, Sobibor trials in Hagen, Belzec trials in Munich, Trawniki trials in Hamburg, Auschwitz trials in Frankfurt, and Dora trials in Essen. It had conducted more than 100,000 investigations and its courts had convicted more than 6,000 Nazis. What more did the rest of the smug, hypocritical world expect of Germany?

• • •

The picture wasn't really that rosy. The German Nazi trials of the 1950s, '60s, and '70s were riddled with acquittals and short sentences that amounted to a rap on the knuckles with a feather. It was true that approximately 180 Nazis got the maximum sentence allowable under German law. For example, Treblinka commandant Kurt Franz and Sobibor commandant Franz Stangl got life.

On the other hand, several thousand SS men working at concentration, labor, and death camps and serving as Einsatzkommandos and T-4 euthanasia workers were sentenced to only one to three years in prison. And hundreds more like Otto Horn, who had supervised the burying of corpses at Treblinka, and Karl Streibel and his top five Trawniki training camp commanders were all acquitted in a liberal—some would say scandalous—interpretation of the German criminal code.

Critics of German war crimes trials are quick to point out that most of the judges and attorneys involved in the early German trials had served the Third Reich during the war. Most had actively participated in the Reich's criminal justice system. Most had been members of the Nazi Party. By 1949, when the responsibility of trying Nazis had shifted from the Allies to the West German judiciary:

- Ninety-three percent of court officials in the German state of Westphalia had been Nazis.
- One hundred percent of the court officers in the city of Schweinfurt had been Nazis.
- Eighty-one percent of the court officers in the large state of Bavaria had been Nazis.
- Only two Nazi lawyers or judges had been convicted of war crimes and they both received light sentences.

It was these former Nazis who provided the legal rationale for the post-Nuremberg war crimes trials, sat on the benches, pronounced judgment, determined sentences, and provided criminal defenses.

Unlike Israel and France, which had included "war crimes" and "crimes against humanity" in their revised penal codes in order to deal with the unique legal problems inherent in trying defendants for war crimes, Germany stood firm on its 1871 criminal code, which did not have statutes covering war crimes or crimes against humanity.

There was a self-serving reason for the steadfast refusal of German jurists to update the penal code as France and Israel had done. Without an update, Nazi war criminals had to be tried for regular murder, which excluded "desk criminals" (*Schreibtischtäter*) like themselves.

As one historian aptly put it: "[They] were loath to institute laws that could hold them accountable as lawmakers during the Nazi period."

Who then could be tried as a war criminal under the 1871 penal code? Only exceptionally sadistic men and women, usually camp guards like Hermine Braunsteiner, who received a life sentence for her brutal murder of women and children. As a result, it was almost impossible to convict the vast majority of Nazi criminals. Under the 1871 statutes, a prosecutor would have to prove beyond a reasonable doubt that the accused both *intended* to kill someone and was *motivated* to kill someone. If he just followed orders, he did not necessarily have intent or motive.

In interpreting that definition of regular murder, German judges and jurists crafted two self-serving guiding principles. *Befehlsnotstand* excused a defendant from the charge of murder if he obeyed a superior officer's command to kill because disobeying it would have endangered his own life. A favorite defense argument, *Befehlsnotstand* was responsible for most post-Nuremberg acquittals. The 1871 code also created the principle of *excess*. In order to be convicted of wartime murder, the defendant had to be an *Exzesstäter*—someone who had committed excessive acts of cruelty in killing someone, like Klaus Barbie, the Butcher of Lyon.

In sum, the postwar German courts interpreted the 1871 code to excuse abettors like SS men who had participated in a killing process but had not directly committed murder. It also freed those who killed on order without committing excessive acts of cruelty.

German Nazi war crimes prosecutors like Ulrich Maas and Thomas Walther were not happy working within the narrow confines of an outmoded, protective, and unfair code.

"We criminal prosecutors have sometimes felt like road workers who are handed a screwdriver instead of a jackhammer," Maas complained. He went on to compare prosecuting low-level Nazi criminals to trying shoplifters. "You feel a certain queasiness. . . . The big economic fraudsters manage to get away scot-free. But the alternative cannot be to let the shoplifter go too."

For months, the German government resisted the efforts of OSI director Eli Rosenbaum to deport John Demjanjuk to Germany to stand trial. Like Poland, Germany didn't want to clean up the mess Israel had made of its prosecution of Demjanjuk. Finally, under pressure from its own prosecutors and out of concern about negative publicity, the German government reluctantly caved in.

Government prosecutors assigned to the Demjanjuk case signaled the Munich court that they were willing to reverse the historical legal trend when they charged John Demjanjuk with *assisting* in the murder of 29,060 Jews at Sobibor. These charges, of course, went beyond the definition of regular murder in the 1871 penal code still in use.

What would the seven judges do? A meld of four legal professionals and three lay people, they were much, much younger than their predecessors and were born after the war. Their memories consisted of, as one observer put it, "islands of knowledge and ignorance." Perhaps their grandfathers had questionable pasts, but they themselves never had to face the moral choices that World War II had imposed on soldiers and civilians alike.

Would they set a precedent and redefine the law because they viewed it as legally unsound? Would they try to correct the mistakes of the past? Would they lower the bar to include non-German Trawniki men? Would they redefine the word "accessory" to include being part of the killing process without directly killing? Would they commit an act of courage that would repudiate sixty years of German war crimes decisions? Or would they commit an act of cowardice and duck their responsibility to right what the rest of the world viewed as a terrible wrong?

CHAPTER FIFTY-FIVE

How Sick is Sick?

On November 30, 2009, the opening day of the trial of John Demjanjuk, there was a quiet desperation outside the Justice Center on Nymphenburger Strasse, a fifteen-minute walk from the main train station in the heart of old Munich. Four hundred people, mostly reporters and Jews, stood on the stone plaza stamping their feet to keep warm. Some had been there since five that morning. Among them was a large contingent from the Netherlands. The trial about to open was painfully relevant to the Dutch. One third of the ninety thousand Dutch Jews who died during the Holocaust were murdered at Sobibor.

On the street bordering the plaza, cable television vans with names like globesat.tv lined the street. In the plaza itself, there was a dignified bustle as TV crews interviewed spectators in German and English. Handheld video cameras scanned the scene looking for anything of interest. Cameras clicked everywhere, marking the day for posterity. There was no shouting or shoving. No songs or spoken prayers. No lighted candles honoring the photo and memory of a relative murdered at Sobibor. A dozen armed police officers were on hand just in case. They appeared watchful but bored.

Surprisingly, there were no Holocaust deniers or neo-Nazi protesters in the crowd as there had been the previous day in the Munich central train station, where a group of about thirty young men waving beer bottles were shouting "Sieg Heil!" at Christmas shoppers celebrating the beginning of Munich's popular holiday season.

As a location for a Nazi collaborator trial, Munich, Bavaria, was both a logical and ironic choice. Bavaria had legal jurisdiction in the Demjanjuk case because he had worked in the district as a civilian after the war. Munich was also the womb of Nazism and its beer halls had once reverberated with the sounds of Brown Shirts singing the Nazi anthem. It was in Munich that Hitler ranted his way into German politics. It was in Munich that he attempted a putsch that landed him in Stadelheim Prison—the same prison complex where John Demjanjuk was being held. And it was in Munich where the Holocaust began, with Kristallnacht. Was Germany sending the world a message?

It all began in Munich and it will end in Munich.

Court administrators had grossly underestimated international interest in the historic opening of the trial. They had set aside only sixty-eight seats in the courtroom for the media. There were 270 accredited reporters vying for them. They had reserved the entire gallery of 147 seats for spectators. There were more than three hundred hoping to get in. The court had promised to open a second room with closed-circuit television to accommodate the overflow, as the Israeli court had done, but apparently it decided not to do so, based on a literal interpretation of a German law forbidding cameras in a courtroom.

Security guards admitted four spectators at a time into the gallery. When all the seats were filled, they turned away those already inside the building and shut the doors to those waiting in the plaza. Spectators who couldn't get in accepted their disappointment with resignation. There was no pushing, shouting, or yelling. Among the rejected were credentialed journalists like the *New York Times* reporter who was next in line to enter the courtroom when the guards blocked the entrance. The morning session on opening day, November 30, produced little of interest to the spectators. By afternoon, there were no lines outside the Justice Center. The plaza was empty and the courtroom gallery was half empty. It would stay that way for most of the trial.

• • •

Courtroom A-101 was a cavernous modern hall with cathedral ceilings and bright white walls. It hummed with anticipation and subdued respect. A single red fire extinguisher gave the room its only spot of color. With the permission of presiding judge Ralph Alt, thirty to forty photographers and TV cameramen were allowed in the well of the courtroom. While they waited for John Demjanjuk to enter for their photo of the day, they snapped pictures of anything that moved.

The panel of seven judges entered the courtroom at eleven o'clock, one hour late. Judge Alt apologized. It had taken longer than anticipated to accommodate all the photographers and cameramen, he explained.

Just before the door to the right of the judges' bench opened, there was an eerie silence, as if two hundred people were holding their breaths. Then there was a loud collective gasp. A medical technician wheeled John Demjanjuk into the courtroom on a hospital gurney. He was draped in a light blue plastic surgical blanket to protect him from courtroom viruses. He wore dark glasses, a blue-gray baseball cap, a black leather jacket, and, under it, a sweatshirt that matched the color of his cap. He lay motionless and his mouth hung open. With his hands crossed on his chest, he looked like a corpse in a coffin.

As soon as Demjanjuk entered, the courtroom lost all semblance of decorum as photographers and TV cameras flooded the accused with lights and surrounded his gurney, snapping picture after picture from every possible angle for fifteen minutes. It was as if he were a freak in a legal circus. Through all the incessant clicking of shutters and the subdued voices of television commentators talking to cameras, Demjanjuk didn't open his eyes or even stir.

A few spectators watched with sympathy. A ninety-year-old man was dying. Was this justice or a travesty of justice? A trial or a spectacle? Wasn't it cruel and unusual punishment? Why didn't the court call off the whole charade?

The majority were cynical. The Simon Wiesenthal Center had exploded the "poor, sick Demjanjuk" myth. It posted a video on YouTube in April 2009—just weeks before Demjanjuk boarded a plane for Munich on a stretcher and looking like death—showing him getting in and out of a car and walking unassisted down a street in Seven Hills, Ohio.

John Demjanjuk might be old, the cynics said. He might be sick. But he was clearly playing to the Munich court, hoping the judges would stop the trial on humanitarian grounds or soften their final judgment.

Efraim Zuroff, a top Nazi hunter at the Simon Wiesenthal Center, was one of the cynics. "[Demjanjuk] has a vested interest in appearing as sick and as frail as possible," Zuroff said, "and he's going to play it up to the hilt. . . . He belongs in Hollywood."

If Demjanjuk was playacting, he was so good at it that it nearly worked. During the course of the eighteen-month trial, dozens of court sessions would be canceled or abbreviated because of real or alleged illness. Under German law, a trial has to start over if it is delayed for more than four weeks. If one added up all the missed court time, it would be close to the four-week limit.

For the next eighteen months, Demjanjuk would arrive at court either on a gurney or in a wheelchair. His appearance would hardly ever change. A female interpreter would sit next to his left ear, constantly talking to him. He gave no indication that he heard or understood her. Every now and then, he would shift to his left side or twitch and wince or move a hand—the only signs that he was still alive.

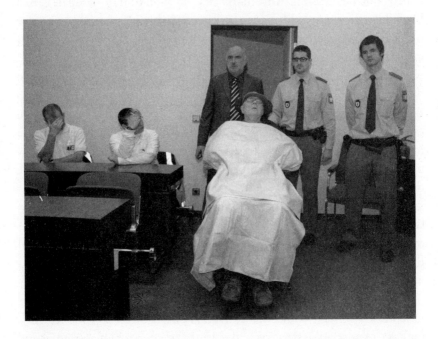

On several occasions, he would complain of chest or back pain or difficulty in breathing. The court-appointed doctor, who was always present when Demjanjuk was in the courtroom, would ask the bench for a recess. The medical technician would wheel the gurney or wheelchair out of the room and into the hallway for a private examination. After five or ten minutes, the doctor would return with a verdict: The session could resume or must be canceled.

When Demjanjuk appeared to be in pain, Judge Alt would ask him what was wrong. He would reply through his interpreter: "All I can say is I need to be brought to the [prison] hospital, not the courtroom."

Asked by Judge Alt if he wanted to examine a document being submitted into evidence, he would say: "That's a joke. With my pain, I cannot look at anything. I can't even listen anymore."

The courtroom health drama raised one of the most important issues of the trial. How sick was John Demjanjuk? How much pain was he really in?

• • •

A team of doctors had examined Demjanjuk when he arrived in Munich in May 2009, six months before the trial opened, to determine if he was physically fit to stand trial and mentally capable of understanding the proceedings. Although he had high blood pressure, which was normal for a man of his age and weight, they found that his heart was in good condition for his age. A battery of psychological tests showed that he could both understand and reason.

Aside from the general fatigue that comes with old age, resulting in a lack of mental stamina, Demjanjuk suffered from two serious medical conditions. He had myelodysplastic syndrome (MDS), a preleukemia bone marrow disease accompanied by severe anemia and fatigue that necessitated blood transfusions every four to six weeks. And he had spinal stenosis, a narrowing of the spinal canal that compresses the spinal cord and pinches the nerves. It was an extremely painful condition that required pain-relief injections. Given his health problems, the medical team recommended courtroom sessions of no longer than ninety minutes and no more than two a day.

Throughout the trial, Demjanjuk's court-appointed defense attorney, Ulrich Busch, would ask the court to terminate the proceedings because his client was too sick and in too much pain to follow them. Presiding judge Alt would consult with the court-appointed doctor, Albrecht Stein, then rule that Demjanjuk was healthy and the trial would continue. It was almost as if Busch were attempting to build a case for a later appeal if the court found Demjanjuk guilty.

CHAPTER FIFTY-SIX

Iwan of Sobibor

John Demjanjuk didn't mince words in his opening statement to the court. He called Germany arrogant in charging him with accessory to murder. Sobibor was a German SS camp, he said, run by German SS officers who forced Soviet POWs to work there. Germans should be on trial, not a low-level Ukrainian slave laborer.

Germany is to blame for the deaths of eleven million Ukrainians, he said.

Germany is to blame for the loss of my home in Ukraine.

Germany is to blame for condemning me to die of starvation in a POW camp.

Germany is to blame for the destruction of my family, my hopes, and my future.

How dare Germany use a former Soviet POW to distract the nation from the real criminals of Sobibor—the men who ordered the execution of innocent Jews and ran the gas chambers!

So began the trial of Iwan of Sobibor. The gallery didn't boo or hiss during Demjanjuk's tirade against Germany. Perhaps it was because his court-appointed attorney, Ulrich Busch, read the statement for him, making it more impersonal and lessening the sting.

• • •

To obtain a guilty verdict from the court, German prosecutors had to prove two things. First, that John Demjanjuk had been at Sobibor, and second, that he had committed a war crime there. That made it very different from the 2001 denaturalization trial in Cleveland, where all OSI prosecutors had to prove was that John Demjanjuk had been at Sobibor and had lied about it on his visa application.

The German prosecutors' task was made more difficult because there still was no credible living eyewitness who could place Demjanjuk at Sobibor and testify to seeing him commit a war crime there. Once again, it appeared that the Munich trial, like the one in Cleveland, would be a trial by archives.

For the *fourth time*, the Trawniki card was on trial, and for the fourth time technical experts debated its authenticity. Most had testified at other Demjanjuk trials in Cleveland and in Jerusalem. None offered compelling new evidence or fresh arguments. The validity of the signature of Iwan Demjanjuk on the ID card was still the main bone of contention. As in Jerusalem, the trial in Munich boiled down to whose expert witnesses—prosecution or defense—appeared more expert.

As U.S. prosecutors had done in the 2001 denaturalization trial, German prosecutors offered into evidence the six documents supporting the authenticity of the Trawniki card, from the Majdanek disciplinary report to the Flossenbürg roster. Once again, the defense argued forgery without offering proof of forgery.

As U.S. prosecutors had done in the 2001 denaturalization trial, German prosecutors entered the Danilchenko Protocol into evidence. The former Sobibor guard had sworn in his statement that he served with Iwan Demjanjuk at Sobibor. His description of Demjanjuk was accurate, and he had positively identified the Trawniki card photo as that of Iwan Demjanjuk. Unfortunately, Danilchenko had died before OSI or anyone else could cross-examine him.

Once again, the defense in Germany argued that Danilchenko's statement was suspect because the KGB had extracted it under torture. German historian Dieter Pohl supported that argument from the stand. He urged the court to treat Danilchenko's statement with "highest caution" since the former Trawniki man appeared to be telling the KGB what it wanted to hear.

In an attempt to rebut Danilchenko, the defense offered into evidence a statement made by Iwan Ivchenko, who had served as an SS guard at Sobibor at the same time Demjanjuk allegedly served there. Ivchenko said he didn't recall a fellow guard named Iwan Demjanjuk.

Whom should the court believe? The Trawniki man who said he saw Demjanjuk at Sobibor or the Trawniki man who said he did not?

• • •

The prosecution was not without potential live witnesses. But they were a mixed blessing. Two former SS guards and a Sobibor survivor had volunteered to testify for the prosecution. Each proved to be a jack-in-the-box—unpredictable and unexpected.

Alex Nagorny, a ninety-three-year-old former Ukrainian Trawniki man, testified that he had worked with and shared a barrack with Iwan Demjanjuk at Flossenbürg. The court asked Nagorny if the man lying on the stretcher in front of him was the Iwan Demjanjuk he had known. Nagorny stepped away from the witness stand, walked over to the gurney, and studied Demjanjuk's face.

"That's definitely not him," he said. "No resemblance."

Nagorny went on to help the defense even more. He testified that when the war was over, the Trawniki men destroyed their ID cards (incriminating evidence) so that the Allies would not deliver them to the Soviets as Nazi collaborators. Wouldn't Iwan Demjanjuk have done the same? If so, where did the Demjanjuk ID card on trial in Munich come from?

Eighty-nine-year-old *Samuel Kunz*, another Trawniki man, volunteered to testify that all SS guards knew what happened to the Jews who entered a death camp even if they didn't work near the gas chambers. They all understood they were part of a killing machine.

Prosecutors had known for several years that Kunz had been a guard at Belzec, but they declined to prosecute him because they had no evidence that he had committed a *specific* murder as defined by the 1871 German penal code. However, during their background check for the Demjanjuk trial, prosecutors learned that Kunz, an ethnic national who had been living in Germany for sixty years, had personally shot at least a dozen Jews at Belzec.

Germany charged Kunz with assisting in the murder of 430,000 Jews at Belzec, but he never faced a panel of judges. Someone was one step ahead of the court. On a cold night in April 2011, assassins entered Kunz's home in Bonn, snatched him from his bed, and left him outside to die of hypothermia.

• • •

Not long after the Demjanjuk trial opened in Munich, a Moscow correspondent for a Czech radio station happened to see a brief item in a Russian newspaper about a former POW from Sobibor named *Alexei Vaitsen*. The news item led her to a cramped apartment in Ryazan, Russia, a picturesque city two hundred miles southeast of Moscow.

Vaitsen was an eighty-seven-year-old former Jewish Red Army officer who had been imprisoned at Sobibor. Assigned an important role in the October 1943 uprising, he escaped during the revolt and fled into the forest. Like the military commander of the uprising, Soviet Army Lieutenant Alexander "Sasha" Pechersky, Vaitsen rejoined the Red Army and survived the war, only to suffer severe discrimination as a Russian Jew in the Soviet Union.

Vaitsen told the correspondent that he had seen Iwan Demjanjuk at Sobibor leading a *Waldkommando* (Forest Kommando) out of the camp into the forest to cut wood. Vaitsen said that he later recognized Iwan Demjanjuk from an old photo published in a Soviet newspaper. The photo Vaitsen was referring to was probably the Trawniki card picture that the KGB released to the Soviet press in 1976.

"It's him," Vaitsen said. "I know him. I'm one hundred percent certain."

German prosecutors did not find Vaitsen credible. Why did he wait thirty years to come forward, they asked.

But Vaitsen hadn't come forward. He had been found and interviewed.

Why didn't he say something during the Israeli trial, they asked.

Assuming he even knew about the Ivan the Terrible trial, Vaitsen suffered from wartime nightmares and never talked about what he had seen and endured during the war, according to family members.

Vaitsen had testified at the Soviet trials of Trawniki men in the 1960s during which he identified several Sobibor guards by name. Why didn't he mention Iwan Demjanjuk, the German prosecutors asked.

Vaitsen knew Demjanjuk's face, but not his name. And no one showed him a picture of Iwan Demjanjuk in the 1960s.

German prosecutors decided not to call Vaitsen to the stand, but they did call two other Sobibor survivors to testify. Neither one recognized Iwan Demjanjuk's name as a Sobibor guard. Neither one could identify his photo or recognize him in court as an SS guard they had seen at Sobibor. Neither one had ever entered camp three, where the Jews were gassed. All they could do from the witness stand was describe the killing process at Sobibor from personal observation and which roles the SS guards played in it.

Thomas "Toivi" Blatt, whose father, mother, and sister were murdered at Sobibor on the day the family arrived there, made an important statement during the trial. Commenting on his failure to identify John Demjanjuk as a Sobibor SS guard, Blatt said: "I can't say I remember Demjanjuk's face. But frankly, I can't even recall [the faces] of my father or mother after so many decades." Blatt testified that he saw SS guards enter camp three through the camouflaged gate. He heard gunshots. He heard the motor start up and rumble. He heard screams. But he couldn't say precisely what the SS guards did once they entered camp three. Did they beat prisoners? Whip them? Force them into the gas chamber? Did they torture them like Ivan the Terrible did at Treblinka? Should the court assume that if the Treblinka SS guards drove Jews into the gas chambers, Sobibor guards must have done the same thing? Furthermore, Blatt could not testify that *every single* SS guard at Sobibor had actually worked in camp three at one time or another.

In sum, all Blatt could testify to was that there were SS guards at Sobibor and they were essential to the killing process.

• • •

The important role of all SS guards in the Sobibor killing process was not lost on the court. But what weight should it give that participation? During the sixteen months of killing at the camp, approximately 250,000 Jews were gassed. As an alleged SS guard at the death camp, John Demjanjuk assisted the SS in murdering them. But how many deaths was he co-responsible for?

Early in the trial, presiding judge Alt took out his calculator and tallied up from transportation records how many Jews arrived at Sobibor between March 1943 and September 1943, when John Demjanjuk allegedly served there. Alt came up with 29,900. Ninety-nine percent of them were Dutch.

Defense attorney Busch objected. The court was assuming, he argued, that Demjanjuk—if he had ever been at Sobibor—was working at the camp seven days a week. Guards had days off and leave time, Busch reminded the court. Shouldn't days away from the camp be factored into the court's murder formula?

Judge Alt agreed and recalculated. He came up with 29,060. Busch accepted the number and the court began the tedious task of reading into the record individual transport numbers and names, if known. Readers spoke rapidly in hushed, flat, monotonous tones:

"From Amsterdam on June 21, 1943, six hundred. . . from Westerbork . . ."

To the spectators in the gallery, it sounded as if the court was reading names and numbers from the Munich white pages. But to the living who lost loved ones at Sobibor, it was an emotional moment. When they heard Alt say the name of their mother or brother, father or sister, they burst into tears.

When Alt finished the reading of names, the testimony of relatives who had lost family at Sobibor began. Under German law, these prosecution witnesses could be co-plaintiffs in the trial and they could be represented by their own attorneys. They testified through their tears and rage about how they suffered because they lost a mother or father, brother or sister at Sobibor. With hands shaking, they read from the last letter they had received from a loved one, or held up a faded picture for the judges to see. Few wanted revenge. All wanted to keep Sobibor alive in the collective memory of the world as a tribute to those who died there. A spiritual gravestone.

• • •

Somewhere along the way—with all the killing process calculations—the court seemed to have lost sight of *why* John Demjanjuk was on trial. The proceedings were about the men, women, and children murdered at Sobibor, not about statistics. *Philip Bialowitz*, the second survivor witness to testify, played an important role in reminding the court of this fact.

Like the Treblinka survivors at the Israeli trial, Bialowitz brought reality into the courtroom. He directed the court's attention away from numbers and relatives and onto the victims themselves. In so doing, he made Sobibor come painfully alive for the seven judges and the packed gallery. Bialowitz's two sisters and a niece were murdered at Sobibor on the day they all arrived. He survived by conning the SS into believing that he had been a pharmacist's assistant before he was captured. That he could be useful at Sobibor if spared.

Bialowitz's first job was cutting the hair of women and girls who had been told that Sobibor was a transit camp. After a delousing, a silver-tongued SS officer announced over a loudspeaker, they would be sent to a work camp along with the rest of their families.

"Many of these women came from Holland and they appeared to believe that this was a resettlement camp," Bialowitz testified. "Before I cut their hair, some of these Dutch women politely asked me not to cut [it] too short. They showed no signs of knowing that they were about to be murdered. Hundreds of women at a time passed through the hair-cutting shed in this manner. Within minutes of cutting their hair, we heard the roar of a motor, mixed with a horrible mass scream, at first loud and strong, then gradually subsiding into silence."

The SS also ordered Bialowitz to help unload passengers and luggage from the boxcars. The Dutch, who had no idea where they were or what would happen to them, would offer him a tip for helping them with their bags. "My heart was bleeding," Bialowitz testified, "because I knew that in less than an hour they would perish."

One experience at the unloading platform gave him a lifetime of nightmares. When he slid open a boxcar door, an overpowering smell of decomposing bodies assaulted him. Half the people crammed inside were dead. The rest were demented and barely alive.

"We began helping the few survivors down from the train," he testified. "Despite being in such pitiful and helpless condition, they were brutally beaten and shot by several German officers and Ukrainian guards.

"Next, we removed the corpses. I tried to pull a dead woman off the train, but her skin came away in my hands. I saw another woman with a baby on top of her. Both were dead and swollen. They were still embracing each other."

• • •

When attorney Ulrich Busch finally began his opening statement for the defense, he raised two critical questions that went to the very heart of the Munich trial. "How can you say that those who gave the orders were innocent," Busch argued, "and the one who received the order is guilty. There is a moral and legal double standard being applied today."

Busch had a valid point. Germany had tried eleven Sobibor SS officers in Hagen in 1965–66. One committed suicide. One was sentenced to life in prison. Five got three to eight years. Four SS officers were acquitted because no one could testify that they had seen them commit a specific murder as required for conviction under the 1871 German penal code.

Busch's second perceptive question drew a hiss from the mostly Jewish spectators in the gallery. How did a Ukrainian SS guard differ from a Jewish Kapo? To even ask the question was viewed by survivors and their families as an anti-Semitic insult. But the question begged for an answer.

Jewish Kapos were prisoners appointed by the Nazis to help manage and discipline their fellow Jews. They didn't volunteer for the job, but many prisoners, if not most, would have done so if asked. The job came with privileges and power and, most important, it increased the chances of survival.

Kapos performed a number of tasks at Sobibor. They were in charge of roll calls and had to tell the SS officer in charge if anyone was missing, usually because of illness. The assignment was far from humanitarian. Sickness meant inability to work. Inability to work meant death. When someone did not show up for roll call, the Kapo had to order a team to go get the missing prisoner. An SS officer or an SS guard would then walk or drag the sick Jew to camp three to be shot.

Kapos served as barracks supervisors or warders. They were supposed to be the eyes and ears of the SS. If a Kapo failed to report a problem, such as talk of escape or eating stolen food, and the SS found out about it later, the Kapo would be punished with a whip or a gun.

Kapos with whips supervised work Kommandos. They accompanied SS men as they made their rounds of the workshops looking for shirkers or hoping to catch some Jew breaking a rule. If a worker was at fault, the Kapo would be ordered to give him or her twenty-five lashes.

Kapos also supervised their fellow Jews who were sorting the clothes and belongings of those who had just been gassed. He was required to report to his SS superior any acts of sabotage, such as cutting up good clothes to make them useless to the Reich, or the theft of tins of milk and sardines or gold coins and jewels. The money and stones could later be traded with the SS guards for food or sewn into prisoners' clothes in case they ever escaped.

Sobibor Jews did not resent or hate their Kapos, who, like them, were merely trying to survive. But they did distinguish between good and bad Kapos. A good Kapo whipped a fellow Jew as lightly as he could get away with. He shared his extra food. He helped tend the bloody welts of those whom he had been forced to beat. He tried to cover for the sick.

Sobibor Jews trusted their good Kapos so much that they invited one to play a critical role in the October 1943 escape.

A bad Kapo was a Nazi sycophant who curried favor in the hope that he would be spared in the end. He whipped fellow Jews with enthusiasm. He reported stolen food. He sought out the sick for execution. He was a stoolie and a snitch. Sobibor prisoners distrusted their bad Kapos so much that they assassinated one—a German Jew whom they called "Berliner"—because he was a snitch and endangered their escape plan.

The Kapo and the Trawniki man had several things in common. They were both prisoners of war. Neither had necessarily volunteered for their death camp job. If they had refused to work with the Nazis, they would have been punished. Both were rewarded with privileges for their collaboration. As part of the killing process, both were ordered to commit acts of brutality. Under the U.S. Supreme Court ruling in the Fedorenko case, neither the guard nor the Kapo was eligible for a U.S. visa because involuntary collaboration was not an extenuating circumstance under the 1948 Displaced Persons Act.

The major difference between the Trawniki man and the Kapo was that the SS planned to kill their Kapos in the end. They had no plans to kill their Trawniki men. Other differences were a matter of degree.

If a prisoner refused to be a Kapo, he most probably would be killed. If a Trawniki man requested not to be posted to camp three or asked for a transfer from a death camp because he could not stomach killing Jews, he probably would not be punished or court-martialed and executed.

The rewards granted to a Sobibor SS guard went far beyond those given to a Kapo. The Trawniki man was paid. He got days off away from the camp. Once he was out of the camp, he was free to move around. He got regular leave, decent food, and clean, warm clothes. And he could earn promotions with better pay.

According to Sobibor survivor accounts, the SS guards at Sobibor did their jobs with sadistic enthusiasm. The good Kapo did his job with a degree of personal pain and compassion.

Survivors were quick to point out that the SS guards at Sobibor could easily desert. Were they applying a double standard? If the SS guard had the moral obligation to take a risk and flee, didn't the Jews at Sobibor also have a moral obligation to take a risk and escape?

There is a huge difference between escaping and deserting. To try to escape from Sobibor was, for the most part, an act of suicide. Philip Bialowitz testified about why he didn't try it until the uprising. "I often thought about escape," he said. "But Sobibor was surrounded by barbed wire, guard towers, a mine field, and a deep forest. Sometimes, in the middle of the night, a wild animal would trigger one of the mines and we were marched out of our beds and counted like diamonds."

The SS guards didn't have to escape. All they had to do was disappear into the forest on their day off and join a partisan group. Many did, as Holocaust historian Peter Black points out. There were 388 known Trawniki men who served at Sobibor over the life of the camp. At least twenty-nine (7.5 percent) either deserted or tried to desert.

There is no record that Iwan Demjanjuk ever tried to desert from Sobibor, assuming he was at Sobibor. Trawniki man Ignat Danilchenko said in his sworn statement that when the SS closed Flossenbürg and reassigned him and Iwan Demjanjuk to another camp safe from the advancing Red Army, he decided to desert. He asked Demjanjuk to join him. Demjanjuk declined.

The SS guards at Sobibor had a second realistic option. There were between 150 and 200 SS guards at the camp and only twenty-five to thirty SS men. How hard would it have been to pick a day and an hour and start shooting? There was a *prisoner* revolt at Sobibor—the largest escape from any European prison camp during World War II—but there was no *SS guard* revolt. In fact, SS guards shot and killed as many escaping Jews as they could during their uprising.

Sobibor survivors argue that Iwan Demjanjuk chose to stay at Sobibor because life there was cushier and safer than life in the forest.

• • •

Those who followed the Munich trial closely have concluded that John Demjanjuk didn't have a chance for acquittal. His court-appointed attorney didn't enjoy a fat defense wallet or an army of researchers at his elbow. He worked diligently, argued even harder, but managed to irritate, if not alienate, the panel of judges with groundless motions to kill or delay the proceedings. His aggressive attitude toward the bench got to associate judge Thomas Lenz during a court session one day.

"You don't have to sneer at me," Lenz yelled at Busch. "Stop doing that."

An analysis of the body language of bored judges, the questions they asked Busch and the defense witnesses, and the constant rejection of defense motions—presiding judge Alt had as many as twelve sitting on his desk at any given time—signaled that the judges were not buying the repetitious arguments of the defense. They appeared to be saying: Who are you trying to kid, Herr Busch? He was at Sobibor.

German trial observer and reporter Gisela Friedrichsen described Busch in unflattering but fair terms. "One doesn't need to like attorney Busch as a person," she wrote in *Der Spiegel*. "One can criticize him for his constant use of abstruse, refuted or unproven arguments. Or for his fruitless motions for rejects, for stay of proceedings or for relief, and his haphazard applications to produce evidence, which numbers in the hundreds and only wasted time. Or his uncontrolled outbursts against the presiding judge Ralph Alt, which truly made his job difficult, as well as against the joint plaintiffs and even against the families of the victims.

"But given the plethora of documents that attest to the detailed record-keeping of the extermination machinery and his client's proximity to that machinery, Busch defended Demjanjuk with his back to the wall. He knew that it was a hopeless case, but he fought nevertheless.

"He should not have to apologize for this."

Given the court's assumption that John Demjanjuk was at Sobibor, would the judges acquit him under the statutes of the criminal code of 1871? Or would the court *set a precedent* and convict him of accessory to murder? If it did convict him, was the German court making John Demjanjuk a scapegoat for sixty years of guilt and selective justice?

The answer to those questions depended on how the panel of seven judges defined the ambiguous word "collaborator."

CHAPTER FIFTY-SEVEN

Who Is a Collaborator?

W*ho is a Nazi collaborator* is such a delicate question in the context of the Holocaust that resistance to examining it and its horrendous implications is fierce and emotional. As a result, the question is so neglected that there isn't a nuanced vocabulary to describe it, as there is for the action of killing.

In both popular and legal language, killing can include, among other things: voluntary or involuntary manslaughter, first-degree or second-degree murder, negligent homicide, accidental death, malpractice, suicide, self-defense, capital punishment, and a soldier's wartime duty. If a man collaborates with an enemy who commits war crimes, however, he is simply a "collaborator."

At the risk of offending Holocaust survivors and their families, it is important to understand and define *who is a collaborator* in the context of World War II in order to establish a framework of reference for the German trial of John Demjanjuk as SS guard Iwan of Sobibor.

Collaboration is a neutral word. It means to work with someone to accomplish a mutually agreed-upon end. In the context of World War II, however, the word *collaboration* has taken on a pejorative meaning—to help an enemy who is engaged in crimes against humanity. Directly or indirectly by association, the collaborator is, or is perceived as, a contributor to the crime of the enemy.

Such an interpretation of collaboration is too broad to be meaningful or useful. Under that definition, tens of millions of Europeans were guilty of collaborating with the occupying Nazi enemy, in every European country from France in the west to Lithuania in the east.

One of the first politicians to use the term *collaboration* in the context of World War II was Marshal Philippe Pétain, who set up the Vichy regime in France in July 1940. Pétain proclaimed collaboration with Germany in implementing its genocidal goals as the foundation of the new Vichy government. Other regimes in German-occupied countries like Croatia and Belorussia, to name just two, also founded their governance on similar collaboration with Germany.

The Nazi occupation of a country presented the citizens of that country with five survival options: flee to another country, sit tight and wait it out, resist the occupiers and their puppet governments, work *for* the occupiers and their puppet governments, or work *with* them.

Flight was not always possible. When it was, it frequently meant jumping from the fire into the frying pan. Sit tight and wait was a more practical option. But to sit tight and survive frequently necessitated compromises like remaining silent in the face of brutality, robbery, and murder, or looking the other way.

The resistance option was a heroic choice that went beyond the dictates of wartime morality. If a civilian chose to resist the enemy at the risk of his own life and the lives of his family, he could do it in a guerilla or partisan movement like the French Resistance, many of whose fighters ended up at Camp Dora. Or a civilian could resist in smaller, less visible ways while trying to survive and protect his family, as thousands did. He could secretly hide a resistance fighter, tend his wounds, feed her, supply him with tactical information, or warn her of danger. He could assist a downed Allied flier, as many did. All these actions were done at great risk. All went beyond the dictates of wartime morality.

The last two survival options, working *for* the enemy and working *with* the enemy, suggest distinctions within the meaning of the term "wartime collaboration." These distinctions encompass an array of blacks and whites and disturbing shades of gray.

Hundreds of thousands of Europeans worked *for* the Nazis without necessarily working *with* them to implement their goals. The word *for* implies a paying job such as cooking for the Nazi occupiers, minding their children, tending their gardens, washing their cars, cleaning the villas they had confiscated for themselves, becoming their girlfriends for jam and nylons, dancing and singing for them, typing their letters, translating their documents, and interpreting for them.

After the war, many who worked *for* the Nazis were stigmatized as Nazi collaborators. They were frequently shunned and suffered discrimination if they chose to remain in the town where they were known and recognized, unless everyone else in the town had done the same thing.

Is cooking for the Nazis collaboration?

Is washing the car of a Nazi officer collaboration? What if the car were used in a roundup of Jews destined for Auschwitz?

Is typing for the Nazis collaboration? What if the secretarial job is in a Gestapo office?

Is translating documents for the Nazis collaboration? What if the document being translated is a list of men, women, and children targeted for roundup and execution?

At the other end of the collaboration spectrum, hundreds of thousands of Europeans in both the west and the east crossed a moral divide and worked *with* the Nazi occupiers. They denounced Jews, Gypsies, resistance fighters, Jehovah's Witnesses, and other Nazi enemies. As paid spies, they infiltrated organizations hostile to the Nazis. They joined Nazi-controlled police forces. They volunteered as Einsatzkommandos. They helped the Germans round up Jews and other civilians. They murdered civilians. They guarded concentration, work, and death camps. They helped gas Jews. They voluntarily joined the German regular army or the Waffen SS.

There were also thousands who stood by and watched the brutal murder of civilians. A German colonel stationed in Kaunas, Lithuania, for example, was passing by a crowd that was jeering, clapping, and shouting "Bravo!" He saw mothers raising their small children over their heads so they could watch whatever was going on. Curious, the officer stopped to investigate.

"On the concrete courtyard," he later wrote, "there was a blonde man aged around twenty-five, of medium height. He was taking a rest and supporting himself on a wooden club which was as thick as an arm and went up to his chest. At his feet lay fifteen, twenty people who were dead or dying. Water poured from a hose and washed their blood into a drain.

"Just a few paces behind this man stood around twenty men who—guarded by several armed civilians—awaited their gruesome execution in silent submission. Beckoned with a curt wave, the next one stepped up silently and was . . . beaten to death with the wooden club, and every blow met with enthusiastic cheers from the audience."

When all the victims were dead, the executioner climbed on the heap of corpses and began playing the Lithuanian national anthem on an accordion. The crowd broke into patriotic song.

Is watching the murder of civilians and doing nothing about it working with the Nazis?

Is cheering and egging on the murderer of Jews working with the Nazis?

Is jeering and spitting on the prisoners marching through the village of Dachau to the SS concentration camp located there working with the Nazis?

Working with the Nazis prompts its own distinction: *criminal or noncriminal*? Dieter Pohl, a historian at the German Institute for Contemporary History, estimated that more than two hundred thousand non-Germans committed war crimes while working with the Nazis. Shooting a Jew is clearly a collaboration crime. But what about:

Denouncing a Jew either gratis or for a kilo of sugar?

Looting the homes of Jews after they have been murdered?

Guarding a factory as a Trawniki man?

Guarding a Nazi labor camp as a Trawniki man without specifically killing a prisoner?

There are many reasons why Europeans worked with the Nazis. They include force, blackmail, greed, or revenge; fear of being killed if one refused; fear of starvation or losing one's job; the need to feed and protect one's family; an opportunity to improve or advance one's career; a chance to buy a better lifestyle; and an opportunity to murder one's ideological and religious enemies—communists, Jews, Poles, Gypsies, Orthodox Serbs—without being punished for the crime.

Motivation for working with the Nazis prompts another distinction: *voluntary or involuntary*. That distinction asks the question: Under what circumstances in wartime is it morally permissible to voluntarily work for the Nazis?

Involuntary collaboration is frequently a simple black-and-white issue. The Nazis conscripted non-German civilians of occupied countries into the Waffen SS. They were never asked, "Would you like to help us kill

Soviet soldiers?" At the death camps, worker Jews were not asked, "Would you like to cut the hair of the girls and women about to die in the gas chambers?" The eighty non-German guards transferred from Trawniki to Sobibor were not asked, "Would you like to work in a death camp?"

Voluntary collaboration is more problematic. What is a morally acceptable reason to voluntarily collaborate with the Nazis? To avoid being shot? To avoid starving to death? To protect one's family from retaliation if one refuses? Out of a need for a paying job to feed one's family?

Where is the moral line in wartime?

When a new prisoner arrives at a death camp and volunteers to work with the Nazis as a tailor, blacksmith, shoemaker, or knitter, is he or she really volunteering?

When a Soviet POW voluntarily agrees to work with the Nazis in an unspecified job, is he really volunteering?

Where one draws the moral line suggests another distinction: *life or death*. If a Jew standing in the selection line at a death camp does not volunteer to make boots for the SS men at the camp, he *will* die. Is his "voluntary" decision under those circumstances really involuntary? Is the law of survival higher than the moral law that forbids working for an enemy who commits crimes against humanity?

If a Soviet POW does not agree to work for the Nazis in an unspecified job, he faces a high probability of either being executed for refusing or of eventually dying from starvation, overwork, or disease. Unlike the death camp prisoner who will *certainly* be killed if he refuses to work for or with the Nazis, the POW does not face certain death. Is he morally justified in working for the Nazis in order to increase his chances of survival?

If a German soldier or a civilian volunteer is ordered to shoot Jews lined up in front of a ditch in a forest in Estonia, he could be executed on the spot for refusing to follow orders. He faces a personal life-or-death decision. Is he morally obligated to be killed rather than to kill? Is it murder to kill someone when the alternative is death for oneself? Is the decision to choose to disobey the order an act of morality or an act of heroism?

If a death camp SS man is ordered by a superior officer to kill a sick old man at the "infirmary" and refuses, is it clear that he will be executed by his SS commander? Is it a life-or-death decision? If it's not clear, is he morally obligated to take the risk and refuse to obey the order?

There were thousands of Nazis and those who worked for them who never personally killed a civilian. Are they war criminals? That question leads to still another distinction clearly defined in the 1871 German criminal code: *specific hands-on crime* or *unspecific abetted crime*.

A civilian denounces a Jew. The Jew is executed. The denouncer did not pull the trigger. He was a voluntary collaborator in the process of killing a Jew without specifically killing him. Is he guilty of a crime? What if he did not know the Jew would be killed? What if he believed the Jew would be sent to a work camp in the east?

A camp commandant like Trawniki boss Karl Streibel never killed a Jew. All he did was train the men who did. He played a major role in the process of killing without specifically killing. Is he guilty of a crime?

A death camp Trawniki man stands in a guard tower. His job is to prevent escapes. There are no escapes, so he doesn't shoot anyone. He is part of the killing process without specifically killing someone. Is he guilty of a crime?

An SS officer works in the death camp office. He has a pistol that he never uses. He is never ordered to drive Jews into a gas chamber. He is never ordered to shoot the old and the sick at the "Infirmary." He is part of the killing process because he helps administer the death camp. Is he guilty of a crime?

Assuming John Demjanjuk trained at Trawniki and served at Sobibor, he may have volunteered to drive a truck for the Nazis without knowing what it would carry. He did not volunteer to be trained at the Trawniki school. He did not request a job at Sobibor. Once at Sobibor, he did not choose which jobs he would and would not do. The SS could order him to perform any of the grim tasks at a death camp:

- Guarding the perimeter or the worker Jews inside the camp or those who worked in Kommandos outside the camp; unloading the new arrivals from boxcars.
- Keeping order at the unloading dock to prevent a revolt; making sure the new arrivals undressed and that the girls and women had their hair shorn.
- Leading or driving the victims up to and then into the gas chambers.
- Supervising the burial or cremation of the corpses and the extraction of gold teeth.
- Shooting or prodding resisters.
- Killing the old and the sick at the "Infirmary."

If John Demjanjuk never specifically killed or severely brutalized anyone at Sobibor but was only a cog in the killing process, did he commit a war crime or a crime against humanity under German law?

• • •

On May 12, 2011, the Munich court issued its ruling. The court found that:

- Without a doubt, John Demjanjuk served as an SS guard at the Sobibor death camp from March 1943 to September 1943.
- As an SS guard, John Demjanjuk knew that the 29,060 Jews who arrived at Sobibor while he served there were murdered.
- As an SS guard, John Demjanjuk assisted the Germans in running a smooth killing machine.

After acknowledging that Demjanjuk had already spent ten years in Israeli and German jails, the court sentenced him to five years in prison. Because he was not a flight risk due to poor health and age, the court freed Demjanjuk from prison until all appeals were settled.

The court decision in Munich came thirty-four years after the United States first charged John Demjanjuk with lying on his visa application about his activities during World War II.

Part Five: Epilogue

After thirty-four years of hearings and trials in the United States, Israel, and Germany, the panel of seven German judges found John Demjanjuk guilty of aiding and abetting the Nazis in the murder of more than 29,000 Jews at the death camp of Sobibor. Although the Munich trial was an important legal benchmark in the search for justice, it did not provide closure.

The *trial* of John Demjanjuk left the *case* of John Demjanjuk legally, intellectually, and emotionally unresolved. Some observers were satisfied with the verdict and sentencing. But more were disappointed. Most were simply relieved that it was over, except for the tears and rants. They took comfort in the thought that in a short time there would be no one left to cry and rail.

For *Sobibor survivors* and *relatives* of the victims who died in the gas chambers there, Munich brought a measure of emotional satisfaction and peace. That the five-year prison sentence was light was irrelevant. Justice was done, and that was all they had asked for in their emotional pleadings before the court.

Munich was the funeral service they never had. Their last good-bye.

For the Treblinka survivors, however, the trial in Germany brought no peace. Those who had died since the Israeli Supreme Court found John Demjanjuk not guilty went to their graves convinced that he was Ivan the Terrible. The Treblinka survivors still alive believe that Ivan of Sobibor *was also* Ivan the Terrible of Treblinka and should have been swinging from a rope, not freed on his own recognizance because he was too old and disabled to run and hide.

The Ukrainians who believed John Demjanjuk was the victim of an international Jewish conspiracy against émigrés still believe that. Jews understandably thirst for revenge, as those Ukrainians still argue, but unfortunately Jews have chosen to vent their blind rage at working-class Americans who also survived the horrors of World War II.

The Jews who believed there is no such thing as an innocent World War II Ukrainian still believe that. Without the complicit silence and active collaboration of Ukrainians, those Jews still argue, the Nazis could never have robbed and murdered nearly a million Ukrainian Jews. They say Ukrainians continue to hide behind their flag, calling the Nazi collaborators among them heroes in the fight against communism and Soviet domination.

Those who believed John Demjanjuk was a pawn in a political game still believe that. They say the Office of Special Investigations used him to buy its continued existence. And Israel used him to educate a new generation of Israelis for whom the Holocaust was only a dry chapter in a history book. And Germany used him to prove that it took seriously its responsibility to try Nazi war criminals, setting a critical legal precedent in the process.

The trial left Demjanjuk supporters, inside and outside the émigré community, bitterly disappointed. To try an old man for something he did in Poland nearly seventy years earlier, when he was a twenty-one-year-old prisoner of war facing starvation, was a form of court-sanctioned torture. How just was it to find a camp guard guilty of assisting in the deaths of thousands, but to acquit four SS officers who ran the camp and issued the orders, as a court had done in Hagen, Germany, in 1965?

Those who believed the KGB duped the United States and framed John Demjanjuk still believe that. In spite of all the tests and expert testimony to the contrary, they still believe that the Trawniki card is a clever KGB forgery, and they continue to point out real or perceived flaws in the card as proof. They will never find satisfaction, however, because their version of the truth will always be just one unexplained blemish away. The simple fact is that, although the United States is still declassifying and releasing Nazi documents, it is unlikely that any significant new evidence relating to John Demjanjuk or the Trawniki card will ever surface.

The lack of closure on the Demjanjuk case, however, does not mean that his trial in Munich was a trivial exercise in belated justice. The highly publicized proceeding has elevated the Demjanjuk case to a larger-than-life status. Like it or not, John Demjanjuk became the coda to the Nazi era. Like Demjanjuk, most alleged war criminals and the witnesses against them are either in their nineties or late eighties. They suffer from health problems, memory lapses, and dementia. More likely than not, that makes Demjanjuk the last major trial of the Nazi war crimes era, which began with the International Military Tribunal in Nuremberg in 1946 and continued in fits and starts until May 2011 in Munich, Germany.

As a coda, John Demjanjuk's trial was no heart-stopping finale. Rather, it ended with a pop and a fizzle.

However disappointed, divided, and emotionally unsatisfied the world may be with the thirty-four-year legal journey of John Demjanjuk and the 2011 Munich verdict, the frustrating ordeal—two denaturalization trials, two deportation hearings, two extradition hearings, and two criminal trials—raised an important question.

John Demjanjuk was no Holocaust architect like Adolf Eichmann, no genocide implementer like Heinrich Himmler, no medical experimenter like Dr. Josef Mengele, no gas chamber operator like Sobibor's Erich Bauer, no anti-Semitic rabble-rouser like Romanian Viorel Trifa, no Nazi puppet mayor like Belorussian Emanuel Jasiuk, no executioner like Karl Linnas, no ethnic cleanser like Croatian Andrija Artukovic, and no sadistic camp guard like Ivan the Terrible of Treblinka.

John Demjanjuk was a poor Ukrainian village boy drafted as an ordinary private into Stalin's Red Army. He was just one of four million Soviet soldiers captured and imprisoned by the Germans. By Holocaust rankings, he was just an ordinary Nazi collaborator who never rose above the rank of private as an SS guard, and just one of more than five thousand Trawniki men who agreed to work with the Nazis in the hope of surviving the war. As fate would have it, John Demjanjuk was one of the few Trawniki men that Nazis hunters caught, simply because his ID card survived the war.

As a very ordinary young man captured by the Germans and facing a high probability of either starving to death, dying from overwork and disease, or being routinely executed, John Demjanjuk poses a final question to his accusers and critics. It is a question that goes to the heart of the human condition—a question that only an ordinary man like John "Iwan" Demjanjuk could ask:

If you had been me in 1942, what would *you* have done?

THE OPEN DOOR

If the Nazi war crimes trials have ended, war crimes revelations have not. The ink on historical documents may have faded and pages may have yellowed, but the content of those pages does not suffer from failing memories or dementia. If there is any disease present, it is that of complacency, arrogance, and incompetence, which continues to shield big government, big money, and big political interests from scrutiny and prosecution.

Fortunately, the further one steps away from the Nazi era and its architects, scoundrels, and sadists, the more light shines on the past. The question is: Will anyone still care when documents now buried in file cabinets, safes, and vaults are finally declassified and released?

As the new revelations about Nazi war criminals and their collaborators find their way into the media, Americans who do care will have Eli Rosenbaum and Elizabeth Holtzman to thank. Beginning in 1980, Rosenbaum devoted almost his entire adult life to prosecuting former Nazis and Nazi collaborators, first as an OSI trial attorney, then as OSI's last director. During the more than thirty years of OSI existence, government prosecutors won 107 cases against Nazi war criminals and prevented hundreds more from entering the United States. And at least seven suspected Nazis and Nazi collaborators facing investigation committed suicide.

In 2009, the Israeli office of the Simon Wiesenthal Center issued a country-by-country report card on how aggressively and well each nation had pursued and prosecuted Nazi war criminals. The center gave the United States straight As every single year from 2000 to date. Despite this "scorecard" success, OSI's 2006 draft internal history of its search for and prosecution of Nazi war criminals in the United States noted that Rosenbaum was "haunted by the belief that additional prosecutions could have been brought had there been more resources—both financial and manpower—available."

Elizabeth Holtzman began chasing former Nazis through legislation beginning in 1974 after she reviewed the Karbach list files in New

York. Over the years, she continued to badger the Justice Department to find and expel Nazis and Nazi collaborators, through her legislative work in Congress and her international network of contacts.

Most recently, Holtzman worked as a consultant in the framing and enactment of the 1998 Nazi War Crimes Disclosure Act, sponsored by Senator Mike DeWine of Ohio and Representative Carolyn Maloney of New York. The 1978 Holtzman Amendment laid the foundation for the disclosure act, which mandated the declassification and release of files and documents dealing with Nazis known to be, or suspected of being, war criminals. The act further mandated that President Clinton create an interagency working group (IWG) to serve as a watchdog over U.S. intelligence agencies and departments that are custodians of Nazi war crimes documents. Clinton appointed Holtzman to the IWG board.

To date, more than eight million pages from the files of agencies under the umbrellas of the departments of State, Justice, and Defense have been declassified, the largest disclosure in U.S. history. Unfortunately, thousands of those pages have been removed from storage boxes and folders under the notice "Access Restricted." Thousands more have been so heavily redacted that they are virtually useless. And there are hundreds of references to files, reports, and documents either missing or still classified.

In spite of their limitations and gaps, however, the newly released documents illustrate how the FBI, the State Department, the military, and the CIA opened a wide door for former Nazis and Nazi collaborators. These documents also reveal the identities of many of the war criminals that U.S. government agencies protected in a cynical perversion of justice. How America welcomed those major war criminals stands in stark contrast to how it hounded minor war criminal John Demjanjuk.

THE F.B.I.

As incomplete as they are, the newly declassified documents lead to several inescapable conclusions about the FBI's role in protecting both proven and alleged Nazi war criminals in America. First, there can be no doubt that J. Edgar Hoover collected Nazis and Nazi collaborators like pennies from heaven. Unlike the military and its highly structured Operation Paperclip—with its specific targets, systematic falsification of visa applications, and creation of bogus biographies—Hoover had no organized program to find, vet, and recruit alleged Nazis and Nazi collaborators as confidential sources, informants, and unofficial spies in émigré communities around the country. America's number-one crime buster was guided only by opportunism and moral indifference.

Each Nazi collaborator that his agents stumbled upon, or learned about from the CIA, was both a potential spy and a potential anticommunist leader. Once they were discovered, Hoover sought them out, used them, and protected them. He had no interest in reporting alleged Nazi war criminals to the INS, the Justice Department, or the State Department for possible deportation or extradition. He appeared smug in his simplistic division of Americans into shadeless categories of bad guys and good guys, communists and anticommunists.

Hoover was careful about the number of former Nazis and Nazi collaborators he placed on the FBI payroll. If Congress or its investigative arm, the GAO, ever insisted on a tally, he could say with a straight face that there were only a handful of paid confidential sources and informants. But if one adds the war criminals he *informally* cultivated and used, the number ranges well into the hundreds.

Although some of the snapshots may be out of focus, the big picture is clear from the newly declassified documents. Hoover and the FBI knew the identities, addresses, and backgrounds of up to a thousand alleged Nazis and Nazi collaborators on whom he had files but did not report to INS, Justice, State, or OSI. Among the newly revealed Nazi collaborators that Hoover and the FBI used and protected were John Avdzej, Laszlo Agh, and Vladimir Sokolov.

During the war, Belorussian *John Avdzej* had been installed as the Nazi's puppet mayor of the Niasvizh district in western Belorussia, once part of Poland. His first mayoral job was to rid his district of all Poles. As a first step, he gave the Gestapo a list of 120 Polish intelligentsia that included journalists, professors, priests, and former military officers, according to recently declassified intelligence files. Then he took part in their execution, as well as in the murder of thousands of Jews under his political jurisdiction. The Polish Home Army condemned him to death in absentia.

The United States was responsible for bringing Avdzej to America. Hoover snapped him up and protected him until 1984, when OSI charged him with visa fraud. Facing trial and possible extradition for war crimes, Avdzej voluntarily left the United States for West Germany, where he died a free man in 1998.

• • •

Laszlo Agh was a wartime member the Hungarian Arrow Cross, an anti-Semitic group of fascists responsible for the murder of ten to fifteen thousand Hungarian Jews and the deportation to Auschwitz of another eighty thousand.

According to twelve eyewitnesses, Agh had personally rounded up, imprisoned, tortured, and killed hundreds of Hungarian Jews. The torture included forced calisthenics to the point of unconsciousness, burial in the ground up to the neck until dead, and orders to jump on ground studded with partially buried bayonets.

Agh intrigued Hoover. A bitterly anticommunist leader had fallen into his lap and Hoover quickly recruited him as an unofficial informant. When the INS began to investigate Agh, the FBI refused to cooperate. As a result, Agh was never tried for visa fraud. Like Avdzej, he died a free man.

Russian *Vladimir Sokolov* (aka Vladimir Samarin) was a senior editor and writer for *Rech* (Speech), a German-controlled, anti-Semitic Russian newspaper. He entered the United States in July 1951. Like Romanian Iron Guardist editor Viorel Trifa, Sokolov penned articles calling for the extermination of Russian Jews as enemies of the people. Jews advised Stalin, he wrote, started the German-Soviet war, and controlled the White House. Only Germany and its allies had the wisdom to understand the international Jewish conspiracy and the courage to fight "the Kikes of the world." After the war, Moscow placed Sokolov on its most-wanted list, claiming it had concrete proof that he had worked with the Gestapo as a propagandist and had personally identified Jews for execution.

The FBI, on the other hand, considered Sokolov a "sincere, outspoken anti-Communist [and] a potential source." At one point, he even taught Russian language and literature at Yale University. "How a man with no high academic credentials suddenly procured such a prestigious position is a mystery," wrote historian Norman Goda. "It is clear that the FBI used him as an informant while at Yale, possibly to report on Russian students."

If Sokolov was spying for a U.S. intelligence agency, he was probably an asset in Redcap, a CIA program to collect information on Soviets living and studying abroad. The CIA as well as the FBI wanted to know if a Soviet alien was a KGB mole and, if not, whether he or she could be flipped. Redcap assets were asked to collect information on selected targets. Besides a photograph and handwriting sample, Redcap wanted: a list of non-Soviet contacts; a description of personality, habits, and hobbies; his or her political vulnerability; and the planned date of return to the Soviet Union. Of particular interest to Redcap was information on extramarital affairs that could be used for blackmail.

OSI filed charges against Sokolov for visa fraud and won its case. A federal court stripped him of his U.S. citizenship. To avoid deportation to the Soviet Union, where he would face a public trial and certain execution, Sokolov fled to Canada. He died a free man in 1992.

• • •

However shocking and reprehensible, Hoover's use of alleged Nazis and Nazi collaborators is just a small part of the FBI story. To focus only on that dimension diverts attention away from a more important issue. In choosing to take the low moral ground, Hoover and the FBI betrayed the trust of Americans, living and dead. And in perpetrating a fifty-year conspiracy of silence, the FBI shamed Americans and made them unwitting hypocrites in the eyes of the world.

Most Americans find morally repugnant—if not criminal—the behavior of European citizens who cheered or merely stood by in silence while Nazis and Nazi collaborators dragged away their neighbors, looted their homes, shot them in the forest, or crammed them into boxcars heading east. How then must Americans judge the cadre of unelected, powerful men who welcomed some of those same murderers to America and helped them escape punishment in the name of national security?

THE STATE DEPARTMENT, THE MILITARY, AND THE CIA

If the newly declassified Nazi documents portray Hoover as an opportunistic Nazi hunter who found and used former Nazis and Nazi collaborators as paid confidential sources—or, more commonly, as unpaid informants—those same documents paint a totally different portrait of the State Department, the military, and the CIA.

Whereas the FBI had no apparent master plan to recruit former Nazis, these three agencies all had ambitious programs to find, vet, train, and fully fund whole strings of spies and guerilla fighters across Europe immediately after the war. Most were former Nazi SS officers like Otto von Bolschwing; members of fascist and anti-Semitic brotherhoods like the Croatian Ustasha, Hungarian Arrow Cross, and Romanian Iron Guard; Nazi puppet politicians like Emanuel Jasiuk and John Avdzej; Einsatzkommando volunteers like Boleslavs Maikovskis; and "freedom fighters" like Mykola Lebed and his fellow Banderists, known for their brutal ethnic cleansing of Jews and Poles.

These war criminals became spies, propagandists, saboteurs, assassins, and guerillas in the early days of the Cold War, paid with hundreds of millions of covert U.S. dollars as well as valuables captured from the Reich as spoils of war. It is a cruel irony that at least some of the loot used to hire Nazis and Nazi collaborators, who killed millions of Jews, must have been stolen from those very Jews.

Besides their postwar programs in Europe, the State Department, the military, and the CIA also had programs to bring former Nazis and Nazi collaborators into the United States. As described earlier, these programs included the CIA one hundred rule; the Displaced Persons National Interest Case; Operation Paperclip (the military and the State Department); Operation Bloodstone; a CIA guerilla army in the United States; CIA Special Forces teams; and project QRPlumb in New York.

The CIA commissioned its historian, Kevin Ruffner, to investigate the agency's use and protection of former Nazis and Nazi collaborators. In his 2003 report, *Swastika and Eagle* (several chapters of which are still classified), Ruffner correctly observed: "The records are scattered, and many were destroyed or otherwise are not readily available. The identification of every single Nazi war criminal or collaborator who came into contact with the CIA is well nigh impossible."

Ruffner's assessment, however, does not preclude a judgment about the scope of America's use and protection of Nazi war criminals. A lot is currently known about the highly structured and White House–approved programs run by the military, State Department, and intelligence organizations. Based on the information currently available, it is safe to say that the United States used, protected, and opened the door to several thousand former SS and SD officers, Gestapo agents and chiefs, Abwehr intelligence officers, Nazi propagandists and scientists,

Einsatzkommandos, Waffen SS volunteers, Vlasov's army soldiers, Nazi quislings, and ethnic cleansers.

There was no megaconspiracy or master plan to use former Nazis and Nazi collaborators for U.S. espionage operations. And there was no government policy to recruit war criminals. Rather, there was no policy *against* hiring them for a series of projects, not necessarily related and sometimes overlapping, that hid behind a mind-numbing number of code names. Often competing with each other, these projects were designed and led by unelected military, State Department, and intelligence officers acting in the name of the United States with the approval of the White House. The creators and implementers of these programs and projects hyped and preyed on the Cold War fears of politicians and citizens alike.

Guided by the principles of unenlightened pragmatism and the end justifying the means, unelected bureaucrats and superspies led the United States down a low road in the name of freedom. They duped Americans and eroded America's moral authority in the world.

If Nazis form the first tier of war criminals and Nazi collaborators the second tier, then the FBI, the State Department, the military, and the CIA have created a third tier—those policy makers, leaders, and implementers who hired, used, and protected thousands of men and women who had committed crimes against humanity.

John Demjanjuk asked the question: "If you had been me in 1942, what would *you* have done?" The story of the U.S. postwar open-door policy also poses a question: How can Americans explain and justify their government's employment and protection of thousands of World War II Nazi criminals and their collaborators:

. . . to the families of half a million American soldiers who died to rid the world of the very Nazis and fascists that the United States began to hire even before the grass had begun to grow over their graves?

. . . to the families of murdered resistance fighters in France, Holland, and Belgium, among others, who risked their lives to save downed American flyers, whose executioners the United States recruited as agents and spies?

. . . to the families of three to four million Soviet POWs murdered by the men the United States later welcomed and recruited into Special Forces and guerilla armies to protect America?

. . . to the families of millions of Polish and Ukrainian civilians exterminated by the ethnic terrorists the United States sought out and hired because of their experience?

. . . to the millions of forced laborers who never returned home, or to those who did return only to become pariahs in their homelands, because of the policies and actions of men the United States was hiding or hiring?

. . . to the nearly four hundred thousand Orthodox Serbian Christians and Gypsies slaughtered by the Catholic Croatians whom the United States later helped escape on the Vatican ratline?

. . . to Holocaust survivors and the families of six million Jewish victims of the anti-Semitic criminals the United States recruited, hired, and protected with war loot and U.S. tax dollars?

. . . and to young Americans for whom World War II is just a chapter in a history book and who ask: How could this be?

Afterword

John Demjanjuk died on March 17, 2012, in a nursing home in southern Germany. Because he died before his final appeal could be heard, he is technically presumed innocent under German law and will have no German criminal record. His body was reportedly buried at a secret location in Ohio because family members feared that his grave would be desecrated by Jewish extremists or become a national shrine to Neo-Nazis.

The Sixth U.S. Court of Appeals in Cleveland rejected the bid of the Demjanjuk estate to restore his U.S. citizenship posthumously. The court ruled that his death made his case moot. As a result, John Demjanjuk remains guilty of lying on his U.S. visa application and hiding from U.S. visa officials his wartime activity as an SS guard.

ACKNOWLEDGMENTS

I would like to thank: Margrit Grubmüller for sharing her Munich trial summaries with me; Alexander Sverdlov for reading a draft of the manuscript for errors in describing Eastern European events and persons; Don Rashke for reviewing and commenting on a draft manuscript; Maja von Oettingen for help in evaluating the John Demjanjuk trial in Munich; Selma Laydesdorff, professor of oral history and culture, Amsterdam, for sharing her contacts; Mickle Beletsky for materials from Kiev; Martin Starger for introducing me to Delphinium Books.

James Yancey at the Jimmy Carter Library and David Clark at the Harry S. Truman Library for their help in retrieving documents; William Davis, archives specialist at the Center for Legislative Archives, U.S. National Archives and Records Administration, for help in finding old legislative documents; the periodicals division of the Broward County Library, Fort Lauderdale, Florida, for help in finding and copying old newspaper articles.

Melissa K. Waterman, paralegal specialist at the National Records Center, Lee's Summit, Missouri; the legal information analysts in the Law Reading Room of the Library of Congress, especially Megan Lulofs; the reference specialists in the European Division of the Library of Congress, especially Taru R. Spiegel; the reference staff in the reading room of the U.S. National Archives, College Park, Maryland.

Special thanks to the historians and archives staff of the U.S. Holocaust Memorial Museum (USHMM), especially Michlean Amir, Peter Black, Ronald Coleman, Vincent Slatt, and Megan Lewis; and to Tom Teicholtz for the use of his Demjanjuk notes and papers held in the USHMM archives.

Very special thanks to Constance and Tim Burr for their careful review of the work in progress, their valuable comments, and their belief in this project; my wife, Paula Kaufmann, for her many edits of an emotionally draining book; Delphinium publishers Cecile Engel and Lori Milken for having the courage to publish this work; Lisl Cade for her advice and enthusiasm; Thomas F. Pitoniak for his careful copyediting; Greg Mortimer for his book design; and Carl Lennertz for shepherding this book through the editorial process.

I would also like to thank the United States Holocaust Memorial Museum for permission to include in this book four photographs from its photo archives. However, the views or opinions expressed in this book, and the context in which the images are used, do not necessarily reflect the views or policy of—nor imply approval or endorsement by—the United States Holocaust Memorial Museum.

ABBREVIATIONS

BIA	Board of Immigration Appeals
CIA	Central Intelligence Agency
CIC	Counter Intelligence Corps, U.S. Army
CROWCASS	Central Registry of War Criminals and Security Suspects
CID	Criminal Investigation Division, U.S. Army
DOJ	U.S. Department of Justice
DP	displaced person
DPA	Displaced Persons Act
DPC	Displaced Persons Commission
FBI	Federal Bureau of Investigation
FHO	Foreign Army–East (Nazi intelligence organization)
FOIA	Freedom of Information Act
GAO	General Accounting Office (since 2004, the Government Accountability Office)
INS	Immigration and Naturalization Service
IRO	International Refugee Organization
JCS	Joint Chiefs of Staff
JDL	Jewish Defense League
NSC	National Security Council
OPC	Office of Policy Coordination, Central Intelligence Agency
OSI	Office of Special Investigations, U.S. Department of Justice
OSS	Office of Strategic Services
OUN	Organization of Ukrainian Nationalists
PPS	Policy Planning Staff, U.S. Department of State
RLA	Russian Liberation Army
ROC	Romanian Orthodox Church
SD	Sicherheitsdienst (SS intelligence organization)
SLU	Special Litigation Unit, U.S. Department of Justice
SS	Schutzstaffel (Nazi paramilitary organization)
SANACC	State–Army–Navy–Air Force Coordinating Committee
SWNCC	State-War-Navy Coordinating Committee
UPA	Ukrainian Insurgent Army
RFE	Radio Free Europe
RL	Radio Liberation/Liberty
VOA	Voice of America

TIMELINE

PRE-WORLD WAR II

1920   April   Iwan Demjanjuk is born.

1932–33   Stalin creates a forced famine in Ukraine.

1938   March   Germany annexes Austria (*Anschluss*).

    July   Evian Conference is held in Evian-les-Bains, France.

    November   Kristallnacht explodes in Germany.

1939   May   German steamer *St. Louis* leaves Hamburg for Havana, Cuba.

    September   Germany invades Poland. Great Britain and France declare war on Germany.

WORLD WAR II

1940   September   Germany, Italy, and Japan sign the Tripartite Pact.

    Winter   U.S. Navy seaman Nathan Schnurman is a victim of mustard gas experiments at the U.S. Army Edgewood Arsenal in Maryland.

1941   January   Iron Guardist Viorel Trifa incites a riot and pogrom in Bucharest, Romania.

    June   Germany invades the Soviet Union.

    Fall   Demjanjuk is seriously wounded in battle at the Dnieper River.

    December   Japan bombs Pearl Harbor. United States declares war on Japan. Nazi Germany and its Axis partners declare war on the United States.

1942   May   Demjanjuk is captured by the German army during the battle of Kerch.

    June   Demjanjuk is imprisoned in Kovno, Ukraine.

	July	Demjanjuk enters the Trawniki training camp.
	September	Demjanjuk serves as a guard at Okszow, Poland.
1943	January	Demjanjuk serves as a guard at Majdanek.
	March	Demjanjuk serves as a guard at Sobibor.
	April	Bermuda Conference opens.
	August	Prisoners at Treblinka revolt.
	October	Demjanjuk is transferred to Regensburg, where he receives the SS blood-type tattoo.
		Prisoners at Sobibor revolt.
1944	June	Allies land on the beaches of Normandy.
	September	Germany launches its first V-2 rocket against London.
1945	February	Yalta Conference is convened.
	April	Private Galione discovers Camp Dora.
		Hitler commits suicide.
		President Roosevelt dies.
	May	Germany surrenders to the Western Allies.
	August	United States drops an atomic bomb on Hiroshima.
	September	Japan surrenders.

POST-WORLD WAR II

1945	May	Demjanjuk enters a DP camp at Landshut, Germany.
	August	President Truman approves Operation Paperclip.
1946	February	George F. Kennan writes the Long Telegram.

1947	July	President Truman signs the National Security Act of 1947, which reorganizes the U.S. military and creates the National Security Council (NSC) and the Central Intelligence Agency (CIA).
	September	Demjanjuk marries Vera Kowlowa in a DP camp in Landshut, Germany.
	November	Demjanjuk receives his German driver's license and begins working for the U.S. Army.
1948	March	Demjanjuk applies for and receives International Refugee Organization (IRO) refugee status.
	June	Congress passes the Displaced Persons Act.
		NSC creates the Office of Policy Coordination (OPC).
	August	White House approves Operation Bloodstone.
1951	December	Demjanjuk applies for a U.S. visa.
1952	February	Demjanjuks arrive in the United States.
	June	Congress passes a new immigration law opening the door for former Nazis and Nazi collaborators.
1958	November	Demjanjuk receives U.S. citizenship and changes his first name to John.
1964	July	*New York Times* finds Nazi collaborator Hermine Braunsteiner hiding in Queens, New York.
1972	November	Elizabeth Holtzman is elected to Congress.
	December	Anthony DeVito and Vincent Schiano blow the whistle on the Immigration and Naturalization Service (INS).
1974	June	*New York Times* publishes the Karbach list.
1975	September	Demjanjuk's name appears on Michael Hanusiak's Ukrainian list.

1976	May	Miriam Radiwker begins investigating Feodor Fedorenko and Demjanjuk in Israel.
1977	August	The U.S. government files charges of immigration fraud against Demjanjuk as Ivan the Terrible.
	September	*News from Ukraine* publishes a story about Demjanjuk as a guard at Sobibor.

THE TRIALS

1978	May	General Accounting Office issues its first report on Nazis in America.
	July	Fedorenko goes on trial in Fort Lauderdale, Florida.
1979	September	First photos of the Trawniki card appear in Ukrainian newspapers.
		Office of Special Investigations (OSI) is created.
	November	OSI receives the Fedorenko Protocol and fails to give it to the Demjanjuk defense.
1981	January	OSI attorney George Parker writes the doubt memo.
		Supreme Court overturns the Fedorenko decision.
	February	Demjanjuk's denaturalization trial opens in Cleveland.
	June	Judge Frank Battisti strips Demjanjuk of his U.S. citizenship.
1982	April	Demjanjuk deportation hearing opens.
	May	John Loftus exposes *The Belarus Secret* on CBS's *60 Minutes.*
	August	Justice Department releases Allan Ryan's report on Klaus Barbie.
1984	May	Immigration court orders Demjanjuk deported to the Soviet Union.

1985	April	Federal judge orders that Demjanjuk be extradited to Israel.
	July	The GAO issues its second Nazis-in-America report.
	August	Collaborator Tscherim Soobzokov is assassinated by a pipe bomb.
	December	Former Nazi guard Ignat Danilchenko dies.
1986	January	Demjanjuk leaves for Israel.
	November	Demjanjuk trial opens in Jerusalem.
1988	April	Demjanjuk is convicted and sentenced to death.
	December	Defense attorney Dov Eitan commits suicide or is murdered. Yoram Sheftel is attacked with acid.
1989	July	First major Dumpster papers are retrieved.
1990	February	Maria Dudek identifies Iwan Marchenko as Ivan the Terrible during a *60 Minutes* interview taped in Poland.
	March	Demjanjuk defense learns about the Fedorenko papers filed in Crimea, which identify Iwan Marchenko as Ivan the Terrible.
	May	Sheftel argues Demjanjuk appeal before the Israeli Supreme Court.
1991	June	Prosecution in Israel releases the Fedorenko files identifying Iwan Marchenko as Ivan the Terrible.
	December	Soviet Union collapses.
1992	June	U.S. Sixth Circuit Court of Appeals agrees to reopen the Demjanjuk denaturalization case and appoints a special master.
1993	July	Israeli Supreme Court acquits Demjanjuk.
	August	U.S. Sixth Circuit court rules that Demjanjuk can return to the United States. Israeli Supreme Court decides not to retry Demjanjuk as Iwan of Sobibor.

	November	U.S. Sixth Circuit court finds OSI guilty of prosecutorial misconduct and fraud upon the court and restores Demjanjuk's U.S. citizenship.
1999	May	Justice Department files a new complaint against Demjanjuk as an SS guard at Sobibor.
2002	May	Second Demjanjuk denaturalization trial opens in Cleveland.
		U.S. Sixth Circuit court strips Demjanjuk of his citizenship a second time.
2005	December	U.S. immigration judge orders Demjanjuk deported to Germany, Poland, or Ukraine.
2009	May	Demjanjuk leaves for Munich to stand trial as Iwan of Sobibor.
	November	Munich trial opens.
2011	May	Munich court finds Demjanjuk guilty of assisting in the murder of 29,060 Jews at Sobibor and sentences him to five years in prison.
		Demjanjuk files an appeal.
2012	March	Demjanjuk dies in a nursing home in Germany.

SOURCES AND NOTES

Much of this book is based on transcripts of trials and hearings. These transcripts are unedited and contain spelling and grammatical errors that appear to be made either by the translator or the transcriber. They also contain inconsistencies in the spelling of names. I have corrected these obvious errors without changing the content of the testimony in any way. The italics in transcript quotations are mine.

The spelling of Eastern European names and places poses a problem. Sometimes, there are several spelling variations for a word. For example, a Ukrainian name will have a Ukrainian spelling, a Russian spelling, and sometimes a Polish spelling. The name of a city or town can have four different variations if one adds the German name for the location. Whenever possible, I have chosen the spelling relevant to the country of origin.

The term "Eastern European," frequently used in this book, encompasses all states once under Soviet influence: Belorussia (today Belarus), Bulgaria, the former Czechoslovakia, Estonia, Hungary, Latvia, Lithuania, Moldova, Poland, Romania, Russia, and Ukraine.

Numbers are a problem. Older sources tend to have larger numbers. More recent sources tend to have smaller numbers based on the latest research. For some numbers, there is no factual base, making them little more than guesses. As scholars find more archival documents, these numbers will continue to be refined. Unless a number is commonly accepted, I have documented the number used, usually presenting it in a sliding scale such as "an estimated three to four million."

Abbreviations

AP	Associated Press
CP	*Cleveland Post*
CPD	*Cleveland Plain Dealer*
CSM	*Christian Science Monitor*
CT	*Chicago Tribune*
DFP	*Detroit Free Press*
JP	*Jerusalem Post*

LAT   *Los Angeles Times*
MH   *Miami Herald*
NA   U.S. National Archives, College Park, Maryland
NYT   *New York Times*
RG   Record Group
WP   *Washington Post*
WSJ   *Wall Street Journal*

INTRODUCTION

Sources

Berkhoff, Karel C. *Harvest of Despair: Life and Death in Ukraine Under Nazi Rule.* Cambridge, MA: Harvard University Press, 2004.

The Encyclopedia of Ukraine. Toronto: Institute of Ukrainian Studies, 2001.

Gottlieb, Mark. "The Hunt for Ivan the Terrible." *Cleveland Magazine*, November 1979.

Hryshko, Vasyl. *The Ukrainian Holocaust of 1933.* Edited and translated by Marco Carynnyk. Toronto: Bahriany Foundation, 1983.

Magosci, Paul Robert. *A History of Ukraine.* Toronto: University of Toronto Press, 1996.

Transcripts of Demjanjuk's Denaturalization Trial in Cleveland in 1981, Deportation Hearing in Cleveland in 1983–84, and Israeli Trial in Jerusalem in 1986.

Notes

This chapter makes no attempt to point out the slightly different versions of and contradictions in Demjanjuk's own story. They will be dealt with in subsequent chapters.

xi   Helped the Nazis murder 29,060 Jews: The number is an estimate taken from the railroad records of Jews transported to Sobibor during the time Demjanjuk worked there as a guard.

xii   Estimates for the number of Ukrainians that Stalin starved to death in the Great Famine range from one million to ten million. The three to four million number comes from *The Encyclopedia of Ukraine.*

xii   Besides Ukraine, the countries that have recognized the Holodomor as an act of genocide include: Australia, Brazil, Canada, Colombia, Ecuador, Estonia, Georgia, Hungary, Latvia, Lithuania, Mexico, Paraguay, Peru, Poland, and the United States.

xii   "You could see each": Hryshko, 96.

xiii   Estimated 3.3 million: Three to four million purged by Stalin is the number generally accepted by scholars.

xiii   Over 160,000 Red Army: This figure comes from German reports on the battle.

xiii   Soviet military law required Iwan to kill himself: This was Demjanjuk's testimony in every trial and hearing. For example, in the 1981 denaturalization trial he said: "I had been a soldier in the Red Army and there was a regulation that if you were going to be taken prisoner, you had to shoot yourself."

xiv During the winter of 1941–42, an estimated two million": Berkhoff, 89.

xvii According to Gottlieb: The Demjanjuk family's American sponsor was Donald Coulter; the last name of the Polish family in Indiana was Underwood; and the last name of family friends in Cleveland was Lishchuk.

PART ONE

CHAPTER ONE

Sources

Adams, Walter. "Extent and Nature of the World Refugee Problem." *Annals of the American Academy of Political and Social Science*, May 1939.

Birnbaum, Ervin. "Evian: The Most Fateful Conference of All Time." *Nativ: A Journal of Politics and the Arts*, February 2009.

Black, Conrad. *Franklin Delano Roosevelt: Champion of Freedom*. New York: Public Affairs, 2003.

Brecher, Frank. *Reluctant Ally: U.S. Foreign Policy Toward Jews from Wilson to Roosevelt*. New York: Greenwood Press, 1991.

Breitman, Richard, and Alan Kraut. *American Refugee Policy and European Jewry 1933–1945*. Bloomington: Indiana University Press, 1987.

Cantril, Hadley, and Mildred Strunk. *Public Opinion, 1935–1946*. Princeton, NJ: Princeton University Press, 1951.

Estorick, Eric. "The Evian Conference and the Intergovernmental Committee." *Annals of the American Academy of Political Science*, vol. 203, May 1939.

Feingold, Henry L. *The Politics of Rescue: The Roosevelt Administration and the Holocaust 1938–1945*. New Brunswick, NJ: Rutgers University Press, 1970.

Meir, Golda. *My Life*. London: Weidenfeld & Nicolson, 1975.

Mendelsohn, John. *The Holocaust: Selected Documents in 18 Volumes*. New York: Garland, 1982.

Morse, Arthur D. *While Six Million Died*. New York: Random House, 1968.

Ogilvie, Sarah A., and Scott Miller. "Jewish Emigration: The SS *St. Louis* Affair and Other Cases." In *Refuge Denied: The* St. Louis *Passengers and the Holocaust*. Madison: University of Wisconsin Press, 2006.

Proceedings of the Intergovernmental Committee, Evian, Switzerland, July 6–15, 1938. New York: Institute for Jewish Research, 1980.

Proudfoot, Malcolm J. *European Refugees: A Study in Forced Movement*. Evanston, IL: Northwestern University Press, 1956.

Rosen, Robert. *Saving the Jews: Franklin Roosevelt and the Holocaust*. New York: Thunder's Mouth Press, 2006.

Sabin, Gloria, and Ernest Honig. *The World's Indifference*. New York: Holocaust Survivors of Auschwitz, n.d.

Shaw, Annette. *The Evian Conference—Hitler's Green Light for Genocide*. Christian Action for Israel, 2001. http://christianactionforisrael.org/antiholo/evian/evian.html/.

Smith, Jean Edward. *FDR*. New York: Random House, 2007.

Thomas, Gordon, and Max Morgan-Witts. *Voyage of the Damned: A Shocking True Story of Hope, Betrayal and Nazi Terror.* New York: Stein & Day, 1974.

Zucker, Bat Ami. *In Search of Refuge: Jews and US Consuls in Nazi Germany, 1933–1941.* London: Vallintine Mitchell, 2001.

"The Voyage of the *St. Louis*." U.S. Holocaust Memorial Museum. www.ushmm. org/wlc/en/article.php?ModuleID=100005267.

Notes

4   "The world seemed": "Settlement of Refugees," *Manchester Guardian*, May 23, 1936. The paper quotes Weizmann's address to a London refugee conference sponsored by the League of Nations.

4   Unemployment statistics for 1938 come from the U.S. Bureau of Labor Statistics.

5   "Should we allow": Cantril and Strunk, 385. The poll was taken on November 22, 1938.

5   Poll data are from Black, Rosen, Smith, and Zucker. For more on anti-Semitism in the United States see Zucker, chap. 2, "Anti-Semitism: The American Scene."

5   "Stop the leak before": Rosen, 63.

5   "It is heart breaking": "The Refugee Question as a Test of Civilization," *NYT*, July 4, 1938.

5   "No country would be": Department of State Bulletin, Press Release, March 24, 1938, as quoted by Brecher, 61.

6   Required a certificate of: Birnbaum, 136.

6   Only granted 18,000: Black, 489.

7   "Viewed as a whole": Adams.

7   "I am satisfied": The July 20, 1938, report to the State Department can be found in Mendelsohn, vol. 5, 245.

8   "I don't think that anyone": Meir, 27.

8   *St. Louis* news stories are from *NYT*: "Fear Suicide Wave on Refugees' Ship," June 1, 1939; Hart Philips, "Cuba Orders Liner and Refugees to Go," June 2, 1939; "Refugee Ship Idles Off Florida Coast," June 5, 1939; "Ship Sails Back with 907 Jews Who Fled Nazis," June 7, 1939; "Cuba Again Asked to Admit Refugees," June 8, 1939.

8   Were 938 paying passengers: Ogilvie lists the names of all the passengers in an appendix.

10   Schroeder sailed north: Schroeder had only 908 passengers at this point. One refugee had died of a heart attack. One had attempted suicide by slitting his wrists and jumping overboard. He was taken to a Havana hospital. Six non-Jews with valid visas were admitted to Cuba as well as twenty-two Jews with valid visas.

10   Unemployment rate was still over seventeen percent: U.S. Bureau of Labor Statistics.

10   "The German refugees": Ogilvie and Miller, 25.

10   "The *St. Louis* will not": Thomas and Witts, 254.

10   "Repeating urgent appeal": Ogilvie and Miller, 23–24.

11   Great Britain accepted 288 refugees, the Netherlands 181, Belgium 214, and France 244.

11   254 weren't so lucky: Ogilvie traced the fate of all the *St. Louis* passengers.

CHAPTER TWO

Sources

Allen, Charles, Jr. *Nazi War Criminals in America: Facts . . . Action.* New York: Highgate House, 1985.

——. "Nazi War Criminals Among Us." *Jewish Currents,* 1963.

Arad, Yitzak. *The Holocaust in the Soviet Union.* Lincoln: University of Nebraska Press, 2009.

——. "Popular Collaboration in the Baltic States: Between Evasion and Facing a Burdensome Past." In *The Refugee Experience: Ukrainian Displaced Persons After World War II,* edited by Wsevolod W. Isajiw, Yury Boshyk, and Roman Senkus. Edmonton: Canadian Institute of Ukrainian Studies Press, University of Alberta, 1992.

Arad, Yitzak, Shmuel Krakowski, and Shmuel Specto. *The Einsatzgruppen Reports.* New York: Holocaust Library, 1989.

Brecher, *Reluctant Ally.*

Cantril and Strunk, *Public Opinion.*

The DP Story: The Final Report of the United States Displaced Persons Act Commission. Washington, DC: U.S. Government Printing Office, 1952.

Gilbert, Martin. *Auschwitz and the Allies.* New York: Holt, Rinehart & Winston, 1981.

Karski, Jan. *The Story of a State Secret.* Boston: Houghton Mifflin, 1944.

Laqueur, Walter. *The Terrible Secret.* Boston: Little, Brown, 1980.

Mendelsohn, John. *The Holocaust: Selected Documents in 18 Volumes.*

Rashke, Richard. *Escape From Sobibor.* Boston: Houghton Mifflin, 1987.

Rosen, *Saving the Jews.*

Sereny, Gita. *Into That Darkness.* New York: Vintage, 1983.

Stauber, Roni, ed. *Collaboration with the Nazis: Public Discourse after the Holocaust.* New York: Routledge Jewish Studies Series, 2011.

Wood, E. Thomas, and Stanislaw Jankowski. *Karski: How One Man Tried to Stop the Holocaust.* New York: John Wiley & Sons, 1994.

Notes

12 The account of the Swedish plan comes from Rashke, chap. 17, and Sereny, 215–17.

13 For details on the Bermuda Conference see: Rashke, chap. 17; Laqueur, 133–34; Gilbert, 131–37; and Reingold, 67–208. Brecher and Rosen have excellent analyses.

13 The Karski story comes from Rashke, Karski, and Wood and Jankowski. Karski mistakenly claimed that Belzec was the death camp he visited disguised as an Estonian guard. Wood and Jankowski have clarified the issue.

13 "I am convinced": Karski's visit to President Roosevelt comes from Karski, Rashke, and the author's 1981 interviews with Karski, who died in 2000.

13 "Absolutely fantastic": S. S. Alden, "Memorandum for Mr. Ladd: Re Bermuda Conference on Refugees," April 13, 1943, NA, RG 65, FBI Subject Files, Box 16.

14 "The 'sob sister' crowd": Rosen, 281.

15   Truman's response to the DP Act can be found in full in "Truman's Statement on Refugee Bill," *NYT*, June 26, 1948. See also *The DP Story* and *NYT*: "Prejudice Blocks DP Legislation, Javits Charges," Feb. 18, 1948; "House Group Acts on DP's, But Quota Cut to 200,000," April 30, 1948; "House Votes 289–291 To Take 200,000 DP's In Next Two Years," June 12, 1948.

15   IOP poll: Cantril and Strunk, 1089.

17   The origins and workings of the Einsatzgruppen are highly documented from hundreds of "situation" and "operation" reports (field reports) discovered by the U.S. Army at the Gestapo headquarters in Berlin as well as testimony from dozens of war crimes trials. For summaries see: Mendelsohn; Arad, *Einsatzgruppen;* Yale F. Edeiken, "An Introduction to the Einsatzgruppen," Holocaust History Project, http://holocaust-history. org/intro-einsatz; "Einsatzgruppen," Nizkor Project, http://www.nizkor. org; and http://www.deathcamp.org/reinhard/hiwis.

17   "We were actually frightened": Quoted by Allen, *Nazi War Criminals*, 10.

17   Einsatzgruppe C engaged: Deposition of Nazi Paul Blobel, Mendelsohn, vol. 10, 131–34.

17   Einsatzgruppe A description and quotes are from: Mendelsohn, vol. 10, 248–49.

18   The Himmler story comes from Edeiken, 2.

18   Although Nazi collaborators may have numbered in the hundreds of thousands, they represented only a minority of citizens from their respective homelands. Furthermore, it would be unfair to single out Balts, Belorussians, and Ukrainians as collaborators. Other occupied countries not annexed by the Soviet Union, such as Croatia and Hungary, also had militia groups that worked closely with the Nazis. Croatia had the Ustashi; Hungary had the Arrow Cross.

18   "As the firing started": Arad, *Einsatzgruppen*, 8.

18   "Indispensable": This conclusion is generally voiced both by Holocaust scholars and by Nazi administrators.

18   Over 70 percent: *The DP Story*, 243. A further breakdown is Poland/Ukraine (34 percent), Latvia (9.3), Lithuania (6.4), and Estonia (2.6). Belorussia is lumped with Russia. From Table Three, 366.

CHAPTER THREE

Sources

Angrick, Andrej, and Peter Klein. *The 'Final Solution' in Riga*. New York: Berghahn Books, 2009.

Dean, Martin. *Collaboration in the Holocaust: Crimes of the Local Police in Belorussia and Ukraine*. New York: St. Martin's Press in association with the U.S. Holocaust Memorial Museum, 2000.

Ezergailis, Andrew, ed. *The German Occupation of Latvia: 1941–1945: What Did America Know?* Riga: Historical Institute of Latvia, 2002.

———. *Symposium of the Commission of Historians of Latvia*. Vol. 5, *The Occupation of Latvia, 1941–1945*. Riga: Historical Institute of Latvia, 2002.

Gilbert, Martin. *Atlas of the Holocaust*. New York: William Morrow, 1993.

Gitelman, Zvi, ed. *Bitter Legacy: Confronting the Holocaust in the USSR*. Bloomington: Indiana University Press, 1997.

———. *The Holocaust: A History of the Jews of Europe During the Second World War*. New York: Henry Holt, 1985.

Hilberg, Raul. *The Destruction of the European Jews*. New York: Holmes and Meier, 1985.

Inimical List. Washington, DC: Displaced Persons Commission, June 21, 1951.

Lowe, Keith. *Savage Continent: Europe in the Aftermath of World War II*. New York: St. Martin's Press, 2012.

Lumans, Valdis O. *Latvia and the Holocaust*. New York: Fordham University Press, 2006.

Press, Bernhard. *The Murder of the Jews in Latvia, 1941–1945*. Translated by Laimdota Mazzarins. Evanston, IL: Northwestern University Press, 2000.

Records of the U.S. Army Adjutant's Office, Classified Decimal File 1948–50, NA, 341–342.1, Box 3659, and Records of the Adjutant General's Office, NA, RG 407.

Sayer, Ian, and Douglas Botting. *America's Secret Army: The Untold Story of the Counter Intelligence Corps*. New York: Franklin Watts, 1989.

Simpson, Christopher. *Blowback*. New York: Macmillan, 1988.

Snyder, Timothy. *The Reconstruction of Nations: Poland, Ukraine, Lithuania, Belarus, 1569-1999*. New Haven and London: Yale University Press, 2003.

U.S. Congress. House. Committee on the Judiciary. Subcommittee on Immigration, Refugees, and International Law. *Alleged Nazi War Criminals*. 95th Cong., first session, August 3, 1977.

———. Public Law 597. *An Act to provide for the enlistment of aliens in the Regular Army*. 81st Cong., 2nd sess., June 30, 1950.

Weiss-Wendt, Anton. *Murder Without Hatred: Estonians and the Holocaust*. Syracuse, NY: Syracuse University Press, 2009.

Notes

20   Special session of Congress reported in *NYT*: "Bill Will Combat DP Discrimination," July 20, 1948; "Senate Bills Seek To Change DP Law," July 29, 1948; *WP*: "Text of Truman Message to Special Session of Congress," July 28, 1948; *CSM*: "President Demands Special Session of Congress," July 27, 1948; Mary Hornaday, "New Measures to AID DP's Revises Rigid Quota Basis," July 27, 1948; AP: "Truman's Box Score," Aug. 13, 1948; *WSJ*: "Congress to Hear Truman Ask Today for Passage of Bills on 11 Subjects," July 27, 1948.

20   "Abhorrent intolerance [and] if Congress": *NYT*: "Truman's Statement in Refugee Bill," June 26, 1948. For a clear analysis of the prewar and postwar DP acts see: "Immigration and Naturalization Law Relevant to Alleged Nazi War Criminals," found in the appendix to the August 3, 1977, *Hearings*.

21   All but swallowed Germany: The description is taken from Sayer, 269. For more detailed descriptions of the chaos and misery at the end of the war see, Lowe, *Savage Continent*.

22   "It is impossible to": Ibid., 270.

22   Inimical List: DPC listed the names of inimical organizations country by country. The list was used by U.S. immigration screening officers. Long

categorized as "Secret," it was declassified in 1980. When statements in the following chapter call an organization "inimical," they are referring to this list. Some of the typed entries are not legible.

23 Latvian Relief, Inc.: NA, Adjutant General (AG), Classified Decimal Files 1948–50, Box 48. Although Latvian Relief was pleased with the DPC decision exempting the Baltic Legions, it was not pleased with DPC's determination that conscription began in January 1944. Latvian Relief argued that conscription actually began in mid-1943. Latvian Relief lost the argument. The chairman of the DPC in 1950 was Ugo Carusi.

24 Besides Hilberg and Gilbert, the Estonia and Latvia summary accounts are based on: Angrick, Dean, Ezergailis, Gitelman, Lumans, Press, and Weiss-Wendt.

25 Didn't bother to wait; and "incite other Latvians": Lumans, 234–35.

25 The following Estonians were convicted in absentia in Estonia in 1961: Ralf Gerrets, Ain-Ervin Mere, Jaan Viik, Juhan Jueiste, Aleksander Laak, and Ervin Vits.

26 "To participate in": Ibid., 237.

26 "Drunken orgies": Ibid., 239–40.

27 "First the policemen": Press, 103.

27 The description of the massacre is from Angrick and Press.

27 Latvian volunteers ringed: Angrick, 144. For an analysis of the current controversy over who was responsible for the genocides in Latvia and Estonia, see the work of Ezergailis.

28 For more information about the armed services support of the Lodge Act see: U.S. Congress. House. *Relating to the Enlistment of Aliens in the Regular Army and Air Force.* 86th Cong., 2nd sess., 1960. Report No. 1776; U.S. Congress. House. *Extending the Authority for the Enlistment of Aliens in the Regular Army.* 85th Cong., 1st session, 1957. Report No. 689; U.S. Congress. Senate. *Providing for the Enlistment of Aliens in the Regular Army.* 81st Cong., 1st sess., 1949. Report No. 946; U.S. Congress. House. *Providing for the Enlistment of Aliens in the Regular Army.* 81st Cong., 2nd sess., 1950. Report No. 2188; U.S. Congress. House. *Extending the Authority for the Enlistment of Aliens in the Regular Army.* 84th Cong., 1st sess., 1955. Report No. 834; U.S. Congress. Senate. *Extending the Authority for the Enlistment of Aliens in the Regular Army.* 85th Cong., 1st sess., 1957. Report No. 541; U.S. Congress. House. *Full Committee Hearing on S 2269, an Act to Provide for the Enlistment of Aliens in the Regular Army.* Committee on Armed Services, Jan. 24, 1950.

28 As an army officer: See Senator Lodge's testimony during the Jan. 24, 1950, hearings.

CHAPTER FOUR

Sources

Blum, Howard. *Wanted! The Search for Nazis in America.* New York: Quadrangle, 1977.

Hersh, Seymour. *The Dark Side of Camelot.* Boston: Little, Brown, 1997.

Higham, Charles. *American Swastika.* Garden City, NY: Doubleday, 1985.

Kowalski, Congressman Frank. Speech on Malaxa. *Congressional Record*, Oct. 5, 1962.

Loftus, John, and Mark Aarons. *The Secret War Against the Jews*. New York: St. Martin's Press, 1994.

Malaxa. NA, RG 263, CIA Name Files, Boxes 60–61, first release, and Boxes 84 and 85, second release; NA, RG 65, FBI Name Files, Boxes 68–71.

Ryan, Allan. *Quiet Neighbors: Prosecuting War Criminals in America*. New York: Harcourt Brace Jovanovich, 1984.

Saidel, Rochelle G. *The Outraged Conscience*. Albany: State University of New York Press, 1984.

Summers, Anthony. *The Arrogance of Power: The Secret World of Richard Nixon*. New York: Viking, 2000.

U.S. Congress. House. Committee on the Judiciary. Subcommittee on Immigration, Refugees, and International Law. *Alleged Nazi War Criminals*. 95th Cong., 1st sess., August 3, 1977.

Notes

31 "I've seen cruel": Ryan, 46.

32 "Periodic and highly": Blum, 24. The INS official quoted was Carl Burrows, Assistant Commissioner for Investigation. Blum does not give a source for the direct quote.

32 For Braunsteiner details, see Blum and Ryan; U.S Holocaust Memorial Museum website (www.ushmm.org), which has several articles on her; and *NYT*: Joseph Lelyveld, "Former Nazi Death Camp Guard is Now a Housewife in Queens," July 15, 1964; Morris Kaplan, "Mrs. Ryan Ordered Extradited for Trial as Nazi War Criminal," May 2, 1973; Joseph Lelyveld, "Breaking Away" (*NYT Magazine*), March 6, 2005.

32 "Wasn't enough evidence": Blum, Ryan, Lelyveld, and Kaplan.

32 The DeVito story is based on his interviews with Blum and his July 1978 testimony before Congress: *Hearings Before the Subcommittee on Immigration*, July 1978. The Schiano story is based on his testimony before Congress in the same hearings and on Ralph Blumenthal, "Ex-Chief Immigration Trial Attorney Quits Abruptly," *NYT*, Dec. 8, 1973.

32 In response to FOIA requests, both the FBI and CIA said they did not have any file(s) on Braunsteiner.

33 Hermine Braunsteiner Defense Fund: Immigration Subcommittee hearings, op.cit., 78. It is not clear whether the fund was a tax-exempt 501(c)3 entity or a private fund.

34 The Maxala story is based on: Blum, Saidel, Hersh, Summers, Lofus and Aarons, and Higham; NA, CIA RG 263 and FBI RG 65; and the speech of Congressman Kowalski. See also *NYT*: "Antonescu Picks Military Cabinet," Jan. 28, 1941; "Nazi Steel Gets Works," Feb. 22, 1941; "Celler Challenges Nixon," Oct. 13, 1952; "U.S. Ouster Move Fought By Exile," Nov. 23, 1957; "U.S. Orders Ouster of a Rumanian," Dec. 18, 1957; "Rumanian Wins Bid To Stay In U.S.," Sept. 10, 1958; "Nixon Is Accused Of Aid To Ex-Nazi," Oct. 7, 1962; "Nixon-Malaxa Link Denied By Attorney," Oct. 10, 1962. *WP:* "Rumania Ties Arms Maker in Guard Revolt," Jan. 29, 1941; Bill Brinkley,"One Agent Planted in Soviet Embassy, Data Introduced in Evidence Imply," Jan. 10, 1949; Drew Pearson, "Ike 2–1 Over Taft in N.H.

Poll," June 10, 1949; Drew Pearson, "A Sidelight on Nixon's Career," Sept. 29, 1952; Drew Pearson, "Malaxa Tries Again to Enter U.S.," Dec. 15, 1955; "Romania's 'Ford' Wins Conditional Reentry to U.S.," Dec. 17, 1955; "Drew Pearson Sued," Dec. 22, 1955; "Malaxa Wins Permanent Home in U.S.," Sept. 10, 1958; "U.S. Probes Said to Clear Malaxa, Oct. 11, 1962; Drew Pearson, "3 War Criminals Remain in U.S.," May 12, 1963; Drew Pearson, "Nixon, Rumania Ready to Do Business," Aug. 2, 1969; Jack Anderson, "Nixon Helped Rich Nazi Stay in U.S.," Nov. 16, 1979. *CSM*: "Rumania Continues Roundup of Iron Guards and Arms," Jan. 30, 1941; "Nazis Get Malaxa Plants," May 15, 1941. *WSJ*: "Romanian Trade Group Due Here Next Week," Aug. 2, 1946. *CT*: "Rumania Tries Arms Maker as Rebels' 'Angel,'" Jan. 29, 1941.

34   Required his five thousand workers: Report 100-2-16-40Y, June 18, 1944, NA, RG 263, CIA Name Files.

34   Based on interviews with former CIA agents, Summers says Malaxa bribed Wisner to get him into the United States. According to T. Vincent Quinn, Assistant Attorney General, Criminal Division, Malaxa bribed Colonel Brady C. McClausen. "Nicolai Malaxa Internal Security," Quinn to FBI, April 8, 1948, NA, RG 263, CIA Name Files. McClausen was chief of the OSS in Romania at the time. It is unlikely that Malaxa bribed Wisner because Wisner was no longer working for the OSS at the time Malaxa came to the United States.

34   There are variations in the spelling of McClausen's name. Sometimes his first name is given as "Brady," sometimes as "Grady." Sometimes his last name is spelled "McClausen," sometimes "McClaussen."

35   Whispers rippled through: Loftus and Aarons, 223.

35   "As Malaxa is extremely clever": Untitled CIA memo, Feb. 14, 1948, NA, RG 263, CIA Name Files.

35   Hundred thousand dollars: Hersh, 159–60. Hersh highly documents the allegation. See also Summers, 133. Hersh further reported that the CIA had a photocopy of the check courtesy of a Romanian on its payroll.

36   Senator Baldwin's bill was S-2942. Representative Lodge's bill was HR-7160. The identical bills were introduced in September 1946. They were voted on in August 1948. According to the FBI, Pennsylvania congressman Francis Walter attempted to save Malaxa as well. The FBI reported that Malaxa bribed him to introduce a private bill. "From: A. Ross . . . To: Director," NA, RG 263, CIA Name Files, Dec. 23, 1959.

36   There are several versions about a congressional bill or resolution to grant Malaxa permanent U.S. residency. One version says Nixon introduced it. A second version says it was Hillings. A third says McClellan. There is also confusion about whether it was a bill or a resolution that was introduced, and whether the bill or resolution contained just Malaxa's name or whether he was part of a longer list. None of the sources actually give a name or a number to the bill/resolution. My version is based on the assumption that the legislation in question was Senate Concurrent Resolution #58 of the 82nd Congress. Drew Pearson ("Malaxa Tries to Enter U.S.," *WP*, Dec. 15, 1955) said Senator Walter got Malaxa's name deleted or killed the bill. Celler said he killed it: *NYT*: "Celler Challenges Nixon," Oct. 13, 1952. Most likely both supported the deletion.

36   Plan B was launched while the Justice Department was trying to get

Congress to grant Malaxa permanent residency. It appears that the strategy was: if one won't work, the other will. Blum and Kowalski describe and document Plan B. Also "To Director . . . From: SAC/NY," NA, RG 65, FBI Name Files, Oct. 10, 1955.

36　According to documents in NA, RG 263, CIA Names Files, Malaxa was the founder of the Iron Guard in Argentina, which became a hotbed of Guardist activity. He went there to build an armament plant.

36　The CIA opposed permanent residency for Malaxa: "In spite of the fact that certain prominent individuals in the country are allegedly sponsoring Mr. Malaxa's cause, the voluminous amount of derogatory information in the CIA files strongly supports the view that it would be undesirable for Mr. Malaxa to obtain permanent residence," Memo: For Deputy Director (Plans), NA, RG 263, CIA Name Files, Feb. 9, 1952. Also "The Agency should take action to prevent naturalization," Untitled Memo for Deputy Chief, SE, NA, CIA RG 263, Feb. 1952, author and specific date not given.

36　Powerful Republicans in Congress supported permanent residency, which raises the question: Were they bribed like Nixon and others? "Some of the GOP's top people have tried to prevent the deportation on the grounds that this industrialist can make a contribution to our national defense. . . . A prominent Midwest Senator is blaming the Justice Department for recommending that he sponsor legislation granting permanent residence to a refugee who worked with the Iron Guard, then the Nazis, and finally made a deal with the communists. The senator's friends say he's too embarrassed to make an issue of it," NA, RG 263, CIA Name Files, Untitled FBI report, Oct. 13, 1953.

36　The Department of Justice also supported permanent residency. "Malaxa's name has been favorably forwarded to the House Judiciary Committee by the Justice Department," NA, RG 263, CIA Name Files, W. Pforzheimer letter to the FBI, Jan. 17, 1952.

36　The threat to have Schiano fired and the INS transfer order to Alaska: "Director/SAC NY," RG 263, CIA Name Files, Oct. 10, 1962.

37　"Around two hundred thousand": Schiano, *Hearings*, 138–39.

37　"What would it take": Schiano, Ibid.

37　Offered twenty thousand: "NY SAC to WAS. SAC," NA, RG 263, CIA Name Files, June 24, 1956; and "NY SAC to FBI Director," ibid., Feb. 10, 1956. The bribe was offered by Malaxa's son-in-law Dr. George Palade.

37　Attorney General Rogers upholds the BIA decision: *NYT*: "Rumanian Wins Bid to Stay in U.S.," Sept. 10, 1958.

37　Double agent working for Romania and Soviets: See NA, RG 263, CIA Name Files: "There are no limits to how far Malaxa will go to ingratiate himself with the Soviets, including sizeable financial aid to Romanian communist activities in the United States," 100-2-16-40y; and "There is no doubt that Malaxa is an agent of the Soviet government and of the Romanian communists in the United States even if he himself is not a commie at heart. . . . As Malaxa is extremely clever, efficient, perfectly self-controlled, very discreet, of an unbelievable perfidy and a master in the art of bribery, he must be considered one of the most dangerous agents," Feb. 24, 1948 (untitled). Also, Malaxa was the only Romanian to receive compensation for property taken over by the Soviets.

37   "Mr. Malaxa is undoubtedly": To Hoover from Department of Navy/ William Abbot. Ibid., Sept. 18, 1953. See also: Department of Navy to Hoover from Carl F. Espe, Rear Admiral, Director of Naval Intelligence, NA, RG 263, CIA Name Files, Oct. 7, 1953.

37   FBI memos suggest that Malaxa was a "highly confidential source" about Bishop Moldovan, who was under investigation by the FBI. "To FBI/SAC WFO," Ibid., Jan. 8, 1957.

CHAPTER FIVE

Sources

Blum, *Wanted!*
Perry, Michael. *Dachau Liberated: The Official Report by the Seventh Army.* Seattle: Inkling Books, 2000.
Zarusky, Juergen. "That is Not the American Way of Fighting: The Shooting of Captured SS-Men During the Liberation of Dachau." In *Dachau and the Nazi Terror 1933–1945*, vol. 2, edited by Wolfgang Benz and Barbara Distel. Dachau: Verlag Dachauer Hefte, 2002.

Notes

41   The Karbach story comes from Blum, 31–35.
42   Operation Clean Sweep comes from *NYT*: "U.S. Schedules an Inquiry Into Immigration Services," Nov. 2, 1972; Martin Tolchin, "Inquiry Hints at Corruption Among Immigration Aides," Nov. 20, 1972; Martin Tolchin, "Union Says Plea Went To Mitchell," Nov. 29, 1972; Martin Waldron, "Wide Abuses Alleged in Texan Border Control," Dec. 19, 1972; "U.S. Indicts Seven In Plot to Smuggle Arms to Mexico," Dec. 23, 1972; Denny Walsh, "Justice Officials Find Corruption Rife among Immigration Aides in Southwest," May 21, 1973; "Trouble on The Border Patrol," May 27, 1973; "INS Seeks to End Patronage Ties," May 30, 1973; Denny Walsh, "Immigration Inquiry Calls Justice Department Aide," June 13, 1973.
42   The Dachau story and description come from DeVito in Blum, Perry, and Zarusky.

CHAPTER SIX

Sources

Blum, *Wanted!*
Breitman, Richard, Norman Goda, Timothy Naftali, and Robert Wolfe. *U.S. Intelligence and the Nazis.* New York: Cambridge University Press, 2005.
Feigin, Judy. *The Office of Special Investigations: Striving for Accountability in the Aftermath of the Holocaust.* Edited by Mark M. Richard. Washington, DC: U.S. Department of Justice, Criminal Division, 2006 (unpublished draft).
*Maikovski*s. NA, RG 263, CIA Name Files, first release, Box 33, and second release, Box 83.
Saidel, *The Outraged Conscience.*

Simpson, *Blowback*.

Soobzokov. NA, RG 263, CIA Name Files, Boxes 49, 123–24; and RG 65, FBI Name Files, Box 167.

U.S. Department of Justice Immigration Court, In the Matter of Boleslavs Maikovskis, A8 194 566. Dec. 14, 1981. Transcripts.

Notes

46   "I saw him lead": *In the Matter of Boleslavs Maikovskis.*

47   Seigel story. See *NYT*, "Deportation Inquiry Reopened in L.I. Alien's War-Crime Case," Feb. 28, 1973.

47   Fifty-five chapters: FBI letterhead memo, NA, RG 263, April 19, 1966.

47   Maikovskis had the support of some segments of the Catholic Church. According to an FBI report, "his files included eighteen letters of recommendation, predominantly from Catholic clergy." FBI letterhead memo, NA, RG 263, Box 33, April 19, 1966.

48   The Fier and Soobzokov story is based on: Blum; Feigin; NA, RG 263, CIA Name Files; and *NYT*: Donald Janson, "Passaic Officials Hail an Employee Accused of Concealing Ties to Nazis," Dec. 8, 1979; Ralph Blumenthal, "Man Accused of Nazi Past Injured by Bomb in New Jersey," Aug. 16, 1985; *WP*: Thomas O'Toole, "CIA 1952 Files Save Ex-Nazi in Deportation Case," July 10, 1980.

49   Liked to show: "From Yusuf Yakar to FBI," NA, RG 65, FBI Name Files, Jan. 1, 1987. The memo is based on the eyewitness testimony of Alem Guetlov.

49   It didn't care if: "Assure NOSTRIL that we are not at all interested in any criminal, moral or other lapses in his past," CIA Chief of Station, NA, RG 263, CIA Name Files, Nov. 6, 1952.

49   Soobzokov's CIA job description: Ibid.

49   The CIA also dangled possible U.S. citizenship as bait to lure spies in Jordan: "An individual who successfully completes a mission into the USSR will stand a good chance of being brought to the US and obtain U.S. citizenship." Ibid.

50   Trained at Fort Meade: This and following description of training and service are from "Summary of Service," NA, RG 65, FBI Name Files, July 16, 1974.

50   "Discrepancies": Ibid.

50   The FBI was pleased with Soobzokov's work: "He furnished information of value . . . concerning numerous individuals of interest to the Bureau." FBI memo prepared by SA John Joseph Reid, FBI, Oct. 20, 1958. Ibid.

50   Resignation of DeVito and Schiano: Ralph Blumenthal, "Ex-Chief Immigration Trial Attorney Quits Abruptly," *NYT*, Dec. 8, 1973.

50   "Romantics": Ibid.

50   Schiano and DeVito had a falling-out after Blum published the DeVito story in *Wanted!* Schiano accused DeVito of lying about the phone calls to his wife and being in it for himself. Saidel describes the tiff.

CHAPTER SEVEN

Sources

Holtzman, Elizabeth. *Who Said It Would Be Easy?* With Cynthia L. Cooper. New York: Arcade, 1996.

Holtzman. Author's interview, April 12, 2010.

Rashke, *Escape From Sobibor.*

U.S. Congress. House. Committee on the Judiciary. Subcommittee on Immigration, Citizenship and International Law. *Immigration and Naturalization Service Oversight.* 93rd Cong., 2nd sess., April 3 and June 25, 1974.

Notes

51 The description of Holtzman's meeting with the whistle-blower comes from Holtzman, chap. 5.

51 "There is a matter": Ibid., 90.

51 "If the man was right": Ibid.

51 DeVito quit in June 1973.

52 Holtzman's version of her encounter with General Chapman is slightly different in her autobiography.

52 Hearing quotes are from U.S. Congress. House. Committee on the Judiciary, 22–26.

54 "Face to face with evil": Holtzman, 97.

54 "I *can't* believe you": Rashke, 128.

55 "Appalling laxness": Ralph Blumenthal, "Rep. Holtzman Calls U.S. Lazy on Nazi Inquiries," *NYT*, May 21, 1974.

CHAPTERS EIGHT AND NINE

Sources

Artukovic. NA, RG 263, CIA Name Files, Boxes 1, 2, and 4; RG 65, FBI Name Files, Boxes 5 and 74–76.

Bolschwing. NA, RG 263, CIA Name Files, Box 7.

Breitman and others, *U.S. Intelligence and the Nazis.*

Feigin, *The Office of Special Investigations.*

Final Report of the International Commission on the Holocaust in Romania, November 11, 2004.

Holtzman, author's interview.

Maclean, Fitzroy. *The Heretic: The Life and Times of Josip Broz Tito.* New York: Harper, 1957.

Ruffner, Kevin Conley. "A Valuable Man We Must Control." In *Eagle and Swastika: CIA and Nazi War Criminals and Collaborators.* History Staff of the CIA, Washington, DC, 2003. Draft Working Paper, Chapter Eight. NA, RG 263, CIA Subject Files, "CIA and Nazi War Criminals and Collaborators," Box 29, folders 1 and 2.

Ryan, *Quiet Neighbors.*

Saidel, *The Outraged Conscience.*

Simpson, *Blowback.*

Summers, *The Arrogance of Power.*

This is Artukovic! New York: Yugoslavian Information Center, 1958.

Trifa. NA, RG 65, FBI Name Files, Boxes 158–160.

United States of America: In the matter of Valerian Trifa, a/k/a, Viorel Trifa. File No. A 7819396. Proceeding transcripts, October 4, 1982.

Notes

57 Most of the important documents referenced in CIA Record Group 263 and FBI Record Group 65 are still classified. Some photocopies that are available are impossible to read.

57 "Some Ustachi collected": Maclean, 125.

57 "Catholic priests were": Ibid., 125–26.

57 No one knows for sure how many Serbs were murdered. Estimates run from 300,000 to 700,000. The latest research places the number between 300,000 and 400,000.

57 The commandant of Jasenovac was "the most notorious butcher" Father Franc Miroslav Majstorovic-Filipevic. The quote comes from *This is Artukovic!*, which took it from survivor Dr. Nikola Mikolic's memoir, *Jasenovac.* When the Yugoslavian embassy published the booklet, the U.S. government dismissed it as communist propaganda.

57 Other Ustashi priests included Zvonko Brekale, Culina (first name unknown), Zvonco Lipovac, Krunoslav Dragonavic, and Simic (first name unknown). After the war, communist Yugoslavia convicted Croatian archbishop Stepinac of war crimes. In Catholic circles, he is considered a martyr.

57 "Himmler of Croatia": The term was used by the government of Yugoslavia to describe Artukovic's crimes.

58 According to the CIA, John Artukovic was a founder of the Iron Guard organization in California. NA, RG 263, CIA Name Files, CIA report 5990 JICAME, April 14, 1944.

58 He and his rich friends: The bill, HR-2185, was repeatedly introduced by California representative James Utt. See NA, RG Group 65, FBI Name Files, "Andrija Artukovic Internal Security-YU," March 10, 1961.

59 The quotations from the Trifa manifesto are taken from a copy of the leaflet handed out at the January 21 demonstration. The handout contains the entire text of the manifesto and ends with the words "Viorel Trifa, President of the National Union of Christian Romanian Students." Researchers found a copy of the leaflet in Romanian archives.

60 "The wretched victims": *Final Report*, 8.

60 According to an eyewitness: This and following allegation are from: NA, RG 65, FBI Name Files. FBI interviews with George Muntean, a student leader in the Iron Guard, Nov. 18, 1955, and Nicholas Martin, Oct. 5, 1955. The eyewitnesses testified during the trial of Trifa in absentia in Yugoslavia after the war. The accounts have not been independently verified by OSI or others. Also see: Washington Field Office/SAC to Director, Subject: "Viorel Donise Trifa," NA, RG 65, FBI Name Files, May 5, 1955. The FBI made no attempt to verify the accounts.

60 Trifa either taught at Rosano or Pesaro under the alias "Chiacu." FBI letter

from Detroit SAC to Director, NA, RG 65, FBI Name Files, April 4, 1952.

62 Ukrainian Metropolitan archbishop John Theodorovich consecrated Trifa bishop in Philadelphia in the Church of the Descent of the Holy Ghost in April 1952. The archbishop acted despite a court injunction against the ordination filed by Bishop Moldovan. Trifa eventually won the lawsuit and was legally recognized as the head of the U.S. ROC. Moldovan's parishioners in Akron expelled him. Moldovan died in 1963.

62 At the recommendation of: Summers, 498, fn 2. For the text of the prayer see *Congressional Record*, May 11, 1955.

62 Trifa was a friend of Malaxa: FBI report from the Washington Field Office to the Director, NA, RG 65, FBI Name Files, May 26, 1954.

62 The Charles Kremer story is based on Blum, Saidel, Ryan, and Ralph Blumenthal, "Dr. Charles Kremer, 89, Dies; Pressed Trifa War Crime Case," *NYT*, May 28, 1987.

62 Moldovan whispered: Saidel, 32.

62 Saidel also names Father Gucherie Moraru as someone who told Kremer about Trifa's true identity. Moldovan got an injunction against Trifa's ordination but he lost: "Judge Cites Bishop for Court Contempt," *NYT*, May 1, 1952.

62 Princess Ileana of Romania testified before Congress against Moldovan, whom she considered a communist collaborator: "Princess Tells of Romanian Plot," *CT*, May 17, 1956.

62 "These charges were": The December 22, 1971, letter is quoted by Saidel, 37–38.

62 Kremer fed the story to the *NYT*: Ralph Blumenthal, "Bishop Under Inquiry on Atrocity Link," Dec. 26, 1973.

63 Bishop Trifa admitted: Hillary H. Ward, "Bishop Admits Past Pro-Fascist Ties," *DFP*, Aug. 27, 1972.

65 Keep communist Romania from: Hoover was worried about communists infiltrating the Iron Guard in America. FBI report 105-478, SAC Detroit to Director, NA, RG 65, FBI Name Files, Jan. 18, 1955.

65 Iron Guard priests as pastors: "Was attempting to infiltrate the Romanian Orthodox parishes in the United States with priests who were former members of the Iron Guard so that the Church would eventually become a political rather than an ecclesiastical entity." FBI Report by Detroit office, G. Maylon Miller, NA, RG 65, FBI Name Files. April 6, 1955. Also, SAC/ Washington Field Office report 105-2153 to Director, May 1, 1955, ibid.

65 "Invaluable information": FBI report, SAC Detroit to Director, NA, RG 65, Oct. 20, 1954.

65 "Trifa is not": Justice Department Memorandum, "Re: U.S. vs Valerian Trifa," NA, RG 65, FBI Name Files, April 6, 1979. This memo is in response to an OSI request for information about the FBI's use of Trifa as a confidential source. See also *NYT*: Ralph Blumenthal, "Bishop is Facing Expanded Inquiry," April 5, 1974; Ralph Blumenthal, "U.S. Accuses Michigan Bishop on Naturalization," July 1, 1975; Ralph Blumenthal, "U.S. Challenging Bishop As Citizen," March 29, 1975; "Rumania Gives U.S. Data in Case Against Bishop Called Ex-Fascist," June 24, 1979; Ari L. Goldman, "Valerian Trifa, an Archbishop With a Fascist Past, Dies at 72," Jan. 29, 1987. See also *DFP*: Aug. 27, 1972; July 6, 1979; July 17, 1983. *Philadelphia Inquirer*: April 30, 1952. *Detroit News*: June 2, 1974. *WP*: April 29, 1983.

65 The Kremer FBI file consists of 136 pages. The quotes dealing with the FBI

investigation of Kremer come from those documents. They are referred to in these chapter notes as "FOIA papers."

65   "Mr. President": Letter to President Johnson from Kremer is dated Jan. 30, 1967. A copy of the letter was in Kremer's FBI file. FOIA papers.

66   "There have been": FBI letter to Marvin Watson, Special Assistant to the President, Feb. 9, 1967. FOIA papers.

66   "The NYO, after careful": "To: Director, FBI (10543011) . . . From: SAC, New York (105-43011) . . . Subject: Charles H. Kremer," June 27, 1961. FOIA papers.

66   "To be covertly sponsored": "To: Director, Federal Bureau of Investigation . . . From: Robert C. Mardian, Assistant Attorney General Internal Security Division . . . Subject: Charles H. Kremer," May 28, 1971. FOIA papers.

67   "Dr. Kremer has two compelling": "To: Director, FBI (105-100575). . . From: SAC, New York (105-4301100) (C) . . . Subject: Dr. Charles H. Kremer," Aug. 8, 1968. FOIA papers.

67   He disclaimed "responsibility": "To: Director, FBI . . . From: SAC, New York (105-43011) . . . Subject: Dr. Charles Kremer," March 23, 1974. FOIA papers.

67   The Holtzman–Radio Free Europe story is based on the author's interview with Holtzman, the Jack Anderson column, "RFE's Bishop Interview is Probed," *WP*, Feb. 28, 1980; and David Binder, "Legislator Assails Radio Free Europe," *NYT*, May 17, 1979.

67   "It is outrageous": Binder, *NYT*, May 17, 1979.

67   "She is blowing this up": "To: Stu Eizenstat . . . From Zbigniew Brzezinski," Feb. 12, 1980. The Brzezinski memo is courtesy of the Carter Library in Atlanta.

67   The National Security Council records are housed in the Carter Library. The collection holds twenty-three documents mentioning Holtzman. I did not visit the Georgia library to examine those pages. I did, however, request and receive from the library a copy of four NSC pages about Trifa.

68   "Clergy and laity": Trifa telegram to Hoover, July 3, 1964. FOIA papers.

68   Personally capturing twenty: Report of Lt. Col. Ray F. Groggin, 71st Infantry, NA, RG 263, CIA Name Files, June 1945.

68   "Virtually indispensable": Letter of Lt. Col. Howard Selk, 410th Infantry Regiment, Aug. 16, 1945, ibid. It is not clear to whom Selk was writing.

68   Most of the Bolschwing material about his work for the CIA is based on Ruffner. Chapters 16 and 17 of Ruffner's report are still classified.

68   The description of Bolschwing's personality and skills comes from Ruffner, 5–7.

69   "A valuable man we must control": Ibid., 6.

69   He was a security risk: Ibid., 14.

69   Uncovered a deeply buried secret": Ibid., 17–18.

69   Cautioned Bolschwing that once: This and following are from ibid., 20.

69   "I wish to express": Ibid., 22.

69   The decision was made to help Bolschwing immigrate to the United States: "Deemed advisable . . . to assist the principal agent to come to the United States with his family," memo from Chief E.I, NA, RG 263, CIA Name Files, Dec. 22, 1953; and "assisted in the immigration and naturalization by CIA," CIA memo for chief of Operation, DDP, May 10, 1961, ibid."

69   Worked on the staff of Adolf Eichmann: Bolschwing worked in Department II, Section 112 of the RSHA. CIA memo, "Otto Albrecht Alfred von Bolschwing,"

NA, RG 263, CIA Name Files, April 10, 1961; and Ruffner and Ryan.

70 Pearson column: "War Criminal Lives in California," *WP*, June 7, 1962.

70 Artukovic was still close to his former boss, Ante Pavelic. Pavelic wanted him to come to Argentina if he was expelled from the United States. CIA Report No: TAB-3191, NA, RG 263, CIA Name Files, Nov. 14, 1951.

70 The New York firm listed as the writer of *This is Artukovic!* was Gaffney, Starcevic, McHough. The Library of Congress and the IWG files at NARA cited above hold copies of the booklet.

71 "If you can't kill": *This is Artukovic!*, 20.

71 Violation of the Foreign Agents: Memo from J. Walter Yeagley, Acting Assistant Attorney General, to FBI Director, Aug. 27, 1958; and SAC/NY to Director memo, Aug. 6, 1958. Both are from NA, RG 263, CIA Name Files.

71 "Appropriate action": Hoover to D. L. Nicholson, Office of Consular Affairs, Department of State, NA, RG 65, FBI Name Files, July 9, 1958: "Artukovic is believed to possess great potential propaganda value inasmuch as appropriate action taken against him would greatly impress Yugoslavian citizens who do not presently trust the Tito regime."

72 Hoover considered Artukovic the "uncrowned leader of the Croatian movement in the United States. Letterhead Memo, NA, RG 65, FBI Name Files, Jan. 31, 1974; FBI Confidential Report, Aug. 17, 1959, ibid.

72 Catholic organizations supporting Artukovic included: Knights of Columbus, United American Croatians, the Catholic Association for International Peace, and the Croatian Catholic Union of the United States. The FBI characterized the Catholic Association for International Peace as a long-standing "friend of the Bureau," NA, RG 65, FBI Name Files, To: L. V. Boardman . . . From: A. H. Belmont, June 26, 1958.

72 Cardinal Spellman's private support of Artukovic comes up several times in the FBI letters and memos of 1958 in NA, RG 65, FBI Name Files.

72 Dozens of Croatian Franciscan priests: John J. Knezevich, *Palos Verdes News*, Jan. 26, 1958.

72 "Considerable knowledge": San Diego SAC to Director, FBI, NA, RG 65, FBI Name Files, Feb. 14, 1951.

72 For the harassment of John Artukovic, see Richard West, "Two Held in Bombing of Auto Owned by Brother of Alleged Nazi War Criminal," *LAT*, Jan. 30, 1975. 000 "His deep appreciation": Breitman, 231. Also: "He advised that he felt a great debt to the United States for refusing to allow him to be extradited to Yugoslavia." FBI Letterhead Memo, RG 65, FBI Name Files, Aug. 14, 1967.

CHAPTER TEN

Sources

Allen, Charles, Jr. "Hubertus Strughold, Nazi in America." *Jewish Currents*, December 1974.

Bower, Tom. *The Paperclip Conspiracy: The Hunt for the Nazi Scientists*. Boston: Little, Brown, 1987.

———. *The Pledge Betrayed: America and Great Britain and the Denazification of Post War Germany*. Garden City, NY: Doubleday, 1982.

The Department of State. *For the President...Subject: Interim Exploitation of*

German and Austrian Specialists in the United States, August 30, l946. Top Secret.

Exploitation of German Scientists and Technicians. NA, RG Group 335, Records of the State–Army–Navy–Air Force Coordinating Committee (SANAAC), Box 20.

Goliszek, Andrew. *In the Name of Science*. New York: St. Martin's Press, 2003.

Hunt, Linda. *Secret Agenda*. New York: St. Martin's Press, 1991.

———. "U.S. Coverup of Scientists." *Bulletin of the Atomic Scientists*, April 1985.

Lasby, Clarence G. *Project Paperclip: German Scientists and the Cold War*. New York: Atheneum, 1971.

Loftus and Aarons, *The Secret War Against the Jews*.

Moreno, Jonathan D. *Undue Risk: Secret State Experiments on Humans*. New York: Routledge, 2001.

Nazi War Crimes and Japanese Imperial Government Records Interagency Working Group: Final Report to the United States Congress, April 2007.

Neufeld, Michael J. *The Rocket and the Reich: Peenemünde and the Coming of the Ballistic Missile Era*. New York: Free Press, 1995.

Operation Paperclip. NA, RG 263, CIA Subject Files, first release, Box 6.

Ordway, Frederick I., and Mitchell R. Sharpe. *The Rocket Team*. New York: Thomas Crowell, 1979.

Policy and Procedure to Facilitate Entry into the United States, in the National Interest, of German and Austrian Scientists and Technicians Sponsored by the War and Navy Departments. NA, RG 335, State-War-Navy Coordinating Committee (SWNCC), 257/14, May 24, 1946, Box 20.

Proposed Policy for Exploitation and Denial of German and Austrian Scientists. NA, RG 335, State-War-Navy Coordinating Committee, (SWNCC), 257/11, May 15, 1946, Appendix F, Box 23.

Sayer and Botting, *America's Secret Army*.

Simpson, *Blowback*.

Spitz, Vivian. *Doctors from Hell*. Boulder, CO: Sentient, 2005.

Strughold, Hubertus. NA, RG 263, CIA Name Files, second release, Box 127.

Trials of War Criminals Before the Nuremberg Military Tribunals, Vol. I. Washington, DC: U.S. Government Printing Office, 1949.

Weindling, Paul J. *Nazi Medicine and the Nuremberg Trials: From Medical War Crimes to Informed Consent*. London: Macmillan, 2004.

Notes

74   T-teams or T-forces: Descriptions are based on Lasby and on Bower, *The Pledge Betrayed*.

74   For a detailed description of the loot, see Lasby, 25–26; and Bower, ibid., 96.

75   Operation Osavakim: Bower, ibid., 97.

75   "Competition is fierce . . . we were even stealing": This and a description of the competition comes from Lasby, 8–30.

76   The description of the denazification program is based on Allied Control Authority Coordinating Committee Directive No. 38, "Arrest and Punishment of War Criminals, Nazis and Militarists and the Internment, Control, and Surveillance of Potentially Dangerous Germans," NA, RG 59, 740.00.119, Box 3692, Oct. 14, 1946.

76   The sheer magnitude of the effort: Sayer, 293.

76   A U.S. denazification tally: "Monthly Denazification Report (MG/PS/13F) Based on Data Submitted by Ministers for Political Liberation as of September 30 1946." Allied Control Authority Coordinating Committee Directive No. 38, ibid.

76   For "intelligence and military reasons": *Nazi War Crimes*, 11. The quote comes from a May 10, 1945, directive from the Joint Chiefs of Staff.

77   "normal Nazis": Simpson, 35. Also Hunt, Bower, and Lasby.

77   "The Secretary of War has": Oct. 1, 1945, as quoted in Goliszek, 99.

77   "The biggest, longest-running": Hunt, 1.

77   Morton Hunt, who worked for the army recruiting scientists for Project Lusty, exposed the name in a two-part article in *Nation*, July 16 and July 23, 1949.

78   "It is the policy of the Government": *Proposed Policy for Exploitation*, NA, RG 335, SWNCC 257/11, #1, Box 23; and *Policy and Procedure to Facilitate Entry*, NA, RG 335, SWNCC 257/14, Box 20. See also SWNCC 257/11, #2 (4).

78   "The War Department": Department of State, "To the President," Aug. 30, 1946.

79   Simpson estimates that as many as 80 percent of the Paperclip scientists were former Nazis.

79   "Some of the world's vilest": Goliszek, 102.

79   The list of universities and industries comes from Lasby, 265.

79   The CIA Act of 1949 (Public Law 81-110) was passed by the 81st Congress. The one-hundred provision is found in section 8.

79   The list of universities and industries comes from Lasby, 265.

79   Neither a Nazi nor a Luftwaffe officer: Weindling, 66. Charles Allen refers to Strughold as a Nazi. The *NYT* incorrectly picked up the label from him.

80   "Jews had crowded": "Strughold, Hubertus," CIA memo A1-2062, NA, RG 263, Box 127, Dec. 28, 1951.

80   Rascher's fellow doctors: Weindling, 75.

80   "Victims screamed in pain": *Trials of War Criminals*, 11.

81   Victims called it the Skyride Machine: Allen, 8.

81   Described the murder of a thirty-seven-year old Jew: Ibid., 39.

81   "Some experiments": Goliszek, 103ff. The author quotes a series of Rascher-to-Himmler reports.

81   He ordered the SS to execute: Hunt, 225.

82   Into a compendium: Ruff coauthored the compendium on aviation medicine with Strughold. The book, *Compendium of Aviation Medicine* (*Grundriss Der Luft-Fahrmedizen*), has an introduction by their boss, Reich Surgeon General, Dr. Erick Hippke, Chief of the Medical Staff of the German Air Corps. The manual has a picture of the high-altitude pressure chamber used in the human experiments as well as tables and charts of the results.

83   Five of those scientists: The scientists were Herman Becker-Freyseng, Hans Romberg, Sigfried Ruff, Oskar Schroeder, and Georg Weltz. The Nuremberg Military Tribunals sentenced Becker-Freyseng to twenty years in prison (commuted to ten) and Schroeder to life (commuted to fifteen years). It acquitted the others because of probable doubt.

83   "Appropriately investigated": Hunt, 232.

83   "Our inquiries about [Dr. Strughold]": Ralph Blumenthal, "Drive on Nazi Suspect a Year Later: No U.S. Legal Steps Have Been Taken," *NYT*, Nov. 23, 1974, which is based on Allen's article in *Jewish Currents*.

CHAPTERS ELEVEN AND TWELVE

Sources

Béon, Yves. *Planet Dora: A Memoir of the Holocaust and the Birth of the Space Age.* New York: Westview Press, 1997.

Biderman, Abraham H. *The World of My Past.* Melbourne: AHB, 1995. Self-published.

von Braun, Wernher. NA, RG 263, CIA Name Files, Boxes 151 and 152.

Dornberger, Walter. NA, RG 330, Foreign Scientists Case Files, Box 32.

Feigin, *The Office of Special Investigations.*

Michel, Jean. *Dora.* With Louis Mucera. Translated by Jennifer Kidd. New York: Holt, Rinehart, and Winston, 1980.

Nahas, Mary. *The Journey of Private Galione: How the Americans Became a Superpower.* Enumclaw, WA: Pleasant World, 2004. Self-published.

Neufeld, *The Rocket and the Reich.*

Ordway and Sharpe, *The Rocket Team.*

Sellier, André. *A History of the Dora Camp.* Translated by Stephen Wright and Susan Taponier. Chicago: Ivan R. Dee, 2003.

Speer, Albert. *Inside the Third Reich.* Translated by Richard and Clara Winston. New York: Macmillan, 1970.

Notes

85   Galione's story is summarized from Nahas's account. Nahas is Galione's daughter and her book is based on her father's recollections as told to her. The story is confirmed by Nelson Eaton, who liberated Dora with Galione.

85   Béon, Biderman, and Sellier are Dora survivors.

87   Michel describes the guards as Hungarian, 277.

87   "Skeletons wrapped in skin": Nahas, 125.

87   Weighing less than: Sellier, 314.

87   "Out of a horror movie" and "you could see": Ibid.

88   French Resistance fighter sang: Ibid.

88   They found about twelve hundred: Ibid., 137.

89   The two other camps were Ellrich and Harzungen.

89   The French and Belgians have established networks of Dora survivors.

91   "The majestic spectacle": Speer, 368.

91   "Decide the war": Ibid.

91   Worst of any SS camp: Michel, 64.

92   "At an infernal speed": Ibid., 6.

92   "He died in agony": Ibid., 105.

92   Sellier describes the lice epidemic and the SS concern about a typhus epidemic, 60.

92   "Over a thousand": Michel, 68.

93   "I had to deal with": Quoted by Sellier, 77–78.

93   "The conditions of these": Speer, 370.

93   "They had to be forcibly": Ibid., 371n.

93   For more details on the nationality breakdown at Dora, see Sellier, chap. 8, "Peoples of Dora."

94 "Most distressing memories": Words of survivor Jean-Pierre Couture, quoted by Sellier, 203.

93 Factory description by survivor Abraham Biderman: Biderman, 250ff.

94 They drowned in shit: Ibid., 223.

95 The SS hung fifty-eight: Ibid., 25.

95 The name of the island near Peenemünde was Greifswalder Oie.

95 "List of faulty rocket details": Neufeld, 225.

95 "blizzard of changes": Ibid.

95 Not five thousand at a crack: Speer, 369.

95 Estimates on how many died at Camp Dora and the other two camps vary. Béon placed the number at 20,000; Michel at 30,000. Sellier doesn't venture an estimate.

96 The involvement of Dornberger, von Braun, and Rudolph comes from analyses by all the sources listed above. Some are based on survivor recollections, some on a short supply of documents.

96 The army swore him to silence: Nahas, 182n10.

97 With a yearly salary of: *Strughold, Hubertus*, NA, RG 330, Box 32.

97 For the Rudolph story see Feigin and *NYT*: "Space Scientist Admitted Role in Nazi Camp," Oct. 6, 1985; Walter Goodman, "The Nazi Connection," *Frontline*, Feb. 24, 1987; John F. Burns, "War-Crimes Suspect Seeks to Stay in Canada," July 10, 1990; "Ex-Nazi Scientist Tries to Renew Citizenship," July 21, 1991; Wolfgang Saxon, "Arthur Rudolph, 89, Developer of Rocket in First Apollo Flight," Jan. 3, 1996; *CT*: Uli Schmetzer, "Former Nazi denies war crimes," Oct. 20, 1984; "'45 report told concerns over ex-Nazi's activities," Nov. 8, 1984; Neal Sher, "Scientist Rudolph and the Justice Department," Nov. 15, 1984; *CSM*: Robert M. Press, "Critics doubt latest US version of rocket scientist's wartime role," Sept. 5, 1985.

97 Dora war crimes trials: Bergen-Belsen, 1945; Dachau, 1947; Essen, 1967–70. The Soviets also held trials in their own zone.

CHAPTER THIRTEEN

Sources

Government Sponsored Testing on Humans: An Overview on Cold War Era Programs. GAO report # T-NSIAD-94-266. Washington, DC: U.S. Government Printing Office, February 1994.

Health Effects from Chemical, Biological, and Radiological Weapons. Washington, DC: U.S. Department of Veterans Affairs, 2003.

Human Experimentation: An Overview on Cold War Era Programs. U.S. General Accounting Office. Washington, DC: U.S. Government Printing Office, September 1994.

Hunt, *Secret Agenda.*

Is Military Research Hazardous to Veterans' Health? Lessons Spanning Half a Century. Staff Report prepared for the Committee on Veterans' Affairs, United States Senate, December 8, 1994.

Moreno, *Undue Risk.*

U.S. Congress. House. Committee on the Judiciary. Subcommittee on Administrative Law and Government Relations. *Government-Sponsored*

Tests on Humans and Possible Compensation for People Harmed in the Tests. February 2, 1994.

U.S. Congress. Senate. Committee on Veterans' Affairs. *Is Military Research Hazardous to Veterans' Health? Lessons from World War II, the Persian Gulf War, and Today.* 103rd Cong., 2nd sess., May 6, 1994.

Notes

100 Schnurman's story is a summary of his 1994 congressional testimony at the hearing before the House Subcommittee on Administrative Law and Government Relations, Feb. 2, 1994.

100 "I was presumed dead": Ibid.

101 "You wouldn't know": Ibid.

101 Two other young seamen who participated in the gas chamber experiments were Rudolph R. Mills and John T. Harrison. Like Schnurman, neither was warned about the danger of the experiments and both were threatened with prison terms if they revealed the experiments to anyone. Mills's and Harrison's sworn statements are recorded in the hearings before the Senate Committee on Veterans' Affairs, May 6, 1994.

101 The mustard gas experiments on seamen like Schnurman, Mills, and Harrison received wide media coverage. In particular: Bruce Reid, "Veterans Fight Military over '40s Chemical Tests," *Baltimore Sun*, Jan. 30, 1994; Tracy Thompson, *WP*, March 7, 1993; "The VA's Sorry, the Army's Silent," *Bulletin of the Atomic Scientists*, March 1993; Jonathan Bor, "Poison Gas 'guinea pig' Helped Others, Victim Exposed Secret U.S. Project," *Baltimore Sun*, Jan. 7, 1993.

101 Experimented on nearly seven thousand: *Health Effects from Chemical, Biological, and Radiological Weapons* summarizes the entire experimentation program.

101 Ten tons of the gases: Hunt, 161.

102 "Precise information on the number": *Human Experimentation*, 1.

102 "Experiments like these": *Government Sponsored Testing*, 239.

102 Hunt, who investigated military experimentation on human subjects, names seven Paperclip scientists who worked at the Edgewood Arsenal: nuclear physicist Herman Donnert; poison gas specialist Friedrich Hoffmann; chemical researcher Theodor Wagner-Jauregg; chemical warfare specialist Albert Pfeiffer; high-frequency electronics specialist Kurt Rahr; toxicologist Hans Turnit; and textile chemist Eduard Wulkow. All but one were members of the Nazi Party or Nazi organizations or worked at Nazi institutions or for the Reich military establishment.

CHAPTERS FOURTEEN AND FIFTEEN

Sources

Civil Action N. C77-923, United States of America, Plaintiff . . . John Demjanjuk, a/k/a, Iwan Demjanjuk, a/k/a, Ivan Grozny (Ivan the Terrible), August 25, 1977.

The Demjanjuk Trial. Consulting editor, Asher Felix Landau. Tel Aviv: Israel Bar Publishing House, 1991. (This three-hundred-page document is the finding of the Israeli Court in the Demjanjuk trial.)

Gottlieb, "The Hunt for Ivan the Terrible."

Hanusiak, Michael. *Lest We Forget*. Toronto: Progress Books, 1976.

Holtzman, *Who Said It Would Be Easy?*

Holtzman, author's interview.

Romerstein, Herbert. "Divide and Conquer: The KGB Disinformation Campaign Against Ukrainians and Jews." *Ukrainian Quarterly*, Fall 2004.

Ryan, *Quiet Neighbors*.

Sheftel, Yoram. *Defending Ivan the Terrible*. Translated by Haim Watzman. Washington, DC: Regnery Publishing, Inc., 1996.

Teicholz, Tom. *The Trial of Ivan the Terrible*. New York: St. Martin's Press, 1990.

U.S. Congress. House. Committee on the Judiciary. Subcommittee on Immigration, Refugees, and International Law. *Alleged Nazi War Criminals*. 95th Cong., 1st session, August 3, 1977.

Widespread Conspiracy to Obstruct Probes of Alleged Nazi War Criminals Not Supported by the Available Evidence—Controversy May Continue. Report by the Comptroller General of the U.S., May 15, 1978.

Notes

105 The many letters of Eilberg and Holtzman to government officials are reprinted in an appendix to the August 1977 hearings, *Alleged Nazi War Criminals*.

105 State Department approach to Bonn: Ryan, 55.

105 The Holtzman-Eilberg meeting with the Soviets in Moscow and Moscow's response is based on: the author's interview with Holtzman; Allan Ryan's later visit described in *Quiet Neighbors*; the Congressional speech of Eilberg (*Congressional Record*, January 29, 1976) and his remarks in the July 1978 subcommittee hearings; and the author's correspondence with Jerry Goodman, a former executive of the National Conference on Soviet Jewry, who attended the Moscow conference.

107 "Making every effort": Holtzman's letter to Kissinger, May 20, 1975.

107 "Plainly dilatory" and following quotes: Blumenthal, "Inquiry on Nazis called lagging," *NYT*, Aug. 25, 1975. See also: Joshua Eilberg speech after the Moscow visit. *Congressional Record*, September 22, 1975, 29727; and *NYT*: May 6, 1975 and May 24, 1976.

107 Kissinger authorized a tentative overture: See Ryan and State Department memo, Jan. 7, 1976.

107 The INS sent four attorneys: INS press release, Aug. 12, 1976.

108 A pro-Soviet rag: Romerstein, 2. Also Gottlieb, Teicholz, and Ryan.

109 Was a member of the communist party: Romerstein, 2. Also *People's World*, Sept. 22, 2007. This article also points out that Hanusiak, who died in October 2006, was awarded the Order of Friendship of the People by the chairman of Ukraine's Supreme Soviet.

110 He claimed he composed: Gottlieb, 162.

111 INS sent two lists of names to the Israeli police. The first list requested information on eighteen alleged Nazi collaborators. The second list had only nine names.

111 The Supreme Court ruling on photo spreads or photo lineups is: *Manson v. Brathwaite*, 432 U.S. 98, 97S. Ct. 2243, 53 L. Ed. 2d 140 [1977]. See "Photo Lineup," in *West's Encyclopedia of Law* for an analysis.

111   INS instructions to Radiwker: NYC 50/40/40.373, "The Following Information Should Be Included As a Minimum When Interviewing a Witness Preparatory to the Taking of a Deposition."

111   The Radiwker story and quotations come from the trial transcripts of her testimony during the Demjanjuk trial in Jerusalem; translated copies of her original depositions; and *The Demjanjuk Trial*, which is the lengthy judgment of the Israeli court.

CHAPTER SIXTEEN

Sources

Fedorenko v. United States, 449 U.S. 490 (1981).
United States v. Fedorenko, 455 F. Supp. 893 (Dist. Court SD, Florida, Ft. Lauderdale Division, 1978).
United States v. Fedorenko, 597 F. 2nd 946 (Court of Appeals, 5th Cir., 1979).

Notes

117   "What do we want": Quoted by Judge Roettger in *United States v. Fedorenko*, 455 F. Also Cathy Grossman Keller, "Nazi Death Camp Recalled," *MH*, May 31, 1978.

117   "Avenging cheerleaders": *MH*, ibid.

117   Roettger told U.S. marshals to arrest him: Ibid.

117   Another excuse to a federal: Cathy Grossman Keller, "I Was Beaten, Forced to Work for Nazis, Fedorenko Says," *MH*, June 13, 1978.

118   "We are Jews": Keller, *MH*, May 31, 1978.

118   "The Jews Live a Lie": This as well as the confrontation incident are from Cathy Grossman Keller, "Fedorenko's Trial Scene of Clash," *MH*, June 2, 1978.

118   "So thick you could almost touch it": Quote from Judge Roettger is from George McVevy, "Fedorenko Innocent Can Stay Here" and "Roettger: Agony of Decision Worst in My Career," *Fort Lauderdale News*, July 26, 1978.

118   The lead prosecution attorneys were U.S. attorney J. V. Eskenazi and INS attorney Alan M. Lubiner.

119   The eyewitnesses were Eugen Turowski, Schalom Kohn, Josef Czarny, Gustav Boraks, Sonja Lewkowicz, and Pinchas Epstein.

119   The former vice-consul who testified was Kempton Jenkins.

119   By 1978, the Zutty team had a five-attorney litigation task force.

121   "This decision is indicative": McVevy, *Fort Lauderdale News*, July 26, 1978.

121   "We are going to start": Ibid.

121   "How can it be": Cathy Grossman Keller, "Guard for Nazis Can Stay in U.S.," *MH*, July 27, 1978.

122   The government had lined up eleven survivors to testify: seven from Israel, two from New York, one from Florida, and one from Montreal.

122   "It was the most gruesome testimony": McVevy, *Fort Lauderdale News*, July 26, 1978.

122   "Armed guard service": Ruth Marcus, "Death Camp Guard In Holocaust Fights To Keep Citizenship," *NYT*, Nov. 9, 1980.

122   "I am happy and satisfied": Ibid.

CHAPTER SEVENTEEN

Sources

Holtzman, *Who Said It Would Be Easy?*
Holtzman, author's interview.
Holtzman Amendment. 8 U.S.C. #1227 (a) (4) (9D), INA #237 (a) (4) (d).
Ryan, *Quiet Neighbors.*
Teicholz, *The Trial of Ivan the Terrible.*
U.S. Congress. House. Committee on the Judiciary. Subcommittee on Immigration, Refugees, and International Law. *Alleged Nazi War Criminals.* 95th Cong., 1st sess., August 3, 1977.
Widespread Conspiracy to Obstruct Probes of Alleged Nazi War Criminals Not Supported by the Available Evidence—Controversy May Continue. Report by the Comptroller of the U.S., May 15, 1978.

Notes

127 Over our dead body: Holtzman interview, April 12, 2010.

CHAPTER EIGHTEEN

Sources

Arad, Yitzhak. *Belzec, Sobibor, Treblinka.* Bloomington: Indiana University Press, 1999.
"At a Different Pole." *Visti z Ukrainy,* August 26, 1976.
Black, Peter. "Askaris in the 'Wild East': The Deployment of Auxiliaries and the Implementation of the Nazi Racial Policy in the Lublin District." In *The Germans and the East,* edited by Charles W. Ingrao and Franz A. J. Szabor. West Lafayette, IN: Purdue University Press, 2008.
———. Author's interview, October 5, 2010.
———. "Foot Soldiers of the Final Solution: The Trawniki Training Camp and Operation Reinhard." *Holocaust and Genocide Studies,* vol. 1, Spring 2011.
Browning, Christopher. *Ordinary Men: Reserve Police Battalion 101 and the Final Solution in Poland.* London: HarperCollins, 2001.
Pohl, Dieter. Demjanjuk Trial Testimony. Munich, January 12–13, 2010, as summarized by Dr. Margrit Grubmueller in a private report made available to the author.
"Punishment Will Come." *News from Ukraine,* September 1977.
Rich, David Alan. "Reinhard's Footsoldiers." In *Remembering for the Future: The Holocaust in an Age of Genocide.* Edited by John K. Roth and Elisabeth Maxwell. New York: Palgrave/St. Martin's Press, 2001.
Ryan, *Quiet Neighbors.*
Teicholz, *The Trial of Ivan the Terrible.*

Notes

129 "Conveyed them to the [gas chamber]": *News from Ukraine* quotes Danilchenko as saying: "conveyed them to the so called 'murder bus.'" This

appears to be a clumsy translation from the article, which was originally written in Ukrainian.

130 Demjanjuk's mother got a letter: Demjanjuk testified about his contacts with his mother at his deportation hearing and at the Israeli trial. There are differences. The account in this chapter is a composite of those testimonies.

132 The Trawniki story is based on Arad, Black ("Foot Soldiers), Browning, Pohl, and Rich.

132 Approximately five thousand: Black puts the number at 5,082.

133 "Because we were all starving": Quoted by Black, "Foot Soldiers," 7.

134 "No one wanted to return": Ibid.

135 Citations for outstanding: Black, "Askaris," 292.

135 For the Lomazy murders see Browning, 78–87.

135 Shoot a Jew eyeball to eyeball: Rich, 691. Quotation is from Black, "Foot Soldiers," 17.

136 At least one thousand: Black, "Askaris," 359, and especially Black, "Foot Soldiers," 12.

136 A monthly salary: Black, "Foot Soldiers," 13.

138 "These units have proved": Quoted in http://www.ushmm.org/wlc/en/article.php?ModuleId=10007397.

CHAPTERS NINETEEN TO TWENTY-ONE

Sources

Arndt, Michael. "The Wrong Man." *Chicago Tribune*, December 2, 1984.

Danylchenko Protocol. November 21, 1979. English translation.

Epstein, Jason. *The Great Conspiracy Trial*. New York: Random House, 1970.

Feigin. "Frank Walus—Lessons Learned by OSI." *The Office of Special Investigations*.

Goulden, Joseph, C. *The Benchwarmers: The Private World of the Powerful Federal Judges*. New York: Weybright & Tally, 1974.

John Demjanjuk. Israeli court decision.

Loftus, John. Author's telephone interview, April 15, 2011.

———. *America's Nazi Secret*. 1st ed. Waterville, OR: Trine Day, 2010.

———. *The Belarus Secret*. New York: Knopf, 1982.

Moscowitz, Norman. Munich trial testimony on June 30, 2010, as summarized by Dr. Margrit Grubmueller in a private report made available to the author.

Parker, George. "To Walter J. Rockler and Allan A. Ryan, Jr., Director/Deputy Director, Litigation, DATE: February 28, 1980, FROM: George Parker, Trial Attorney, SUBJECT: Demjanjuk—A Reappraisal."

Ryan, *Quiet Neighbors*.

Sereny, *Into That Darkness*.

———. *The German Trauma: Experiences and Reflections 1938–2001*. London: Penguin, 2000.

Tillery, Julia. Author's interviews and correspondence with Rockler's daughter, August–October 2010.

Civil Action N. C77-923, United States of America, Plaintiff . . . John Demjanjuk, a/k/a, Iwan Demjanjuk, a/k/a, Ivan Grozny (Ivan the Terrible), August 25, 1977.

United States of America v. Frank Walus, 453 F. Supp. 699 (N.D. Ill 1978). Argued April 26, 1979, and decided February 13, 1980.

Wiseman, Thomas A. *Report of the Special Master*. June 30, 1993. Report to the

United States Court of Appeals for the Sixth Circuit, *John Demjanjuk v. Joseph Petrovsky, et, al.*, No. 85-3435.

Notes

140   A list of thirteen Wall Street banks: The only source for this statement is John Loftus, author's interview, April 15, 2001.

140   "Welcome to the Justice Department": Loftus, *America's Nazi Secret*, 2.

141   "He believed was withholding materials": Wiseman, 8.

141   Rockler-Mendelson flap: Robert Pear, "Justice Department to Oust Nazi Hunter," *NYT*, Jan. 6, 1980.

141   Ryan's story is from his book, *Quiet Neighbors*.

142   "Forget [job] security": Ryan, 67.

142   "Gotcha, you son-of-a-bitch": Ryan, 107. There are several variations of the quotation.

143   Nazi hunter Simon Wiesenthal triggered: Bill Grady, "Walus Target of Nazi Hunter Wiesenthal," *CT*, April 2, 1978.

143   "It's a dirty, dirty, dirty trick": Robert Enstad, "Nazi Link Vehemently Denies," *CT*, Jan. 27, 1977.

143   "Because I'm a Jew": "Alleged War Criminal is Attacked in Loop," *CT*, Feb. 2, 1977.

144   "A Jewish witch hunt": Lee Strobel, "Nazis Offer to Aid Defense in Atrocity Trial," *CT*, Dec. 6, 1977. The neo-Nazi group was the National Socialist White People's Party.

144   "If the devil would give": Michael Hirsley, "Walus Sought Aid Through Neo-Nazis," *CT*, June 3, 1978.

144   "Pig . . . Julius Hitler": Robert Enstad, "Riot 7 Hit Judge With Tirades," *CT*, Feb. 6, 1970; Anthony Lucas, "Judge Hoffman Is Taunted at Trial of the Chicago 7 After Silencing Defense Counsel," *NYT*, Feb. 6, 1970.

144   "Sadistic old bastard": Goulden, 139.

144   Survey of the Chicago Council of Lawyers and quotes: Ibid., 116–18.

144   "Her daughter came running": Bill Grady, "Witness Says Walus Killed Two," *CT*, March 29, 1978. The witness was Simon Mlodinow.

145   "Walus motioned with his hand": Bill Grady, "Witness Links Walus to Deaths of Three Poles," *CT*, March 23, 1978. The witness was Meylich Rosenwald.

145   "He took them to a nearby": Bill Grady, "Walus Led Youth's Death March: Nurse," *CT*, March 25, 1978. The witness was Sara Leichter.

145   "Here is the murderer!": Ibid.

145   "It is remarkable how I look": Bill Grady, "Hoffman's a Star, and He Loves It," *CT*, May 31, 1978.

146   "In the face of the case presented by": *U.S. v. Frank Walus*, 3.

146   "It's a terrible conspiracy": Bill Grady, "Walus Loses Citizenship," *CT*, May 31, 1978.

146   "Are the atrocities charged against": "Why Was Walus Tried?" *CT*, June 5, 1978.

146   "Prevent a miscarriage of justice": Jay Branegan, "3 New Witnesses Confirm Slave Labor Story: Walus," *CT*, Sept. 19, 1978.

146   "Inflammatory" in-court statements: Bill Grady, "Walus' Lawyer Seeks New Citizenship Trial," *CT*, June 9, 1978.

147 "Let's not waste our time": This and following quotes are from *U.S. v. Frank Walus.*

148 "There is no question of retrying": Feigin analyzes the Walus case, 82–100.

148 OSI offered to pay: "U.S. Drops Case Against Suspected Nazi Criminal," *NYT*, Nov. 27, 1980.

148 Ordered the government to pay Walus $31,000: "U.S. Must Pay $31,000 for Labeling Man a Nazi," *CT*, Feb. 15, 1981.

148 Russek's letter to Ryan, Dec. 1, 1980.

149 "It was a terrible nightmare": "Nazi Accusation Turns Life Into a Nightmare," *NYT*, May 1, 1983. For a fuller description of Walus's feelings see Grady, "Walus Loses Citizenship," and Arndt, "The Wrong Man," *CT*, Dec. 2, 1984.

149 "His age and complaints": "Julius Hoffman," *Academic Dictionaries and Encyclopedia*, http://en.academic.ru.

149 He discussed his concerns with a colleague: Wiseman, 102. Her name was Kathleen Coleman.

153 The description of the OSI meeting comes from the depositions of Rockler, Ryan, Parker, and Moscowitz as summarized in the Special Master's Report. Wiseman, 105ff.

154 The Mendelsohn conflict comes from: Robert Pear, *NYT*, Jan. 6, 1980.

155 "We only wanted to question him": Sereny, *Into That Darkness*, 338.

157 Kolesnikova was convinced: Ibid.

PART ONE: EPILOGUE

Sources

The Soobzokov and JDL story is based on more than one thousand pages of FBI reports released under a freedom of information request and on Feigin, *The Office of Special Investigations.*

Aarons, Leroy. "Jewish Defense League Resists Extremists of the Left and Right." *WP*, June 28, 1969.

"Anonymous Caller Says He Sent Bombs to Ex-Nazis Living in the U.S." AP, June 3, 1979.

Arnett, Earl. "Blum in Pursuit of Former Nazis Who Are Now Living the Good Life Here in the United States." *Baltimore Sun*, January 24, 1977.

Anderson, Jack. "Long Memories in New Jersey about 3rd Reich." *WP*, July 11, 1981.

———. "U.S. Gives Ex-Nazis Security Blanket." *WP*, June 5, 1981.

Baier, Don. "Seek Special Prosecutor in Soobzokov Bomb Case." *New Solidarity*, September 2, 1985.

Blumenthal, Ralph. "Man Accused of Nazi Past Injured by Bomb in Jersey." *WP*, August 16, 1985.

Bunch, William, and Joseph Gambardello. "Rabbi Kahane Assassinated in City... Arab Man Blamed in Hotel Attack." *Newsday*, November 6, 1990.

Cummings, Judith. "F.B.I. Says Jewish Defense League May Have Planted Fatal Bombs." *NYT*, November 9, 1985.

David, Gunther. "Woman Spied on U.S. Nazis." *Philadelphia Bulletin*, July 7, 1979.

Engelberg, Stephen. "F.B.I. Moving on Blasts Laid to Jewish Extremists." *NYT,* July 17, 1986.

Jalon, Allan. "Bomb Hits Home of Man Who Calls Holocaust Myth." *LAT,* May 15, 1985.

Janson, Donald. "Passaic Officials Hail an Employee Accused of Concealing Ties to Nazis." *NYT,* December 8, 1979.

Lidman, Melanie. "1,000 Gather in Jerusalem to Mark Twentieth Anniversary of Kahane's Assassination." *JP,* October 27, 2010.

McFadden, Robert. "Blast at Home of Ex–War Crimes Suspect Injures One." *NYT,* September 7, 1985.

O'Toole, Thomas. "CIA 1952 Files Save Ex-Nazi in Deportation Case." *WP,* July 10, 1980.

Palermo, Dave. "'85 Northridge Blast 1 of 4 Linked by FBI to 'Elements' of JDL." *LAT,* July 6, 1986.

———. "FBI Links JDL to Bomb Death of Arab Leader." *LAT,* November 8, 1985.

———. "FBI Links JDL 'Elements' to 4 '85 Terror Bombs." *LAT,* July 3, 1986.

———. "FBI Probes Tie to Southland Arab's Death." *LAT,* October 24, 1985.

Parish, Albert. "Pipe Bomb Death." *NYT,* September 15, 1985.

Quindlen, Anna. "Without Kahane, Jewish Defense Seems to Decline." *NYT,* June 20, 1980.

Richey, Warren. "US Has a Home-Grown Brand of Terrorism." *CSM,* November 15, 1985.

Sasaki, Laralyn. "FBI Attributes Fatal Bombing in Santa Ana to 'Extremists.'" *LAT,* July 17, 1986.

Shenon, Philip. "F.B.I. Chief Warns Arabs of Danger." *NYT,* December 11, 1985.

"Suit to Revoke Citizenship Dismissed." AP, July 10, 1980.

Unger, Arthur. "Powerful 'ABC Closeup' Documentary on Nazi Fugitives." *CSM,* January 11, 1980.

"U.S. Says Man Hid His SS Service." *Hartford Courant,* December 6, 1979.

Notes

163 JDL descriptions are based on: FBI report NK-174A-2754 (undated); and on Lidman, Quindlen, and Richey.

163 "If we see guns": Aarons.

164 "Soobzokov—you are a Nazi butcher": FBI report 174-8375, Nov. 28, 1979. The letter was postmarked Sept. 13, 1979.

164 "Unless you drop": FBI report NK 9-3262, May 18, 1978.

164 "What happened": FBI report NY 174-2958, June 4, 1979.

164 Rape of JDL woman: David.

165 "One doesn't ignore": FBI report NK 174A-2754 U (undated). The meeting was held at Young Israel of Passaic-Clifton Temple.

165 "You better not mix up": The letter was postmarked Paterson, NJ, June 25, 1969.

165 "You are barking up": To Sheriff Engelhardt, postmarked Paterson, NJ, Aug. 26, 1985.

166 Police interview is based on FBI report Newark, 174A-2754, Aug. 23, 1985.

167 "Listen carefully": McFadden.

167 "It is absolutely absurd": Palermo, "FBI Links JDL to Bomb Threat of Arab Leader."

PART TWO

CHAPTER TWENTY-TWO

Sources

Brentar, Jerome. "My Campaign for Justice for John Demjanjuk." *Journal of Historical Review*, November–December 1993.

Davis, Brett. "Nazi Hunters: Are They Detectives or Zealots?" *The Huntsville Times*, October 27, l991.

———. "'Ivan the Terrible' Case Pivotal for Both OSI, Critics." *The Huntsville Times*, October 28, l991.

———. "Rocket Scientist is a Controversial Target for OSI." *The Huntsville Times*, October 29, l991.

———. "Case Against Artukovic Questions the Power of OSI." *The Huntsville Times*, October 30, l991.

"Hearing on Nazi War Crimes Relights Spark of Ethnic Hatred." *CT*, March 1, 1981.

Himka, John-Paul. "Letters: Ukrainians Who Resisted." *NYT*, December 23, 1984.

Hryshko, *Ukrainian Holocaust of 1933*.

Kuropas, Myron B. "Voice of the People: A Ukrainian Reply to Book on Nazis in U.S." *CT*, March 23, 1985.

Mathews, Jay. "Nazi-Hunt Methods Protested." *WP*, March 23, 1985.

"Mr. Ryan's Letter." *WP* editorial, May 5, 1987.

O'Connor, Mark J. "Injustice Delayed Is Justice." *WSJ*, August 12, 1985.

———. "A Nazi Hunt and a Conspiracy Accusation." *CT*, October 26, 1985.

Romerstein, Herbert. "Divide and Conquer: The KGB Disinformation Campaign against Ukrainians and Jews." *Ukrainian Quarterly*, Fall 2004.

Sheftel, Yoram. "Attempted Murder of John Demjanjuk." *New Federalist Weekly*, Oct. 16, 1995. This was trial testimony before the Schiller Institute convened in Vienna, Virginia, August 31 and September 1, 1995, to investigate the gross misconduct of the U.S. Department of Justice.

Szaz, Z. Michael. "Justice or Witch Hunt?" *CT*, September 14, 1985.

U.S. Congress. House. Permanent Select Committee on Intelligence. Subcommittee on Oversight. *Soviet Covert Action*. 96th Cong., 2nd sess., February 6, 1980.

Notes

171   "Short life span...unrelenting attack": The 1991 series of articles by Bret Davis in *The Huntsville Times* gives rich detail about the attacks on OSI. Davis's October 28 story, "'Ivan the Terrible' Case Pivotal for Both OSI, Critics," quotes Ryan as saying: "Looking back now, if we had lost the case, it would have been a blow to our credibility, but that probably would have been true of any case...It was one of the first cases we tried. And we were very much on line. If we had blown that case, we probably would have had a very short life span." OSI critics frequently cite that statement as proof that the choice to try John Demjanjuk in Cleveland as Ivan the Terrible was political.

172   All quotes in the Romerstein summary are from his article.

173 "Evidence from Soviet sources": *Congressional Record*, May 28, 1981, 10929–30.
174 "Major weapons": U.S. Congress, *Soviet Covert Action*, 8–9.
174 "Forgeries are a preferred": Ibid., 63–64.
175 "Soviet evidence and witnesses": "450 Attend Rally at Parma Church to Support Demjanjuk," *CPD*, Feb. 9, 1981; and "Ukrainian V Moroz Declares Courts Should Not Admit Evidence," *CPD*, March 5, 1981.
175 A nun with a large cross: She may have been a fraud. She claimed that her name was Sister Eugenia and that she was associated with the Carmelite Church of the Holy Face. The *Plain Dealer* determined that the Church of the Holy Face was not associated in any way with the Carmelite order. "Demjanjuk Seems Calm as Trial Gets Underway," *CPD*, Feb. 11, 1981.
175 "All Ukrainians kill Jews": "Hearing on Nazi War Crimes Relights Spark of Ethnic Hatred," *CT*, March 1, 1981.
175 "Russia murdered": *CPD*, Feb. 11, 1981.
175 "We are protesting against": "Ohio Man Accused of Nazi Crimes," *NYT*, Feb. 11, 1981.
176 Some Ukrainian scholars refer to it: For example, Hryshko, *The Ukrainian Holocaust of 1933*.
176 Ukraine had one Einsatzgruppe operating in the area. Hillberg and others estimate that one thousand of the Kommandos in the group were Ukrainian volunteers. Ukrainian critics are correct. Historians like Hillberg do not distinguish between Ukrainians and *Volksdeutsche*.

CHAPTERS TWENTY-THREE TO THIRTY-ONE

Sources

These chapters are based on more than two thousand pages of transcripts from Demjanjuk's 1981 denaturalization trial. All quotations come from those transcripts. Needless to say, these chapters provide only a summary, and not every witness who testified is summarized. The italics within the quotations are the author's.

Alfreds Berzins. NA, RG 263, CIA Name Files, second release, Box 12.
Arad, *Belzec, Sobibor, Treblinka.*
Blatt, Thomas. *From the Ashes of Sobibor: A Story of Survival.* Evanston, IL: Northwestern University Press, 1997.
———. *Sobibor: The Forgotten Revolt.* Issaquath, WA: H.E.P., 1998. Self-published.
Birnbaum, "Evian: The Most Fateful Conference."
Brentar. "My Campaign for Justice."
Davidson, Susie. "The Bush Family—Third Reich Connection: Fact or Fiction?" *Jewish Advocate*, Boston, April 19, 2001.
The Demjanjuk Trial, Landau, ed.
Hoehne, Heinz. *The Order of the Death's Head.* Translated by Richard Barry. London: Penguin, 2000.
Memorandum Decision and Order. United States of America, Plaintiff v. John Demjanjuk, Defendant. No. C77-923, June 23, 1981.
O'Connor, Edward M. "Our Open Society Under Attack by the Despotic State." *Ukrainian Quarterly*, Spring 1984.
Rashke, *Escape From Sobibor.*

Simpson, *Blowback*.

Stein, George H. *The Waffen SS: Hitler's Elite Guard at War 1939–1945*. Ithaca, NY: Cornell University Press, 1966.

Sydnor, Charles W., Jr. *Soldiers of Destruction: The SS Death's Head Division, 1933–1945*. Princeton, NJ: Princeton University Press, 1977.

Williamson, Gordon. *The SS: Hitler's Instrument of Terror*. London: Sidgwick & Jackson, 1995.

Notes

178   "He withstood much of the hostility": Battisti's obituary, *CPD*, Oct. 20, 1994.

179   John Martin's obituary, *CPD*, Dec. 3, 2009. The article quotes Demjanjuk's son-in-law, Ed Nishnic, as saying: "I love John Martin. Nobody would take this case in the beginning except for John Martin. John went well over and above what any lawyer would do."

183   Schefler spoke through an interpreter and some of the translation was awkward and confusing. The original German transcript was not available for comparison purposes. Some minor editing was required.

194   Heinrich Schaefer affidavit, Oct. 17, 1983. English translation.

215   Michael Pap's background is taken from his John Carroll University curriculum vitae and from his pretrial deposition taken by OSI on April 30, 1980. Civil Action No. C77-923.

215   A Michael Pap (born in Tirma, Czechoslovakia, on July 24, 1920) entered the United States at Boston on June 3, 1949, alien registration No. 71644796. This appears to be the same Michael S. Pap who testified at the Demjanjuk trial. Pap's son Charles did not respond to several requests for information about his father's date and place of birth, and how his father survived the war.

216   The Reich had passed a law requiring all ethnic Germans: "From: Document Center, US Army Berlin . . . Subject: Waffen SS in the Balkans . . . To: US Displaced Persons Commission . . . Attn: M. M. DeCapua," Sept. 12, 1951, NA, RG 278, "Displaced Persons Commission Administration File," Box 72.

216   "Absurdities and contradictions": See Mark Weber's introduction to Jerome Brentar's article, "My Campaign for Justice for John Demjanjuk." The Institute of Historical Research is considered a Holocaust revisionist organization.

216   An anti-Semitic Holocaust denier: Brentar was dismissed as cochairman of an ethnic coalition supporting George H. W. Bush's 1988 presidential campaign, on charges of anti-Semitism. See also: Birnbaum, Brentar, and *NYT*, Sept. 9, 1999. Until his death in 2006 at age eighty-four, Brentar steadfastly denied those allegations.

216   The radio interview aired on the John McCulloch show at WJW in Cleveland. Quotes come from "Demjanjuk Case Evokes Anti-Semitism," *American Israelite*, Jan. 9, 1986.

217   "Forced through": Simpson, 207.

217   The details of O'Connor's life before 1949 are taken from his thirty-eight-page FBI background investigation file. The investigation was mandated because he was under consideration for a presidential appointment to the Displaced Persons Commission.

217   O'Connor's FBI file details his deeply Catholic roots: He graduated from

St. Joseph's Collegiate High School in Buffalo; studied at the Jesuit-run Niagara University; received a BS and MA from the University of Notre Dame; served as superintendant of Catholic Charities in Buffalo and as a case consultant for the Buffalo St. Vincent DePaul Society; was a member of the Supreme Council of the Knights of Columbus; and served as Executive Assistant, War Relief Services, National Catholic Welfare Conference. As a result of his relief work in Europe, O'Connor was decorated by France, Netherlands, and Luxembourg.

217   "It is altogether desirable": "To All State Commissions and Committees and Voluntary Agencies . . . From: Ugo Carusi, Chairman," Displaced Persons Commission, December 21, 1950. NA, RG 278, "Administrative Files of the Displaced Persons Commission," Box 72.

217   "The single most important activist": This and the description of ABN are from Simpson, 269–70.

217   For background on Alfreds Berzins see Simpson, *Blowback;* and NA, RG 263, Box 12.

225   "Gave him the temporary rank of": "Dr. Edward M. O'Connor, 77, Former NSC Staffer, Dies," *NYT*, Nov. 27, 1985.

251   "We categorically reject guilt by association": "Jews, Ukrainians Unite on Human Rights Violation on Ruling of Demjanjuk," *CPD*, June 23, 1981.

PART TWO: EPILOGUE

Sources

Feigin, "Karl Linnas: Cold War Politics and OSI Litigation." *The Office of Special Investigations.*

———. "Klaus Barbie: The Butcher of Lyon." *The Office of Special Investigations.*

Holtzman, *Who Said It Would Be Easy?*

Legge, Jerome S., Jr. "The Karl Linnas Deportation Case, the Office of Special Investigations and American Ethnic Politics." *Holocaust and Genocide Studies*, Spring 2010.

Linnas, Karl. NA, RG 263, CIA Name Files, first release, Box 33; and second release, Box 81.

Ryan, *Quiet Neighbors.*

Soodla. NA, RG 263, CIA Name Files, first release, Box 49; and second release, Box 124.

Walter, Guy. *Hunting Evil: The Nazi War Criminals Who Escaped and the Quest to Bring Them to Justice.* New York: Broadway Books, 2009.

Notes

252   Murdered between thirty-five hundred: Legge, 31.

253   "Linnas frequently travelled to the execution site": "From: Moscow . . . to Secretary of State," No: 215, October 11, 8 PM, NA, RG 263, first release, Box 33.

253   "Murderers" and "German Fascist handymen": "Memorandum For: Chief, SR . . . Via: Chief, SR . . . Subject: Karl Linnas," Oct. 13, 1961, NA, RG 263, first release, Box 33. Secret.

253   The CIA files apparently show that Linnas had no CIA connections: "It is

believed that LINNAS had no past contact with CIA and there seems to be no need for CIA action in this matter. . . . CIA files contain only a single reference to LINNAS and this document has been destroyed." Ibid.

254 "Soodla worked for the CIA in Trieste": Ibid.

254 For more on Soodla see: NA, RG 263; Joachim Joeston, "Baltic Legions," *WP*, May 27, 1943; "Six in the West Accused of Crimes by Soviet," *NYT*, May 23, 1961; and Legge, who conducted exhaustive research on the Karl Linnas case. The CIA deemed a "suitable candidate" for espionage work: "From: Chief of Station . . . To: Chief Foreign Division W," Dispatch No. WSSA-2397, March 5, 1951, NA, RG 263, Soodla, second release, Box 124.

254 Legge presents and documents the following breakdown of the 7,798 Estonians killed during the Nazi occupation: native Estonian (69.4 percent), Russian (15.2), Jewish (11.9), Romany (3.1), and other (0.4), 27.

256 "Live out his life peacefully": Holtzman, 95. See also *NYT*: Ralph Blumenthal, "Delays Charged in Nazi Inquiry," July 1, 1974; Kenneth B. Noble, "U.S. Deports Man Condemned to Die by Soviet Union," April 21, 1987; *CT*: "Reagan fights Nazi-case Deportation," March 18, 1987; Thom Shanker, "Linnas Dies in Soviet Union," July 3, 1987.

257 The Barbie account is based on Ryan, chap. 9, and Feigin, "Klaus Barbie: The Butcher of Lyon."

261 "How rare it is": *NYT* editorial, Aug. 18, 1983.

PART THREE

CHAPTERS THIRTY-TWO AND THIRTY-THREE

Sources

These chapters are based on the Demjanjuk deportation trial transcript, *John Demjanjuk aka Iwan Demjanjuk aka Ivan Demjanjuk, United States Department of Justice Immigration Court*, A8 237417, October 26, 1983.

Arndt, "The Wrong Man."

Birnbaum, Susan. "Letter From Demjanjuk Backer Supports Charges Against Him." *Jewish Telegraphic Agency*, December 10, 1992.

Brentar, "My Campaign for Justice for John Demjanjuk."

Davidson, "The Bush Family—Third Reich Connection: Fact or Fiction?"

"Demjanjuk Case Evokes Anti-Semitism." *American Israelite*, January 9, 1986.

Medoff, Rafael. "Bush Puts Politics Above Concern for Holocaust Legacy." *Jewish Bulletin of Northern California*, June 6, 2003.

Teicholz, *The Trial of Ivan the Terrible.*

"Teicholz Collection." U.S. Holocaust Memorial Museum archives.

Notes

265 Background information on Mark O'Connor and John Gill comes from Teicholz.

266 "It took me almost six months": "Three Lawyers in Israel Entwined Over 'Ivan the Terrible,'" *CPD*, May 18, 1987. Also: Teicholz interview with O'Connor, April 30, 1987, "Teicholz Collection."

270 Bandera assassination is from "On the 50th Anniversary of Stepan Bandera's Murder," *Ukrainian Weekly*, Oct. 18, 2009. See also: *NYT*, Oct. 17 and 20, 1959.

276 "Key figure": "Demjanjuk's Defender JA Brentar Spends Thousands to Clear Him," *CPD*, May 1, 1985.

276 Brentar's search for evidence comes from Brentar, "My Campaign for Justice for John Demjanjuk."

276 "Russek was as eager": Ibid.

276 The trial testimony of Brentar and Reiss is quoted from the deportation hearing transcripts, op. cit.

277 Frank Walus's reaction to his trial comes from Arndt.

CHAPTERS THIRTY-FOUR TO THIRTY-SEVEN

Sources

Boshyk, Yury. "Ukrainian DPs in Germany and Austria." In *The Refugee Experience: Ukrainian Displaced Persons After World War II*. Edited by Wsevolod W. Isajiw, Yury Boshyk, and Roman Senkus. Edmonton: Canadian Institute of Ukrainian Studies Press, University of Alberta, 1992.

Elliott, Mark R. *Pawns of Yalta*. Urbana: University of Illinois Press, 1982.

———. "The Soviet Repatriation Campaign." In *The Refugee Experience: Ukrainian Displaced Persons After World War II*.

Epstein, Julius. *Operation Keelhaul*. Old Greenwich Village, CT: Devin-Adair, 1973.

In the Matter of John Demjanjuk Respondent. United States Department of Justice, Executive Office for Immigration Review, Office of the Immigration Judge, Cleveland, Ohio, File A8 237 417, May 23, 1984.

Isajiw, Wsevolod, and Michael Palij. "Refugees and the DP Problem in Postwar Europe." In *The Refugee Experience: Ukrainian Displaced Persons After World War II*.

Polskaya, Eugenia Borisovna. "Death on the Drava." In *Forced Repatriation: The Tragedy of the 'Civilized' World*. Edited by Nicholas V. Feodoroff. Commack, NY: Nova Science, 1997.

Proudfoot, Malcolm. *European Refugees*.

Stauber, Roni, ed. *Collaboration with the Nazis*.

Stein, George. *The Waffen SS*.

Tolstoy, Nicolai. *The Secret Betrayal 1944–1947*. New York: Scribner's, 1977.

Trachevsky, George. "For the Right to Live." In *Forced Repatriation*.

Notes

282 In staggering round numbers: Elliott, *Pawns of Yalta*, 2.

283 Legal . . . because the 1929 Geneva Convention: See Epstein, chap. 2, "International Law and Forced Repatriation."

283 "In Hitler's camps": Quoted in Elliot, *Pawns of Yalta*, 192.

284 "Russians [are] a considerable charge": Ibid., 43–44.

285 Red Army representatives": Ibid., 2.

285 The Camp Rupert story comes from Epstein, 32–33, and Tolstoy, 88 and 192.

286 Soviet POWs were immediately imprisoned: Tolstoy, 88–89.

286 Twenty-five (sixty percent): Stein, Appendix II.
286 One hundred *Osttruppen*: Ibid., 17.
287 Roosevelt was both disinterested and uninformed: Elliott, *Pawns of Yalta*, 48.
288 As a crime against humanity: Argument of Epstein and Tolstoy.
289 The Fort Dix story comes from Elliott, *Pawns of Yalta*; Epstein; Tolstoy; and *NYT*: "Russians Captured With Nazis Riot at Fort Dix; 3 Commit Suicide," June 30, 1945; "U.S. Halts Return of 150 to Russia," July 1, 1945.
289 To a Soviet ship anchored at Seattle: Epstein, 103. His story is based on his interviews with former Soviet POWs.
291 "Three tombstones there": Elliott, *Pawns of Yalta*, 90.
291 The Dachau/Plattling story: Ibid., Epstein, and Tolstoy.
292 "The scene inside": Elliott, 93.
292 "It just wasn't human": Ibid.
292 "What happened at Plattling": Ibid. Quoted from Juergen Thorwald, *Whom They Wanted to Destroy: Report of the Great Treason* (Stuttgart: Steingrueben-Verlag, 1952).
292 "For about two weeks day and night": Epstein, 100. From a letter to him written by Sinclair J. Hoffman, April 22, 1969.
294 The Kempton roundup comes from Tolstoy and from Elliott, *Pawns of Yalta*.
295 The Linz roundup comes from Polskaya and Trachevsky.
296 "The soldiers scurried, taking away": Ibid., 129.
296 "Oh my god, the river was full": Polskaya, 129.
296 A medical doctor strapped her child: Trachevsky, 211.
297 "Who is going to" have to answer: Elliott, *Pawns of Yalta*, 92.
298 "My part in the Plattling": Ibid., 104. Quoted from Coffin's memoir, *Once to Every Man*.
298 "The cries of these": Ibid., 104. Quoted from Howley's introduction to Nikolai Krasnov's book, *The Hidden Russia: My Ten Years as a Slave Laborer*. New York: Henry Holt, 1960.

PART THREE: EPILOGUE

Sources

Allen, Charles R., Jr. "How Not to Pursue War Criminals." *Jewish Currents*, April 1984.

Breitman, Richard. *Historical Analysis of 20 Name Files from CIA Records*. Washington, DC: IWG, April 2001.

Breitman et al., *U.S. Intelligence and the Nazis*.

Chirovsky, Nicholas. *Ukraine and the Second World War*. New York: Ukrainian Congress of America, 1985.

CIA Memorandum for the State-War-Navy Coordinating Committee . . . Subject: Psychological Warfare in Reference to SWNCC 304/6, October 22, 1947. Secret.

Darling, Arthur B. *The Central Intelligence Agency: An Instrument of Government to 1950*. Langley, VA: Central Intelligence Agency. Approved for release Oct. 5, 1989. Typewritten. Secret.

Dean, Martin. *Collaboration in the Holocaust: Crimes of the Local Police in Belorussia and Ukraine*. New York: St. Martin's Press, in association with the U.S. Holocaust Memorial Museum, 2000.

Directive to the Director of the Central Intelligence Agency. NSC 4A, December 9, 1947. Top Secret.

Enlisted Personnel in the Regular Army of Aliens. NA, RG 407. Records of the Adjutant General's Office, 342.118, Box 8, July 28, 1952.

Etzhold, Thomas H., and John Lewis Gaddis, eds. *Containment: Documents on American Policy and Strategy 1945–1950*. New York: Columbia University Press, 1978.

Exploitation of Defectors and Other Aliens Within the United States. National Security Directive No. 14, March 3, 1950. Top Secret.

Exploitation of Soviet and Satellite Defectors Outside the United States. National Security Council Intelligence Directive No. 13, January 19, 1950. Top Secret.

Feigin, "Belarus Conspiracy—Sensationalism vs Reality." *The Office of Special Investigations.*

Gaddis, John Lewis. *George F. Kennan: An American Life*. New York: Penguin Press, 2011.

Gilbert, *Atlas of the Holocaust*.

Hersh, Burton. *The Old Boys: The American Elite and the Origins of the CIA*. New York: Charles Scribner's Sons, 1992.

Hilger, Gustav. NA, RG 263, CIA Name Files, first release, Box 22.

Jasiuk, Emanuel. NA, RG 65, FBI Name Files, Boxes 62 and 76.

Johnson, A. Ross. *Radio Free Europe and Radio Liberty: The CIA Years and Beyond*. Stanford, CA: Stanford University Press, 2010.

Kennan, George F. "Moscow Embassy Telegram #511," February 22, 1946. Secret.

Loftus, John. *America's Nazi Secret*.

———. *The Belarus Secret*.

Mickelson, Sig. *America's Other Voice: The Story of Radio Free Europe and Radio Liberty*. New York: Praeger, 1983.

Miscamble, Wilson D. *George F. Kennan and the Making of American Foreign Policy, 1947–1950*. Princeton, NJ: Princeton University Press, 1992.

National Security Council Directive on Office of Special Projects. NSC 10/2, June 18, 1948. Top Secret.

Poppe, Nikolai. NA, RG 263, CIA Name Files, first release, Box 41.

Powers, Thomas. *The Man Who Kept Secrets: Richard Helms and the CIA*. New York: Knopf, 1979.

Proposal for the Establishment of a Guerilla Warfare School and a Guerilla Warfare Corps. NA, RG 319, Joint Strategic Plans Committee, JSPC 862/3, P&O 352 TS (Section 1, Case 1), Box 79. Top Secret.

Psychological Operations. National Security Council NSC 4A, December 9, 1947. Top Secret.

Rein, Leonid. *The Kings and the Pawns: Collaboration in Byelorussia During World War II*. New York: Berghan Books, 2011.

Ruffner, Kevin Conley, "Belorussians, *60 Minutes*, and the GAO's Second Investigation." Chap. 18 in *Eagle and Swastika*.

———. "Could He Not Be Brought to This Country and Used?" Chap. 7 in *Eagle and Swastika*.

———. "A Valuable Man Whom We Must Control." Chap. 10 in *Eagle and Swastika*.

Screening of Lodge Bill Personnel for Special Forces Activities. NA, Classified Decimal File 1948–50, 342.18, Box 3659, April 13, 1954. Box 3659.

592 • *Sources and Notes*

Sher, Neal, Aron Goldberg, and Elizabeth White. *Robert Jan Verbelen and the United States Government: A Report to the Assistant Attorney General, Criminal Division, U.S. Department of Justice.* OSI Report, June 16, 1988.

Simpson, *Blowback.*

State–Army–Navy–Air Force Coordinating Committee. Actions and Decisions 1947–1949. NA, RG 334, Boxes 5–7, 11–12, and 14–17.

————. Numbered Papers Security Classified 1944–1949. NA, RG 335, Box 29.

————. P1-Actions and Decisions 1947–1949. NA, RG 0334, Interservice Agencies, Boxes 1–9.

————. SANAAC 395, March 17, 1948; and SANAAC 395/1, May 25, 1948. All Secret.

State Department Policy Planning Staff Papers. New York: Garland, 1983.

Thomas, Evan. *The Very Best Men: Four Who Dared—The Early Years of the CIA.* New York: Simon & Schuster, 1995.

Training of Individuals and Units of the Army in Special Forces Operations. . . To: Chief of Army Field Forces, Fort Monroe, Virginia. NA, RG 407, Records of the Adjutant General's Office, AG553, Box 8, July 16, 1951. Top Secret.

U.S. Congress. House. Committee on the Judiciary. Subcommittee on Immigration, Refugees, and International Law. *GAO Report on Nazi War Criminals in the United States.* 99th Cong., 1st sess., October 17, 1985.

————. Senate. Select Committee to Study Government Operations with Respect to Intelligence Activities. *Final Report: Supplementary Detailed Staff Reports on Foreign and Military Intelligence: Book IV.* 94th Cong., 2nd sess. Washington, DC: U.S. Government Printing Office, 1976.

Use of European Nationals in U.S. Occupation Forces. NA, RG 335, State-War-Navy Coordinating Committee (SWNCC) 222, Box 16, November 15, 1945. Secret.

Utilization of Refugees from the Soviet Union in U.S. National Interest. PPS 22/1, March 11, 1948.

Vakar, Nicholas P. *Belorussia: The Making of a Nation.* Cambridge, MA: Harvard University Press, 1956.

Winks, Robin W. *Cloak and Gown: Scholars in the Secret War, 1939–1961.* New York: Morrow, 1987.

Zaprudnik, Jan. *Belarus: At a Crossroads in History.* Boulder, CO: Westview Press, 1993.

Notes

314   "The Nazi Connection." *60 Minutes*, CBS, May 16, 1982.

315   "Mr. Loftus persistently made": Feigin, 361.

316   "Totally inadequate": 1985 AAO Report/Hearing.

316   "The action of U.S. Intelligence": Ibid., 56.

316   "No one had the faintest idea": Loftus, *The Belarus Secret*, 4.

316   The declassification process of 400 million pages: Peter Finn, "Archives' Major Task: Declassification," *WP*, Dec. 4, 2011.

317   "Defense material NOT cleared": Loftus, *America's Nazi Secret*, 244.

318   "Mayors, governors and other officials": Loftus, *The Belarus Secret*, 6.

318   Loftus's OSI reports are still classified. As a result, it is not known how many Belorussian quislings he investigated and who they were. It is known that he

asked the CIA for files on Emanuel Jasiuk, Jan Avdzej, Radoslaw Ostrowsky, Frank Kushel, George Sabolewski, John Kosiak, and Dr. Nicholas Scors. Ruffner, chap. 18, 2.

318 OSI was about to file a denaturalization action against Jan Avdzej (John Awsziej), a regional mayor in Belorussia, when he voluntarily left the United States in 1984 for Germany. He admitted that he "carried out the orders of Nazi occupation authorities." OSI flipped Basil Artischenko. He agreed to help investigate fellow Belorussian quislings if OSI dropped charges against him. From Feigin, who lists OSI investigations and outcomes in her appendix.

320 "Of a highly confidential nature": Ibid., 117. According to a 1951 FBI report on Jasiuk, the two State Department representatives were C. E. Collier and Arndt Wagner. "These men were aware of his background in the Byelorussian Central Council during the war years." Stanley A. Lewczyk memo to Internal Security, #100-34393 MHM, September 14, 1951, NA, RG 65, Box 62.

321 "Not to arrest": According to the FBI memo cited above, the FBI knew Jasiuk was a war criminal: "Subject became well known for his cruelty and persecution of the Polish populace in the area and was responsible for sending many persons to forced labor in Germany. In 1942, during the liquidation of the Polish intelligentsia, subject submitted a list . . . to the [SD] and, as a result, a number of these persons were shot."

322 Description of CIA's response to Loftus is from Ruffner, chap. 18, 6–9.

322 It had 3,500 separate files: Ibid., 11.

323 "It's bad history": Feigin, 362.

325 "The policemen were sitting on top": Dean, 48.

325 "A prominent role in the persecution": Rein, 138.

326 "The Germans made it clear": Ibid., 132.

326 "In most cases": Ibid., 402.

328 "Over the next two years": Gaddis, *George F. Kennan*, 287.

328 For background on Wisner see: Thomas, Hersh, Powers, Miscamble, Mickelson, and "Frank Gardiner Wisner Dead; Former Top Official of C.I.A." *NYT*, Oct. 30, 1965.

328 "Secretive, insular, elitist": Thomas, 17. The description of Wisner draws heavily on the work of Thomas.

330 "To initiate and conduct": NSC 4A, #2.

330 "Promptly begin in Free Europe": SANAAC 395, March 17, 1948, recommendation two.

331 "Fifty aliens": PPS 22/1, March 4, 1948, recommendation two.

331 "Conducting espionage and counter espionage": NSC 10/2, June 18, 1948, #2.

331 For a discussion of the power struggle over OPC, see Darling's internal history of the CIA, "OPC," 55–69; also Gaddis and Miscamble.

331 "An instrument of U.S. Policy": Miscamble, 109.

331 "Operate independently": NSC 10/2, 3c.

332 Guerilla Warfare School: "Proposal for the Establishment of a Guerilla Warfare School," J.C.S. 1807/1, August 17, 1948.

332 Authorize the FBI and CIA to work together: NSCID No. 14, number one, March 3, 1950.

332 "In the case of those who are *excludible*": SANAAC 395/1, May 25, 1948, p. 8. Top Secret.

333 "Extralegal character": Miscamble, 110.
333 "Membership in the SS": Sher et al., 387.
333 "We would have slept:" 1985 GAO report, 15.
333 "Who had a new idea every ten minutes": Powers, 93.
333 OPC was managing seventeen: Hersh, 319. Also Ruffner, chap. 10, 4.
333 "Wisner pragmatically overloaded the books": Ibid., 5.
334 "Was so influential that the government": Ibid., 287.
334 The Organization was a secret intelligence group established by the War Department and run by John V. Grumbach, an army officer. The State Department took it over in September 1947 and the CIA took it over in April 1951. The organization folded in 1954.
334 Project Solarium: See memorandum by the President to the Secretary of State . . . Subject: Project Solarium, May 20, 1953. Top Secret. The memo is reproduced in *Foreign Relations, 1952–1954*, vol. 2, 341–42.
335 An initial 250 Nazi collaborators: Simpson, 100–1.
335 "They were the cream of Nazi collaborators": Ibid., 150.
335 Poppe and Hilger are based on Simpson, Ruffner (chap. 7), and their CIA files in NA, RG 263, CIA Name Files.
335 "Played leading roles in Nazi Germany": Ruffner, 7.
337 To wave its required examination: Ibid., 17.
337 "The fact that the Office of Policy Coordination": Ibid., 24.
338 "Special consideration": *Alien Enlistment Program*, 6.
338 The army estimated its Guerilla Army requirements as: AG 553, no. 4, p. 1.
338 Provided the following estimates: SWNCC 222, p. 2.
338 The description of the role of the guerila-army-in-waiting is from Simpson, chap. 10, "Guerillas for World War Three."
339 He asked for authorization to bring 15,000: This and other Bloodstone descriptions are from Simpson, chap. 8, "Bloodstone."
340 "Organizers, fomenters, and operational nuclei": Proposal for the Establishment of a Guerilla Warfare School, J.C.S. 1807/1, "Enclosure B," #2.
340 "The entry for Liber Pokorny, for example": *Screening of Lodge Bill Personnel.*
340 The National War College, and the State Department: Proposal for the Establishment of a Guerilla Warfare School, J.C.S. 1807/1, "Enclosure A," 16.
340 "The primary interest in guerilla warfare": Proposal for the Establishment of a Guerilla Warfare School, J.C.S. 1807/1, "Enclosure A," 15.
341 A series of classified, top secret records of Camp Kilmer: *Screening of Lodge Bill Personnel.*
341 "Some of these guys": Ibid.; see also 158–75.
341 "The biggest mistake he ever made": Miscamble's interview with Kennan, 109.
341 "It didn't work out at all the way": Anne Karalekas, "History of the Central Intelligence Agency," in *Final Report: Supplementary Detailed Staff Reports on Foreign and Military Intelligence: Book IV*, U.S. Congress, Senate Select Committee to Study Government Operations. 26n.

PART FOUR

CHAPTERS THIRTY-EIGHT TO FORTY-EIGHT

Sources

These chapters are based on more than eight thousand pages of transcripts from Demjanjuk's Jerusalem trial. All trial quotes come from the transcripts. Italics are the author's.

John Demjanjuk. Israeli court decision.
Demjanjuk, John. Letter to Mark J. O'Connor, June 30, 1987.
———. Letter to the Honorable District Court of Jerusalem, June 30, 1987.
Feigin, "Case Studies of Bohdan Koziy and Harry Maennil." *The Office of Special Investigations.*
Frankel, Glenn. "Demjanjuk Trial Caught in Dispute Over Defense." *WP*, July 16, 1987.
Friedman, Thomas L. "War Crimes Trial in Turmoil On Move to Change Lawyers." *NYT*, July 13, 1987.
Loftus, Elizabeth. *Eyewitness Testimony.* Cambridge, MA: Harvard University Press, 1979.
NYT and *JP*, 1987–1993.
O'Connor, Mark J. Letter to the Honorable District Court of Jerusalem, July 14, 1987.
———. Letter to the Honorable District Court of Jerusalem, July 17, 1987.
Ryan, *Quiet Neighbors.*
Schelvis, Jules. *Sobibor: A History of a Nazi Death Camp.* Translated by Karin Dixon. New York: Berger Publishers, in association with the U.S. Holocaust Memorial Museum, 2007.
Segev, Tom. *The Seven Million: The Israelis and the Holocaust.* New York: Henry Holt, 1991.
Sheftel, *Defending Ivan the Terrible.*
Teicholz, *The Trial of Ivan the Terrible.*
Wagenaar, Willem A. *Identifying Ivan: A Case Study in Legal Psychology.* Cambridge, MA: Harvard University Press, 1988.

Notes

345 "Kiss the ground of the Holy Land": A.E. Ilan, "Ex-Nazi Arrives in Israel for Trial," *CT*, March 1, 1986.
345 "They don't understand": Teicholz, 82.
346 "A dust of indifference has settled": Annette Dulzin, "Israel, Don't Try Nazis," *NYT*, May 6, 1984.
346 "Enough! We know it already": Jonathan Broder, "Ivan a Terrible Bore to Israelis," *CT*, Feb. 18, 1987.
347 The Koziy account is taken from Ryan and Feigin.
348 "Historic justice": Ilan. The survivor's name is Mordechi Fuchs.
349 "That Israel does not have to feel": Thomas Friedman, "Treblinka Becomes an Israeli Obsession," *NYT*, March 13, 1987.
349 "Restaging a funeral in order to add": Dulzin, *NYT*, May 6, 1984.
352 There was no defense team: Based on Sheftel, who details the bickering, confusion, secrecy, lack of planning, and friction among defense attorneys.

See also Frankel, Friedman, Mark O'Connor, and John Demjanjuk, op. cit.

354 Israeli school children loved him: "Three Lawyers in Israel Entwined Over 'Ivan the Terrible,'" *CPD*, May 17, 1987.

360 The description of Sheftel comes from: Francis X. Clines, "An Israeli Lawyer Dares Defend an Accused Nazi," *NYT*, March 2, 1987; *CPD*, May 17, 1987; and *Cleveland Jewish News*, Feb. 13, 1987.

361 Sheftel's thoughts and observations about Judge Levin come from his own account of the trial in *Defending Ivan the Terrible*.

361 "Kapo, Nazi...piece of filth": Sheftel, 9.

365 "This is probably the last time": Friedman, "Treblinka Trial Becomes an Israeli Obsession."

366 "I want her to hear something that": Ibid.

366 "You're a liar": Jonathan Broder, "Nazi War Crimes Trial Underway," *CT*, Feb. 17, 1987.

371 "No way will I cross-examine": *CPD*, May 17, 1987.

373 "Every nation has its heroes": Michael Dobbs, "Nazi Trial Rekindles Émigré Groups' Tensions," *WP*, March 24, 1987.

373 "People talk about how we Ukrainians": Ibid.

373 "This case has created": Ibid.

373 "My concern is that when": Rogers Worthingon, "'Ivan's' Trial Opens Old Wounds,'" *CT*, April 19, 1987.

373 "It is not only John on trial": Ibid.

379 "It is very frustrating that after five months": Quoted by Thomas Friedman in "War Crimes Trial in Turmoil on Move to Change Lawyers," *NYT*, July 13, 1987.

380 "Ed and I spent a lot of time": Sheftel, 91–92.

380 The defense had no defense: Ibid.

382 "I don't understand why the court": Ibid., 77–78.

383 "I would never buy a used car": Ibid., 17.

383 "You're fired.": Ibid., 109.

384 "Impartial, huh?": Teicholz, 183.

386 He considered them to be ant-Semitic *goyim*: Sheftel, 118.

388 Disbarment of O'Connor: *Matter of Mark J. O'Connor, an Attorney, Respondent . . . Grievance Committee of the Eighth Judicial District, Petitioner.* Supreme Court of the State of New York, Appellate Division, Fourth Judicial Department, December 30, 2004.

393 "They have humiliated me in front of": *Yediot Ahronot*, Aug. 14, 1987.

395 Made his direct testimony worthless," Sheftel, 157.

399 There is some confusion about what kind of pills Pritchard took and how many. A Reuters story in the *NYT* reported that she had consumed fifty aspirin and cut her wrists ("A Witness for Demjanjuk Reported to Try Suicide," Aug. 22, 1987). Sheftel reported that she had consumed pain pills and tranquilizers but said nothing about slitting her wrists. Since Sheftel is not always reliable, the report in *NYT*/Reuters seemed a better choice.

405 Camp Dorohucza. See "Dorohucza," *Holocaust Research Project*, at http//:www. holocaustresearchproject.org., and Schelvis, who is a Dorohucza survivor.

414 Wagenaar's testimony is reinforced by his book, *Identifying Ivan*.

423 "Liars . . . You're all liars": Carol Rosenberg (UPI), "Lawyer Asks Acquittal for Accused Nazi," *WP*, Feb. 19, 1988.

424 "All I know is that if": Wolf Blitzer and Ernie Meyer, "Cleveland Ukrainians Criticize Court for Convicting Demjanjuk," *JP*, April 20, 1988.

432 The courtroom erupted in joy: Ernie Meyer, "Death for 'Ivan the Terrible,' " *JP*, April 26, 1988.
433 Reaction in Ohio: Dirk Johnson, "Anger in Ohio Over a Death Camp Conviction," *NYT*, April 27, 1988.

PART FOUR: EPILOGUE

Sources

Aerodynamic. NA, RG 263, CIA Subject Files, second release, Box 7.
Armstrong, John Alexander. *Ukrainian Nationalism.* New York: Columbia University Press, 1963.
Army/CIC Nets in Eastern Europe. NA, RG 263, CIA Subject Files, first release, Box 26.
Breitman, Richard. *Historical Analysis of 20 Name Files from CIA Records.* Washington, DC: U.S. National Archives, April 2001.
Breitman, Richard, and Norman J.W. Goda. *Hitler's Shadow: Nazi War Criminals, U.S. Intelligence, and the Cold War.* Washington, DC: U.S. National Archives, 2010.
Breitman et al., *U.S. Intelligence and the Nazis.*
Chirovsky, *Ukraine and the Second World War.*
Feigin, "Robert Verbelen—Another Barbie?" *The Office of Special Investigations.*
Gilbert, *Atlas of the Holocaust.*
Goda, Norman. "Nazi Collaborators in the United States: What did the FBI Know?" In Breitman et al., *U.S. Intelligence and the Nazis.*
Hoehne, Heinz, and Hermann Zolling. *The General Was a Spy: The Truth about General Gehlen—20th Century Superspy.* New York: Coward, McCann & Geoghegan, 1972.
Lebed, Mykola. NA, RG 65, FBI Name Files, Boxes 128 and 129; and RG 263, CIA Name Files, Box 80.
Loftus, author's interview.
Lowe. *Savage Continent.*
Magocsi, *A History of Ukraine.*
Naftali, Timothy. "Reinhard Gehlen and the United States." In Breitman et al., *U.S. Intelligence and the Nazis.*
Nazi War Crimes and Japanese Imperial Government Records Interagency Working Group: Final Report to the United States Congress, April 2007.
Outline Plan for Project NO. 2B-34, Code Name PBCRUET. NA, RG 263, Aerodynamic, CIA Subject Files, Vol. 1, Development and Plans, second release, Box 7, March 27, 1950.
QRPlumb. NA, RG 263, CIA Subject Files, second release, Boxes 58–59.
Ruffner, *Eagle and Swastika,* chapters 5 and 6.
Sher et al., *Robert Jan Verbelen and the United States Government: A Report to the Assistant Attorney General, Criminal Division, U.S. Department of Justice.*
Simpson, *Blowback.*
Snyder, *The Reconstruction of Nations.*
Verbelen, Jan Robert. NA, RG 263, CIA Name Files, Box 132.
Yekelchyk, Serhy. *Ukraine: Birth of a Modern Nation.* New York: Oxford University Press, 2007.

Notes

435 Release of Soviet files: Charles Mohr, "Soviets Agree to Open Files on the Nazi Genocide to U.S. Scholars," *NYT*, Aug. 25, 1988.

435 Conviction of Fedorenko: "Soviets Find Nazi Guard Guilty," *CT*, June 20, 1986.

437 During the nine years he worked for the United States, Verbelen had five different CIC handlers and used as many as five aliases. It is beyond the scope of this book to give the details of each.

437 "Could not make public": Sher et al., 5.

437 Resistance fighters murdered his family instead: CIC memo: "From Chief of Base, Pullach . . . To Chief, CLS . . . Operational Upswing, Robert Verbelen, aka, Alfred H. Schwab," NA, RG 263, Verbelen, CIA Name Files, Box 132, Aug. 24, 1956.

438 "Handed over to Yugoslavian authorities": Sher et al., 85.

439 "Nearly all the former CIC agents": Ibid., 19.

439 "Succeeded in developing a large net": Ibid., 32.

439 Would later brag that his net: Ralph Blumenthal, "Robert Jan Verbelen Dies at 79," *NYT*, Jan. 8, 1991.

440 The material on Mount Vernon, Montgomery, and Los Angeles is from "Net Project Mount Vernon," in Army/CIC Nets in Eastern Europe and from Breitman and Goda, *Hitler's Shadow*, 60–64.

440 For more on the *Spinne*, see Breitman and Goda, *Hitler's Shadow*, 60–64. For more on Hoettl, see Goda, "The Nazi Peddler: Wilhem Hoettl and Allied Intelligence," in Breitman et al., *U.S. Intelligence and the Nazis*, 265–78.

441 The CIC decided not to tell Belgium: Sher et al., 79. "The Army instructed that 'the information pertaining to Verbelen's past association with the USI [United States Intelligence] is not, repeat, is not for release to the public or Belgian Government because of potential embarrassment to the United States."

441 "Without prejudice . . . .suitable of intelligence re-employment": Ibid., 81.

441 The Austrian police considered Verbelen their best informant. U.S. Embassy report, Vienna: "Vienna Police Support of the Belgian War Criminal, Verbelen," NA, RG 263, Verbelen, CIA Name Files, Box 132, "Report n: EAV-8131," April 20, 1962.

441 The murder of seven named Belgian Resistance fighters: The Vienna trial is covered by Sher et al., 77–79; and "Ex-SS Colonel, a Belgian, Put on Trial in Seven Murders," *NYT*, Nov. 30, 1965.

442 John Loftus stumbled across Lebed's records: Author's interview with Loftus.

442 Whom the CIA considered "dangerous": Breitman and Goda, *Hitler's Shadow*, 77.

443 "The mere mention of the name 'Bandera'": Ruffner, chap. 5, 17.

443 He personally supervised the torture: Simpson, 163.

443 "Rendered valuable services": 1950 CIA summary of a report titled "The Ukrainian Nationalist Movement: An Interim Study," October 1946, NA, RG 263, Lebed, CIA Name Files, Box 80, 1.

444 "Death to Jews and Communists": Ibid., 164.

444 "Killed all the Jews they could find": Breitman and Goda, *Hitler's Shadow*, 75. For a detailed account of Polish and Ukrainian ethnic cleansing, see Snyder

and Lowe, chap. 18, "Ethnic Cleansing." Lowe provides the estimates of 90,000 Poles and 20,000 Ukrainians.

444 "Long Live greater Independent Ukraine": Quoted by Goda in Breitman et al., *U.S. Intelligence and the Nazis*, 250.

444 "Cleanse the entire revolutionary territory": Breitman and Goda, *Hitler's Shadow*, 75.

444 "Bandera men...are not discriminating": Ibid.

445 "Killing up to 10,000 Poles": Ibid.

445 They looted and raped and destroyed: Simpson, 163–64.

445 "Extremely dangerous": Breitman and Goda, *Hitler's Shadow*, 79.

445 "British intelligence hired": Ibid., 78–84.

446 "Ruthless . . . cunning": Goda in Breitman et al., *U.S. Intelligence and the Nazis*, 251.

447 In Operation Ohio, for example: Simpson, 151.

447 Descriptions of QRPlumb, Redsox, and Aerodynamic are based on: Ruffner, chap. 6, "Approval of Operational Activity"; and QRPLUMB and Aerodynamic, NA, RG 263, CIA Subject Files.

447 "There are at least twenty former": Ruffner, chap. 6, 28.

447 "One of the most important Bandera terrorists": Ibid., 22.

448 Allen Dulles made a strong case, and also quotes: "Allen W. Dulles Deputy Director CIA to Argyle R. Mackey Commissioner of INS," NA, RG 263, Lebed, CIA Name Files, Box 80, May 5, 1952; and CIA JL-668, "Memorandum for the Commissioner of INS, Attn: Mr. W. W. Wiggins. . . Subject: Mykola Lebed, aka Roman Turan," Oct. 3, 1951, ibid.

448 "We have always cooperated with": Quoted by Goda in Breitman et al., *U.S. Intelligence and the Nazis*, 253.

448 "Expressed German appreciation": FBI memo, "To Mr. Belmont from Mr. Hennrich. Subject: Mikola Lebed, AKA Internal Security—Ukrainian," NA, RG 65, Lebed, FBI Name Files, Boxes 128–129, June 5, 1950.

449 "To produce and infiltrate into the Soviet Union": In "Memorandum for: Deputy Director for Operations . . . From Chief, Political and Psychological Staff . . . Subject: OSI investigation with Potential Consequences of QRPLUMB Operation," NA, RG 263, QRPLUMB, CIA Subject Files, Box 80, Oct. 21, 1985.

450 "QRPLUMB is one of the oldest": *QRPlumb. Approval of Operational Activity QRPLUMB*, Tab. B.

450 "His office does not have a file": "OSI Investigation with Potential for Compromise of QRPLUMB Operation," NA, RG 263, Box 80, October 21, 1985. See also summary of a meeting between OSI head Neal Sher and CIA: "QRPOOL . . . Memo for the Record . . . Subject: Potential Impact of GAO Investigation on QRPOOL: Ibid., Aug. 15, 1985. Also see "GAO Report with Potential for Compromise of QRPLUMB Operation," Ibid., Oct. 7, 1985.

450 "Indirectly involved in the planning" and "He was protecting live persons": NA, RG 263, Box 59, vol. 5, March 29, 1990.

450 "Provide for a more natural": *QRPlumb*.

451 "Typical KGB-sponsored disinformation": Chirovsky, 55.

453 "At least one hundred of Gehlen's": Naftali in Breitman et al., *U.S. Intelligence and the Nazis*, 377.

453 The Brunner story is based on Simpson; "Brunner, Alois," Yad Vashem

Holocaust Resource Center; and "The Eichmann Henchmen," http://www.holocaustrearchproject.org

454   "His best man": Simpson, 249.
454   "The Jews deserved to die": "The Eichmann Henchmen," 1.
455   Streiber (eager beaver): Simpson, 47.
455   "One of the biggest swine": Ibid., 49.
455   "Extraordinary results…in special tasks": Ibid., 49.
455   The Augsburg account is based on Simpson and on Breitman, *Historical Analysis of 20 Name Files from CIA Records.*
456   "A shining star…a godsend": Breitman, ibid., 5.
456   The Deppner account is based on Goda in Breitman et al.; "Westerbork Transit Camp," Holocaust Research Project, http://www.holocaustresearchproject.org.; and Gilbert, *Atlas of the Holocaust.*
457   "The Gehlen organization provided nothing worthwhile": Quoted by Simpson, 65.

PART FIVE

CHAPTER FORTY-NINE

Sources

Court, Andy. "Holoclaust Survivor Hurls Acid at Sheftel." *JP*, December 2, 1988.
———. "J'lem Man Guilty of Hurling Acid at Lawyer." *JP*, March 14, 1989.
———. "No Clues in Apparent Suicide of Former Judge." *JP*, November 30, 1988.
———. "Opening Up Old Wounds." *JP*, February 3, 1989.
Hadzewycz, Roma. "Interview: Yoram Sheftel, Israeli Defender of John Demjanjuk." *Ukrainian Weekly*, July 7, 1996.
Keinon, Herb. "Ex-Judge's Suicide Baffles Colleagues." *JP*, December 2, 1988.
Meyer, Ernie. "Assailant's Threat." *JP*, December 14, 1988.
"Nazi's Lawyer Killed in Plunge in Jerusalem." AP, November 30, 1988.
Reine, Marcus. "Sheftel: Rebel With an Unpopular Cause." *JP*, August 6, 1993.
"Sheftel Assailant Freed." *JP*, December 16, 1988.
Sheftel, *Defending Ivan the Terrible.*
"Survivor Charged." *JP*, December 11, 1988.

Notes

460   He signed a left-wing petition: The left-wing group was Yesh Gvul.
460   "Levin is disgracing Israeli justice": Sheftel, 268.
462   "I want to tell you as clearly as possible": Ibid., 268.
462   "They say he committed suicide": Ibid., 287.
463   "How can you allow your son": Reine.
463   "His face looked like that of": Keinon.
464   "I went into shock": Sheftel, 292. See also Andy Court, "Holocaust Survivor Hurls Acid at Sheftel," *JP*, December 2, 1988: "J'lem Man Guilty of Hurling Acid at Lawyer," *JP*, March 14, 1989; "Opening Up Old Wounds," *JP*, Feburary 3, 1989.
464   "All the Jews are happy for what I did": Keinon and Court, "Opening up Old Wounds."

464   "Send a man to the gallows": Reine.
464   "To disturb, disrupt, spoil and explode": Sheftel, 292.
464   "Physical bond uniting": Reine.

CHAPTERS FIFTY AND FIFTY-ONE

Sources

Battisti, John. *Memorandum Decision and Order. United States of America, Plaintiff v. John Demjanjuk, Defendant.* No. C77-923, June 23, 1981.
Fletcher, Elaine Ruth. "Survivors Weep." *Cleveland Plain Dealer,* July 30, 1993.
Friedman, Ina. "Obscuring the Lessons of the Holocaust." *Baltimore Jewish Times,* August 6, 1993.
Gordon, Evelyn. "Petitions to Retry Demjanjuk Rejected." *JP,* August 19, 1993.
Greenberg, Joel. "Israeli Court Bars Demjanjuk Leaving." *NYT,* August 2, 1993.
Haberman, Clyde. "Acquittal in Jerusalem: A Painful Case is Closed." *NYT,* July 30, 1993.
———. "Demjanjuk is Free to Return to U.S." *NYT,* September 20, 1993.
———. "Israeli Judges Hear Demjanjuk Charge Conspiracy." *NYT,* December 24, 1991.
Hoffman, David. "Demjanjuk Held in Israel As Prosecutors Consider New Charges." *NYT,* August 2, 1993.
"Ivan the Terrible." *60 Minutes,* CBS, February 25, 1990.
Kuropas, Myron. "Faces and Places: American Jewish Committee Applauds OSI." *Ukrainian Weekly,* August 29, 1993.
Labaton, Stephen. "U.S. Vows to Close Doors to Demjanjuk." *WP,* July 30, 1993.
Lesie, Michele. "Demjanjuk Drama: Rage and Relief." *CPD,* July 30, 1993.
McIntyre, Michael. "Family Rejoices." *CPD,* July 30, 1993.
Parks, Michael. "Court Rejects New Demjanjuk Trial in Israel." *LAT,* August 19, 1993.
Reine, Marcus. "Sheftel: Rebel With an Unpopular Cause." *JP,* August 6, 1993.
Shapiro, Allan. "Harish, Sub Judice, and Demjanjuk." *JP,* December 1, 1989.
Sheftel, *Defending Ivan the Terrible.*
"Summary Court Ruling." *NYT,* July 30, 1993.
"What Now for Ivan the Acquitted." *NYT,* July 31, 1993.

Notes

466   Visit with Dudek: Sheftel, chap. 14, "The Turning Point."
467   "I made a big mistake when": Sheftel, 342.
468   "There in the [Fedorenko] case file": Ibid., 346.
468   Had confessed "without shame": Ibid., 347.
470   The appeal arguments and quotes are from Sheftel, chap. 13, "The Appeal," and from the 1990 *JP* and *NYT* coverage of the appeal.
472   Clipping service story comes from Sheftel, chap. 12, "A Precedent."
473   The *sub judice* story is based on Sheftel and Shapiro. The author of the questioned articles was Noah Klieger, the newspaper was *Yediot Ahrono;* and the editor was Dov Yudkovsky.
474   The trip to Ukraine comes from Sheftel, chap. 14, "Turning Point."
474   "In many of the statements attached to the file": Sheftel, 352.

476 "He [Iwan Marchenko]": Quoted in ibid., 359.
478 "The translation and typing": Ibid., 367.
478 "I was trembling with emotion": Ibid.
478 "Iwan Marchenko—I do not know his father's": Quoted in ibid., 373–74.
480 Quotes from the Israeli Supreme Court appeal decision come from excerpts published in "Summary Court Ruling."
480 "Had I known that such a thing": A composite quote taken from Haberman, "Acquittal in Jerusalem," and from Friedman.
480 "I...I...Czarny Yosef": Haberman, "Acquittal in Jerusalem."
480 "I lost my whole family": Ibid.
480 "Why should a survivor come forward": Ibid.
481 "It's a great day": Ibid.
481 "I am not looking for justice": Kuropas.
481 "In retrospect, perhaps it would have been better": Haberman, "Acquittal in Jerusalem."
481 "The Israeli Supreme Court showed": "What Now for Ivan the Acquitted?"
481 "The decision was impressive": Lesie.
481 "His nationality is enough to make him guilty:" This and following quotes are from Kuropas, Lesie, Fletcher, and McIntyre.
482 "On a technicality": Labaton.
483 "Reasonable is not the same as correct": Gordon.
483 "We have no choice but": Ibid.
484 "You bring shame to the Jewish people": Ibid.
484 "I had two acids": Reine and Gordon.
484 "We will make justice": Gordon.
484 "As far as I am concerned": Haberman, "Acquittal in Jerusalem," is quoting Hagai Merom.
484 "I am very sad": Parks.
484 "[Israelis] are fed up": Haberman, "Demjanjuk is Free to Return to U.S."
484 "Preposterous": Hoffman and Haberman, "Israeli Judges Hear Demjanjuk Charge Conspiracy."

CHAPTER FIFTY-TWO

Sources

Bernard J. Dougherty, Jr., to Arthur Sinai, Deputy Director, OSI. Subject: Horn, Otto—Report of Interview. Undated OSI memo.

Excerpt of the KGB interrogation of Nikolay Petrovich Malagon, March 18, 1978, and Oct. 2, 1979. From the "Fedorenko Protocol." English translation.

Excerpt of the KGB interrogation of Pavel Vladimirovich Leleko, Feb. 20, 1945. From the "Fedorenko Protocol." English translation.

Feigin, "John Demjanjuk—An Appropriate Prosecution Initially Brought, in Part, Under the Wrong Factual Predicate." *The Office of Special Investigations.*

Garland, George W., Historian, to Arthur Sinai, Deputy Director, OSI. Subject: Horn, Otto. Report of Interview. Undated OSI memo.

Memorandum To: Walter J. Rockler and Allan A. Ryan, Jr., Deputy Director, Litigation. Date: February 28, 1980. #146-2-47-43 SI. From: George Parker, Trial Attorney. OSI memo.

United States Court of Appeals for the Sixth Circuit. *John Demjanjuk, Petitioner-*

Appellant, v. Joseph Petrovsky, et al., Respondents-Appellees, No. 85-3435. Argued September 3, 1993, decided November 17, 1993. And *Judgement Entry . . . Supplemental Opinion . . . Findings of Fact*. Case No. 1:99CV1193.

United States Court of Appeals for the Sixth Circuit. *United States of America v. John Demjanjuk*, 367 F. 623. Argued December 10, 2003, decided April 30, 2004.

United States District Court for the Northern District of Ohio, Eastern Division. *United States of America v. John Demjanjuk a/k/a Iwan Demjanjuk*, Case No. 1:99CV1193. May 29, 2001. Transcripts.

Wiseman. *Report of the Special Master*.

Zazak, W. W. *Critique of Wiseman's Report*, October 12, 1993.

Notes

487   The Cleveland mistrial petition is based on Battisti, *Memorandum Decision and Order*.

489   The first was a cable about: The cable read: "Embassy has received material from MFA [Ministry of Foreign Affairs] concerning Fedorenko under a cover note dated August 11. Among these materials are excerpts from the minutes of interrogations of . . ." Sheftel has reproduced copies of this and other cables, 382–89.

490   The author of the Polish list of former Treblinka guards was Stanislaw Wojtczak.

493   "Deceived the court by being *intentionally* false": Wiseman, 151.

493   "Failing to ask questions regarding": Ibid., 165.

493   Quotations and analysis of the Sixth Circuit Court of Appeals are from: *John Demjanjuk, Petitioner-Appellant v. Joseph Petrovsky, et al., Respondents-Appellees*.

494   The American Bar Association reviewed: Feigin, "John Demjanjuk," 165–67.

495   OPR overturned the findings: Ibid.

CHAPTERS FIFTY-THREE TO FIFTY-SEVEN

Sources

Much of the Munich trial testimony is based on trial summaries provided by Dr. Margrit Grubmüller. They are used with her permission.

"As Demjanjuk Trial Opens, Defense Presents Him As a Victim," *Deutsche Welle*, Nov. 30, 2009.

Author's interviews and correspondence with German defense attorney Maja von Oettingen.

"Demjanjuk Presents German Law With An Almost Impossible Problem." *Deutsche Welle*, December 12, 2009.

"Nazi Crimes on Trial (West German Trials) Defendants." *Justiz Und NS-Verbrechen*, June 9, 2011.

Wittmann, Rebecca. "Q & A—Rebecca Wittmann . . . A Front Row Seat at Demjanjuk's Nazi War Crimes Trial," CBC News, December 12, 2009.

———. "The West German Judiciary and the Prosecution of Nazi War Criminals."

Atrocities on Trial: Historical Perspective on the Politics of Prosecuting War Crimes. Edited by Patricia Heberer and Jügen Matthäus. Lincoln: University of Nebraska Press, 2008.

Notes

508 "By 1949": Wittmann, "The West German Judiciary and the Prosecution of Nazi War Criminals," 212.

509 "They were loath": Ibid., 215.

509 "*Befehlsnotstand . . . Exzesstäter*": Wittmann, "Q & A."

509 "We criminal prosecutors have sometimes felt": "I Have Never Seen Remorse: Interview With Nazi War Crimes Prosecutor Ulrich Maas." *Spiegel Online*, May 5, 2011.

510 "Islands of knowledge and ignorance": Yitzhak Laor, "Germany Shouldn't Have Tried Ivan the Miserable." *Haaretz*, Jan. 14, 2010.

513 "[Demjanjuk] has a vested interest": "'Justice Takes a Long Time,' Says Plaintiff at Start of Demjanjuk Trial," *Haaretz*, Jan. 22, 2010; "As Demjanjuk Trial Opens, Defense Presents him as a Victim," *Deutsche Welle*, Nov. 30, 2009; and "Demjanjuk Presents German Law With an Almost Impossible Problem," *Deutsche Welle*, Dec. 12, 2009.

518 The Samuel Kunz story is from: Georg Boensch, "Witness in War Crimes Trial Could Face Indictment," *Spiegel Online International*, Nov. 6, 2009; Zeev Avrahami, "The Man Next Door," *Haeretz.com*, Aug. 13, 2010; Allan Hall, "Nazi Death Camp Guard Who Died Before Answering Charges of Killing 430,000 Jews 'May Have Been Assassinated,'" *Daily Mail*, April 4, 2011.

518 The Alex Nagorny story comes from "Alex Nagorny Under Investigation in Germany for Nazi Killings," *Huffington Post*, Feb. 18, 2011.

519 "It's him...I know him": Megan Stack, "For Elderly Russian, Man Accused as Camp Guard is Vivid Memory," *LAT*, Feb. 6, 2010. The name of the Czech radio correspondent was Kbrhelova.

519 Sobibor survivor Esther Raab told the *Atlantic City Press* (Dec. 1, 2009) that she recognized Demjanjuk as the Sobibor guard who came into the armory building where she worked cleaning captured Soviet weapons and ammunition. She said Demjanjuk would bring in the empty machine gun ammo belts and refill them. She told the *Press* that she would testify if asked. She was never asked. German prosecutors noted that she was shown a Demjanjuk photo spread in the early 1980s and failed to identify Demjanjuk. At that time she also said that she did not recognize the name Demjanjuk.

522 Four SS officers were acquitted: See Blatt, *Sobibor*, chap. 15, "Fate of the Sobibor Nazis."

526 "One doesn't need to like": Gisela Friedrichsen, "Families of Sobibor Victims Value Memories over Malice," *Spiegel Online*, May 5, 2011.

529 "On the concrete courtyard": The story comes from "Hitler's European Holocaust Helpers," *Spiegel Online International*, Dec. 17, 2009.

PART FIVE: EPILOGUE

Sources

Breitman, *Historical Analysis of 20 Name Files.*

Breitman and Goda. *Hitler's Shadow.*

Breitman et al., *U.S. Intelligence and the Nazis.*

Feigin, "Conclusion." *The Office of Special Investigations.*

———. "Kurt Waldheim—A Prominent International Figure." *The Office of Special Investigations.*

———. "Vladimir Sokolov—A Persecutor Who Found a Home in Academia." *The Office of Special Investigations.*

Goda, "Nazi Collaborators in the United States: What did the FBI Know?" In Breitman et al., *U.S. Intelligence and the Nazis.*

Nazi War Crimes and Japanese Imperial Government Records Interagency Working Group: Final Report to the United States Congress, April 2007.

Office of Special Investigations. Washington, DC: U.S. Department of Justice, Executive Office for United States' Attorneys, USA Bulletin, January 2006.

Rosenbaum, Eli. *Betrayal: The Untold Story of the Kurt Waldheim Investigation and Cover-up.* With William Hoffer. New York: St. Martin's Press, 1993.

Simpson, *Blowback.*

Zuroff, Dr. Efraim. *Worldwide Investigation and Prosecution of Nazi War Criminals (April 1, 2008–March 31, 2009).* Jerusalem: Simon Wiesenthal Center, November 2009.

Notes

537 OSI died quietly during the Munich trial. During its thirty years of Nazi hunting, it successfully denaturalized eighty-three Nazis and Nazi collaborators, forced another sixty-two to leave the United States voluntarily, and triggered the suicide of at least seven who were facing trial. Through its Watch List containing the names of eighty thousand alleged Nazis and Nazi collaborators, OSI blocked more than 170 from entering the United States. Among those denied entry—at the insistence of Elizabeth Holtzman—was Kurt Waldheim, the president of Austria. Nazi hunters had collected compelling evidence that Waldheim committed atrocities or was complicit with atrocities committed against Jews and POWs as a senior German intelligence officer in the Balkans during the years 1942–45. See Rosenbaum, *Betrayal*, and Feigin, "Kurt Waldheim—A Prominent International Figure."

537 For more on OSI prosecution statistics see Feigen, "Conclusion." Her appendix lists the names and status of all the suspected Nazis and Nazi collaborators that OSI prosecuted.

537 "Straight A's": Zuroff, 39.

540 The Avdzej, Agh, and Sokolov summaries are based on Feigin and on Goda, "Nazi Collaborators in the United States: What the FBI Knew," in Breitman et al., *U.S. Intelligence and the Nazis.*

541 Fight "Kikes of the world": Goda, 245.

541 "A sincere, outspoken anti-communist": Ibid.

541 "How a man with no high academic crecdentials": Ibid.
541 Description of Redcap is from: *Redcap*. NA, RG 263, CIA Subject Files, second release, "From: Chief, SR . . . Subject: Redcap/LCimprove— Acquisition and Reporting on Information on Soviet Students Abroad," Book Dispatch No. 2396, undated, Box 60, folder two/draft; and "To: Chiefs of Certain Stations and Bases . . . From: Chief, SR . . . Subject REDCAP/ operational," Book Dispatch File No. 74-120-64, undated, Box 60, folder two.
542 "The records are scattered": Ruffner, Introduction, 10–11.

INDEX

ABOUT THE AUTHOR

Richard Rashke is the author of several controversial nonfiction books, including *The Killing of Karen Silkwood* and *Escape from Sobibor*. His books have been translated into eleven languages and have been the subject of movies for screen and television. His play *Dear Esther* has been produced every year since its premiere at the United States Holocaust Memorial Museum in 1998.